LP

F
CLA

Clancy, Tom   414 752

Clear and present
danger

101475

$21.95 Ⓑⓣ

DATE		
APR 10 1992	MAR 26 '94	
4/24/92	MAY 3 '94	
NOV 25	MAY 17 '94	
Dec 8	NOV 17 '99	
JAN 20 1993	JAN 20 2000	
MAR 22 1993	SEP 09 '03	
JAN 25 '99		
MAR 1 '94	DEC 30 '03	
Mar. 15		

Clear
and Present
Danger

Also by Tom Clancy
in Thorndike Large Print

Red Storm Rising
The Cardinal of the Kremlin

Clear and Present Danger

Tom Clancy

THORNDIKE~MAGNA
Thorndike, Maine U.S.A.
North Yorkshire, England

Library of Congress Cataloging-in-Publication Data:
Clancy, Tom.
  Clear and present danger / Tom Clancy.
  p. cm.
ISBN 0-89621-930-5 (alk. paper : lg. print)
ISBN 0-89621-942-9 (pbk. alk. paper : lg. print)
1. Large type books. I. Title
[PS3553.L245C5   1990]   89-27153
813'.54--dc20   CIP

British Library Cataloging in Publication Data:

Clancy, Tom
  Clear and present danger.
  I. Title
  813'.54[F]

  ISBN 1-85057-853-2

Thorndike Press Large Print edition published in 1990
by arrangement with G. P. Putnam's Sons.

Large Print edition available in the British
Commonwealth by arrangement with William
Collins, Ltd.

Cover design copyright © 1989 by
Lawrence Ratzkin.

This book is printed on acid-free, high opacity paper. ∞

ACKNOWLEDGMENTS

As always, there are many people to thank. To "The Great Geraldo" for his friendship; to Russ for his second installment of wise counsel and amazing breadth of knowledge; to Carl and Colin, who never knew what they were starting, but then, neither did I; to Bill for his wisdom; to Rich for his contemplation of what matters; to Tim, Ninja-Six, for more than a few tips on fieldcraft; to Ed, commander of warriors, and Patricia, who named the Cabbage Patch Hat, for their gracious hospitality; to Pete, former headmaster of the world's most exciting school (the passing grade is life); to Pat, who teaches the same course at yet another school; to Harry, mentee, for his most serious irreverence; to W.H., who does his best in a hopeless, thankless job; and of course to a dozen or so warrant officers who could teach astronauts a thing or two; and so many others — would that America served you as faithfully as you serve her.

To the memory of John Ball,
Friend and teacher,
The professional who took the last plane out

Law, without force, is impotent.
— PASCAL

It is the function of police to exercise force, or to threaten it, in execution of the state's purpose, internally and under normal conditions. It is the function of armed forces to exercise force, or the threat of it, externally in normal times and internally only in times that are abnormal. . . .

[T]he degree of force which the state is prepared to apply in the execution of its purpose . . . is as much as the government of the day considers it necessary or expedient to use to avoid a breakdown in its function and a surrender of its responsibilities.
— GENERAL SIR JOHN HACKETT

Prologue:

Situation

The room was still empty. The Oval Office is in the southeast corner of the White House West Wing. Three doors lead into it, one from the office of the President's personal secretary, another from a small kitchen which leads in turn to the President's study, and a third into a corridor, directly opposite the entrance to the Roosevelt Room. The room itself is of only medium size for a senior executive, and visitors always remark afterward that it seemed smaller than they expected. The President's desk, set just in front of thick windows of bullet-resistant polycarbonate that distort the view of the White House lawn, is made from the wood of HMS *Resolute*, a British ship that sank in American waters during the 1850s. Americans salvaged and returned it to the United Kingdom, and a grateful Queen Victoria ordered a desk made from its oaken timbers by way of official thanks. Made in

11

an age when men were shorter than today, the desk was increased somewhat in height during the Reagan presidency. The President's desk was laden with folders and position papers capped with a printout of his appointment schedule, plus an intercom box, a conventional push-button multiline telephone, and another ordinary-looking but highly sophisticated secure instrument for sensitive conversations.

The President's chair was custom-made to fit its user, and its high back included sheets of DuPont Kevlar — lighter and tougher than steel — as additional protection against bullets that some madman might fire through the heavy windows. There were, of course, about a dozen Secret Service agents on duty in this part of the Presidential Mansion during business hours. To get here most people had to pass through a metal detector — in fact all did, since the obvious ones were a little *too* obvious — and everyone had to pass the quite serious scrutiny of the Secret Service detail, whose identity was plain from the flesh-toned earpieces that coiled out from under their suit jackets, and whose politeness was secondary to their real mission of keeping the President alive. Beneath the jacket of each was a powerful handgun, and each of these agents was trained to view everyone and everything as a potential threat to WRANGLER, which was the President's current code-name. It had no meaning beyond being easy to say and easily recognizable on a radio circuit.

Vice Admiral James Cutter, USN, was in an office on the opposite, northwest corner of the West Wing and had been since 6:15 that morning. The job of Special Assistant to the President for National Security Affairs requires a man to be an early riser. At a quarter to eight he finished off his second cup of morning coffee — it was good here — and tucked his briefing papers into a leather folder. He walked through the empty office of his vacationing deputy, turned right down the corridor past the similarly vacant office of the Vice President, who was in Seoul at the moment, and turned left past the office of the President's Chief of Staff. Cutter was one of the handful of real Washington insiders — the Vice President was not among them — who didn't need the permission of the Chief of Staff to walk into the Oval Office whenever he felt the need, though he'd generally call ahead first to give the secretaries a heads-up. The Chief of Staff didn't like anyone to have that privilege, but that made his unlimited access all the more pleasant for Cutter to exercise. Along the way four security personnel nodded good morning to the Admiral, who returned the gestures as he would greet any skilled menial. Cutter's official code-name was LUMBERJACK, and though he knew that the Secret Service agents called him something else among themselves, Cutter was past caring what little people thought of him. The secretaries' anteroom was already up and running, with three secretaries and a Secret Service agent

13

sitting in their appointed places.

"Chief on time?" he asked.

"WRANGLER is on the way down, sir," Special Agent Connor said. He was forty, a section chief of the Presidential Detail, didn't give a goddamn who Cutter was, and could care less what Cutter thought of him. Presidents and aides came and went, some liked, some loathed, but the professionals of the Secret Service served and protected them all. His trained eyes swept over the leather folder and Cutter's suit. No guns there today. He was not being paranoid. A king of Saudi Arabia had been killed by a family member, and a former prime minister of Italy had been betrayed by a daughter to the terrorist kidnappers who'd ultimately murdered him. It wasn't just kooks he had to worry about. Anyone could be a threat to the President. Connor was fortunate, of course, that he only had to worry about physical security. There were other sorts; those were the concerns of others less professional than he.

Everyone stood when the President arrived, of course, followed by his personal bodyguard, a lithe, thirtyish woman whose dark tresses neatly concealed the fact that she was one of the best pistol shots in government service. "Daga" — her Service nickname — smiled good morning at Pete. It would be an easy day. The President wasn't going anywhere. His appointment list had been thoroughly checked — the Social Security numbers of all nonregulars are run through the

14

FBI's crime computers — and the visitors themselves would, of course, be subjected to the most thorough searches that can be made without an actual pat-down. The President waved for Admiral Cutter to follow him in. The two agents went over the appointment list again. It was routine, and the senior agent didn't mind that a man's job had been taken by a woman. Daga had earned her job on the street. If she were a man, everyone agreed, she'd have two big brass ones, and if any would-be assassin mistook her for a secretarial type, that was his bad luck. Every few minutes, until Cutter left, one or the other of the agents would peer through the spy-hole in the white-painted door to make sure that nothing untoward was happening. The President had held office for over three years, and was used to the constant observation. It hardly occurred to the agents that a normal man might find it oppressive. It was their job to know everything there was to know about the President, from how often he visited the bathroom to those with whom he slept. They didn't call the agency the Secret Service for nothing. Their antecedents had concealed all manner of peccadillos. The President's wife was not entitled to know what he did every hour of the day — at least, some presidents had so decided — but his security detail was.

Behind the closed door, the President took his seat. From the side door a Filipino mess steward carried in a tray with coffee and croissants and

15

came to attention before leaving. With this the morning's preliminary routine was complete, and Cutter began his morning intelligence briefing. This had been delivered from CIA to his Fort Myer, Virginia, home before dawn, which allowed the Admiral to paraphrase it. The brief didn't take long. It was late spring, and the world was a relatively quiet place. Those wars underway in Africa and elsewhere were not of great import to American interests, and the Middle East was as tranquil as it ever seemed to be. That left time for other issues.

"What about SHOWBOAT?" the President asked while buttering his croissant.

"It's underway, sir. Ritter's people are already at work," Cutter replied.

"I'm still worried about security on the operation."

"Mr. President, it's as tight as one could reasonably expect. There are risks — you can't avoid them all — but we're keeping the number of people involved to an absolute minimum, and those people have been carefully selected and recruited."

That earned the National Security Adviser a grunt. The President was trapped — and as with nearly every president, it had come about from his own words. Presidential promises and statements . . . the people had this annoying way of remembering them. And even if they didn't there were journalists and political rivals who never passed on a chance to make the necessary

16

reminders. So many things had gone right in this presidency. But so many of those were secret — and, annoyingly to Cutter, those secrets had somehow been kept. Well, they had to be, of course. Except that in the political arena no secret was truly sacred, most especially in an election year. Cutter wasn't supposed to be concerned with that. He was a professional naval officer, and therefore supposed to be apolitical in his outlook on the ins and outs of national security, but whoever had formulated that particular guideline must have been a monk. Members of the senior executive service did not take vows of poverty and chastity, however — and obedience was also a sometime thing.

"I promised the American people that we'd do something about this problem," the President observed crossly. "And we haven't accomplished shit."

"Sir, you cannot deal with threats to national security through police agencies. Either our national security is threatened or it is not." Cutter had been hammering that point for years. Now, finally, he had a receptive audience.

Another grunt: "Yeah, well, I said that, too, didn't I?"

"Yes, Mr. President. It's time they learned a lesson about how the big boys play." That had been Cutter's position from the beginning, when he'd been Jeff Pelt's deputy, and with Pelt now gone it was his view that had finally prevailed.

"Okay, James. It's your ball. Run with it. Just

17

remember that we need results."

"You'll get 'em, sir. Depend on that."

"It's time those bastards were taught a lesson," the President thought aloud. He was certain that the lessons would be hard ones. On that he was correct. Both men sat in a room in which was focused and from which emanated the ultimate power of the most powerful nation in the history of civilization. The people who selected the man who occupied that room did so above all for their protection. Protection against the vagaries of foreign powers and domestic bullies, against all manner of enemies. Those enemies came in many forms, some of which the founding fathers had not quite anticipated. But one sort that had been anticipated existed in this very room . . . though it was not the one the President had in mind.

The sun rose an hour later on the Caribbean coast, and unlike the climate-controlled comfort of the White House, here the air was thick and heavy with humidity on what promised to be yet another sultry day under a lingering high-pressure system. The forested hills to the west reduced the local winds to a bare whisper, and the owner of *Empire Builder* was past being ready to go to sea, where the air was cooler and the breezes unrestricted.

His crewmen arrived late. He didn't like their looks, but he didn't have to. Just so long as they behaved themselves. After all, his family was aboard.

"Good morning, sir. I am Ramón. This is Jesús," the taller one said. What troubled the owner was that they were so obviously tidied-up versions of . . . of what? Or had they merely wanted to look presentable?

"You think you can handle this?" the owner asked.

"*Sí*. We have experience with large motor craft." The man smiled. His teeth were even and brushed. This was a man who took care with his appearance at all times, the owner thought. He was probably being overly cautious. "And Jesús, you will see, is a fine cook."

Charming little bastard. "Okay, crew quarters are forward. She's tanked up, and the engines are already warm. Let's get out where it's cool."

"*Muy bien, Capitán.*" Ramón and Jesús unloaded their gear from the jeep. It took several trips to get it all stowed, but by nine in the morning, MY *Empire Builder* slipped her mooring lines and stood out to sea, passing a handful of party boats heading out with *yanqui* tourists and their fishing rods. Once in open waters, the yacht turned north. It would take three days.

Ramón already had the wheel. That meant he sat in a wide, elevated chair while the autopilot — "George" — handled the steering. It was an easy ride. The Rhodes had fin stabilizers. About the only disappointment was in the crew accommodations, which the owner had neglected. So typical, Ramón thought. A multimillion-dollar yacht

19

with radar and every possible amenity, but the crew who operated it didn't have so much as a television set and VCR to amuse themselves when off duty. . . .

He moved forward on the seat, craning his neck to look on the fo'c'sle. The owner was there, asleep and snoring, as though the work of taking the yacht out to sea had exhausted him. Or perhaps his wife had tired him out? She was beside her husband, lying facedown on her towel. The string for her bikini top was untied so as to give her back an even tan. Ramón smiled. There were many ways for a man to amuse himself. But better to wait. Anticipation made it all the better. He heard the sound of a taped movie in the main salon, aft of the bridge, where their children were watching some movie or other. It never occurred to him to feel pity for any of the four. But he was not completely heartless. Jesús was a good cook. They both approved of giving the condemned a hearty meal.

It was just light enough to see without the night-vision goggles, the dawn twilight that the helicopter pilots hated because the eye had to adapt itself to a lightening sky and ground that was still in shadows. Sergeant Chavez's squad was seated and strapped in with four-point safety belts, and between the knees of each was a weapon. The UH-60A Blackhawk helicopter swooped high over one of the hills and then dropped hard when past the crest.

"Thirty seconds," the pilot informed Chavez over the intercom.

It was supposed to be a covert insertion, which meant that the helicopters were racing up and down the valleys, careful that their operational pattern should confuse any possible observer. The Blackhawk dove for the ground and pulled up short as the pilot eased back on the cyclic control stick, which gave the aircraft a nose-up attitude, signaling the crew chief to slide the right-side door open and the soldiers to twist the release dials on their safety-belt buckles. The Blackhawk could touch down only for a moment.

"Go!"

Chavez went out first, moving perhaps ten feet from the door before he fell flat to the ground. The squad did the same, allowing the Blackhawk to lift off immediately, and rewarding each of its former passengers with a faceful of flying grit as it clawed its way back into the sky. It would reappear around the southern end of a hill as though it had never stopped. Behind it, the squad assembled and moved out into the treeline. Its work had just begun. The sergeant gave his commands with hand motions and led them off at a dead run. It would be his last mission, then he could relax.

At the Navy's weapons testing and development facility, China Lake, California, a team of civilian technicians and some Navy ordnance experts hovered over a new bomb. Built with roughly the same dimensions as the old two-thousand-pounder, it weighed nearly seven hundred pounds less. This resulted from its construction. Instead of a steel skin, the bombcase was made of Kevlar-reinforced cellulose — an idea borrowed from the French, who made shell casings from the naturally produced fibers — with only enough metal fittings to allow attachment of fins, or the more extensive hardware that would convert it into an "LGB," able to track in on a specific point target. It was little known that a smart-bomb is generally a mere iron bomb with the guidance equipment bolted on.

"You're not going to get fragments worth a damn," a civilian objected.

"What's the point of having a Stealth bomber," another technician asked, "if the bad guys get a radar return off the ordnance load?"

"Hmph," observed the first. "What's the point of a bomb that just pisses the other guy off?"

"Put it through his front door and he won't live long enough to get pissed, will he?"

"Hmph." But at least he knew what the bomb was actually for. It would one day hang on the ATA, the Advanced Tactical Aircraft, a carrier-based attack bomber with stealth technology built in. Finally, he thought, the Navy's getting on board that program. About time. For the moment, however, the job at hand was to see if this new bomb with a different weight and a different center of gravity would track in on a target with a standard LGB guidance pack. The bomb hoist came over and lifted the streamlined shape off its pallet. Next the operator maneuvered it under the center-line hard-point of an A-6E Intruder attack bomber.

The technicians and officers walked over to the helicopter that would take them to the bombing range. There was no rush. An hour later, safely housed in a bunker that was clearly marked, one of the civilians trained an odd-looking device at a target four miles away. The target was an old five-ton truck that the Marines had given up on, and which would now, if everything went according to plan, die a violent and spectacular death.

"Aircraft is inbound over the range. Start the music."

"Roger," the civilian replied, squeezing the trigger on the GLD. "On target."

"Aircraft reports acquisition — stand by . . . " the communicator said.

At the other end of the bunker, an officer was watching a television camera locked onto the inbound Intruder. "Breakaway. We have a nice, clean release off the ejector rack." He'd check that view later with one off an A-4 Skyhawk fighter-bomber that was flying chase on the A-6. Few people realized that the mere act of dropping a bomb off an airplane was a complex and potentially dangerous exercise. A third camera followed the bomb down.

"Fins are moving just fine. Here we go . . . "

The camera on the truck was a high-speed one. It had to be. The bomb was falling too fast for anyone to catch it on the first run-through, but by the time the crushing bass note of the detonation reached the bunker, the operator had already started rewinding the tape. The replay was done one frame at a time.

"Okay, there's the bomb." Its nose appeared forty feet over the truck. "How was it fused?"

"VT," one of the officers answered. VT stood for variable time. The bomb had a miniradar transceiver in its nose, and was programmed to explode within a fixed distance of the ground; in this case, five feet, or almost the instant it hit the truck. "Angle looks just fine."

"I thought it would work," an engineer observed quietly. He'd suggested that since the bomb was essentially a thousand pounder, the guidance equipment could be programmed for the lighter weight. Though it was slightly heavier than that, the reduced density of the cellulose bombcase made for a similar ballistic performance. "Detonation."

As with any high-speed photos of such an event, the screen flashed white, then yellow, then red, then black, as the expanding gasses from the high-explosive filler cooled in the air. Just in front of the gas was the blast wave: air compressed to a point at which it was denser than steel, moving faster than any bullet. No machine press could duplicate the effect.

"We just killed another truck." It was a wholly

unnecessary observation. Roughly a quarter of the truck's mass was pounded straight down into a shallow crater, perhaps a yard deep and twenty across. The remainder was hurled laterally as shrapnel. The gross effect was not terribly different, in fact, from a large car bomb of the sort delivered by terrorists, but a hell of a lot safer for the deliverymen, one of the civilians thought.

"Damn — I didn't think it'd be that easy. You were right, Ernie, we don't even have to reprogram the seeker," a Navy commander observed. They'd just saved the Navy over a million dollars, he thought. He was wrong.

And so began something that had not quite begun and would not soon end, with many people in many places moving off in directions and on missions which they all mistakenly thought they understood. That was just as well. The future was too fearful for contemplation, and beyond the expected, illusory finish lines were things fated by the decisions made this morning — and, once decided, best unseen.

1.

The King of SAR

You couldn't look at her and not be proud, Red
Wegener told himself. The Coast Guard cutter
Panache was one of a kind, a design mistake of
sorts, but she was his. Her hull was painted the
same gleaming white found on an iceberg —
except for the orange stripe on the bow that
designated the ship as part of the United States
Coast Guard. Two hundred eighty feet in length,
Panache was not a large ship, but she was his
ship, the largest he'd ever commanded, and certainly the last he would ever have. Wegener was
the oldest lieutenant-commander in the Coast
Guard, but Wegener was The Man, the King of
Search-and-Rescue missions.

His career had begun the same way many
Coast Guard careers had. A young man from a
Kansas wheat farm who'd never seen the sea,
he'd walked into a Coast Guard recruiting station
the day after graduating from high school. He

hadn't wanted to face a life driving tractors and combines, and he'd sought out something as different from Kansas as he could find. The Coast Guard petty officer hadn't made much of a sales pitch, and a week later he'd begun his career with a bus ride that ended at Cape May, New Jersey. He could still remember the chief petty officer that first morning who'd told them of the Coast Guard creed. "You have to go out. You don't have to come back."

What Wegener found at Cape May was the last and best true school of seamanship in the Western world. He learned how to handle lines and tie sailor knots, how to extinguish fires, how to go into the water after a disabled or panicked boater, how to do it right the first time, every time — or risk not coming back. On graduation he was assigned to the Pacific Coast. Within a year he had his rate, Boatswain's Mate Third Class.

Very early on it was recognized that Wegener had that rarest of natural gifts, the seaman's eye. A catch-all term, it meant that his hands, eyes, and brain could act in unison to make his boat perform. Guided along by a tough old chief quartermaster, he soon had "command" of his "own" thirty-foot harbor patrol boat. For the really tricky jobs, the chief would come along to keep a close eye on the nineteen-year-old petty officer. From the first Wegener had shown the promise of someone who only needed to be shown things once. His first five years in uniform now seemed to have passed in the briefest instant as he learned his craft. Nothing really dramatic, just a succession of jobs that he'd done as the book prescribed, quickly and smoothly. By the time he'd considered and opted for re-enlistment, it was evident that when a tough job had to be done, his name was the one that came up first. Before the end of his second hitch, officers routinely asked his opinion of things. By this time he was thirty, one of the youngest chief bosun's mates in the service, and he was able to pull a few strings, one of which ended with command of *Invincible*, a forty-eight-footer which had already garnered a reputation for toughness and dependability. The stormy California coast was her home, and it was here that Wegener's name first became known outside of his service. If a fisherman or a yachtsman got into trouble, *Invincible* always seemed to be there, often roller-coastering across thirty-foot seas with her crewmen held in place with ropes and safety belts — but there and ready to do the job with a red-haired chief at the wheel, an unlit briar pipe in his teeth. In that first year he saved the lives of at least fifteen people.

The number grew to fifty before he'd ended his tour of duty at the lonely station. After a couple of years, he was in command of his own station, and the holder of a title craved by all seamen — Captain — though his rate was that of Senior Chief. Located on the banks of a small stream that fed into the world's largest ocean, he ran his station as tautly as any ship, and inspecting officers had come there not so much to see how Wegener ran things as to see how things should be run.

For good or ill, Wegener's career plan had changed with one epic winter storm on the Oregon Coast. Commanding a larger rescue station now near the mouth of the Columbia River and its infamous bar, he'd received a frantic radio call from a deep-sea fisherman named *Mary-Kat*: engines and rudder disabled, being driven toward a lee shore that devoured ships. His personal flagship, the eighty-two-foot *Point Gabriel* was away from the dock in ninety seconds, her mixed crew of veterans and apprentices hooking their safety belts into place while Wegener coordinated the rescue efforts on his own radio channels.

It had been an epic battle. After a six-hour ordeal, Wegener had rescued the *Mary-Kat*'s six fishermen, but just barely, his ship assaulted by wind and furious seas. Just as the last man had been brought in, the *Mary-Kat* had grounded on a submerged rock and snapped in half.

As luck would have it, Wegener had had a reporter on board that day, a young feature writer for the *Portland Oregonian* and an experienced yachtsman, who thought he knew what there was to know about the sea. As the cutter had tunneled through the towering breakers at the Columbia bar, the reporter had vomited on his notebook, then wiped it on his Mustang suit and kept writing. The series of articles that had followed was entitled "The Angel of the Bar," and won the journalist a Pulitzer Prize for feature writing.

The following month, in Washington, the senior United States Senator from the State of Oregon, whose nephew had been a crewman on the *Mary-Kat*, wondered aloud why someone as good as Red Wegener was not an officer, and since the commandant of the Coast Guard was in that room to discuss the service's budget, it was an observation to which a four-star admiral had decided to pay heed. By the end of the week Red Wegener was commissioned as lieutenant — the senator had also observed that he was a little too old to be an ensign. Three years later he was recommended for the next available command.

There was only one problem with that, the commandant considered. He did have an available command — *Panache* — but it might seem a mixed blessing. The cutter was nearly completed. She was to have been the lead ship for a new class, but funding had been cut, the yard had gone bankrupt, and the commissioning skipper had been relieved for bungling his job. That left the Coast Guard with an unfinished ship whose engines didn't work, in an out-of-business shipyard. But Wegener was supposed to be a miracle worker, the commandant decided at his desk. To make it a fair chance, he made sure that Wegener got some good chiefs to back up the inexperienced wardroom.

His arrival at the shipyard gate had been delayed by the picket line of disgruntled workers and by the time he'd gotten through that, he was sure things couldn't get worse. Then he'd seen what was supposed to have been a ship. It was a steel artifact, pointed at one end and blunt at the other, half painted, draped with cables, piled with crates, and generally looking like a surgical patient who'd died on the table and been left there to rot. If that hadn't been bad enough, *Panache* couldn't even be towed from her berth — the last thing a worker had done was to burn out the motor on a crane, which blocked the way.

The previous captain had already left in disgrace. The commissioning crew, assembled on the helicopter deck to receive him, looked like children forced to attend the funeral of a disliked uncle, and when Wegener tried to address them, the microphone didn't work. Somehow that broke the evil spell. He waved them toward himself with a smile and a chuckle.

"People," he'd said, "I'm Red Wegener. In six months this will be the best ship in the United States Coast Guard. In six months you will be the best crew in the United States Coast Guard. I'm not the one who's going to make that happen. You will — and I'll help a little. For right now, I'm cutting everybody as much liberty as we can stand while I get a handle on what we have to do. Have yourselves a great time. When you get back, we all go to work. Dismissed."

There was a collective "oh" from the assembled multitude, which had expected shouts and screams. The newly arrived chiefs regarded one another with raised eyebrows, and the young officers who'd been contemplating the abortion of their service careers retired to the wardroom in a state of bemused shock. Before meeting with them, Wegener took his three leading chiefs aside.

"Engines first," Wegener said.

"I can give you fifty-percent power all day long, but when you try to use the turbochargers, everything goes to hell in fifteen minutes," Chief Owens announced. "An' I don't know why." Mark Owens had been working with marine diesels for sixteen years.

"Can you get us to Curtis Bay?"

"As long as you don't mind taking an extra day, Cap'n."

Wegener dropped the first bomb. "Good — 'cause we're leaving in two weeks, and we'll finish the fitting-out up there."

"It'll be a month till the new motor's ready for that crane, sir," Chief Boatswain's Mate Bob Riley observed.

"Can the crane turn?"

"Motor's burned out, Cap'n."

"When the time comes, we'll snake a line from the bow to the back end of the crane. We have seventy-five feet of water in front of us. We set the clutch on the crane and pull forward real gentle-like, and turn the crane ourselves, then back out," the captain announced. Eyes narrowed.

"Might break it," Riley observed after a moment.

"That's not my crane, but, by God, this is my ship."

Riley let out a laugh. "Goddamn, it's good to see you again, Red — excuse me, Captain Wegener!"

"Mission Number One is to get her to Baltimore for fitting-out. Let's figure out what we have to do, and take it one job at a time. I'll see you oh-seven-hundred tomorrow. Still make your own coffee, Portagee?"

"Bet your ass, sir," Chief Quartermaster Oreza replied. "I'll bring a pot."

And Wegener had been right. Twelve days later, *Panache* had indeed been ready for sea, though not much else, with crates and fittings lashed down all over the ship. Moving the crane out of the way was accomplished before dawn, lest anyone notice, and when the picket line showed up that day, it had taken a few minutes to notice that the ship was gone. Impossible, they'd all thought. She hadn't even been fully painted yet.

The painting was accomplished in the Florida Strait, as was something even more important. Wegener had been on the bridge, napping in his leather chair during the forenoon watch when the growler phone rang, and Chief Owens invited him to the engine room. Wegener arrived to find the only worktable covered with plans, and an engineman-apprentice hovering over them, with his engineering officer standing behind him.

"You ain't gonna believe it," Owens announced. "Tell him, sonny."

"Seaman Obrecki, sir. The engine isn't

installed right," the youngster said.

"What makes you think that?" Wegener asked.

The big marine diesels were of a new sort, perversely designed to be very easy to operate and maintain. To aid in this, small how-to manuals were provided for each engine-room crewman, and in each manual was a plastic-coated diagram that was far easier to use than the builder's plans. A blow-up of the manual schematic, also plastic-coated, had been provided by the drafting company, and was the laminated top of the worktable.

"Sir, this engine is a lot like the one on my dad's tractor, bigger, but — "

"I'll take your word for it, Obrecki."

"The turbocharger ain't installed right. It matches with these plans here, but the oil pump pushes the oil through the turbocharger backwards. The plans are wrong, sir. Some draftsman screwed up. See here, sir? The oil line's supposed to come in here, but the draftsman put it on the wrong side of this fitting, and nobody caught it, and — "

Wegener just laughed. He looked at Chief Owens: "How long to fix?"

"Obrecki says he can have it up and running this time tomorrow, Cap'n."

"Sir." It was Lieutenant Michelson, the engineering officer. "This is all my fault. I should have — " The lieutenant was waiting for the sky to fall.

"The lesson from this, Mr. Michelson, is that

you can't even trust the manual. Have you learned that lesson, Mister?"

"Yes, sir!"

"Fair enough. Obrecki, you're a seaman-first, right?"

"Yes, sir."

"Wrong. You're a machinist-mate third."

"Sir, I have to pass a written exam . . . "

"You think Obrecki's passed that exam, Mr. Michelson?"

"You bet, sir."

"Well done, people. This time tomorrow I want to do twenty-three knots."

And it had all been downhill from there. The engines are the mechanical heart of any ship, and there is no seaman in the world who prefers a slow ship to a fast one. When *Panache* had made twenty-five knots and held that speed for three hours, the painters painted better, the cooks took a little more time with the meals, and the technicians tightened their bolts just a little more. Their ship was no longer a cripple, and pride broke out in the crew like a rainbow after a summer shower — all the more so because one of their own had figured it out. One day early, *Panache* came into the Curtis Bay Coast Guard Yard with a bone in her teeth. Wegener had the conn and pushed his own skill to the limit to make a fast "one-bell" approach to the dock. "The Old Man," one line handler noted on the fo'c'sle, "really knows how to drive this fuckin' boat!"

The next day a poster appeared on the ship's bulletin board: PANACHE: DASHING ELEGANCE OF MANNER OR STYLE. Seven weeks later, the cutter was brought into commission and she sailed south to Mobile, Alabama, to go to work. Already she had a reputation that exactly matched her name.

It was foggy this morning, and that suited the captain, even though the mission didn't. The King of SAR was now a cop. The mission of the Coast Guard had changed more than halfway through his career, but it wasn't something that you noticed much on the Columbia River bar, where the enemy was still wind and wave. The same enemies lived in the Gulf of Mexico, but added to them was a new one. Drugs. Drugs were not something that Wegener thought a great deal about. For him drugs were something a doctor prescribed, that you took in accordance with the directions on the bottle until they were gone, and then you tossed the bottle. When Wegener wanted to alter his mental state, he did so in the traditional seaman's way — beer or hard liquor — though he found himself doing so less now that he was approaching fifty. He'd always been afraid of needles — every man has his private dread — and the idea that people would voluntarily stick needles into their arms had always amazed him. The idea of sniffing a white powder into one's nose — well, that was just too much to believe. His attitude wasn't so much naïveté as a reflection of the age in which he'd grown up. He knew that the problem was real. Like everyone else in uniform, every few months he had to provide a urine sample to prove that he was not using "controlled substances." Something that the younger crewmen accepted as a matter of course, it was a source of annoyance and insult to people of his age group.

The people who ran the drugs were his more immediate concern, but the most immediate of all was a blip on his radar screen.

They were a hundred miles off the Mexican coast, far from home. And the Rhodes was overdue. The owner had called in several days earlier, saying that he was staying out a couple of days extra . . . but his business partner had found that odd, and called the local Coast Guard office. Further investigation had determined that the owner, a wealthy businessman, rarely went more than three hours offshore. The Rhodes cruised at fifteen knots.

The yacht was sixty-two-feet long, big enough that you'd want a few people to help you sail it . . . but small enough that real master's papers were not required by law. The big motor-yacht had accommodation for fifteen, plus two crewmen, and was worth a couple of million dollars. The owner, a real-estate developer with his own little empire outside Mobile, was new to the sea, and a cautious sailor. That made him smart, Wegener thought. Too smart to stray this far offshore. He knew his limitations, which was rare in the yachting community, especially the richer segment. He'd gone south two weeks earlier, tracing the coast and making a few stops, but he was late coming back, and he'd missed a business meeting. His partner said that he would not have missed it unnecessarily. A routine air patrol had spotted the yacht the day before, but not tried to contact it. The district commander had decided that something smelled about this one. *Panache* was the closest cutter and Wegener got the call.

"Sixteen thousand yards. Course zero-seven-one," Chief Oreza reported from the radar plot. "Speed twelve. He ain't heading for Mobile, Cap'n."

"Fog's going to burn off in another hour, maybe hour and a half," Wegener decided. "Let's close in now. Mr. O'Neil, all ahead full. Intercept course, Chief?"

"One-six-five, sir."

"That's your course. If the fog holds, we'll adjust when we get within two or three miles and come up dead astern."

Ensign O'Neil gave the proper rudder orders. Wegener went to the chart table.

"Where do you figure he's headed, Portagee?"

The chief quartermaster projected the course, which appeared to go nowhere in particular. "He's on his most economical speed setting . . . not any port on the Gulf, I'll bet." The captain picked up a pair of dividers and started walking them across the chart.

"That yacht has bunkerage for . . ." Wegener

38

frowned. "Let's say he topped off at the last port. He can get to the Bahamas easily enough. Refill there, and then anyplace he wants to go on the East Coast."

"Cowboys," O'Neil opined. "First one in a long time."

"Why do you think that?"

"Sir, if I owned a boat that big, I sure wouldn't run it through fog with no radar. His isn't operating."

"I hope you're wrong, son," the captain said. "How long since the last one, Chief?"

"Five years? Maybe more. I thought that sort of thing was all behind us."

"We'll know in an hour." Wegener turned to look at the fog again. Visibility was under two hundred yards. Next he looked into the hooded radar display. The yacht was the closest target. He thought for a minute, then flipped the set from active to standby. Intelligence reports said that druggies now had ESM gear to detect radar transmissions.

"We'll flip it back on when we get within, oh, say, four miles or so."

"Aye, Cap'n," the youngster nodded.

Wegener settled in his leather chair and extracted the pipe from his shirt. He found himself filling it less and less now, but it was part of an image he'd built. A few minutes later the bridge watch had settled down to normal. In keeping with tradition, the captain came topside to handle two hours of the morning watch — the one

with the youngest junior officer of the watch —
but O'Neil was a bright young kid and didn't
need all that much supervision, at least not with
Oreza around. "Portagee" Oreza was the son
of a Gloucester fisherman and had a reputation
approaching his captain's. With three tours at
the Coast Guard Academy, he'd helped educate a
whole generation of officers, just as Wegener had
once specialized in bringing enlisted men along.

Oreza was also a man who understood the
importance of a good cup of coffee, and one thing
about coming to the bridge when Portagee was
around was that you were guaranteed a cup of his
personal brew. It came right on time, served in
the special mug the Coast Guard uses, shaped
almost like a vase, wide at the rubber-coated bottom, and narrowed down near the top to prevent
tipping and spillage. Designed for use on small
patrol craft, it was also useful on *Panache*, which
had a lively ride. Wegener hardly noticed.

"Thanks, Chief," the captain said as he took
the cup.

"I figure an hour."

" 'Bout right," Wegener agreed. "We'll go to
battle stations at zero-seven-forty. Who's on the
duty boat section?"

"Mr. Wilcox. Kramer, Abel, Dowd, and
Obrecki."

"Obrecki done this yet?"

"Farm boy. He knows how to use a gun, sir.
Riley checked him out."

"Have Riley replace Kramer."

40

"Anything wrong, sir?"

"Something feels funny about this one," Wegener said.

"Probably just a busted radio. There hasn't been one of those since — jeez, I don't even remember when that was, but, yeah. Call Riley up here?"

The captain nodded. Oreza made the call, and Riley appeared two minutes later. The two chiefs and the captain conferred out on the bridge wing. It only took a minute by Ensign O'Neil's watch. The young officer thought it very odd that his captain seemed to trust and confide in his chiefs more than his wardroom, but mustang officers had their own ways.

Panache rumbled through the waves at full speed. She was rated at twenty-three knots, and though she'd made just over twenty-five a few times, that was in light-ship conditions, with a newly painted bottom on flat seas. Even with the turbochargers pounding air into the diesels, top speed now was just over twenty-two knots. It made for a hard ride. The bridge crew compensated for this by standing with their feet a good distance apart, and in O'Neil's case by walking around as much as possible. Condensation from the fog cluttered up the bridge windows. The young officer flipped on the wipers. Back out on the bridge wing, he stared out into the fog. He didn't like traveling without radar. O'Neil listened, but heard nothing more than the muted rumblings of *Panache*'s own engines. Fog did

41

that. Like a wet shroud, it took away your vision and absorbed sound. He listened for another minute, but in addition to the diesels, there was only the whisper of the cutter's hull passing through the water. He looked aft just before going back into the wheelhouse. The cutter's white paint job would help her disappear from view.

"No foghorns out there. Sun's burning through," he announced. The captain nodded.

"Less than an hour until it's gone. Gonna be a warm one. Weather forecast in yet?"

"Storms tonight, sir. The line that went through Dallas around midnight. Did some damage. Couple of tornadoes clobbered a trailer park."

Wegener shook his head. "You know, there must be something about trailers that attract the damned things. . . . " He stood and walked to the radar. "Ready, Chief?"

"Yes, sir."

Wegener flipped the set from standby to active, then bent his eyes down to the top of the rubber hood. "You called it close, Chief. Contact bearing one-six-zero, range six thousand. Mr. O'Neil, come right to one-eight-five. Oreza, give me a time to come left up behind him."

"Aye, Cap'n. Take a minute."

Wegener flipped the radar off and stood back up. "Battle stations."

As planned, the alarm got people moving after everyone had had a chance to eat breakfast. The word was already out, of course. There was a possible druggie out in the fog. The duty boat section assembled at the rubber Zodiac. Everyone had a weapon of some sort: one M-16 automatic rifle, one riot shotgun, and the rest Beretta 9mm automatics. Forward, a crew manned the 40mm gun on the bow. It was a Swedish-designed Bofors that had once sat on a Navy destroyer and was older than anyone aboard except the captain. Just aft of the bridge, a sailor pulled the plastic cover off an M-2 .50-caliber machine gun that was almost as old.

"Recommend we come left now, sir," Chief Oreza said.

The captain flipped the radar on again. "Come left to zero-seven-zero. Range to target is now three-five-zero-zero. We'll want to approach from the target's port side."

The fog was thinning out. Visibility was now at about five hundred yards, a little more or a little less as the mist became visibly patchy. Chief Oreza got on the radar as the bridge filled up with the normal battle watch. There was a new target twenty miles out, probably a tanker inbound for Galveston. Its position was plotted as a matter of course.

"Range to our friend is now two thousand yards. Bearing constant at zero-seven-zero. Target course and speed are unchanged."

"Very well. Should have him visual in about five minutes." Wegener looked around the wheelhouse. His officers were using their binoculars. It was a waste of energy, but they didn't know that yet. He walked out on the starboard bridge wing and looked aft to the boat station. Lieutenant Wilcox gave him a thumbs-up gesture. Behind him, Chief Boatswain's Mate Riley nodded agreement. An experienced petty officer was at the winch controls. Launching the Zodiac into these sea conditions was no big deal, but the sea had a way of surprising you. The .50-caliber was pointed safely skyward, a box of ammo hanging on its left side. Forward he heard the metallic clash as a round was racked into the 40mm cannon.

Used to be we pulled alongside to render assistance. Now we load up, Wegener thought. *Goddamned drugs . . .*

"I see him," a lookout said.

Wegener looked forward. The white-painted yacht was hard to pick out within the fog, but a moment later the squared-off transom stern was clearly visible. Now he used his glasses to read the name. *Empire Builder*. That was the one. No flag at the staff, but that wasn't unusual. He couldn't see any people yet, and the yacht was motoring along as before. That was why he'd approached from dead astern. For as long as men had gone to sea, he thought, no lookout ever bothered looking aft.

"He's in for a surprise," O'Neil thought, coming out to join the captain. "The Law of the Sea."

Wegener was annoyed for a moment, but shook it off. "Radar isn't turning. Of course,

44

maybe he broke it."

"Here's the picture of the owner, sir."

The captain hadn't looked at it before. The owner was in his middle forties. Evidently he'd married late, because he reportedly had two children aboard, ages eight and thirteen, in addition to his wife. Big man, six-three or so, bald and overweight, standing on some dock or other next to a fair-sized swordfish. *He must have had to work hard for that one*, Wegener thought, judging by the sunburn around the eyes and below the shorts. . . . The captain brought the glasses back up.

"You're coming in too close," he observed. "Bear off to port, Mister."

"Aye aye, sir." O'Neil went back into the wheelhouse.

Idiots, Wegener thought. *You ought to have heard us by now.* Well, they had a way to make sure of that. He poked his head into the wheelhouse: "Wake 'em up!"

Halfway up *Panache*'s mast was a siren of the sort used on police cars and ambulances, but quite a bit larger. A moment later its whooping sound nearly made the captain jump. It did have the expected effect. Before Wegener had counted to three a head appeared out of the yacht's wheelhouse. It wasn't the owner. The yacht began a hard right turn.

"You jackass!" the captain growled. "Close up tight!" he ordered next.

The cutter turned to the right, as well. The

45

yacht settled a bit at the stern as more power was applied, but the Rhodes didn't have a prayer of outrunning *Panache*. In another two minutes the cutter was abeam of the yacht, which was still trying to turn. They were too close to use the Bofors. Wegener ordered the machine gun to fire across the *Empire Builder*'s bow.

The .50-caliber crackled and thundered for a five-round burst. Even if they hadn't seen the splashes, the noise was unmistakable. Wegener went inside to get the microphone for his ship's loudhailer.

"This is the United States Coast Guard. Heave to immediately and prepare to be boarded!"

You could almost see the indecision. The yacht came back left, but the speed didn't change for a minute or two. Next a man appeared at the stern and ran up a flag — the Panamanian flag, Wegener saw with amusement. Next the radio would say that he didn't have authority to board. His amusement stopped short of that point.

"*Empire Builder*, this is the U.S. Coast Guard. You are a U.S.-flag ship, and we are going to board you. Heave to — *now!*"

And she did. The yacht's stern rose as engine power dropped off. The cutter had to back down hard to avoid surging past the Rhodes. Wegener went back outside and waved at the boat crew. When he had their attention, he mimicked pulling back the slide on an automatic pistol. That was his way of telling the crew to be careful. Riley patted his holster twice to let the captain

46

know that the boat crew wasn't stupid. The Zodiac was launched. The next call on the loud-hailer told the yacht's crew to get into the open. Two people came out. Again, neither looked like the owner. The cutter's machine gun was trained on them as steadily as the rolling allowed. This was the tense part. The only way *Panache* could protect the boat crew was to fire first, but that was something they couldn't do. The Coast Guard hadn't lost anyone that way yet, but it was only a matter of time, and waiting for it only made it worse.

Wegener kept his glasses fixed on the two men while the Zodiac motored across. A lieutenant did the same next to the machine gun. Though no obvious weapons were visible, a pistol wasn't that hard to hide under a loose shirt. Someone would have to be crazy to fight it out under these conditions, but the captain knew that the world was full of crazy people — he'd spent thirty years rescuing them. Now he arrested them, the ones whose craziness was more malignant than simple stupidity.

O'Neil came to his side again. *Panache* was dead in the water, with her engines turning at idle, and with the seas now on the beam she took on a heavier but slower roll. Wegener looked aft to the machine gun again. The sailor had it aimed in about the right direction, but his thumbs were well off the firing switch, just the way they were supposed to be. He could hear the five empty cases rolling around on the deck. Wegener frowned for a moment. The empties were a safety hazard. He'd have someone rig a bag to catch them. The kid on the gun might stumble on one and shoot by mistake. . . .

He turned back. The Zodiac was at the yacht's stern. Good. They were going aboard there. He watched Lieutenant Wilcox go aboard first, then wait for the rest. The coxswain pulled back when the last was aboard, then scooted forward to cover their advance. Wilcox went forward on the portside, with Obrecki backing him up, the shotgun pointed safely at the sky. Riley went inside with his backup. The lieutenant got to the two men in under a minute. It was odd to see them talking, but not to hear what they were saying. . . .

Somebody said something. Wilcox's head turned quickly one way, then back the other. Obrecki stepped to the side and brought the shotgun down. Both men went down on their faces, dropping from view.

"Looks like a bust, sir," Ensign O'Neil noted. Wegener took one step into the wheelhouse.

"Radio!" A crewman tossed him a Motorola portable. Wegener listened but didn't make a call. Whatever his people had just found, he didn't want to distract them. Obrecki stayed with the two men while Wilcox went inside the yacht. Riley had sure as hell found something. The shotgun was definitely aimed at them, and the tension in the boy's arms radiated across the water to the cutter. The captain turned to the machine-

48

gunner, whose weapon was still aimed at the yacht.

"Safe that gun!"

"Aye!" the sailor answered at once, and dropped his hands to point it at the sky. The officer next to him winced with embarrassment. Another lesson learned. A few words would accompany it in an hour or two. This had been a mistake with a gun.

Wilcox reappeared a moment later, with Chief Riley behind him. The bosun handed over two pairs of handcuffs to the officer, who bent down to work them. They had to be the only two aboard; Riley holstered his pistol a moment later, and Obrecki's shotgun went up to the sky again. Wegener thought he saw the youngster reset the safety. The farm boy knew his guns, all right, had learned to shoot the same way his skipper had. Why had he taken the safety off . . . ? The radio crackled just as Wegener's mind asked the question.

"Captain, this is Wilcox." The lieutenant stood to speak, and both men faced each other, a hundred yards apart.

"I'm here."

"It's a bad one, sir . . . sir, there's blood all over the place. One of 'em was scrubbing the salon down, but — it's a real mess here, sir."

"Just the two of them?"

"Affirmative. Only two people aboard. We've cuffed 'em both."

"Check again," Wegener ordered. Wilcox read

the captain's mind: he stayed with the prisoners and let Chief Riley do the search. The bosun appeared three minutes later, shaking his head. His face looked pale through the binoculars, Wegener saw. What would make Bob Riley go pale?

"Just these two, sir. No ID on them. I don't think we want to do much of a search, I think — "

"Correct. I'll send you another man and leave you Obrecki. Can you get the yacht to port?"

"Sure, Captain. We got plenty of fuel."

"There's going to be a little blow tonight," Wegener warned.

"I checked the weather this morning. No sweat, sir."

"Okay, let me call this one in and get things organized. Stand by."

"Roger that. Sir, I recommend that you send the TV camera across for a permanent record to back up the stills."

"Okay, it'll be over in a few minutes."

It took half an hour for the Coast Guard base to get the FBI and DEA agreed on things. While they waited for word, the Zodiac took another crewman over with a portable TV camera and tape recorder. One of the boarding party shot off sixty frames with a Polaroid camera, while the TV recorded everything on half-inch tape. The Coast Guardsmen restarted *Empire Builder*'s engines and headed northwest for Mobile, with the cutter holding station on her portside. It was finally decided that Wilcox and Obrecki could take the yacht back to Mobile, and that a helicopter would pick up the two "yachtsmen" that afternoon — weather permitting. It was a long way to the helicopter base. *Panache* was supposed to have her own helicopter, but the Coast Guard didn't have the funding to buy enough. A third seaman was landed on the yacht, and it was time to bring the prisoners back to *Panache*.

Chief Riley took the prisoners aft. Wegener watched the bosun fairly throw them into the Zodiac. Five minutes later it was hoisted aboard. The yacht headed northwest, and the cutter turned away to continue her patrol. The first man from the boarding party to reach the bridge was the seaman who'd worked the Polaroid. He handed over half a dozen of the color frames.

"The chief collected some stuff for you to look at, Cap'n. It's worse'n it looks here. Wait till you see the TV tape. It's already set up for copying."

Wegener handed the photos back. "Okay — it all goes into the evidence locker. You join up with the others. Have Myers set up a new tape in the VCR, and I want you all to tell the camera what you saw. You know how it goes. Let's make sure we get it all right."

"Yes, sir!"

Riley appeared a minute later. Robert Timothy Riley was a man in the traditional pattern of the chief boatswain's mate. Six-two and over two hundred pounds, he had the hairy arms of a gorilla, the gut of a man who knew his way

51

around a beer can, and the rumbling voice to outscream a winter gale. His oversized right hand grasped a couple of plastic food bags. His face showed that anger was now replacing the shock.

"It's a fuckin' slaughterhouse, sir. Like somebody exploded a couple cans of brown paint — 'cept it ain't paint. Jesus." One bag came up. "The little one was cleaning up when we pulled 'em over. There's a trash can in the saloon with maybe a half dozen cartridge cases. I pulled these two off the rug — just like they taught us, Cap'n. Picked 'em up with my ball-point and shuffled 'em into the baggie. Two guns I left aboard. I bagged them, too. That ain't the worst of it."

The next baggie contained a small, framed photograph. It had to be the yacht's owner and his family. The baggie after that contained a . . .

"Found it under a table. Rape, too. She must've been havin' her period, but they didn't let that stop 'em. Maybe just the wife. Maybe the little girl, too. In the galley there's some butcher knives, all bloodied up. I figure they carved the bodies up and tossed 'em over the side. These four people are shark-shit now."

"Drugs?"

"Twenty or so keys of white powder stowed in the crew's quarters. Some marijuana, too, but that just looks like a personal stash." Riley shrugged. "I didn't even bother using the test kit, sir. Don't matter. This is straight piracy-and-murder. I saw one bullet hole in the deck, a through-and-through. Red, I ain't seen nothing

52

like this in my whole life. Like something in a movie, but worse." He let out a long breath. "You have to have been there, sir."

"What do we know about the prisoners?"

"Nothing. They ain't done nothing more'n grunt, leastways not when I was around. No ID on them, and I didn't want to go messing around things looking for passports an' stuff. Figured I'd leave that for the real cops. The wheelhouse is clean. So's one of the heads. Mr. Wilcox won't have much trouble taking her back, and I heard him tell Obrecki and Brown not to touch anything. Plenty of fuel aboard, he can run her at full speed. He'll have her in Mobile 'fore midnight if the weather holds off. Nice boat." Another shrug.

"Bring 'em up here," Wegener said after a moment.

"Aye aye." Riley went aft.

Wegener filled his pipe, then had to remember where he'd left his matches. The world had changed while he'd been off doing other things, and Wegener didn't like it. It was dangerous enough out here. Wind and wave were as deadly an enemy as man needed. The sea was always waiting for her chance. It didn't matter how good you thought you were; you only had to forget once, just once, that you could never trust her. Wegener was a man who never forgot, and devoted his life to protecting those who had. Remembering that one hazard, and protecting those who forgot, had given him a full and satisfying life. He liked being the guardian angel in the snow-white boat. You were never lost if Red Wegener was around. You always had a chance, a good chance, that he could reach into the wet, stormy grave and pull you out with his bare hands . . . but sharks were feasting on four people now. Wegener loved the sea for all her moods, but sharks were something to loathe, and the thought that they were now eating people that he might have saved . . . four people who'd forgotten that not all sharks live in the sea, Wegener told himself. That's what had changed. Piracy. He shook his head. That's what you called it on the water. Piracy. Something that Errol Flynn had made movies about in Wegener's boyhood. Something that had ended two centuries earlier. Piracy and murder, the part that the movies had usually left out. Piracy and murder and rape, each of them a capital offense in the old days. . . .

"Stand up straight!" Riley snarled. He had both by the arm. Both were still cuffed, and Riley's hands kept them from straying. Chief Oreza had come along to keep an eye on things.

Both were in their mid-twenties, both were thin. One was tall, about six feet, and arrogant, which struck the captain as odd. He had to know the trouble he was in, didn't he? His dark eyes burned at Wegener, who regarded the younger man dispassionately from behind his pipe. There was something odd about his eyes, but Wegener didn't know what it was.

"What's your name?" the captain asked. There was no reply. "You have to tell me your name," Wegener pointed out quietly.

Then something very unusual happened. The tall one spat on Wegener's shirt. There was a strangely long fragment of time in which the captain refused to believe what had happened, his face not even showing surprise. Riley was the first to react to the blasphemy.

"You son of a bitch!" The bosun lifted the prisoner up like a rag doll, spinning him in the air and smashing him down on the bridge rail. The young man landed on his belt, and for a second it seemed that he'd break in half. The air whooshed out of his mouth, and his legs kicked, trying to find the deck before he dropped into the water.

"Christ, Bob!" Wegener managed to say as Riley picked him back up. The bosun spun him around, his left hand clamped on the man's throat as he lifted him clear of the deck with one arm. "Put him down, Riley!"

If nothing else, Riley had broken through the arrogance. For a moment there was genuine fear in those eyes as the prisoner fought for breath. Oreza had the other one on the deck already. Riley dropped his man beside him. The pirate — Wegener was already thinking of him in those terms — pitched forward until his forehead touched the deck. He gagged and struggled for breath while Chief Riley, just as pale, rediscovered his self-control.

"Sorry, Captain. Guess I just lost it for a sec-

55

ond." The bosun made it clear that he was apologizing only for embarrassing his commanding officer.

"Brig," Wegener said. Riley led both aft.

"Damn." Oreza observed quietly. The quartermaster fished out his handkerchief and wiped his captain's shirt. "Jesus, Red, what's the world comin' to?"

"I don't know, Portagee. I think we're both too old to answer that one." Wegener finally found his matches and managed to light his pipe. He stared out at the sea for several seconds before finding the right words. "When I joined up I got broke in by an old chief who told stories about Prohibition. Nothing nasty like this — he made it all sound like a great big game."

"Maybe people were more civilized back then," Oreza thought.

"More likely you couldn't carry a million bucks' worth of booze on a motorboat. Didn't you ever watch 'The Untouchables'? The gang wars they had back then were as nasty as the ones we read about now. Maybe worse. Hell, I don't know. I didn't join up to be a cop, Chief."

"Me neither, Cap'n." Oreza grunted. "We went an' got old, and the world went an' changed on us. One thing I wish didn't change, though."

"What's that, Portagee?"

The master chief quartermaster turned to look at his commanding officer. "Something I picked up at New London a few years back. I used to sit in on some classes when I had nothing better to

56

do. In the old days when they caught a couple of pirates, they had the option of doing a court-martial on the spot and settlin' things right then an' there — and you know something? It worked." Oreza grunted again. "I s'pose that's why they stopped doin' it that way."

"Give 'em a fair trial — then hang 'em?"

"Hell, why not, sir?"

"That's not the way we do things anymore. We're civilized now."

"Yeah, civilized." Oreza opened the door to the wheelhouse. "I can tell. I seen the pictures."

Wegener smiled, then wondered why. His pipe had gone out. He wondered why he didn't just quit entirely as he fished for his matches again, but the pipe was part of the image. The old man of the sea. He'd gotten old, all right, Wegener thought. A puff of wind caught the match as he tried to toss it, dropping it on the deck. How did you ever forget to check the wind? he asked himself as he bent down to retrieve it.

There was a pack of cigarettes there, halfway out the scupper. Wegener was a fanatic on ship-cleanliness and was ready to snarl at whoever had tossed the empty pack when he realized that it hadn't come from one of his crewmen. The name on the pack was "Calvert," and that, he remembered vaguely, was a Latin American brand-name from a U.S. tobacco company. It was a hard pack, with a flip-top, and out of simple curiosity he opened it.

They weren't cigarettes. At least, they weren't

57

tobacco cigarettes. Wegener fished one out. They weren't hand-rolled, but neither were they as neatly manufactured as something from a real American cancer factory. The captain smiled in spite of himself. Some clever entrepreneur had come up with a cute way of disguising — joints, wasn't it? — as real cigarettes. Or maybe it was just more convenient to carry them this way. It must have pitched out of his shirt when Riley flipped him around, Wegener realized belatedly. He closed the pack and pocketed it. He'd turn it over to the evidence locker when he got a chance. Oreza returned.

"Weather update. That squall line'll be here no later'n twenty-one hundred. The squalls are upgraded some. We can expect gusts up to forty knots. Gonna be a fair blow, sir."

"Any problem for Wilcox and the yacht?" There was still time to recall him.

"Shouldn't be, sir. It turned south. A high-pressure system is heading down from Tennessee. Mr. Wilcox oughta have it pretty smooth all the way in, Cap'n, but it might be a little dicey for the helicopter. They didn't plan to get it to us until eighteen hundred, and that's cutting it a little close. They'll be bucking the front edge of the line on the way back."

"What about tomorrow?"

"Supposed to clear off about dawn, then the high-pressure system takes over. We're in for some rollin' tonight, but then we got four days of good weather." Oreza didn't actually voice his

58

recommendation. He didn't have to. The two old pros communicated with glances.

Wegener nodded agreement. "Advise Mobile to put the pickup off until noon tomorrow."

"Aye aye, Cap'n. No sense risking a helicopter to haul garbage."

"Right on that, Portagee. Make sure Wilcox gets the word on the weather in case that system changes course." Wegener checked his watch. "Time for me to get my paperwork done."

"Pretty full day already, Red."

"True enough."

Wegener's stateroom was the largest aboard, of course, and the only private accommodation aboard, since privacy and loneliness were the traditional luxuries accorded a skipper. But *Panache* wasn't a cruiser, and Wegener's room was barely over a hundred square feet, albeit with a private head, which on any ship was something worth fighting for. Throughout his Coast Guard career, paperwork was something Wegener had avoided whenever possible. He had an executive officer, a bright young lieutenant whom the captain stuck with as much of it as his conscience could justify. That left him with two or three hours' worth per day. The captain attacked it with the enthusiasm of a man on his way to a hanging. Half an hour later he realized that it seemed harder than usual. The murders were pulling at his consciousness. Murder at sea, he thought, as he looked at the porthole on the

59

starboard bulkhead. It wasn't unknown, of course. He'd heard of a few during his thirty years, though he'd never been directly involved. There had been a case off the Oregon coast when a crewman had gone berserk and nearly killed a mate — turned out that the poor guy had developed a brain tumor and he'd later died from it, Red remembered. *Point Gabriel* had gone out and collected the man, already hog-tied and sedated. That was the extent of Wegener's experience with violence at sea. At least the man-made kind. The sea was dangerous enough without the need for that sort of thing. The thought came back to him like the recurring theme of a song. He tried to get back to his work, but failed.

Wegener frowned at his own indecision. Whether he liked paperwork or not, it was part of the job. He relit the pipe in the hope that it would aid his concentration. That didn't work either. The captain muttered a curse at himself, partly in amusement, partly in annoyance, as he walked into his head for a drink of water. The paperwork still beckoned. He looked at himself in the mirror and realized that he needed a shave. And the paperwork wasn't getting done.

"You're getting old, Red," he told the face in the mirror. "Old and senile."

He decided that he had to shave. He did it in the old-fashioned way, with a shaving cup and brush, the disposable razor his only concession to modernity. He had his face lathered and halfway shaved when someone knocked at the door.

"Come!" It opened to reveal Chief Riley.

"Sorry, Cap'n, didn't know you were — "

"No problem, Bob, what's up?"

"Sir, I got the first-draft of the boarding report. Figured you'd want to go over it. We got everyone's statement on tape, audio, and TV. Myers made a copy of the tape from the boarding. The original's in with the evidence, in a lockbox inside the classified-materials safe, as per orders. I got the copy if you wanna see it."

"Okay, just leave it. Anything from our guests?"

"No, sir. Turned into a pretty day outside."

"And me stuck with all this damned paper."

"A chief may work from sun to sun, but the skipper's work is never done," Riley observed.

"You're not supposed to pick on your commanding officer, Master Chief." Wegener managed to stop himself from laughing only because he still had the razor to his throat.

"I humbly beg the captain's pardon. And, by your leave, sir, I also have work to do."

"The kid we had on the fifty-cal this morning was part of the deck division. He needs a talk about safety. He was slow taking his gun off the yacht this morning. Don't tear his head all the way off," Wegener said as he finished shaving. "I'll talk to Mr. Peterson myself."

"We sure don't need people fucking around with those things. I'll talk with the lad, sir, right after I do my walk-around."

"I'm going to do one after lunch — we have some weather coming in tonight."

"Portagee told me. We'll have everything lashed down tight."

"See you later, Bob."

"Aye." Riley withdrew.

Wegener stowed his shaving gear and went back to his desk. The preliminary draft of the boarding and arrest report was on the top of his pile. The full version was being typed now, but he always liked to see the first version. It was generally the most accurate. Wegener scanned it as he sipped at some cold coffee. The Polaroid shots were tucked into pockets on a plastic page. They hadn't gotten any better. Neither had the paperwork. He decided to slip the videotape into his personal VCR and view it before lunch.

The quality of the tape was several steps down from anything that could be called professional. Holding the camera still on a rolling yacht was nearly impossible, and there hadn't been enough light for decent picture quality. For all that, it was disturbing. The sound caught snippets of conversations, and the screen occasionally flared when the Polaroid's flash went off.

It was plain that four people had died aboard *Empire Builder,* and all they had left behind were bloodstains. It didn't seem very much of a legacy, but imagination supplied the rest. The bunk in what had probably been the son's cabin was sodden with blood — a lot of it — at the top end of the bed. Head shot. Three other sets of bloodstains decorated the main salon. It was the part of the yacht with the most space, the place where the entertainment had gone on. *Entertainment,* Wegener thought. Three sets of bloodstains. Two close together, one distant. The man had an attractive wife, and a daughter of thirteen . . . they'd made him watch, hadn't they?

"Jesus," Wegener breathed. That had to be it, didn't it? *They made him watch, and then they killed them all . . . carved up the bodies and tossed them over the side.*

"Bastards."

2.

Creatures of the Night

The name on this passport said J.T. Williams, but he had quite a few passports. His current cover was as a representative for an American pharmaceuticals firm, and he could give a lengthy discourse on various synthetic antibiotics. He could similarly discuss the ins and outs of the heavy-equipment business as a special field representative for Caterpillar Tractor, and had two other "legends" that he could switch in and out of as easily as he changed his clothes. His name was not Williams. He was known in CIA's Operations Directorate as Clark, but his name wasn't Clark either, even though that was the name under which he lived and raised his family. Mainly he was an instructor at CIA's school for field officers, known as "The Farm," but he was an instructor because he was pretty good at what he did, and for the same reason he often returned to the field.

Clark was a solidly built man, over six feet tall, with a full head of black hair and a lantern jaw that hinted at his ancestry, along with the blue eyes that twinkled when he wanted them to, and burned when he did not. Though well over forty, Clark did not have the usual waistline flab that went along with a desk job, and his shoulders spoke volumes about his exercise program. For all that, in an age of attention to physical fitness he was unremarkable enough, save for one distinguishing mark. On his forearm was the tattoo of a grinning red seal. He ought to have had it removed, but sentiment did not allow it. The seal was part of the heritage he'd once chosen for himself. When asked about it during a flight, he'd reply, honestly, that he'd once been in the Navy, then go on to lie about how the Navy had financed his college education in pharmaceuticals, mechanical engineering, or some other field. Clark actually had no college or graduate degree, though he'd accumulated enough special knowledge along the way to qualify for a half dozen of them. The lack of a degree would have — should have — disqualified him for the position which he held in the Agency, but Clark had a skill that is curiously rare in most of the Western intelligence agencies. The need for it was also rare, but the need *was* occasionally real, and a senior CIA official had once recognized that someone like Clark was useful to have on the payroll. That he'd blossomed into a very effective field officer — mainly for special, short, dangerous jobs — was all the better for the Agency. Clark was something of a legend, though only a handful of people at Langley knew why. There was only one Mr. Clark.

"What brings you to our country, Señor Williams?" the immigration official asked.

"Business. And I'm hoping to do a little fishing before I go home," Clark replied in Spanish. He was fluent in six languages, and could pass for a native with three of them.

"Your Spanish is excellent."

"Thank you. I grew up in Costa Rica," Clark lied. He was particularly good at that, too. "My father worked there for years."

"Yes, I can tell. Welcome to Colombia."

Clark went off to collect his bags. The air was thin here, he noted. His daily jogging helped him with that, but he reminded himself to wait a few days before he tried anything really strenuous. It was his first time in this country, but something told him that it wouldn't be the last. All the big ones started with reconnaissance. That was his current mission. Exactly what he was supposed to recon told him what the real mission would probably be. He'd done such things before, Clark told himself. In fact, one such mission was the reason that CIA had picked him up, changed his name, and given him the life that he'd led for nearly twenty years.

One of the singular things about Colombia was

that the country actually allowed people to bring firearms in with very little in the way of hassle. Clark had not bothered this time. He wondered if the next time might be a little different. He knew that he couldn't work through the chief of station for that. After all, the chief of station didn't even know that he was here. Clark wondered why, but shrugged it off. That didn't concern him. The mission did.

The United States Army had reinstituted the idea of the Infantry Division (Light) only a few years before. The units had not been all that hard to make. It was simply a matter of selecting an Infantry Division (Mechanized) and removing all of its (Mechanized) equipment. What then remained behind was an organization of roughly 10,500 people whose TOE (Table of Organization and Equipment) was even lighter than that of an airborne division, traditionally the lightest of them all, and therefore able to be air-transported by a *mere* five hundred flights of the Air Force's Military Airlift Command. But the light infantry divisions, or "LIDs" as they came to be known, were not as useless as the casual observer might imagine, however. Far from it.

In creating the "light-fighters," the Army had decided to return to the timeless basics of history. Any thinking warrior will testify that there are two kinds of fighters: the infantry, and those who in one way or another support the infantry. More than anything else, the LIDs were post-graduate institutions for advanced infantry skills. Here was where the Army grew its sergeants the old-fashioned way. In recognizing this, the Army had carefully assigned some of its best officers to command them. The colonels commanding the brigades, and the generals commanding the divisions, were veterans of Vietnam whose memories of that bitter conflict included admiration for their enemies — most especially the way in which the Viet Cong and NVA had converted their lack of equipment and firepower into an asset. There was no reason, the Army's thinkers decided, that American soldiers should not have the same degree of skill in fieldcraft that Vo Nguyen Giap's soldiers had developed; better still that those skills should be mated to America's traditional fascination with equipment and firepower. What had resulted were four elite divisions, the 7th in the green hills of Fort Ord, California, the 10th Mountain at Fort Drum, New York, the 25th at Schofield Barracks, Hawaii, and the 6th at Fort Wainwright, Alaska. Perversely, each had problems holding on to its sergeants and company-grade officers, but that was part of the overall plan. Light-fighters live a strenuous life, and on reaching thirty even the best of them would think longingly of being able to ride to battle in a helicopter or an armored personnel carrier, and maybe being able to spend a reasonable amount of time with their young wives and children instead of climbing hills. Thus the best of them, the ones that stayed and completed the difficult

NCO schools that each division ran, having learned that sergeants must occasionally act without their lieutenants' direction, then joined the heavy formations that comprised the rest of the Army, bringing with them skills that they'd never quite forget. The LIDs were, in short, factory institutions, where the Army built sergeants with exceptional leadership ability and mastery of the unchanging truths of warfare — it always came down to a few people with muddy boots and smelly uniforms who could use the land and the night as allies to visit death on their fellow-men.

Staff Sergeant Domingo Chavez was one of these. Known as "Ding" by his squad, he was twenty-six. Already a nine-year veteran, he'd begun as a gang kid in Los Angeles whose basic common sense had overcome his ineffectual education — he'd decided that there was no future in the *Bandidos* when a close friend had died in a drive-by shooting whose purpose he'd never quite figured out. The following Monday morning he'd taken the bus to the nearest Army Recruiting Office after the Marines had turned him down. Despite his near illiteracy, the recruiting sergeant had signed him up in a moment — his quota had been short, and the kid had expressed a willingness to go infantry, thus fulfilling two blank spots on the sergeant's monthly reporting sheet. Most of all, the youngster wanted to go right in. It could not have been better for the recruiter.

Chavez hadn't had many ideas what military service would be like, and most of those had turned out to be wrong. After losing his hair and a rat-faced beard, he'd learned that toughness is worthless without discipline, and that the Army doesn't tolerate insolence. That lesson had come behind a white-painted barracks at the hands of a drill sergeant whose face was as black as a jungle night. But Chavez's life had never known an easy lesson; as a result he hadn't learned to resent the hard ones. Having discovered that the Army was also a hierarchy with strict hierarchical rules, he stayed within them and gradually turned into an above-average recruit. Former gang kid that he was, he'd already known about camaraderie and teamwork, and redirecting these traits into positive directions had come easily enough. By the time basic training had ended, his small frame was as lean and taut as a steel cable, his physical appearance was something in which he took inordinate pride, and he was already well on his way to mastering every weapon that an infantryman can carry. Where else, he asked himself once a day, do they give you a machine gun and pay you to shoot it?

But soldiers are grown, not born. Chavez's first posting was to Korea, where he learned about hills, and just how deadly enemy gangs could be, since duty on the DMZ has never been anything that one might call safe. Discipline, he learned there once and for all, had a real purpose. It kept you alive. A small team of North Korean

70

infiltrators had picked a rainy night to go through his unit's piece of the line for purposes known only to their commanders. On the way they'd stumbled on an unmarked listening post whose two American occupants had decided to sleep through the night, and never awoke. ROK units had later intercepted and killed the invaders, but Chavez was the one who'd discovered the men from his own platoon, throats cut in the same way he'd seen in his own neighborhood. Soldiering, he'd decided then and there, was a serious business, and one which he wanted to master. The platoon sergeant noticed first, then the lieutenant. Chavez paid attention to lectures, even trying to take notes. On realizing his inability to read and write beyond things he'd carefully memorized in advance, the platoon leader had gotten the young PFC help. Working hard on his own time, before the end of the year Chavez had passed a high-school equivalency test — on his first try! he told everyone who would listen that night — and made Specialist Fourth Class, which earned him an extra $58.50 per month. His lieutenant didn't fully understand, though the platoon sergeant did, that Domingo Chavez had been forever changed by that combination of events. Though he'd always had the Latino's deep pride, part of the eighteen-year-old soldier now understood that he had truly done something to be proud about. For this he deemed himself to be in the Army's debt, and with the deep sense of personal honor which was also part of his cultural heritage, it was a debt that he would forever after work to repay.

Some things never left. He cultivated physical toughness. Part of that came from his small size — just five-eight — but he also came to understand that the real world was not a football field: the tough ones who made the long haul were most often the compact, lean fighters. Chavez came to love running, and enjoyed a good sweat. Because of this, assignment to the 7th Infantry Division (Light) was almost inevitable. Though based at Fort Ord, near Monterey on the California coast, the 7th trains farther down the coast at Hunter-Liggett Military Reservation, once the sprawling rancho of the Hearst family. A place of magnificent green hills in the moist winters, Hunter-Liggett becomes a blistering moonscape in the California summer, a place of steep, topless hills, gnarled, shapeless trees, and grass that crumbles to dust under one's boots. For Chavez it was home. He arrived as a brand-new buck sergeant E-5, and was immediately sent to the division's two-week Combat Leaders Course, a prep school for squad sergeants that also paved the way for his entry into Ranger School at Fort Benning, Georgia. On his return from that most rigorous of Army training courses, Chavez was leaner and more confident than ever. His return to Fort Ord coincided with the arrival of a new "cohort" of recruits for his battalion. Ding Chavez was assigned to command a squad of slick-sleeved privates fresh from Advanced Infantry

Training. It was the first payback time for the young sergeant. The Army had invested considerable time and training in him, and now it was time for him to pass it along to nine raw recruits — and also time for the Army to see if Chavez had the stuff that leaders are made of. He took command of his squad as a stepfather of a large and unruly family faces his newly acquired children. He wanted them to turn out properly because they were his, and because they were his, he was damned sure going to see that they did.

At Fort Ord, he'd also learned the real art of soldiering, for infantry tactics are precisely that for the light-fighters — an art form. Assigned to Bravo Company, 3rd Battalion of the 17th Infantry Regiment, whose somewhat ambitious motto was "Ninja! We Own the Night!" Chavez went into the field with his face coated in camouflage paint — in the 7th LID even the helicopter pilots wear camouflage paint — and learned his profession in full even while he taught his men. Most of all, he came to love the night. Chavez learned to move himself and his squad through cover as quietly as a whispering breeze. The objective of such missions was generally the same. Unable to match a heavy formation force-on-force, Chavez trained to do the close, nasty work that has always characterized light infantrymen: raids and ambushes, infiltration and intelligence gathering. Stealth was their means, and surprise was their tool, to appear where least expected, to strike with close-quarter ferocity, then to escape into the darkness before the other side could react. Such things had been tried on Americans once, and it was only fair that Americans should learn to return the favor. All in all, SSG Domingo Chavez was a man whom the Apaches or the Viet Cong would have recognized as one of their own — or one of their most dangerous enemies.

"Hey, Ding!" the platoon sergeant called. "The ell-tee wants you."

It had been a long one at Hunter-Liggett, ending at the dawn now two hours old. The exercise had lasted nearly nine days, and even Chavez was feeling it. He wasn't seventeen anymore, his legs were telling him with some amusement. At least it was his last such job with the Ninjas. He was rotating out, and his next assignment was to be a drill sergeant with the Army's basic-training school at Fort Benning, Georgia. Chavez was immensely proud of that. The Army thought enough of him that he would now be an example to young recruits. The sergeant got to his feet, but before walking over to where the lieutenant was, he reached into his pocket and took out a throwing star. Ever since the colonel had taken to calling his men Ninjas, the nasty little steel projectiles had become *de rigueur* to the men — somewhat to the concern of the powers-that-were. But there was always a little slack cut for the good ones, and Chavez was one of these. He flipped the star with a deceptively powerful flick of the wrist and buried it an inch deep in a tree fifteen feet away. He collected it on the way to see the boss.

"Yes, sir!" Chavez said, standing at attention.

"At ease, Sergeant," Lieutenant Jackson said. He was sitting against a tree to take the strain off his blistered feet. A West Point graduate and only twenty-three, he was learning how hard it could be to keep up with the soldiers he was supposed to lead. "Got a call. They need you back at headquarters. Something to do with the paperwork on your transfer. You can go in on a resupply flight out of battalion trains. The chopper'll be down there in an hour. Nice work last night, by the way. I'm going to be sorry to lose you, Ding."

"Thank you, sir." Jackson wasn't bad for a young officer, Chavez thought. Green, of course, but he tried pretty hard and learned fast. He saluted the younger man snappily.

"You take care of yourself, Sergeant." Jackson rose to return it properly.

"We own the night, sir!" Chavez replied in the manner of the Ninjas, 3rd Battalion, 17th Infantry. Twenty-five minutes later he climbed aboard a Sikorsky UH-60A Blackhawk helicopter for the fifty-minute ride back to Ord. The battalion sergeant-major handed him a message as he got aboard. Chavez had an hour to get cleaned up before appearing at the divisional G-1 or personnel office. It took a long shower to erase the salt and "war paint," but he managed to arrive early in his best set of BDU camouflage fatigues.

"Hey, Ding," said another staff sergeant, who was working in G-1 while his broken leg healed. "The man's waiting for you in the conference room, end of the hall on the second floor."

"What's it all about, Charlie?"

"Damned if I know. Some colonel asked to see you is all."

"Damn — I need a haircut, too," Chavez muttered as he trotted up the wooden stairs. His boots could have used a little more work also. Hell of a way to appear before some friggin' colonel, but then Chavez was entitled to a little more warning than he'd been given. That was one of the nice things about the Army, the sergeant thought. The rules applied to everyone. He knocked on the proper door, too tired to be worried. He wouldn't be around much longer, after all. His orders for Fort Benning were already cut, and he was wondering what the loose womenfolk in Georgia were like. He'd just broken up with a steady girlfriend. Maybe the more stable life-style that went with a drill sergeant would allow him to —

"Come!" a voice boomed in reply to his knock.

The colonel was sitting behind a cheap wooden desk. He was dressed in a black sweater over a lime-green shirt, and had a name tag that said SMITH. Ding came to attention.

"Staff Sergeant Domingo Chavez reporting as ordered, sir."

"Okay, relax and sit down, Sergeant. I know you've been on the go for a while. There's coffee in the corner if you want."

"No, thank you, sir." Chavez sat down and almost relaxed a bit until he saw his personnel jacket lying on the desk. Colonel Smith picked it up and flipped it open. Having someone rip through your personnel file was usually worrisome, but the colonel looked up with a relaxed smile. Chavez noticed that Colonel Smith had no unit crest above his name tag, not even the hourglass-bayonet symbol of the 7th LID. Where did he come from? Who was this guy?

"This looks pretty damned good, Sergeant. I'd say you're a good bet for E-7 in two or three years. You've been down south, too, I see. Three times, is it?"

"Yes, sir. We been to Honduras twice and Panama once."

"Did well all three times. It says here your Spanish is excellent."

"It's what I was raised with, sir." As his accent told everyone he met. He wanted to know what this was all about, but staff sergeants do not ask such questions of bird-colonels. He got his wish in any case.

"Sergeant, we're putting a special group together, and we want you to be part of it."

"Sir, I got new orders, and — "

"I know that. We're looking for people with a combination of good language skills and — hell, we're looking for the best light-fighters we can find. Everything I see about you says you're one of the best in the division." There were other

77

criteria that "Colonel Smith" did not go into. Chavez was unmarried. His parents were both dead. He had no close family members, or at least was not known to write or call anyone with great frequency. He didn't fit the profile perfectly — there were some other things that they wished he had — but everything they saw looked good. "It's a special job. It might be a little dangerous, but probably not. We're not sure yet. It'll last a couple of months, six at the most. At the end, you make E-7 and have your choice of assignments."

"What's this special job all about, sir?" Chavez asked brightly. The chance of making E-7 a year or two early got his full and immediate attention.

"That I can't say, Sergeant. I don't like recruiting people blind," "Colonel Smith" lied, "but I have my orders, too. I can say that you'll be sent somewhere east of here for intensive training. Maybe it'll stop there, maybe not. If it does stop there, the deal holds on the promotion and the assignment. If it goes farther, you will probably be sent somewhere to exercise your special kind of skills. Okay, I *can* say that we're talking some covert intelligence-gathering. We're not sending you to Nicaragua or anything like that. You're not being sent off to fight a secret war." That statement was technically not a lie. "Smith" didn't know exactly what the job was all about, and he wasn't being encouraged to speculate. He'd been given the mission requirements, and his nearly completed job was to find people who could do it — whatever the hell it was.

"Anyway, that's all I can say. What we have discussed to this point does not leave the room — meaning that you do not discuss it with anybody without my authorization, understood?" the man said forcefully.

"Understood, sir!"

"Sergeant, we've invested a lot of time and money in you. It's payback time. The country needs you. We need what you know. We need what you know how to do."

Put that way, Chavez knew he had little choice. "Smith" knew that, too. The young man waited about five seconds before answering, which was less than expected.

"When do I leave, sir?"

Smith was all business now. He pulled a large manila envelope from the desk's center drawer. CHAVEZ was scrawled on it in Magic Marker. "Sergeant, I've taken the liberty of doing a few things for you. In here are your medical and finance records. I've already arranged to clear you through most of the post agencies. I've also scratched in a limited power of attorney form so that you can have somebody ship your personal effects — where 'to' shows on the form."

Chavez nodded, though his head swam slightly. Whoever this Colonel Smith was, he had some serious horsepower to run paperwork through the Army's legendary bureaucracy so quickly. Clearing post ordinarily took five days of sitting and waiting. He took the envelope from the colonel's hand.

"Pack your gear and be back here at eighteen hundred. Don't bother getting a haircut or anything. You're going to let it grow for a while. I'll handle things with the people downstairs. And remember: you do not discuss this with anybody. If someone asks, you got orders to report to Fort Benning a little early. That's your story, and I expect you to stick to it." "Colonel Smith" stood and extended his hand while he told another lie, mixed with some truth. "You did the right thing. I knew we could count on you, Chavez."

"We own the night, sir!"

"Dismissed."

"Colonel Smith" replaced the personnel folder in his briefcase. That was that. Most of the men were already on their way to Colorado. Chavez was one of the last. "Smith" wondered how things would work out. His real name was Edgar Jeffries, and he had once been an Army officer, long since seconded to, then hired by, the Central Intelligence Agency. He found himself hoping that things would go as planned, but he'd been with the Agency too long to place much store in that train of thought. This wasn't his first recruiting job. Not all of them had gone well, and fewer still had gone as planned. On the other hand, Chavez and all the rest had volunteered to join the country's military service, had voluntarily re-enlisted, and had voluntarily decided to accept his invitation to do something new and different. The world was a dangerous place, and these forty men had made an informed decision to join one of its more dangerous professions. It was some consolation to him, and because Edgar Jeffries still had a conscience, he needed the consolation.

"Good luck, Sarge," he said quietly to himself.

Chavez had a busy day. First changing into civilian clothes, he washed his field uniform and gear, then assembled all of the equipment which he'd be leaving behind. He had to clean the equipment also, because you were supposed to give it back better than you got it, as Sergeant First Class Mitchell expected. By the time the rest of the platoon arrived from Hunter-Liggett at 1300, his tasks were well underway. The activity was noted by the returning NCOs, and soon the platoon sergeant appeared.

"Why you packed up, Ding?" Mitchell asked.

"They need me at Benning early — that's, uh, that's why they flew me back this morning."

"The lieutenant know?"

"They musta told him — well, they musta told the company clerk, right?" Chavez was a little embarrassed. Lying to his platoon sergeant bothered him. Bob Mitchell had been a friend and a teacher for his nearly four years at Fort Ord. But his orders came from a colonel.

"Ding, one thing you still have to learn about is paperwork. Come on, son. The ell-tee's in his office."

Lieutenant Timothy Washington Jackson, Infantry, hadn't cleaned up yet, but was almost ready to leave for his place in the bachelor officers' quarters, called the BOQ or merely The Q. He looked up to see two of his senior NCOs.

"Lieutenant, Chavez here's got orders to skip off to Fort Benning PDQ. They're picking him up this evening."

"So I hear. I just got a call from the battalion sergeant major. What the hell gives? We don't do things this way," Jackson growled. "How long?"

"Eighteen hundred, sir."

"Super. I gotta go and get cleaned up before I see the S-3. Sergeant Mitchell, can you handle the equipment records?"

"Yes, sir."

"Okay, I'll be back at seventeen hundred to finish things up. Chavez, don't leave before I get back."

The rest of the afternoon passed quickly. Mitchell was willing to handle shipping — there wasn't that much to ship — and squared the younger man away, with a few lessons tossed in on the better ways to expedite paperwork. Lieutenant Jackson was back on time, and brought both men into his office. It was quiet. Most of the platoon was already gone for a well-deserved night on the town.

"Ding, I ain't ready to lose you yet. We haven't decided who takes the squad over. You were talking about Ozkanian, Sergeant Mitchell?"

"That's right, sir. What d'you think, Chavez?"

"He's about ready," Ding judged.

"Okay, we'll give Corporal Ozkanian a shot at it. You're lucky, Chavez," Lieutenant Jackson said next. "I got caught up on all my paperwork right before we went into the field. You want me to go over your evaluation with you?"

"Just the high spots'll be fine, sir." Chavez grinned. The lieutenant liked him, and Chavez knew it.

"Okay, I say you're damned good, which you are. Sorry to lose you this quick. You going to need a lift?" Jackson asked.

"No problem, sir. I was planning to walk over."

"Crap. We all did enough walking last night. Load your stuff into my car." The lieutenant tossed him the keys. "Anything else, Sergeant Mitchell?"

"Nothin' that can't wait until Monday, sir. I figure we earned ourselves a nice restful weekend."

"As always, your judgment is impeccable. My brother's in town, and I'm gone till 0600 Monday morning."

"Roger that. Have a good one, sir."

Chavez didn't have much in the way of personal gear, and, unusually, didn't even have a car. In fact he was saving his money to buy a Chevy Corvette, the car that had fascinated him since boyhood, and was within five thousand dollars of being able to pay cash for one. His baggage was already loaded into the back of Jackson's Honda CVCC when the lieutenant emerged from

83

the barracks. Chavez tossed him the keys back.

"Where they picking you up?"

"Division G-1 is what the man said, sir."

"Why there? Why not Martinez Hall?" Jackson asked as he started up. Martinez was the customary processing facility.

"Lieutenant, I just go where they tell me."

Jackson laughed at that. "Don't we all?"

It only took a couple of minutes. Jackson dropped Chavez off with a handshake. There were five other soldiers there, the lieutenant noted briefly. All sergeants, which was something of a surprise. All looked hispanic, too. He knew two of them. León was in Ben Tucker's platoon, 4th of the 17th, and Muñoz was with divisional recon. Those were two good ones, too. Lieutenant Jackson shrugged it off as he drove away.

3.

The *Panache* Procedure

Wegener's inspection came before lunch instead of after. There wasn't much to complain about. Chief Riley had been there first. Except for some paint cans and brushes that were actually in use — painting a ship is something that never begins or ends; it just is — there was no loose gear in view. The ship's gun was properly trained in and secured, as were the anchor chains. Lifelines were taut, and hatches dogged down tight in anticipation of the evening storm. A few off-duty sailors lounged here and there, reading or sunning themselves. These leapt to their feet at Riley's rumbling "Attention on deck!" One third-class was reading a *Playboy*. Wegener informed him good-naturedly that he'd have to watch out for that on the next cruise, as three female crewmen were scheduled to join the ship in less than two weeks' time, and it wouldn't do to offend their sensibilities. That *Panache* had none aboard at the moment was a statistical anomaly, and the change didn't trouble the captain greatly, though his senior chiefs were skeptical to say the least. There was also the problem of who got to use the plumbing when, since female crewmen had not been anticipated by the cutter's designers. It was the first time today that Red Wegener had had something to smile about. The problems of taking women to sea . . . and the smile died again as the images from the videotape came back to him. Those two women — no, a woman and a little girl — had gone to sea, too, hadn't they . . . ?

It just wouldn't go away.

Wegener looked around and saw the questions forming on the faces of the men around him. The skipper was pissed about something. They didn't know what it was, but knew that you don't want to be around the captain when he was mad about something. Then they saw his face change. The captain had just asked himself a question, they thought.

"Looks all right to me, people. Let's make sure we keep it that way." He nodded and walked forward to his stateroom. Once there he summoned Chief Oreza.

The quartermaster arrived within a minute. *Panache* wasn't big enough to allow a longer walk than that. "You called, Captain?"

"Close the door, Portagee, and grab a seat."

The master chief quartermaster was of Portuguese extraction, but his accent was New England. Like Bob Riley he was a consummate seaman, and like his captain he was also a gifted instructor. A whole generation of Coast Guard officers had learned the use of the sextant from this swarthy, overweight professional. It was men like Manuel Oreza who really ran the Coast Guard, and Wegener occasionally regretted leaving their ranks for officer status. But he hadn't left them entirely, and in private Wegener and Oreza still communicated on a first-name basis.

"I saw the tape of the boarding, Red," Oreza said, reading his captain's mind. "You shoulda let Riley snap the little fucker in half."

"That's not the way we're supposed to do things," Wegener said somewhat lamely.

"Piracy, murder, and rape — toss in the drugs for fun." The quartermaster shrugged his shoulders. "I know what we oughta do with people like that. Problem is, nobody ever does."

Wegener knew what he meant. Although there was a new federal death-penalty law to deal with drug-related murders, it had only rarely been invoked. The problem was simply that every drug dealer arrested knew someone bigger who was even more desirable a target — the really big ones never placed themselves in a position where the supposed long arm of the law could reach. Federal law-enforcement agencies might have been omnipotent within U.S. borders, and the Coast Guard might have plenipotentiary powers at sea — even to the point where they were

87

allowed to board and search numerous foreign-flag ships at will — but there were always limits. There had to be. The enemy knew what those limits were, and it was really a simple thing to adapt to them. This was a game whose fixed rules applied only to one side; the other was free to redefine its own rules at will. It was simple for the big boys in the drug trade to keep clear, and there were always plenty of smaller fry to take their chances on the dangerous parts — especially since their pay exceeded that of any army in history. These foot soldiers were dangerous and clever enough to make the contest difficult — but even when you caught them, they were always able to trade their knowledge for partial immunity.

The result was that nobody ever seemed to pay in full. Except the victims, of course. Wegener's train of thought was interrupted by something even worse.

"You know, Red, these two might get off entirely."

"Hold it, Portagee, I can't — "

"My oldest girl is in law school, skipper. You want to know the really bad news?" the chief asked darkly.

"Go on."

"We get these characters to port — well, the helo brings them in tomorrow — and they ask for a lawyer, right? Anybody who watches American TV knows that much. Let's say that they keep their mouths shut till then. Then their lawyer says that his clients saw a drifting yacht yesterday morning and boarded it. The boat they were on headed back to wherever it came from, and they decide to take it to port to claim the salvage rights. They didn't use the radio because they didn't know how to work it — you see that on the tape? It was one of those gollywog computer-driven scanners with the hundred-page manual — and our friends don't reada da Eenglish so good. Somebody on the fishing boat will corroborate part of the story. It's all a horrible misunderstanding, see? So the U.S. Attorney in Mobile decides that he might not have a good-enough case, and our friends cop to a lesser charge. That's how it works." He paused.

"That's hard to believe."

"We got no bodies. We got no witnesses. We have weapons aboard, but who can say who fired them? It's all circumstantial evidence." Oreza smiled for a grim moment. "My daughter gave me a good brief last month on how all this stuff works. They whistle up someone to back up their version of how they got aboard — somebody clean, no criminal record — and all of a sudden the only real witnesses are on the other side, and we got shit, Red. They cop to some little piddly-ass charge, and that's it."

"But if they're innocent, why don't they — "

"Talk very much? Oh, hell, that's the easy part. A foreign-flag warship pulls up alongside and puts an armed boarding party aboard. The boarding party points a bunch of guns at them,

89

roughs them up a bit, and they're so scared that they didn't say anything — that's what the lawyer'll say. Bet on it. Oh, they prob'ly won't walk, but the prosecutor will be so afraid of losing the case that he'll look for an easy way out. Our friends will get a year or two in the can, then they get a free plane ticket home."

"But they're murderers."

"Sure as hell," Portagee agreed. "To get off, all they have to be is smart murderers. And there might even be some other things they can say. What my girl taught me, Red, is that it's never as simple as it looks. Like I said, you shoulda let Bob handle it. The kids would have backed you up, Captain. You oughta hear what they're saying about this thing."

Captain Wegener was quiet for a moment. That made sense, didn't it? Sailors didn't change much over the years, did they? On the beach they'd work mightily to get into every pair of female pants in sight, but on the question of murder and rape, the "kids" felt the same way the old-timers did. Times hadn't changed all that much after all. Men were still men. They knew what justice was, courts and lawyers to the contrary.

Red thought about that for a few seconds. Then he rose and walked to his bookshelf. Next to his current copy of the *Uniform Code of Military Justice* and *The Manual of Courts Martial* was a much older book better known by its informal title, "Rocks and Shoals." It was the old refer-

90

ence book of regulations whose ancestry went back to the 18th century, and which had been replaced by the UCMJ soon after World War II. Wegener's copy was an antique. He'd found it gathering dust in a cardboard box fifteen years before at an old boat station on the California coast. This one had been published in 1879, when the rules had been very different. It had been a safer world then, the captain told himself. It wasn't hard to understand why. All you had to do was read what the rules had once been. . . .

"Thanks, Portagee. I've got a little work to do. I want you and Riley here at fifteen hundred."

Oreza stood. "Aye aye, sir." The quartermaster wondered for a moment what the captain had thanked him for. He was skilled at reading the skipper's mind, but it didn't work this time. He knew that something was going on in there. He just didn't know what it was. He also knew that he'd find out at fifteen hundred. He could wait.

Wegener had lunch with his officers a few minutes later. He sat quietly at the end of the table reading over some message traffic. His wardroom was young and informal. Table talk was as lively as usual. The talk today was on the obvious subject, and Wegener allowed it to go on as he flipped through the yellow sheets generated by the ship's printer. The thought that had come to him in his stateroom was taking shape. He weighed the pluses and minuses in silence. What could they really do to him? Not much, he judged. Would his people go along with him?

"I heard Oreza say that in the old days, they knew what to do about bastards like this," a lieutenant (j.g.) observed at the far end of the table. There were affirmative grunts all around the table.

"Ain't 'progress' a bitch?" another noted. The twenty-four-year-old officer didn't know that he had just made a decision for his commanding officer.

It would work, Wegener decided. He glanced up from his messages to look at the faces of his officers. He'd trained them well, the captain thought. He'd had them for ten months now, and their performance was as nearly perfect as any commander could ask. They'd been a sorry, dejected lot when he'd arrived at the shipyard, but now they sparkled with enthusiasm. Two had grown mustaches, the better to look like the seamen they'd become. All of them lounged in their hard-backed chairs, radiating competence. They were proud of their ship and proud of their captain. They'd back him up. Red joined the conversation, just to make sure, just to test the waters, just to decide who would play a part and who would not.

He finished his lunch and returned to his cabin. The paperwork was still there, and he raced through it as quickly as he could, then opened his "Rocks and Shoals." At fifteen hundred Oreza and Riley arrived, and he outlined his plan. The two master chiefs were surprised at first, but fell into line quickly.

"Riley, I want you to take this down to our guests. One of 'em dropped it on the bridge." Wegener fished the cigarette pack out of his pocket. "There's a vent in the brig, isn't there?"

"Sure is, skipper," the bosun answered in some surprise. He didn't know about the "Calverts."

"We start at twenty-one hundred," the captain said.

"About the time the weather gets here," Oreza observed. "Fair enough, Red. You know you wanna be real careful how you — "

"I know, Portagee. What's life without a few risks?" he asked with a smile.

Riley left first. He walked forward to a ladder, then down two levels and aft until he got to the brig. The two were there, inside the ten-foot-square cage. Each lay on a bunk. They might have been speaking before, but stopped when the door to the compartment opened. It seemed to the bosun that someone might have included a microphone in the brig, but the district legal officer had once explained that such an installation would be a violation of constitutional rights, or a violation of search-and-seizure, or some such legalistic bullshit, the chief thought.

"Hey, Gomer," he said. The one on the lower bunk — the one he'd cracked across the bridge rail — looked around to see who it was. He was rewarded with widening eyes. "You guys get lunch?" the bosun asked.

"Yes." There was an accent there, but a funny one, the master chief thought.

"You dropped your smokes on the bridge awhile back." Riley tossed the pack through the bars. They landed on the deck, and Pablo — the chief thought he looked like a Pablo — snatched them up with a surprised look on his face.

"Thank you," the man said.

"Uh-huh. Don't you boys go anywhere without letting me know, hear?" Riley chuckled and walked away. It was a real brig. The designers had gotten that part right, the master chief thought. Even had its own head. That offended Riley. A prison cell on a Coast Guard cutter. Hmph. But at least that meant you didn't have to detail a couple of men to guard the gomers. At least not yet, Riley smiled to himself. *Are you boys in for a surprise.*

Weather at sea is always impressive. Perhaps it looks that way sweeping across a uniform surface, or maybe the human mind simply knows that weather has a power at sea that it lacks on land. There was a three-quarter moon tonight, allowing Wegener to watch the line squalls approach at over twenty knots. There were sustained twenty-five-knot winds in there, and gusts almost double that. Experience told him that the gentle four-foot swells that *Panache* rode through would soon be whipped to a maniacal series of breaking waves and flying spray. Not all that much, really, but enough to give his cutter an active ride. Some of his younger crewmen would presently regret dinner. Well, that was something you had to learn about the sea. She didn't like people to overeat.

Wegener welcomed the storm. In addition to giving him the atmosphere he wanted, it also gave him an excuse to fiddle with his watch bill. Ensign O'Neil had not yet conned the ship through heavy weather and tonight would be his chance.

"Any problems, Mister?" the skipper asked the junior officer.

"No, sir."

"Okay, just remember that if anything comes up, I'll be in the wardroom." One of Wegener's standing orders read: *No watch officer will ever be reprimanded for calling the captain to the bridge. Even if you only want to check the correct time: CALL ME!* It was a common hyperbole. You had to say such things, lest your junior officers be so afraid to bother the skipper that they rammed a tanker by way of protecting his sleep — and ending his career. The mark of a good officer, Wegener repeatedly told his youngsters, was willingness to admit he had something yet to learn.

O'Neil nodded. Both men knew that there was nothing to worry about. It was just that the kid had never learned first-hand that a ship handles a little differently with sea and wind on the beam. Besides, Chief Owens was standing by. Wegener walked aft, and the boatswain's mate of the watch announced, "Captain off the bridge."

In the crew's mess the enlisted men were settling down to watch a movie. It was a new tape, with a "Hard R" notation on the plastic box. Riley had seen to that. Lots of T&A to keep their attention. The same movie was available to the wardroom TV; young officers had the same hormonal drives, but they wouldn't be exercised tonight.

The onrushing storm would serve to keep people off the weather decks, and the noise wouldn't hurt either. Wegener smiled to himself as he pulled open the door to the wardroom. He couldn't have planned it any better.

"Are we ready?" the captain asked.

The initial enthusiasm for the plan was gone. The reality of things had sunk in a little. That was to be expected, Wegener thought. The youngsters were sober, but they weren't backing away either. They needed someone to say something, and they got it.

"Ready here, sir," Oreza said from his seat at the far end of the table. The officers all nodded agreement. Red walked to his seat in the center of the mess table. He looked at Riley.

"Bring 'em up here."

"Aye aye, sir."

The bosun left the room and proceeded down to the brig. On opening the door again, he caught the acrid stink that made him think at first that there was a fire in the rope locker — but an instant later the truth sprang on him.

"Shit," he growled disgustedly. *On my ship!*

"Stand up, Gomer!" his voice boomed, adding, "Both of ya'!"

The one on the lower bunk flipped his butt into the toilet and stood slowly, an arrogant smile on his face. Riley answered it, and produced a key. That changed Pablo's smile, but didn't erase it.

"We're taking a little walk, children." The bosun also produced a pair of handcuffs. He figured that he could handle both of them easily enough, especially stoned, but the skipper had been clear on his instructions. Riley reached through the bars to yank one toward him. On a rough order to turn around, the man complied, and allowed himself to be cuffed. So did the other. The lack of resistance surprised the master chief. Next Riley unlocked the brig door and waved them out. As "Pablo" passed, Riley removed the pack from his pocket and for want of something better, tossed it back on the lower bunk.

"Come on." Riley grabbed each by the arm and led them forward. They walked unevenly — the increased rolling of the ship didn't help, but there was more to it than that. It took three or four minutes to reach the wardroom.

"The prisoners will be seated," Wegener announced when they arrived. "The court is called to order."

Both of them stopped cold on hearing that, which told everybody something. Riley steered them to their seats at the defense table after a

97

moment. It is hard for a person to endure the stares of his fellowman in silence, particularly when one knows that something is going on, but not quite what it is. The big one broke the silence after a minute or so.

"What's happening?"

"Sir," Wegener replied evenly, "we are holding a summary court-martial." That only earned him a curious look, and he went on, "The trial judge advocate will read the charges."

"Mr. President, the defendants are charged under the Eleventh Article of War with piracy, rape, and murder. Each of these is a capital offense. Specifications: that on or about the fourteenth of this month, the defendants did board the motor yacht *Empire Builder;* that while aboard they did murder the four people aboard the vessel, that is, the owner and master, his wife, and their two minor children; further, that in the course of these events the defendants did rape the wife and daughter of the owner and master; further that the defendants did dismember and dispose of the bodies of the victims prior to our boarding the vessel on the morning of the fifteenth. The prosecution will show that these actions took place in the course of drug-running operations. Murder in the course of drug-related activities is a capital offense under United States Code, Annotated. Further, murder in the course of piracy, and rape in the course of piracy, are capital crimes under the Articles of War. As the court is aware, piracy is a crime under the doctrine of *jus gentium*, and falls under the jurisdiction of any interested warship. Further, murder attending piracy is, as I have stated, a capital crime. Although as a ship of the United States Coast Guard we have *de jure* rights to board and seize any American-flag vessel, that authority is not strictly necessary in a case of this kind. Therefore, this court has full jurisdiction to try and, if necessary, execute the prisoners. The prosecution announces herewith its intention to request the death penalty in this case."

"Thank you," Wegener said, turning to the defense table. "Do you understand the charges?"

"Huh?"

"What the trial judge advocate just said was that you are being tried for piracy, rape, and murder. If you are found guilty, the court will then decide whether or not to execute you. You have the right to legal counsel. Lieutenant Alison, sitting there at the table with you, is your defending officer. Do you understand?" It took a few more seconds for things to sink in, but he understood all right. "Does the defense waive full reading of charges and specifications?"

"Yes, Mr. President. Sir, the defense moves that the cases be tried individually, and begs the indulgence of the court to confer with his clients."

"Sir, the prosecution objects to splitting the cases."

"Argument?" the captain asked. "Defense first."

"Sir, since, as the trial judge advocate has told us, this is to be a capital case, I beg the court's indulgence to allow me to defend my clients as best I can under the circumstances, and — "

Wegener stopped him with a wave of the hand. "The defense correctly points out that, since this is a capital case, it is customary to grant the utmost leeway to the defense. The court finds this a persuasive argument and grants the motion. The court also grants the defense five minutes to confer with his clients. The court suggests that the defense might instruct his clients to identify themselves properly to the court."

The lieutenant took them to a corner of the room, still in handcuffs, and started talking to them quietly.

"Look, I'm Lieutenant Alison, and I'm stuck with the job of keeping you two characters alive. For starters, you'd better damned sight tell me who the hell you are!"

"What is this bullshit?" the tall one asked.

"This bullshit is a court-martial. You're at sea, mister, and in case nobody ever told you, the captain of an American warship can do any goddamned thing he wants. You shouldn't have pissed him off."

"So?"

"So, this is a *trial,* you asshole! You know, a judge, a jury. They can sentence you to death and they can do it right here aboard the ship."

"Bullshit!"

"What's your name, for God's sake?"

100

"Yo' mama," the tall one said contemptuously. The other one looked somewhat less sure of himself. The lieutenant scratched the top of his head. Eighteen feet away, Captain Wegener took note of it.

"What the hell did you do aboard that yacht?"

"Get me a real lawyer!"

"Mister, I'm all the lawyer you're gonna get," the lieutenant said. "Haven't you figured that out yet?"

The man didn't believe him, which was precisely what everyone had expected. The defending officer led his clients back to their table.

"The court is back in session," Wegener announced. "Do we have a statement for the defense?"

"May it please the court, neither defendant chooses to identify himself."

"That does not please the court, but we must take that fact at face value. For the purposes of the trial, we will identify your clients as John Doe and James Doe." Wegener pointed to designate which was which. "The court chooses to try John Doe first. Is there any objection? Very well, the trial judge advocate will begin presenting his case."

Which he did over the next twenty minutes, calling only one witness, Master Chief Riley, who recounted the boarding and gave a color commentary to the videotape record of the boarding.

"Did the defendant say anything?"

"No, sir."

"Could you describe the contents of this evidence bag?" the prosecutor asked next.

"Sir, I think that's called a tampon. It appears to be used, sir," Riley said with some embarrassment. "I found that under the coffee table in the yacht's main salon, close to a bloodstain — actually these two on the photograph, sir. I don't use the things myself, you understand, sir, but in my experience women don't leave them around on the floor. On the other hand, if someone was about to rape a lady, this thing would be in the way, sort of, and he might just remove it and toss it out of the way so's he could get on with it, like. If you see where I picked it up, and where the bloodstains are, well, it's pretty obvious what happened there, sir."

"No further questions. The prosecution rests."

"Very well. Before the defense begins its case, the court wishes to ask if the defense intends to call any witnesses other than the defendant."

"No, Mr. President."

"Very well. At this point the court will speak directly to the defendant." Wegener shifted his gaze and leaned forward slightly in his chair. "In your own defense, sir, you have the right to do one of three things. First, you can choose not to make any statement at all, in which case the court will draw no inferences from your action. Second, you are allowed to make a statement not under oath and not subject to cross-examination. Third, you may make a statement under oath and subject to cross-examination by the trial judge advocate. Do you understand these rights, sir?"

"John Doe," who had watched the preceding hour or so in amused silence, came awkwardly to his feet. With his hands cuffed behind his back, he leaned slightly forward, and since the cutter was now rolling like a log in a flume, he had quite a bit of trouble keeping his feet.

"What is all this shit?" he demanded, again making people wonder about his accent. "I want to go back to my room and be left alone till I can get my own fucking lawyer."

"Mr. Doe," Wegener replied, "in case you haven't figured it out yet, you are on trial for piracy, rape, and murder. This book" — the captain lifted his "Rocks and Shoals" — "says I can try you here and now, and this book says that if we find you guilty, we can decide to hang you from the yardarm. Now, the Coast Guard hasn't done this in over fifty years, but you better believe that I can damned well do it if I want to! They haven't bothered changing the law. So now things are different from what you expected, aren't they? You want a lawyer — you have Mr. Alison right there. You want to defend yourself? Here's your chance. But, Mr. Doe, there is no appeal from this court, and you'd better think about that real hard and real fast."

"I think this is all bullshit. Go fuck yourself!"

"The court will disregard the defendant's statement," Wegener said, struggling to keep his face straight and sober, as befitting the presiding

103

officer in a capital case.

Counsel for the defense spoke for fifteen minutes, making a valiant but futile attempt to counter the weight of evidence already presented by the trial judge advocate. Case summaries took five minutes each. Then it was time for Captain Wegener to speak again.

"Having heard the evidence, the members of the court will now vote on the verdict. This will be by secret written ballot. The trial judge advocate will pass out the voting papers, and collect them."

This took less than one minute. The prosecutor handed each of the five members a slip of note paper. The members of the court all looked at the defendant before and after marking their votes. The prosecutor then collected the ballots, and after shuffling them in his hand about as adroitly as a five-year-old with his Old Maid cards, handed them to the captain. Wegener unfolded the ballots and set them on the table in front of him. He made a note in his yellow pad before speaking.

"Defendant will stand and face the court. Mr. Doe, do you have anything to say before sentence is passed?"

He didn't, an amused, disbelieving smirk on his face.

"Very well. The court having voted, two-thirds of the members concurring, finds the defendant guilty, and sentences him to death by hanging. Sentence to be carried out within the hour. May God have mercy on your soul. Court is adjourned."

"Sorry, sir," the defense counsel said to his client. "You didn't give me much to work with."

"Now get me a lawyer!" Mr. Doe snarled.

"Sir, you don't need a lawyer just now. You need a priest." As if to emphasize that fact, Chief Riley took him by the arm.

"Come on, sweetheart. You got a date with a rope." The master chief led him out of the room.

The other prisoner, known as James Doe, had watched the entire proceeding in fascinated disbelief. The disbelief was still there, everyone saw, but it was more the sort of disbelief that you'd expect to see on the face of a man stuck in front of an onrushing train.

"Do *you* understand what's going on here?" the lieutenant asked.

"This ain't real, man," the prisoner said, his voice lacking much of the conviction it might have held an hour or so earlier.

"Hey, man, aren't you paying attention? Didn't they tell you guys that some of your kind just sort of disappear out here? We've been doing this for almost six months. The prisons are all full up, and the judges just don't want to be bothered. If we bag somebody and we have the evidence we need, they let us handle things at sea. Didn't anybody tell you that the rules have changed some?"

"You can't do this!" he almost screamed in reply.

"Think so? Tell you what. In about ten minutes I'll take you topside, and you can watch. I'm telling you, if you don't cooperate, we are not going to fuck around with you, pal. We're tired of that. Why don't you just sit quiet and think it over, and when the time comes, I'll let you see how serious we are." The lieutenant helped himself to a cup of coffee to pass the time, not speaking at all to his client. About the time he finished, the door opened again.

"Hands topside to witness punishment," Chief Oreza announced.

"Come on, Mr. Doe. You'd better see this." The lieutenant took him by the arm and led him forward. Just outside the wardroom door was a ladder that led upward. At the top of it was a narrow passageway, and both men headed aft toward the cutter's vacant helicopter deck.

The lieutenant's name was Rick Alison. A black kid from Albany, New York, and the ship's navigator, Alison thanked God every night for serving under Red Wegener, who was far and away the best commander he'd ever met. He'd thought about leaving the service more than once, but now planned on staying in as long as he could. He led Mr. Doe aft, about thirty feet from the festivities.

The seas were really rough now, Alison noted. He gauged the wind at over thirty knots, and the seas at twelve or fourteen feet. *Panache* was taking twenty-five-degree rolls left and right of the vertical, snapping back and forth like a kids' see-saw. Alison remembered that O'Neil had the conn, and hoped that Chief Owens was keeping an eye on the boy. The new ensign was a good enough kid, but he still had a lot to learn about ship handling, thought the navigator, who was a bare six years older himself. Lightning flashed occasionally to starboard, flash-lighting the sea. Rain was falling in solid sheets, the drops flying across the deck at a sharp angle and driven hard enough by the wind to sting the cheeks. All in all it was the sort of night to make Edgar Allan Poe salivate at its possibilities. There were no lights visible, though the cutter's white paint gave them a sort of ghostly outline as a visual reference. Alison wondered if Wegener had decided to do this because of the weather, or was it just a fortunate coincidence?

Captain, you've pulled some crazy shit since you came aboard, but this one really takes it.

There was the rope. Someone had snaked it over the end of the cutter's radio/radar mast. That must have been fun, Alison thought. Had to have been Chief Riley. Who else would be crazy enough to try?

Then the prisoner appeared. His hands were still behind his back. The captain and XO were there, too. Wegener was saying something official, but they couldn't hear it. The wind whistled across the deck, and through the mast structure with its many signal halyards — oh, that's what Riley did, Alison realized. He'd used a halyard as a messenger line to run the one-inch hemp

107

through the block. Even Riley wasn't crazy enough to crawl the mast top in this weather.

Then some lights came on. They were the deck floods, used to help guide a helo in. They had the main effect of illuminating the rain, but did give a slightly clearer picture of what was happening. Wegener said one more thing to the prisoner, whose face was still set in an arrogant cast. He still didn't believe it, Alison thought, wondering if that would change. The captain shook his head and stepped back. Riley then placed the noose around his neck.

John Doe's expression changed at that. He still didn't believe it, but all of a sudden things were slightly more serious. Five people assembled on the running end of the line. Alison almost laughed. He'd known that was how it was done, but hadn't quite expected the skipper to go that far. . . .

The final touch was the black hood. Riley turned the prisoner to face aft toward Alison and his friend — there was another reason, as well — before surprising him with it. And finally it got through to Mr. Doe.

"Noooooo!" The scream was perfect, a ghostly sort of cry that matched the weather and the wind better than anyone might have hoped. His knees buckled as expected, and the men on the running end of the line took the strain and ran aft. The prisoner's feet rose clear of the black no-skid deck as the body jerked skyward. The legs kicked a few times, then were still before the line

was tied off on a stanchion.

"Well, that's that," Alison said. He took the other Mr. Doe by the arm and led him forward. "Now it's your turn, sport."

Lightning flashed close aboard just as they reached the door leading back into the superstructure. The prisoner stopped cold, looking up one last time. There was his companion, body limp, swinging like a pendulum below the yard, hanging there dead in the rain.

"You believe me now?" the navigator asked as he pulled him inside. Mr. Doe's trousers were already soaked from the falling rain, but they were wet for another reason as well.

The first order of business was to get dried off. When the court reconvened, everyone had changed to fresh clothing. James Doe was now in a set of blue Coast Guard coveralls. His handcuffs had been taken off and left off, and he found a hot cup of coffee waiting for him on the defense table. He failed to note that Chief Oreza was no longer at the head table, nor was Chief Riley in the wardroom at the moment. The entire atmosphere was more relaxed than it had been, but the prisoner scarcely noticed that. James Doe was anything but calm.

"Mr. Alison," the captain intoned, "I would suggest that you confer with your client."

"This one's real simple, sport," Alison said. "You can talk or you can swing. The skipper doesn't give a shit one way or the other. For starters, what's your name?"

Jesús started talking. One of the officers of the court picked up a portable TV camera — the same one used in the boarding, in fact — and they asked him to start again.

"Okay — do you understand that you are not required to say anything?" someone asked. The prisoner scarcely noticed, and the question was repeated.

"Yeah, right, I understand, okay?" he responded without turning his head. "Look, what do you want to know?"

The questions were already written down, of course. Alison, who was also the cutter's legal officer, ran down the list as slowly as he could, in front of the video camera. His main problem was in slowing the answers down enough to be intelligible. The questioning lasted forty minutes. The prisoner spoke rapidly, but matter-of-factly, and didn't notice the looks he was getting from the members of the court.

"Thank you for your cooperation," Wegener said when things were concluded. "We'll try to see that things go a little easier for you because of your cooperation. We won't be able to do much for your colleague, of course. You do understand that, don't you?"

"Too bad for him, I guess," the man answered, and everyone in the room breathed a little easier.

"We'll talk to the U.S. Attorney," the captain promised. "Lieutenant, you can return the prisoner to the brig."

"Aye aye, sir." Alison took the prisoner out of

the room as the camera followed. On reaching the ladder to go below, however, the prisoner tripped. He didn't see the hand that caused it, and didn't have time to look, as another unseen hand crashed down on the back of his neck. Next Chief Riley broke the unconscious man's forearm, while Chief Oreza clamped a patch of ether-soaked gauze over his mouth. The two chiefs carried him to sick bay, where the cutter's medical corpsman splinted the arm. It was a simple green-stick fracture and required no special assistance. His undamaged arm was secured to the bunk in sick bay, and he was allowed to sleep there.

The prisoner slept late. Breakfast was brought in to him from the wardroom, and he was allowed to clean himself up before the helicopter arrived. Oreza came to collect him, leading him topside again, and aft to the helo deck, where he found Chief Riley, who was delivering the other prisoner to the helicopter. What James Doe — his real name had turned out to be Jesús Castillo — found remarkable was the fact that John Doe — Ramón José Capati — was alive. A pair of DEA agents seated them as far apart as possible, and had instructions to keep the prisoners separate. One had confessed, the captain explained, and the other might not be overly pleased with that. Castillo couldn't take his eyes off Capati, and the amazement in his eyes looked enough like fear that the agents — who liked the idea of a confession in a capital case — resolved to keep the prisoners as far apart as circumstances allowed. Along with them went all the physical evidence and several videotape cassettes. Wegener watched the Coast Guard Dolphin helo power up, wondering how the people on the beach would react. The sober pause that always follows a slightly mad act had set in, but Wegener had anticipated that also. In fact, he figured that he'd anticipated everything. Only eight members of the crew knew what had taken place, and they knew what they were supposed to say. The executive officer appeared at Wegener's side.

"Nothing's ever quite what it seems, is it?"

"I suppose not, but three innocent people died. Instead of four." *Sure as hell the owner wasn't any angel*, the captain reflected. *But did they have to kill his wife and kids, too?* Wegener stared out at the changeless sea, unaware of what he had started or how many people would die because of it.

4.

Preliminaries

Chavez's first indication of how unusual this job really was came at San José airport. Driven there in an unmarked rental van, they ended up in the general-aviation part of the facility and found a private jet waiting for them. Now, that was really something. "Colonel Smith" didn't board. He shook every man's hand, told them that they'd be met, and got back into the van. The sergeants all boarded the aircraft which, they saw, was less an executive jet than a mini-airliner. It even had a stewardess who served drinks. Each man stowed his gear and availed himself of a drink except Chavez, who was too tired even to look at the young lady. He barely noted the plane's takeoff, and was asleep before the climb-out was finished. Something told him that he ought to sleep while he had the time. It was a common instinct for soldiers, and usually a correct one.

Lieutenant Jackson had never been at the Monterey facility, but his older brother had given him the necessary instructions, and he found the O-Club without difficulty. He felt suddenly lonely. As he locked his Honda he realized that his was the only Army uniform in view. At least it wasn't hard to figure out whom to salute. As a second lieutenant, he had to salute damned near everybody.

"Yo, Timmy!" his brother called, just inside the door.

"Hiya, Rob." The two men embraced. Theirs was a close family, but Timmy hadn't seen his big brother, Commander Robert Jefferson Jackson, USN, in almost a year. Robby's mother had died years before. Only thirty-nine, she'd complained of a headache, decided to lie down for a few minutes, and never stirred again, the victim of a massive stroke. It had later been determined that she was an undiagnosed hypertensive, one of many American blacks cursed by the symptomless malady. Her husband, the Reverend Hosiah Jackson, mourned her loss along with the community in which both had raised their family. But pious man that Reverend Jackson was, he was also a father whose children needed a mother. Four years later he'd remarried, to a twenty-three-year-old parishioner, and started afresh. Timothy was the first child of his second union. His fourth son had followed a path similar to the first's. An Annapolis graduate, Robby Jackson flew fighter aircraft for the Navy.

Timmy had won an appointment at West Point, and looked forward to a career in the infantry. Another brother was a physician, and the fourth was a lawyer with political ambitions. Times had changed in Mississippi.

It would have been hard for an observer to determine which brother was prouder of the other. Robby, with three gold stripes on his shoulder boards, bore on his breast pocket the gold star that denoted a former command at sea — in his case, VF-41, a squadron of F-14 Tomcat fighters. Now working in the Pentagon, Robby was on his way to command of a Carrier Air Wing, and after that perhaps his own carrier. Timothy, on the other hand, had been the family runt for quite a few years, but West Point had changed that with a vengeance. He had two solid inches on his older brother, and at least fifteen more pounds of muscle. There was a Ranger flash on his shoulder above the hourglass insignia of his division. Another boy had been turned into a man, the old-fashioned way.

"Lookin' good, boy," Robby observed. "How 'bout a drink?"

"Not too many, I've been up for a while."

"Long day?"

"Long week, as a matter of fact," Tim replied, "but I did get a nap yesterday."

"Nice of 'em," the elder Jackson observed with some fraternal concern.

"Hey, if I wanted an easy life, I woulda joined the Navy." The brothers had a good laugh on the way to the bar. Robby ordered John Jameson, a taste introduced to him by a friend. Tim settled for a beer. Conversation over dinner, of course, began with catching up on family matters, then turned to shop talk.

"Not real different from what you do," Timmy explained. "You try to get in close and smoke a guy with a missile before he knows you're there. We try to get in close and shoot him in the head before he knows where we are. You know about that, don't you, big brother?" Timmy asked with a smile that was touched with envy. Robby had been there once.

"Once was enough," Robby answered soberly. "I leave that close-quarter crap to idiots like you."

"Yeah, well, last night we were the forward element for the battalion. My lead squad went in beautiful. The OPFOR — excuse me, Opposing Force — was a bunch from the California Guard, mainly tanks. They got careless about how they set up, and Sergeant Chavez was inside the laager before they knew about it. You oughta see this guy operate. I swear, Rob, he's nearly invisible when he wants to be. It's going to be a bitch to replace him."

"Huh?"

"Just transferred out this afternoon. I was going to lose him in a couple weeks anyway, but they lifted him early to go to Fort Benning. Whole bunch of good sergeants moved out today." Tim paused for a moment. "All Spanish ones. Coincidence." Another pause. "That's funny, wasn't León supposed to go to Fort Benning, too?"

"Who's León?"

"Sergeant E-6. He was in Ben Tucker's platoon — Ben and I played ball together at the Point. Yeah, he was supposed to be going to Ranger School as an instructor in a couple of weeks. I wonder why him and Chavez left together? Ah, well, that's the Army for you. So how do you like the Pentagon?"

"Could be worse," Robby allowed. "Twenty-five more months, and thank God Almighty, I'll be free at last. I'm in the running for a CAG slot," the elder brother explained. He was at the career stage where things got really sticky. There were more good men than jobs to be filled. As with combat operations, one of the determining factors now was pure luck. Timmy, he saw, didn't know about that yet.

The jet landed after a flight of just under three hours. Once on the ground it taxied to the cargo terminal at the small airport. Chavez didn't know which one. He awoke still short of the sleep he needed when the plane's door was wrenched open. His first impression was that there wasn't much air here. It seemed an odd observation to make, and he wrote it off to the usual confusion following a nap.

"Where the hell are we?" another sergeant asked.

"They'll tell you outside," the attendant replied. "Y'all have a nice time here." The smile that accompanied the answer was too charming to merit a further challenge.

The sergeants collected their bags and shuffled out of the aircraft, finding yet another van waiting for them. Chavez got his question answered before he boarded it. The air was very thin here, all right, and in the west he saw why. The last glow of sunset illuminated the jagged outline of mountains to the west. Easterly course, three hours' flight time, and mountains: he knew at once they were somewhere in the Rockies, even though he'd never really been there. His last view of the aircraft as the van rolled off showed a fueling truck moving toward it. Chavez didn't quite put it together. The aircraft would be leaving in less than thirty minutes. Few people would have noticed that it had even been there, much less trouble themselves to wonder why.

Clark's hotel room was a nice one, befitting his cover. There was an ache at the back of his head to remind him that he was still not fully adjusted to the altitude, but a couple of Tylenol caplets went to work on that, and he knew that his job didn't involve much in the way of physical activity. He ordered breakfast sent up and went through some setting-up exercises to work the kinks out of his muscles. The morning jog was definitely out, however. Finished, he showered and shaved. Service was good here. Just as he got his clothes on, breakfast arrived, and by nine o'clock he was ready for work. Clark took the elevator down to the lobby, then went outside. The car was waiting. He got in the front.

"*Buenos días,*" the driver said. "There may be rain this afternoon."

"If so, I have my coat."

"A cold rain, perhaps."

"The coat has a liner," Clark said, finishing the code sequence.

"Whoever thought that one up was bright enough," the man said. "There is rain in the forecast. The name's Larson."

"Clark." They didn't shake hands. It just wasn't done. Larson, which probably wasn't his real name either, Clark thought, was about thirty, with dark hair that belied his vaguely Nordic surname. Locally, Carlos Larson was thought to be the son of a Danish father and a Venezuelan mother, and he ran a flying school, a service much in demand. He was a skilled pilot who taught what he knew and didn't ask many questions, which appealed to his clientele. He didn't really need to ask questions — pilots, especially student pilots, talk a good deal — and he had a good memory for every sort of detail, plus the sort of professional expertise that invited lots of requests for advice. It was also widely believed that he'd financed his business by making a few highly illegal flights, then semiretired to a life of luxury. This legend created bona fides for the people in whom he had interest, but did so with-

119

out making him any sort of adversary. He was a man who'd done what was needed to get what he wanted, and now lived the sort of life that he'd wanted to live. That explained the car, which was the most powerful BMW made, and the expensive apartment, and the mistress, a stewardess for Avianca whose real job was as a courier for CIA. Larson thought it all a dream assignment, the more so because the stewardess really was his lover, a fringe benefit that might not have amused the Agency's personnel directorate. The only thing that bothered him was that his placement in Colombia was also unknown to the station chief. A relatively inexperienced agent, Larson — Clark would have been surprised to learn that that was his real name — knew enough about how the Agency worked to realize that separate command loops generally denoted some sort of special operation. His cover had been established over a period of eighteen months, during which he'd been required to do not very much in return. Clark's arrival was probably the signal that all of that was about to change. Time to earn his pay.

"What's the plan of the day?" Clark asked.

"Do a little flying. We'll be down before the weather goes bad," Larson added.

"I know you have an instrument rating."

"I will take that as a vote of confidence," the pilot said with a smile as he drove toward the airport. "You've been over the photos, of course."

"Yeah, about three days' worth. I'm just old-fashioned enough that I like to eyeball things myself. Maps and photos don't tell you everything."

"They told me the mission profile is just to fly around straight and level, no buzzing or circling to get people mad." The nice thing about having a flying school was that its aircraft were expected to be all over the place, but if one showed specific interest in specific people, they might take note of your registration number, and they might come down to the airport to ask why. The people who lived in Medellín were not known to ask such questions politely. Larson was not afraid of them. So long as he maintained his cover, he knew that he had little to worry about. At the same time, he was a pro, and pros are careful, especially if they want to last.

"Sounds okay to me." Clark knew the same things. He'd gotten old in a dangerous business by taking only the necessary risks. Those were bad enough. It wasn't very different from playing the lottery. Even though the odds were against one's hitting the number, if you played the game long enough, the right — or wrong — number would appear, no matter how careful you were. Except in this lottery the prize wasn't money. It was an unmarked, shallow grave, and you got that only if the opposition remembered something about religion.

He couldn't decide if he liked the mission or not. On the one hand, the objective was worthy enough. On the other . . . But Clark wasn't paid

121

to make that sort of evaluation. He was paid to do, not to think very much about it. That was the main problem with covert operations. You had to risk your life on the judgment of others. It was nice to know why, but the decision-makers said knowing why often had the effect of making the job all the more dangerous. The field operators didn't always believe that. Clark had that problem right now.

The Twin-Beech was parked in the general-aviation section of El Dorado International Airport. It didn't require too much in the way of intelligence to make an accurate assessment of what the aircraft were used for. There were too many expensive cars, and far too many expensive aircraft to be explained by the Colombian gentry. These were toys for the newly rich. Clark's eyes swept over them, his face showing neutral interest.

"Wages of sin ain't bad, are they?" Larson chuckled.

"What about the poor bastards who're paying the wages?"

"I know about that, too. I'm just saying that they're nice airplanes. Those Gulfstreams — I'm checked out on 'em — that's one sweet-handlin' bird."

"What do they cost?" Clark asked.

"A wise man once said, if you have to ask the price, you can't afford it."

"Yeah." Clark's mouth twisted into a smile. *But some things carry a price that's not measured in dollars*. He was already getting into the proper frame of mind for the mission.

Larson preflighted the Beech in about fifteen minutes. He'd just flown in ninety minutes earlier, and few private pilots would have bothered to run through the whole checklist, but Larson was a good pilot, which meant he was before all things a careful one. Clark took the right-side cockpit seat, strapping in as though he were a student pilot on his first hop. Commercial traffic was light at this hour, and it was easy to taxi into the takeoff pattern. About the only surprise was the long takeoff roll.

"It's the altitude," Larson explained over the intercom headset as he rotated off the runway. "It makes the controls a little mushy at low speed, too. No problem. Like driving in the snow — you just have to pay attention." He moved the lever to bring the gear up, leaving the aircraft at full power to claw up to altitude as quickly as possible. Clark scanned the instruments and saw nothing obviously awry, though it did seem odd to show nine thousand feet of altitude when you could still pick out individual people on the ground.

The aircraft banked to the left, taking a northwesterly heading. Larson backed off on the throttles, commenting that you also had to pay close attention to engine temperatures here, though the cooling systems on the twin Continental engines were beefed up to allow for it. They were heading toward the country's mountainous spine. The sky was clear and the sun was bright.

"Beautiful, isn't it?"

"It is that," Clark agreed. The mountains were covered with emerald-green trees whose leaves shimmered with moisture from the night's rain. But Clark's trained eyes saw something else. Walking these hills would be a cast-iron bitch. About the only good thing to be said was that there was good cover under which people could conceal themselves. The combination of steep hills and thin air would make this place an arduous one. He hadn't been briefed on what exactly was going to happen, but he knew enough to be glad that the hard part of the job would not be his.

The mountain ranges in Colombia run on a southwest-to-northeast vector. Larson picked a convenient pass to fly over, but the winds off the nearby Pacific Ocean made the crossing bumpy.

"Get used to it. Winds are picking up today because of the weather front that's moving in. They really boil around these hills. You ought to see what real bad weather is like."

"Thanks, but no thanks! Not much in the way of places to land in case things — "

"Go bad?" Larson asked. "That's why I pay attention to the checklist. Besides, there are more little strips down there than you might imagine. Of course, you don't always get a welcome when you decide to use one. Don't sweat it. I just put new engines on this bird a month ago. Sold the old ones to one of my students for his old King

Air. It belongs to the Bureau of Customs now," Larson explained.

"Did you have any part in that?"

"Negative! Look, they expect me to know why all these kids are taking lessons. I'm not supposed to be dumb, right? So I also teach them standard evasion tactics. You can read them in any decent book, and they expect me to be able to do that. Pablo wasn't real big on reading. Hell of a natural pilot, though. Too bad, really, he was a nice enough kid. They bagged him with fifty keys. I understand he didn't talk much. No surprise there. Gutsy little bastard."

"How well motivated are these folks?" Clark had seen lots of combat once, and he knew that the measure of an enemy is not to be found by counting his weapons.

Larson frowned at the sky. "Depends on what you mean. If you change the word from 'motivated' to 'macho,' that about covers it. You know, the cult of manliness, that sort of thing. Part of it's kinda admirable. These people have a funny sense of honor. For example, the ones I know socially treat me just fine. Their hospitality is impressive, especially if you show a little deference, which everyone does. Besides, I'm not a business rival. What I mean is, I know these people. I've taught a bunch of them to fly. If I had a money problem, I could probably go to them for help and get it. I'm talking like half a million in cash on a handshake — and I'd walk out of the hacienda with the cash in a briefcase. I'd have to

125

make some courier flights to square things, of course. And I'd never have to pay the money back. On the other hand, if I screwed them, well, they'd make damned sure that I paid for that, too. They have rules. If you live by them, you're fairly safe. If not, you'd better have your bags packed."

"I know about the ruthlessness. What about the brains?"

"They're as smart as they have to be. What smarts they don't have, they buy. They can buy anything, anybody. Don't underestimate them. Their security systems are state-of-the-art, like what we put on ICBM silos — shit, maybe better than that. They're protected as tightly as we protect the President, except their shooters are less restrained by rules of engagement. I suppose the best indicator on how smart they are is the fact that they've banded together to form the cartel. They're smart enough to know that gang wars cost everybody, so they formed a loose alliance. It ain't perfect, but it works. People who try to break into the business mostly end up dead. Medellín is an easy town to die in."

"Cops? Courts?"

"The locals have tried. Lots of dead cops, lots of dead judges to prove it," Larson said with a shake of the head. "Takes a lot for people to keep plugging away when they can't see any results. Then toss in the money angle. How often can a man walk away from a suitcase full of tax-free hundred-dollar bills? Especially when the alternative is certain death for himself and his family. The cartel is smart, my friend, and it's patient, and it has all the resources it needs, and it's ruthless enough to scare a veteran Nazi. All in all, that's some enemy." Larson pointed to a gray smudge in the distance. "There's Medellín. Drugs 'R Us, all in that one little city in the valley. One nuke could settle things, say about two megatons, air-burst four thousand feet AGL. I wonder if the rest of the country would really mind . . . ?"

That earned Larson a glance from his passenger. Larson lived here, knew a lot of these people, and even liked some, as he'd just said. But his hatred for them occasionally peeked through his professional detachment. The best sort of duplicity. This kid had a real future in the Agency, Clark decided. Brains and passion both. If he knew how to maintain a proper balance of the two, he could go places. Clark reached into his bag for a camera and a pair of binoculars. His interest wasn't in the city itself.

"Nice places, aren't they?"

The drug chieftains were growing increasingly security-conscious. The hilltops around the city were all being cleared of trees. Clark counted over a dozen new homes already. Homes, he thought with a snort. Castles was more like it. Walled fortresses. Enormous dwelling structures surrounded by low walls, surrounded in turn by hundreds of yards of clear, steep slopes. What people found picturesque about Italian villages and Bavarian castles was always the elegant setting. Always on the top of a hill or mountain. You could easily imagine the work that went into such a beautiful place — clearing the trees, hauling the stone blocks up the slopes, and ending up with a commanding view of the countryside that extended for miles. But the castles and villages hadn't been built in such places for fun, and neither had these houses. The heights meant that no one could approach them unobserved. The cleared ground around those houses was known in terse military nomenclature as a killing zone, a clear field of fire for automatic weapons. Each house had a single road up to a single gate. Each house had a helipad for a fast evacuation. The wall around each was made of stone that would stop any bullet up to fifty caliber. His binoculars showed that immediately inside each wall was a gravel or concrete path for guards to walk. A company of trained infantrymen would have no easy time assaulting one of these haciendas. *Maybe a helicopter assault, supported by mortars and gunships . . . Christ,* Clark thought to himself, *what am I thinking about?*

"What about house plans?"

"No problem. Three architectural firms have designed these places. Security isn't all that good there. Besides, I've been in that one for a party — just two weeks ago, as a matter of fact. I guess that's one area they're not too smart in. They like to show their places off. I can get you floor plans. The satellite overheads will show guard strength,

128

vehicle garaging, all that sort of thing."

"They do." Clark smiled.

"Can you tell me exactly what you're here for?"

"Well, they want an evaluation of the physical characteristics of the terrain."

"I can see that. Hell, I could do that easy enough from memory." Larson's question was not so much curiosity as his slight offense at not being asked to do this job himself.

"You know how it is at Langley," was the statement Clark used to dismiss the observation.

You're a pilot, Clark didn't say. *You've never humped a field pack in the boonies. I have.* If Larson had known his background, he could have made an intelligent guess, but what Clark did for the Agency, and what he'd done before joining, were not widely known. In fact, they were hardly known at all.

"Need-to-know, Mr. Larson," Clark said after another moment.

"Roger that," the pilot agreed over the intercom.

"Let's do a photo pass."

"I'll do a touch-and-go at the airport first. We want to make it look good."

"Fair enough," Clark agreed.

"What about the refining sites?" Clark asked after they headed back to El Dorado.

"Mainly southwest of here," Larson answered, turning the Beech away from the valley. "I've never seen one myself — I'm not in that part of the business, and they know it. If you want to scout them out, you go around at night with imaging IR equipment, but they're hard to track in on. Hell, they're portable, easy to set up, and easy to move. You can load the whole assembly on a medium truck and set it up ten miles away the next day."

"Not that many roads. . . . "

"What you gonna do, search every truck that comes along?" Larson asked. "Besides, you can man-pack it if you want. Labor's cheap down here. The opposition is smart, and adaptable."

"How much does the local army get involved?" Clark had been fully briefed, of course, but he also knew that a local perspective might not agree with Washington's — and might be correct.

"They've tried. Biggest problem they have is sustaining their forces — their helicopters don't spend twenty percent of their time in the air. That means they don't do many ops. It means that if anyone gets hit he might get medical attention very fast — and that hurts performance when they do run ops. Even then — you can guess what the government pays a captain, say. Now imagine that somebody meets that captain at a local bar, buys him a drink, and talks to him. He tells the captain that he might want to be in the southwestern corner of his sector tomorrow night — well, *anywhere but* the northeastern sector, okay? If he decides to patrol one part of his area, but not another, he gets a hundred thousand dollars. Okay, the other side has enough money that they can pay him up front just to see if he'll cooperate. Seed money, kind of. Once he shows he can be bought, they settle down to a smaller but regular payment. Also, the other side has enough product that they can let him do some real seizures once in a while, once they know he's theirs, to make him look good. Someday that captain grows up and becomes a colonel who controls a lot more territory. . . . It's not because they're bad people, it's just that things are so fucking hopeless. Legal institutions are fragile down here and — hell, look at the way things are at home, for Christ's sake. I — "

"I'm not criticizing anybody, Larson," Clark said. "Not everybody can take on a hopeless mission and keep at it." He turned to look out the side window and smiled to himself. "You have to be a little crazy to do that."

5.

Beginnings

Chavez awoke with the headache that accompanies initial exposure to a thin atmosphere, the sort that begins just behind the eyes and radiates around the circumference of one's head. For all that, he was grateful. Throughout his career in the Army, he'd never failed to awaken a few minutes before reveille. It allowed him an orderly transition from sleep to wakefulness and made the waking-up process easier to tolerate. He turned his head left and right, inspecting his environment in the orange twilight that came through the uncurtained windows.

The building would be called a barracks by anyone who did not regularly live in one. To Chavez it seemed more of a hunting camp, a guess that was wholly accurate. Perhaps two thousand square feet in the bunk room, he judged, and he counted a total of forty single metal-frame bunks, each with a thin GI mattress and brown GI blanket. The sheets, however, were fitted, with elastic at the corners; so he decided that there wouldn't be any of the bouncing-quarter bullshit, which was fine with him. The floor was bare, waxed pine, and the vaulted ceiling was supported by smoothed-down pine trunks in lieu of finished beams. It struck the sergeant that in hunting season people — rich people — actually paid to live like this: proof positive that money didn't automatically confer brains on anyone. Chavez didn't like barracks life all that much, and the only reason he'd not opted for a private apartment in or near Fort Ord was his desire to save up for that Corvette. To complete the illusion, at the foot of each bed was a genuine Army-surplus footlocker.

He thought about getting up on his elbows to look out the windows, but knew that the time for that would come soon enough. It had been a two-hour drive from the airport, and on arrival each man had been assigned a bunk in the building. The rest of the bunks had already been filled with sleeping, snoring men. Soldiers, of course. Only soldiers snored like that. It had struck him at the time as ominous. The only reason why young men would be asleep and snoring just after ten at night was fatigue. This was no vacation spot. Well, that was no surprise either.

Reveille came in the form of an electric buzzer, the kind associated with a cheap alarm clock. That was good news. No bugle — he hated bugles in the morning. Like most professional soldiers, Chavez knew the value of sleep, and waking up was not a cause for celebration. Bodies stirred around him at once, to the accompaniment of the usual wake-up grumbles and profanity. He tossed off the blanket and was surprised to learn how cold the floor was.

"Who're you?" the man in the next bunk said while staring at the floor.

"Chavez, Staff Sergeant. Bravo, 3rd of the 17th."

"Vega. Me, too. Headquarters Company, 1st/22nd. Get in last night?"

"Yep. What gives here?"

"Well, I don't really know, but they sure did run us ragged yesterday," Staff Sergeant Vega said. He stuck his hand out. "Julio."

"Domingo. Call me Ding."

"Where you from?"

"L.A."

"Chicago. Come on." Vega rose. "One good thing about this place, you got all the hot water you want, and no Mickey Mouse on the housekeeping. Now, if they could just turn the fucking heat on at night — "

"Where the hell are we?"

"Colorado. I know that much. Not much else, though." The two sergeants joined a loose trail of men heading for the showers.

Chavez looked around. Nobody was wearing glasses. Everybody looked pretty fit, even accounting for the fact that they were soldiers. A few were obvious iron-pumpers, but most, like

134

Chavez, had the lean, wiry look of distance runners. One other thing that was so obvious it took him half a minute to notice it. They were all Latinos.

The shower helped. There was a nice, tall pile of new towels, and enough sinks that everyone had room to shave. And the toilet stalls even had doors. Except for the thin air, Chavez decided, this place had real possibilities. Whoever ran the place gave them twenty-five minutes to get it together. It was almost civilized.

Civilization ended promptly at 0630. The men got into their uniforms, which included stout boots, and moved outside. Here Chavez saw four men standing in a line. They had to be officers. You could tell from the posture and the expressions. Behind the four was another, older man, who also looked and acted like an officer, but . . . not quite, Chavez told himself.

"Where do I go?" Ding asked Vega.

"You're supposed to stick with me. Third squad, Captain Ramirez. Tough mother, but a good guy. Hope you like to run, *'mano*."

"I'll try not to crap out on ya'," Chavez replied.

Vega turned with a grin. "That's what I said."

"Good morning, people!" boomed the voice of the older one. "For those of you who don't know me, I am Colonel Brown. You newcomers, welcome to our little mountain hideaway. You've already gotten to your proper squads, and for everyone's information, our TO and E is now

135

complete. This is the whole team."

It didn't surprise Chavez that Brown was the only obvious non-Latino to be seen. But he didn't know why he wasn't surprised. Four others were walking toward the assembly. They were PT instructors. You can always tell from the clean, white T-shirts and the confidence that they could work anyone into the ground.

"I hope everyone got a good night's sleep," Brown went on. "We will start our day with a little exercise — "

"Sure," Vega muttered, "might as well die before breakfast."

"How long you been here?" Ding asked quietly.

"Second day. Jesus, I hope it gets easier. The officers musta been here a week at least — they don't barf after the run."

" — and a nice little three-mile jog through the hills," Brown ended.

"That's no big deal," Chavez observed.

"That's what I said yesterday," Vega replied. "Thank God I quit smokin'."

Ding didn't know how to react to that. Vega was another light infantryman from the 10th Mountain, and like himself was supposed to be able to move around all day with fifty pounds of gear on his back. But the air was pretty thin, thin enough that Chavez wondered just how high they were.

They started off with the usual daily dozen, and the number of repeats wasn't all that bad, though Chavez found himself breaking a slight sweat. It was the run that told him how tough things would get. As the sun rose above the mountains, he got a feel for what sort of country it was. The camp was nestled in the bottom of a valley, and comprised perhaps fifty acres of almost flat ground. Everything else looked vertical, but on inspection proved to be slopes of less than forty-five degrees, dotted with scruffy-looking little pine trees that would never outgrow the height for Christmas decorations. The four squads, each led by an instructor and a captain, moved in different directions, up horse trails worn into the mountainside. In the first mile, Chavez reckoned, they had climbed over five hundred feet, snaking their way along numerous switchbacks toward a rocky knoll. The instructor didn't bother with the usual singing that accompanied formation running. There wasn't much of a formation anyway, just a single-file of men struggling to keep pace with a faceless robot whose white shirt beckoned them on toward destruction. Chavez, who hadn't run a distance less than three miles, every day for the last two years of his life, was gasping for breath after the first. He wanted to say something, like, "There isn't any fuckin' air!" But he didn't want to waste the oxygen. He needed every little molecule for his bloodstream. The instructor stopped at the knoll to make sure everyone was there, and Chavez, jogging doggedly in place, had the chance to see a vista worthy of an Ansel Adams photograph — all the better in the full light of a morning sun. But his only thought on being able to see over forty miles was terror that he'd have to run it all.

God, I thought I was in shape!

Hell, I am in shape!

The next mile traced a ridgeline to the east, and the sun punished eyes that had to stay alert. This was a narrow trail, and going off it could involve a painful fall. The instructor gradually picked up the pace, or so it seemed, until he stopped again at another knoll.

"Keep those legs pumpin'!" he snarled at those who'd kept up. There were two stragglers, both new men, Chavez thought, and they were only twenty yards back. You could see the shame on their faces, and the determination to catch up. "Okay, people, it's downhill from here."

And it was, mostly, but that only made it more dangerous. Legs rubbery from the fatigue that comes from oxygen deprivation had to negotiate a downward slope that alternated from gradual to perilously steep, with plenty of loose rocks for the unwary. Here the instructor eased off on the pace, for safety as everyone guessed. The captain let his men pass, and took up the rear to keep an eye on things. They could see the camp now. Five buildings. Smoke rose from a chimney to promise breakfast. Chavez saw a helipad, half a dozen vehicles — all four-wheel-drives — and what could only be a rifle range. There was no other sign of human habitation in sight, and the

138

sergeant realized that even the wide view he'd had earlier hadn't shown any buildings closer than five or six miles. It wasn't hard to figure out why the area was sparsely settled. But he didn't have time or energy for deep thoughts at the moment. His eyes locked on the trail, Ding Chavez concentrated on his footing and the pace. He took up a position alongside one of the erstwhile stragglers and kept an eye on him. Already Chavez was thinking of this as his squad, and soldiers are supposed to look out for one another. But the man had firmed up. His head was high now, his hands balled into tight, determined fists, and his powerfully exhaled breaths had purpose in them as the trail finally flattened out and they approached the camp. Another group was coming in from the far side.

"Form up, people!" Captain Ramirez called out for the first time. He passed his men and took the place of the instructor, who peeled off to let them by. Chavez noted that the bastard wasn't even sweating. Third Squad formed into a double line behind their officer.

"Squad! Quick-time, march!" Everyone slowed to a regular marching pace. This took the strain off lungs and legs, told them that they were now the custody of their captain, and reminded them that they were still part of the Army. Ramirez delivered them in front of their barracks. The captain didn't order anyone to sing a cadence, though. That made him smart, Chavez thought, smart enough to know that nobody had enough breath to do so. Julio was right, probably. Ramirez might be a good boss.

"Squad, halt!" Ramirez turned. "At ease, people. Now, that wasn't so bad, was it?"

"*Madre de Dios!*" a voice noted quietly. From the back rank, a man tried to vomit but couldn't find anything to bring up.

"Okay." Ramirez grinned at his men. "The altitude is a real bitch. But I've been here two weeks. You get used to it right quick. Two weeks from now, we'll be running five miles a day with packs, and you'll feel just fine."

Bullshit. Chavez shared the thought with Julio Vega, knowing that the captain was right, of course. The first day at boot camp had been harder than this . . . hadn't it?

"We're taking it easy on you. You have an hour to unwind and get some breakfast. Go easy on the chow: we'll have another little run this afternoon. At 0800 we assemble here for training. Dismissed."

"Well?" Ritter asked.

They sat on the shaded veranda of an old planter's house on the island of St. Kitts. Clark wondered what they'd planted here once. Probably sugarcane, though there was nothing now. What had once been a plantation manor was obviously supposed to look like the island retreat of a top-drawer capitalist and his collection of mistresses. In fact it belonged to CIA, which used it as an informal conference center, a particularly nice safe house for the debriefing of VIP defectors, and other, more mundane uses — like a vacation spot for senior executives.

"The background info was fairly accurate, but it underestimated the physical difficulties. I'm not criticizing the people who put the package together. You just have to see it to believe it. It's very tough country." Clark stretched in the wicker chair and reached for his drink. His personal seniority at the Agency was many levels below Ritter's, but Clark was one of a handful of CIA employees whose position was unique. That, plus the fact that he often worked personally for the Deputy Director (Operations), gave him the right to relax in the DDO's presence. Ritter's attitude toward the younger man was not one of deference, but he did show Clark considerable respect. "How's Admiral Greer doing?" Clark asked. It was James Greer who'd actually recruited him, many years before.

"Doesn't look very good. Couple of months at most," Ritter replied.

"Damn." Clark stared into his drink, then looked up. "I owe that man a lot. Like my whole life. They can't do anything?"

"No, it's spread too much for that. They can keep him comfortable, that's about all. Sorry. He's my friend, too."

"Yes, sir, I know." Clark finished off his drink and went back to work. "I still don't know exactly what you have in mind, but you can forget about going after them in their houses."

"That tough?"

Clark nodded. "That tough. It's a job for real infantry with real support, and even then you're going to take real casualties. From what Larson tells me, the security troops these characters have are pretty good. I suppose you might try to buy a few off, but they're probably well paid already, so that might just backfire." The field officer didn't ask what the real mission was, but he assumed it was to snatch some warm bodies and whisk them off stateside, where they'd arrive gift-wrapped in front of some FBI office, or maybe a U.S. courthouse. Like everyone else, he was making an incorrect guess. "Same thing with bagging one on the move. They take the usual precautions — irregular schedules, irregular routes, and they have armed escorts everywhere they go. So bagging one on the fly means having good intel, which means having somebody on the inside. Larson is as close to being inside as anybody we've ever run, and he's not close enough. Trying to get him in closer will get him killed. He's gotten us some good data — Larson's a pretty good kid — and the risks of trying that are just too great. I presume the local people have tried to — "

"They have. Six of them ended up dead or missing. Same thing with informers. They disappear a lot. The locals are thoroughly penetrated. They can't run any sort of op for long without risking their own. You do that long enough and people stop volunteering."

Clark shrugged and looked out to seaward. There was a white-hulled cruise ship inbound on the horizon. "I suppose I shouldn't have been surprised at how tough these bastards are. Larson was right, what brains they don't already have they can buy. Where do they hire their consultants?"

"Open market, mainly Europe, and — "

"I mean the intel pros. They must have some real spooks."

"Well, there's Félix Cortez. That's only a rumor, but the name's come up half a dozen times in the past few months."

"The DGI colonel who disappeared," Clark observed. The DGI was Cuba's intelligence service, modeled on the Soviet KGB. Cortez had been reported working with the Macheteros, a Puerto Rican terrorist group that the FBI had largely run to ground in the past few years. Another DGI colonel named Filiberto Ojeda had been arrested by the Bureau, after which Cortez had disappeared. So he'd decided to remain outside his country's borders. Next question: had Cortez decided to opt for this most vigorous branch of the free-enterprise system or was he still working under Cuban control? Either way, DGI was Russian-trained. Its senior people were graduates of the KGB's own academy. They were, therefore, opponents worthy of respect. Certainly Cortez was. His file at the Agency spoke of a genius for compromising people to get information.

"Larson know about this?"

"Yeah. He caught the name at a party. Of course, it would help if we knew what the hell Cortez looks like, but all we have is a description that fits half the people south of the Rio Grande. Don't worry. Larson knows how to be careful, and if anything goes wrong, he's got his own airplane to get out of Dodge with. His orders are fairly specific on that score. I don't want to lose a trained field officer doing police work." Ritter added, "I sent you down for a fresh appraisal. You know what the overall objective is. Tell me what you think is possible."

"Okay. You're probably right to go after the airfields and to keep it an intelligence-gathering operation. Given the necessary surveillance assets, we *could* finger processing sites fairly easily, but there's a lot of them and their mobility demands a rapid reaction time to get there. I figure that'll work maybe a half-dozen times, max, before the other side wises up. Then we'll take casualties, and if the bad guys get lucky, we might lose a whole assault force — if you've got people thinking in those terms. Tracking the finished product from the processing sites is probably impossible without a whole lot of people on the ground — too many to keep it a covert op for very long — and it wouldn't buy us very much anyway. There are a lot of little airfields on the northern part of the country to keep an eye on, but Larson thinks that they may be victims of their own success. They've been so successful buying off the military and police in that district that they might be falling into a regular pattern of airfield use. If the insertion teams keep a low profile, they could conceivably operate for two months — that may be a little generous — before we have to yank them out. I need to see the teams, see how good they are."

"I can arrange that," Ritter said. He'd already decided to send Clark to Colorado. Clark was the best man to evaluate their capabilities. "Go on."

"What we're setting up will go all right for a month or two. We can watch their aircraft lift off and call it ahead to whoever else is wrapped up in this." This was the only part of the op that Clark knew about. "We can inconvenience them for that long, but I wouldn't hope for much more."

"You're painting a fairly bleak picture, Clark."

Clark leaned forward. "Sir, if you want to run a covert operation to gather usable tactical intelligence against an adversary who's this decentralized in his own operations — yes, it's possible, but only for a limited period of time and only for a limited return. If you increase the assets to try and make it more effective, you're going to get blown sure as hell. You can run an operation like that, but it can't be for long. I don't know why we're even bothering." That wasn't quite true. Clark figured, correctly, that the reason was that it was an election year, but that wasn't the sort of observation a field officer was allowed to make — especially when it was a correct one.

"Why we're bothering isn't strictly your concern," Ritter pointed out. He didn't raise his voice. He didn't have to, and Clark was not a man to be intimidated.

"Fine, but this is not a serious undertaking. It's an old story, sir. Give us a mission we can do, not one we can't. Are we serious about this or aren't we?"

"What do you have in mind?" Ritter asked.

Clark told him. Ritter's face showed little in the way of emotion at the answer to his question. One of the nice things about Clark, Ritter thought to himself, was that he was the only man in the Agency who could discuss these topics calmly and dispassionately — and really mean it. There were quite a few for whom such talk was an interesting intellectual exercise, unprofessional speculation, really, gotten consciously or subconsciously from reading spy fiction. *Gee, wouldn't it be nice if we could* . . . It was widely believed in the general public that the Central Intelligence Agency employed a goodly number of expert professionals in this particular field. It didn't. Even the KGB had gotten away from such things, farming this kind of work out to the Bulgarians — regarded by their own associates as uncouth barbarians — or genuine third-parties like terrorist groups in Europe and the Middle East. The political cost of such operations was too high, and despite the mania for secrecy cultivated by every intelligence service in the world, such things always got out eventually. The world had gotten far more civilized since Ritter had graduated from The Farm on the York River, and while he thought that a genuinely good thing, there were times when a return to the good old days beckoned with solutions to problems that hadn't quite gone away.

"How hard would it be?" Ritter asked, interested.

"With the proper backup and some additional assets — it's a snap." Clark explained what special assets were needed. "Everything they've done plays into our hands. That's the one mistake they've made. They're conventional in their defensive outlook. Same old thing, really. It's a matter of who determines the rules of the game. As things now stand, we both play by the same rules, and those rules, as applied here, give the advantage to the opposition. We never seem to learn that. We always let the other side set the rules. We can annoy them, inconvenience them, take away some of their profit margin, but, hell, given what they already make, it's a minor business loss. I only see one thing changing that."

"Which is?"

"How'd you like to live in a house like that one?" Clark asked, handing over one of his photographs.

"Frank Lloyd Wright meets Ludwig the Mad," Ritter observed with a chuckle.

"The man who commissioned that house is growing quite an ego, sir. They have manipulated whole governments. Everyone says that they *are* a government for all practical purposes. They said the same thing in Chicago during Prohibition, that Capone really ran the town — just one city, right? Well, these people are on their way to running their own *country*, and renting out others. So let's say that they do have the *de facto* power of a government. Factor ego into that. Sooner or later they're going to start acting like one. I know we won't break the rules. But it wouldn't surprise me if they stepped outside them once or twice, just to see what they might get away with. You see what I mean? They keep expanding their own limits, and they haven't found the brick wall yet, the one that tells them where to stop."

"John, you're turning into a psychologist," Ritter noted with a thin smile.

"Maybe so. These guys peddle addictive drugs, right? Mostly they do not use the stuff themselves, but I think they're getting themselves hooked on the most powerful narcotic there is."

"Power."

Clark nodded. "Sooner or later, they're going to OD. At that point, sir, somebody's going to think seriously about what I just proposed. When you get into the majors, the rules change some. That's a political decision, of course."

He was master of all he surveyed. At least that was the phrase that came to mind, and with all such aphorisms it could be both true and false at the same time. The valley into which he looked did not all belong to him; the parcel of land on which he stood was less than a thousand hectares, and his vista included millions. But not one person who lived within his view could continue to live were he to decide otherwise. That was the only sort of power that mattered, and it was a form of power that he had exercised on occasions too numerous to count. A flick of the wrist, a casual remark to an associate, and it was done. It wasn't that he had ever been casual about it — death was a serious business — but he knew that he could be. It was the sort of power that might make a man mad, he knew. He'd seen it happen among his own business associates, to their sorrow on several occasions. But he was a student of the world, and a student of history. Unusually, for someone in his chosen trade, he was the beneficiary of a good education, something forced on him by his late father, one of the pioneers. One of the greatest regrets of his life was that he'd never expressed his gratitude for it. Because of it he understood economics as well as any university professor. He understood market forces and trends. And he understood the historical forces that brought them about. He was a student of Marxism; though he rejected the Marxist outlook for a multiplicity of reasons, he knew that it contained more than one grain of truth intermixed with all the political gibberish. The rest of his professional education had been what Americans called "on-the-job training." While his father had helped invent a whole new way of doing business, he had watched and advised, and taken

149

action. He'd explored new markets, under his father's direction, and formed the reputation of a careful, thorough planner, often sought after but never apprehended. He'd been arrested only once, but after two of the witnesses had died, the others had grown forgetful, ending his direct experience with police and courts.

He deemed himself a carry-over from another age — a classic robber-baron capitalist. A hundred years before, they'd driven railroads across the United States — he was a genuine expert on that country — and crushed anything in their path. Indian tribes — treated like a two-legged version of the plains buffalo and swatted aside. Unions — neutralized with hired thugs. Governments — bribed and subverted. The press — allowed to bray on . . . until too many people listened. He'd learned from that example. The local press was no longer terribly outspoken, not after learning that its members were mortal. The railroad barons had built themselves palatial homes — winter ones in New York, and summer "cottages" at Newport. Of course, he had problems that they'd not faced, but any historical model broke down if you took it too far. He also chose to ignore the fact that the Goulds and the Harrimans had built something that was useful, not destructive, to their societies. One other lesson he had learned from the previous century was that cutthroat competition was wasteful. He had persuaded his father to seek out his competitors. Even then his powers of persuasion had been impressive. Cleverly, it had been done at a time when danger from outside forces made cooperation attractive. Better to cooperate, the argument had gone, than to waste time, money, energy, and blood — and increase their own personal vulnerabilities. And it had worked.

His name was Ernesto Escobedo. He was one of many within the Cartel, but most of his peers would acknowledge that his was a voice to which all listened. They might not all agree, not all bend to his will, but his ideas were always given the attention they deserved because they had proven to be effective ones. The Cartel had no head as such, since the Cartel was not a single enterprise, but rather a collection of leaders who operated in close confederation — almost a committee, but not quite; almost friends, but not that either. The comparison to the American Mafia suggested itself, but the Cartel was both more civilized and more savage than that. Escobedo would have chosen to say that the Cartel was more effectively organized, and more vigorous, both attributes of a young and vital organization, as opposed to one that was older and feudal.

He knew that the sons of the robber barons had used the wealth accumulated by their antecedents to form a power elite, coming to rule their nation with their "service." He was unwilling to leave such a legacy to his sons, however. Besides, he himself was technically one of the second generation. Things moved more quickly now. The accumulation of great wealth no longer

151

demanded a lifetime, and, therefore, Ernesto told himself, he didn't have to leave that to his sons. He could have it all. The first step in accomplishing any goal was deciding that it was possible. He had long since come to that decision.

It was his goal to see it done. Escobedo was forty, a man of uncommon vigor and confidence. He had never used the product which he provided for others, instead altering his consciousness with wine — and that rarely, now. A glass or two with dinner; perhaps some hard liquor at business meetings with his peers, but more often Perrier. This trait earned him more respect among his associates. Escobedo was a sober, serious man, they all knew. He exercised regularly, and paid attention to his appearance. A smoker in his youth, he'd broken the habit young. He watched his diet. His mother was still alive and vigorous at seventy-three; her mother was the same at ninety-one. His father would have been seventy-five last week, he knew, except for . . . but the people who'd ended his father's life had paid a savage price for their crime, along with all of their families, mostly at Escobedo's own hand. It was something he remembered with filial pride, taking the last one's wife while her dying husband watched, killing her and the two little ones before his eyes closed for the last time. He took no pleasure in killing women and children, of course, but such things were necessary. He'd shown that one who was the better man, and as word of the feat spread, it had become unlikely that his family would ever be troubled again. He took no pleasure from it, but history taught that harsh lessons made for long memories. It also taught that those who failed to teach such lessons would not be respected. Escobedo demanded respect above all things. His personal involvement in settling that particular account, instead of leaving it to hirelings, had earned him considerable prestige within the organization. Ernesto was a thinker, his associates said, but he knew how to get things done.

His wealth was so great that counting it had no point. He had the godlike power of life and death. He had a beautiful wife and three fine sons. When the marriage bed palled, he had a choice of mistresses. Every luxury that money could purchase, he had. He had homes in the city below him, this hilltop fortress, and ranches near the sea — both seas, in fact, since Colombia borders on two great oceans. At the ranches were stables full of Arabian horses. Some of his associates had private bull rings, but that sport had never interested him. A crack shot, he had hunted everything that his country offered — including men, of course. He told himself that he ought to be satisfied. But he was not.

The American robber barons had traveled the world, had been invited to the courts of Europe, had married off their progeny to that of noble houses — a cynical exercise, he knew, but somehow a worthy one that he fully understood. The

153

freedoms were denied him, and though the reason for it was plain enough, he was nevertheless offended that a man of his power and wealth could be denied anything. Despite everything that he had accomplished, there were still limits on his life — worse still, the limits were placed there by others of lesser power. Twenty years earlier he had chosen his path to greatness, and despite his obvious success, the fact that he'd chosen that particular path denied him the fruits that he wanted, because lesser men did not approve of it.

It had not always been so. "Law?" one of the great railroad men had said once. "What do I care about law?" And he had gotten away with it, had traveled about at will, had been recognized as a great man.

So why not me? Escobedo asked himself. Part of him knew the answer, but a more powerful part rejected it. He was not a stupid man, far less a foolish one, but he had not come so far to have others set rules upon his life. Ernesto had, in fact, violated every rule he wished, and prospered from it. He had gotten here by making his own rules, the businessman decided. He would have to learn to make some new ones. They would learn to deal with him, on terms of his own choosing. He was tired of having to accommodate the terms of others. Having made the decision, he began to explore methods.

What had worked for others?

The most obvious answer was — success. That

which one could not defeat, one had to acknowledge. International politics had as few rules as any other major enterprise, except for the only one that mattered — success. There was not a country in the world that failed to make deals with murderers, after all; it was just that the murderers in question had to be effective ones. Kill a few million people and one was a statesman. Did not every nation in the world kowtow to the Chinese — and had they not killed millions of their own? Didn't America seek to accommodate the Russians — and had they not killed millions of their own? Under Carter, the Americans had supported the regime of Pol Pot, which had killed millions of its own. Under Reagan, America had sought to reach a *modus vivendi* with the same Iranians who had killed so many of their own, including most of those who thought of America as a friend — and been abandoned. America befriended dictators with bloody hands — some on the right and some on the left — in the name of *realpolitik*, while refusing to support moderates — left or right — because they might not be quite moderate enough. Any country so lacking in principle could come to recognize him and his associates, couldn't it? That was the central truth about America in Ernesto's view. While he had principles from which he would not deviate, America did not.

The corruption of America was manifest to Ernesto. He, after all, fed it. For years now, forces in his largest and most important market had lobbied to legalize his business there. Fortunately they had all failed. That would have been disaster for the Cartel, and was yet another example of how a government lacked the wit to act in its own self-interest. The American government could have made billions from the business — as he and his associates did — but lacked the vision and the good sense to do so. And they called themselves a great power. For all their supposed strength, the *yanquis* had no will, no manhood. He could regulate the goings-on where he lived, but they could not. They could range over oceans, fill the air with warplanes — but use them to protect their own interests? He shook his head with amusement.

No, the Americans were not to be respected.

6.

Deterrence

Félix Cortez traveled with a Costa Rican passport. If someone noted his Cuban accent, he'd explain that his family had left that country when he was a boy, but by carefully selecting his port of entry, he avoided that notice. Besides, he was working on the accent. Cortez was fluent in three languages — English and Russian in addition to his native Spanish. A raffishly handsome man, his tropical complexion was barely different from a vacationer's tan. The neat mustache and custom-tailored suit proclaimed him a successful businessman, and the gleaming white teeth made him a pleasant one at that. He waited in the immigration line at Dulles International Airport, chatting with the lady behind him until he got to the INS inspector, as resignedly unhurried as any frequent traveler.

"Good afternoon, sir," the inspector said, barely looking up from the passport. "What brings you to America?"

"Business," Cortez replied.

"Uh-huh," the inspector grunted. He flipped through the passport and saw numerous entry stamps. The man traveled a lot, and about half his trips in the previous . . . four years were to the States. The stamps were evenly split between Miami, Washington, and Los Angeles. "How long will you be staying?"

"Five days."

"Anything to declare?"

"Just my clothes, and my business notes." Cortez held up his briefcase.

"Welcome to America, Mr. Díaz." The inspector stamped the passport and handed it back.

"Thank you." He moved off to collect his bag, a large and well-used two-suiter. He tried to come through American airports at slack hours. This was less for convenience than because it was unusual for someone who had something to hide. At slack times the inspectors had all the time they needed to annoy people, and the sniffer dogs weren't rushed along the rows of luggage. It was also easier to spot surveillance when the airport concourses were uncrowded, of course, and Cortez/Díaz was an expert at countersurveillance.

His next stop was the Hertz counter, where he rented a full-size Chevy. Cortez had no love for Americans, but he did like their big cars. The routine was down pat. He used a Visa card. The young lady at the counter asked the usual question about joining the Hertz Number One Club, and he took the proffered brochure with feigned interest. The only reason he used a rental car company more than once was that there weren't enough to avoid repetition. Similarly, he never used the same passport twice, nor the same credit cards. At a place near his home he had an ample supply of both. He had come to Washington to see one of the people who made that possible.

His legs were still stiff as he walked out to get his car — he could have taken the courtesy van, but he'd been sitting for too long. The damp heat of a late spring day reminded him of home. Not that he remembered Cuba all that fondly, but his former government had, after all, given him the training that he needed for his current job. All the school classes on Marxism-Leninism, telling people who scarcely had food to eat that they lived in paradise. In Cortez's case, they'd had the effect of telling him what he wanted out of life. His training in the DGI had given him the first taste of privilege, and the unending political instruction had only made his government look all the more grotesque in its claims and its goals. But he'd played the game, and learned what he'd needed to learn, exchanging his time for training and field work, learning how capitalist societies work, learning how to penetrate and subvert them, learning their strong points and weak ones. The contrast between the two was entertaining to the former colonel. The relative poverty in Puerto Rico had looked like paradise to him, even while working along with fellow Colonel

Ojeda and the Machetero savages to overthrow it — and replace it with Cuba's version of socialist realism. Cortez shook his head in amusement as he walked toward the parking lot.

Twenty feet over the Cuban's head, Liz Murray dropped her husband off behind a vanload of travelers. There was barely time for a kiss. She had errands to run, and they'd call Dan's flight in another ten minutes.

"I ought to be back tomorrow afternoon," he said as he got out.

"Good," Liz replied. "Remember the movers."

"I won't." Dan closed the door and took three steps. "I mean, I won't forget, honey . . . " He turned in time to see his wife laughing as she drove off; she'd done it to him again. "It's not fair," he grumbled to himself. "Bring you back from London, big promotion, and second day on the job they drop you in the soup." He walked through the self-opening doors into the terminal and found a TV monitor with his flight information. He had only one bag, and that was small enough to carry on. He'd already reviewed the paperwork — it had all been faxed to Washington by the Mobile Field Office and was the subject of considerable talk in the Hoover Building.

The next step was getting through the metal detector. Actually he bypassed it. The attendant gave out the usual, "Excuse me, sir," and Murray held up his ID folder, identifying himself as Daniel E. Murray, Deputy Assistant Director of the Federal Bureau of Investigation. There was no way he could have passed through the magnetometer, not with the Smith & Wesson automatic clipped to his belt, and people in airports tended to get nervous if he showed what he was carrying. Not that he shot that well with it. He hadn't even requalified yet. That was scheduled for the next week. They weren't so strict about that with top-level FBI management — his main workplace hazard now came from staple pullers — but though Murray was a man with few vanities, shooting skill was one of them. For no particular reason, Murray was worried about that. After four years in London as the legal attaché, he knew that he needed some serious practice before he would shoot "expert" with either hand again, especially with a new gun. His beloved stainless-steel Colt Python .357 was in retirement. The Bureau was switching over to automatics, and on his arrival in his new office he'd found the engraved S&W gift-wrapped on his desk, a present arranged by his friend Bill Shaw, the newly appointed executive assistant director (Investigations). Bill always had been a class act. Murray switched the bag to his left hand and surreptitiously checked to see that the gun was in place, much as an ordinary citizen might check for his wallet. The only bad thing about his London duty was being unarmed. Like any American cop, Murray felt slightly naked without a gun, even though he'd never had cause to use one in anger. If nothing else, he could make sure that this flight didn't go to Cuba. He wouldn't have much chance to do hands-on law enforcement anymore, of course. Now he was part of management, another way of saying that he was too old to be useful, Murray told himself as he selected a seat close to the departure gate. The problem at hand was about as close as he was going to get to handling a real case, and it was happening only because the Director had got hold of the file and called in Bill Shaw who, in turn, had decided that he wanted someone he knew to take a look at it. It promised to be ticklish. They were really starting him off with a cute one.

The flight took just over two hours of routine boredom and a dry meal. Murray was met at the gate by Supervisory Special Agent Mark Bright, assistant special-agent-in-charge of the Mobile Field Office.

"Any other bags, Mr. Murray?"

"Just this one — and the name's Dan," Murray replied. "Has anybody talked to them yet?"

"Not in yet — that is, I don't think so." Bright checked his watch. "They were due in about ten, but they got called in on a rescue last night. Some fishing boat blew up and the cutter had to get the crew off. It made the morning TV news. Nice job, evidently."

"Super," Murray observed. "We're going in to grill a friggin' hero, and he's gone and done it again."

"You know this guy's background?" Bright asked. "I haven't had much chance to — "

162

"I've been briefed. Hero's the right word. This Wegener's a legend. Red Wegener's called the King of SAR — that means search-and-rescue. Half the people who've ever been to sea, he's saved at one time or another. At least that's the word on the guy. He's got some big-time friends on The Hill, too."

"Like?"

"Senator Billings of Oregon." Murray explained why briefly.

"Chairman of Judiciary. Why couldn't he just have stayed with Transportation?" Bright asked the ceiling. The Senate Judiciary Committee had oversight duties for the FBI.

"How new are you on this case?"

"I'm here because DEA liaison is my job. I didn't see the file until just before lunch. Been out of the office for a couple of days," Bright said as he walked through the door. "We just had a baby."

"Oh," Murray noted. You couldn't blame a man for that. "Congratulations. Everyone all right?"

"Brought Marianne home this morning, and Sandra is the cutest thing I ever saw. Noisy, though."

Murray laughed. It had been quite a while since he'd had to handle an infant. Bright's car turned out to be a Ford whose engine purred like a well-fed tiger. Some paperwork on Captain Wegener lay on the front seat. Murray leafed through it while Bright picked his way out of the

163

airport parking lot. It fleshed out what he'd heard in Washington.

"This is some story."

"How 'bout that." Bright nodded. "You don't suppose this is all true, do you?"

"I've heard some crazy ones before, but this one would be the all-time champ." Murray paused. "The funny thing is — "

"Yeah," the younger agent agreed. "Me, too. Our DEA colleagues believe it, but what broke loose out of this — I mean, even if the evidence is all tossed, what we got out of this is so — "

"Right." Which was the other reason Murray was involved in the case. "How important was the victim?"

"Big-time political connections, directorships of banks, the University of Alabama, the usual collection of civic groups — you name it. This guy wasn't just a solid member of the community, he was goddamned Stone Mountain." Both men knew that was in Georgia, but the point was made. "Old family, back to a Civil War general. His grandfather was a governor."

"Money?"

Bright grunted. "More than I'd ever need. Big place north of town, still a working farm — plantation, I guess you'd call it, but that's not where it comes from. He put all the family money into real-estate development. Very successfully as far as we can tell. The development stuff is a maze of small corporations — the usual stuff. We've got a team working, but it'll take awhile to sort through it. Some of the corporate veils are over-seas, though, and we may never get it all. You know how that goes. We've barely begun to check things out."

" 'Prominent local businessman tied to drug kingpins.' Christ, he hid things real well. Never had a sniff?"

"Nary a one," Bright admitted. "Not us, not DEA, not the local cops. Nothing at all."

Murray closed the file and nodded at the traf-fic. This was only the opening crack in a case that could develop into man-years of investigative work. *Hell, we don't even know exactly what we're looking for yet,* the deputy assistant director told himself. *All we do know is that there was a cold mil-lion dollars in used twenties and fifties aboard the good ship* Empire Builder. So much cash could only mean one thing — but that wasn't true. It could mean lots of things, Murray thought.

"Here we are."

Getting onto the base was easy enough, and Bright knew the way to the pier. *Panache* looked pretty big from the car, a towering white cliff with a bright-orange stripe and some dark smudgemarks near midships. Murray knew that she was a small ship, but one needed a big ocean to tell. By the time he and Bright got out of the car, someone got on the phone at the head of the gangway, and another man appeared there within seconds. Murray recognized him from the file. It was Wegener.

The man had the muddy remains of what had

once been red hair, but was now sprinkled with enough gray to defy an accurate description. He looked fit enough, the FBI agent thought as he came up the aluminum brow, a slight roll at the waist, but little else. A tattoo on his forearm marked him for a sailorman, and the impassive eyes marked the face of a man unaccustomed to questioning of any kind.

"Welcome aboard. I'm Red Wegener," the man said with enough of a smile to be polite.

"Thank you, Captain. I'm Dan Murray and this is Mark Bright."

"They told me you were FBI," the captain observed.

"I'm a deputy assistant director, down from Washington. Mark's the assistant special-agent-in-charge of the Mobile Office." Wegener's face changed a bit, Murray saw.

"Well, I know why you're here. Let's go to my cabin to discuss things."

"What's with all the scorching?" Dan asked as the captain led off. There was something about the way he'd said that. Something . . . odd.

"Shrimp boat had an engine fire. Happened five miles away from us last night while we were on the way in. The fuel tanks blew just as we came alongside. Got lucky. Nobody killed, but the mate was burned some."

"How about the boat?" Bright asked.

"Couldn't save her. Getting the crew off was pretty tricky." Wegener held open the door for his visitors. "Sometimes that's the best you can do. You gentlemen want any coffee?"

Murray declined. His eyes really bored in on the captain now. More than anything else, Dan thought, he looked embarrassed. Wrong emotion. Wegener got his guests seated, then took his chair behind the desk.

"I know why you're here," Red announced. "It's all my fault."

"Uh, Captain, before you go any farther —" Bright tried to say.

"I've pulled some dumb ones in my time, but this time I really fucked up," Wegener went on as he lit his pipe. "You don't mind if I smoke, do you?"

"No, not at all," Murray lied. He didn't know what was coming, but he knew that it wasn't what Bright thought. He knew several other things that Bright didn't know, also. "Why don't you tell us about it?"

Wegener reached into his desk drawer and pulled something out. He tossed it to Murray. It was a pack of cigarettes.

"One of our friends dropped this on the deck and I had one of my people give this back to them. I figured — well, look at it. I mean, it looks like a pack of cigarettes, right? And when we have people in custody, we're supposed to treat 'em decent, right? So, I let 'em have their smokes. They're joints, of course. So, when we questioned them — especially the one who talked — well, he was high as a kite. That screws it all up, doesn't it?"

167

"That's not all, Captain, is it?" Murray asked innocently.

"Chief Riley roughed one of 'em up. My responsibility. I talked to the chief about it. The, uh, I forget his name — the obnoxious one — well, he spit on me, and Riley was there, and Riley got a little pissed and roughed him up some. He should not have done it, but this is a military organization, and when you spit on the boss, well, the troops might not like it. So Riley got a little out of hand — but it happened on my ship and it's my responsibility."

Murray and Bright exchanged a look. The suspects hadn't talked about that at all.

"Captain, that's not why we're here exactly," Murray said after a moment.

"Oh?" Wegener said. "Then why?"

"They say that you executed one of them," Bright replied. The stateroom was quiet for a moment. Murray could hear someone hammering on something, but the loudest noise came from the air-conditioning vent.

"They're both alive, aren't they? There were only two of them, and they're both alive. I sent that tape on the helicopter when we searched the yacht. I mean, if they're both alive, which one did we shoot?"

"Hanged," Murray said. "They say you hanged one."

"Wait a minute." He lifted the phone and punched a button. "Bridge, captain speaking. Send the XO to my stateroom. Thank you." The

168

phone went back into place, and Wegener looked up. "If it's all right with you, I want my executive officer to hear this also."

Murray managed to keep his face impassive. *You should have known, Danny,* he told himself. *They've had plenty of time to work out the little details, and Mr. Wegener is nobody's fool. He's got a U.S. senator to hide behind, and he handed us two cold-blooded killers. Even without the confession, there's enough evidence for a capital murder case, and if you trash Wegener, you run the risk of losing that. The prominence of the victim — well, the U.S. Attorney won't go for it. No chance. . . .* There wasn't a United States Attorney in all of America who lacked political ambition, and putting these two in the electric chair was worth half a million votes. Murray couldn't run the risk of screwing this case up. FBI Director Jacobs had been a federal prosecutor, and he'd understand. Murray decided that it might make things a lot easier.

The XO appeared a moment later, and after introductions were exchanged, Bright went on with his version of what the subjects had told the local FBI office. It took about five minutes during which Wegener puffed on his pipe and let his eyes go slightly wide.

"Sir," the XO told Bright when he was finished. "I've heard a couple of good sea stories, but that one's the all-time champ."

"It's my fault," Wegener grumbled with a shake of the head. "Lettin' 'em have their pot back."

"How come nobody noticed what they were smoking?" Murray asked, less with curiosity for the answer than for the skill with which it was delivered. He was surprised when the XO replied.

"There's an A/C return right outside the brig. We don't keep a constant watch on prisoners — these were our first, by the way — because that's supposed to be unduly intimidating or something. Anyway, it's in our procedure book that we don't. Besides, we don't have all that many people aboard that we can spare 'em. What with the smoke getting sucked out, nobody noticed the smell until that night. Then it was too late. When we brought them into the wardroom for questioning — one at a time; that's in the book, too — they were both kinda glassy-eyed. The first one didn't talk. The second one did. You have the tape, don't you?"

"Yes, I've seen it," Bright answered.

"Then you saw that we read them their rights, right off the card we carry, just like it says. But — hung 'em? Damn. That's crazy. I mean, that's really crazy. We don't — I mean, we can't. I don't even know when it was legal to do it."

"The last time I know about was 1843," the captain said. "The reason there's a Naval Academy at Annapolis is because some people got strung up on USS *Somers*. One of them was the son of the Secretary of War. Supposedly it was an attempted mutiny, but there was quite a stink about it. We don't hang people anymore,"

Wegener concluded wryly. "I've been in the service a long time, but I don't go that far back."

"We can't even have a general court-martial," the XO added. "Not by ourselves, I mean. The manual for that weighs about ten pounds. Gawd, you need a judge, and real lawyers, all that stuff. I've been in the service for almost nine years, and I've never even seen a real one — just the practice things in law classes at the Academy. All we ever do aboard is Captain's Mast, and not much of that."

"Not a bad idea, though. I wouldn't have minded hanging those sons of bitches," Wegener observed. It struck Murray as a very strange, and very clever, thing to say. He felt a little sorry for Bright, who'd probably never had a case go this way. In that sense Murray was grateful for his time as legal attaché in London. He understood politics better than most agents.

"Oh?"

"When I was a little kid, they used to hang murderers. I grew up in Kansas. And you know, there weren't many murders back then. Course, we're too civilized to do that now, and so we got murders every damned day. Civilized," Wegener snorted. "XO, did they ever hang pirates like this?"

"I don't think so. Blackbeard's crew was tried at Williamsburg — ever been there? — the old courthouse in the tourist part of the place. I remember hearing that they were actually hung where one of the Holiday Inns is. And Captain

171

Kidd was taken home to England for hanging, wasn't he? Yeah, they had a place called Execution Dock or something like that. So — no, I don't think they really did it aboard ship, even in the old days. Damn sure we didn't do it. Christ, what a story."

"So it never happened," Murray said, not in the form of a question.

"No, sir, it did not," Wegener replied. The XO nodded to support his captain.

"And you're willing to say that under oath."

"Sure. Why not?"

"If it's all right with you, I also need to speak to one of your chiefs. It's the one who 'assaulted' the — "

"Is Riley aboard?" Wegener asked the XO.

"Yeah. Him and Portagee were working on something or other down in the goat locker."

"Okay, let's go see 'em." Wegener rose and waved for his visitors to follow.

"You need me, sir? I have some work to do."

"Sure thing, XO. Thanks."

"Aye aye. See you gentlemen later," the lieutenant said, and disappeared around a corner.

The walk took longer than Murray expected. They had to detour around two work parties who were repainting bulkheads. The chiefs' quarters — called the goat locker for reasons ancient and obscure — was located aft. Riley and Oreza, the two most senior chiefs aboard, shared the cabin nearest the small compartment where they and their peers ate in relative privacy. Wegener got to

172

the open door and found a cloud of smoke. The bosun had a cigar clamped in his teeth while his oversized hands were trying to manipulate a ridiculously small screwdriver. Both men came to their feet when the captain appeared.

"Relax. What the hell you got there?"

"Portagee found it." Riley handed it over. "It's a real old one and we've been trying to fix it."

"How does 1778 grab you, sir?" Oreza asked. "A sextant made by Henry Edgworth. Found it in an old junk shop. It might be worth a few bucks if we can get it cleaned up."

Wegener gave it a close look. "1778, you said?"

"Yes, sir. That makes it one of the oldest-model sextants. The glass is all broke, but that's easy to fix. I know a museum that pays top dollar for these — but then I might just keep it myself, of course."

"We got some company," Wegener said, getting back to business. "They want to talk about the two people we picked up."

Murray and Bright held up their ID cards. Dan noticed a phone in the compartment. The XO, he realized, might have called to warn them what was coming. Riley's cigar hadn't dropped an ash yet.

"No problem," Oreza said. "What are you guys going to do with the bastards?"

"That's up to the U.S. Attorney," Bright said. "We're supposed to help put the case together, and that means we have to establish what you people did when you apprehended them."

"Well, you want to talk to Mr. Wilcox, sir. He was in command of the boarding party," Riley said. "We just did what he told us."

"Lieutenant Wilcox is on leave," the captain pointed out.

"What about after you brought them aboard?" Bright asked.

"Oh, that," Riley admitted. "Okay, I was wrong, but that little cocksucker — I mean, he spit on the captain, sir, and you just don't do that kinda shit, y'know? So I roughed him up some. Maybe I shouldn't have done it, but maybe that little prick oughta have manners, too."

"That's not what we're here about," Murray said after a moment. "He says you hanged him."

"Hung him? What from?" Oreza asked.

"I think you call it the yardarm."

"You mean — hang, like in, well, *hang?* Around the neck, I mean?" Riley asked.

"That's right."

The bosun's laugh rumbled like an earthquake. "Sir, if I ever hung somebody, he wouldn't go around bitchin' about it the next day."

Murray repeated the story as he'd heard it, almost word for word. Riley shook his head.

"That's not the way it's done, sir."

"What do you mean?"

"You say that the little one said that the last thing he saw was his friend swinging back and forth, right? That ain't the way it's done."

"I still don't understand."

"When you hang somebody aboard ship, you

tie his feet together and run a downhaul line —
you tie that off to the rail or a stanchion so he
don't swing around. You gotta do that, sir. You
have something that weight — well, over a hundred pounds — swinging around like that, it'll
break things. So what you do is, you two-block
him — that means you run him right up to the
block — that's the pulley, okay? — and you got
the downhaul to keep him in place real snug like.
Otherwise it just ain't shipshape. Hell, everybody knows that."

"How do *you* know that?" Bright asked, trying
to hide his exasperation.

"Sir, you lower boats into the water, or you rig
stuff on this ship, and that's my job. We call it
seamanship. I mean, say you had some piece of
gear that weighs as much as a man, okay? You
want it swinging around loose like a friggin'
chandelier on a long chain? Christ, it'd eventually hit the radar, tear it right off the mast. We
had a storm that night, too. Nah, the way they
did it in the old days was just like a signal hoist —
line on top of the hoist and a line on the bottom,
tie it off nice and tight so it don't go noplace.
Hey, somebody in the deck division leaves stuff
flapping around like that, I tear him a new asshole. Gear is expensive. We don't go around
breaking it for kicks, sir. What do you think,
Portagee?"

"He's right. That was a pretty good blow we
had that night — didn't the captain tell you? —
the only reason we still had the punks aboard was

that we waved off the helo pickup 'cause of the weather. We didn't have any work parties out on deck that night, did we?"

"No chance," Riley said. "We buttoned up tight that night. What I mean, sir, is we can go out and work even in a damned hurricane if we have to, but unless you gotta, you don't go screwin' around on the weather decks during a gale. It's dangerous. You lose people that way."

"How bad was it that night?" Murray asked.

"Some of the new kids spent the night with their heads in the thunderjugs. The cook decided to serve chops that night, too." Oreza laughed. "That's how we learned, ain't it, Bob?"

"Only way," Riley agreed.

"So there wasn't a court-martial that night either?"

"Huh?" Riley appeared genuinely puzzled for a moment, then his face brightened. "Oh, you mean we gave 'em a fair trial, then hung 'em, like in the old beer commercial?"

"Just one of them," Murray said helpfully.

"Why not both? They're both fuckin' murderers, ain't they? Hey, sir, I was aboard that yacht, all right? I seen what they did — have you? It's a real mess. You see something like that all the time, maybe. I never have, and — well, I don't mind tellin' you, sir, it shook me up some. You want 'em hung, yeah, I'll do it and they won't bitch about it the next day, either. Okay, maybe I shouldn't 'a snapped the one over the rail — lost my cool, and I shouldn't have — okay, I'm sorry about that. But those two little fucks took out a whole family, probably did some rapin', too. I got a family, too, y'know? I got daughters. So does Portagee. You want us to shed tears over those two fuckers, you come to the wrong place, sir. You sit 'em in the electric chair and I'll throw the switch for you."

"So you didn't hang him?" Murray asked.

"Sir, I wish I'd'a thought of it," Riley announced. It was, after all, Oreza who'd thought of it.

Murray looked at Bright, whose face was slightly pink by this time. It had gone even more smoothly than he'd expected. Well, he'd been told that the captain was a clever sort. You didn't give command of a ship to a jerk — at least you weren't supposed to.

"Okay, gentlemen, I guess that answers all the questions we have for the moment. Thank you for your cooperation." A moment later, Wegener was leading them away.

The three men stopped at the gangway for a moment. Murray motioned for Bright to head for the car, then turned to the captain.

"You actually operate helicopters off that deck up there?"

"All the time. I just wish we had one of our own."

"Could I see it before I leave? I've never been aboard a cutter before."

"Follow me." In less than a minute, Murray was standing in the center of the deck, directly on

177

the crossed yellow lines painted on the black no-skid deck coating. Wegener was explaining how the lights at the control station worked, but Murray was looking at the mast, drawing an imaginary line from the yardarm to the deck. *Yeah*, he decided, *you could do it easy enough.*

"Captain, for your sake I hope you never do anything this crazy again."

Wegener turned in surprise. "What do you mean?"

"We both know what I mean."

"You believe what those two — "

"Yes, I do. A jury wouldn't — at least I don't think one would, though you can never really tell what a jury will believe. But you did it. I know — you can't say anything. . . . "

"What makes you think — "

"Captain, I've been in the Bureau for twenty-six years. I've heard lots of crazy stories, some real, some made up. You gradually get a feel for what's real and what isn't. The way it looks to me, you could run a piece of rope from that pulley up there, down to here pretty easy, and if you're taking the seas right, having a man swing wouldn't matter much. It sure wouldn't hurt the radar antenna that Riley was so worried about. Like I said, don't do it again. This one's a freebie because we can prosecute the case without the evidence you got for us. Don't push it. Well, I'm sure you won't. You found out that there was more to this one than you thought, didn't you?"

"I was surprised that the victim was — "

"Right. You opened a great big can of worms without getting your hands too dirty. You were lucky. Don't push it," Murray said again.

"Thank you, sir."

One minute after that, Murray was back in the car. Agent Bright was still unhappy.

"Once upon a time, when I was a brand-new agent fresh out of the Academy, I was assigned to Mississippi," Murray said. "Three civil-rights workers disappeared, and I was a very junior member of the team that cleared the case. I didn't do much of anything other than hold Inspector Fitzgerald's coat. Ever hear about Big Joe?"

"My dad worked with him," Bright answered.

"Then you know that Joe was a character, a real old-time cop. Anyway, the word got to us that the local Klukkers were mouthing off about how they were gonna kill a few agents — you know the stories, how they were harassing some families and stuff like that. Joe got a little pissed. Anyway, I drove him out to see — forget the mutt's name, but he was the Grand Kleagle of the local Klavern and he was the one with the biggest mouth. He was sitting under a shady tree in his front lawn when we pulled up. He had a shotgun next to the chair, and he was half in the bag from booze already. Joe walks up to him. The mutt starts to pick up the shotgun, but Joe just stared him down. Fitzgerald could do that; he put three guys in the ground and you could see in his face that he'd done it. I got a little worried, had my hand on my revolver, but Joe just stared him

179

down and told him if there was any more talk about offing an agent, or any more shitty phone calls to wives and kids, Big Joe was going to come back and kill him, right there in his front yard. Didn't shout or anything, just said it like he was ordering breakfast. The Kleagle believed him. So did I. Anyway, all that loose talk ended.

"What Joe did was illegal as hell," Murray went on. "Sometimes the rules get bent. I've done it. So have you."

"I've never — "

"Don't get your tits in a flutter, Mark. I said 'bent,' not broken. The rules do not anticipate all situations. That's why we expect agents to exercise judgment. That's how society works. In this case, those Coasties broke loose some valuable information, and the only way we can use it is if we ignore how they got it. No real harm was done, because the subjects will be handled as murderers, and all the evidence we need is physical. Either they fry or they cop to the murders and cooperate by again giving us all the information that the good Captain Wegener scared out of 'em. Anyway, that's what they decided in D.C. It's too embarrassing to everyone to make an issue of what we discussed aboard the cutter. Do you really think a local jury would — "

"No," Bright admitted at once. "It wouldn't take much of a lawyer to blow it apart, and even if he didn't — "

"Exactly. We'd just be spinning our wheels. We live in an imperfect world, but I don't think that Wegener will ever make that mistake again."

"Okay." Bright didn't like it, but that was beside the point.

"So what we do now is figure out exactly why this poor bastard and his family got themselves murdered by a *sicario* and his spear-carrier. You know, when I was chasing wise guys up in New York, nobody messed with families. You didn't even kill a guy in front of his family except to make a special kind of point."

"Not much in the way of rules for the druggies," Bright pointed out.

"Yeah — and I used to think terrorists were bad."

It was so much easier than his work with the Macheteros, Cortez thought. Here he was, sitting in the corner booth of a fine, expensive restaurant with a ten-page wine list in his hands — Cortez thought himself an authority on wines — instead of a rat-infested barrio shack eating beans and mouthing revolutionary slogans with people whose idea of Marxism was robbing banks and making heroic taped pronouncements that the local radio stations played between the rock songs and commercials. America had to be the only place in the world, he thought, where poor people drove their own cars to demonstrations and the longest lines they stood in were at the supermarket check-out.

He selected an obscure estate label from the Loire Valley for dinner. The wine steward clicked his ballpoint in approval as he retrieved the list.

Cortez had grown up in a place where the poor people — which category included nearly everyone — scrounged for shoes and bread. In America, the poor areas were the ones where people indulged drug habits that required hundreds of cash dollars per week. It was more than bizarre to the former colonel. In America drugs spread from the slums to the suburbs, bringing prosperity to those who had what others wanted.

Which was essentially what happened on the international scale also, of course. The *yanquis*, ever niggardly in their official aid to their less prosperous neighbors, now flooded them with money, but on what the Americans liked to call a people-to-people basis. That was good for a laugh. He didn't know or care how much the *yanqui* government gave to its friends, but he was sure that ordinary citizens — so bored with their comfortable lives that they needed chemical stimulation — gave far more, and did so without strings on "human rights." He'd spent so many years as a professional intelligence officer, trying to find a way to demean America, to damage its stature, lessen its influence. But he'd gone about it in the wrong way, Félix had come to realize. He'd tried to use Marxism to fight capitalism despite all the evidence that showed what worked and what did not. He could, however, use capitalism against itself, and fulfill his original mission while enjoying all the benefits of the very system that he was hurting. And the oddest part of all: his former employers thought him a traitor because he had found a way that worked. . . .

The man opposite him was a fairly typical American, Cortez thought. Overweight from too much good food, careless about cleaning his expensive clothing. Probably didn't polish his shoes either. Cortez remembered going barefoot for much of his youth, and thinking himself fortunate to have three shirts to call his own. This man drove an expensive car, lived in a comfortable flat, had a job that paid enough for ten DGI colonels — and it wasn't enough. That was America right there — whatever one had, it was never enough.

"So what do you have for me?"

"Four possible prospects. All the information is in my briefcase."

"How good are they?" Cortez asked.

"They all meet your guidelines," the man answered. "Haven't I always — "

"Yes, you are most reliable. That is why we pay you so much."

"Nice to be appreciated, Sam," the man said with a trace of smugness.

Félix — Sam to his dinner partner — had always appreciated the people with whom he worked. He appreciated what they could do. He appreciated the information they provided. But he despised them for the weaklings they were. Still, an intelligence officer — and that remained the way he thought of himself — couldn't be too picky. America abounded with people like this

183

one. Cortez did not reflect on the fact that he, too, had been bought. He deemed himself a skilled professional, perhaps something of a mercenary, but that was in keeping with an honored tradition, wasn't it? Besides, he was doing what his former masters had always wanted him to do, more effectively than had ever been possible with the DGI, and someone else was doing the paying. In fact, ultimately the Americans themselves paid his salary.

Dinner passed without incident. The wine was every bit as excellent as he'd expected, but the meat was overdone and the vegetables disappointing. Washington, he thought, was overrated as a city of restaurants. On his way out he simply picked up his companion's briefcase and walked to his car. The drive back to his hotel took twenty leisurely minutes. After that, he spent several hours going over the documents. The man was reliable, Cortez reflected, and earned his appreciation. Each of the four was a solid prospect.

His recruiting effort would begin tomorrow.

7.

Knowns and Unknowns

It had taken a week to get accustomed to the altitude, as Julio had promised. Chavez eased out of the suspenders pack. It wasn't a fully loaded one yet, only twenty-five pounds, but they were taking their time, almost easing people into the conditioning program instead of using a more violent approach. That suited the sergeant, still breathing a little hard after the eight-mile run. His shoulders hurt some, and his legs ached in the usual way, but around him there was no sound of retching, and there hadn't been any dropouts this time around. Just the usual grumbles and curses.

"That wasn't so bad," Julio said without gasping. "But I still say that getting laid is the best workout there is."

"You got that one right," Chavez agreed with a laugh. "All those unused muscle groups, as the

185

free-weight guys say."

The best thing about the training camp was the food. For lunch in the field they had to eat MRE packs — "Meal Ready to Eat," which was three lies for the price of one — but breakfast and supper selections were always well prepared in the camp's oversized kitchen. Chavez invariably selected as large a bowl of fresh fruits as he could get away with, heavily laced with white sugar for energy, along with the usual Army coffee whose caffeine content always seemed augmented to give you that extra wake-up punch. He laid into his bowl of diced grapefruit, oranges, and damned near everything else with gusto while his tablemates attacked their greasy eggs and bacon. Chavez went back to the line for some hash-browns. He'd heard that carbohydrates were also good for energy, and now that he was almost accustomed to the altitude, the thought of grease for breakfast didn't bother him that much.

Things were going well. Work here was hard, but there was nothing in the way of Mickey Mouse bullshit. Everyone here was an experienced pro, and they were being treated as such. No energy was being wasted on bed-making; the sergeants all knew how, and if a blanket corner wasn't quite tucked in, peer pressure set things right without the need for shouting from a superior officer. They were all young men, as serious about their work as they knew how to be, but there was a spirit of fun and adventure. They still didn't know exactly what they were training for.

There was the inevitable speculation, whispering between bunks that gradually transformed to a symphony of snoring at night after agreement on some wildly speculative idea.

Though an uneducated man, Chavez was not a stupid one. Somehow he knew that all of the theories were wrong. Afghanistan was all over; they couldn't be going there. Besides, everyone here spoke fluent Spanish. He mulled over it again while chewing a mouthful of kiwi fruit — a treat he hadn't known to exist a week before. High altitude — they weren't training them here for the fun of it. That eliminated Cuba and Panama. Nicaragua, perhaps. How high were the mountains there? Mexico and the other Central American nations had mountains, too. Everyone here was a sergeant. Everyone here had led a squad, and had done training at one level or other. Everyone here was a light infantryman. Probably they'd be dispatched on some special training mission, therefore, training other light-fighters. That made it counterinsurgency. Of course, every country south of the Rio Grande had one sort of guerrilla problem or other. They resulted from the inequities of the individual governments and economies, but to Chavez the explanation was simpler and to the point — those countries were all fucked up. He'd seen enough of that in his trips with his battalion to Honduras and Panama. The local towns were dirty — they'd made his home barrio seem paradise on earth. The police — well, he'd never thought

187

that he would come to admire the LAPD. But it was the local armies that had earned his *especial* contempt. Bunch of lazy, incompetent bullies. Not much different from street gangs, as a matter of fact, except that they all carried the same sort of guns (the L.A. gangs tended toward individualism). Weapons skills were about the same. It didn't require very much for a soldier to buttstroke some poor bastard with his rifle. The officers — well, he hadn't seen anyone to compare with Lieutenant Jackson, who loved to run with his men and didn't mind getting all dirty and smelly like a real soldier. But inevitably it was the sergeants down there who earned his fullest contempt. It had been that paddy Sergeant McDevitt in Korea who'd shown Ding Chavez the light — skill and professionalism equaled pride. And, when you got down to it, pride truly earned was all there was to a man. Pride was what kept you going, what kept you from caving in on those goddamned mountainside runs. You couldn't let down your friends. You couldn't let your friends see you for something less than you wanted to be. That was the short version of everything he had learned in the Army, and he knew that the same could be said of all the men in this room. What they were preparing for, therefore, was to train others to do the same. So their mission was a fairly conventional Army mission. For some reason or other — probably political, but Chavez didn't worry about political stuff; never made much sense

188

anyway — it was a secret mission. He was smart enough to know that this kind of hush-hush preparation meant CIA. He was correct on that judgment. It was the mission he was wrong on.

Breakfast ended at the normal time. The men rose from their tables, taking their trays and dishes to the stacking table before proceeding outside. Most made pit stops and many, including Chavez, changed into clean, dry T-shirts. The sergeant wasn't overly fastidious, but he did prefer the crisp, clean smell of a newly washed shirt. There was an honest-to-God laundry service here. Chavez decided that he'd miss the camp, altitude and all. The air, if thin, was clean and dry. Each day they'd hear the lonely wail of diesel horns from the trains that entered the Moffat Tunnel, whose entrance they'd see on their twice-daily runs. Often in the evening they'd catch the distant sight of the double-deck cars of an Amtrak train heading east to Denver. He wondered what hunting was like here. What did they hunt? Deer, maybe? They'd seen a bunch of them, big mule deer, but also the curious white shapes of mountain goats racing up sheer rock walls as the soldiers approached. Now, *those* fuckers were really in shape, Julio had noted the previous day. But Chavez dismissed the thought after a moment. The animals he hunted had only two legs. And shot back if you weren't careful.

The four squads formed up on time. Captain Ramirez called them to attention and marched them off to their separate area, about half a mile east of the main camp at the far end of the flat bottom of the high valley. Waiting for them was a black man dressed in T-shirt and dark shorts, both of which struggled to contain bulging muscles.

"Good morning, people," the man said. "I am Mr. Johnson. Today we will begin some real mission-oriented training. All of you have had training in hand-to-hand combat. My job is to see how good you are, and to teach you some new tricks that your earlier training may have left out. Killing somebody silently isn't all that hard. The tricky part is getting close enough to do it. We all know that." Johnson's hands slipped behind his back as he talked on for a moment. "This is another way to kill silently."

His hands came into view holding a pistol with a large, canlike device affixed to the front. Before Chavez had told himself that it was a silencer, Johnson brought it around in both hands and fired it three times. It was a very good silencer, Ding noted immediately. You could barely hear the metallic clack of the automatic's slide — quieter, in fact, than the tinkle of glass from the three bottles that disintegrated twenty feet away — and you couldn't hear the sound of the shot at all. Impressive.

Johnson gave them all a mischievous grin. "You don't get your hands all bruised, either. Like I said, you all know hand-to-hand, and we're going to work on that. But I've been around the block a few times, just like you people, and let's not dick around the issue. Armed combat beats unarmed any day of the week. So today we're going to learn a whole new kind of fighting: silent *armed* combat." He bent down and flipped the blanket off a submachine gun. It, too, appeared to have a silencer on the muzzle. Chavez reproached himself for his earlier speculation. Whatever the mission was, it wasn't about training.

Vice Admiral James Cutter, USN, was a patrician. At least he looked like one, Ryan thought — tall and spare, his hair going a regal silver, and a confident smile forever fixed on his pink-scrubbed face. Certainly he acted like one — or thought he did, Jack corrected himself. It was Ryan's view that truly important people didn't go out of their way to act like it. It wasn't as though being the President's Special Assistant for National Security Affairs was the same as a peerage. Ryan knew a few people who actually had them. Cutter came from one of those old swamp-Yankee families which had grown rocks on their New England farmsteads for generations, then turned to the mercantile trade, and, in Cutter's case, sent its surplus sons to sea. But Cutter was the sort of sailor for whom the sea was a means to an end. More than half of his career had been spent in the Pentagon, and that, Ryan thought, was no place for a proper sailor. He'd had all the necessary commands, Jack knew. First a destroyer, then a cruiser. Each time he'd done his job well — well enough to be noticed, which must have been the important part. Plenty of outstanding officers' careers stopped cold at captain's rank because they'd failed to be noticed by a high-enough patron. What had Cutter done to make him stick out from the crowd . . . ?

Polished up the knocker faithfully, perhaps? Jack wondered as he finished his briefing.

Not that it mattered now. The President had noticed him on Jeff Pelt's staff, and on Pelt's return to academia — the International Relations chair at the University of Virginia — Cutter had slipped into the job as neatly as a destroyer coming alongside the pier. He sat behind his desk in a neatly tailored suit, sipping his coffee from a mug with USS BELKNAP engraved on it, the better to remind people that he'd commanded that cruiser once. In case the casual visitor missed that one — there were few casual visitors to the National Security Adviser's office — the wall on the left was liberally covered with plaques of the ships he'd served on, and enough signed photographs for a Hollywood agent's office. Naval officers call this phenomenon the I LOVE ME! wall, and while most of them have one, they usually keep it at home.

Ryan didn't like Cutter very much. He hadn't liked Pelt either, but the difference was that Pelt was almost as smart as he thought he was. Cutter was not even close. The three-star Admiral was in over his head, but had not the sense to know it. The bad news was that while Ryan was also a

Special Assistant To, it was not To the President. That meant he had to report to Cutter whether he liked it or not. With his boss in the hospital, that task would be a frequent occurrence.

"How's Greer?" the man asked. He spoke with a nasal New England accent that ought to have died a natural death long before, though it was one thing that Ryan didn't mind. It reminded him of his undergraduate days at Boston College.

"They're not through with the tests yet." Ryan's voice betrayed his worries. It looked like pancreatic cancer, the survival rate for which was just about zero. He'd checked with Cathy about that, and had tried to get his boss to Johns Hopkins, but Greer was Navy, which meant going to Bethesda. Though Bethesda Naval Medical Center was the Navy's number-one hospital, it wasn't Johns Hopkins.

"And you're going to take over for him?" Cutter asked.

"That is in rather poor taste, Admiral," Bob Ritter answered for his companion. "In Admiral Greer's absence, Dr. Ryan will represent him from time to time."

"If you handle that as well as you've handled this briefing, we ought to get along just fine. Shame about Greer. Hope things work out." There was about as much emotion in his voice as one needed to ask directions.

You're a warm person, aren't you? Ryan thought to himself as he closed his briefcase. *I bet the crew of the* Belknap *just loved you.* But Cutter wasn't

193

paid to be warm. He was paid to advise the President. And Ryan was paid to brief him, not to love him.

Cutter wasn't a fool. Ryan had to admit that also. He was not an expert in the area of Ryan's own expertise, nor did he have Pelt's cardsharp's instinct for political wheeling and dealing behind the scene — and, unlike Pelt, Cutter liked to operate without consulting the State Department. He sure as hell didn't understand how the Soviet Union worked. The reason he was sitting in that high-back chair, behind that dark-oak desk, was that he was a reputed expert in other areas, and evidently those were the areas in which the President had most of his current interest. Here Ryan's intellect failed him. He came back to his brief on what KGB was up to in Central Europe instead of following that idea to its logical conclusion. Jack's other mistake was more basic. Cutter knew that he wasn't the man Jeff Pelt had been, and Cutter wanted to change all that.

"Nice to see you again, Dr. Ryan. Good brief. I'll bring that matter to the President's attention. Now if you'll excuse us, the DDO and I have something to discuss."

"See you back at Langley, Jack," Ritter said. Ryan nodded and left. The other two waited for the door to close behind him. Then the DDO presented his own brief on Operation SHOWBOAT. It lasted twenty minutes.

"So how do we coordinate this?" the Admiral asked Ritter.

194

"The usual. About the only good thing that came out of the Desert One fiasco was that it proved how secure satellite communications were. Ever see the portable kind?" the DDO asked. "It's standard equipment for the light forces."

"No, just the ones aboard ship. They're not real portable."

"Well, it has a couple of pieces, an X-shaped antenna and a little wire stand that looks like it's made out of a couple of used coat hangers. There's a new backpack only weighs fifteen pounds, including the handset, and it even has a Morse key in case the sender doesn't want to talk too loud. Single sideband, super-encrypted UHF. That's as secure as communications get."

"But what about keeping them covert?" Cutter was worried about that.

"If the region was heavily populated," Ritter explained tiredly, "the opposition wouldn't be using it. Moreover, they operate mainly at night for the obvious reason. So our people will belly-up during the day and only move around at night. They are trained and equipped for that. Look, we've been thinking about this for some time. These people are very well trained already, and we're — "

"Resupply?"

"Helicopter," Ritter said. "Special-ops people down in Florida."

"I still think we should use Marines."

"The Marines have a different mission. We've

been over this, Admiral. These kids are better trained, they're better equipped, most of them have been into areas like this one, and it's a hell of a lot easier to get them into the program without anybody noticing," Ritter explained for what must have been the twentieth time. Cutter wasn't one to listen to the words of others. His own opinions were evidently too loud. The DDO wondered how the President fared, but that question needed no answer. A presidential whisper carried more weight that a scream from anyone else. The problem was, the President so often depended on idiots to make his wishes a reality. Ritter would not have been surprised to learn that his opinion of the National Security Adviser matched that of Jack Ryan; it was just that Ryan could not know why.

"Well, it's your operation," Cutter said after a moment. "When does it start?"

"Three weeks. Just had a report last night. Things are going along just fine. They already had all the basic skills we needed. It's only a matter of honing a few special ones and adding a few refinements. We've been lucky so far. Haven't even had anybody hurt up there."

"How long have you had that place, anyway?"

"Thirty years. It was supposed to have been an air-defense radar installation, but the funding got cut off for some reason or other. The Air Force turned it over to us, and we've been using it to train agents ever since. It doesn't show up on any of the OMB site lists. It belongs to an offshore corporation that we use for various things. During the fall we occasionally lease it out as a hunting camp, would you believe? It even shows a profit for us, which is another reason why it doesn't show on the OMB list. Is that covert enough? Came in real useful during Afghanistan, though, doing the same thing we're doing now, and nobody ever found out about it. . . . "

"Three weeks."

Ritter nodded. "Maybe a touch longer. We're still working on coordinating the satellite intelligence, and our assets on the ground."

"Will it all work?" Cutter asked rhetorically.

"Look, Admiral, I've told you about that. If you want some magical solution to give to the President, we don't have it. What we can do is sting them some. The results will look good in the papers, and, hell, maybe we'll end up saving a life or two. Personally, I think it's worth doing even if we don't get much of a return."

The nice thing about Ritter, Cutter thought, was that he didn't state the obvious. There would be a return. Everyone knew what that was all about. The mission was not an exercise in cynicism, though some might see it as such.

"What about the radar coverage?"

"There are only two aircraft coming on line. They're testing a new system called LPI — Low Probability of Intercept — radar. I don't know all the details, but because of a combination of frequency agility, reduced side-lobes, and relatively low power output, it's damned hard to

197

detect the emissions from the set. That will invalidate the ESM equipment that the opposition has started using. So we can use our assets on the ground to stake out between four and six of the covert airfields, and let us know when a shipment is en route. The modified E-2s will establish contact with them south of Cuba and pace them all the way in till they're intercepted by the F-15 driver I told you about. He's a black kid — hell of a fighter jock, they say. Comes from New York. His mother got mugged by a druggie up there. It was a bad one. She got all torn up, and eventually died. She was one of those ghetto success stories that you never hear about. Three kids, all of them turned out pretty well. The fighter pilot is a very angry kid at the moment. He'll work for us, and he won't talk."

"Right," Cutter said skeptically. "What about if he develops a conscience later on and — "

"The boy told me that he'd shoot all the bastards down if we wanted him to. A druggie killed his *mother*. He wants to get even, and he sees this as a good way. There are a lot of sensitive projects underway at Eglin. His fighter is cut loose from the rest as part of the LPI Radar project. It's two Navy airplanes carrying the radar, and we've picked the flight crews — pretty much the same story on them. And remember — after we have lock-on from the F-15, the radar aircraft shuts down and leaves. So if Bronco — that's the kid's name — does have to splash the inbound druggie, nobody'll know about it. Once we get them on the ground, the flight crews will have the living shit scared out of them. I worked out the details on that part myself. If some people have to disappear — I don't expect it — that can be arranged, too. The Marines there are all special-ops types. One of my people will pretend he's a fed, and the judge we take them to is the one the President — "

"I know that part." It was odd, Cutter thought, how ideas grow. First the President had made an intemperate remark after learning that the cousin of a close friend had died of a drug overdose. He'd talked about it with Ritter, gotten an idea, and mentioned it to the President. A month after that, a plan had started to grow. Two months more and it was finalized. A secret Presidential Finding was written and in the files — there were only four copies of it, each of which was locked up tight. Now things were starting to move. It was past the time for second thoughts, Cutter told himself weakly. He'd been involved in all the planning discussions, and still the operation had somehow leaped unexpectedly to full flower. . . .

"What can go wrong?" he asked Ritter.

"Look, in field operations anything can go wrong. Just a few months ago a crash operation went bad because of an illegal turn — "

"That was KGB," Cutter said. "Jeff Pelt told me about that one."

"We are not immune. Shit happens, as they say. What we can do, we've done. Every aspect of the operation is compartmentalized. On the air part, for example, the fighter pilot doesn't know the radar aircraft or its people — for both sides it's just call signs and voices. The people on the ground don't know what aircraft are involved. The people we're putting in-country will get instructions from satellite radios — they won't even know where from. The people who insert them won't know why they're going or where the orders come from. Only a handful of people will know everything. The total number of people who know anything at all is less than a hundred, and only ten know the whole story. I can't make it any tighter than that. Now, either it's a Go-Mission or it's not. That's your call, Admiral Cutter. I presume," Ritter added for effect, "that you've fully briefed the President."

Cutter had to smile. It was not often, even in Washington, that a man could speak the truth and lie at the same time: "Of course, Mr. Ritter."

"In writing," Ritter said next.

"No."

"Then I call the operation off," the DDO said quietly. "I won't be left hanging on this one."

"But I will?" Cutter observed. He didn't allow anger to creep into his voice, but his face conveyed the message clearly enough. Ritter made the obvious maneuver.

"Judge Moore requires it. Would you prefer that he ask the President himself?"

Cutter was caught short. His job, after all, was to insulate the President. He'd tried to pass that onus to Ritter and/or Judge Moore, but found himself outmaneuvered in his own office. Someone had to be responsible for everything; bureaucracy or not, it always came down to one person. It was rather like a game of musical chairs. Someone was always left standing. That person was called the loser. For all his skills, Vice Admiral Cutter had found himself without a seat on that last chair. His naval training, of course, had taught him to take responsibilities, but though Cutter called himself a naval officer, and thought of himself as one — without wearing the uniform, of course — responsibility was something he'd managed to avoid for years. Pentagon duty was good for that, and White House duty was better still. Now responsibility was his again. He hadn't been this vulnerable since his cruiser had nearly rammed a tanker during replenishment operations — his executive officer had saved him with a timely command to the helmsman, Cutter remembered. A pity that his career had ended at captain's rank, but Ed just hadn't had the right stuff to make Flag. . . .

Cutter opened a drawer to his desk and pulled out a sheet of paper whose letterhead proclaimed "The White House." He took a gold Cross pen from his pocket and wrote a clear authorization for Ritter in his best Palmer Method penmanship. *You are authorized by the President* . . . The Admiral folded the sheet, tucked it into an envelope, and handed it across.

"Thank you, Admiral." Ritter tucked the envelope into his coat pocket. "I'll keep you posted."

"You be careful who sees that," Cutter said coldly.

"I do know how to keep secrets, sir. It's my job, remember?" Ritter rose and left the room, finally with a warm feeling around his backside. His ass was covered. It was a feeling craved by many people in Washington. It was one he didn't share with the President's National Security Adviser, but Ritter figured it wasn't his fault that Cutter hadn't thought this one through.

Five miles away, the DDI's office seemed a cold and lonely place to Ryan. There was the credenza and the coffee machine where James Greer made his Navy brew, there the high-backed judge's chair in which the old man leaned back before making his professorial statements of fact and theory, and his jokes, Jack remembered. His boss had one hell of a sense of humor. What a fine teacher he might have made — but then he really was a teacher to Jack. What was it? Only six years since he'd started with the Agency. He'd known Greer for less than seven, and the Admiral had in large part become the father he'd lost in that airplane crash at Chicago. It was here he had come for advice, for guidance. How many times?

The trees outside the seventh-floor windows were green with the leaves of summer, blocking the view of the Potomac Valley. The really crazy things had all happened when there were no leaves, Ryan thought. He remembered pacing around on the lush carpet, looking down at the piles of snow left by the plows while trying to find answers to hard questions, sometimes succeeding, sometimes not.

Vice Admiral James Greer would not live to see another winter. He'd seen his last snow, his last Christmas. Ryan's boss lay in a VIP suite at Bethesda Naval Medical Center, still alert, still thinking, still telling jokes. But his weight was down by fifteen pounds in the last three weeks, and the chemotherapy denied him any sort of food other than what came through tubes stuck in his arms. And the pain. There was nothing worse, Ryan knew, than to watch the pain of others. He'd seen his wife and daughter in pain, and it had been far worse than his own hospital stays. It was hard to go and see the Admiral, to see the tightness around the face, the occasional stiffening of limbs as the spasms came and went, some from the cancer, some from the medications. But Greer was as much a part of his family as — God, Ryan thought, I am thinking of him like my father. And so he would, until the end.

"Shit," Jack said quietly, without knowing it.

"I know what you mean, Dr. Ryan."

"Hmph?" Jack turned. The Admiral's driver (and security guard) stood quietly by the door while Jack retrieved some documents. Even though Ryan was the DDI's special assistant and *de facto* deputy, he had to be watched when going over documents cleared DDI-eyes-only. CIA's security rules were tough, logical, and inviolable.

"I know what you mean, sir. I've been with him eleven years. He's as much a friend as a boss. Every Christmas he has something for the kids. Never forgets a birthday, either. You think there's any hope at all?"

"Cathy had one of her friends come down. Professor Goldman. Russ is as good as they come, professor of oncology at Hopkins, consultant to NIH, and a bunch of other things. He says one chance in thirty. It's spread too far, too fast, Mickey. Two months, tops. Anything else would be a miracle." Ryan almost smiled. "I got a priest working on that."

Murdock nodded. "I know he's tight with Father Tim over at Georgetown. He was just at the hospital for some chess last night. The Admiral took him in forty-eight moves. You ever play chess with him?"

"I'm not in his class. Probably never will be."

"Yes, sir, you are," Murdock said after a moment or two. "Leastways, that's what he says."

"He would." Ryan shook his head. Damn it, Greer wouldn't want either of them to talk like this. There was work to be done. Jack took the key and unlocked the file drawer in the desk. He set the key chain on the desk blotter for Mickey to retrieve and reached down to pull the drawer, but goofed. Instead he pulled out the sliding board you could use as a writing surface, though this one was marked with brown rings from the

DDI's coffee mug. Near the inside end of it, Ryan saw, was a file card, taped in place. Written on the card, in Greer's distinctive hand, were two safe combinations. Greer had a special office safe and so did Bob Ritter. Jack remembered that his boss had always been clumsy with combination locks, and he probably needed the combination written down so he wouldn't forget it. He found it odd that the Admiral should have combinations for both his and Ritter's, but decided after a moment that it made sense. If somebody had to get into the DDO's safe in a hurry — for example, if Ritter were kidnapped, and someone had to see what really classified material was in the current file — it had to be someone very senior, like the DDI. Probably Ritter had the combination to the DDI's personal safe, as well. Jack wondered who else did. Shrugging off the thought, he slid the board back into place and opened the drawer. There were six files there. All related to long-term intelligence evaluations that the Admiral wanted to see. None were especially critical. In fact, they weren't all that sensitive, but it would give the Admiral something to occupy his mind. A rotating team of CIA security personnel guarded his room, with two on duty at all times, and he could still do work in the time he had left.

Damn! Jack snarled at himself. *Get your mind off of it. Hell, he does have a chance. Some chance is better than none at all.*

Chavez had never handled a submachine gun. His personal weapon had always been the M-16 rifle, often with an M-203 grenade launcher slung under the barrel. He also knew how to use the SAW — the Belgian-made squad automatic weapon that had recently been added to the Army's inventory — and had shot expert with pistol once. But submachine guns had long since gone out of favor in the Army. They just weren't serious weapons of the sort a soldier would need.

Which was not to say that he didn't like it. It was a German gun, the MP-5 SD2 made by Heckler & Koch. It was decidedly unattractive. The matte-black finish was slightly rough to the touch, and it lacked the sexy compactness of the Israeli Uzi. On the other hand, it wasn't made to look good, he thought, it was made to shoot good. It was made to be reliable. It was made to be accurate. Whoever had designed this baby, Chavez decided as he brought it up for the first time, knew what shooting was all about. Unusually for a German-made weapon, it didn't have a huge number of small parts. It broke down easily and quickly for cleaning, and reassembly took less than a minute. The weapon nestled snugly against his shoulder, and his head dropped automatically into the right place to peer through the ring-aperture sight.

"Commence firing," Mr. Johnson commanded.

Chavez had the weapon on single-shot. He squeezed off the first round, just to get a feel for

206

the trigger. It broke cleanly at about eleven pounds, the recoil was straight back and gentle, and the gun didn't jump off the target the way some weapons did. The shot, of course, went straight through the center of the target's silhouetted head. He squeezed off another, and the same thing happened, then five in rapid fire. The repeated shots rocked him back an inch or two, but the recoil spring ate up most of the kick. He looked up to see seven holes in a nice, tight group, like the nose carved into a jack-o'-lantern. Okay. Next he flipped the selector switch to the burst position — it was time for a little rock and roll. He put three rounds at the target's chest. This group was larger, but any of the three would have been fatal. After another one Chavez decided that he could hold a three-round burst dead on target. He didn't need full-automatic fire. Anything more than three rounds just wasted ammunition. His attitude might have seemed strange for a soldier, but as a light infantryman he understood that ammunition was something that had to be carried. To finish off his thirty-round magazine he aimed bursts at unmarked portions of the target card, and was rewarded with hits exactly where he'd wanted them.

"Baby, where have you been all my life?" Best of all, it wasn't much noisier than the rustle of dry leaves. It wasn't that it had a silencer; the barrel *was* a silencer. You heard the muted clack of the action, and the swish of the bullet. They were using a subsonic round, the instructor told them. Chavez picked one out of the box. The bullet was a hollow-point design; it looked like you could mix a drink in it, and on striking a man it probably spread out to the diameter of a dime. Instant death from a head shot, nearly as quick in the chest — but if they were training him to use a silencer, he'd be expected to go for the head. He figured that he could take head shots reliably from fifty or sixty feet — maybe farther under ideal circumstances, but soldiers don't expect ideal circumstances. On the face of it, he'd be expected to creep within fifteen or twenty yards of his target and drop him without a sound.

Whatever they were preparing for, he thought again, it sure as hell wasn't a training mission.

"Nice groups, Chavez," the instructor observed. Only three other men were on the firing line. There would be two submachine gunners per squad. Two SAWs — Julio had one of those — and the rest had M-16s, two of them with grenade launchers attached. Everyone had pistols, too. That seemed strange, but despite the weight Chavez didn't mind.

"This baby really shoots, sir."

"It's yours. How good are you with a pistol?"

"Just fair. I don't usually — "

"Yeah, I know. Well, you'll all get practice. Pistol ain't really good for much, but there's times when it comes in right handy." Johnson turned to address the whole squad. "All right, you four come on up. We want everyone to know how all these here weapons work. Everybody's gotta be an expert."

Chavez relinquished his weapon to another squad member and walked back from the firing line. He was still trying to figure things out. Infantry combat is the business of death, at the personal level, where you could usually see what you were doing and to whom you were doing it. The fact that Chavez had not actually done it yet was irrelevant; it was still his business, and the organization of his unit told him what form the mission would take. Special ops. It had to be special ops. He knew a guy who'd been in the Delta Force at Bragg. Special operations were merely a refinement of straight infantry stuff. You had to get in real close, usually you had to chop down the sentries, and then you hit hard and fast, like a bolt of lightning. If it wasn't over in ten seconds or less — well, then things got a little too exciting. The funny part to Chavez was the similarity with street-gang tactics. There was no fair play in soldiering. You sneaked in and did people in the back without warning. You didn't give them a chance to protect themselves — none at all. But what was called cowardly in a gang kid was simply good tactics to a soldier. Chavez smiled to himself. It hardly seemed fair, when you looked at it like that. The Army was just better organized than a gang. And, of course, its targets were selected by others. The whole point to an Army, probably, was that what it did made sense to someone. That was true of gangs, too, but Army activity was supposed to make sense to someone important, someone who knew what he was really doing. Even if what he was doing didn't make much sense to him — a frequent occurrence for soldiers — it did make sense to somebody.

Chavez wasn't old enough to remember Vietnam.

Seduction was the saddest part of the job.

With this, as with all parts of his profession, Cortez had been trained to be coldly objective and businesslike. But there wasn't a way to be coldly intimate — at least not if you wanted to accomplish anything. Even the KGB Academy had recognized that. There had been hours of lectures on the pitfalls, he remembered with an ironic smile — Russians trying to tell a Latin about romantic entanglements. Probably the climate worked against them. You adapted your approach to the individual peculiarities of your target subject, in this case a widow who at forty-six retained surprising good looks, who had enough remaining of her youth to need companionship after the children retired for the evening or went out on their own dates, whose bed was a lonely place of memories grown cold. It wasn't his first such subject, and there was always something brave about them, as well as something pathetic. He was supposed to think — as his training had taught him — that their problems were their business and his opportunity. But how does a man become intimate with such a woman without feeling her pain? The KGB instructors hadn't had an answer to that one, though they did give him the proper technique. He, too, had to have suffered a recent loss.

His "wife" had also died of cancer, he'd told her. He'd married late in life, the story went, after getting the family business back on track — all that time working, flying around to secure the business his father had spent his life founding — and then married his María only three years before. She'd become pregnant, but when she'd visited the doctor to confirm the joyous news, the routine tests . . . only six months. The baby hadn't had a chance, and Cortez had nothing left of María. Perhaps, he'd told his wineglass, it was God's punishment on him for marrying so young a girl, or for his many dalliances as a footloose playboy.

At that point Moira's hand had come across the table to touch his. Of course it wasn't his fault, the woman told him. And he looked up to see the sympathy in the eyes of someone who'd asked herself questions not so different from those he'd just ostensibly addressed to himself. People were so predictable. All you had to do was press the right buttons — and have the proper feelings. When her hand had come to his, the seduction was accomplished. There had been a flush of warmth from the touch, the feeling of simple humanity. But if he thought of her as a simple target, how could he return the emotions — and how could he accomplish the mission? He felt her pain, her loneliness. He would be good to her.

And so he was, now two days later. It would have been comical except for how touching it was, how she'd prepared herself like a teenage girl on a date — something she hadn't done for over twenty years; certainly her children had found it entertaining, but there had been enough time since the death of their father that they didn't resent their mother's needs and had smiled bemused encouragement at her as she walked out to her car. A quick, nervous dinner, then the short ride to his hotel. Some more wine to get over the nerves that were real for both of them, if more so for her. But it had certainly been worth the wait. She was out of practice, but her responses were far more genuine than those he got from his usual bedmates. Cortez was very good at sex. He was proud of his abilities and gave her an above-average performance: an hour's work, building her up slowly, then letting her back down as gently as he knew how.

Now they lay side by side, her head on his shoulder, tears dripping slowly from her eyes in the silence. A fine woman, this one. Even dying young, her husband had been a lucky man to have a woman who knew that silence could be the greatest passion of all. He watched the clock on the end table. Ten minutes of silence before he spoke.

"Thank you, Moira . . . I didn't know . . . it's been." He cleared his throat. "This is the first time since ... since ..." Actually it had been a week since the last one, which had cost him thirty thousand pesos. A young one, a skilled one. But —

The woman's strength surprised him. He was barely able to take his next breath, so powerful was her embrace. Part of what had once been his conscience told him that he ought to be ashamed, but the greater part reported that he'd given more than he'd taken. This was better than purchased sex. There were feelings, after all, that money couldn't buy; it was a thought both reassuring and annoying to Cortez, and one which amplified his sense of shame. Again he rationalized that there would be no shame without her powerful embrace, and the embrace would not have come unless he had pleased her greatly.

He reached behind himself to the other end table and got his cigarettes.

"You shouldn't smoke," Moira Wolfe told him.

He smiled. "I know. I must quit. But after what you have done to me," he said with a twinkle in his eye, "I must gather myself." Silence.

"*Madre de Dios*," he said after another minute.

"What's the matter?"

Another mischievous smile. "Here I have given myself to you, and I hardly know who you are!"

"What do you want to know?"

A chuckle. A shrug. "Nothing important — I mean, what could be more important than what

213

you have already done?" A kiss. A caress. More silence. He stubbed out the cigarette at the half-way point to show that her opinion was important to him. "I am not good at this."

"Really?" It was her turn to chuckle, his turn to blush.

"It is different, Moira. I — when I was a young man, it was understood that when — it was understood that there was no importance, but . . . now I am grown, and I cannot be so . . . " Embarrassment. "If you permit it, I wish to know about you, Moira. I come to Washington frequently, and I wish . . . I am tired of the loneliness. I am tired of . . . I wish to know you," he said with conviction. Then, tentatively, haltingly, hopeful but afraid, "If you permit it."

She kissed his cheek gently. "I permit it."

Instead of his own powerful hug, Cortez let his body go slack with relief not wholly feigned. More silence before he spoke again.

"You should know about me. I am wealthy. My business is machine tools and auto parts. I have two factories, one in Costa Rica, the other in Venezuela. The business is complicated and — not dangerous, but . . . it is complicated dealing with the big assemblers. I have two younger brothers also in the business. So . . . what work do you do?"

"Well, I'm an executive secretary. I've been doing that kind of work for twenty years."

"Oh? I have one myself."

"And you must chase her around the office . . . "

"Consuela is old enough to be my mother. She worked for my father. Is that how it is in America? Does your boss chase you?" A hint of jealous outrage.

Another chuckle. "Not exactly. I work for Emil Jacobs. He's the Director of the FBI."

"I do not know the name." A lie. "The FBI, that is your *federales*, this I know. And you are the chief secretary for them all, then?"

"Not exactly. Mainly my job is to keep Mr. Jacobs organized. You wouldn't believe his schedule — all the meetings and conferences to keep straight. It's like being a juggler."

"Yes, it is that way with Consuela. Without her to watch over me . . . " Cortez laughed. "If I had to choose between her and one of my brothers, I would choose her. I can always hire a factory manager. What sort of man is this — Jacobs, you say? You know, when I was a boy, I wanted to be a policeman, to carry the gun and drive the car. To be the chief police officer, that must be a grand thing."

"Mainly his job is shuffling papers — I get to do a lot of the filing, and dictation. When you are the head, your job is mainly doing budgets and meetings."

"But surely he gets to know the — the good things, yes? The best part of being a policeman — it must be the best thing, to know the things that other people do not. To know who are the criminals, and to hunt them."

"And other things. It isn't just police work.

215

They also do counterespionage. Chasing spies," she added.

"That is CIA, no?"

"No. I can't talk about it, of course, but, no, that is a Bureau function. It's all the same, really, and it's not like television at all. Mainly it's boring. I read the reports all the time."

"Amazing," Cortez observed comfortably. "All the talents of a woman, and also she educates me." He smiled encouragement so that she would elaborate. That idiot who'd put him onto her, he remembered, suggested that he'd have to use money. Cortez thought that his KGB training officers would have been proud of his technique. The KGB was ever parsimonious with funds.

"Does he make you work so hard?" Cortez asked a minute later.

"Some of the days can go long, but really he's pretty good about that."

"If he makes you work too hard, we will speak, Mr. Jacobs and I. What if I come to Washington and I cannot see you because you are working?"

"You really want . . . ?"

"Moira." His voice changed its timbre. Cortez knew that he'd pressed too hard for a first time. It had gone too easily, and he'd asked too many questions. After all, lonely widow or not, this was a woman of substance and responsibility — therefore a woman of intellect. But she was also a woman of feelings, and of passion. He moved his hands and his head. He saw the question on her face: Again? He smiled his message: Again.

This time he was less patient, no longer a man exploring the unknown. There was familiarity now. Having established what she liked, his ministrations had direction. Within ten minutes she'd forgotten all of his questions. She would remember the smell and the feel of him. She would bask in the return of youth. She would ask herself where things might lead, but not how they had started.

Assignations are conspiratorial by their nature. Just after midnight he returned her to where her car was parked. Yet again she amazed him with her silence. She held his hand like a schoolgirl, yet her touch was in no way so simple. One last kiss before she left the car — she wouldn't let him get out.

"Thank you, Juan," she said quietly.

Cortez spoke from the heart. "Moira, because of you I am again a man. You have done more for me. When next I come to Washington, we must — "

"We will."

He followed her most of the way home, to let her know that he wished to protect her, breaking off before getting so close to her home that her children — surely they were waiting up — would notice. Cortez drove back to the apartment with a smile on his face, only partly because of his mission.

Her co-workers knew at once. With little more than six hours' sleep, Moira bounced into the office wearing a suit she hadn't touched in a year. There was a sparkle in her eye that could not be hidden. Even Director Jacobs noticed, but no one said anything. Jacobs understood. He'd buried his wife only a few months after Moira's loss, and learned that such voids in one's life could never quite be filled with work. *Good for her*, he thought. She still had children at home. He'd have to go easier on her schedule. She deserved another chance at a real life.

8.

Deployment

The amazing thing was how smoothly things had gone, Chavez thought. After all, they were all sergeants, but whoever had set this thing up had been a clever man because there had been no groping around for which man got which function. There was an operations sergeant in his squad to assist Captain Ramirez with planning. There was a medical corpsman, a good one from the Special Forces who already had his weapons training. Julio Vega and Juan Piscador had once been machine-gunners, and they got the SAWs. The same story applied to their radioman. Each member of the team fit neatly into a preselected slot, all were sufficiently trained that they respected the expertise of one another, and further cross-training enhanced that respect even more. The rugged regime of exercises had extended the pride with which each had arrived, and within two weeks the team had meshed together like a finely made machine. Chavez, a Ranger School graduate, was point man and scout. His job was to probe ahead, to move silently from one place of concealment to another, to watch and listen, then report his observations to Captain Ramirez.

"Okay, where are they?" the captain asked.

"Two hundred meters, just around that corner," Chavez whispered in reply. "Five of them. Three asleep, two awake. One's sitting by the fire. The other one's got an SMG, walking around some."

It was cool in the mountains at night, even in summer. A distant coyote howled at the moon. There was the occasional whisper from a deer moving through the trees, and the only sound associated with man was the distant noise of jets. The clear night made for surprisingly good visibility, even without the low-light goggles with which they were normally equipped. In the thin mountain air, the stars overhead didn't sparkle, but shone as constant, discrete points of light. Ordinarily Chavez would have noticed the beauty, but this was a work night.

Ramirez and the rest of the squad were wearing four-color camouflage fatigues of Belgian manufacture. Their faces were painted with matching tones from sticks of makeup (understandably the Army didn't call it that) so that they blended into the shadows as perfectly as Wells' invisible man. Most importantly, they were totally at home in the darkness. Night was their best and most powerful friend. Man was a

220

day-hunter. All of his senses, all of his instincts, and all of his inventions worked best in the light. Primordial rhythms made him less efficient at night — unless he worked very hard to overcome them, as these soldiers had. Even American Indian tribes living in close partnership with nature had feared the night, had almost never fought at night, had not even guarded their encampments at night — thus giving the U.S. Army its first useful doctrine for operations in darkness. At night man built fires as much for vision as for warmth, but in doing so reduced that vision to mere feet, whereas the human eye, properly conditioned, can see quite well in the darkness.

"Only five?"

"That's all I counted, sir."

Ramirez nodded and gestured for two more men to come forward. A few quiet orders were given. He went with the other two, moving to the right to get above the encampment. Chavez went back forward. His job was to take the sentry down, along with the one dozing at the fire. Moving quietly in the dark is harder than seeing. The human eye is better at spotting movement in the dark than in identifying stationary objects. He put each foot down carefully, feeling for something that might slide or break, thus making noise — the human ear is much underestimated. In daylight his method of moving would have appeared comical, but stealth has its price. Worst of all, he moved slowly, and Ding was no more patient than any man still in his twenties. It was a weakness against which he'd trained himself. He walked in a tight crouch. His weapon was up and ready to guard against surprise, and as the moment approached, his senses were fully alerted, as though an electric current ran across his skin. His head swiveled slowly left and right, his eyes never quite locking on anything, because when one stares at an object in the darkness, it tends to disappear after a few seconds.

Something bothered Chavez, but he didn't know what it was. He stopped for a moment, looking around, searching with all his senses over to his left for about thirty seconds. Nothing. For the first time tonight he found himself wishing for his night goggles. Ding shook it off. Maybe a squirrel or some other night forager. Not a man, certainly. No one could move in the dark as well as a Ninja, he smiled to himself, and got back to the business at hand. He reached his position several minutes later, just behind a scrawny pine tree, and eased down to a kneeling position. Chavez slid the cover off the green face of his digital watch, watching the numbers march slowly toward the appointed moment. There was the sentry, moving in a circle around the fire, never more than thirty feet from it, trying to keep his eyes turned away from it to protect his night vision. But the light reflected off the rocks and the pines would damage his perceptions badly enough — he looked straight at Chavez twice, but saw nothing.

Time.

Chavez brought up his MP-5 and loosed a single round into the target's chest. The man flinched with the impact, grasped the spot where he'd been hit, and dropped to the ground with a surprised gasp. The MP-5 made only a slight metallic clack, like a small stone rolling against another, but in the still mountain night, it was something out of the ordinary. The drowsy one by the fire turned around, but only made it halfway when he too was struck. Chavez figured himself to be on a roll and was taking aim on one of the sleeping men when the distinctive ripping sound of Julio's squad automatic weapon jolted them from their slumber. All three leapt to their feet, and were dead before they got there.

"Where the hell did you come from?" the dead sentry demanded. The place on his chest where the wax bullet had struck was very sore, all the more so from surprise. By the time he was standing again, Ramirez and the others were in the camp.

"Kid, you are very good," a voice said behind Chavez, and a hand thumped down on his shoulder. The sergeant nearly jumped out of his skin as the man walked past him into the encampment. "Come on."

A rattled Chavez followed the man to the fire. He cleared his weapon on the way — the wax bullets could do real harm to a man's face.

"We'll score that one a success," the man said. "Five kills, no reaction from the bad guys. Captain, your machine-gunner got a little carried away. I'd go easier on the rock and roll; the sound of an automatic weapon carries an awful long way. I'd also try to move in a little closer, but — I guess that rock there was about the best you could do. Okay, forget that one. My mistake. We can't always pick the terrain. I liked your discipline on the approach march, and your movement into the objective was excellent. This point man you have is terrific. He almost picked me up." The last struck Chavez as faint praise indeed.

"Who the fuck are you!" Ding asked quietly.

"Kid, I was doing this sort of thing for-real when you were playing with guns made by Mattel. Besides, I cheated." Clark held up his night goggles. "I picked my route carefully, and I froze every time you turned your head. What you heard was my breathing. You almost had me. I thought I blew the exercise. Sorry. My name's Clark, by the way." A hand appeared.

"Chavez." The sergeant took it.

"You're pretty good, Chavez. Best I've seen in a while. I especially like the footwork. Not many have the patience you do. We could have used you in the 3rd SOG." It was Clark's highest praise, and rarely given.

"What's that?"

A grunt and a chuckle. "Something that never existed — don't worry about it."

Clark walked over to examine the two men Chavez had shot. Both were rubbing identical places on their flak jackets, right over their hearts.

"You know how to shoot, too."

"Anybody can hit with this."

Clark turned to look at the young man. "Remember, when it's for-real, it's not quite the same."

Chavez recognized genuine meaning in that statement. "What should I do different, sir?"

"That's the hard part," Clark admitted as the rest of the squad approached the fire. He spoke as a teacher to a gifted pupil. "Part of you has to pretend it's the same as training. Another part has to remember that you don't get many mistakes anymore. You have to know which part to listen to, 'cause it changes from one minute to the next. You got good instincts, kid. Trust 'em. They'll keep you alive. If things don't feel right, they probably aren't. Don't confuse that with fear."

"Huh?"

"You're going to be afraid out there, Chavez. I always was. Get used to the idea, and it can work for you 'stead of against you. For Christ's sake, don't be ashamed of it. Half the problem out in Indian Country is people afraid of being afraid."

"Sir, what the hell are we training for?"

"I don't know yet. Not my department." Clark managed to conceal his feelings on that score. The training wasn't exactly in accord with what he thought the mission was supposed to be. Ritter might be having another case of the clevers. There was nothing more worrisome to Clark than a clever superior.

"You're going to be working with us, though."

It was an exceedingly shrewd observation, Clark thought. He'd asked to come out here, of course, but realized that Ritter had maneuvered him into asking. Clark was the best man the Agency had for this sort of thing. There weren't many men with similar experience anywhere in government service, and most of those, like Clark, were getting a little old for the real thing. Was that all? Clark didn't know. He knew that Ritter liked to keep things under his hat, especially when he thought he was being clever. Clever men outsmart themselves, Clark thought, and Ritter wasn't immune from that.

"Maybe," he admitted reluctantly. It wasn't that he minded associating with these men, but Clark worried about the circumstances that might make it necessary, later on. *Can* you *still cut it, Johnny boy?*

"So?" Director Jacobs asked. Bill Shaw was there, too.

"So he did it, sure as hell," Murray replied as he reached for his coffee. "But taking it to trial would be nasty. He's a clever guy, and his crew backed him up. If you read up on his file, you'll see why. He's some officer. The day I went down, he rescued the crew of a burning fishing boat — talk about perfect timing. There were scorch marks on the hull, he went in so close. Oh, sure, we could get them all apart and interview them, but just figuring out who was involved would be tricky. I hate to say this, but it probably isn't worth the hassle, especially with the senator looking over our shoulder, and the local U.S. Attorney probably won't spring for it either. Bright wasn't all that crazy about it, but I calmed him down. He's a good kid, by the way."

"What about the defense for the two subjects?" Jacobs asked.

"Slim. On the face of it the case against them is pretty damned solid. Ballistics has matched the bullet Mobile pulled out of the deck to the gun recovered on the boat, with both men's fingerprints on it — that was a real stroke of luck. The blood type around where the bullet was found was AB-positive, which matches the wife. A carpet stain three feet away from that confirms that she was having her period, which along with a couple of semen stains suggests rape rather strongly. Right now they're doing the DNA match downstairs on semen samples recovered from the rug — anybody here want to bet against a positive match? We have a half-dozen bloody fingerprints that match the subjects ten points' worth or more. There's a lot of good physical evidence. It's more than enough to convict already," Murray said confidently, "and the lab boys haven't got halfway through their material yet. The U.S. Attorney is going to press for capital punishment. I'll think he'll get it. The only question is whether or not we allow them to trade information for a lighter sentence. But it's not exactly my case." That earned Murray a smile from the Director.

"Pretend it is," Jacobs ordered.

"We'll know in a week or so if we need anything they can tell us. My instincts say no. We ought to be able to figure out who the victim was working for, and that'll be the one who ordered the hit — we just don't know why yet. But it's unlikely that the subjects know why either. I think we have a couple of *sicarios* who hoped to parlay their hit into an entrée to the marketing side of the business. I think they're throwaways. If that's correct, they don't know anything that we can't figure out for ourselves. I suppose we have to give them a chance, but I would recommend against mitigation of sentence. Four murders — bad ones at that. We have a death-penalty statute, and to this brick-agent, I think the chair would fit them just fine."

"Getting nasty in your old age?" Shaw asked. It was another inside joke. Bill Shaw was one of the Bureau's leading intellectuals. He had won his spurs cracking down on domestic terrorist groups, and had accomplished that mission by carefully rebuilding the FBI's intelligence-gathering and analysis procedures. A quintessential chess player with a quiet, organized demeanor, this tall, spare man was also a former field agent who advocated capital punishment in a quiet, organized, and well-reasoned way. It was a point on which police opinion was almost universal. All you had to do to understand capital punishment was to see a crime scene in all its vile spectacle.

"The U.S. Attorney agrees, Dan," Director Jacobs said. "These two druggies are out of the business for keeps."

As if it matters, Murray thought to himself. What mattered to him was that two murderers would pay the price. Because a sufficiently large stash of drugs had been found aboard the yacht, the government could invoke the statute that allowed the death penalty in drug-related murders. The relationship was probably a loose one in this case, but that didn't matter to the three men in the room. The fact of murder — brutal and premeditated — was enough. But to say, as both they and the United States Attorney for the Southern District of Alabama would tell the TV cameras, that this was a fight against the drug trade, was a cynical lie.

Murray's education had been a classical one at Boston College, thirty years before. He could still recite passages in Latin from Virgil's *Aeneid*, or Cicero's opening salvo against Catiline. His study of Greek had been only in translation — foreign languages were one thing to Murray; different alphabets were something else — but he remembered the legend of the Hydra, the mythical beast that had seven or more heads. Each time you cut one off, two would grow to take its place. So it was with the drug trade. There was just too much money involved. Money beyond the horizon of greed. Money to purchase anything a simple man — most of them were — could desire. A single deal could make a man wealthy for life, and there were many who would willingly and consciously risk their lives for that one deal. Having decided to wager their lives on a toss of the dice — what value might they attach to the lives of others? The answer was the obvious one. And so they killed as casually and as brutally as a child might stamp down his foot on an anthill. They killed their competitors because they didn't wish to have competition. They killed their competitors' families whole because they didn't want a wrathful son to appear five, ten, twenty years later with vendetta on his mind; and also because, like nation-states armed with nuclear weapons, the principle of deterrence came into play. Even a man willing to wager his own life might quail before the prospect of wagering those of his children.

So in this case they'd cut off two heads from the Hydra. In three months or so the government would present its case in Federal District Court. The trial would probably last a week. The defense would do its best, but as long as the feds were careful with their evidence, they'd win. The defense would try to discredit the Coast Guard, but it wasn't hard to see what the prosecutor had already decided: the jury would look at Captain Wegener and see a hero, then look at the defendants and see scum. The only likely tactic of the defense would almost certainly be counterproductive. Next, the judge had to make the proper rulings, but this was the South, where even federal judges were expected to have simple, clear ideas about justice. Once the defendants had been found guilty, the penalty phase of the trial would proceed, and again, this was the South, where people read their Bibles. The jury would listen to the aggravating circumstances: mass murder of a family, probability of rape, murder of children, and drugs. But there was a million dollars aboard, the defense would counter. The principal victim was involved in the drug trade. What proof of that is there? the prosecutor would inquire piously — and what of the wife and children? The jury would listen quietly, soberly, almost reverently, would get their instructions from the same judge who had told them how to find the defendants guilty in the first place. They'd deliberate a reasonable period of time, going through the motions of thorough consideration for a decision made days earlier, and report back: death. The criminals, no longer defendants, would be remanded to federal custody. The case would automatically be appealed, but a reversal was unlikely so long as the judge hadn't made any serious procedural errors, which the physical evidence made unlikely. It would take years of appeals. People would object to the sentence on philosophical grounds — Murray disagreed but respected them for their views. The Supreme Court would have to rule sooner or later, but the Supremes, as the police called them, knew that, despite earlier rulings to the contrary, the Constitution clearly contemplated capital punishment, and the will of the People, expressed through Congress, had directly mandated death in certain drug-related cases, as the majority opinion would make clear in its precise, dry use of the language. So, in about five years, after all the appeals had been heard and rejected, both men would be strapped into a wooden chair and a switch would be thrown.

That would be enough for Murray. For all his experience and sophistication, he was before all things a cop. He was an adulthood beyond his graduation from the FBI Academy, when he'd thought that he and his classmates — mostly retired now — would really change the world. The statistics said that they had in many ways, but statistics were too dry, too remote, too inhuman. To Murray the war on crime was an endless series of small battles. Victims were robbed alone, kidnapped alone, or killed alone, and were individuals to be saved or avenged by the warrior-priests of the FBI. Here, too, his outlook was shaped by the values of his Catholic education, and the Bureau remained a bastion of Irish-Catholic America. Perhaps he hadn't changed the world, but he had saved lives, and he had avenged deaths. New criminals would arise as they always did, but his battles had all ended in victories, and ultimately, he had to believe, there would be a net difference for his society, and the difference would be a positive one. He believed as truly as he believed in God that every felon caught was probably a life saved, somewhere down the line.

In this case he had helped to do so again.

But it wouldn't matter a damn to the drug business. His new post forced him to assume a longer view that ordinary agents contemplated only over drinks after their offices closed. With these two out of circulation, the Hydra had already grown two new heads, Murray knew, perhaps more. His mistake was in not pursuing the myth to its conclusion, something others were already doing. Heracles had slain the Hydra by changing tactics. One of the people who had remembered that fact was in this room. What Murray had not yet learned was that at the policy-making level, one's perspective gradually changed one's views.

Cortez liked the view also, despite the somewhat thinner air of this eyrie. His newly acquired boss knew the superficial ways to communicate his power. His desk faced away from the wide window, making it hard for those opposite the massive desk to read the expression on his face. He spoke with the calm, quiet voice of great power. His gestures were economical, his words generally mild. In fact he was a brutal man, Cortez knew, and despite his education a less sophisticated man than he deemed himself to be, but that, Félix knew, was why he'd been hired. So the former colonel trained in Moscow Center adjusted the focus of his eyes to examine the green vista of the valley. He allowed Escobedo to play his eye-power games. He'd played them with far more dangerous men than this one.

"So?"

"I have recruited two people," Cortez replied. "One will feed us information for monetary considerations. The other will do so for other reasons. I also examined two other potential prospects, but discarded them as unsuitable."

"Who are they — who are the ones you will use?"

"No." Cortez shook his head. "I have told you that the identity of my agents must remain secret. This is a principle of intelligence operations. You have informers within your organization, and loose talk would compromise our ability to gather the information which you require. *Jefe*," he said fawningly. This one needed that sort of thing. "*Jefe*, you have hired me for my expertise and experience. You must allow me to do my work properly. You will know the quality of my sources from the information which I give you. I understand how you feel. It is normal. Castro himself has asked me that question, and I gave him the same answer. It must be so."

That earned Cortez a grunt. Escobedo liked to be compared with a chief of state, better still one who had defied the *yanquis* so successfully for a generation. There would be a satisfied smile now on the handsome face, Félix knew without bothering to check for it. His answer was a lie for two reasons: Castro had never asked the question, and neither Félix nor anyone else on that island would ever have dared to deny him the information.

234

"So what have you learned?"

"Something is afoot," he said in a matter-of-fact voice that was almost taunting. After all, he had to justify his salary. "The American government is putting together a new program designed to enhance their interdiction efforts. My sources have no specifics as yet, though what they have heard has come from multiple sources and is probably true. My other source will be able to confirm what information I receive from the first." The lesson was lost on Escobedo, Félix knew. Recruiting two complementary sources on a single mission would have earned him a flowery commendation letter from any real intelligence service.

"What will the information cost us?"

Money. It is always money with him, Cortez told himself with a stifled sigh. No wonder he needed a professional with his security operations. Only a fool thinks that he can buy everything. On the other hand, there were times when money was helpful, and though he didn't know it, Escobedo paid more money to his American hirelings and traitors than the entire Communist intelligence network.

"It is better to spend a great deal of money on one person at a high level than to squander it on a large number of minor functionaries. A quarter of a million dollars will do nicely to get the information which we require." Cortez would be keeping most of that, of course. He had expenses of his own.

"That is all?" Escobedo asked incredulously. "I pay more than that to — "

"Because your people have never used the proper approach, *jefe*. Because you pay people on the basis of where they are, not what they know. You have never adopted a systematic approach to dealing with your enemies. With the proper information, you can utilize your funds much more efficiently. You can act strategically instead of tactically," Cortez concluded by pushing the proper button.

"Yes! They must learn that we are a force to be reckoned with!"

Not for the first time, Félix thought that his main objective was to take the money and run . . . perhaps a house in Spain . . . or, perhaps, to supplant this egomaniacal buffoon. That was a thought. . . . But not for now. Escobedo was an egomaniac, but he was also a shrewd one, capable of rapid action. One difference between this man and those who ran his former agency was that Escobedo wasn't afraid to make a decision, and do it quickly. No bureaucracy here, no multiplicity of desks for messages to pass. For that he respected *El Jefe*. At least he knew how to make a decision. KGB had probably been that way once, maybe even the American intelligence organs. But no longer.

"One more week," Ritter told the National Security Adviser.

"Nice to hear that things are moving," the

236

Admiral observed. "Then what?"

"Why don't you tell me? Just to keep things clear," the DDO suggested. He followed it with a reminder. "After all, the operation was your idea in the first place."

"Well, I sold Director Jacobs on the idea," Cutter replied with a smile at his own cleverness. "When we're ready to proceed — and I mean ready to push the button — Jacobs will fly down there to meet with their Attorney General. The ambassador says that the Colombians will go along with almost anything. They're even more desperate than we are and — "

"You didn't — "

"No, Bob, the ambassador doesn't know. Okay?" *I'm not the idiot you take me for,* his eyes told the CIA executive. "If Jacobs can sell the idea to them, we insert the teams ASAP. One change I want to make."

"What's that?"

"The air side of it. Your report says that practice tracking missions are already turning up targets."

"Some," Ritter admitted. "Two or three per week."

"The wherewithal to handle them is already in place. Why not activate that part of the operation? I mean, it might actually help to identify the areas we want to send the insertion teams to, develop operational intelligence, that sort of thing."

"I'd prefer to wait," Ritter said cautiously.

"Why? If we can identify the most frequently used areas, it cuts down on the amount of moving around they'll have to do. That's your greatest operational risk, isn't it? This is a way to develop information that enhances the entire operational concept."

The problem with Cutter, Ritter told himself, was that the bastard knew just enough about operations to be dangerous. Worse, he had the power to enforce his will — and a memory of the Operations Directorate's recent history. What was it he'd said a few months back? *Your best operations in the last couple of years actually came out of Greer's department.* . . . By which he meant Jack Ryan, James's bright rising star — possibly the new DDI the way things looked. That was too bad. Ritter was genuinely fond of his counterpart at the head of the Intelligence Directorate, but less so of Greer's ingratiating protégé. But it was nevertheless true that the Agency's two best coups in recent years had begun in the "wrong" department, and it was time for Operations to reassert its primacy. Ritter wondered if Cutter was consciously using that as a prod to move him to action. Probably not, he decided. Cutter didn't know enough about infighting yet. Not that he wouldn't learn, of course.

"Going too early is a classic error in field operations," the DDO offered lamely.

"But we're not. Essentially we have two separate operations, don't we?" Cutter asked. "The air part can operate independently of the in-country part. I admit it'll be less effective, but it can still operate. Doesn't this give us a chance to check out the less tricky side of the plan before we commit to the dangerous part? Doesn't it give us something to take to the Colombians to show that we're really serious?"

Too soon, the voice in Ritter's head said urgently, but his face showed indecision.

"Look, do you want me to take it to the President?" Cutter asked.

"Where is he today — California?"

"Political trip. I would prefer not to bother him with this sort of thing, but — "

It was a curious situation, the DDO thought. He had underestimated Cutter, while the National Security Adviser seemed quite able to overestimate himself. "Okay, you win. EAGLE EYE starts day after tomorrow. It'll take that long to get everyone up and running."

"And SHOWBOAT?"

"One more week to prep the teams. Four days to get them to Panama and meet up with the air assets, check communications systems and all that."

Cutter grinned as he reached for his coffee. It was time to smooth some ruffled feathers, he thought. "God, it's nice to work with a real pro. Look on the bright side, Bob. We'll have two full weeks to interrogate whatever turns up in the air net, and the insertion teams will have a much better idea of where they're needed."

You've already won, you son of a bitch. Do you

have to rub it in? Ritter wanted to ask. He wondered what would have happened if he'd called Cutter's cards. What would the President have said? Ritter's position was a vulnerable one. He'd grumbled long and loud within the intelligence community that CIA hadn't run a serious field operation in . . . fifteen years? It depended on what you meant by "serious," didn't it? Now he was being given the chance, and what had been a nice line to be spoken at the coffee sessions during high-level government conferences was now a gray chicken come home to roost. Field operations like this were dangerous. Dangerous to the participants. Dangerous to those who gave the orders. Dangerous to the governments that sponsored them. He'd told Cutter that often enough, but like many, the National Security Adviser was mesmerized by the glamour of field ops. It was known in the trade as the *Mission: Impossible* Syndrome. Even professionals could confuse a TV drama with reality, and, throughout government, people tended to hear only that which they wished to hear, and to ignore the unpleasant parts. But it was somewhat late for Ritter to give out his warnings. After all, he'd complained for years that such a mission was possible, and occasionally a desirable adjunct to international policy. And he'd said often enough that his directorate still knew how to do it. The fact that he'd had to recruit field operatives from the Army and Air Force had escaped notice. Time had been when the Agency had been able to use its own private air force and its own private army . . . and if this worked out, perhaps those times would come again. It was a capability the Agency and the country needed, Ritter thought. Here, perhaps, was his chance to make it all happen. If putting up with amateur power-vendors like Cutter was the price of getting it, then that was the price he'd have to pay.

"Okay, I'll get things moving."

"I'll tell the boss. How soon do you expect we'll have results . . . ?"

"Impossible to say."

"But before November," Cutter suggested lightly.

"Yeah, probably by then." Politics, too, of course. Well, that was what kept traffic circling around the beltway.

The 1st Special Operations Wing was based at Hurlburt Field, at the west end of the Eglin Air Force Base complex in Florida. It was a unique unit, but any military unit with "Special" in its name was unique by its very nature. The adjective was used for any number of meanings. "Special weapons" most often meant nuclear weapons, and here the word was used to avoid offending the sensibilities of those for whom "nuclear" connoted mushroom clouds and mega-deaths; it was as though a change of wording could effect a change of substance, yet another characteristic of governments all over the world. "Special Operations," on the other hand, meant something else. Generally it denoted covert business, getting people into places where they ought not to be, supporting them while they were there, and getting them out after concluding business that they ought not to have done in the first place. That, among other things, was the business of the 1st.

Colonel Paul Johns — "PJ" — didn't know everything the wing did. The 1st was rather an odd grouping where authority didn't always coincide with rank, where the troops provided support for the aircraft and crews without always knowing why they did so, where aircraft came and went on irregular schedules, and where people weren't encouraged to speculate or ask questions. The wing was divided into individual fiefdoms that interacted with others on an *ad hoc* basis. PJ's fiefdom included half a dozen MH-53J "Pave Low III" helicopters. Johns had been around for quite a while, and somehow had managed to spend nearly all of his Air Force career in the air. It was a career path that guaranteed him both a fulfilling, exciting career, and precisely zero chance at ever wearing general's stars. But on that score he didn't give much of a damn. He'd joined the Air Force to fly; something generals don't get to do very much. He'd kept his part of the bargain, and the service had kept its, which wasn't quite as common an arrangement as some would imagine. Johns had early on eschewed fixed-wing aircraft, the fast-movers that dropped bombs or shot down other aircraft.

A people-person all of his life, Johns had started off in the Jolly Green Giants, the HH-3 rescue helicopters of Vietnam fame, then graduated to the Super Jolly HH-53, part of the Air Rescue Service. As a brash young captain he'd flown in the Song Tay Raid, copilot of the aircraft that had deliberately crashed into the prison camp twenty miles west of Hanoi as part of the effort to rescue people who, it turned out, had been moved just a short time before. That had been one of the few failures in his life. Colonel Johns was not a man accustomed to such things. If you went down, PJ would come get you. He was the third-ranking all-time rescue specialist in the Air Force. The current Chief of Staff and two other general officers had been excused a stay in the Hanoi Hilton because of him and his crews. PJ was a man who only rarely had to buy himself a drink. He was also a man whom general officers saluted first. It was a tradition that went along with the Medal of Honor.

Like most heroes, he was grossly ordinary. Only five-six and a hundred thirty pounds, he looked like any other middle-aged man picking up a loaf of bread in the base exchange. The reading glasses he now had to wear made him look rather like a friendly suburban banker, and he did not often raise his voice. He cut his own grass when he had the time, and his wife did it when he didn't. His car was a fuel-efficient Plymouth Horizon. His son was studying engineering at Georgia Tech, and his daughter had won a scholarship to Princeton, leaving him and his wife an overly quiet house on post in which to contemplate the retirement that lay a few years in the future.

But not now. He sat in the left seat of the Pave Low helicopter checking out a bright young captain who, everyone thought, was ready to be a command pilot himself. The multimillion-dollar helicopter was skimming treetops at a hair under two hundred knots. It was a dark, cloudy night over the Florida panhandle, and this part of the Eglin complex wasn't brightly lit, but that didn't matter. Both he and the captain wore special helmets with built-in low-light goggles, not terribly unlike what Darth Vader wore in *Star Wars*. But these worked, converting the vague darkness ahead into a green and gray display. PJ kept his head moving around, and made sure that the captain did the same. One danger with the night-vision gear was that your depth perception — a matter of life and death to a low-level flyer — was degraded by the artificial picture generated by the masks. Perhaps a third of the squadron's operational losses, Johns thought, could be traced to that particular hazard, and the technical wizards hadn't come up with a decent fix yet. One problem with the Pave Lows was that operational and training losses were relatively high. It was a price of the mission for which they trained, and there was no answer to that but more training.

The six-bladed rotor spun overhead, driven by

the two turboshaft engines. Pave Low was about as big as helicopters got, with a full combat crew of six and room for over forty combat-equipped passengers. The nose bulged at various places with radar, infrared, and other instruments — the general effect was of an insect from another planet. At doors on each side of the airframe were mounts for rotary miniguns, plus another at the tail cargo door, because their primary mission, covert insertion and support of special-operations forces, was a dangerous business — as was the secondary role they practiced tonight, combat search-and-rescue. During his time in Southeast Asia, PJ had worked with A-1 Skyraider attack bombers, the Air Force's last piston-engine attack aircraft, called SPADs or Sandys. Exactly who would support them today was still something of an open question. To protect herself, in addition to the guns the aircraft carried flare and chaff pods, IR jamming and suppression gear . . . and her crew of madmen.

Johns smiled within his helmet. This was real flying, and there wasn't much of that left. They had the option of flying with the aid of an auto-pilot-radar-computer system that hedgehopped automatically, but tonight they were simulating a system failure. Autopilot or not, the pilot was responsible for flying the airplane, and Willis was doing his best to keep the helicopter down on the treetops. Every so often Johns would have to stop himself from flinching as an errant tree branch seemed certain to slap against the chopper's underside, but Captain Willis was a competent young man, keeping the aircraft low, but not too low. Besides, as PJ knew from long experience, the top branches on trees were thin, fragile things that did nothing more than mar the paint. More than once he'd brought home a helicopter whose underside bore green stains like those on a child's jeans.

"Distance?" Willis asked.

Colonel Johns checked the navigation display. He had a choice of Doppler, satellite, or inertial, plus the old-fashioned plotting board that he still used, and still insisted that all his people learn.

"Two miles, zero-four-eight."

"Roger." Willis eased off on the throttle.

For this training mission, an honest-to-God fighter pilot had "volunteered" to be trucked out to the boonies, where another helicopter had draped a parachute over a tree to simulate a genuinely shot-down airman, who had in turn activated a genuine rescue-beacon radio. One of the new tricks was that the chute was coated with a chemical that fluoresced on ultraviolet light. Johns did the copilot's job of activating a low-power UV laser that scanned ahead, looking for the return signal. Whoever had come up with this idea deserved a medal, PJ thought. The worst, scariest, and always seemingly the longest part of any rescue mission was actually getting eyeballs on the victim. That was when the gomers on the ground, who were also out hunting, would hear the sound of the rotor and decide that they might as well bag two aircraft on the same day. . . . His Medal of Honor had come on such a mission over eastern Laos, when the crew of an F-105 Wild Weasel had attracted a platoon of NVA. Despite aggressive support from the Sandy team, the downed airmen hadn't dared to reveal their position. But Johns had coldly decided not to go home empty, and his Jolly had absorbed two hundred rounds in a furious gunfight before getting both men out. Johns often wondered if he'd ever have the courage — lunacy — to try that again.

"I got a chute at two o'clock."

"X-Ray Two-Six, this is Papa Lima; we have your chute. Can you mark your position?"

"Affirmative, tossing smoke, tossing green smoke."

The rescuee was following proper procedure in telling the chopper crew what sort of smoke grenade he was using, but you couldn't tell in the dark. On the other hand, the heat of the pyrotechnic device blazed like a beacon on the infrared display, and they could see their man.

"Got him?"

"Yep," Willis answered, and spoke next to the crew chief. "Get ready, we have our victim."

"Standing by, sir." In the back the flight engineer, Senior Master Sergeant Buck Zimmer — he and the colonel went way back together — activated his winch controls. At the end of the steel cable was a heavy steel device called a penetrator. Heavy enough to fall through the foliage of any forest, its bottom unfolded like the petals of a flower, providing a seat for the victim, who would then be pulled back up through the branches, an experience which remarkably enough had never quite killed anyone. In the event that the victim was injured, it was the job of Sergeant Zimmer or a rescue paramedic to ride it down, attach the victim to the penetrator, and take the elevator ride himself. That job sometimes entailed physically searching for the victim, often under fire. It was for this reason that the people who flew the rescue choppers treated their crewmen with considerable respect. Nothing so horrifies a pilot as the idea of being on the ground, with people shooting at you.

But not this time. Since it was peacetime and safety rules applied, training or not, the pickup was being made from a small clearing. Zimmer worked the winch controls. The victim unfolded the seat-petals and hooked himself securely aboard, knowing what was to follow. The flight engineer started hoisting the cable, made sure that the victim was firmly attached, and so notified the flight crew.

On the flight deck, forward, Captain Willis immediately twisted the throttle control to full power and moved upward. Within fifteen seconds, the "rescued" fighter pilot was three hundred feet over the ground, hanging by a quarter-inch steel cable and wondering why in the hell he'd been so fucking idiotic to volunteer for this. Five seconds later, the burly arm of Sergeant Zimmer yanked him into the aircraft.

"Recovery complete," Zimmer reported.

Captain Willis pushed his cyclic control forward, diving the helicopter at the ground. He'd climbed too much on the extraction, he knew, and tried to compensate by showing Colonel Johns that he could get back down to the safety of the treetops very quickly. He accomplished this, but he could feel the eyes of his commander on the side of his head. He'd made a mistake. Johns did not tolerate mistakes. People died of mistakes, the colonel told them every goddamned day, and he was tired of having people die.

"Can you take it for a minute?" Willis asked.

"Copilot's airplane," Johns acknowledged, taking the stick and easing the Sikorsky down another foot or so. "You don't want to climb so much winching the guy in, not with possible SAMs out there."

"At night you'd expect more guns than SAMs." Willis was right, sort of. It was a hard call. And he knew the answer that would come.

"We're protected against small-caliber guns. The big ones are as dangerous as SAMs. You keep it closer to the ground next time, Captain."

"Yes, sir."

"Other than that, not bad. Arm a little stiff?"

"Yes, sir."

"It might be the gloves. Unless your fingers fit in just right, you end up gripping too hard, and that translates back into the wrist and upper arm after a while. You end up with a stiff arm, stiff movements on the stick, and sloppy handling. Get yourself a good set of gloves. My wife makes mine for me special. You might not always have a copilot to take the airplane, and this sort of thing is tough enough that you don't want any more distractions than you gotta have."

"Yes, sir."

"By the way, you passed."

It wouldn't do to thank the colonel, Captain Willis knew. He did the next best thing after flexing his hand for a minute.

"I got the airplane."

PJ took his hand off the stick. "Pilot's airplane," he acknowledged. "By the way . . . "

"Yes, sir?"

"I've got a special job coming up in a week or so. Interested?"

"Doing what?"

"You're not supposed to ask that," the colonel told him. "A little TDY. Not too far away. We'll be flying this bird down. Call it Spec-Ops."

"Okay," Willis said. "Count me in. Who's cleared to — "

"In simple terms, nobody is. We're taking Zimmer, Childs, and Bean, and a support team. Far as everybody knows, we're TDY for some practice missions out on the California coast. That's all you need to know for now."

Inside his helmet, Willis's eyebrow went up. Zimmer had worked with PJ all the way back to Thailand and the Jolly Green days, one of the few enlisted men left with real combat experience. Sergeant Bean was the squadron's best gunner. Childs was right behind him. Whatever this TDY — temporary detached duty — assignment was, it was for-real. It also meant that Willis would remain a copilot for a little while longer, but he didn't mind. It was always a treat flying with the champion of Combat Search and Rescue. That was where the colonel got his call sign. C-SAR, in PJ's lexicon, it came out "Caesar."

Chavez traded a look with Julio Vega: *Jesucristo!*

"Any questions?" the briefer asked.

"Yes, sir," a radio operator said. "What happens after we call it in?"

"The aircraft will be intercepted."

"For-real, sir?"

"That's up to the flight crew. If they don't do what they're told, they're going swimming. That's all I can say. Gentlemen, everything you've heard is Top Secret. Nobody — I mean *nobody!* — ever hears what I just said. If the wrong folks ever learn about this, people will get hurt. The objective of this mission is to put a crimp in the way people move drugs into the United States. It may get a little rough."

"About fucking time," a quiet voice observed.

"Okay, now you know. I repeat, gentlemen, this mission is going to be dangerous. We are going to give each of you some time to think about it. If you want out, we'll understand. We're

251

dealing with some pretty bad folks. Of course"
— the man smiled and went on after a moment —
"we got some pretty bad people here, too."

"Fuckin' A!" another voice said.

"Anyway, you have the rest of the night to
think this one over. We move out at eighteen-
hundred hours tomorrow. There is no turning
back at that point. Everybody understand?
Good. That is all for now."

"Ten-Hut!" Captain Ramirez snapped. Everyone in the room jumped to attention as the briefer
left. Then it was the captain's turn: "Okay, you
heard the man. Give this one a real good think,
people. I want you to come along on this one —
hell, I need every one of you — but if you're not
comfortable with the idea, I don't want you. You
got any questions for me?" There weren't. "Okay.
Some of you know people who got fucked up
because of drugs. Maybe friends, maybe family,
I don't know. What we have here is a chance to
get even. Those bastards are fucking up our
country, and it's time we taught 'em a little lesson. Think it over. If anyone has any problems,
let me know right away. If anybody wants out,
that's okay." His face and tone said something
else entirely. Anyone who opted out would be
seen by his officer as something less than a man,
and that would be doubly painful since Ramirez
had led his men, shared every hardship, and
sweated with them through every step of training. He turned and left.

"Damn," Chavez observed finally. "I figured

this was going to be a strange one, but ... damn."

"I had a friend died of an OD," Vega said. "He was just playing around, y'know, not a regular user like, but I guess it was bad stuff. Scared the shit outa me. I never touched it again. I was pissed when that happened. Tomás was a friend, 'mano. The fucker sold him the shit, man, I wouldn't mind introducin' him to my SAW."

Chavez nodded as thoughtfully as his age and education allowed. He remembered the gangs who had been vicious enough in his early childhood, but that activity seemed almost playful in retrospect. Now the turf fights were not the mere symbolism over who dwelt on what block. Now it was over marketing position. There was serious money involved, more than enough to kill for. That was what had transformed his old neighborhood from a zone of poverty to an area of open combat. Some people he knew were afraid to walk their own streets because of other people with drugs and guns. Wild rounds came through windows and killed people in front of televisions, and the cops were often afraid to visit the projects unless they came with the numbers and weapons of an invading army ... all because of drugs. And the people who caused it all were living high and safe, fifteen hundred miles away. . . .

Chavez didn't begin to grasp how skillfully he and his fellows — even Captain Ramirez — had been manipulated. They were all soldiers who trained constantly to protect their country against its enemies, products of a system that took their youth and enthusiasm and gave it direction; that rewarded hard work with achievement and pride; that most of all gave their boundless energy purpose; that asked only for allegiance in return. Since enlisted soldiers most often come from the poorer strata of society, they all had learned that minority status did not matter — the Army rewarded performance without consideration to one's color or accent. All of these men were intimately aware of the social problems caused by drugs, and were part of a subculture in which drugs were not tolerated — the military's effort to expunge its ranks of drug users had been painful, but it had succeeded. Those who stayed in were people for whom the use of drugs was beyond the pale. They were the achievers from their neighborhoods. They were the success stories. They were the adventurous, the brave, the disciplined graduates of the mean streets for whom obstacles were things to be overcome, and for whom every instinct was to help others to do the same.

And that was the mission they all contemplated. Here was a chance to protect not only their country, but also the barrios from which they had all escaped. Already marked as achievers within the ranks of the Army's most demanding units, then given training to make them prouder still, they could no more decline participation in this mission than they could deny their manhood. There was not a man here who had not once in his life contemplated taking down a drug dealer. But the Army was letting them do something even better. Of course they'd do it.

"Blow the fuckers right out of the sky!" the squad's radio operator said. "Put a Sidewinder missile right up his ass! You got the right to remain *dead*, sucker!"

"Yeah," Vega agreed. "I wouldn't mind seeing that. Hell, I wouldn't mind it if we got to go after the big shots where they fucking live! Think we could get them, Ding?"

Chavez grinned. "You shittin' me, Julio? Who you suppose they got working for them, soldiers? Shit. Punks with machine guns, probably don't even keep 'em clean. Against us? Shit. Maybe against what they got down there, maybe, but against us? No chance, man. I'm talking dead meat. I just get in close, pop the sentries nice an' quiet with my H and K, an' let you turkeys do the easy stuff."

"More Ninja shit," a rifleman said lightly.

Ding pulled one of his throwing stars from his shirt pocket and flicked it into the doorframe fifteen feet away.

"Smile when you say that, boy." Chavez laughed.

"Hey, Ding, could you teach me to do that?" the rifleman asked. There was no further discussion of the mission's dangers, only of its opportunities.

They called him Bronco. His real name was

Jeff Winters, and he was a newly promoted captain in the United States Air Force, but because his job was flying fighter aircraft he had to have a special name, known as a call sign. His resulted from a nearly forgotten party in Colorado — he'd graduated from the United States Air Force Academy — at which he'd fallen from a horse so gentle that the animal had nearly died of fright. The six-pack of Coors had contributed to the fall, along with the laughter that followed from his amused classmates, and one of them — the asshole was flying trash-haulers now, Winters told himself with a tight smile — assigned him the name on the spot. The classmate knew how to ride horses, Bronco told the night, but he hadn't made the grade to fly F-15-Charlies. The world wasn't exactly overrun with justice, but there was some to be found.

Which was the whole purpose of his special mission.

Winters was a small man, and a young one. Twenty-seven, to be exact, he already had seven hundred hours in the McDonnell-Douglas fighter. As some men were born to play baseball, or to act, or to drive race cars, Bronco Winters had entered the world for the single purpose of flying fighter planes. He had the sort of eyesight to make an ophthalmologist despair, coordination that combined the best of a concert pianist and the man on the flying trapeze, and a much rarer quality known in his tight community as SA — situational awareness. Winters always knew what was happening around him. His airplane was as natural a part of the young man as the muscles in his arm. He transmitted his wishes to the airplane and the F-15C complied at once, precisely mimicking the mental image in the pilot's mind. Where his mind went, the airplane followed.

At the moment he was orbiting two hundred miles off the Florida Gulf Coast. He'd taken off from Eglin Air Force Base forty minutes earlier, topped off his fuel from a KC-135 tanker, and now he had enough JP-5 aboard to fly for five hours if he took things easy, as he had every intention of doing. FAST-pack conformal fuel cells were attached along the sides of his aircraft. Ordinarily they were hung with missiles as well — the F-15 can carry as many as eight — but for this evening's mission the only ordnance aboard were the rounds for his 20mm rotary cannon, and these were always kept aboard the aircraft because their weight was a convenience in maintaining the Eagle's flying trim.

He flew in a racetrack pattern, his engines throttled down to loitering speed. Bronco's dark, sharp eyes swept continuously left and right, searching for the running lights of other aircraft but finding none among the stars. He wasn't the least bit bored. He was, rather, a man quietly delighted that the taxpayers of his country were actually foolish enough to give him over $30,000 per year to do something for which he would have been grateful to pay. Well, he told himself, I guess that's what I'm doing tonight.

"Two-Six Alpha, this is Eight-Three Quebec, do you read, over?" his radio crackled. Bronco squeezed the trigger on his stick.

"Eight-Three Quebec, this is Two-Six Alpha. I read you five by five, over." The radio channel was encrypted. Only the two aircraft were using the unique encoding algorithm for this evening; all that anyone trying to listen in would hear would be the warbling rasp of static.

"We have a target on profile, bearing one-nine-six, range two-one-zero your position. Angels two. Course zero-one-eight. Speed two-six-five. Over." There was no command to accompany this information. Despite the secure radios, chatter was kept to a minimum.

"Roger, copy. Out."

Captain Winters moved his stick left. The proper course and speed for his intercept sprang into his mind unbidden. The Eagle changed over to a southerly heading. Winters dropped the nose a touch as he brought the fighter to a course of one hundred eighty degrees and increased power a fraction to bring his speed up. It actually seemed that he was abusing the airplane to fly her this slow, but that was not actually the case.

It was a twin-engined Beech, Captain Winters saw, the most common aircraft used by the druggies. That meant cocaine rather than the bulkier marijuana, and that suited him, since it was probably a cokehead who'd mugged his mom. He pulled his F-15 level behind it, about half a mile back.

This was the eighth time he'd intercepted a drug runner, but it was the first time he'd be allowed to do something about it. On the previous occasions he'd not even been allowed to call the information in to the Customs boys. Bronco verified the course of the target — for fighter pilots anything other than a friendly was a target — and checked his systems. The directional radio transmitter hanging in the streamlined container under the fighter's centerline slaved itself to the radar tracking Beech. He made his first radio call, and flipped on his landing lights, transfixing the small executive aircraft in the night. Immediately the Beech dived for the wave tops, and the Eagle followed it down. He called again, giving his order and getting no response. He moved the button on the top of his stick to the "guns" position. The next call was accompanied by a burst from his cannon. This started the Beech in a series of radical evasive turns. Winters decided that the target was not going to do what it was told.

Okay.

An ordinary pilot might have been startled by the lights and turned to evade a collision, but an ordinary pilot would not do what the druggies did. The Beech dived for the wave tops, reduced power, and popped his flaps, slowing the aircraft down to approach speed, which was far slower than the F-15 could do without stalling out. This maneuver often forced the DEA and Coast Guard planes to break contact. But Bronco's job wasn't

259

to follow the guy in. As the Beech turned west to run for the Mexican coast, Captain Winters killed his lights, added power, and zoomed up to five thousand feet. There he executed a smart hammerhead turn and took a nose-down attitude, the Eagle's radar sweeping the surface of the sea. There: heading due west, speed 85 knots, only a few feet over the water. A gutsy pilot, Bronco thought, holding that close to a stall and that low. Not that it mattered.

Winters extended his own speed brakes and flaps, taking the fighter down. He felt to make sure that the selector button was still in the "guns" position and watched the Head-Up Display, bringing the pipper right on the target and holding it there. It might have been harder if the Beech had kept speed up and tried to maneuver, but it wouldn't really have mattered. Bronco was just too good, and in his Eagle, he was nearly invincible. When he got within four hundred yards, his finger depressed the button for a fraction of a second.

A line of green tracers lanced through the sky.

Several rounds appeared to miss the Beech ahead, but the rest hit right in the cockpit area. He heard no sound from the kill. There was only a brief flash of light, followed by a phosphorescent splash of white foam when the aircraft hit.

Winters reflected briefly that he had just killed one man, maybe two. That was all right. They wouldn't be missed.

9.

Meeting Engagement

"So?" Escobedo eyed Larson as coldly as a biology professor might look at a caged white rat. He had no special reason to suspect Larson of anything, but he was angry, and Larson was the nearest target for that anger.

But Larson was used to that. "So I don't know, *jefe*. Ernesto was a good pilot, a good student. So was the other one, Cruz. The engines in the aircraft were practically new — two hundred hours on each. The airframe was six years old, but that's nothing unusual; the aircraft was well maintained. Weather was okay all the way north, some scattered high clouds over the Yucatan Channel, nothing worse than that." The pilot shrugged. "Aircraft disappear, *jefe*. One cannot always know why."

"He is my cousin! What do I tell his mother?"

"Have you checked with any airfields in Mexico?"

"Yes! And Cuba, and Honduras, and Nicaragua!"

"No distress calls? No reports from ships or aircraft in the vicinity?"

"No, nothing." Escobedo moderated somewhat as Larson went through the possibilities, professional as ever.

"If it was some sort of electrical failure, he might be down somewhere, but . . . I would not be hopeful, *jefe*. If they had landed safely, they would have let us know by now. I am sorry, *jefe*. He is probably lost. It has happened before. It will happen again."

One other possibility was that Ernesto and Cruz had made their own arrangements, had landed somewhere other than their intended destination, had sold their cargo of forty kilograms, and had decided to disappear, but that was not seriously considered. The question of drugs had not even been mentioned, because Larson was not really part of the operation, merely a technical consultant who had asked to be cut out of that aspect of the business. Escobedo trusted Larson to be honest and objective because he had always been so in the past, taking his money and doing his job well, and also because Larson was no fool — he knew the consequences of lying and double-dealing.

They were in Escobedo's expensive condominium in Medellín. It occupied the entire top

262

floor of the building. The floor immediately under this was occupied by Escobedo's vassals and retainers. The elevator was controlled by people who knew who could pass and who could not. The street outside the building was watched. Larson reflected that at least he didn't have to worry about somebody stealing the hubcaps off his car. He also wondered what the hell had happened to Ernesto. Was it simply an accident of some sort? Such things had happened often enough. One reason for his position as flying instructor was that past smuggling operations had lost quite a few airplanes, often through the most prosaic of causes. But Larson was not a fool. He was thinking about recent visitors and recent orders from Langley; training at The Farm didn't encourage people to believe in coincidences. Some sort of op was about to run. Might this have been the opening move?

Larson didn't think so. CIA was years past that sort of thing, which was too bad, he thought, but a fact nonetheless.

"He was a good pilot?" Escobedo asked again.

"I taught him myself, *jefe*. He had four hundred hours, good mechanical skills, and he was as good on instruments as a young pilot can be. The only thing that worried me about him was that he liked flying low."

"Yes?"

"Flying low over water is dangerous, especially at night. It is too easy to become disoriented. You forget where the horizon is, and if you keep looking out of the windows instead of checking your instruments. . . . Experienced pilots have driven their airplanes right into the water that way. Unfortunately, flying very low is fun and many pilots, especially the young ones, think that it is also a test of manhood. That is foolish, as pilots learn with time."

" 'A good pilot is a cautious pilot'?" Escobedo asked.

"That is what I tell every student," Larson replied seriously. "Not all of them believe me. It is true everywhere. You can ask instructors in any air force in the world. Young pilots make foolish mistakes because they are young and inexperienced. Judgment comes with experience — most often through a frightening experience. Those who survive learn, but some do not survive."

Escobedo considered that for a few seconds.

"He was a proud one, Ernesto." To Larson it sounded like an epitaph.

"I will recheck the maintenance log of the aircraft," the pilot offered. "And I will also review the weather data."

"Thank you for coming in so quickly, Señor Larson."

"I am at your service, *jefe*. If I learn anything, I will let you know."

Escobedo saw him to the door, then returned to his desk. Cortez entered the room from a side door.

"Well?"

"I like Larson," Cortez said. "He speaks the truth. He has pride, but not too much."

Escobedo nodded agreement. "A hireling, but a good one."

. . . *like you.* Cortez didn't react to the implied message. "How many flights have been lost over the years?"

"We didn't even keep records until eighteen months ago. Since then, nine. That's one reason we took Larson on. I felt that the crashes were due to pilot error and poor maintenance. Carlos has proven to be a good instructor."

"But never wished to become involved himself?"

"No. A simple man. He has a comfortable life doing what he enjoys. There is much to be said for that," Escobedo observed lightly. "You have been over his background?"

"*Sí.* Everything checks out, but . . ."

"But?"

"But if he were something other than what he appears to be, things would also check out." This was the point at which an ordinary man would say something like, *But you can't suspect everyone.* Escobedo did not, and that was a measure of his sophistication, Cortez noted. His employer had ample experience with conspiracy and knew that you had to suspect everyone. He wasn't exactly a professional, but he wasn't exactly a fool either.

"Do you think —"

"No. He was nowhere near the place the flight left from, had no way of knowing that it was happening that night. I checked: he was in Bogotá with his lady friend. They had dinner alone and retired early. Perhaps it was a flying accident, but coming so soon after we learn that the *norteamericanos* are planning something, I do not think we should call it such a thing. I think I should return to Washington."

"What will you find out?"

"I will attempt to discover something of what they are doing."

"Attempt?"

"Señor, gathering sensitive intelligence information is an art — "

"You can buy anything you need!"

"There you are incorrect," Cortez said with a level stare. "The best sources of information are never motivated by money. It is dangerous — foolish — to assume that allegiance can be purchased."

"And what of you?"

"That is a question you must consider, but I am sure you already have." The best way to earn trust with this man was always to say that trust did not exist. Escobedo thought that whatever allegiance money could not buy could be maintained with fear instead. In that sense, his employer was foolish. He assumed that his reputation for violence could cow anyone, and rarely considered that there were those who could give him lessons in applied violence. There was much to admire about this man, but so much also to merit disdain. Fundamentally he was an amateur

— though a gifted one — who learned from his mistakes readily enough, but lacked the formal training that might have enabled him to learn from the mistakes of others — and what was intelligence training but the institutional memory of lessons from the mistakes of others? He didn't so much need an intelligence and security adviser as one in covert operations per se, but that was an area in which none of these men would solicit or accept advice. They came from generations of smugglers, and their expertise in corrupting and bribing was real enough. It was just that they'd never learned how to play the game against a truly organized and formidable adversary — the Colombians didn't count. That the *yanquis* had not yet discovered within themselves the courage to act in accordance with their power was nothing more than good fortune. If there was one thing the KGB had drilled into Cortez, it was that good fortune did not exist.

Captain Winters viewed his gunsight videotape with the men from Washington. They were in a corner office of one of the Special Ops buildings — Eglin had quite a few — and the other two wore Air Force uniforms, both bearing the rank of lieutenant colonel, a convenient middle grade of officer, many of whom came and went in total anonymity.

"Nice shooting, son," one observed.

"He could have made it harder," Bronco replied without much in the way of emotion. "But he didn't."

"How about traffic on the surface?"

"Nothing within thirty miles."

"Put up the Hawkeye tape," the senior man ordered. They were using three-quarter-inch tape, which was preferred by the military for its higher data capacity. The tape was already cued. It showed the inbound Beechcraft, marked as XX1 on the alphanumeric display, one of many contacts, most of which were clearly marked as airliners, and had been high over the shoot-down. There were also numerous surface contacts, but all of them were a good distance away from the area of the attack, and this tape ended prior to the shoot-down. The Hawkeye crew, as planned, had no direct knowledge of what had transpired after handing over the contact to the fighter. The guidelines for the mission were clear, and the intercept area was calculated to avoid frequently used shipping channels. The low-altitude path taken by the drug smugglers helped, of course, insofar as it limited the distance at which someone might see a flash or an explosion, neither of which had happened here.

"Okay," said the senior one. "That was well within mission parameters." They switched tapes again.

"How many rounds expended?" the junior one asked Winters.

"A hundred 'n eight," the captain replied. "With a Vulcan it's kinda hard to keep it down, y'know? The critter shoots right quick."

"It did that plane like a chainsaw."

"That's the idea, sir. I could have been a little faster on the trigger, but you want me to try 'n avoid the fuel tanks, right?"

"That's correct." The cover story, in case anyone saw a flash, was that there was a Shoot-Ex out of Eglin — exercises killing target drones are not uncommon there — but so much the better if no one noticed at all.

Bronco didn't like the secrecy stuff. As far as he was concerned, shooting the bastards down made perfectly good sense. The point of the mission, they'd told him during the recruiting phase, was that drug trafficking was a threat to U.S. national security. That phrasing made everything legitimate. As an air-defense fighter pilot, he was trained to deal with threats to national security in this specific way — to shoot them out of the sky with as much emotion as a skeet-shooter dispatched clay birds thrown out from the traps. Besides, Bronco thought, if it's a real threat to national security, why shouldn't the people know about it? But that wasn't his department. He was only a captain, and captains are operators, not thinkers. Somebody up the line had decided that this was okay, and that was all he needed to know. Dispatching this Twin-Beech had been the next thing to murder, but that was as accurate a description of combat operations as any other. After all, giving people a fair chance was what happened at the Olympics, not where your life was on the line. If somebody was dumb enough to let his ass get killed, that wasn't Bronco's lookout, especially if he happened to be committing an act of war against Bronco's country. And *that* was what "threat to national security" meant, wasn't it?

Besides, he *had* given Juan — or whatever the bastard's name had been — a fair warning, hadn't he? If the asshole'd thought he could outfly the best fucking fighter plane in the whole world, well, he'd learned different. Tough.

"You got any problems to this point, Captain?" the senior one asked.

"Problems with what, sir?" *What a dumbass question!*

The airstrip at which they had arrived wasn't big enough for a proper military transport. The forty-four men of Operation SHOWBOAT traveled by bus to Peterson Air Force Base, a few miles east of the Air Force Academy at Colorado Springs. It was dark, of course. The bus was driven by one of the "camp counselors," as the men had taken to calling them, and the ride was a quiet one, with many of the soldiers asleep after their last day's PT. The rest were alone with their own thoughts. Chavez watched the mountains slide by as the bus twisted its way down the last range. The men were ready.

"Pretty mountains, man," Julio Vega observed sleepily.

"Especially in a bus heading downhill."

"Fuckin' A!" Vega chuckled. "You know, someday I'm gonna come back here and do some skiing." The machine-gunner adjusted himself in the seat and faded out.

They were roused thirty-five minutes later after passing through the gate at Peterson. The bus pulled right up to the aft ramp of an Air Force C-141 Starlifter transport. The soldiers rose and assembled their gear in an orderly fashion, with each squad captain checking to make sure that everyone had everything he'd been issued as they filed off. A few looked around on the way to the aircraft. There was nothing unusual about the departure, no special security guards, merely the ground crew fueling and preflighting the aircraft for an immediate departure. In the distance a KC-135 aerial tanker was lifting off, and though no one thought much about it, they'd be meeting that bird in a little while. The Air Force sergeant who was loadmaster for this particular aircraft took them aboard and seated them as comfortably as the spartan appointments allowed — this mainly involved giving everyone ear protectors.

The flight crew went through the usual startup procedures, and presently the Starlifter began moving. The noise was grating despite the earmuffs, but the aircraft had an Air Force Reserve crew, all airline personnel, who gave them a decent ride. Except for the mid-air refueling, that is. As soon as the C-141 had climbed to altitude, it rendezvoused with the KC-135 to replace the fuel burned off during the climb-out. For the passengers this involved the usual roller-coaster buffet which, amplified by the near total absence of windows, made a few stomachs decidedly queasy, though all looked quietly inured to it. Half an hour after lifting off, the C-141 settled down on a southerly course, and from a mixture of fatigue and sheer boredom, the soldiers drifted off to sleep for the remainder of the ride.

The MH-53J left Eglin Air Force Base at about the same time, all of its fuel tanks topped off after engine warm-up. Colonel Johns took it to one thousand feet and a course of two-one-five for the Yucatan Channel. Three hours out, an MC-130E Combat Talon tanker/support aircraft caught up with the Pave Low, and Johns decided to let the captain handle the midair refueling. They'd have to tank thrice more, and the tanker would accompany them all the way down, bringing a maintenance and support crew and spare parts.

"Ready to plug," PJ told the tanker commander.

"Roger," answered Captain Montaigne in the MC-130E, holding the aircraft straight and level.

Johns watched Willis ease the nose probe into the drogue. "Okay, we got plug."

In the cockpit of the -130E, Captain Montaigne took note of the indicator light and keyed the microphone. *"Ohhh!"* she said in her huskiest voice. *"Nobody* does it like you, Colonel!"

Johns laughed out loud and keyed his switch

twice, generating a *click-click* signal, which meant Affirmative. He switched to intercom. "Why spoil it for her?" he asked Willis, who was regrettably strait-laced. The fuel transfer took six minutes.

"How long do you think we'll be down there?" Captain Willis wondered after it was done.

"They didn't tell me that, but if it goes too long, they say we'll get relief."

"That's nice," the captain observed. His eyes shifted back and forth from his flight instruments to the world outside the armored cockpit. The aircraft had more than its full load of combat gear aboard — Johns was a firm believer in firepower — and the electronic countermeasures racks were gone. Whatever they'd be doing, they wouldn't have to worry about unfriendly radar coverage, and that meant that the job, whatever it was, didn't involve Nicaragua or Cuba. It also made for more passenger room in the aircraft and deleted the second flight engineer from the crew. "You were right about the gloves. My wife made up a set and it does make a difference."

"Some guys just fly without 'em, but I don't like to have sweaty hands on the stick."

"Is it going to be that warm?"

"There's warm, and there's warm," Johns pointed out. "You don't get sweaty hands just from the outside temperature."

"Oh. Yes, sir." *Gee, he gets scared, too — just like the rest of us?*

"Like I keep telling people, the more thinking

you do before things get exciting, the less exciting things will be. And they get plenty exciting enough."

Another voice came onto the intercom circuit: "You keep talking like that, sir, and *we* might get a little scared."

"Sergeant Zimmer, how are things in the back?" Johns asked. Zimmer's regular spot was just aft of the two pilots, hovering over an impressive array of instruments.

"Coffee, tea, or milk, sir? The meals for this flight are Chicken Kiev with rice, Roast Beef au Jus with baked potato, and for the weight-watchers among us, Orange Ruffy and stir-fried veggies — and if you believe that, sir, you've been staring at the instrument panel too long. Why the hell don't we have a stewardess along with us?"

" 'Cause you and I are both too old for that shit, Zimmer!" PJ laughed.

"It ain't bad in a chopper, sir. What with all the vibration and all . . . "

"I've been trying to reform him since Korat," Johns explained to Captain Willis. "How old are the kids now, Buck?"

"Seventeen, fifteen, twelve, nine, six, five, and three, sir."

"Christ," Willis noted. "Your wife must be some gal, Sarge."

"She's afraid I'll run around, so she robs me of my energy," Zimmer explained. "I fly to get away from her. It's the only thing that keeps me alive."

"Her cooking must be all right, judging by your uniform."

"Is the colonel picking on his sergeant again?" Zimmer asked.

"Not exactly. I just want you to look as good as Carol does."

"No chance, sir."

"Roger that. Some coffee would be nice."

"On the way, Colonel, sir." Zimmer was on the flight deck in less than a minute. The instrument console for the Pave Low helicopter was large and complex, but Zimmer had long since installed gimbaled cup holders suitable for the spillproof cups that Colonel Johns liked. PJ took a quick sip.

"She makes good coffee, too, Buck."

"Funny how things work out, isn't it?" Carol Zimmer knew that her husband would share it with his colonel. Carol wasn't her original given name. Born in Laos thirty-six years earlier, she was the daughter of a Hmong warlord who'd fought long and hard for a country that was no longer his. She was the only survivor of a family of ten. PJ and Buck had lifted her and a handful of others off a hilltop at the final stages of a North Vietnamese assault in 1972. America had failed that man's family, but at least it hadn't failed his daughter. Zimmer had fallen in love with her from the first moment, and it was generally agreed that they had the seven cutest kids in Florida.

"Yep."

It was late in Mobile, somewhere between the two southbound aircraft, and jails — especially Southern jails — are places where the rules are strictly applied. For lawyers, however, the rules are often rather lenient, and paradoxically they were very lenient indeed in the case of these two. These two had an as-yet-undetermined date with "Old Sparky," the electric chair at Admore Prison. The jailors at Mobile therefore didn't want to do anything to interfere with the prisoners' constitutional rights, access to counsel, or general comfort. The attorney, whose name was Edward Stuart, had been fully briefed going in, and was fully fluent in Spanish.

"How did they do it?"

"I don't know."

"You screamed and kicked, Ramón," Jesús said.

"I know. And you sang like a canary."

"It doesn't matter," the attorney told them. "They're not charging you with anything but drug-related murder and piracy. The information Jesús gave them is not being used at all in this case."

"So do your lawyer shit and get us off!"

The look on Stuart's face was all the response either man needed.

"You tell our friends that if we don't get off on this one, we start talking."

The jail guards had already told both men in loving detail what fate had in store for them. One had even shown Ramón a poster of the chair itself with the caption REGULAR OR EXTRA CRISPY. Though a hard man and a brutal one, the idea of being strapped into a hard-backed wooden chair, then having a copper band affixed to his left leg, and a small metal cap set on a bald spot that the prison barber would shave on his head the day before, and the small sponge soaked in a saline solution to facilitate electrical conductivity, the leather mask to keep his eyes from flying out of his head . . . Ramón was a brave man when he had the upper hand, and that hand held a gun or a knife directed at an unarmed or bound person. Then he was quite brave. It had never occurred to him that one day he might be the helpless one. Ramón had lost five pounds in the preceding week. His appetite was virtually nil and he took an inordinate interest in light bulbs and wall sockets. He was afraid, but more than that he was angry, at himself for his fear, at the guards and police for giving him that fear, and at his former associates for not getting him free of this mess.

"I know many things, many useful things."

"It does not matter. I have spoken with the *federales*, and they do not care what you know. The U.S. Attorney claims to have no interest in what you might tell him."

"That is ridiculous. They always trade for information, they always — "

"Not here. The rules have changed."

"What do you tell us?"

"I will do my best for you." *I'm supposed to tell*

you to die like men, Stuart could not say. "There are many things that can happen in the next few weeks."

The attorney was rewarded with skeptical expressions not entirely devoid of hope. He himself had no hope at all. The U. S. Attorney was going to handle this one himself, the better to get his face on the 5:30 and 11:00 Eyewitness News broadcasts. This would be a very speedy trial, and a U.S. Senate seat would be available in just over two years. So much the better that the prosecutor could point to his law-and-order record. Frying some druggie-pirate-rapist-murderers would surely appeal to the citizens of the sovereign state of Alabama, Stuart knew. The defense attorney objected to capital punishment on principle, and had spent much of his time and money working against it. He'd successfully taken one case to the Supreme Court and on a five-to-four decision managed to get his client a new trial, where the death sentence had been bargained down to life plus ninety-nine years. Stuart regarded that as a victory even though his client had survived precisely four months in the prison's general population until someone who disliked child-murderers had put a shank into his lumbar spine. He didn't have to like his clients — and most often he didn't. He was occasionally afraid of them, especially the drug runners. They quite simply expected that in return for however much cash — it was generally cash — they paid for his services they would get their freedom in return. They did not understand that in law there are no guarantees, especially for the guilty. And these two were guilty as hell. But they did not deserve death. Stuart was convinced that society could not afford to debase itself to the level of . . . his clients. It was not a popular opinion in the South, but Stuart had no ambition to run for public office.

In any case, he was their lawyer, and his job was to provide them with the best possible defense. He'd already explored the chances of a plea-bargain; life imprisonment in exchange for information. He'd already examined the government's case. It was all circumstantial — there were no witnesses except his own clients, of course — but the physical evidence was formidable, and that Coast Guard crew had scrupulously left the crime scene intact except for removing some evidence, all of which had been carefully locked up for a proper chain-of-evidence. Whoever had briefed and trained those people had done it right. Not much hope there. His only real hope, therefore, was to impeach their credibility. It was a slim hope, but it was the best he had.

Supervisory Special Agent Mark Bright was also working late. The crew had been busy. For starters there had been an office and a home to search, a lengthy procedure that was just the opening move in a process to last months, probably, since all the documents found, all the phone numbers scribbled in any of eleven places, all the photographs on desks and walls, and everything else found would have to be investigated. Every business acquaintance of the deceased would be interviewed, along with neighbors, people whose offices adjoined his, members of his country club, and even parishioners at his church. For all that, the major break in the case had come in the second hour of the fourth home search, fully a month after the case had begun. Something had told them all that there *had to be* something else. In his den, the deceased had a floor safe — with no record of its purchase or installation — neatly hidden by an untacked segment of the wall-to-wall carpeting. Discovering it had required thirty-two days. Tickling it open took nearly ninety minutes, but an experienced agent had done it by first experimenting with the birthdays of the deceased's whole family, then playing variations on the theme. It turned out that the three-element combination came from taking the month of the man's birth and adding one, taking the day of his birth and adding two, then taking the year of his birth and adding three. The door of the expensive Mosler came open with a whisper as it rubbed against the rug flap.

No money, no jewels, no letter to his attorney. Inside the safe had been five computer disks of a type compatible with the businessman's IBM personal computer. That told the agents all they wanted. Bright had at once taken the disks and the deceased's computer to his office, which was also equipped with IBM-compatible machines.

Mark Bright was a good investigator, which meant that he was a patient one. His first move had been to call a local computer expert who assisted the FBI from time to time. A free-lance software consultant, he'd first protested that he was busy, but he'd only needed to hear that there was a major criminal investigation under-way to settle that. Like many such people who informally assist the FBI, he found police work most exciting, though not quite exciting enough to take a full-time job for the FBI Laboratory. Government service didn't come close to paying what he earned on the outside. Bright had antici-pated his first instruction: bring in the man's own computer and hard-disk.

After first making exact copies of the five disks using a program called CHASTITY BELT, he had Bright store the originals while he went to work on the copies. The disks were encrypted, of course. There were many ways of accomplishing that, and the consultant knew them all. As he and Bright had anticipated, the encrypting algorithm was permanently stored on the deceased's hard disk. From that point it was merely a question of what option and what personal encrypting key had been used to secure the data on the disks. That took nine nonstop hours, with Bright feed-ing coffee and sandwiches to his friend and won-dering why he did it all for free.

"Gotcha!" A scruffy hand punched the PRINT command, and the office laser printer started humming and disgorging papers. All five disks were packed with data, totaling over seven hundred single-spaced pages of text. By the time the third one was printed, the consultant had left. Bright read it all, over a period of three days. Then he made six Xerox copies for the other senior agents in the case. They were now flipping through the pages around the conference table.

"Christ, Mark, this stuff is fantastic!"

"That's what I said."

"Three hundred million dollars!" another exclaimed. "Christ, I shop there myself . . ."

"What's the total involved?" a third asked more soberly.

"I just skimmed through this stuff," Bright answered, "but I got close to seven hundred million. Eight shopping malls spread from Fort Worth to Atlanta. The investments go through eleven different corporations, twenty-three banks, and — "

"My life insurance is with this company! They do my IRA, and — "

"The way he set it up, he was the only one who knew. Talk about an artist, this guy was like Leonardo. . . ."

"Sucker got greedy, though. If I read this right, he skimmed off about thirty million . . . God almighty . . ."

The plan, as with all great plans, was an elegantly simple one. There were eight real-estate-development projects. In each case the deceased had set up himself as the general partner representing foreign money — invariably described as

Persian Gulf oil money or Japanese industrial money, with the funds laundered through an incredible maze of non-American banks. The general partner had used the "Oil Money" — the term was almost generic in the venture capital field — to purchase land and set the project in motion, then solicited further development funds from limited partners who had no say in the executive management of the individual projects, but whose profits were almost guaranteed by the syndicate's previous performance. Even the one in Fort Worth had made money, despite the recent slowdown in the local oil industry. By the time ground was broken on every project, actual ownership was further disguised by majority investment from banks, insurance companies, and wealthy private investors, with much of the original overseas investment fully recovered and gone back to the Bank of Dubai and numerous others — but with a controlling interest remaining in the project itself. In this way, the overseas investors speedily recouped their initial investment with a tidy profit, and continued to get much of the profits from the project's actual operations, further looking forward to the eventual sale of the project to local interests for more profit still. For each hundred million dollars invested, Bright estimated, one hundred fifty million fully laundered dollars were extracted. And that was the important part. The hundred million put in, and the fifty million profit taken out were as clean as the marble on the Washington Monument.

Except for these computer disks.

"Every one of these projects, and every dime of investment and profits, went through IRS, SEC, and enough lawyers to fill the Pentagon, and *nobody* ever caught a sniff. He kept these records in case somebody ever burned him — but he must have expected to trade this information for a crack at the Witness Protection Program — "

"And he'd be the richest guy in Cody, Wyoming," Mike Schratz observed. "But the wrong people got a sniff. I wonder what tipped them off? What did our friends say?"

"They don't know. Just that they pulled the job of killing them all off and making it look like a disappearance. The bosses clearly anticipated losing them and compartmentalized the information. How hard is it to get one of these mutts to take a contract? It's like filling out a girl's dance card at the cotillion."

"Roger that. Headquarters know about this yet?"

"No, Mike, I wanted you guys to see it first," Bright said. "Opinions, gentlemen?"

"If we move fast . . . we could seize a whole shitload of money . . . unless they've moved the money on us," Schratz thought aloud. "I wonder if they have? As clever as this stuff is . . . I got a buck says they haven't. Takers?"

"Not from me," another agent announced. This one was a CPA and a lawyer. "Why should they bother? This is the closest thing I've ever seen to — hell, it *is* a perfect plan. I suppose we

284

ought to show some appreciation, what with all the help they're giving our balance-of-payments problem. In any case, folks, this money is exposed. We can bag it all."

"There's the Bureau's budget for the next two years — "

"And a squadron of fighters for the Air Force. This is big enough to sting them pretty good. Mark, I think you ought to call the Director," Schratz concluded. There was general agreement. "Where's Pete today?" Pete Mariano was the special-agent-in-charge of the Mobile Field Office.

"Probably Venice," an agent said. "He's going to be pissed he was away for this one."

Bright closed the ring binder. He was already booked on an early-morning flight to Dulles International Airport.

The C-141 landed ten minutes early at Howard Field. After the clean, dry air of the Colorado Rockies, and the cleaner, thinner, and drier air of the flight, the damp oven of the Isthmus of Panama was like walking into a door. The soldiers assembled their gear and allowed themselves to be herded off by the loadmaster. They were quiet and serious. The change in climate was a physical sign that playtime was over. The mission had begun. They immediately boarded yet another green bus which took them to some dilapidated barracks on the grounds of Fort Kobbe.

The MH-53J helicopter landed several hours

later at the same field, and was rolled unceremoniously into a hangar, which was surrounded with armed guards. Colonel Johns and the flight crew were taken to nearby quarters and told to stay put.

Another helicopter, this one a Marine CH-53E Super Stallion, lifted off the deck of USS *Guadalcanal* just before dawn. It flew west over the Bay of Panama to Corezal, a small military site near the Gaillard Cut, the most difficult segment of the original Panama Canal construction project. The helicopter-carrier's flight-deck crew attached a bulky item to a sling dangling from the helicopter's underside, and the CH-53E headed awkwardly toward shore. After a twenty-minute flight, the helicopter hovered over its predetermined destination. The pilot killed his forward speed and gently eased toward the ground, coached by instructions from the crew chief, until the communications van touched down on a concrete pad. The sling was detached and the helicopter flew off at once to make room for a second aircraft, a smaller CH-46 troop carrier which deposited four men before returning to its ship. The men went immediately to work setting up the van.

The van was quite ordinary, looking most of all like a cargo container with wheels, though it was painted in the mottled green camouflage scheme of most military vehicles. That changed rapidly as the communications technicians began erecting various radio antennas, including one four-foot satellite dish. Power cables were run in from a generator vehicle already in place, and the van's air-conditioning systems were turned on to protect the communications gear, rather than the technicians. They wore military-style dress, though none of them were soldiers. All the pieces were now in place.

Or almost all. At Cape Canaveral, a Titan-IIID rocket began its final countdown. Three senior Air Force officers and half a dozen civilians watched the hundred or so technicians go through the procedure. They were unhappy. Their cargo had been bumped at the last minute for this less important one (they thought). The explanation for the change was not to their collective satisfaction, and there weren't enough launch rockets to play this sort of game. But nobody had bothered telling them what the game actually was.

"Tallyho, tallyho. I have eyeballs on target," Bronco reported. The Eagle bottomed out half a mile astern and slightly below the target. It seemed to be a four-engined Douglas. A DC-4, -6, or -7, a big one — the biggest he'd yet intercepted. Four piston engines and a single rudder made it a Douglas product, certainly older than the man who was now chasing it. Winters saw the blue flames from the exhaust ports on the big radial engines, along with the moonlight shimmering from the propellers. The rest was mainly guesswork.

The flying became harder now. He was closing on the target and had to slough off his airspeed lest he overtake it. Bronco throttled his Pratt & Whitney engines back and put on some flaps to increase both lift and drag as he watched his airspeed drop to a scant two-hundred forty knots.

He matched speed when he was a hundred yards aft of the target. The heavy fighter rocked slightly — only the pilot would have noticed — from the larger plane's wake turbulence. Time. He took a deep breath and flexed his fingers once around the stick. Captain Winters switched on his powerful landing lights. They were alert, he saw. The wingtips rocked a second after his lights transfixed the former airliner in the sky.

"Aircraft in view, please identify, over," he called over the guard frequency.

It started turning — it was a DC-7B, he thought now, the last of the great piston-engine liners, so quickly brushed aside by the advent of the jetliners in the late fifties. The exhaust flames grew brighter as the pilot added power.

"Aircraft in view, you are in restricted airspace. Identify immediately, over," Bronco called next. *Immediately* is a word that carries a special meaning for flyers.

The DC-7B was diving now, heading for the wave tops. The Eagle followed almost of its own accord.

"Aircraft in view, I repeat — you are in restricted airspace. Identify *at once!*"

Turning away now, heading east for the Florida peninsula. Captain Winters eased back on the stick and armed his gun system. He checked the surface of the ocean to make sure that there were no ships or boats about.

"Aircraft in view, if you do not identify I will open fire, over." No reaction.

The hard part now was that the Eagle's gun system, once armed, did everything possible to facilitate the pilot's task of hitting the target. But they wanted him to bring one in alive, and Bronco had to concentrate to make sure he'd miss, then squeezed the trigger for a fraction of a second.

Half the rounds in the magazine were tracers, and the six-barrel cannon spat them out at a rate of almost a hundred per second. What resulted was a streak of green-yellow light that looked like one of the laser beams in a science-fiction movie, and hung for a sizable portion of infinity a bare ten yards from the DC-7B's cockpit window.

"Aircraft in view: level out and identify or you'll eat the next burst. Over."

"Who is this? What the hell are you doing?" The DC-7B leveled out.

"Identify!" Winters commanded tersely.

"Carib Cargo — we're a special flight, inbound from Honduras."

"You are in restricted airspace. Come left to new course three-four-seven."

"Look, we didn't know about the restriction. Tell us where to go and we're out of here, okay? Over."

"Come left to three-four-seven. I will be following you in. You got some big-league explaining to do, Carib. You picked a bad place to be flying without lights. I hope you got a good story, 'cause the colonel is not pleased with you. Bring that fat-assed bird left — now!"

Nothing happened for a moment. Bronco was a little bit peeved that they were not taking him seriously enough. He eased his fighter over to the right and triggered off another burst to encourage the target.

And it came left to a heading of three-four-seven. And the anticollision lights came on.

"Okay, Carib, maintain course and altitude. Stay off your radio. I repeat, maintain radio silence until instructed otherwise. Don't make it any worse than it already is. I'll be back here to keep an eye on you. Out."

It took nearly an hour — each second like driving a Ferrari in Manhattan rush-hour traffic. Clouds were rolling in from the north, he saw as they approached the coast, and there was lightning in them. They'd land first, Winters thought. On cue, a set of runway lights came on.

"Carib, I want you to land on that strip right in front of you. You do exactly what they tell you. Out." Bronco checked his fuel state. Enough for several more hours. He indulged himself by throttling up and rocketing to twenty thousand as he watched the DC-7's strobe lights enter the blue rectangle of the old airstrip.

"Okay, he's ours," the radio told the fighter pilot.

Bronco did not acknowledge. He brought the Eagle around for Eglin AFB, and figured that he'd beat the weather in. Another night's work.

The DC-7B rolled to a stop at the end of the runway. As it halted, a number of lights came on. A jeep rolled to within fifty yards of the aircraft's nose. On the back of the jeep was an M-2 .50-caliber machine gun, on the left side of which hung a large box of ammunition. The gun was pointed right at the cockpit.

"Out of the fuckin' airplane, *amigo!*" an angry voice commanded over some loudspeakers.

The forward door opened on the left side of the aircraft. The man who looked down was white and in his forties. Blinded by the lights that were aimed at his face, he was still disoriented. Which was part of the plan, of course.

"Down on the pavement, *amigo*," a voice said from behind a light.

"What gives? I — "

"*Down on the fuckin' pavement — right the fuck now!*"

There were no stairs. The pilot was joined by another man, and one at a time they sat down on the doorsill, and stretched down to hang from their hands, then dropped the four feet or so to the cracked concrete. They were met by strong arms in rolled-up camouflage fatigues.

"*Face on the cement, you fuckin' commie spy!*" a young voice screamed at them.

291

"Hot diggity damn, we finally bagged one!" another voice called. "We got us a fuckin' Cuban spy plane!"

"What the hell — " one of the men on the cement started to say. He stopped talking when the three-pronged flash suppressor on an M-16 rifle came to rest on the back of his neck. Then he felt a hot breath on the side of his face.

"I want any shit out of you, *amigo,* I'll fuckin' blow it outa ya!" said the other voice. It sounded older than the first one. "Anybody else on the airplane, *amigo?*"

"No. Look, we're — "

"Check it out! And watch your ass!" the gunnery sergeant added.

"Aye aye, Gunny," answered the Marine corporal. "Give me some cover on the door."

"You got a name?" the gunnery sergeant asked. He punctuated the question by pressing his muzzle into the pilot's neck.

"Bert Russo. I'm — "

"You picked a bad time to spy on the exercise, *Rob*ert*o.* We was ready for y'all this time, boy! I wonder if Fidel'll want your ass back . . . ?"

"He don't look Cuban to me, Gunny," a young voice observed. "You s'pose he's a Russian?"

"Hey, I don't know what you're talking about," Russo objected.

"Sure, *Rob*ert*o.* I — over here, Cap'n!" Footsteps approached. And a new voice started talking.

"Sorry I'm late, Gunny Black."

"We got it under control, sir. Putting people into the plane now. Finally bagged that Cuban snooper, we did. This here's Ro*bert*o. Ain't talked to the other one yet."

"Roll him over."

A rough hand flipped the pilot faceup like a rag doll and he saw what the hot breath came from. The biggest German Shepherd dog he'd ever seen in his life was staring at him from a distance of three inches. When he looked at it, it started growling.

"Don't you go scarin' my dog, Roberto," Gunnery Sergeant Black warned him unnecessarily.

"You have a name?"

Bert Russo couldn't see any faces. Everyone was backlit by the perimeter lights. He could see the guns, and the dogs, one of which stood next to his copilot. When he started to speak, the dog over his face moved, and that froze the breath in his throat.

"You Cubans ought to know better. We warned you not to come snooping into our exercise last time, but you had to come bother us again, didn't you?" the captain observed.

"I'm not a Cuban — I'm an American. And I don't know what you're talking about," the pilot finally managed to say.

"You got some ID?" the captain asked.

Bert Russo started moving his hand toward his wallet, but then the dog really let loose a snarl.

"Don't scare the dog," the captain warned. "They're a little high-strung, y'know?"

293

"Fuckin' Cuban spies," Gunny Black observed. "We could just waste them, sir. I mean, who really gives a damn?"

"Hey, Gunny!" a voice called from the airplane. "This ain't no spy-bird. It's full of drugs! We got us a drug runner!"

"Son of a bitch!" The gunny sounded disappointed for a moment. "Fuckin' druggie is all? Shit!"

The captain just laughed. "Mister, you really picked the wrong place to drive that airplane tonight. How much, Corp?"

"A whole goddamned pisspot full, sir. Grass and coke both. Plane's like full of it, sir."

"Fuckin' druggie," the gunny observed. He was quiet for a moment. "Cap'n?"

"Yeah?"

"Sir, all the time, sir, these planes land, and the crew just bugs the hell out, and nobody ever finds 'em, sir."

As though on cue, they all heard a guttural sound from the swamp that surrounded the old airstrip. Albert Russo came from Florida and knew what the sound was.

"I mean, sir, who'd ever know the difference? Plane landed, and the crew ran off 'fore we could catch up, and they got into the swamp over yonder, and like we heard some screams, y'know . . . ?" A pause. "I mean, they're just druggies. Who's really gonna care, sir? Make the world a better place, y'know? Hell, it even feeds them 'gators. They sound right hungry to me, sir."

"No evidence , . . ." the captain mused.

"Ain't nobody gonna give a good goddamn, sir," the sergeant persisted. "Just us be out here, sir."

"*No!*" the copilot screamed, speaking for the first time and startling the dog at the back of his neck.

"Y'all be quiet now, we be talking business here," the gunny observed.

"Gentlemen, I find that the sergeant makes a pretty good case," the captain said after a moment's contemplation. "And the 'gators do sound hungry. Kill 'em first, Sergeant. No sense being cruel about it, and the 'gators don't care one way or the other. Be sure you take all their IDs, though."

"Aye aye, skipper," the gunnery sergeant replied. He and the remainder of the duty section — there were only eight of them — came from the Special Operations Center at MacDill. They were Recon Marines, for whom unusual activities were the rule rather than the exception. Their helicopter was half a mile away.

"Okay, sport," Black said as he bent down. He hoisted Russo to his feet with one brutal jerk. "You sure did pick the wrong time to run drugs, boy."

"Wait a minute!" the other one screamed. "We didn't — I mean, we can tell you — "

"You talk all you want, boy. I *got* my orders. Come on, now. Y'all want to pray or something, now be the time."

"We came in from Colombia — "

"That's a real surprise, ain't it?" Black observed as he frog-marched the man toward the trees. "You best be doing your talking to the Lord, boy. He might listen. Then again, He might not. . . ."

"I can tell you everything," Russo said.

"I ain't *int'rested!*"

"But you can't — "

"Sure I can. What do you think I do for a livin', boy?" Black said with amusement. "Don't worry. It'll be quick and clean. I don't make people suffer like your kind does with drugs. I just do it."

"I have a family . . ." Russo was whimpering now.

"Most people do," Black agreed. "They'll get along. You got insurance, I 'spect. Lookie there!"

Another Marine pointed his flashlight into the bushes. It was as large an alligator as Russo had ever seen, over twelve feet long. The large eyes blazed yellow in the darkness, while the rest of the reptile's body looked like a green log. With a mouth.

"This is far enough," Black judged. "Keep them dogs back, goddammit!"

The alligator — they called him Nicodemus — opened his mouth and hissed. It was a thoroughly evil sound.

"Please . . ." Russo said.

"I can tell you everything!" the copilot offered again.

"Like *what?*" the captain asked disgustedly. *Why can't you just die like a man?* he seemed to ask instead.

"Where we came from. Who gave us the load. Where we're going. Radio codes. Who's supposed to meet us. Everything!"

"Sure," the captain noted. "Get their IDs. Pocket change, car keys, everything. As a matter of fact, just strip 'em naked before you shoot 'em. Let's try to be neat."

"I know everything!" Russo screamed.

"He knows everything," Gunny Black said. "Isn't that nice? Take off your clothes, boy."

"Hold it a minute, Gunny." The captain came forward and shined his light right in Russo's face.

"What do you know that would interest us?" It was a voice they hadn't heard before. Though dressed in fatigues, he was not a Marine.

Ten minutes later it was all on tape. They already knew most of the names, of course. The location of the airstrip was new information, however, as were the radio codes.

"Do you waive the right to counsel?" the civilian asked.

"Yes!"

"You willing to cooperate?"

"Yes!"

"Good." Russo and the copilot, whose name was Bennett, were blindfolded and led to a helicopter. By noon the next day they'd be taken before a U.S. Magistrate, then a judge of the

297

Federal District Court; by sundown to a remote part of Eglin Air Force Base, a newly built structure with a high fence. It was guarded by serious-looking men in uniform.

They didn't know that they were the lucky ones. Five downed planes qualified a pilot as an ace. Bronco was well on his way there.

10.

Dry Feet

Mark Bright checked in with Deputy Assistant Director Murray, just as a matter of courtesy, before going in to see the Director.

"You must have caught the first bird out. How's the case coming?"

"The Pirates Case — that's how the papers are treating it — is just fine. I'm up here because of what spun off of it. The victim was dirtier than we thought." Bright explained on for several minutes, pulling one of the ring binders from his briefcase.

"How much?"

"We're not sure. This one's going to take some careful analysis by people with expertise in the world of high finance, but . . . well, probably on the order of seven hundred million dollars."

Murray managed to set down his coffee without spilling any. "Say that again?"

"You heard right. I didn't know that until day before yesterday, and I didn't finish reading this until about twenty-four hours ago. Christ, Dan, I just skimmed it. If I'm wrong, I'm off on the low side. Anyway, I figured the Director needed to see this PDQ."

"Not to mention the AG and the President. What time you going in to see Emil?"

"Half an hour. Want to tag along? You know this international shuffle better than I do."

The Bureau had a lot of deputy assistant directors, and Murray's post had a vague definition that he jokingly called "utility outfielder." The Bureau's leading authority on terrorism, Murray was also the agency's in-house expert on how various international groups moved people, arms, and money from point to point. That, added to his wide experience as a street agent, gave him the brief of overseeing certain important cases for the Director or for Bill Shaw, the executive assistant director (Investigations). Bright hadn't walked into this office entirely by accident.

"How solid is your information?"

"Like I said, it's not all collated yet, but I got a bunch of account numbers, transaction dates, amounts, and a solid trail all the way back to the point of origin."

"And all of this because that Coast Guard — "

"No, sir." Bright hesitated. "Well, maybe. Knowing the victim was dirty made us search his background a little more thoroughly. We probably would have gotten this stuff eventually anyway. As it was, I kept going back to the house. You know how it is."

"Yeah." Murray nodded. One mark of a good agent was tenacity. Another was instinct. Bright had returned to the home of the victims for as long as his mind kept telling him that something else had to be there. "How'd you find the safe?"

"The guy had one of those Rubbermaid sheets for his swivel chair to ride on. You know how they tend to drift away when you move your chair back and forth? I must have sat at that desk for an hour, all told, and I noticed that it had moved. I rolled the chair away, so I could slide the mat back, and then it hit me — what a perfect hiding place. I was right." Bright grinned. He had every right to do so.

"You should write that one up for *The Investigator*" — that was the Justice Department's in-house newsletter — "so everybody'll know to look for it."

"We have a good safe-man in the office. After that, it was just a matter of cracking the code on the disks. We have a guy in Mobile who helps us out on that — and, no, he doesn't know what's on the disks. He knows not to pay close attention, and he's not all that interested anyway. I figure we'll want to keep this one pretty tight until we move to seize the funds."

"You know, I don't think we've ever owned a shopping mall. I remember when we seized that topless bar, though." Murray laughed as he lifted

301

his phone and tapped in the number for the Director's office. "Morning, Moira, this is Dan Murray. Tell the boss that we have something really hot for him. Bill Shaw will want to come in for this, too. Be there in two minutes." Murray hung up. "Come on, Agent Bright. It's not often that you hit a grand slam on your first major-league at-bat. You ever meet the Director?"

"Just to say hi to him twice at receptions."

"He's good people," Murray assured him on the way out the door. It was a short walk down the carpeted corridor. Bill Shaw met them on the way.

"Hi, Mark. How's your dad?"

"Catching a lot of fish."

"Living down in the Keys now, isn't he?"

"Yes, sir."

"You're going to love this one, Bill," Murray observed as he opened the door. He led them in and stopped cold when he saw the Director's secretary. "My God, Moira, you're beautiful!"

"You watch that, Mr. Murray, or I'll tell your wife!" But there was no denying it. Her suit was lovely, her makeup was perfect, and her face positively glowed with what could only be new love.

"I most humbly beg your pardon, ma'am," Murray said gallantly. "This handsome young man is Mark Bright."

"You're five minutes early, Agent Bright," Mrs. Wolfe noted without checking the appointment calendar. "Coffee?"

"No, thank you, ma'am."

302

"Very well." She checked to see that the Director wasn't on the phone. "You can go right in."

The Director's office was large enough for conferences. Emil Jacobs had come to the Bureau after a distinguished career as a United States Attorney in Chicago, and to take this job he'd declined a seat on the U.S. Circuit Court of Appeals there. It went without saying that he could have held a partner's chair in any criminal-law firm in America, but from the day he'd passed the bar exam, Emil Jacobs had dedicated his life to putting criminals in jail. Part of that resulted from the fact that his father had suffered during the beer wars of Prohibition. Jacobs never forgot the scars his father bore for once having talked back to a South Side Gang enforcer. A small man, like his father, Emil Jacobs viewed his mission in life as protecting the weak from the evil. He pursued that mission with a religious fervor that hid behind a brilliant analytical mind. A rare Jew in a largely Irish-Catholic agency, he'd been made an honorary member of seventeen Hibernian lodges. While J. Edgar Hoover had been known in the field as "Director Hoover," to the current crop of agents, Director Jacobs was "Emil."

"Your dad worked for me once," Jacobs said as he extended his hand to Agent Bright. "He's down on Marathon Key, isn't he? Still fishing for tarpon?"

"Yes, sir. How'd you know?"

303

"Every year he sends me a Chanukah card."
Jacobs laughed. "It's a long story. I'm surprised
he hasn't told you that one. So what's the story?"

Bright sat down and opened his briefcase,
handing out the bound copies of his documents.
He started talking, awkwardly at first, but in ten
minutes he was fully warmed to the subject.
Jacobs was flipping rapidly through the binder,
but didn't miss a spoken word.

"We're talking over half a billion dollars,"
Bright concluded.

"More than that from what I see here, son."

"I haven't had time to give it a detailed analysis, sir. I figured you'd want to see this right
quick."

"You figured right," Jacobs replied without
looking up. "Bill, who's the best guy at Justice to
get in on this?"

"Remember the guy who headed the savings-
and-loan thing? He's a whiz for following money
from place to place. Marty something," Shaw
said. "Young guy. He has a real nose for it. I
think Dan ought to be involved also."

Jacobs looked up. "Well?"

"Fine with me. Shame we can't get a commission on what we seize. We're going to want
to move fast on this. The first inkling they
have . . . "

"That might not matter," Jacobs mused. "But
there's no reason to drag our feet. This sort of
loss will sting them pretty good. And with the
other things we're . . . excuse me. Right, Dan,

304

let's set this up to move fast. Any complications on the piracy case?"

"No, sir. The physical evidence is enough for a conviction. The U.S. Attorney tossed the confession entirely when the defense lawyer started grumbling about how it had been obtained. Says he smiled when he did it. Told the other guy no deals of any kind, that he had enough evidence to fry them, which is exactly what he plans to do. He's pressing for an early trial date, going to try the case himself. The whole thing."

"Sounds like we have a budding political career on our hands," Jacobs observed. "How much show and how much substance?"

"He's been pretty good to us down in Mobile, sir," Bright said.

"You can never have too many friends on The Hill," Jacobs agreed. "You're fully satisfied with the case?"

"Yes, sir. It's solid. What's spun off of it can stand pretty much on its own."

"Why was there so much money on the boat if they just planned to kill him?" Murray asked.

"Bait," Agent Bright answered. "According to the confession that we trashed, they were actually supposed to deliver it to a contact in the Bahamas. As you can see from this document, the victim occasionally handled large cash transactions himself. That's probably the reason he bought the yacht in the first place."

Jacobs nodded. "Fair enough. Dan, you did tell that captain — "

"Yes, sir. He learned his lesson."

"Fine. Back to the money. Dan, you coordinate with Justice and keep me informed through Bill. I want a target date to start the seizures — give you three days for that. Agent Bright and the Mobile Field Office are to get full credit for turning this one — *but*, this one is code-word until we're ready to move." Code-word meant that the case would be classified right up with CIA operations. It wasn't all that unusual for the Bureau, which ran most of America's counterintelligence operations. "Mark, pick a code-word."

"*Tarpon.* Dad always has been crazy about chasing after them, and they're good fighters."

"I'm going to have to go down there and see. I've never caught anything bigger than a pike." Jacobs was quiet for a moment. He was thinking about something, Murray thought, wondering what it was. Whatever it was, it gave Emil a very crafty look. "The timing couldn't be better. Shame I can't tell you why. Mark, say hi to your dad for me." The Director stood, ending the meeting.

Mrs. Wolfe noted that everyone was smiling when they came out of the room. Shaw even gave her a wink. Ten minutes later she'd opened a new file in the secure cabinet, an empty folder with the name TARPON typed on the paper label. It went in the drug section, and Jacobs told her that further documentation would follow in a few days.

Murray and Shaw walked Agent Bright down

306

to his car and saw him off.

"What's with Moira?" Dan asked as the car pulled out.

"They think she's got a boyfriend."

"About time."

At 4:45, Moira Wolfe placed the plastic cover over her computer keyboard and another over her typewriter. Before leaving the office, she checked her makeup one last time and then walked out with a spring in her step. The oddest thing was that she didn't realize that everyone else in the office was rooting for her. The other secretaries and executive assistants, even the Director's security detail, had avoided comment for fear of making her self-conscious. But tonight had to be a date. The signs were clear, even though Moira thought that she was concealing it all.

As a senior executive secretary, Mrs. Wolfe rated a reserved parking space, one of many things that made her life easier. She drove out a few minutes later onto 10th Street, Northwest, then turned right onto Constitution Avenue. Instead of her normal southward course toward Alexandria and home, she headed west across the Theodore Roosevelt Bridge into Arlington. It seemed as though the rush-hour traffic was parting before her, and twenty-five minutes later she pulled up to a small Italian restaurant in Seven Corners. Before going in she checked her makeup again in the rearview mirror. Her children would be getting dinner from McDonald's tonight, but they understood. She told them that she'd be working very late, and she was sure that they believed her, though she ought to have known that they saw through her lies as easily as she had once seen through theirs.

"Excuse me," she said to the hostess upon entering.

"You must be Mrs. Wolfe," the young lady replied at once. "Please come with me. Mr. Díaz is waiting for you."

Félix Cortez — Juan Díaz — was sitting in a corner booth at the rear of the restaurant. Moira was sure that he'd picked the dark place for privacy, and that he had his back to the wall so that he could see her coming. She was partially correct on both counts. Cortez was wary of being in this area. CIA headquarters was less than five miles away, thousands of FBI personnel lived in this area, and who could say whether a senior counterintelligence officer might also like this restaurant? He didn't think that anyone there knew what he looked like, but intelligence officers do not live to collect their pensions by assuming anything. His nervousness was not entirely feigned. On the other hand, he was unarmed. Cortez was in a business where firearms caused far more problems than they solved, public perceptions to the contrary.

Félix rose as she approached. The hostess departed as soon as she realized the nature of this "business dinner," leaving the two lovers — she

308

thought it was kind of cute — to grab each other's hands and exchange kisses that were oddly passionate despite their being restrained for so public a place. Cortez seated his lady, pouring her a glass of white wine before resuming his place opposite her. His first words were delivered with sheepish embarrassment.

"I was afraid you wouldn't come."

"How long have you been waiting?" Moira asked. There were a half-dozen stubbed-out cigarettes in the ashtray.

"Almost an hour," he answered with a funny look. Clearly he was amused at himself, she thought.

"But I'm early."

"I know." This time he laughed. "You make me a fool, Moira. I do not act in such a way at home."

She misread what he was trying to say. "I'm sorry, Juan, I didn't mean — "

A perfect response, Cortez's mind reported. *Exactly right.* He took her hand across the table and his eyes sparkled. "Do not trouble yourself. Sometimes it is good for a man to be a fool. Forgive me for calling you so abruptly. A small business problem. I had to fly to Detroit on short notice, and since I was in the neighborhood, as you say, I wanted to see you before I went home."

"Problem . . . ?"

"A change in the design for a carburetor. Something to do with fuel economy, and I must change some tools in my factories." He waved his hand. "The problem is solved. These things are not uncommon — and, it gave me an excuse to make an extra trip here. Perhaps I should thank your EPA, or whatever government office complains about air pollution."

"I will write the letter myself, if you wish."

His voice changed. "It is *so* good to see you again, Moira."

"I was afraid that — "

The emotion on his face was manifest. "No, Moira, it was I who was afraid. I am a foreigner. I come here so seldom, and surely there must be many men who — "

"Juan, where are you staying?" Mrs. Wolfe asked.

"At the Sheraton."

"Do they have room service?"

"Yes, but why — "

"I won't be hungry for about two hours," she told him, and finished off her wine. "Can we leave now?"

Félix dropped a pair of twenties on the table and led her out. The hostess was reminded of a song from *The King and I*. They were in the lobby of the Sheraton in less than six minutes. Both walked quickly to the elevators, and both looked warily about, both hoping that they wouldn't be spotted, but for different reasons. His tenth-floor room was actually an expensive suite. Moira scarcely noticed on entering, and for the next hour knew of nothing but a man whose name she mistakenly thought was Juan Díaz.

"So wonderful a thing," he said at last.

"What's that?"

"So wonderful a thing that there was a problem with the new carburetor."

"Juan!"

"I must now create quality-control problems so that they call me every week to Detroit," he suggested lightly, stroking her arm as he did so.

"Why not build a factory here?"

"The labor costs are too high," he said seriously. "Of course, drugs would be less of a problem."

"There, too?"

"Yes. They call it *basuco*, filthy stuff, not good enough for export, and too many of my workers indulge." He stopped talking for a moment. "Moira, I try to make a joke, and you force me to speak of business. Have you lost interest in me?"

"What do you think?"

"I think I need to return to Venezuela while I can still walk."

Her fingers did some exploring. "I think you will recover soon."

"That is good to know." He turned his head to kiss her, and let his eyes linger, examining her body in the rays of the setting sun that spilled through the windows. She noticed his stares and reached for the sheet. He stopped her.

"I am no longer young," she said.

"Every child in all the world looks upon his mother and sees the most beautiful woman in the world, even though many mothers are not beautiful. Do you know why this is so? The child looks with love, and sees love returned. Love is what makes beauty, Moira. And, truly, you are beautiful to me."

And there it was. The word was finally out in the open. He watched her eyes go somewhat wider, her mouth move, and her breaths deepen for a moment. For the second time, Cortez felt shame. He shrugged it off. Or tried to. He'd done this sort of thing before, of course. But always with young women, young, single ones with an eye for adventure and a taste for excitement. This one was different in so many ways. Different or not, he reminded himself, there was work to be done.

"Forgive me. Do I embarrass you?"

"No," she answered softly. "Not now."

He smiled down at her. "And now, are you ready for dinner?"

"Yes."

"That is good."

Cortez rose and got the bathrobes from the back of the bathroom door. Service was good. Half an hour later, Moira stayed in the bedroom while the dinner cart was rolled into the sitting room. He opened the connecting door as soon as the waiter left.

"You make of me a dishonest man. The look he gave me!"

She laughed. "Do you know how long it's been since I had to hide in the other room?"

"And you didn't order enough. How can you live on this tiny salad?"

"If I grow fat, you will not come back to me."

"Where I come from, we do not count a woman's ribs," Cortez said. "When I see someone who grows too thin, I think it is the *basuco* again. Where I live, they are the ones who forget even to eat."

"Is it that bad?"

"Do you know what *basuco* is?"

"Cocaine, according to the reports I see."

"Poor quality, not good enough for the criminals to send to the *norteamericanos,* and mixed with chemicals that poison the brain. It is becoming the curse of my homeland."

"It's pretty bad here," Moira said. She could see that it was something that really worried her lover. Just like it was with the Director, she thought.

"I have spoken to the police at home. How can my workers do their jobs if their minds are poisoned by this thing? And what do the police do? They shrug and mumble excuses — and people die. They die from the *basuco*. They die from the guns of the dealers. And no one does anything to stop it." Cortez made a frustrated gesture. "You know, Moira, I am not merely a capitalist. My factories, they give jobs, they bring money into my country, money for the people to build houses and educate their children. I am rich, yes, but I help to build my country — with these hands, I do it. My workers, they come to me and tell me that their children — ah! I can do nothing. Someday, the dealers, they will come to me and try to take my factory," he went on. "I will go to the police, and the police will do nothing. I will go to the army, and the army will do nothing. You work for your *federales*, yes? Is there nothing anyone can do?" Cortez nearly held his breath, wondering what the answer would be.

"You should see the reports I have to type for the Director."

"Reports," he snorted. "Anyone can write reports. At home, the police write many reports, and the judges do their investigations — and nothing happens. If I ran my factory in this way, soon I would be living in a hillside shack and begging for money in the street! Do your *federales* do anything?"

"More than you might think. There are things going on right now that I cannot speak about. What they're saying around the office is that the rules are changing. But I don't know what that means. The Director is flying down to Colombia soon to meet with the Attorney General, and — oh! I'm not supposed to tell anybody that. It's supposed to be a secret."

"I will tell no one," Cortez assured her.

"I really don't know that much anyway," she went on carefully. "Something new is about to start. I don't know what. The Director doesn't like it very much, whatever it is."

"If it hurts the criminals, why should he not like it?" Cortez asked in a puzzled voice. "You could shoot them all dead in the street, and I would buy your *federales* dinner afterwards!"

Moira just smiled. "I'll pass that along. That's what all the letters say — we get letters from all sorts of people."

"Your director should listen to them."

"So does the President."

"Perhaps he will listen," Cortez suggested. *This is an election year. . .*

"Maybe he already is. Whatever just changed, it started there."

"But your director doesn't like it?" He shook his head. "I do not understand the government in my country. I should not try to understand yours."

"It *is* funny, though. This is the first time that I don't know — well, I couldn't tell you anyway." Moira finished her salad. She looked at her empty wineglass. Félix/Juan filled it for her.

"Can you tell me one thing?"

"What?"

"Call me when your director leaves for Colombia," he said.

"Why?" She was too taken aback to say no.

"For state visits one spends several days, no?"

"Yes, I suppose. I don't really know."

"And if your director is away, and you are his secretary, you will have little work to do, no?"

"No, not much."

"Then I will fly to Washington, of course." Cortez rose from his chair and took three steps around the table. Moira's bathrobe hung loosely around her. He took advantage of that. "I must fly home early tomorrow morning. One day with you is no longer enough, my love. Hmm, you are ready, I think."

"Are you?"

"We will see. There is one thing I will never understand," he said as he helped her from the chair.

"What is that?"

"Why would any fool use powder for pleasure when he can have a woman?" It was, in fact, something that Cortez never would understand. But it wasn't his job to understand it.

"Any woman?" she said, heading for the door.

Cortez pulled the robe from her. "No, not any woman."

"My God," Moira said, half an hour later. Her chest glistened with perspiration, hers and his.

"I was mistaken," he gasped facedown at her side.

"What?"

"When your director of *federales* flies to Colombia, do not call me!" He laughed to show that he was kidding. "Moira, I do not know that I can do this for more than one day a month."

A giggle. "Perhaps you should not work so hard, Juan."

"How can I not?" He turned to look at her. "I have not felt like this since I was a boy. But I am no longer a boy. How can women stay young when men cannot?" She smiled with amusement at the obvious lie. He had pleased her greatly.

"I cannot call you."

"What?"

"I do not have your number." She laughed. Cortez leaped from the bed and pulled the wallet from his coat pocket, then muttered something that sounded profane.

"I have no cards — ah!" He took the pad from the night table and wrote the number. "This is for my office. Usually I am not there — I spend my days on the shop floor." A grunt. "I spend my nights in the factory. I spend weekends in the factory. Sometimes I sleep in the factory. But Consuela will reach me, wherever I might be."

"And I must leave," Moira said.

"Tell your director that he must make it a weekend trip. We will spend two days in the country. I know of a small, quiet place in the mountains, just a few hours from here."

"Do you think you can survive it?" she asked with a hug.

"I will eat sensibly and exercise," he promised her. A final kiss, and she left.

Cortez closed the door and walked into the bathroom. He hadn't learned all that much, but what he had found out might be crucial. "The rules are changing." Whatever they were changing to, Director Jacobs didn't like it, but was evidently going along. He was going to Colombia to discuss it with the Attorney General. Jacobs, he remembered, knew the Attorney General quite well. They had been classmates together in college, over thirty years before. The Attorney General had flown to America for the funeral of Mrs. Jacobs. Something with a presidential seal on it, also. Well. Two of Cortez's associates were in New Orleans to meet with the attorney for the two fools who'd botched the killing on the yacht. The FBI had certainly played a part in that, and whatever had happened there would give him a clue.

Cortez looked up from washing his hands to see the man who had obtained those intelligence tidbits and decided that he didn't like the man who had done it. He shrugged off the feeling. It wasn't the first time. Certainly it wouldn't be the last.

The shot went off at 23:41 hours. The Titan-IIID's two massive solid-rocket boosters ignited at the appointed time, over a million tons of thrust was generated, and the entire assembly leapt off the pad amid a glow that would be seen from Savannah to Miami. The solid boosters burned for 120 seconds before being discarded. At this point the liquid-fuel engines on the booster's center section ignited, hurling the remaining package higher, faster, and farther downrange. All the while onboard instruments relayed data from the booster to ground station at the Cape. In fact, they were also radioing their data to a Soviet listening post located on the northern tip of Cuba, and to a "fishing trawler" which kept station off Cape Canaveral, and also flew a red flag. The Titan-IIID was a bird used exclusively for

318

military launches, and Soviet interest in this launch resulted from an unconfirmed GRU report that the satellite atop the launcher had been specially modified to intercept very weak electronic signals — exactly what kind the report didn't specify.

Faster and higher. Half of the remaining rocket dropped off now, the second-stage fuel expended, and the third stage lit off about a thousand miles downrange. In the control bunkers at the Cape, the engineers and technicians noted that everything was still going as planned, as befitted a launch vehicle whose ancestry dated back to the late 1950s. The third stage burned out on time and on profile. The payload, along with the fourth, or transstage, now awaited the proper time to ignite, kicking the payload to its intended geosynchronous height, from which it would hover over a specific piece of the earth's equator. The hiatus allowed the control-room crew to top off their coffee, make necessary pit stops, and review the data from the launch, which, they all agreed, had been about as perfect as an engineer had any right to expect.

The trouble came half an hour later. The transstage ignited early, seemingly on its own, boosting the payload to the required height, but not in the expected place; also, instead of being perfectly placed in a stationary position, the payload was left in an eccentric path, meandering in a lopsided figure-eight that straddled the equator. Even if it had been over the right longitude, the path would negate its coverage of the higher latitudes for brief but annoying periods of time. Despite everything that had gone right, all the thousands of parts that had functioned exactly as designed, the launch was a failure. The engineering crew who managed the lower stages shook their heads in sympathy with those whose responsibility had been the transstage, and who now surveyed launch control in evident dejection. The launch was a failure.

The payload didn't know that. At the appointed time, it separated itself from the transstage and began to perform as it had been programmed. Weighted arms ten meters in length extended themselves. Gravity from an earth over twenty thousand miles away would act on them through tidal forces, keeping the satellite forever pointed downward. Next the solar panels deployed to convert sunlight into electricity, charging the onboard batteries. Finally, an enormous dish antenna began to form. Made of a special metal-ceramic-plastic material, its frame "remembered" its proper configuration, and on being heated by sunlight unfolded itself over a three-hour period until it formed a nearly perfect parabolic dish fully thirty meters in diameter. Anyone close enough to view the event would have noticed the builder's plate on the side of the satellite. Why this was done was itself an anachronism, since there would never be anyone close enough to notice, but it was the custom. The plate, made of gold foil, designated the prime contractor as TRW, and the name of the satellite as Rhyolite-J. The last of an obsolete series of such satellites, it had been built in 1981 and sat in storage — at the cost of over $100,000 per year — awaiting a launch that had never actually been expected, since CIA and NSA had developed newer, less cumbersome electronic-reconnaissance birds that used advanced signal-gathering equipment. In fact, some of the new equipment had been attached to this obsolete bird, made even more effective by the massive receiving dish. Rhyolite had been originally designed to eavesdrop on Soviet electronic emissions, telemetry from missile tests, side-lobes from air-defense radars, scatterings from microwave towers, even for signals from spy devices dropped off by CIA officers and agents at sensitive locations.

That didn't matter to the people at the Cape. An Air Force public affairs officer released a statement to the general effect that the (classified) launch had not achieved proper orbit. This was verified by the Soviets, who had fully expected the satellite to take a place over the Indian Ocean when, in fact, it was now oscillating over the Brazilian-Peruvian border, from which it couldn't even see the Soviet Union. Curious, they thought, that the Americans had even allowed it to switch itself on, but from yet another "fishing trawler" off the California coast, they monitored intermittent scatterings of encrypted transmissions from the satellite down to some earth station or other. Whatever it was sending down, however, was of little concern to the Soviet Union.

Those signals were received at Fort Huachuca, Arizona, where technicians in yet another nondescript communications van, with a satellite dish set outside, began calibrating their instruments. They didn't know that the launch was supposedly a failure. They just knew that everything about it was secret.

The jungle, Chavez thought. It smelled, but he didn't mind the smell so much as the snakes. Chavez had never told anyone about it, but he hated and feared snakes. All kinds of snakes. He didn't know why — and it troubled him that fear of snakes was associated with women, not men — but even the thought of the slithering, slimy things made his skin crawl, those legless lizards with flicking tongues and lidless eyes. They hung from branches and hid under fallen trees, waiting for him to pass so that they could strike at whatever part of his anatomy offered itself. He knew that they would if they got the chance. He was sure that he would die if they did. So he kept alert. No snake would get him, not so long as he stayed alert. At least he had a silenced weapon. That way he could kill them without making noise. *Fuckin' snakes*.

He finally made the road, and he really ought to have stayed in the mud, but he wanted to lie down on a dry, clear place, which he first scanned with his AN/PVS-7 night scope. No snakes. He took a deep breath, then removed the plastic canteen from its holder. They'd been on the move for six hours, covering nearly five miles — which was really pushing it — but they were supposed to get to this road before dawn, and get there unseen by the OPFOR — the opposing force — who were warned of their presence. Chavez had spotted them twice, each time, he thought, a pair of American MPs, who weren't really soldiers, not to his way of thinking. Chavez had led his squad around them, moving through the swamp as quietly as . . . as a snake, he told himself wryly. He could have double-tapped all four of them easily enough, but that wasn't the mission.

"Nice job, Ding." Captain Ramirez came down beside him. They spoke in whispers.

"Hell, they were asleep."

The captain grinned in the darkness. "I hate the fuckin' jungle. All these bugs."

"Bugs ain't so bad, sir. It's the snakes I don't like."

Both men scanned the road in both directions. Nothing. Ramirez clapped the sergeant on the shoulder and went to check on the rest of the squad. He'd scarcely left when a figure emerged from the treeline three hundred yards away. He was moving directly toward Chavez. *Uh-oh*.

Ding moved backward under a bush and set down his submachine gun. It wasn't loaded anyway, not even with the wax practice bullets. A second one came out, but he walked the other way. Bad tactics, Chavez thought. Pairs are supposed to support each other. Well, that was too bad. The last sliver of moon was dropping below the top level of the triple-canopy forest, and Chavez still had the advantage of his night scope as the figure walked toward him. The man walked quietly — at least he knew how to do that — and slowly, keeping his eyes on the edge of the road and listening as much as looking. Chavez waited, switching off the scope and removing it from his head. Then he removed his fighting knife from its sheath. Closer, only about fifty yards now, and the sergeant coiled up, drawing his legs under his chest. At thirty feet, he stopped breathing. If he could have willed his heart to stop, he'd have done that to reduce the noise. This was for fun. If this had been for-real, a 9mm bullet would now reside in the man's head.

The sentry walked right past Ding's position, looking but not seeing the form under the bush. He made it another step before he heard a swishing sound, but then it was too late. By that time, he was facedown on the gravel, and he felt the hilt of a knife at the back of his neck.

"Ninja owns the night, boy! You're history."

"You got me, sure as hell," the man whispered in reply.

Chavez rolled him over. It was a major, and his headgear was a beret. Maybe the OPFOR wasn't MPs after all.

"Who are you?" the victim asked.

"Staff Sergeant Domingo Chavez, sir."

"Well, you just killed a jungle-warfare instructor, Chavez. Good job. Mind if I get a drink? It's been a long night." Chavez allowed the man to roll into the bushes, where he, too, took a pull off his canteen. "What outfit you from — wait a minute, 3rd of the 17th, right?"

"We own the night, sir," Chavez agreed. "You been there?"

"Going there, for a battalion staff job." The major wiped some blood from his face. He'd hit the road a little hard.

"Sorry about that, sir."

"My fault, Sergeant, not yours. We have twenty guys out there. I never thought you'd make it this far without being spotted."

The sound of a vehicle came down the road. A minute later the wide-set lights of a Hummer — the new and larger incarnation of the venerable jeep — appeared, announcing that the exercise was over. The "dead" major marched off to collect his men, while Captain Ramirez did the same.

"That was the final exam, people," he told the squad. "Get a good day's sleep. We go in tonight."

"I don't believe it," Cortez said. He'd hopped the first flight from Dulles to Atlanta. There he met an associate in a rented car, and now they discussed their information in the total anonymity of an automobile driving at the posted limit on the Atlanta beltway.

"Call it psychological warfare," the man

answered. "No plea-bargain, no nothing. It's being handled as a straight murder trial. Ramón and Jesús will not get any consideration."

Cortez looked at the passing traffic. He didn't give a damn about the two *sicarios,* who were as expendable as any other terrorists and who didn't know the reason for the killings. What he was considering now was a series of seemingly disjointed and unconnected bits of information on American interdiction operations. An unusual number of courier aircraft were disappearing. The Americans were treating this legal case in an unusual way. The Director of the FBI was doing something that he didn't like, and that his personal secretary didn't know about yet. "The rules are changing." That could mean anything at all.

Something fundamental. It had to be. But what?

There were a number of well-paid and highly reliable informants throughout the American government, in Customs, DEA, the Coast Guard, none of whom had reported a single thing. The law-enforcement community was in the dark — except for the FBI Director, who didn't like it, but would soon go to Colombia. . . .

Some sort of intelligence operation was — no. Active Measures? The phrase came from KGB, and could mean any of several things, from feeding disinformation to reporters to "wet" work. Would the Americans do anything like that? They never had. He glowered at the passing scenery. He was an experienced intelligence officer, and his profession was to determine what people were doing from bits and pieces of random data. That he was working for someone he detested was beside the point. This was a matter of pride and besides, he detested the Americans even more.

What were they doing now?

Cortez had to admit to himself that he didn't know, but in one hour he'd board a plane, and in six hours he'd have to tell his employer that he didn't know. That did not appeal to him.

Something fundamental. The rules are changing. The FBI Director didn't like it. His secretary didn't know. The trip to Colombia was clandestine.

Cortez relaxed. Whatever it was, it was not an immediate threat. The Cartel was too secure. There would be time to analyze and respond. There were many people in the smuggling chain who could be sacrificed, who would fight for the chance, in fact. And after a time, the Cartel would adapt its operations to the changing conditions as it always had. All he had to do was convince his employer of that simple fact. What did *el jefe* really care about Ramón and Jesús or any of the underlings who ran the drugs and did the killings that became necessary? It was continuing the supply of drugs to the consumers that mattered.

His mind came back to the vanishing airplanes. Historically, the Americans had managed to intercept one or two per month, that small a number despite all their radars and aircraft. But recently — four in the last two weeks, wasn't it? — had disappeared. What did that mean? Unknown to the Americans, there had always been "operational" losses, a military term that meant nothing more mysterious than flying accidents. One of the reasons that his boss had taken Carlos Larson on was to mitigate that wastage of resources, and it had, initially, shown promise — until very recently. Why the sudden jump in losses? If the Americans had somehow intercepted them, the air crews would have shown up in courtrooms and jails, wouldn't they? Cortez had to dismiss that thought.

Sabotage, perhaps? What if someone were placing explosives in the aircraft, like the Arab terrorists did . . . ? Unlikely . . . or was it? Did anyone check for that? It wouldn't take much. Even minor damage to a low-flying aircraft could face the pilot with a problem whose solution required more time than he had in altitude. Even a single blasting cap could do it, not even a cubic centimeter . . . he'd have to check that out. But, then, who would be doing it? The Americans? But what if it became known that the Americans were placing bombs on aircraft? Would they take that political risk? Probably not. Who else, then? The Colombians might. Some senior Colombian military officer, operating entirely on his own . . . or in the pay of the *yanquis?* That was possible. It couldn't be a government operation, Cortez was sure. There were too many informants there, too.

Would it have to be a bomb? Why not contaminated gasoline? Why not minor tampering with an engine, a frayed control cable . . . or a flight instrument. What was it that Larson had said about having to watch instruments at low level? What if some mechanic had altered the setting on the artificial horizon . . . ? Or merely arranged for it to stop working . . . something in the electrical system, perhaps? How hard was it to make a small airplane stop flying? Whom to ask? Larson?

Cortez grumbled to himself. This was undirected speculation, decidedly unprofessional. There were countless possibilities. He knew that *something* was probably happening, but not what it was. And only probably, he admitted to himself. The unusually large number of missing aircraft could merely be a statistical anomaly — he didn't believe that, but forced himself to consider the possibility. A series of coincidences — there was not an intelligence academy in the world that encouraged its students to believe in coincidences, and yet how many strange coincidences had he encountered in his professional career?

"The rules are changing," he muttered to himself.

"What?" the driver asked.

"Back to the airport. My Caracas flight leaves in less than an hour."

"*Sí, jefe.*"

Cortez lifted off on time. He had to travel to

Venezuela first for the obvious reasons. Moira might get curious, might want to see his ticket, might ask his flight number, and besides, American agents would be less interested in people who flew there than those who flew directly to Bogotá. Four hours later he made his Avianca connection to El Dorado International Airport, where he met a private plane for the last hop over the mountains.

Equipment was issued as always, with a single exception. Chavez noted that nobody was signing for anything. That was a real break from routine. The Army always had people sign for their gear. If you broke it or lost it, well, though they might not make you pay for it, you had to account for it in one way or another.

But not now.

The load-outs differed slightly from one man to the next. Chavez, the squad scout, got the lightest load, while Julio Vega, one of the machine-gunners, got the heaviest. Ding got eleven magazines for his MP-5 submachine gun, a total of 330 rounds. The M-203 grenade launchers that two squad members had attached to their rifles were the only heavy firepower they'd be carrying in.

His uniform was not the usual stripe-and-splotch Army fatigue pattern, but rather rip-stop khaki because they weren't supposed to look like Americans to the casual observer, if any. Khaki clothing was not the least unusual in Colombia.

Jungle fatigues were. A floppy green hat instead of a helmet, and a scarf to tie over his hair. A small can of green spray paint and two sticks of facial camouflage "makeup." A waterproof map case with several maps; Captain Ramirez got one also. Twelve feet of rope and a snaplink, issued to everyone. A short-range FM radio of an expensive commercial type that was nonetheless better and cheaper than the one the Army used. Seven-power compact binoculars, Japanese. American-style web gear of the type used by every Army in the world, actually made in Spain. Two one-quart canteens to hang on the web belt, and a third two-quart water bottle for his rucksack, American, commercial. A large supply of water-purification tablets — they'd resupply their own water, which wasn't a surprise.

Ding got a strobe light with an infrared cover lens because one of his jobs would be to select and mark helicopter landing zones, plus a VS-17 panel for the same purpose. A signaling mirror for times when a radio might not be appropriate (steel mirrors, moreover, do not break). A small flashlight; and a butane cigarette lighter, which was far better than carrying matches. A large bottle of extra-strength Tylenol, also known as "light-fighter candy." A bottle of prescription cough medicine, heavily laced with codeine. A small bottle of Vaseline petroleum jelly. A small squeeze bottle of concentrated CS tear gas. A weapons-cleaning kit, which included a tooth-brush. Spare batteries for everything. A gas mask.

Chavez would travel light with but four hand grenades — Dutch NR-20 C1 type — and two smokes, also of Dutch manufacture. The rest of the squad got the Dutch frags, and some CS tear-gas grenades, also Dutch. In fact, all of the weapons carried by the squad and all of their ammunition had been purchased at Colón, Panama, in what was fast becoming the hemisphere's most convenient arms market. For anyone with cash there were weapons to be had.

Rations were the normal MREs. Water was the main hygienic concern, but they'd already been fully briefed about using their water-purification tablets. Whoever forgot had a supply of antidiarrhea pills that would follow a serious chewing from Captain Ramirez. Every man had gotten a new series of booster shots while still in Colorado against the spectrum of tropical diseases endemic to the area, and all carried an odorless insect repellent made for the military by the same company that produced the commercial product called "Off." The squad medic carried a full medical kit, and each rifleman had his own morphine Syrette and a plastic bottle of IV fluids for use as a blood-expander.

Chavez had a razor-sharp machete, a four-inch folding knife, and, of course, his three nonregulation throwing stars that Captain Ramirez didn't know about. With other sundry items, Chavez would be carrying a load of exactly fifty-eight pounds. That made his load the lightest in the squad. Vega and the other SAW gunner had the heaviest, with seventy-one pounds. Ding jostled the load around on his shoulders to get a feel for it, then adjusted the straps on his ruck to make it as comfortable as possible. It was a futile exercise. He was packing a third of his body weight, which is about as much as a man can carry for any length of time without risking a physical breakdown. His boots were well broken-in, and he had extra pairs of dry socks.

"Ding, could you give me a hand with this?" Vega asked.

"Sure, Julio." Chavez took some slack in on one of the machine gunner's shoulder straps. "How's that?"

"Just right, 'mano. Jeez, carrying the biggest gun do have a price."

"Roger that, Oso." Julio, who'd demonstrated the ability to pack more than anyone in the squad, had a new nickname, Oso: Bear.

Captain Ramirez came down the line, walking around each man to check the loads. He adjusted a few straps, bounced a few rucks, and generally made sure that every man was properly loaded, and that all weapons were clean. When he was finished, Ding checked the captain's load, and Ramirez took his place in front of the squad.

"Okay — anybody got aches, pains, or blisters?"

"No, sir!" the squad replied.

"We ready to go do it?" Ramirez asked with a wide grin that belied the fact that he was as nervous as everyone else in the squad bay.

"Yes, sir!"

One more thing left to do. Ramirez walked down the line and collected dog tags from each man. Each set went into a clear plastic bag along with wallets and all other forms of identification. Finished, he removed his own, counted the bags a last time, and left them on the table in the squad bay. Outside, each squad boarded a separate five-ton truck. Few waves were exchanged. Though friendships had sprouted up in training, they were mainly limited within the structure of the squads. Each eleven-man unit was a self-contained community. Every member knew every other, knew all there was to know, from stories of sexual performance to marksmanship skills. Some solid friendships had blossomed, and some even more valuable rivalries. They were, in fact, already closer than friends could ever be. Each man knew that his life would depend on the skill of his fellows, and none of them wished to appear weak before his comrades. Argue as they might among themselves, they were now a team; though they might trade barbed comments, over the past weeks they had been forged into a single complex organism with Ramirez as their brain, Chavez as their eyes, Julio Vega and the other machine-gunner as their fists, and all the others as equally vital components. They were as ready for their mission as any soldiers had ever been.

The trucks arrived together behind the helicopter and the troops boarded by squads. The first thing Chavez noticed was the 7.62mm mini-gun on the right side of the aircraft. There was an

Air Force sergeant standing next to it, his green coveralls topped by a camouflage-painted flight helmet, and a massive feed line of shells leading to an even larger hopper. Ding had no particular love for the Air Force — a bunch of pansy truck drivers, he'd thought until now — but the man on that gun looked serious and competent as hell. Another such gun was unmanned on the opposite side of the aircraft, and there was a spot for another at the rear. The flight engineer — his name tag said ZIMMER — moved them all into their places and made sure that each soldier was properly strapped down to his particular piece of floor. Chavez didn't trade words with him, but sensed that this man had been around the block a few times. It was, he belatedly realized, the biggest goddamned helicopter he'd ever seen.

The flight engineer made one final check before going forward and plugging his helmet into the intercom system. A moment later came the whine from the helicopter's twin turbine engines.

"Looking good," PJ observed over the headset. The engines had been pre-warmed and the fuel tanks topped off. Zimmer had repaired a minor hydraulic problem, and the Pave Low III was as ready as his skilled men could make it. Colonel Johns keyed his radio.

"Tower, this is Night Hawk Two-Five requesting permission to taxi. Over."

"Two-Five, tower, permission granted. Winds are one-zero-niner at six knots."

"Roger. Two-Five is rolling. Out."

Johns twisted the throttle grip on his collective control and eased the cyclic stick forward. Due to the size and engine power of the big Sikorsky, it was customary to taxi the aircraft toward the runway apron before actually lifting off. Captain Willis swiveled his neck around, checking for other ground traffic, but there was none this late at night. One ground crewman walked backward in front of them as a further safety measure, waving for them to follow with lighted wands. Five minutes later they were at the apron. The wands came together and pointed to the right. Johns gave the man a last look, returning the ceremonial salute.

"Okay, let's get this show on the road." PJ brought the throttle to full power, making a last check of his engine instruments as he did so. Everything looked fine. The helicopter lifted at the nose a few feet, then dipped forward as it began to move forward. Next it started to climb, leaving behind a small tornado of dust, visible only in the blue runway perimeter lights.

Captain Willis put the navigations systems on line, adjusting the electronic terrain display. There was a moving map display not unlike that used by James Bond in *Goldfinger*. Pave Low could navigate from a Doppler-radar system that interrogated the ground, from an inertial system using laser-gyroscopes, or from navigational satellites. The helicopter initially flew straight down the Canal's length, simulating the regular security patrol. They unknowingly flew within a mile of the SHOWBOAT's communications nexus at Corezal.

"Lot of pick-and-shovel work down there," Willis observed.

"Ever been here before?"

"No, sir, first time. Quite a job for eighty-ninety years ago," he said as they flew over a large container ship. They caught a little buffet from the hot stack-gas of the ship. PJ came to the right to get out of it. It would be a two-hour flight, and there was no sense in jostling the passengers any more than necessary. In an hour their MC-130E tanker would lift off to refuel them for the return leg.

"Lot of dirt to move," Colonel Johns agreed after a moment. He moved a little in his seat. Twenty minutes later they went "feet wet," passing over the Caribbean Sea for the longest portion of the flight on a course of zero-nine-zero, due east.

"Look at that," Willis said half an hour later. On their night-vision sets, they spotted a twin-engine aircraft on a northerly heading, perhaps six miles away. They spotted it from the infrared glow of the two piston engines.

"No lights," PJ agreed.

"I wonder what he's carrying?"

"Sure as hell isn't Federal Express." *More to the point, he can't see us unless he's wearing the same goggles we got.*

"We could pull up alongside and take the miniguns —"

"Not tonight." *Too bad. I wouldn't especially mind. . . .*

"What do you suppose our passengers — "

"If we were supposed to know, Captain, they would have told us," Johns replied. He was wondering, too, of course. *Christ, but they're loaded for bear,* the colonel thought. Not wearing standard-issue uniforms . . . obviously a covert insertion — *hell, I've known that part of the mission for weeks* — but they were clearly planning to stay awhile. Johns hadn't heard that the government had ever done that. He wondered if the Colombians were playing ball . . . *probably not. And we're staying down here for at least a month, so they're planning for us to support them, maybe extract them if things get a little hot . . . Christ, it's Laos all over again,* he concluded. *Good thing I brought Buck along. We're the only real vets left.* Colonel Johns shook his head. Where had his youth gone?

You spent it with a helicopter strapped to your back, doing all sorts of screwy things.

"I got a ship target on the horizon at about eleven o'clock," the captain said, and altered course a few degrees to the right. The mission brief had been clear on that. Nobody was supposed to see or hear them. That meant avoiding ships, fishing boats, and inquisitive dolphins, staying well off the coast, no more than a thousand feet up, and keeping their anticollision lights off. The mission profile was precisely what they'd fly in wartime, with some flight-safety rules set aside. Even in the special-operations business, that last fact was somewhat out of the ordinary, Johns reminded himself. Hot guns and all.

They made the Colombian coast without further incident. As soon as it was in view, Johns alerted his crew. Sergeants Zimmer and Bean powered up their electrically driven miniguns and slid open the doors next to them.

"Well, we just invaded a friendly foreign country," Willis noted as they went "feet dry" north of Tolú. They used their low-light instruments to search for vehicular traffic, which they were also supposed to avoid. Their course track was plotted to avoid areas of habitation. The six-bladed rotor didn't make the fluttering *whops* associated with smaller helicopters. Its sound, at a distance, wasn't terribly different from turbopowered aircraft; it was also directionally deceptive — even if you heard the noise, it was hard to figure where it came from. Once past the Pan American Highway, they curved north, passing east of Plato.

"Zimmer, LZ One in five minutes."

"Right, PJ," the flight engineer replied. It had been decided to leave Bean and Childs on the guns, while Zimmer handled the dropoff.

It must be a combat mission. Johns smiled to himself. *Buck only calls me that when he expects to get shot at.*

Aft, Sergeant Zimmer walked down the center of the aircraft, telling the first two squads to unbuckle their safety belts and holding up his hand

339

to show how many more minutes there were. Both captains nodded.

"LZ One in sight," Willis said soon thereafter.

"I'll take her."

"Pilot's airplane."

Colonel Johns orbited the area, spiraling into the clearing selected from satellite photos. Willis scanned the ground for the least sign of life, but there was none.

"Looks clear to me, Colonel."

"Going in now," Johns said into the intercom.

"Get ready!" Zimmer shouted as the helicopter's nose came up.

Chavez stood up with the rest of his squad, facing aft to the opening cargo door. His knees buckled slightly as the Sikorsky touched down.

"*Go!*" Zimmer waved them out, patting each man on the shoulder to keep a proper count.

Chavez went out behind his captain, turning left to avoid the tail rotor as soon as his feet were on the dirt. He went ten steps and dropped to his face. Above his head, the rotor was still turning at full power, holding the lethal blades a safe fifteen feet off the ground.

"Clear, clear, clear!" Zimmer said when he'd seen them all off.

"Roger," Johns replied, twisting the throttle again to lift off.

Chavez turned his head as the whine of the engines increased. The blacked-out helicopter was barely visible, but he saw the spectral outline lift off and felt the dirt stinging his face as the hundred-knot downwash from the rotor subsided, and stopped. It was gone.

He ought to have expected it, but the feeling came to Chavez as a surprise. He was in enemy territory. It was real, not an exercise. The only way he had out — had just flown away, already invisible. Despite the fact that there were ten men around him, he was momentarily awash in a sense of loneliness. But he was a trained man, a professional soldier. Chavez grasped his loaded weapon and took strength from it. He wasn't quite alone.

"Move out," Captain Ramirez told him quietly.

Chavez moved toward the treeline in the knowledge that behind him the squad would follow.

11.

In-Country

Three hundred miles away from SSG Ding Chavez, Colonel Félix Cortez, formerly of the Cuban DGI, sat dozing in *el jefe*'s office. *El jefe*, he'd been told on his arrival several hours before, was occupied at present — probably entertaining a mistress. *Maybe even his wife,* Cortez thought; unlikely but possible. He'd drunk two cups of the fine local coffee — previously Colombia's most valuable export crop — but it hadn't helped. He was tired from the previous night's exertions, from the travel, and now from readjusting yet again to the high altitude of the region. Cortez was ready for sleep, but had to stay awake to debrief his boss. Inconsiderate bastard. At least in the DGI he could have submitted a hastily written report and taken a few hours to freshen up before normal office hours began. But the DGI was composed of professionals, and he'd chosen to work for an amateur.

Just after 1:30 in the morning he heard feet coming down the corridor. Cortez stood and shook off the sleep. The door opened, and there was *el jefe*, his visage placid and happy. One of his mistresses.

"What have you learned?" Escobedo asked without preamble.

"Nothing specific as of yet," Cortez replied with a yawn. He proceeded to speak for about five minutes, going over what things he had discovered.

"I pay you for results, Colonel," Escobedo pointed out.

"That is true, but at high levels such results require time. Under the methods for gathering information which you had in place before I arrived, you would still know nothing other than the fact that some aircraft are missing, and that two of your couriers have been apprehended by the *yanquis*."

"Their story about the interrogation aboard the ship?"

"Most unusual, perhaps all a fabrication on their part." Cortez settled into his chair, wishing for another cup of coffee. "Or perhaps true, though I doubt it. I do not know either man and cannot evaluate the reliability of their claims."

"Two men from Medellín. Ramón's older brother served me well. He was killed in the battles with M-19. He died bravely. Ramón has also served me. I had to give him a chance," Escobedo said. "It was a matter of honor. He is not very

343

intelligent, but he is faithful."

"And his death is not overly troublesome?"

Escobedo shook his head without a moment's pause. "No. He knew what the chances were. He did not know why it was necessary to kill the American. He can tell them nothing about that. As for the American — he was a thief, and a foolish thief. He thought that we would not discover his thievery. He was mistaken. So we eliminated him."

And his family, Cortez noted. Killing people was one thing. Raping children . . . that was something else. But such things were not his concern.

"You are sure that they cannot tell the Americans — "

"They were told to get aboard the yacht, using the money as their bona fides and concealing their cache of drugs. Once the killings were accomplished, they were instructed to go to the Bahamas, turn the money over to one of my bankers, destroy the yacht discreetly, and then smuggle the drugs in normally, into Philadelphia. They knew that the American had displeased me, but not how he had done so."

"They must know that he was laundering money, and they must have told the Americans this," Cortez pointed out patiently.

"*Sí.* Fortunately, however, the American was very clever in how he did this. We were careful, Colonel. Beforehand we made sure that no one could learn exactly what the thief had done."

Escobedo smiled, still in the afterglow of Pinta's services. "He was so very clever, that American."

"What if he left behind a record?"

"He did not. A police officer in that city searched his office and home for us — so carefully that the American *federales* never noticed that he had been there — *before* I authorized the killings."

Cortez took a deep breath before speaking. "*Jefe*, do you not understand that you *must tell me about such things as this beforehand!* Why do you employ me if you have no wish to make use of my knowledge?"

"We have been doing things such as this for years. We can manage our affairs without — "

"The Russians would send you to Siberia for such idiocy!"

"You forget your place, Señor Cortez!" Escobedo snarled back.

Félix bit off his own reply and managed to speak reasonably. "You think the *norteamericanos* are fools because they are unable to stop your smuggling. Their weakness is a political failing, not one of professional expertise. You do not understand that, and so I will explain it to you. Their borders are easy to violate because the Americans have a tradition of open borders. You confuse that with inefficiency. It is not. They have highly efficient police with the best scientific methods in the world — do you know that the Russian KGB reads American police textbooks? And copies their techniques? The Ameri-

345

can police are hamstrung because their political leadership does not allow them to act as they wish to act — and as they could act, in a moment, if those restrictions were ever eased. The American FBI — the *federales* — have resources beyond your comprehension. I know — they hunted me in Puerto Rico and came within a hair of capturing me along with Ojeda — and I am a trained intelligence officer."

"Yes, yes," Escobedo said patiently. "So what are you telling me?"

"Exactly what did this dead American do for you?"

"He laundered vast sums of money for us, and it continues to generate clean income for us. He set up a laundering scheme that we continue to use and — "

"Get your money out at once. If this *yanqui* was as efficient as you say, it is very likely that he left evidence behind. If he did so, then it is likely that those records were found."

"If so, then why have the *federales* not acted? They've had over a month now." Escobedo turned around to grab a bottle of brandy. He rarely indulged, but this was a time for it. Pinta had been especially fine tonight, and he enjoyed telling Cortez that his expertise, while useful, was not entirely crucial.

"*Jefe*, perhaps it will not happen this time, but someday you will learn that chances such as you took in this case are foolish."

Escobedo waved the snifter under his nose.

"As you say, Colonel. Now, what about these new rules you speak of?"

Chavez was already fully briefed, of course. They'd had a "walk-through/talk-through" on a sand table as part of their mission brief, and every man in the unit had the terrain and their way through it committed to memory. The objective was an airfield designated RENO. He'd seen satellite and low-oblique photos of the site. He didn't know that it had been fingered by someone named Bert Russo, confirming an earlier intelligence report. It was a gravel strip about five thousand feet long, easy enough for a twin-engine aircraft, and marginally safe for a larger one, if it were lightly loaded — with grass, for instance, which was bulky but not especially heavy. The sergeant navigated by the compass strapped to his wrist. Every fifty yards he'd check the compass, sight on a tree or other object on the proper line of bearing, and head for it, at which time the procedure would begin again. He moved slowly and quietly, listening for any vaguely human noise and looking around with the night-vision scope that he wore on his head. His weapon was loaded and locked, but the selector switch was on "safe." Vega, the second or "slack" man in the line, was the buffer between Chavez's point position and the main body of the unit, fifty meters behind Vega. His machine gun made for a formidable buffer. If contact were made, their first thought would be evasion, but if evasion proved impossible, then they were to eliminate whatever stood in their path as quickly and violently as possible.

After two hours and two kilometers, Ding picked a spot to rest, a preselected rally point. He raised his hand and twirled it around in a lasso-motion to communicate what he was doing. They could have pushed a little harder, but the flight, as all lengthy helicopter flights, had been tiring, and the captain hadn't wanted to press too hard. They were not in fact expected to reach the objective until the following night. Every other word in the mission brief had been "Caution!" He remembered smirking every time he'd heard that. Now the amusement had left him. That guy Clark had been right. It was different in Indian Country. The price of failure here would not be the embarrassment of having your "MILES" beeper go off.

Chavez shook his head to clear away the thought. He had a job. It was a job for which he was fully trained and equipped, and it was a job which he wanted to do.

His rest spot was a small, dry knoll, which he scanned for snakes before sitting down. He made one last scan of the area before switching off his goggles to save battery time, and pulled out his canteen for a drink. It was hot, but not terribly so. High eighties, he thought, and the humidity was well up there also. If it was this hot at night, he didn't want to think about the daytime heat. At least they'd be bellied up during daylight. And Chavez was accustomed to heat. At Hunter-Liggett he'd marched over hills through temperatures over a hundred-ten degrees. He didn't much like it, but he could do it easily enough.

"How we doin', Chavez?"

"Muy bien, Capitán," Chavez replied. "I figure we've made two miles, maybe two and a half — three klicks. That's Checkpoint WRENCH right over there, sir."

"Seen anything?"

"Negative. Just birds and bugs. Not even a wild pig or anything . . . you suppose people hunt here?"

"Good bet," Ramirez said after a moment's thought. "That's something we'll want to keep in mind, Ding."

Chavez looked around. He could see one man, but the rest blended in with the ground. He'd worried about the khaki clothing — not as effective camouflage as what he was accustomed to — but in the field it seemed to disappear just fine. Ding took another drink, then shook his canteen to see how noisy it was. That was a nice thing about the plastic canteens. Water sloshing around wasn't as noisy as with the old aluminum ones. It was still something to worry about. Any kind of noise was, in the bush. He popped a cough drop to keep his mouth moist and made ready to head out.

"Next stop, Checkpoint CHAINSAW. Captain, who thinks those dumbass names up?"

Ramirez chuckled quietly. "Why, I do, Sergeant. Don't feel bad. My ex didn't much like my taste either, so she went and married a real-estate hustler."

"Ain't broads a bitch?"

"Mine sure was."

Even the captain, Chavez thought. *Christ, nobody has a girl or a family behind.* . . . The thought was distantly troubling, but the issue at hand was getting past WRENCH to CHAINSAW in less than two hours.

The next hop involved crossing a road — what they called a road. It was a straight dirt-gravel track that stretched off to infinity in both directions. Chavez took his time approaching and crossing it. The rest of the squad halted fifty meters from the roadway, allowing the point man to move left and right of the crossing point to make sure it was secure. That done, he made a brief radio transmission to Captain Ramirez, in Spanish:

"The crossing is clear." His answer was a double click of static as the captain keyed the transmit key on his radio, but without saying anything. Chavez answered in kind and waited for the squad to cross.

The terrain here was agreeably flat, enough so that he was wondering why their training had been in towering, airless mountains. Probably because it was well hidden, he decided. The forest, or jungle, was thick, but not quite as bad as it had been in Panama. There was ample evi-

dence that people occasionally farmed here, probably slash-and-burn operations, judging from the
numerous small clearings. He'd seen half a dozen
crumbling shacks where some poor bastard had
tried to raise a family, or farm for beans, or something that hadn't worked out. The poverty that
such evidence spoke of was depressing to Chavez.
The people who lived in this region had names
not unlike his, spoke a language differing only in
accent from that spoken in his childhood home.
Had his great-grandfather not decided to come to
California and pick lettuce, might he have grown
up in such a place? If so, how might he have
turned out? Might Ding Chavez have ended up
running drugs or being a shooter for the Cartel
bigshots? That was a truly disturbing thought.
His personal pride was too great to consider the
possibility seriously, but its basic truth hovered
at the edges of his conscious thoughts. There was
poverty here, and poor people seized at whatever
opportunity presented itself. How could you face
your children and say that you could not feed
them without doing something illegal? You could
not, of course. What would a child understand
other than an empty belly? Poor people had poor
options. Chavez had found the Army almost by
accident, and had found in it a true home of security and opportunity and fellowship and respect.
But down here . . . ?

Poor bastards. But what about the people from
his own barrio? Their lives poisoned, their neighborhoods corrupted. Who was to blame for it all?

351

Less thinkin' and more workin', 'mano, he told himself. Chavez switched on his night scope for the next part of the trek.

He moved standing straight up, not crouched as one would expect. His feet caressed the ground carefully, making sure that there wasn't a twig to snap, and he avoided bushes that might have leaves or thorns to grasp at his clothing and make their own rustling noise. Wherever possible he cut across clearings, skirting the treelines to keep from being silhouetted against the cloudy sky. But the main enemy at night was noise, not sight. It was amazing how acute your hearing got in the bush. He thought he could hear every bug, every birdcall, each puff of breeze in the leaves far over his head. But there were no human sounds. No coughs or mutters, none of the distinctive metallic noises that only men make. While he didn't exactly relax, he moved with confidence, just like on field-training exercises, he realized. Every fifty meters he'd stop and listen for those behind him. Not a whisper, not even *Oso* with his machine gun and heavy load. In their quiet was safety.

How good was the opposition? he wondered. Well equipped, probably. With the sort of money they had, you could buy any sort of weapons — in America or anyplace else. But trained soldiers? No way.

So how good are they? Ding asked himself. Like the members of his old gang, perhaps. They'd cultivate physical toughness, but not in a structured way. They'd be bullies, tough when they had the edge in weapons or numbers. Because of that they wouldn't be skilled in weapons use or fieldcraft; they'd rely on intimidation, and they'd be surprised when people failed to be intimidated. Some might be good hunters, but they wouldn't know how to move as a team. They wouldn't know about overwatch, mutual support, and grazing fire. They might know ambushes, but the finer points of reconnaissance would be lost on them. They would not have proper discipline. Chavez was sure that when they got to their objective, he'd find men smoking on guard. The arts of soldiering took time to acquire — time and discipline and desire. No, he was up against bullies. And bullies were cowards. These were mercenaries who acted for money. Chavez, on the other hand, took great pride that he performed his *duties* for love of country and, though he didn't quite think of it in those terms, for love of his fellow soldiers. His earlier uneasiness at the departure of the helicopter faded away. Though his mission was reconnaissance — intelligence-gathering — he found himself hoping that he'd have his chance to use the MP-5 SD2.

He reached CHAINSAW right on schedule. There the squad rested again, and Chavez led off to the final objective for the night's march, Checkpoint RASP. It was a small wooded knoll, five kilometers from their objective. Ding took his time checking RASP out. He looked especially for evidence of animals that might be hunted, and the tracks of men who might be doing the hunting. He found nothing. The squad arrived twenty minutes after he called them in by radio, having "hooked" and reversed their path to make sure that there were no trailers. Captain Ramirez examined the site as carefully as Chavez had done and came to the same positive conclusion. The squad members paired off to find places to eat and sleep. Ding teamed with Sergeant Vega, taking a security position along the most likely threat axis — northeast — to site one of the squad's two SAW machine guns. The squad medic — Sergeant Olivero — took a man to a nearby stream to replenish canteens, taking special care that everyone used his water-purification tablets. A latrine site was agreed upon, and men used that as well to dump the trash left over from their daily rations. But cleaning weapons came first, even though they hadn't been used. Each pair of soldiers cleaned their weapons one at a time, then worried about food.

"That wasn't so bad," Vega said as the sun climbed over the trees.

"Nice and flat," Chavez agreed with a yawn. "Gonna be a hot fucker down here, though."

"Have one o' these, 'mano." Vega passed over an envelope of Gatorade concentrate.

"All right!" Chavez loved the stuff. He tore open the envelope and dumped the contents into his canteen, swishing it around to get the powder mixed in properly. "Captain know about this?"

"Nah — why worry him?"

"Right." Chavez pocketed the empty envelope. "Shame they don't make instant beer, isn't it?" They traded a chuckle. Neither man would do something so foolish, but both agreed that a cold beer wasn't all that bad an idea in the abstract.

"Flip you for first sleep," Vega said next. It turned out that he had a single U.S. quarter for the task. They'd each been issued five hundred dollars' equivalent in local currency, but all in paper, since coins make noise. It came up heads. Chavez got to stand watch on the gun while Vega curled up for sleep.

Ding settled down in the position. Julio had selected a good one. It was behind a spreading bush of one kind or another, with a shallow berm of dirt in front of him that could stop bullets but didn't obstruct his view, and the SAW had a good field of fire out to nearly three hundred meters. Ding checked that the weapon had a round chambered, but that the selector switch was also on "safe." He took out his binoculars to survey the area.

"How do things look, Sergeant?" Captain Ramirez asked quietly.

"Nothing moving at all, sir. Why don't you catch some Zs? We'll keep watch for ya'." Officers, Ding knew, have to be looked after. And if sergeants didn't do it, who would?

Ramirez surveyed the position. It had been well selected. Both men had eaten and refreshed

355

themselves as good soldiers do, and would be well rested by sundown — over ten hours away. The captain patted Chavez on the shoulder before returning to his own position.

"All ready, sir," the communications sergeant — Ingeles — reported. The satellite-radio antenna was set up. It was only two bits of steel, about the size and shape of grade-school rulers, linked together in a cross, with a bit of wire for a stand. Ramirez checked his watch. It was time to transmit.

"VARIABLE, this is KNIFE, over." The signal went twenty-two thousand miles to a geosynchronous communications satellite, which relayed it back down toward Panama. It took about one-third of a second, and two more seconds passed before the reply came down. The circuit was agreeably free of static.

"KNIFE, this is VARIABLE. Your signal is five by five. Over."

"We are in position, Checkpoint RASP. All is quiet, nothing to report, over."

"Roger, copy. Out."

In the hilltop communications van, Mr. Clark occupied a seat in the corner by the door. He wasn't running the operation — far from it — but Ritter wanted his tactical expertise available in case it was needed. On the wall opposite the racks of communications gear was a large tactical map which showed the squads and their various checkpoints. All had made them on schedule. At least whoever had set this operation up had known — or listened to people who did — what men in the bush could and could not do. The expectations for time and distance were reasonable.

That's nice for a change, Clark thought. He looked around the van. Aside from the two communicators, there were two senior people from the Directorate of Operations, neither of whom had what Clark would call expertise in this particular sort of operation — though they were close to Ritter and dependable. *Well,* he admitted, *people with my sort of experience are mostly retired now.*

Clark's heart was out there in the field. He'd never operated in the Americas, at least not in the jungles of the Americas, but for all that he'd "been there" — out in the boonies, alone as a man could be, your only lifeline back to friendly forces a helicopter that might or might not show, tethered by an invisible thread of radio energy. The radios were far more reliable now; that was one positive change. For what it was worth. If something went wrong, these radios would not, however, bring in a flight of "fast-movers" whose afterburning engines rattled the sky and whose bombloads shook the ground fifteen minutes after you called for help. No, not this time.

Christ, do they know that? Do they really know what that fact means?

No, they don't. They can't. They're all too young. Kids. They're all little kids. That they were older, bigger, and tougher than his own children was for the moment beside the point. Clark was a man who'd operated in Cambodia and Vietnam — North and South. Always with small teams of men with guns and radios, almost always trying to stay hidden, looking for information and trying to get the hell away without being noticed. Mostly succeeding, but some of them had been very, very close.

"So far, so good," the senior Operations guy observed as he reached for a coffee mug. His companion nodded agreement.

Clark merely raised an eyebrow. *And what the hell do you two know about this?*

The Director, Moira saw, was excited about TARPON. As well he might be, she thought as she made her notes. It would take about a week, but already the seizure notices were being scratched in. Four Justice Department specialists had spent more than a day going through the report Mark Bright had delivered. Electronic banking, she realized, had made the job much easier. Somewhere in the Department of Justice there was someone who could access the computerized records of every bank in the world. Or maybe not in Justice. Maybe one of the intelligence agencies, or maybe a private contractor, because the legality of the matter was slightly vague. In any case, comparing records of the Securities and Exchange Commission with the numerous bank transactions, they had already identified the drug money used to finance the projects in which the "victim" — at least his family had been real victims, Moira told herself — had sought to launder it. She'd never known the wheels of justice to turn so quickly.

What arrogant people they must be, thinking they can invest and launder their dirty money right here! Juan was right about them and their arrogance, Moira thought. Well, this would wipe the smiles off their faces. There was at least six hundred million dollars of equity that the government could seize, and that didn't count the profits that they expected to make when the properties were rolled over. Six hundred million dollars! The amount was astounding. Sure, she'd heard about how "billions" in drug money poured out of the country, but the actual estimates were about as reliable as weather reports. It was plain, the Director said in dictation, that the Cartel was unhappy with its previous laundering arrangements and/or found that bringing the cash directly back to their own country created as many problems as it solved. Therefore, it appeared that after laundering the primary funds — plus making a significant profit on their money — they were setting up their accounts in such a way as to establish an enormous investment trust fund which could legitimately begin to take over all commercial businesses in their home country or any other country in which they wished to establish a political or economic position. What made this interesting, Emil went on, was that it might presage an attempt to launder themselves — the old American criminal phraseology: "to go legit" — to a degree that would be fully acceptable in the local, Latin American political context.

"How soon do you need this, sir?" Mrs. Wolfe asked.

"I'm seeing the President tomorrow morning."

"Copies?"

"Five, all numbered. Moira, this is code-word material," he reminded her.

"Soon as I finish, I'll eat the computer disk," she promised. "You have Assistant Director Grady coming in for lunch, and the AG canceled on dinner tomorrow night. He has to go out to San Francisco."

"What does the Attorney General want in San Francisco?"

"His son decided to get married on short notice."

"That's short, all right," Jacobs agreed. "How far away are you from that?"

"Not very. Your trip to Colombia — do you know when yet, so I can rework your appointments?"

"Sorry, still don't know. It shouldn't hurt the schedule too much, though. It'll be a weekend trip. I'll get out early Friday, and I ought to be back by lunch on the following Monday. So it shouldn't hurt anything important."

"Oh, okay." Moira left the room with a smile.

"Good morning." The United States Attorney was a thirty-seven-year-old man named Edwin Davidoff. He planned to be the first Jewish United States senator from Alabama in living memory. A tall, fit, two hundred pounds of former varsity wrestler, he'd parlayed a Presidential appointment into a reputation as a tough, effective, and scrupulously honest champion of the people. When handling civil-rights cases, his public statement always referred to the Law Of The Land, and all the things that America Stands For. When handling a major criminal case, he talked about Law And Order, and the Protection That The People Expect. He spoke a lot, as a matter of fact. There was scarcely a Rotary or Optimists group in Alabama to which he had not spoken in the past three years, and he hadn't missed any police departments at all. His post as the chief government lawyer for this part of Alabama was mainly administrative, but he did take the odd case, which always seemed to be a high-profile one. He'd been especially keen on political corruption, as three state legislators had discovered to their sorrow. They were now raking the sand traps at the Officers' Club Golf Course at Eglin Air Force Base.

Edward Stuart took his seat opposite the desk. Davidoff was a polite man, standing when Stuart arrived. Polite prosecutors worried Stuart.

"We finally got confirmation on your clients' identity," Davidoff said in a voice that might have feigned surprise, but instead was fully businesslike. "It turns out that they're both Colombian citizens with nearly a dozen arrests between them. I thought you said that they came from Costa Rica."

Stuart temporized: "Why did identification take so long?"

"I don't know. That factor doesn't really matter anyway. I've asked for an early trial date."

"What about the consideration the Coast Guard offered my client?"

"That statement was made after his confession — and in any case, we are not using the confession because we don't need it."

"Because it was obtained through flagrantly — "

"That's crap and you know it. Regardless, it will not play in this case. Far as I'm concerned, the confession does not exist, okay? Ed, your clients committed mass murder and they're going to pay for that. They're going to pay in full."

Stuart leaned forward. "I can give you information — "

"I don't care what information they have," Davidoff said. "This is a murder case."

"This isn't the way things are done," Stuart objected.

"Maybe that's part of the problem. We're sending a message with this case."

"You're going to try to execute my clients just to send a message." It was not a question.

"I know we disagree on the deterrent value of capital punishment."

"I'm willing to trade a confession to murder

362

and all their information for life."

"No deal."

"Are you really that sure you'll win the case?"

"You know what our evidence is," Davidoff replied. Disclosure laws required the prosecution to allow the defense team to examine everything they had. The same rule was not applied in reverse. It was a structural means of ensuring a fair trial to the defendants, though it was not universally approved of by police and prosecutors. It was, however, a rule, and Davidoff always played by the rules. That, Stuart knew, was one of the things that made him so dangerous. He had never once lost a case or an appeal on procedural grounds. Davidoff was a brilliant legal technician.

"If we kill these two people, we've sunk to the same level that we say they live at."

"Ed, we live in a democracy. The people ultimately decide what the laws should be, and the people approve of capital punishment."

"I will do everything I can to prevent that."

"I would be disappointed in you if you didn't."

Christ, but you'll be a great senator. So even-handed, so tolerant of those who disagree with you on principle. No wonder the papers love you.

"So that's the story on Eastern Europe for this week," Judge Moore observed. "Sounds to me like things are quieting down."

"Yes, sir," Ryan replied. "It does look that way for the present."

The Director of Central Intelligence nodded and changed subjects. "You were in to see James last night?"

"Yes, sir. His spirits are still pretty good, but he knows." Ryan hated giving these progress reports. It wasn't as though he were a physician.

"I'm going over tonight," Ritter said. "Anything he needs, anything I can take over?"

"Just work. He still wants to work."

"Anything he wants, he gets," Moore said. Ritter stirred slightly at that, Ryan saw. "Dr. Ryan, you are doing quite well. If I were to suggest to the President that you might be ready to become the next DDI — look, I know how you feel about James; remember that I've worked with him longer than you have, all right? — and — "

"Sir, Admiral Greer isn't dead," Jack objected. He'd almost said *yet*, and cursed himself for even having thought that word.

"He's not going to make it, Jack," Moore said gently. "I'm sorry about that. He's my friend, too. But our business here is to serve our country. That is more important than personalities, even James. What's more, James is a pro, and he would be disappointed in your attitude."

Ryan managed not to flinch at the rebuke. But it wounded him, all the more so because the Judge was correct. Jack took a deep breath and nodded agreement.

"James told me last week that he wants you to succeed him. I think you might be ready.

What do you think?"

"Judge, I think I am fitted technically, but I lack the political sophistication needed for the office."

"There's only one way to learn that part of the job — and, hell, politics aren't supposed to have much place in the Intelligence Directorate." Moore smiled to punctuate the irony of that statement. "The President likes you, and The Hill likes you. As of now you're acting Deputy Director (Intelligence). The slot won't be officially filled until after the election, but as of now the job is yours on a provisional basis. If James recovers, well and good. The additional seasoning you get from working under him won't hurt. But even if he recovers, it will soon be time for him to leave. We are all replaceable, and James thinks you're ready. So do I."

Ryan didn't know what to say. Still short of forty, he now had one of the premiere intelligence posts in the world. As a practical matter, he'd had it for several months — even for several years, some might say — but now it was official, and somehow that made it different. People would now come to him for opinions and judgments. That had been going on for a long time, but he'd always had someone to fall back on. Now he would not. He'd present his information to Judge Moore and await final judgment, but from this moment the responsibility for being right was his. Before, he'd presented opinions and options to his superiors. Beginning now, he'd present policy decisions directly to the ultimate decision-makers. The increase in responsibility, though subtle, was vast.

"Need-to-know still applies," Ritter pointed out.

"Of course," Ryan said.

"I'll tell Nancy and your department heads," Moore said. "James ginned up a letter I'll read. Here's your copy."

Ryan stood to take it.

"I believe you have work to do, Dr. Ryan," Moore said.

"Yes, sir." Jack turned and left the room. He knew that he should have felt elated, but instead felt trapped. He thought he knew why.

"Too soon, Arthur," Ritter said after Jack had left.

"I know what you're saying, Bob, but we can't have Intelligence go adrift just because you don't want him in on SHOWBOAT. We'll keep him out of that, at least isolated from what Operations is doing. He'll have to get in on the information that we're developing. For Christ's sake, his knowledge of finance will be useful to us. He just doesn't have to know how the information gets to us. Besides, if the President says 'go' on this, and he gets approval from The Hill, we're home free."

"So when do you go to The Hill?"

"I have four of them coming here tomorrow afternoon. We're invoking the special- and hazardous-operations rule."

SAHO was an informal codicil of the oversight rules. While Congress had the right under law to oversee all intelligence operations, in a case two years earlier, a leak from one of the select committees had caused the death of a CIA station chief and a high-ranking defector. Instead of going public, Judge Moore had approached the members of both committees and gotten written agreement that in special cases the chairman and co-chairman of each committee would alone be given access to the necessary information. It was then their responsibility to decide if it should be shared with the committees as a whole. Since members of both political parties were present, it had been hoped that political posturing could be avoided. In fact, Judge Moore had created a subtle trap for all of them. Whoever tried to decide that information had to be disseminated ran the risk of being labeled as having a political agenda. Moreover, the higher selectivity of the four SAHO-cleared members had already created an atmosphere of privilege that militated directly against spreading the information out. So long as the operation was not politically sensitive, it was a virtual guarantee that Congress would not interfere. The remarkable thing was that Moore had managed to get the committees to agree to this. But bringing the widow and children of the dead station chief to the executive hearings hadn't hurt one bit. It was one thing to carp abstractly about the majesty of law, quite another to have to face the results of a mistake —

the more so if one of them was a ten-year-old girl without a father. Political theater was not solely the domain of elected officials.

"And the Presidential Finding?" Ritter asked.

"Already done. 'It is determined that drug-smuggling operations are a clear and present danger to U.S. national security. The President authorizes the judicious use of military force in accord with established operational guidelines to protect our citizens,' *et cetera*."

"The political angle is the one I don't like."

Moore chuckled. "Neither will the people from The Hill. So we have to keep it all secret, don't we? If the President goes public to show that he's 'really doing something,' the opposition will scream that he's playing politics. If the opposition burns the operation, then the President can do the same thing. So both sides have a political interest in keeping this one under wraps. The election-year politics work in our favor. Clever fellow, that Admiral Cutter."

"Not as clever as he thinks," Ritter snorted. "But who is?"

"Yeah. Who is? You know, it's a shame that James never got in on this."

"Gonna miss him," Ritter agreed. "God, I wish there was something I could take him, something to make it a little easier."

"I know what you mean," Judge Moore agreed. "Sooner or later, Ryan has to get in on this."

"I don't like it."

"What you don't like, Bob, is the fact that Ryan's been involved in two highly successful field operations in addition to all the work he's done at his desk. Maybe he did poach on your territory, but in both cases he had your support when he did so. Would you like him better if he'd failed? Robert, I don't have Directorate chiefs so that they can get into pissing contests like Cutter and those folks on The Hill."

Ritter blinked at the rebuke. "I've been saying for a long time that we brought him along too fast — which we have. I'll grant you that he's been very effective. But it's also true that he doesn't have the necessary political savvy for this sort of thing. He's yet to establish the capacity needed for executive oversight. He has to fly over to Europe to represent us at the NATO intel conference. No sense dropping SHOWBOAT on him before he leaves, is there?"

Moore almost replied that Admiral Greer was out of the loop because of his physical condition, which was mainly, but only partly, true. The presidential directive mandated an extremely tight group of people who really knew what the counter-drug operations were all about. It was an old story in the intelligence game: sometimes security was so tight that people who might have had something important to offer were left out of the picture. It was not unknown, in fact, for those left out to have had knowledge crucial to the operation's successful conclusion. But it was equally true that history was replete with examples of the disasters that resulted from making an operation so broadly based as to paralyze the decision-making process and compromise its secrecy. Drawing the line between operational security and operational efficiency was historically the most difficult task of an intelligence executive. There were no rules, Judge Moore knew, merely the requirement that such operations must succeed. One of the most persistent elements of spy fiction was the supposition that intelligence chiefs had an uncanny, infallible sixth sense of how to run their ops. But if the world's finest surgeons could make mistakes, if the world's best test pilots most often died in crashes — for that matter, if a pro-bowl quarterback could throw interceptions — why should a spymaster be any different? The only real difference between a wise man and a fool, Moore knew, was that the wise man tended to make more serious mistakes — and only because no one trusted a fool with really crucial decisions; only the wise had the opportunity to lose battles, or nations.

"You're right about the NATO conference. You win, Bob. For now." Judge Moore frowned at his desk. "How are things going?"

"All four teams are within a few hours' march of their surveillance points. If everything goes according to plan, they'll be in position by dawn tomorrow, and the following day they'll begin feeding us information. The flight crew we bagged the other day coughed up all the preliminary information we need. At least two of the airfields we staked out are 'hot.' Probably at least one of the others is also."

"The President wants me over tomorrow. It seems that the Bureau has tumbled to something important. Emil's really hot about it. Seems that they've identified a major money-laundering operation."

"Something we can exploit?"

"It would seem so. Emil's treating it as code-word material."

"Sauce for the goose," Ritter observed with a smile. "Maybe we can put a real crimp in their operations."

Chavez awoke from his second sleep period an hour before sundown. Sleep had come hard. Daytime temperatures were well over a hundred, and the high humidity made the jungle seem an oven despite being in shade. His first considered act was to drink over a pint of water — Gatorade — from his canteen to replace what he'd sweated off while asleep. Next came a couple of Tylenol. Light-fighters lived off the things to moderate the aches and pains that came with their normal physical regimen of exertion. In this case, it was a heat-induced headache that felt like a low-grade hangover.

"Why don't we let 'em keep this fucking place?" he muttered to Julio.

"Roger that, 'mano." Vega chuckled in return.

Sergeant Chavez wrenched himself to a sitting position, shaking off the cobwebs as he did so.

371

He rubbed a hand over his face. The heavy beard he'd had since puberty was growing with its accustomed rapidity, but he wouldn't shave today. That merited a grunt. Normal Army routine was heavy on personal hygiene, and light infantrymen, as elite soldiers, were supposed to be "pretty" troops. Already he stank like a basketball team after double overtime, but he wouldn't wash, either. Nor would he don a clean uniform. But he would, of course, clean his weapon again. After making sure that Julio had already serviced his SAW, Chavez stripped his MP-5 down to six pieces and inspected them all visually. The matte-black finish resisted rust quite well. Regardless, he wiped everything down with oil, ran a toothbrush along all operation parts, checked to see that all springs were taut and magazines were not fouled with dirt or grit. Satisfied, he reassembled the weapon and worked the action quietly to make certain that it functioned smoothly. Finally, he inserted the magazine, chambered a round, and set the safety. Next he checked that his knives were clean and sharp. This included his throwing stars, of course.

"The captain's gonna be pissed if he sees them," Vega observed quietly.

"They're good luck," Chavez replied as he put them back in his pocket. " 'Sides, you never know. . . . " He checked the rest of his gear. Everything was as it should be. He was ready for the day's work. Next the maps came out.

"That where we're goin'?"

"RENO." Chavez pointed to the spot on the tactical map. "Just under five klicks." He examined the map carefully, making several mental notes and again committing the details to memory. The map had no marks on it, of course. If lost or captured, such marks would tell the wrong people things that they ought not to know.

"Here." Captain Ramirez joined the two, handing over a satellite photograph.

"These maps must be new, sir."

"They are. DMA" — he referred to the Defense Mapping Agency — "didn't have good maps of this area until recently. They were drawn up from the satellite photos. See any problems?"

"No, sir." Chavez looked up with a smile. "Nice and flat, lots of thinned-out trees — looks easier than last night, Cap'n."

"When we get in close, I want you to approach from this angle here into the objective rally point." Ramirez traced his hand across the photo. "I'll make the final approach with you for the 'leader's recon.' "

"You the boss, sir," Ding agreed.

"Plan the first break point right here, Checkpoint SPIKE."

"Right."

Ramirez stuck his head up, surveying the area. "Remember the briefing. These guys may have very good security, and be especially careful for booby traps. You see something, let me know immediately — as long as it's safe to do so. When in doubt, remember the mission is covert."

"I'll get us there, sir."

"Sorry, Ding," Ramirez apologized. "I must sound like a nervous woman."

"You ain't got the legs for it, sir," Chavez pointed out with a grin.

"You up to carrying that SAW another night, *Oso?*" Ramirez asked Vega.

"I carried heavier toothpicks, *jefe.*"

Ramirez laughed and made off to check the next pair.

"I've known worse captains than that one," Vega observed when he was gone.

"Hard worker," Chavez allowed. Sergeant Olivero appeared next.

"How's your water?" the medic asked.

"Both a quart low," Vega replied.

"Both of you, drink a quart down right now."

"Come on, doc," Chavez protested.

"No dickin' around, people. Somebody gets heatstroke and it's my ass. If you ain't gotta piss, you ain't been drinking enough. Pretend it's a Corona," he suggested as both men took out their canteens. "Remember that: if you don't have to piss, you need a drink. Damn it, Ding, you oughta know that, you spent time at Hunter-Liggett. This fucking climate'll dry your ass out in a heartbeat, and I ain't carrying your ass, dried-out or not."

Olivero was right, of course. Chavez emptied a canteen in three long pulls. Vega followed the medic off to the nearby stream to replenish the empty containers. He reappeared several minutes later. *Oso* surprised his friend with a couple more envelopes of Gatorade concentrate. The medic, he explained, had his own supply. About the only bad news was that the water-purification pills did not mix well with the Gatorade, but that was for electrolytes, not taste.

Ramirez assembled his men just at sundown, repeating the night's brief already delivered to the individual guard posts. Repetition was the foundation of clarity — some manual said that, Chavez knew. The squad members were all dirty. The generally heavy beards and scraggly hair would enhance their camouflage, almost obviating the need for paint. There were a few aches and pains, mainly from the rough sleeping conditions, but everyone was fit and rested. And eager. Garbage was assembled and buried. Olivero sprinkled CS tear-gas powder before the dirt was smoothed over the hole. That would keep animals from scratching it up for a few weeks. Captain Ramirez made a final check of the area while there was still light. By the time Chavez moved out at point, there was no evidence that they'd ever been here.

Ding crossed the clearing as quickly as safety allowed, scanning ahead with his low-light goggles. Again using compass and landmarks, he was able to travel rapidly, now that he had a feel for the country. As before, there was no sound other than what nature provided, and better still, the forest wasn't quite as dense. He made better than a kilometer per hour. Best of all, he had yet to spot a snake.

He made Checkpoint SPIKE in under two hours, feeling relaxed and confident. The walk through the jungle had merely served to loosen up his muscles. He stopped twice along the way for water breaks, more often to listen, and still heard nothing unexpected. Every thirty minutes he checked in by radio with Captain Ramirez.

After Chavez picked a place to belly-up, it took ten minutes for the rest of the squad to catch up. Ten more minutes and he was off again for the final checkpoint, MALLET. Chavez found himself hoping that they'd run out of tool names.

He was more careful now. He had the map committed to memory, and the closer he got to the objective, the more likely that he'd encounter somebody. He slowed down almost without thinking about it. Half a klick out of SPIKE he heard something moving off to his right. Something quiet, but a land creature. He waved the squad to halt while he checked it out — Vega did the same, aiming his SAW in that direction — but whatever it was, it moved off heading southwest. Some animal or other, he was sure, though Ding waited another few minutes before he felt totally safe moving off. He checked the wind, which was blowing from his left rear, and wondered if his pungent odor was detectable to men — probably not, he decided. The rank smells of the jungle were pretty overpowering. On the other hand, maybe washing once in a while was worth the effort. . . .

He arrived at MALLET without further incident. He was now one kilometer off the objective. Again the squad assembled. There was a creek less than fifty meters from the checkpoint, and water was again replenished. The next stop was the objective rally point, picked for its easy identifiability. Ding got them there in just under an hour. The squad formed yet another defensive perimeter while the point man and commander got together.

Ramirez took out his map again. Chavez and his captain turned on the infrared lights that were part of the goggle-sets and traced ideas on the map and the accompanying photos. Also present was the operations sergeant, appropriately named Guerra. The road to the airfield came in from the opposite direction, looping around a stream that the squad had followed into the rally point. The only building visible on the photo was also on the far side of the objective.

"I like this way in, sir," Chavez observed.

"I think you're right," Ramirez replied. "Sergeant Guerra?"

"Looks pretty good to me, sir."

"Okay, people, if there's going to be contact, it'll be in this here neighborhood. It is now post time. Chavez, I'm going in with you. Guerra, you bring the rest of the squad in behind us if there's any trouble."

"Yes, sir," both sergeants replied.

Out of habit, Ding pulled out his camouflage

377

stick and applied some green and black to his face. Next he put on his gloves. Though sweaty hands were a nuisance, the dark leather shells would darken his hands. He moved out, with Captain Ramirez close behind. Both men had their goggles on, and both moved very slowly now.

The stream they'd followed in for the last half a klick made for good drainage in the area, and that made for dry, solid footing — the same reason that someone had decided to bulldoze a landing strip here, of course. Chavez was especially wary for booby traps. With every step he checked the ground for wires, then up at waist and eye level. He also checked for any disturbance of ground. Again he wondered about game in the area. If there were some, it, too, would set off the booby traps, wouldn't it? So how would the bad guys react if one got set off? Probably they'd send somebody out to look . . . that would be bad news regardless of what he expected to find, wouldn't it?

Let's be cool, 'mano, Chavez told himself.

Finally: noise. It carried against the breeze. The low, far-off murmuring of talking men. Though too sporadic and confused even to guess the language, it was human speech.

Contact.

Chavez turned to look at his captain, pointing to the direction from which it seemed to come and tapping his ear with a finger. Ramirez nodded and motioned for the sergeant to press on.

Not real smart, people, Chavez thought at his quarry. *Not real smart talking so's a guy can hear you a couple hundred meters away. You are making my job easier.* Not that the sergeant minded. Just being here was hard enough.

Next, a trail.

Chavez knelt down and looked for human footprints. They were here, all right, coming out and going back. He took a very long step to pass over the narrow dirt path, and stopped. Ramirez and Chavez were now a tight two-man formation, far enough apart that the same burst wouldn't get both, close enough that they could provide mutual support. Captain Ramirez was an experienced officer, just off his eighteen-month tour in command of a light-infantry company, but even he was in awe of Chavez's woodcraft skills. It was now post time, as he'd told them a few minutes earlier, and his were the greatest worries of the unit. He was in command. That meant that the mission's success was his sole responsibility. He was similarly responsible for the lives of his men. He'd brought ten men in-country, and he was supposed to bring all ten men out. As the single officer, moreover, he was supposed to be at least as good as any of his men — preferably better — in every specialty. Even though that was not realistic, it was expected by everyone. Including Captain Ramirez, who was old enough to know better. But watching Chavez, ten meters ahead, in the gray-green image of his night goggles, moving like a ghost, as quietly as a puff of breeze,

Ramirez had to shake off a feeling of inadequacy. It was replaced a moment later with one of elation. This was better than command of a company. Ten elite specialists, each one of them among the best the Army had, and they were his to command. . . . Ramirez distantly realized that he was experiencing the emotional roller-coaster common to combat operations. A bright young man, he was now learning another lesson that history talked about but never quite conveyed: it was one thing to talk and think and read about this sort of thing, but there would never be a substitute for doing it. Training could attenuate the stress of combat operations, but never remove it. It amazed the young captain that everything seemed so clear to him. His senses were as fully alert as they had ever been, and his mind was working with speed and clarity. He recognized the stress and danger, but he was ready for it. In that recognition came elation as the roller coaster rolled on. A far-off part of his intellect watched and evaluated his performance, noting that as in a contact sport, every member of the squad needed the shock of real contact before settling down fully to work. The problem was simply that they were supposed to avoid that contact.

Chavez's hand went up, Ramirez saw, and then the scout crouched down behind a tree. The captain passed around a thicket of bushes and saw why the sergeant had stopped.

There was the airfield.

Better yet, there was an aircraft, several hundred yards away, its engines off but glowing on the infrared image generated by the goggles.

"Looks like we be in business, Cap'n," Ding noted in a whisper.

Ramirez and Chavez moved left and right, well inside the treeline, to search for security forces. But there were none. The objective, RENO, was agreeably identical to what they'd been told to expect. They took their time making sure, of course, then Ramirez went back to the rally point, leaving Chavez to keep an eye on things. Twenty minutes later the squad was in place on a small hill just northwest of the airfield, covering a front of two hundred yards. This had probably once been some peasant's farm, with the burned-off fields merely extended into the strip. They all had a clear view of the airstrip. Chavez was on the extreme right with Vega, Guerra on the far left with the other SAW gunner, and Ramirez stayed in the center, with his radio operator, Sergeant Ingeles.

12.

The Curtain on SHOWBOAT

"VARIABLE, this is KNIFE. Stand by to copy, over."

The signal off the satellite channel was as clear as a commerical FM station. The communications technician stubbed out his cigarette and keyed his headset.

"KNIFE, this is VARIABLE, your signal is five by five. We are ready to copy, over." Behind him, Clark turned in his swivel chair to look at the map.

"We are at Objective RENO, and guess what — there's a twin-engine aircraft in view with some people loading cardboard boxes into it. Over."

Clark turned to look in surprise at the radio rack. Was their operational intel *that good?*

"Can you read the tail number, over."

"Negative, the angle's wrong. But he's going

to take off right past us. We are right in the planned position. No security assets are evident at this time."

"Damn," observed one of the Operations people. He lifted a handset. "This is VARIABLE. RENO reports bird in the nest, time zero-three-one-six Zulu . . . Roger. Will advise. Out." He turned to his companion. "The stateside assets are at plus-one hour."

"That'll do just fine," the other man thought.

As Ramirez and Chavez watched through their binoculars, two men finished loading their boxes into the aircraft. It was a Piper Cheyenne, both men determined, a midsize corporate aircraft with reasonably long range, depending on load weights and flight profile. Local shops could fit it with ferry tanks, extending the range designed into the aircraft. The cargo flown into America by drug smugglers had little to do with weight or — except in the case of marijuana — bulk. The limiting factor was money. A single aircraft could carry enough refined cocaine, even at wholesale value, to wipe out the cash holdings of most federal reserve banks.

The pilots boarded the aircraft after shaking hands with the ground crews — that part seemed to their covert observers just as routine as any aircraft departure. The engines began turning, and their roar swept across the open land toward the light-fighters.

"Jesus," Sergeant Vega noted with bemusement. "I could smoke the bird right here and now. Damn." His gun was on "safe," of course.

"Might make our life a little too exciting," Chavez noted. "Yeah, that makes sense, *Oso*. The security guys were all around the airplane. They're spreading out now." He grabbed his radio. "Captain — "

"I see it. Heads up in case we have to move out."

The Piper taxied to the end of the runway, moving like a crippled bird, bouncing and bobbing on the landing-gear shocks. The airstrip was illuminated by a mere handful of small flares, far fewer lights than were normally used to outline a real runway. It struck all who looked as dangerous, and suddenly Chavez realized that if the aircraft crashed on takeoff, some squad members would end up eating the thing. . . .

The aircraft's nose dropped as the pilot pushed the engines to full throttle preparatory to takeoff, then reduced power to make sure the motors wouldn't quit when he did so. Satisfied, they ran up again, and the aircraft slipped its brakes and started moving. Chavez set his binoculars down to watch. Heavily loaded with fuel, it cleared the trees to his right by a mere twenty yards. Whoever the pilot was, he was a daredevil. The term that sprang into the sergeant's mind seemed appropriate enough.

"Just took off now. It's a Piper Cheyenne," Ramirez's voice read off the tail number. It had American registration. "Course about three-

384

three-zero." Which headed for the Yucatan Channel, between Cuba and Mexico. The communicator took the proper notes. "What can you tell me about RENO?"

"I count six people. Four carry rifles, can't tell about the rest. One pickup truck and a shack, like on the satellite overheads. Truck's moving now, and I think — yeah, they're putting out the runway lights. They're using flares, just putting dirt over on top of them. Stand by, we have a truck heading this way."

Off to Ramirez's left, Vega had his machine gun up on its bipod, the sight tracking the pickup as it moved down the east side of the runway. Every few hundred meters, it stopped, and the passenger jumped out and shoveled dirt on one of the sputtering flares.

"Reach out, reach out and touch someone . . . " Julio murmured.

"Be cool, *Oso*," Ding cautioned.

"No problem." Vega's thumb was on the selector switch — still set on "safe" — and his finger was on the trigger guard, not the trigger itself.

The flares went out one by one. The truck was briefly within one hundred fifty meters of the two soldiers, but never approached them directly. They merely happened to be in a place the truck had to pass by. Vega's gun stayed on the truck until well after it turned away. As he set the butt-stock back down on the dirt, he turned to his comrade.

"Aw, shit!" he whispered in feigned disappointment.

Chavez had to stifle a giggle. Wasn't this odd,
he thought. Here they were in enemy territory,
loaded for fucking bear, and they were playing
a game no different from what children did on
Christmas Eve, peeking around corners. The
game was serious as hell, they all knew, but the
form it took was almost laughable. They also
knew that could change in an instant. There
wasn't anything funny about training a machine
gun on two men in a truck. Was there?

Chavez reactivated his night goggles. At the far
end of the runway, people were lighting cigarettes. The faint images on his display flared
white with the heat energy. That would kill their
night vision, Ding knew. He could tell from the
way they moved that they were just bullshitting
around now. Their day's — night's — work was
complete. The truck drove off, leaving two men
behind. These, it would seem, were the security
troops for this airstrip. Only two, and they
smoked at night. Armed or not — they seemed to
be carrying AK-47s or a close copy thereof —
they were not serious opposition.

"What do you suppose they're smoking?"
Vega asked.

"I didn't think about that," Chavez admitted
with a grunt. "You don't suppose they're that
dumb, do you?"

"We ain't dealing with soldiers, man. We
coulda moved in and snuffed those fuckers no

386

sweat. Maybe ten seconds' worth of firefight."

"Still gotta be careful," Chavez whispered in reply.

"Roge-o," Vega agreed. "That's where you get the edge."

"KNIFE, this is Six," Ramirez called on the radio net. "Fall back to the rally point."

"Move, I'll cover," Chavez told Vega.

Julio stood and shouldered his weapon. There was a slight but annoying tinkle from the metal parts as he did so — the ammo belt, Ding thought. *Have to keep that in mind.* He waited in place for several minutes before moving out.

The rally point was a particularly tall tree close to the stream. Again, people replenished their canteens at Olivero's persistent urging. It turned out that one man had had his face slashed by a low branch, requiring attention from the medic, but otherwise the squad was fully intact. They'd camp five hundred meters from the airfield, leaving two men at an observation point — the one Chavez had staked out for himself — around the clock. Ding took the first watch, again with Vega, and would be relieved at dawn by Guerra and another man armed with a silenced MP-5. Either a SAW or a soldier armed with a grenade launcher would always be at the OP in case the opposition got rambunctious. If there was to be a firefight, the idea was to end it as quickly as possible. Light-fighters weren't especially big on tanks and heavy guns, but American soldiers think in terms of firepower, which, after all, had been largely an American invention in the first place.

It amazed Chavez how easily one could slip into a routine. An hour before dawn, he and Vega surveyed the landing strip from their little knoll. Of the two men in the permanent security team, only one was moving around. The other was sitting with his back against the shack, still smoking something or other. The one up and moving didn't stray far.

"What's happening, Ding?" the captain asked.

"I heard you coming, sir," Chavez said.

"I tripped. Sorry."

Chavez ran down the situation briefly. Ramirez put his binoculars on the enemy to check things for himself.

"Supposedly they aren't being bothered by the local police and army," the captain observed.

"Bought off?" Vega asked.

"No, just they got discouraged, mainly. So the druggies have settled down to a half-dozen or so regular airfields. Like this one. We're gonna be here awhile." A pause. "Anything happens — "

"We'll call you right off, sir," Vega promised.

"See any snakes?" Ramirez asked.

"No, thank God." The captain's teeth flared in the darkness. He clapped Chavez on the shoulder and disappeared back into the bushes.

"What's wrong with snakes?" Vega asked.

Captain Winters felt the pangs of disappointment as he watched the Piper touch down. It was two in a row now. The big one from the other night was gone already. Exactly where they flew them off to, he didn't know. Maybe the big boneyard in the desert. One more old piston bird would hardly be noticed. On the other hand, you could sell one of these Pipers easily enough.

The .50-caliber machine gun looked even more impressive at eye level, though with dawn coming up, the spotlights were less overpowering. They didn't use the spy-plane ploy this time. The Marines treated the smugglers just as roughly as before, however, and their actions again had the desired effect. The CIA officer running the operation had formerly been with DEA, and he enjoyed the difference in interrogation methods. Both pilots were Colombians, the aircraft's registration to the contrary. Despite their machismo, it took only one look at Nicodemus. To be brave in the face of a bullet, or even an attack dog, was one thing. To be brave before a living carnosaur was something else entirely. It took less than an hour for them to be processed, then taken off to the tame federal district judge.

"How many planes don't make it here?" Gunnery Sergeant Black asked as they were driven away.

"What d'you mean, Gunny?"

"I seen the fighter, sir. It figures that he told the dude, 'Fly this way or else!' An' we been called here more times 'n airplanes have showed up, right? What I'm saying, sir, is it stands to

389

reason, like, that some folks didn't take the hint, and the boy driving the fighter showed them the 'or else.' "

"You don't need to know that, Gunny Black," the CIA officer pointed out.

"Fair enough. Either way, it's cool with me, sir. My first tour in 'Nam, I seen a squad get wiped because some of 'em were doped up. I caught a punk selling drugs in my squad, back in '74–75, and I damned near beat the little fuck to death. Almost got in trouble over it, too."

The CIA officer nodded as though that statement surprised him. It didn't.

" 'Need-to-know,' Gunny," he repeated.

"Aye aye, sir." Gunnery Sergeant Black assembled his men and walked off toward the waiting helicopter.

That was the problem with "black" operations, the CIA officer thought as he watched the Marines leave. You want good people, reliable people, smart people, to be part of the op. But the good, reliable, and smart people all had brains and imagination. And it really wasn't all that hard for them to figure things out. After enough of that happened, "black" operations tended to become gray ones. Like the dawn that had just risen. Except that light wasn't always a good thing, was it?

Admiral Cutter met Directors Moore and Jacobs in the lobby of the office wing, and took them straight to the Oval Office. Agents Connor and D'Agostino were on duty in the secretarial office and gave all three the usual once-over out of habit. Unusually, for the White House, they walked straight in to see WRANGLER.

"Good afternoon, Mr. President," all three said in turn.

The President rose from his desk and took his place in an antique chair by the fireplace. This was where he usually sat for "intimate" conversations. The President regretted this. The chair he sat in was nowhere near as comfortable as the custom-designed one behind his desk, and his back was acting up, but even presidents have to play by the rules of others' expectations.

"I take it that this is to be a progress report. You want to start off, Judge?"

"SHOWBOAT is fully underway. We've had a major stroke of luck, in fact. Just as we got a surveillance team in place, they spotted an aircraft taking off." Moore favored everyone with a smile. "Everything worked exactly as planned. The two smugglers are in federal custody. That was luck, pure and simple, of course. We can't expect that to happen too often, but we intercepted ninety kilos of cocaine, and that's a fair night's work. All four covert teams are on the ground and in place. None have been spotted."

"How's the satellite working out?"

"Still getting parts of it calibrated. That's mainly a computer problem, of course. The thing we're planning to use the Rhyolite for will take another week or so. As you know, that element of the plan was set up rather late, and we're playing it by ear at the moment. The problem, if I can call it that, is setting up the computer software, and they need another couple of days."

"What about The Hill?"

"This afternoon," Judge Moore answered. "I don't expect that to be a problem."

"You've said that before," Cutter pointed out.

Moore turned and examined him with a tired eye. "We've laid quite a bit of groundwork. I don't invoke SAHO very often, and I've never had any problems from them when I did."

"I don't expect any active opposition there, Jim," the President agreed. "I've laid some groundwork, too. Emil, you're quiet this morning."

"We've been over that aspect of the operation, Mr. President. I have no special legal qualms, because there really is no law on this issue. The Constitution grants you plenipotentiary powers to use military force to protect our national security once it is determined — by you, of course — that our security is, in fact, threatened. The legal precedents go all the way back to the Jefferson presidency. The political issues are something else, but that's not really my department. In any case, the Bureau has broken what appears to be a major money-laundering operation, and we're just about ready to move on it."

"How major?" Admiral Cutter asked, annoying the President, who wanted to ask the same question.

"We can identify a total of five hundred eighty-eight million dollars of drug money, spread through twenty-two different banks all the way from Liechtenstein to California, invested in a number of real-estate ventures, all of which are here in the United States. We've had a team working 'round the clock all week on this."

"How much?" the President asked, getting in first this time. He wasn't the only person in the room who wanted that number repeated.

"Almost six hundred million," the FBI Director repeated. "It was just over that figure two days ago, but a sizable block of funds was transferred on Wednesday — it looks like it was a routine transfer, but we are keeping an eye on the accounts in question."

"And what will you be doing?"

"By this evening we'll have complete documentation on all the accounts. Starting tomorrow, the legal attachés in all our embassies overseas, and the field divisions covering the domestic banks, will move to freeze the accounts and — "

"Will the Swiss and the Europeans cooperate?" Cutter interrupted.

"Yes, they will. The mystique about numbered accounts is over-rated, as President Marcos found out a few years ago. If we can prove that the deposits result from criminal operations, the governments in question will freeze the funds. In Switzerland, for example, the money goes to the state — 'canton' — government for domestic applications. Aside from the moral issue, it's simple self-interest, and we have treaties to cover this. It hardly hurts the Swiss economy, for example, to keep that money in Switzerland, does it? If we're successful, as I have every right to expect, the total net loss to the Cartel will be on the order of one billion dollars. That figure is just an estimate on our part which includes loss of equity in the investments and the expected profits from rollover. The five eighty-eight, on the other hand, is a hard number. We're calling this Operation TARPON. Domestically, the law is entirely on our side, and on close inspection, it's going to be very hard for anyone to liberate the funds, ever. Overseas the legal issues are more muddied, but I think we can expect fairly good cooperation. The European governments are starting to notice drug problems of their own, and they have a way of handling the legal issues more . . . oh, I guess the word is pragmatically," Jacobs concluded with a smile. "I presume you'll want the Attorney General to make the announcement."

You could see the sparkle in the President's eyes. The press release would be made in the White House Press Room. He'd let the Justice Department handle it, of course, but it would be done in the White House so that journalists could get the right spin. *Good morning, ladies and gentlemen. I have just informed the President that we have made a major break in the continuing war against . . .*

"How badly will this hurt them?" the President asked.

"Sir, exactly how much money they have has always been a matter of speculation on our part. What's really interesting about this whole scheme is that the laundering operation may actually be designed to legitimize the money once it gets into Colombia. That's hard to read, but it would seem that the Cartel is trying to find a less overtly criminal way in which to infiltrate their own national economy. Since that is not strictly necessary in economic terms, the presumptive goal of the operation would seem to be political. To answer your question, the monetary loss will sting them rather badly, but will not cripple them in any way. The political ramifications, however, may be an extra bonus whose scope we cannot as yet evaluate."

"A billion dollars. . . . " the President said. "That really gives you something to tell the Colombians about, doesn't it?"

"I do not think they'll be displeased. The political rumblings they've been getting from the Cartel are very troubling to them."

"Not troubling enough to take action," Cutter observed.

Jacobs didn't like that at all. "Admiral, their Attorney General is a friend of mine. He travels with a security detail that's double the size of the President's, and he has to deal with a security threat that'd make most people duck for cover every time a car backfired. Colombia is trying damned hard to run a real democracy in a region where democracies are pretty rare — which historically happens to be our fault, in case you've forgotten — and you expect them to do — what? Trash what institutions they do have, do what Argentina did? For Christ's sake, the Bureau and DEA combined don't have the manpower to go after the drug rings that we already know about, and we have a thousand times their resources. So what the hell do you expect, that they'll go fascist again to hunt down the druggies just because it suits us? We *did* expect that and we *got* that, for over a hundred years, and look where it's gotten *us!*" *This clown is supposed to be an expert on Latin America,* Jacobs didn't say out loud. *Says who? I bet you couldn't even drive boats worth a damn!*

The bottom line, Judge Moore noted, *is that Emil doesn't like this whole operation, does he?* On the other hand, it did rock Cutter back in his chair. A small man, Jacobs had dignity and moral authority measured in megaton quantities.

"You're trying to tell us something, Emil," the President said lightly. "Spit it out."

"Terminate this whole operation," the FBI Director said. "Stop it before it goes too far. Give me the manpower I need, and I can accomplish more right here at home, entirely within the law, than we'll ever accomplish with all this covert-operations nonsense. TARPON is the proof of that. Straight police work, and it's the biggest success we've ever had."

"Which happened only because some Coast Guard skipper got a little off the reservation," Judge Moore noted. "If that Coastie hadn't broken the rules himself, your case would have looked like simple piracy and murder. You left that part out, Emil."

"Not the first time something like that has happened, and the difference, Arthur, is that that wasn't planned by anyone in Washington."

"That captain isn't going to be hurt, is he?" the President asked.

"No, sir. That's already been taken care of," Jacobs assured him.

"Good. Keep it that way. Emil, I respect your point of view," the President said, "but we have to try something different. I can't sell Congress on the funding to double the size of the FBI, or DEA. You know that."

You haven't tried, Jacobs wanted to say. Instead he nodded submission.

"And I thought we had your agreement on this operation."

"You do, Mr. President." *How did I ever rope myself into this?* Jacobs asked himself. This road, like so many others, was paved with good intentions. What they were doing wasn't quite illegal; in the same sense that skydiving wasn't quite dangerous — so long as everything went according to plan.

"And when are you heading down to Bogotá?"

"Next week, sir. I've messengered a letter to the legal attaché, and he'll deliver it by hand to the AG. We'll have good security for the meeting."

"Good. I want you to be careful, Emil. I need you. I especially need your advice," the President said kindly. "Even if I don't always take it."

The President has to be the world's champ at setting people down easy, Moore told himself. But part of that was Emil Jacobs. He'd been a team player since he joined the U.S. Attorney's office in Chicago, lo, those thirty years ago.

"Anything else?"

"I've made Jack Ryan the acting DDI," Moore said. "James recommended him, and I think he's ready."

"Will he be cleared for SHOWBOAT?" Cutter asked immediately.

"He's not that ready, is he, Arthur?" the President opined.

"No, sir, your orders were to keep this one tight."

"Any change with Greer?"

"It does not look good, Mr. President," Moore replied.

"Damned shame. I have to go into Bethesda to have my blood pressure looked at next week. I'll stop in to see him."

"That would be very kind of you, sir."

Everyone was supportive as hell, Ryan noted. He felt like a trespasser in this office, but Nancy Cummings — secretary to the DDI from long before the time Greer arrived here — did not treat him as an interloper, and the security detail that he now rated called him "sir" even though two of them were older than Jack was. The really good news, he didn't realize until someone told him, was that he now rated a driver also. The purpose of this was simply that the driver was a security officer with a Beretta Model 92-F automatic pistol under his left armpit (there was something even more impressive under the dash), but for Ryan it meant that he'd no longer have to make the fifty-eight-minute drive himself. From now on he'd be one of those Important People who sat in the back of the speeding car talking on a secure mobile phone, or reading over Important Documents, or, more likely, reading the paper on the way into work. The official car would be parked in CIA's underground garage, in a reserved space near the executive elevator, which would whisk him directly to the seventh floor without having to pass through the customary security-gate routine, which was such a damned nuisance. He'd eat in the executive dining room with its mahogany furniture and discreetly elegant silverware.

The increase in salary was also impressive, or would have been if it had matched what his wife, Cathy, was making from the surgical practice that supplemented her associate professorship at Johns Hopkins. But there was not a single government salary — not even the President's — that matched what a good surgeon made. Ryan also had the equivalent rank of a three-star general or admiral, even though his capacity in the job was merely "acting."

His first task of the day, after closing the office door, had been to open the DDI safe. There was nothing in it. Ryan memorized the combination, again noting that the DDO's combination was scribbled on the same sheet of paper. His office had that most precious of government perks: a private bathroom; a high-definition TV monitor on which he could watch satellite imagery come in without going to the viewing room in the building's new north wing; a secure computer terminal over which he could communicate to other offices if he so wished — there was dust on the keys; Greer had almost never used it. Most of all, there was *room*. He could get up and pace if he wanted. His job gave him unlimited access to the Director. When the Director was away — and even if he were not — Ryan could call the White House for an immediate meeting with the President. He'd have to go through the Chief of Staff — bypassing Cutter, if he felt the need — but if Ryan now said, "I have to see the President, right now!" he'd get in, right now. Of course he'd have to have a very good reason for doing so.

Jack sat in the high-backed chair, facing away from the plate-glass windows, and realized that he had gotten there. This was as far as he had ever expected to rise in the Agency. Not even forty yet. He'd made his money in the brokerage business — and the money was still growing; he needed his CIA salary about as much as he needed a third shoe — gotten his doctor's degree, written his books, taught some history, made himself a new and interesting career, and worked his way to the top. Not even forty yet. He would have awarded himself a gentle, satisfied smile except for the fatherly gentleman who was now at Bethesda Naval Medical Center, dying the lingering and painful death that had put him in this chair, in this office, in this position.

It's not worth it. It sure as hell isn't worth that, Jack told himself. He'd lost his parents to an airliner crash at Chicago, and remembered the sudden, wrenching loss, the impact that had come like a thrown punch. For all that, it had come with merciful speed. He hadn't realized it at the time, but he did now. Ryan made a point of seeing Admiral Greer three times a week, watching his body shrink, draw in on itself like a drying plant, watching the pain lines deepen in his dignified face as the man fought valiantly in a battle he knew to be hopeless. He'd been spared the ordeal of watching his parents fade away, but Greer had become a new father to him, and Ryan was now observing his filial duty for his surrogate parent. Now he understood why his wife had chosen eye surgery. It was tough, technically demanding work in which a slip could cause blindness, but Cathy didn't have to watch people die. What could be harder than this — but Ryan knew that answer. He'd seen his daughter hover near death, saved by chance and some especially fine surgeons.

Where do they get the courage? Jack wondered. It was one thing to fight against people. Ryan had done that. But to fight against Death itself, knowing that they must ultimately lose, but still fighting. Such was the nature of the medical profession.

Jesus, you're a morbid son of a bitch this morning. What would the Admiral say?

He'd say to get on with the goddamned job.

The point of life was to press on, to do the best you can, to make the world a better place. Of course, Jack admitted, CIA might seem to some a most peculiar place in which to do that, but not to Ryan, who had done some very odd but also very useful things here.

A smell got his attention. He turned to see that the coffee machine on the credenza was turned on. Nancy must have done it, he realized. But Admiral Greer's mugs were gone, and some "generic" CIA-logoed cups sat on the silver tray. Just then came a knock on the door. Nancy's head appeared.

"Your department-head meeting starts in two minutes, Dr. Ryan."

"Thanks, Mrs. Cummings. Who did the coffee?" Jack asked.

"The Admiral called in this morning. He said you would need some on your first day."

"Oh. I'll thank him when I go over tonight."

"He sounded a little better this morning," Nancy said hopefully.

"Hope you're right."

The department heads appeared right on schedule. He poured himself a cup of coffee, offering the same to his visitors, and in a minute

402

was down to work. The first morning report, as always, concerned the Soviet Union, followed by the others as CIA's interests rotated around the globe. Jack had attended these meetings as a matter of routine for years, but now he was the man behind the desk. He knew how the meetings were supposed to be run, and he didn't break the pattern. Business was still business. The Admiral wouldn't have had it any other way.

With presidential approval, things moved along smartly. Overseas communications were handled, as always, by the National Security Agency, and only the time zones made things inconvenient. An earlier heads-up signal had been dispatched to the legal attachés in several European embassies, and at the appointed time, first in Bern, teletype machines operating off encrypted satellite channels began punching out paper. In the communications rooms in all the embassies, the commo-techs took note of the fact that the systems being used were the most secure lines available. The first, or register, sheet prepped the technicians for the proper one-time-pad sequence, which had to be retrieved from the safes which held the cipher keys.

For especially sensitive communications — the sort that might accompany notice that war was about to start, for example — conventional cipher machines simply were not secure enough. The Walker-Whitworth spy ring had seen to that. Those revelations had forced a rapid and radical change in American code policy. Each embassy had a special safe — actually a safe within yet another, larger safe — which contained a number of quite ordinary-looking tape cassettes. Each was encased in a transparent but color-coded plastic shrink-wrap. Each bore two numbers. One number — in this case 342 — was the master registration number for the cassette. The other — in the Bern embassy; it was 68 — designated the individual cassette within the 342 series. In the event that the plastic wrap on any of the cassettes, anywhere in the world, was determined to be split, scratched, or even distorted, all cassettes on that number series were immediately burned on the assumption that the cassette might have been compromised.

In this case, the communications technician removed the cassette from its storage case, examined its number, and had his watch supervisor verify that it had the proper number: "I read the number as three-four-two."

"Concur," the watch supervisor confirmed. "Three-four-two."

"I am opening the cassette," the technician said, shaking his head at the absurd solemnity of the event.

The shrink-wrap was discarded in the low-tech rectangular plastic waste can next to his desk, and the technician inserted the cassette in an ordinary-looking but expensive player that was linked electronically to another teletype machine ten feet away.

The technician set the original printout on the clipboard over his own machine and started typing.

The message, already encrypted on the master 342 cassette at NSA headquarters, Fort Meade, Maryland, had been further encrypted for satellite transmission on the current maximum-security State Department cipher, called STRIPE, but even if someone had the proper keys to read STRIPE, all he would have gotten was a message that read DEERAMO WERAC KEWJRT, and so on, due to the super-encipherment imposed by the cassette system. That would at the least annoy anyone who thought that he'd broken the American communications systems. It certainly annoyed the communications technician, who had to concentrate as hard as he knew on how to type things like DEERAMO WERAC KEWJRT instead of real words that made some sort of sense.

Each letter passed through the cassette player, which took note of the incoming letter and treated it as a number from 1 (A) to 26 (Z), and then added the number on the tape cassette. Thus, if 1 (A) on the original text corresponded to another 1 (A) on the cassette, 1 was added to 1, making 2 (B) on the clear-text message. The transpositions on the cassette were completely random, having been generated from atmospheric radio noise by a computer at Fort Meade. It was a completely unbreakable code system, technically known as a One-Time Pad. There was, by definition, no way to order or predict random behavior. So long as the tape cassettes were uncompromised, no one could break this cipher system. The only reason that this system, called TAPDANCE, was not used for all communications was the inconvenience of making, shipping, securing, and keeping track of the thousands of cassettes that would be required, but that would soon be made easier when a laser-disc format replaced the tape cassettes. The code-breaking profession had been around since Elizabethan times, and this technical development threatened to render it as obsolete as the slide rule.

The technician pounded away on the keyboard, trying to concentrate as he grumbled to himself about the late hours. He ought to have been off work at six, and was looking forward to dinner in a nice little place a couple of blocks from the embassy. He could not, of course, see the clear-text message coming up ten feet away, but the truth was that he didn't give a good goddamn. He'd been doing this sort of thing for nine years, and the only reason he stuck with it was the travel opportunity. Bern was his third posting overseas. It wasn't as much fun as Bangkok had been, but it was far more interesting than his childhood home in Ithaca, New York.

The message had seventeen thousand characters, which probably corresponded to about twenty-five hundred words, the technician thought. He blazed through the message as quickly as he could.

"Okay?" he asked when he was finished. The last "word" had been ERYTPESM.

"Yep," the legal attaché replied.

"Great." The technician took the telex print-out he'd just typed from and fed it into the code room's own shredder. It came out as flat pasta. Next he removed the tape cassette from the player and, getting a nod from the watch supervisor, walked to the corner of the room. Here, tied to a cable fixed to the wall — actually it was just a spiraled telephone cord — was a large horseshoe magnet. He moved this back and forth over the cassette to destroy the magnetic information encoded on the tape inside. Then the cassette went into the burn-bag. At midnight, one of the Marine guards, supervised by someone else, would carry the bag to the embassy's incinerator, where both would watch a day's worth of paper and other important garbage burned to ashes by a natural-gas flame. Mr. Bernardi finished scanning the message and looked up.

"I wish my secretary could type that fast, Charlie. I count two — only two! — mistakes. Sorry we kept you late." The legal attaché handed over a five-franc note. "Have a couple of beers on me."

"Thank you, Mr. Bernardi."

Chuck Bernardi was a senior FBI agent, whose civil-service rank was equivalent to that of brigadier general in the United States Army, in which he had served as an infantry officer, long ago and far away. He had two more months to serve here, after which he'd rotate home to FBI Headquarters and maybe a job as special-agent-in-charge of a medium-sized field division. His specialty was in the Bureau's OC — Organized Crime — Directorate, which explained his posting to Switzerland. Chuck Bernardi was an expert on tracking mob money, and a lot of it worked its way through the Swiss banking system. His job, half police officer and half diplomat, put him in touch with all of the top Swiss police officials, with whom he had developed a close and friendly working relationship. The local cops were smart, professional, and damned effective, he thought. A little old lady could walk the streets of Bern with a shopping bag full of banknotes and feel perfectly secure. And some of them, he chuckled to himself on the walk to his office, probably did.

Once in his office, Bernardi flipped on his reading light and reached for a cigar. He hadn't shaken off the first ash when he leaned back in his chair to stare at the ceiling.

"Son of a *bitch!*" He reached for his telephone and called the most senior cop he knew.

"This is Chuck Bernardi. Could I speak to Dr. Lang, please? Thank you. . . . Hi, Karl, Chuck here. I need to see you . . . right away if possible . . . it's pretty important, Karl, honest. . . . In your office would be better. . . . Not over the phone, Karl, if you don't mind. . . . Okay, thanks, pal. It's worth it, believe me. I'll be there in fifteen minutes."

He hung up the phone. Next he walked out to the office Xerox machine and made a copy of the document, signing off that it was he who had used the machine and how many copies had been run off. Before leaving, he put the original in his personal safe and tucked the copy in his coat pocket. Karl might be pissed about missing dinner, he thought, but it wasn't every day that somebody enriched your national economy to the tune of two hundred million dollars. The Swiss would freeze the accounts. That meant that six of their banks would, by law, keep all the accrued interest — and maybe the principal also, as the identity of the government which was entitled to get the funds might never be clear, "forcing" the Swiss to keep the funds, which would ultimately be turned over to the canton governments. And people wondered why Switzerland was such a wealthy, peaceful, charming little country. It wasn't just the skiing and the chocolate.

Within an hour, six embassies had the word, and as the sun marched across the earth, special agents of the FBI also visited the executive suites of several American commercial — "full-service" — banks. They handed over the identifying numbers or names of several accounts, all of whose considerable funds would be immediately frozen by the simple expedient of putting a computer lock on them. In all cases, it was done quietly. No one had to know, and the importance of secrecy was conveyed in very positive terms — in America and elsewhere — by serious, senior government employees, to bank presidents who were fully cooperative in every instance. (After all, it wasn't *their* money, was it?) In nearly all cases, the police officials learned, the accounts were not terribly active, averaging two or three transactions per month; always large ones, of course. Deposits would still be accepted, and it was suggested by a Belgian official that if the FBI had the account information for other such accounts, transfers from one monitored account to another would be allowed — only within the same country, of course, the Belgian pointed out — to prevent tipping off the depositors. After all, he said, drugs were the common enemy of all civilized men, and most certainly of all police officers. That suggestion was immediately ratified by Director Jacobs, with the concurrence of the AG. Even the Dutch went along, despite the fact that the Netherlands government itself sold drugs in approved stores to its more jaded younger citizens. It was, all in all, a clear case of capitalism in action. There was dirty money around, money that had not been rightly earned, and governments did not approve of such money. Which was why they seized it for their own approved ends. In the case of the banks, the secrecy to which they were sworn was every bit as sacred as that by which they guarded the identity of their depositors.

By the close of business hours on Friday, all had been accomplished. The banks' computer systems stayed up and running. The law-enforcement people now had two full additional days to give the money trails further examination. If they found any more money related to the accounts already seized, those funds would also be frozen, and, in the case of the European banks, confiscated. The first hit here was in Luxembourg. Though Swiss banks are those known internationally for their confidentiality laws, the only real difference in security between their operation and those of banks in most other European countries was the fact that Belgium, for example, wasn't surrounded by the Alps, and that Switzerland hadn't been overrun by foreign armies quite as recently as her European neighbors. Otherwise, the integrity of the banks was identical, and accordingly the non-Swiss bankers actually resented the Alps for giving their Swiss brethren such an additional and accidental business advantage. But in this case, international cooperation was the rule. By Sunday evening, six new "dirty" accounts had been identified, and one hundred thirty-five million additional dollars were put under computer lock.

Back in Washington, Director Jacobs, Deputy Assistant Director Murray, the specialists from the organized-crime office, and the Justice Department left their offices for a well-deserved dinner at the Jockey Club Restaurant. While the Director's security detail watched, the ten men proceeded to have themselves a superb meal at government expense. Perhaps a passing reporter or Common Cause staffer might have objected, but this one had been well and truly earned. Operation TARPON was the greatest single success in the War on Drugs. It would go public, they agreed, by the end of the week.

"Gentlemen," Dan Murray said, rising with his — he didn't remember how many glasses of Chablis had accompanied this fish — of course — dinner. "I give you the United States Coast Guard!"

They all rose with a chorus of laughter that annoyed the other customers in the restaurant. "The United States Coast Guard!" It was a pity, one of the Justice Department attorneys noted, that they didn't know the words to "Semper Paratus."

The party broke up about ten o'clock. The Director's security men shared looks. Emil didn't hold his liquor all that well, and he'd be a gruff, hungover little bear tomorrow morning — though he'd apologize to them all before lunch.

"We'll be flying down to Bogotá Friday afternoon," he told them in the sanctity of his official car, an Oldsmobile. "Make your plans but don't tell the Air Force until Wednesday. I don't want any leaks on this."

"Yes, sir," the chief of the detail answered. He wasn't looking forward to this one either. Especially now. The druggies were going to be pissed. But this visit would catch them unawares. The news stories would say that Jacobs was remaining in D.C. to work on the case, and they wouldn't expect him to show up in Colombia. Even so, the security for this one would be tight. He and his fellow agents would be spending some extra time in the Hoover Building's own weapons range, honing their skills with their automatic pistols and submachine guns. They couldn't let anything happen to Emil.

Moira found out Tuesday morning. By this time she, too, knew all about TARPON, of course. She knew that the trip was supposed to be secret, and she had no doubt that it would also be dangerous. She wouldn't tell Juan until Thursday night. After all, she had to be careful. She spent the rest of the week wondering what special place he had in the Blue Ridge Mountains.

It no longer mattered that the uniform clothing was khaki instead of woodland pattern Battle Dress Uniform. Between the sweat stains and the dirt, the squad members were now exactly the same color as the ground on which they hid. They had all washed once in the stream from which they took their water, but no one had used soap for fear that suds or smell or something might alert someone downstream. Under the circumstances, washing without soap wasn't even as good as kissing your sister. It had cooled them off, however, and that for Chavez was a most pleasant memory. For — what was it? — ten glorious minutes he'd been comfortable. Ten minutes after which, he'd sweated again. The climate was beastly, with temperatures reaching to one hundred twenty degrees on one cloudless afternoon. If this was a goddamned jungle, Chavez asked himself, why the hell doesn't it rain? The good news was that they didn't have to move around a great deal. The two jerks who guarded this airstrip spent most of their time sleeping, smoking — probably grass, Chavez thought — and generally jerking off. They had, once, startled him by firing their weapons at tin cans that they'd set up on the runway. That might have been dangerous, but the direction of fire hadn't been toward the observation post, and Chavez had used the opportunity to evaluate the weapons skills of the opposition. Shitty, he'd told Vega at once. Now they were up to it again. They set up three bean cans — big ones — perhaps a hundred meters from the shack, and just blazed away, shooting from the hip like movie actors.

"Christ, what fuck-ups," he observed, watching through his binoculars.

"Lemme see." Vega got to watch just as one of them knocked a can down on his third try. "Hell, I could hit the damned things from here. . . . "

"Point, this is Six, what the fuck is going on!" the radio squawked a moment later. Vega answered the call.

"Six, this is Point. Our friends are doing some plinkin' again. Their axis of fire is away from us, sir. They're punchin' holes in some tin cans. They can't shoot for shit, Cap'n."

414

"I'm coming over."

"Roger." Ding set down the radio. "The Cap'n's coming. I think the noise made him nervous."

"He sure does worry a lot," Vega noted.

"That's what they pay officers for, ain't it?"

Ramirez appeared three minutes later. Chavez made to hand over his binoculars, but the captain had brought his own pair this time. He fell to a prone position and got his glasses up just in time to watch another can go down.

"Oh."

"Two cans, two full magazines," Chavez explained. "They like to go rock-and-roll. I guess ammo's cheap down here."

Both of the guards were still smoking. The captain and the sergeant watched them laugh and joke as they shot. Probably, Ramirez thought, they're as bored as we are. After the first aircraft, there had been no activity at all here at RENO, and soldiers like boredom even less than ordinary citizens. One of them — it was hard to tell them apart since they were roughly the same size and wore the same sort of clothing — inserted another magazine into his AK-47 and blazed off a ten-round burst. The little fountains of dirt walked up to the remaining can, but didn't quite hit it.

"I didn't know it would be this easy, sir," Vega observed from behind the sights of his machine gun. "What a bunch of fuck-ups!"

"You think that way, *Oso*, you turn into one

yourself," Ramirez said seriously.

"Roger that, Cap'n, but I can't help seein' what I'm seein'."

Ramirez softened his rebuke with a smile. "I suppose you're right."

The third can finally went down. They were averaging thirty rounds per target. Next the guards used their weapons to push the cans around the runway.

"You know," Vega said after a moment, "I ain't seen 'em clean their weapons yet." For the squad members, cleaning their weapons was as regular a routine as morning and evening prayers were for clergymen.

"The AK'll take a lot of abuse. It's good for that," Ramirez pointed out.

"Yes, sir."

Finally the guards, too, grew bored. One of them retrieved the cans. As he was doing so, a truck appeared. With little in the way of warning, Chavez was surprised to note. The wind was wrong, but even so it hadn't occurred to him that he wouldn't have at least a minute or two worth of warning. Something to remember. There were three people in the truck, one of whom was riding in the back. The driver dismounted and walked out to the two guards. In a moment he was pointing at the ground and yelling — they could hear it from five hundred yards away even though they hadn't heard the truck, which really seemed strange.

"What's that all about?" Vega asked.

Captain Ramirez laughed quietly. "FOD. He's pissed off at the FOD."

"Huh?" Vega asked.

"Foreign Object Damage. You suck one of those cartridge cases into an aircraft engine, like a turbine engine, and it'll beat the hell out of it. Yeah — look, they're picking up their brass."

Chavez turned his binoculars back to the truck. "I see some boxes there, sir. Maybe we got a pickup tonight. How come no fuel cans — yeah! Captain, last time we were here, they didn't fuel the airplane, did they?"

"The flight originates from a regular airstrip twenty miles off," Ramirez explained. "Maybe they don't have to top off . . . Does seem odd, though."

"Maybe they got fuel drums in the shack . . . ?" Vega wondered.

Captain Ramirez grunted. He wanted to send a couple of men in close to check the area out, but his orders didn't permit that. Their only patrolling was to check the airfield perimeter for additional security troops. They never got closer than four hundred meters to the cleared area, and it was always done with an eye on the two guards. His operational orders were not to take the slightest risk of making contact with the opposition. So they weren't supposed to patrol the area even though it would have told them more about the opposition than they knew — would tell them things that they might need to know. That was just good basic soldiering, he thought, and the order not to do it was a dumb order, since it ran as many — or more — risks than it was supposed to avoid. But orders were still orders. Whoever had generated them didn't know much about soldiering. It was Ramirez's first experience with that phenomenon, since he, too, was not old enough to remember Vietnam.

"They're gonna be out there all day," Chavez said. It appeared that the truck driver was making them count their brass, and you never could find all of the damned things. Vega checked his watch.

"Sundown in two hours. Anybody wanna bet we'll have business tonight? I got a hundred pesos says we get a plane before twenty-two hundred."

"No bet," Ramirez said. "The tall one by the truck just opened a box of flares." The captain left. He had a radio call to make.

It had been a quiet couple of days at Corezal. Clark had just returned from a late lunch at the Fort Amador Officers' Club — curiously, the head of the Panamanian Army had an office in the same building; most curious, since he was not overly popular with the U.S. military at the moment — followed by a brief siesta. Local customs, he decided, made sense. Especially sleeping through the hottest part of the day. The cold air of the van — the air conditioning was to protect the electronics gear, mainly from the oppressive humidity here — gave him the wakeup shock he needed.

Team KNIFE had scored on their first night with a single aircraft. Two of the other squads had also had hits, but one of the aircraft had made it all the way to its destination when the F-15 had lost its radar ten minutes after takeoff much to everyone's chagrin. But that was the sort of problem you had to expect with an operation this short of assets. Two for three wasn't bad at all, especially when you considered what the odds had been like a bare month before, when the Customs people were lucky to bag a single aircraft in a month. One of the squads, moreover, had drawn a complete blank. Their airfield seemed totally inactive, contradicting intelligence data that had looked very promising only a week before. That also was a hazard of real-world operations.

"VARIABLE, this is KNIFE, over," the speaker said without preamble.

"KNIFE, this is VARIABLE. We read you loud and clear. We are ready to copy, over."

"We have activity at RENO. Possible pickup this evening. We will keep you advised. Over."

"Roger, copy. We'll be here. Out."

One of the Operations people lifted the handset to another radio channel.

"EAGLE'S NEST, this is VARIABLE . . . Stand to . . . Roger. We'll keep you posted. Out." He set the instrument down and turned. "They'll get everyone up. The fighter is back on line. Seems the radar was overdue for some part replacement or other. It's up and running, and the Air Force offers its apology."

"Damned well ought to," the other Operations man grumbled.

"You guys ever think that maybe an operation can go too right?" Clark asked from his seat in the corner.

The senior one wanted to say something snotty, Clark saw, but knew better.

"They must know that something odd is happening. You don't want to make it too obvious," Clark explained for the other one. Then he leaned back and closed his eyes. Might as well get another piece of that siesta, he told himself. It might be a long night.

Chavez got his wish just after sundown. It started to rain lightly, and clouds moving in from the west promised an even heavier downpour. The airfield crew set out their flares — quite a few more than the last time, he saw — and the aircraft arrived soon after that.

Rain made visibility difficult. It seemed to Chavez that someone ran a fuel hose out from the shack. Maybe there were some fuel drums in there, and maybe a hand-crank pump, but his ability to see the five or six hundred yards came and went with the rain. Something else happened. The truck drove down the center of the strip, and the driver tossed out at least ten additional flares to mark the centerline. The aircraft took off twenty minutes after it arrived, and Ramirez was already on his satellite radio.

"Did you get the tail number?" VARIABLE asked.

"Negative," the captain replied. "It's raining pretty heavy now. Visibility is dogshit. But he got off at twenty-fifty-one Lima, heading north-northwest."

"Roger, copy. Out."

Ramirez didn't like the effect that the reduced visibility might have on his unit. He took another pair of soldiers forward to the OP, but he just as well might not have bothered. The guards didn't bother extinguishing the flares this time, letting the rain wet things down. The truck left soon after the aircraft took off, and the two chastised runway guards retired to the shack to keep dry. All in all, he thought, it couldn't be much easier.

Bronco was bored, too. It wasn't that he minded what he was doing, but there really wasn't much challenge in it. And besides, he was stuck at four kills, and needed only one more to be an ace. The fighter pilot was sure that the mission was better accomplished with live prisoners — but, damn it, killing the sons of bitches was . . . satisfying, even though there wasn't much challenge to it. He was flying an aircraft designed to mix it up with the best fighters the Russians could make. Taking out a Twin-Beech was about as difficult as driving to the O-Club for a couple of brews. Maybe tonight he'd do something different . . . but what?

That gave him something to think about as

he orbited north of the Yucatan Channel, just behind the E-2C, and of course out of normal airliner tracks. The contact call came in at about the right time. He turned south to get on the target, which took just over ten minutes.

"Tallyho," he told the Hawkeye. "I have eyeballs on target."

Another two-engine, therefore another coke smuggler. Captain Winters was still angry about the other night. Someone had forgotten to check the maintenance schedule on his Eagle, and sure enough, that damned widget had failed right when the contractor said it would, at five hundred three hours. Amazing that they could figure it that close. Amazing that an umpty-million-dollar fighter plane went tits-up because of a five-dollar widget, or diode, or chip, or whatever the hell it was. It cost five bucks. He knew that because the sergeant had told him.

Well, there he was. Twin engines, looked like a Beech King Air. No lights, cruising a lot lower than his most efficient cruise altitude.

Okay, Bronco thought, slowing his fighter down, then lighting him up and making the first radio call.

It was a druggie, all right. He did the same dumbass thing they all did, reducing power, lowering flaps, and diving for the deck. Winters had never gotten past the fourth level of Donkey Kong, but popping a real airplane under these circumstances was a hell of a lot easier than that, and you didn't even have to put in a quarter . . .

but he was bored.

Okay, let's try something different.

He let the aircraft go down, maintaining his own altitude and power setting to pass well ahead of it. He checked to make sure that all of his flying lights were off, then threw the Eagle into a tight left-hand turn. This brought his fire-control radar in on the target, and that allowed him to spot the King Air on his infrared scanner, which was wired in to a videotape recorder the same way his gun systems were.

You think you've lost me, don't you. . . .

Now for the fun part. It was a really dark one tonight. No stars, no moon, solid overcast at ten or twelve thousand feet. The Eagle was painted in a blue-gray motif that was supposed to blend in with the sky anyway, and at night it was even better than flat-matte black. He was invisible. The crew in the Beech must be looking all over creation for him, he knew. Looking everywhere but directly forward.

They were flying at fifty feet, and on his screen Captain Winters saw that their propwash was throwing up spray from the waves — five- or six-footers, he thought — just over a mile away. He came straight in at one hundred feet and five hundred knots. Exactly a mile from the target, he put on his lights again.

It was so predictable. The Beech pilot saw the incoming, sunbright lights, seemingly dead-on, and instinctively did what any pilot would do. He banked hard right and dove — *exactly fifty feet* —

cartwheeling spectacularly into the sea. Probably didn't even have time to realize what he'd done wrong, Bronco thought, then he laughed out loud as he yanked back on the stick and rolled to give it a last look. *Now that was a class kill*, Captain Winters told himself as he turned for home. The Agency people would really love that one. And best of all, he was now an ace. You didn't have to shoot them down for it to count. You just had to get the kill.

13.

The Bloody Weekend

It really wasn't fair to make him wait, was it? Moira thought on her drive home Wednesday afternoon. What if he couldn't come? What if he needed notice in advance? What if he had something important scheduled in for the weekend? What if he couldn't make it?

She had to call him.

Mrs. Wolfe reached into the purse at her side and felt for the scrap of hotel stationery — it was still there in the zipper pocket — and the numbers written on it seemed to burn into her skin. She had to call him.

Traffic was confused today. Somebody had blown a tire on the 14th Street Bridge, and her hands sweated on the plastic steering wheel. What if he couldn't make it?

What about the kids? They were old enough to

look after themselves, that was the easy part — but how to explain to them that their mother was going off for a weekend to — what was the phrase they used? To "get laid." *Their mother.* How would they react? It hadn't occurred to her that her horrible secret was nothing of the kind, not to her children, not to her co-workers, not to her boss, and she would have been dumbfounded to know that all of them were rooting for her . . . *to get laid.* Moira Wolfe had missed the sexual revolution by only a year or two. She'd taken her fearful-hopeful-passionate-frightened virginity to the marriage bed, and always thought that her husband had done the same. He must have, she'd told herself then and later, because they'd both botched things so badly the first time. But within three days they'd had the basics figured out — youthful vigor and love could handle almost anything — and over the next twenty-two years the two newlyweds had truly become one.

The void left in her life by the loss of her husband was like an open sore that would not heal. His picture was at her bedside, taken only a year before his death, working on his sailboat. No longer a young man when it had been taken, love handles at his waist, much of his hair gone, but the smile. What was it Juan said? You look with love, and see love returned. *Such a fine way of putting it,* Moira thought.

My God, What would Rich think? She'd asked herself that question more than once. Every time she looked at the photograph before sleep. Every time she looked at her children on the way in or out of the house, hoping that they didn't suspect, knowing in a way conscious thought did not touch that they must know. But what choice did she have? Was she supposed to wear widow's weeds — that was a custom best left in the distant past. She'd mourned for the appropriate time, hadn't she? She'd wept alone in her bed when a phrase crossed her mind, on the anniversaries of all the special dates that acquire meaning in the twenty-two years that two lives merge into one, and, often enough, just from looking at that picture of Rich on the boat that they'd saved years for. . . .

What do people expect of me? she asked herself in sudden anguish. *I still have a life. I still have needs.*

What would Rich say?

He hadn't had time to say anything at all. He'd died on his way to work, two months after a routine physical that had told him that he should lose a few pounds, that his blood pressure was a touch high, but nothing to worry about really, that his cholesterol was pretty good for somebody in his forties, and that he should come back for the same thing next year. Then, at 7:39 in the morning, his car had just run off the road into a guardrail and stopped. A policeman only a block away had come and been puzzled to see the driver still in the car, and wondered whether or not someone might be driving drunk this early in the morning, then realized that there was no pulse. An ambu-

427

lance had been summoned, its crew finding the officer pounding on Rich's chest, making the assumption of a heart attack that they'd made themselves, doing everything they'd been trained to do. But there had never been a chance. Aneurysm in the brain. A weakening in the wall of a blood vessel, the doctor had explained after the postmortem. Nothing that could have been done. Why did it happen . . . ? Maybe hereditary, probably not. No, blood pressure had nothing to do with it. Almost impossible to diagnose under the best of circumstances. Did he complain of headaches? Not even that much warning? The doctor had walked away quietly, wishing he could have said more, not so much angry as saddened by the fact that medicine didn't have all the answers, and that there never was much you could say. (*Just one of those things*, was what doctors said among themselves, but you couldn't say that to the family, could you?) There hadn't been much pain, the doctor had said — not knowing if it were a lie or not — but that hardly mattered now, so he'd said confidently that, no, she could take comfort in the fact that there would not have been much pain. Then the funeral. Emil Jacobs there, already anticipating the death of his wife; she'd come from the hospital herself to attend the event with the husband she'd soon leave. All the tears that were shed. . . .

It wasn't fair. Not fair that he'd been forced to leave without saying goodbye. A kiss that tasted of coffee on the way to the door, something about

428

stopping at the Safeway on the way home, and she'd turned away, hadn't even seen him enter the car that last time. She'd punished herself for months merely because of that.

What would Rich say?

But Rich was dead, and two years was long enough.

The kids already had dinner going when she got home. Moira walked upstairs to change her clothes, and found herself looking at the phone that sat on the night table. Right next to the picture of Rich. She sat down on the bed, looking at it, trying to face it. It took a minute or so. Moira took the paper from her purse, and with a deep breath began punching the number into the phone. There were the normal chirps associated with an international call.

"Díaz y Díaz," a voice answered.

"Could I speak to Juan Díaz, please?" Moira asked the female voice.

"Who is calling, please?" the voice asked, switching over to English.

"This is Moira Wolfe."

"Ah, Señora Wolfe! I am Consuela. Please hold for a *momento.*" There followed a minute of static on the line. "Señora Wolfe, he is somewhere in the factory. I cannot locate him. Can I tell him to call you?"

"Yes. I'm at home."

"*Sí,* I will tell him — Señora?"

"Yes?"

"Please excuse me, but there is something I

must say. Since the death of his María — Señor Juan, he is like my son. Since he has met you, Señora, he is happy again. I was afraid he would never — please, you must not say I tell you this, but, thank you for what you have done. It is a good thing you have done for Señor Juan. We in the office pray for both of you, that you will find happiness."

It was exactly what she needed to hear. "Consuela, Juan has said so many wonderful things about you. Please call me Moira."

"I have already said too much. I will find Señor Juan, wherever he is."

"Thank you, Consuela. Goodbye."

Consuela, whose real name was María — from which Félix (Juan) had gotten the name for his dead wife — was twenty-five and a graduate of a local secretarial school who wanted to make better money than that, and who, as a consequence, had smuggled drugs into America, through Miami and Atlanta, on half a dozen occasions before a close call had decided her on a career change. Now she handled odd jobs for her former employers while she operated her own small business outside Caracas. For this task, merely waiting for the phone to ring, she was being paid five thousand dollars per week. Of course, that was only one half of the job. She proceeded to perform the other half, dialing another number. There was an unusual series of chirps as, she suspected, the call was skipped over from the number she'd dialed to another she didn't know about.

"Yes?"

"Señor Díaz? This is Consuela."

"Yes?"

"Moira called a moment ago. She wishes for you to call her at home."

"Thank you." And the connection broke.

Cortez looked at his desk clock. He'd let her wait . . . twenty-three minutes. His place was yet another luxury condominium in Medellín, two buildings down from that of his boss. Was this the call? he wondered. He remembered when patience had come hard to him, but it was a long time since he'd been a fledgling intelligence officer, and he went back to his papers.

Twenty minutes later he checked the time again and lit a cigarette, watching the hands move around the dial. He smiled, wondering what it was like for her to have to wait, two thousand miles away. What was she thinking? Halfway through the cigarette, it was time to find out. He lifted the phone and dialed in the number.

Dave got to the phone first. "Hello?" He frowned. "We have a bad connection. Could you repeat that? Oh, okay, hold on." Dave looked over to see his mother's eyes on him. "For you, Mom."

"I'll take it upstairs," she said at once, and moved toward the stairs as slowly as she could manage.

Dave put his hand over the receiver. "Guess who?" There were knowing looks around the dining room.

"Yes," Dave heard her say on the other phone. He discreetly hung up. *Good luck, Mom.*

"Moira, this is Juan."

"Are you free this weekend?" she asked.

"This weekend? Are you sure?"

"I'm free from lunch Friday to Monday morning."

"So . . . let me think . . ." Two thousand miles away, Cortez stared out the window at the building across the street. *Might it be a trap? Might the FBI Intelligence Division . . . might the whole thing be a . . . ?* Of course not. "Moira, I must talk to someone here. Please hold for another minute. Can you?"

"Yes!"

The enthusiasm in her voice was unmistakable as he punched the hold button. He let her wait two minutes by his clock before going back on the line.

"I will be in Washington Friday afternoon."

"You'll be getting in about the time — about the right time."

"Where can we meet? At the airport. Can you meet me at the airport?"

"Yes."

"I don't know what flight I'll be on. I'll meet you at . . . at the Hertz counter at three o'clock. You will be there, yes?"

"I will be there."

"As will I, Moira. Goodbye, my love."

Moira Wolfe looked again at the photograph. The smile was still there, but she decided it was not an accusing smile.

Cortez got up from his desk and walked out of the room. The guard in the hall stood when he came out of the door.

"I am going to see *el jefe*," he said simply. The guard lifted his cellular phone to make the call.

The technical problems were very difficult. The most basic one was power. While the base stations cranked out about five hundred watts, the mobile stations were allowed less than seven, and the battery-powered hand-held sets that everyone likes to use were three hundred milliwatts, and even with a huge parabolic dish receiving antenna, the signals gathered were like whispers. But the Rhyolite-J was a highly sophisticated instrument, the result of uncounted billions of research-and-development dollars. Supercooled electronics solved part of the problem. Various computers worked on the rest. The incoming signals were broken down into digital code — ones and zeroes — by a relatively simple computer and downlinked to Fort Huachuca, where another computer of vastly greater power examined the bits of raw information and tried to make sense of them. Random static was eliminated by a mathematically simple but still massively repetitive procedure — an algorithm

— that compared neighboring bits to one another and through a process of averaging numerical values filtered out over 90 percent of the noise. That enabled the computer to spit out a recognizable conversation from what it had downloaded from the satellite. But that was only the beginning.

The reason the Cartel used cellular phones for its day-to-day communications was security. There were roughly six hundred separate frequencies, all in the UHF band from 825 to 845 and 870 to 890 megahertz. A small computer at the base station would complete a call by selecting an available frequency at random, and in the case of a call from a mobile phone, changing that frequency to a better one when performance wavered. Finally, the same frequency could be used simultaneously for different calls on neighboring "cells" (hence the name of the system) of the same overall network. Because of this operating feature, there was not a police force in the world that could monitor phone calls made on cellular-phone equipment. Even without scrambling, the calls could be made in the clear, without even the need for code.

Or that's what everyone thought.

The United States government had been in the business of intercepting foreign radio communications since the days of Yardley's famous Black Chamber. Technically known as comint or sigint — for communications or signals intelligence — there was no better form of information possible than your enemy's own words to his own people. It was a field in which America had excelled for generations. Whole constellations of satellites were deployed to eavesdrop on foreign nations, catching snippets of radio calls, side-lobe signals from microwave relay towers. Often encoded in one way or another, the signals were most often processed at the headquarters of the National Security Agency, on the grounds of Fort Meade, Maryland, between Washington and Baltimore, whose acres of basement held most of the super-computers in the world.

The task here was to keep constant track of the six hundred frequencies used by the cellular phone net in Medellín. What was impossible for any police agency in the world was less than a light workout for NSA, which monitored literally tens of thousands of radio and other electronic channels on a continuous basis. The National Security Agency was far larger than CIA, far more secretive, and much better funded. One of its stations was on the grounds of Fort Hua-chuca, Arizona. It even had its own supercom-puter, a brand-new Cray connected by fiberoptic cable to one of many communications vans, each of which performed functions that those in the loop knew not to ask about.

The next problem was making the computer work. The names and identities of many Cartel figures were fully known to the U.S. govern-ment, of course. Their voices had been recorded, and the programmers had started there. Using voiceprints of the known voices, they established an algorithm to recognize those voices, whichever cellular frequency they used. Next, those who called *them* had their voices electronically identified. Soon the computer was automatically keying and recording over thirty known voices, and the number of known voice-targets was expanding on a daily basis. Source-power considerations made voice identification difficult on occasion, and some calls were inevitably missed, but the chief technician estimated that they were catching over 60 percent, and that as their identification data-base grew larger, that their performance would grow to 85 percent.

Those voices that did not have names attached were assigned numbers. Voice 23 had just called Voice 17. Twenty-three was a security guard. He had been identified because he had called 17, who was also known to be a security guard for Subject ECHO, as Escobedo was known to the comint team. "He's coming over to see him," was all the recorded signal told them. Exactly who "he" was they didn't know. It was a voice they had either not yet heard or, more likely, not yet identified. The intelligence specialists were patient. This case had gone a lot quicker than normal. For all their sophistication, the targets never dreamed that someone could tap in on them in this way and as a consequence had taken no precautions against it. Within a month the comint team would have enough experience with the targets to develop all sorts of usable tactical

436

intelligence. It was just a matter of time. The technicians wondered when actual operations would begin. After all, setting up the sigint side was always the precursor to putting assets in the field.

"What is it?" Escobedo asked as Cortez entered the room.

"The American FBI Director will be flying to Bogotá tomorrow. He leaves Washington sometime after noon. It is to be a covert visit. I would expect him to be using an official aircraft. The Americans have a squadron of such aircraft at Andrews Air Force Base. There will be a flight plan filed, probably covered as something else. Anything from four tomorrow afternoon to eight in the evening could be the flight. I expect it to be a twin-engine executive jet, the G-Three, although another type is possible. He will be meeting with the Attorney General, undoubtedly to discuss something of great importance. I will fly to Washington immediately to find out what I can. There is a flight to Mexico City in three hours. I'll be on it."

"Your source is a good one," Escobedo observed, impressed for once.

Cortez smiled. "*Sí, jefe.* Even if you are unable to determine what is being discussed here, I hope to find out over the weekend. I make no promises, but I will do my best."

"A woman," Escobedo observed. "Young and beautiful, I am sure."

"As you say. I must be off."

"Enjoy your weekend, Colonel. I will enjoy mine."

Cortez had been gone only an hour when a telex came in, informing him that last night's courier flight had failed to arrive at its destination in southwestern Georgia. The amusement that invariably accompanies receipt of top-secret information changed at once to anger. *El jefe* thought to call Cortez on his mobile phone, but remembered that his hireling refused to discuss substantive matters over what he called a "non-secure" line. Escobedo shook his head. This *colonel* of the DGI — he was an old woman! *El jefe*'s phone twittered its own signal.

"Bingo," a man said in a van, two thousand miles away.

VOX IDENT, his computer screen announced: SUBJECT BRAVO INIT CALL TO SUBJECT ECHO FRQ 848.970MHZ CALL INIT 2349Z INTERCEPT IDENT 345.

"We may have our first big one here, Tony."

The senior technician, who'd been christened Antonio forty-seven years earlier, put on his headphones. The conversation was being taken down on high-speed tape — it was actually a three-quarter-inch videotape because of the nature of the system used to intercept the signal. Four separate machines recorded the signal. They were Sony commercial recorders, only slightly modified by the NSA technical staff.

"Ha! Señor Bravo is pissed!" Tony observed as he caught part of the conversation. "Tell Meade that we finally caught a frozen rope down the left-field line." A "frozen rope" was the current NSA nickname for a very important signal intercept. It was baseball season, and the Baltimore Orioles were coming back.

"How's the signal?"

"Clear as a church bell. Christ, why don't I ever buy TRW stock?" Antonio paused, struggling not to laugh. "God, is he pissed!"

The call ended a minute later. Tony switched his headphone input to one of the tape machines and crab-walked his swivel chair to a teleprinter, where he started typing.

FLASH
TOP SECRET ★★★★★ CAPER
2358Z
SIGINT REPORT
INTERCEPT 345 INIT 2349Z FRQ 836.970 MHZ

INIT: SUBJECT BRAVO
RECIP: SUBJECT ECHO

B: WE'VE LOST ANOTHER DELIVERY. [AGITATION]

E: WHAT HAPPENED?

B: THE CURSED THING DIDN'T APPEAR. WHAT DO YOU THINK? [AGITATION].

E: THEY'RE DOING SOMETHING DIFFERENT. I TOLD YOU THAT. WE'RE TRYING TO FIND OUT WHAT IT IS.

B: SO WHEN ARE YOU GOING TO KNOW?

E: WE'RE WORKING ON THAT. OUR MAN IS TRAVELING TO WASHINGTON TO FIND OUT. THERE ARE SOME OTHER THINGS HAPPENING ALSO.

B: WHAT? [AGITATION]

E: I PROPOSE WE MEET TOMORROW TO DISCUSS IT.

B: THE REGULAR MEETING IS TUESDAY.

E: THIS IS IMPORTANT, EVERYONE MUST HEAR IT, PABLO.

B: CAN'T YOU TELL ME ANYTHING?

E: THEY ARE CHANGING THE RULES, THE NORTH AMERICANS. EXACTLY HOW THEY ARE CHANGING THEM WE DO NOT YET KNOW.

B: WELL, WHAT ARE WE PAYING THAT CUBAN RENEGADE FOR? [AGITATION]

E: HE IS DOING VERY WELL. PERHAPS HE WILL LEARN MORE ON HIS TRIP TO WASHINGTON. BUT WHAT WE HAVE LEARNED TO THIS POINT WILL BE THE SUBJECT OF OUR MEETING.

B: VERY WELL. I WILL SET UP THE MEETING.

E: THANK YOU, PABLO.

END CALL. DISCONNECT SIGNAL. END INTERCEPT.

"What's this 'agitation' business?"

"I can't put 'pissed' in an official TWX," Antonio pointed out. "This one's hot. We have some operational intel here." He pressed the transmit key on his terminal. The signal was addressed to a code-word destination — CAPER

— which was all anyone who worked in the van knew.

Bob Ritter had just left for home, and was only a mile up on the George Washington Parkway when his secure carphone made its distinctive and, to him, irritating noise.

"Yeah?"

"CAPER traffic," the voice said.

"Right," the Deputy Director (Operations) said with a suppressed sigh. To his driver: "Take me back."

"Yes, sir."

Getting back, even for a top CIA executive, meant finding a place to reverse course, and then fight the late D.C. rush-hour traffic which, in its majesty, allows rich, poor, and important to crawl at an equal twenty miles per hour. The gate guard waved the car through, and he was in his seventh-floor office five minutes after that. Judge Moore was already gone. There were only four watch officers cleared for this operation. That was the minimum number required merely to wait for and evaluate signal traffic on the operation. The current watch officer had just come on duty. He handed over the signal.

"We have something hot," the officer said.

"You're not kidding. It's Cortez," Ritter observed after scanning the message form.

"Good bet, sir."

"Coming here . . . but we don't know what he looks like. If only the Bureau had gotten a picture of the bastard when he was in Puerto Rico. You know the description we have of him." Ritter looked up.

"Black and brown. Medium height, medium build, sometimes wears a mustache. No distinguishing marks or characteristics," the officer recited from memory. It wasn't hard to memorize nothing, and nothing was exactly what they had on Félix Cortez.

"Who's your contact at the Bureau?"

"Tom Burke, middle-level guy in the Intelligence Division. Pretty good man. He handled part of the Henderson case."

"Okay, get this to him. Maybe the Bureau can figure a way to bag the bastard. Anything else?"

"No, sir."

Ritter nodded and resumed his trip home. The watch officer returned to his own office on the fifth floor and made his call. He was in luck this night; Burke was still at his office. They couldn't discuss the matter over the phone, of course. The CIA watch officer, Paul Hooker, drove over to the FBI Building at 10th and Pennsylvania.

Though CIA and FBI are sometimes rivals in the intelligence business, and always rivals for federal budget funds, at the operational level their employees get along well enough; the barbs they trade are good-natured ones.

"There's a new tourist coming into D.C. in the next few days," Hooker announced once the door was closed.

"Like who?" Burke inquired, gesturing to his coffee machine.

Hooker declined. "Félix Cortez." The CIA officer handed over a Xerox of the telex. Portions of it had been blacked out, of course. Burke didn't take offense at this. As a member of the Intelligence Division, charged with catching spies, he was accustomed to "need-to-know."

"You're assuming that it's Cortez," the FBI agent pointed out. Then he smiled. "But I wouldn't bet against you. If we had a picture of this clown, we'd stand a fair chance of bagging him. As it is . . . " A sigh. "I'll put people at Dulles, National, and BWI. We'll try, but you can guess what the odds are." *If the Agency had gotten a photo of this mutt while he was in the field — or while he was at the KGB Academy — it would make our job a hell of a lot easier. . . .* "I'll assume that he's coming in over the next four days. We'll check all flights directly in from down there, and all connecting flights."

The problem was more one of mathematics than anything. The number of direct flights from Colombia, Venezuela, Panama, and other nearby countries directly into the D.C. area was quite modest and easy to cover. But if the subject made a connecting flight through Puerto Rico, the Bahamas, Mexico, or any number of other cities, including American ones, the number of possible connections increased by a factor of ten. If he made one more intermediary stop in the United States, the number of possible flights for the FBI to monitor took a sudden jump into the hundreds. Cortez was a KGB-trained pro, and he knew that fact as well as these two men did. The task wasn't a hopeless one. Police play for breaks all the time, because even the most skilled adversaries get careless or unlucky. But that was the game here. Their only real hope was a lucky break.

Which they would not get. Cortez caught an Avianca flight to Mexico City, then an American Airlines flight to Dallas–Fort Worth, where he cleared customs and made yet another American connection to New York City. He checked into the St. Moritz Hotel on Central Park South. By this time it was three in the morning, and he needed some rest. He left a wakeup call for ten and asked the concierge to have him a first-class ticket for the eleven o'clock Metroliner into Union Station, Washington, D.C. The Metroliners, he knew, had their own phones. He'd be able to call ahead if something went wrong. Or maybe . . . no, he decided, he didn't want to call her at work; surely the FBI tapped its own phones. The last thing Cortez did before collapsing onto the bed was to shred his plane-ticket receipts and the baggage tags on his luggage.

The phone awoke him at 9:56. *Almost seven hours' sleep*, he thought. It seemed like only a few seconds, but there was no time to dawdle. Half an hour later he appeared at the desk, tossed in his express check-out form, and collected his train ticket. The usual Manhattan midtown traffic nearly caused him to miss the train, but he made it, taking a seat in the last row of the three-across club-car smoking section. A smiling, red-vested attendant started him off with decaffeinated coffee and a copy of *USA Today,* followed by a breakfast that was no different — though a little warmer — from what he'd have gotten on an airliner. By the time the train stopped in Philadelphia, he was back asleep. Cortez figured that he'd need his rest. The attendant noted the smile on his sleeping face as he collected the breakfast tray and wondered what dreams passed through the passenger's head.

At one o'clock, while Metroliner 111 approached Baltimore, the TV lights were switched on in the White House Press Room. The reporters had already been prepped with a "deep background, not for attribution" briefing that there would be a major announcement from the Attorney General, and that it would have something to do with drugs. The major networks did not interrupt their afternoon soap operas — it was no small thing to cut away from "The Young and the Restless" — but CNN, as usual, put up their "Special Report" graphic. This was noticed at once by the intelligence watch officers in the Pentagon's National Military Command Center, each of whom had a TV on his desk tuned into CNN. That was perhaps the most eloquent comment possible on the ability of America's intelligence agencies to keep its government informed, but one on which the major networks, for obvious reasons, had never commented.

The Attorney General strode haltingly toward the lectern. For all his experience as a lawyer, he was not an effective public speaker. You didn't need to be if your practice was corporate law and political campaigning. He was, however, photogenic and a sharp dresser, and always good for a leak on a slow news day, which explained his popularity with the media.

"Ladies and gentlemen," he began, fumbling with his notes. "You will soon be getting handouts concerning Operation TARPON. This represents the most effective operation to date against the international drug cartel." He looked up, trying to see the reporters' faces past the glare of the lights.

"Investigation by the Department of Justice, led by the FBI, has identified a number of bank accounts both in the United States and elsewhere which were being used for money-laundering on an unprecedented scale. These accounts range over twenty-nine banks from Liechtenstein to California, and their deposits exceed, at our current estimates, over six hundred fifty million dollars." He looked up again as he heard a *Goddamn!* from the assembled multitude. That elicited a smile. It was never easy to impress the White House press corps. The autowind cameras were really churning away now.

"In cooperation with six foreign governments,

we have initiated the necessary steps to seize all of those funds, and also to seize eight real-estate joint-venture investments here in the United States which were the primary agency in the actual laundering operation. This is being done under the RICO — the Racketeer-Influenced and Corrupt Organization — statute. I should emphasize on that point that the real-estate ventures involve the holdings of many innocent investors; their holdings will not — I repeat *not* — be affected in any way by the government's action. They were used as dupes by the Cartel, and they will not be harmed by these seizures."

"Excuse me," Associated Press interrupted. "You did say six hundred fifty *million* dollars?"

"That is correct, more than half a *billion* dollars." The AG described generally how the information had been found, but not the way in which the first lead had been obtained, nor the precise mechanisms used to track the money. "As you know, we have treaties with several foreign governments to cover cases such as this. Those funds identified as drug-related and deposited in foreign banks will be confiscated by the governments in question. In Swiss accounts, for example, are approximately . . . " He checked his notes again. "It looks like two hundred thirty-seven million dollars, all of which now belongs to the Swiss government."

"What's our take?" *The Washington Post* asked.

"We don't know yet. It's difficult to describe the complexity of this operation — just the accounting is going to keep us busy for weeks."

"What about cooperation from the foreign governments?" another reporter wanted to know.

You gotta be kidding, the journalist next to him thought.

"The cooperation we've received on this case is simply outstanding." The Attorney General beamed. "Our friends overseas have moved with dispatch and professionalism."

Not every day you can steal this much money and call it something for the Public Good, the quiet journalist told herself.

CNN is a worldwide service. The broadcast was monitored in Colombia by two men whose job it was to keep track of the American news media. They were journalists themselves, in fact, who worked for the Colombian TV network, Inravision. One of them excused himself from the control room and made a telephone call before returning.

Tony and his partner had just come back on duty in the van, and there was a telex clipped to the wall, telling them to expect some activity on the cellular-phone circuits at about 1800 Zulu time. They weren't disappointed.

"Can we talk to Director Jacobs about this?" a reporter asked.

"Director Jacobs is taking a personal interest in the case, but is not available for comment," the AG answered. "You'll be able to talk to him next

448

week, but at the moment he and his team are all pretty busy." That didn't break any rules. It gave the impression that Emil was in town, and the reporters, recognizing exactly what the Attorney General had said and how he had said it, collectively decided to let it slide. In fact, Emil had taken off from Andrews Air Force Base twenty-five minutes earlier.

"Madre de Dios!" Escobedo observed. The meeting had barely gotten past the usual social pleasantries so necessary for a conference of cutthroats. All the members of the Cartel were in the same room, which happened rarely enough. Even though the building was surrounded with a literal wall of security people, they were nervous about their safety. The building had a satellite dish on the roof, and this was immediately tuned into CNN. What was supposed to have been a discussion of unexpected happenings in their smuggling operations was suddenly sidetracked onto something far more troubling. It was especially troubling for Escobedo, moreover, since he'd been one of the three Cartel members who had urged this money-laundering scheme on his colleagues. Though all had complimented him on the efficiency of the arrangement over the last two years, the looks he was getting now were somewhat less supportive.

"There is nothing we can do?" one asked.

"It is too early to tell," replied the Cartel's equivalent of a chief financial officer. "I remind

449

you that the money we have already taken completely through the arrangements nearly equals what our normal returns would be. So you can say that we have lost very little other than the gain we expected to reap from our investments." That sounded lame even to him.

"I think we have tolerated enough interference," Escobedo said forcefully. "The Director of the American *federales* will be here in Bogotá later today."

"Oh? And how did you discover this?"

"Cortez. I told you that hiring him would be to our benefit. I called this meeting to give you the information that he has gotten for us."

"This is too much to accept," another member agreed. "We should take action. It must be forceful."

There was general agreement. The Cartel had not yet learned that important decisions ought never to be taken in anger, but there was no one to counsel moderation. These men were not known for that quality in any case.

Train 111, Metroliner Service from New York, arrived a minute early at 1:48 P.M. Cortez walked off, carrying his two bags, and walked at once to the taxi stand at the front of the station. The cabdriver was delighted to have a fare to Dulles. The trip took just over thirty minutes, earning the cabbie what for Cortez was a decent tip: $2.00. He entered the upper level, walked to his left, took the escalator down, where he found the

Hertz counter. Here he rented another large Chevy and took the spare time to load his bags. By the time he returned inside, it was nearly three. Moira was right on time. They hugged. She wasn't one to kiss in so public a place.

"Where did you park?"

"In the long-term lot. I left my bags in the car."

"Then we will go and get them."

"Where are we going?"

"There is a place on Skyline Drive where General Motors occasionally holds important conferences. There are no phones in the rooms, no televisions, no newspapers."

"I know it! How did you ever get a reservation at this late notice?"

"I've been reserving a suite for every weekend since we were last together," Cortez explained truthfully. He stopped dead in his tracks. "That sounds . . . that sounds improper?" He had the halting embarrassment down pat by this time.

Moira grabbed his arm. "Not to me."

"I can tell that this will be a long weekend." Within minutes they were on Interstate 66, heading west toward the Blue Ridge Mountains.

Four embassy security officers dressed in airline coveralls gave the area a final look, then one of them pulled out a sophisticated satellite-radio phone and gave the final clearance.

The VC-20A, the military version of the G-III executive jet, flew in with a commercial setting on its radar transponder, landing at 5:39 in the afternoon at El Dorado International Airport, about eight miles outside of Bogotá. Unlike most of the VC-20As belonging to the 89th Military Airlift Wing at Andrews Air Force Base, Maryland, this one was specially modified to fly into high-threat areas and carried jamming gear originally invented by the Israelis to counter surface-to-air missiles in the hands of terrorists . . . or businessmen. The aircraft flared out and made a perfect landing into gentle westerly winds, then taxied to a distant corner of the cargo terminal, the one the cars and jeeps were heading for. The aircraft's identity was no longer a secret to anyone who'd bothered to look, of course. It had barely stopped when the first jeeps formed up on its left side. Armed soldiers dismounted and spread out, their automatic weapons pointed at threats that might have been imaginary, or might not. The aircraft's door dropped down. There were stairs built into it, but the first man off the plane didn't bother with them. He jumped, with one hand hidden in the right side of a topcoat. He was soon joined by another security guard. Each man was a special agent of the FBI, and the job of each was the physical safety of their boss, Director Emil Jacobs. They stood within the ring of Colombian soldiers, each of whom was a member of an elite counterinsurgency unit. Every man there was nervous. There was nothing routine about security in this country. Too many had died proving otherwise.

Jacobs came out next, accompanied by his own special assistant, and Harry Jefferson, Administrator of the Drug Enforcement Administration. The last of the three stepped down just as the ambassador's limousine pulled up. It didn't stop for long. The ambassador did step out to greet his guests, but all of them were inside the car a minute later. Then the soldiers remounted their jeeps, which moved off to escort the ambassador. The aircraft's crew chief closed the Gulfstream's door, and the VC-20A, whose engines had never stopped turning, immediately taxied to take off again. Its destination was the airfield at Grenada, thoughtfully built for the Americans by the Cubans only a few years before. It would be easier to guard it there.

"How was the flight, Emil?" the ambassador asked.

"Just over five hours. Not bad," the Director allowed. He leaned back on the velvet seat of the stretch limo, which was filled to capacity. In front were the ambassador's driver and bodyguard. That made a total of four machine guns in the car, and he was sure Harry Jefferson carried his service automatic. Jacobs had never carried a gun in his life, didn't wish to bother with the things. And besides, if his two bodyguards and his assistant — another crack shot — didn't suffice to protect him, what would? It wasn't that Jacobs was an especially courageous man, just that after nearly forty years of dealing with criminals of all sorts — the Chicago mob had once threatened him quite seriously — he was tired of it all. He'd grown as comfortable as any man can be with such a thing: it was part of the scenery now, and like a pattern in the wallpaper or the color of a room's paint, he no longer noticed it.

He did notice the altitude. The city of Bogotá sits at an elevation of nearly 8,700 feet, on a plain among towering mountains. There was no air to breathe here and he wondered how the ambassador tolerated it. Jacobs was more comfortable with the biting winter winds off Lake Michigan. Even the humid pall that visited Washington every summer was better than this, he thought.

"Tomorrow at nine, right?" Jacobs asked.

"Yep." The ambassador nodded. "I think they'll go along with nearly anything we want." The ambassador, of course, didn't know what the meeting was about, which did not please him. He'd worked as chargé d'affaires at Moscow, and the security *there* wasn't as tight as it was here.

"That's not the problem," Jefferson observed. "I know they mean well — they've lost enough cops and judges proving that. Question is, will they play ball?"

"Would we, under similar circumstances?" Jacobs mused, then steered the conversation in a safer direction. "You know, we've never been especially good neighbors, have we?"

"How do you mean?" the ambassador asked.

"I mean, when it suited us to have these countries run by thugs, we let it happen. When democracy finally started to take root, we often

454

as not stood at the sidelines and bitched if their ideas didn't agree fully with ours. And now that the druggies threaten their governments because of what our own citizens want to buy — we blame them."

"Democracy comes hard down here," the ambassador pointed out. "The Spanish weren't real big on — "

"If we'd done our job a hundred years ago — or even fifty years ago — we wouldn't have half the problems we have now. Well, we didn't do it then. We sure as hell have to do it now."

"If you have any suggestions, Emil — "

Jacobs laughed. "Hell, Andy, I'm a cop — well, a lawyer — not a diplomat. That's your problem. How's Kay?"

"Just fine." Ambassador Andy Westerfield didn't have to ask about Mrs. Jacobs. He knew Emil had buried his wife nine months earlier after a courageous fight with cancer. He'd taken it hard, of course, but there were so many good things to remember about Ruth. And he had a job to keep him busy. Everyone needed that, and Jacobs more than most.

In the terminal, a man with a 35mm Nikon and a long lens had been snapping pictures for the past two hours. When the limousine and its escorts started moving off the airport grounds, he removed the lens from the body, set both in his camera case, and walked off to a bank of telephones.

The limousine moved quickly, with one jeep in

front and another behind. Expensive cars with armed escorts were not terribly unusual in Colombia, and they moved out from the airport at a brisk clip. You had to spot the license plate to know that the car was American. The four men in each jeep had not known of their escort job until five minutes before they left, and the route, though predictable, wasn't a long one. There shouldn't have been time for anyone to set up an ambush — assuming that anyone would be crazy enough to consider such a thing.

After all, killing an American ambassador was crazy; it had only happened recently in the Sudan, Afghanistan, Pakistan. . . . And no one had ever made a serious attempt on an FBI Director.

The car they drove in was a Cadillac Fleetwood chassis. Its special equipment included thick Lexan windows that could stop a machine-gun bullet, and Kevlar armor all around the passenger compartment. The tires were foam-filled against flattening, and the gas tank of a design similar to that used on military aircraft as protection against explosion. Not surprisingly, the car was known in the embassy motor pool as the Tank.

The driver knew how to handle it as skillfully as a NASCAR professional. He had engine power to race at over a hundred miles per hour; he could throw the three-ton vehicle into a bootlegger turn and reverse directions like a movie stunt driver. His eyes flickered between the road ahead and the rearview mirror. There had been one car following them, for two or three miles, but it turned off. Probably nothing, he judged. Somebody else coming home from the airport. . . . The car also had sophisticated radio gear to call for help. They were heading to the embassy. Though the ambassador had a separate residence, a pretty two-story house set on six sculpted acres of garden and woodland, it wasn't secure enough for his visitors. Like most contemporary American embassies, this one looked to be a cross between a low-rise office block and part of the Siegfried Line.

VOX IDENT, his computer screen read, two thousand miles away: VOICE 34 INIT CALL TO UNKNOWN RECIP FRQ 889.980MHZ CALL INIT 2258Z INTERCEPT IDENT 381.

Tony donned the headphones and listened in on the tape-delay system.

"Nothing," he said a moment later. "Somebody's taking a drive."

At the embassy, the legal attaché paced nervously in the lobby. Special Agent Pete Morales of the FBI should have been at the airport. It was *his* director coming in, but the security pukes said only one car because it was a surprise visit — and surprise, everyone knew, was better than a massive show of force. The everybodies who knew did not include Morales, who believed in showing force. It was bad enough having to live down here. Morales was from California; though his surname was Hispanic, his family had been in the San Francisco area when Major Frémont had arrived, and he'd had to brush up on his somewhat removed mother tongue to take his current job, which job also meant leaving his wife and kids behind in the States. As his most recent report had told headquarters, it was dangerous down here. Dangerous for the local citizens, dangerous for Americans, and very dangerous indeed for American cops.

Morales checked his watch. About two more minutes. He started moving to the door.

"Right on time," a man noted three blocks from the embassy. He spoke into a hand-held radio.

Until recently, the RPG-7D had been the standard-issue Soviet light antitank weapon. It traces its ancestry to the German Panzerfaust, and was only recently replaced by the RPG-18, a close copy of the American M-72 LAW rocket. The adoption of the new weapon allowed millions of the old ones to be disposed of, adding to the already abundant supply in arms bazaars all over the world. Designed to punch holes in battle tanks, it is not an especially easy weapon to use. Which was why there were four of them aimed at the ambassador's limousine.

The car proceeded south, down Carrera 13 in the district known as Palermo, slowing now because of the traffic. Had the Director's bodyguards known the name of the district and designation of the street, they might have objected merely on grounds of superstition. The slow speed of the traffic here in the city itself made everyone nervous, especially the soldiers in the escort jeeps who craned their necks looking up into the windows of various buildings. It is a fact so obvious as to be misunderstood that one cannot ordinarily look into a window from outside. Even an open window is merely a rectangle darker than the exterior wall, and the eye adjusts to ambient light, not to light in a specific place. There was no warning.

What made the deaths of the Americans inevitable was something as prosaic as a traffic light. A technician was working on a balky signal — people had been complaining about it for a week — and while checking the timing mechanism, he flipped it to red. Everyone stopped on the street, almost within sight of the embassy. From third-floor windows on both sides of the street, four separate RPG-7D projectiles streaked straight down. Three hit the car, two of them on the roof.

The flash was enough. Morales was moving even before the noise reached the embassy gates, and he ran with full knowledge of the futility of the gesture. His right hand wrenched his Smith & Wesson automatic from the waist holster, and he carried it as training prescribed, pointed straight up. It took just over two minutes.

The driver was still alive, thrown from the car and bleeding to death from holes that no doctor could ever patch in time. The soldiers in the lead jeep were nowhere to be seen, though there was blood on a rear seat. The trail jeep's driver was still at the wheel, his hands clutching at a face shredded with broken glass, and the man next to him was dead, but again the other two were gone —

Then Morales knew why. Automatic weapons fire erupted in a building to his left. It started, stopped, then began again. A scream came from a window, and that also stopped. Morales wanted to race into the building, but he had no jurisdiction, and was too much a professional to risk his life so foolishly. He moved up to the smashed limousine. He knew that this, too, was futile.

They'd all died instantly, or as quickly as any man might die. The Director's two bodyguards had worn Kevlar armor. That would stop bullets, but not fragments from a high-explosive warhead, and had proven no more effective than the armor in the Tank. Morales knew what had hit the car — weapons designed to destroy tanks. Real ones. For those inside, the only remarkable thing was that you could tell that they had once been human. There was nothing anyone could do, except a priest . . . or rabbi. Morales turned away after a few seconds.

He stood alone in the street, still operating on his professional training, not letting his humanity affect his judgment. The one living soldier in view was too injured to move — probably had no idea where he was or what had happened to him. None of the people on the sidewalk had come to help . . . but some of them, he saw, were hurt, too, and their injuries occupied the attention of the others. Morales realized that the damage to the car told everyone else in view where they might best spend their efforts. The agent turned to scan up and down the street. He didn't see the technician at the light-control box. The man was already gone.

Two soldiers came out of a building, one carrying what looked like an RPG-7 launcher unit. Morales recognized one of them, Captain Edmundo Garza. There was blood on his khaki shirt and pants, and in his eyes the wild look that Morales hadn't seen since his time in the Marine Corps. Behind him, two more men dragged yet another who'd been shot in the arms and the groin. Morales holstered his automatic before going over, slowly, his hands visible until he was sure he'd been recognized.

"*Capitán* . . . " Morales said.

"One more dead upstairs, and one of mine. Four teams. Getaway cars in the alleys." Garza looked at the blood on his upper arm with annoyance that was rapidly changing to appreciation of his wounds. But there was something more than shock to postpone the pain. The captain looked at the car for the first time in several minutes, hoping that his immediate impression might have been wrong and knowing that it could not be. His

461

handsome, bloody face looked at the American and received a shake by way of reply. Garza was a proud man, a professional soldier dedicated to his country as thoroughly as any man could be, and he'd been chosen for this assignment for his combination of skill and integrity. A man who did not fear death, he had just suffered the thing all soldiers fear more. He had failed in his mission. Not knowing why only made it worse.

Garza continued to ignore his wounds, turning to their one prisoner. "We will talk," the captain promised him just before he collapsed into Morales' arms.

"Hi, Jack!" Dan and Liz Murray had just arrived at the Ryan house. Dan had to remove his automatic and holster, which he set on the shelf in the closet with something of a sheepish look.

"I figured you for a revolver," Jack said with a grin. It was the first time that they'd had the Murrays over.

"I miss my Python, but the Bureau's switching over to automatics. Besides, I don't chase bad guys anymore. I chase memos, and position papers, and budget estimates." A rueful shake of the head. "What fun."

"I know the feeling," Ryan agreed, leading Murray to the kitchen. "Beer?"

"Sounds good to me."

They'd first met in London, at St. Thomas's Hospital to be precise, some years earlier when Murray had been legal attaché to the American

Embassy, and Ryan had been a shooting victim. Still tall and spare, his hair a little thinner but not yet gray, Murray was an affable, free-spirited man whom one would never pick for a cop, much less one of the best around. A gifted investigator, he'd hunted down every sort of criminal there was, and though he now chafed at his absence from hands-on police work, he was handling his administrative job as skillfully as all his others.

"What's this sting I heard about?" Jack asked.

"TARPON? The Cartel murdered a guy who was laundering money for them on a very big scale — and doing some major-league skimming, too. He left records behind. We found them. It's been a busy couple of weeks running all the leads down."

"I heard six-hundred-plus-million bucks."

"It'll go higher. The Swiss cracked open a new account this afternoon."

"Ouch." Ryan popped open a couple of beers. "That's a real sting, isn't it?"

"I think they'll notice this one," Murray agreed. "What's this I hear about your new job?"

"You probably heard right. It's just that you don't want to get a promotion this way."

"Yeah. I've never met Admiral Greer, but the Director thinks a lot of him."

"Two of a kind. Old-fashioned honorable gentlemen," Jack observed. "Endangered species."

"Hello, Mr. Murray," Sally Ryan said from the door.

"Mister Murray?"

"Uncle Dan!" Sally raced up and delivered a ferocious hug. "Aunt Liz says that you and Daddy better get out there," she said with a giggle.

"Why do we let them push us warriors around, Jack?"

" 'Cause they're tougher than we are?" Ryan wondered.

Dan laughed. "Yeah, that explains it. I —" Then his beeper went off. Murray pulled the small plastic box from his belt. In a moment the LCD panel showed the number he was supposed to call. "You know, I'd like to waste the bastard who invented these things."

"He's already dead," Jack replied deadpan. "He came into a hospital emergency room with chest pains, and after the doc figured out who he was, they were a little slow getting around to treating him. The doc explained later that he had had an important phone call come in, and . . . oh, well. . . . " Ryan's demeanor changed. "You need a secure line? I have one in the library."

"Color me important," Murray observed. "No. Can I use this one?"

"Sure, the bottom button's a D.C. line."

Murray punched in the number without referring to his beeper. It was Shaw's office. "Murray here. You rang, Alice? Okay . . . Hi, Bill, what gives?"

It was as though the room took a sudden chill. Ryan felt it before he understood the change in Murray's face.

"No chance that — oh, yeah, I know Pete." Murray checked his watch. "Be there in forty minutes." He hung up.

"What happened?"

"Somebody killed the Director," Dan answered simply.

"What — where?"

"Bogotá. He was down for a quiet meeting, along with the head of DEA. Flew down this afternoon. They kept it real quiet."

"No chance that — "

Murray shook his head. "The attaché down there's Pete Morales. Good agent, I worked OC with him once. He said they were all killed instantly. Emil, Harry Jefferson, the ambassador, all the security guys." He stopped and read the look on Jack's face. "Yeah, somebody had some pretty good intel on this."

Ryan nodded. "This is where I came in. . . . "

"I don't think there's a street agent in the Bureau who doesn't love that man." Murray set his beer down on the counter.

"Sorry, pal."

"What was it you said? Endangered species?" Murray shook his head and went to collect his wife. Ryan hadn't even closed the door behind them when his secure phone started ringing.

The Hideaway, located only a few miles from the Luray Caverns, was a modern building despite its deliberate lack of some modern amenities. While there was no in-room cable television, no pay-for-view satellite service, no complimentary paper outside the door every morning, there was air conditioning, running water, and the room-service menu was six pages long, supplemented by ten full pages of wine listings. The hotel catered to newlyweds who needed few distractions and to others trying to save their marriages from distractions. Service was on the European model. The guest wasn't expected to do anything but eat, drink, and rumple the linen, though there were saddle horses, tennis courts, and a swimming pool for those few whose suite didn't include a bathtub large enough for the purpose. Moira watched her lover tip the bellman ten dollars — far more than he ever tipped anyone — before she thought to ask the most obvious question.

"How did you register?"

"Mr. and Mrs. Juan Díaz." Another embarrassed look. "Forgive me, but I didn't know what else to say. I didn't think" — he lied haltingly. "And I didn't want — what could I say without embarrassing myself?" he finally asked with a frustrated gesture.

"Well, I need a shower. Since we are husband and wife, you may join me. It looks big enough for two." She walked from the room, dropping her silk blouse on the bed as she went.

Five minutes later, Cortez decided that the shower was easily big enough for four. But as things turned out, that was just as well.

The President had flown to Camp David for the weekend, and had barely showered himself when his junior military aide — a Marine lieutenant had the duty — brought him the cordless phone.

"Yes — what is it?"

The lieutenant's first reaction on seeing the President's expression was to wonder where his pistol was.

"I want the Attorney General, Admiral Cutter, Judge Moore, and Bob Ritter flown here immediately. Tell the press secretary to call me in fifteen minutes to work on the statement. I'll be staying here for the time being. What about bringing them back home? Okay — we have a couple of hours to think about that. For now, the usual protocol. That's right. No, nothing from State. I'll handle it from here, then the secretary can have his say. Thank you." The President pushed the kill button on the phone and handed it back to the Marine.

"Sir, is there anything that the guard detail needs — "

"No." The President explained briefly what had happened. "Carry on, Lieutenant."

"Aye aye, sir." The Marine left.

The President put on his bathrobe and walked over to the mirror to comb his hair. He had to use the terrycloth of his sleeve to wipe the condensation off the glass. Had he noticed, he would have wondered why the look in his eyes didn't shatter it.

"Okay," the President of the United States told the mirror. "So you bastards want to play. . . ."

The flight from Andrews to Camp David was made in one of the new VH-60 Blackhawk helicopters that the 89th Military Airlift Wing had just acquired. Plushly appointed to carry VIPs from place to place, it was still too noisy for anything approximating a normal conversation. Each of the four passengers stared out the windows on the sliding doors, watching the western Maryland hills slide beneath the aircraft, each alone with his grief and his anger. The trip took twenty minutes. The pilot had been told to hurry.

On touching down, the four men were loaded into a car for the short drive to the President's cabin on the grounds. They found him hanging up the phone. It had taken half an hour to locate his press secretary, further exacerbating the President's already stormy mood.

Admiral Cutter started to say something about how sorry everyone was, but the President's expression cut him short.

The President sat down on a couch opposite the fireplace. In front of him was what most people ordinarily took to be a coffee table, but now, with the top removed, it was a set of computer screens and quiet thermal printers that tapped into the major news wire services and other government information channels. Four television sets were in the next room, tuned into CNN and the major networks. The four visitors stared down at him, watching the anger come off the President like steam from a boiling pot.

"We will not let this one slip past with us standing by and deploring the event," the President said quietly as he looked up. "They killed my friend. They killed my ambassador. They have directly challenged the sovereign power of the United States of America. They want to play with the big boys," the President went on in a voice that was grotesquely calm. "Well, they're going to have to play by the big boys' rules. Peter," he said to the AG, "there is now an informal Presidential Finding that the drug Cartel has initiated an undeclared war against the government of the United States. They have chosen to act like a hostile nation-state. We will treat them as we would treat a hostile nation-state. As President, I am resolved to carry the fight to the enemy as we would carry it to any other originator of state-sponsored terrorism."

The AG didn't like that, but nodded agreement anyway. The President turned to Moore and Ritter.

"The gloves come off. I just made the usual wimpy-ass statement for my press secretary to deliver, but the fucking gloves come off. Come up with a plan. I want these bastards hurt. No more of this 'sending a message' crap. I want them to get the message whether the phone rings or not. Mr. Ritter, you have your hunting license, and there's no bag limit. Is that sufficiently clear?"

"Yes, sir," the DDO answered. Actually, it wasn't. The President hadn't said "kill" once, as the tape recorders that were surely somewhere in this room would show. But there were some things that you didn't do, and one of them was that you did not force the President to speak clearly when clarity was something he wished to avoid.

"Find yourselves a cabin and come up with a plan. Peter, I want you to stay here with me for a while." The next message: the Attorney General, once having acceded to the President's desire to Do Something, didn't need to know exactly what was going to be done. Admiral Cutter, who was more familiar with Camp David than the other two, led the way to one of the guest cabins. Since he was in front, Moore and Ritter could not see the smile on his face.

Ryan was just getting to his office, having driven himself in, a habit which he had just unlearned. The senior intelligence watch officer was waiting for him in the corridor as Jack got off the elevator. The briefing took a whole four minutes, after which Ryan found himself sitting in the office with nothing at all to do. It was strange. He was now privy to everything the U.S. government knew about the assassination of its people — not much more than what he'd heard on the car radio coming in, actually, though he now had names to put on the "unnamed sources." Sometimes that was important, but not this time. The

DCI and DDO, he learned at once, were up at Camp David with the President.

Why not me? Jack asked himself in surprise.

It should have occurred to him immediately, of course, but he was not yet used to being a senior executive. With nothing to do, his mind went along that tangent for several minutes. The conclusion was an obvious one. He didn't need to know what was being talked about — but that had to mean that something was *already* happening, didn't it . . . ? If so, what? And for how long?

By noon the next day, an Air Force C-141B Starlifter transport had landed at El Dorado International. Security was like nothing anyone had seen since the funeral of Anwar Sadat. Armed helicopters circled overhead. Armored vehicles sat with their gun tubes trained outward. A full battalion of paratroops ringed the airport, which was shut down for three hours. That didn't count the honor guard, of course, all of whom felt as though they had no honor at all, that it had been stripped away from their army and their nation by . . . *them.*

Esteban Cardinal Valdéz prayed over the coffins, accompanied by the chief rabbi of Bogotá's small Jewish community. The Vice President attended on behalf of the American government, and one by one the Colombian Army handed the caskets over to enlisted pallbearers from all of the American uniformed services. The usual, predictable speeches were made, the most eloquent being a brief address by Colombia's Attorney General, who shed unashamed tears for his friend and college classmate. The Vice President boarded his aircraft and left, followed by the big Lockheed transport.

The President's statement, already delivered, spoke of reaffirming the rule of law to which Emil Jacobs had dedicated his life. But that statement seemed as thin as the air at El Dorado International even to those who didn't know better.

In the town of Eight Mile, Alabama, a suburb of Mobile, a police sergeant named Ernie Braden was cutting his front lawn with a riding mower. A burglary investigator, he knew all the tricks of the people whose crimes he handled, including how to bypass complex alarm systems, even the sophisticated models used by wealthy investment bankers. That skill, plus the information he picked up from office chatter — the narcs' bullpen was right next to the burglary section — enabled him to offer his services to people who had money with which to pay for the orthodonture and education of his children. It wasn't so much that Braden was a corrupt cop as that he'd simply been on the job for over twenty years and no longer gave much of a damn. If people wanted to use drugs, then the hell with them. If druggies wanted to kill one another off, then so much the better for the rest of society. And if some arrogant prick of a banker turned out to be a crook among crooks, then that also was too bad; all Braden had been asked to do was shake the man's house to make sure that he'd left no records behind. It was a shame about the man's wife and kids, of course, but that was called playing with fire.

Braden rationalized the damage done to society simply by continuing to investigate his burglaries, and even catching a real hood from time to time, though that was rare enough. Burglary was a pretty safe crime to commit. It never got the attention it deserved. Neither did the people whose job it was to track them down — probably the most unrewarded segment of the law-enforcement profession. He'd been taking the lieutenant's exam for nine years, and never quite made it. Braden needed or at least wanted the money that the promotion would bring, only to see the promotions go to the hotshots in Narcotics and Homicide while he slaved away . . . and why not take the goddamned money? More than anything else, Ernie Braden was tired of it all. Tired of the long hours. Tired of the crime victims who took their frustration out on him when he was just trying to do his job. Tired of being unappreciated within his own community of police officers. Tired of being sent out to local schools for the *pro forma* anticrime lectures that nobody ever listened to. He was even tired of coaching little-league baseball, though that had once been the single joy of his life. Tired of just about everything. But he couldn't afford to retire, either. Not yet, anyway.

The noise from the Sears riding mower crackled through the hot, humid air of the quiet street on which he and his family lived. He wiped a handkerchief across his sweaty brow and contemplated the cold beer he'd have as soon as he was finished. It could have been worse. Until three years ago he'd pushed a goddamned Lawn-Boy across the grass. At least now he could sit down as he did his weekly chore, cutting the goddamned grass. His wife had a real thing about the lawn and garden. As if it mattered, Braden grumbled.

He concentrated on the job at hand, making sure that the spinning blades had at least two sweeps over every square inch of the green crap that, this early in the season, grew almost as fast as you cut it. He didn't notice the Plymouth minivan coming down the street. Nor did he know that the people who paid him his supplementary income were most unhappy with a recent clandestine effort he'd made on their behalf.

Braden had several eccentricities, as do many men and most police officers. In his case, he never went anywhere unarmed. Not even to cut the grass. Under the back of his greasy shirt was a Smith & Wesson Chief's Special, a five-shot stainless steel revolver that was as close as he'd ever get to something with "chief" written on it. When he finally noticed the minivan pull up behind his Chevy Citation, he took little note of it, except that there were two men in it, and they seemed to be looking at him.

His cop's instinct didn't entirely fail him, however. They were looking real hard at him. That made him look back, mainly in curiosity. Who'd be interested in him on a Saturday afternoon? When the passenger-side door opened and he saw the gun, that question faded away.

When Braden rolled off the mower, his foot came off the brake pedal, which had the opposite effect as in a car. The mower stopped in two feet, its blades still churning away on the bluegrass-and-fescue mix of the policeman's front yard. Braden came off just at the ejection port of the mower assembly, and felt tiny bits of grit and sand peppering his knees, but that, too, was not a matter of importance at the moment. His revolver was already out when the man from the van fired his first round.

He was using an Ingram Mac-10, probably a 9-millimeter, and the man didn't know how to use it well. His first round was roughly on target, but the next eight merely decorated the sky as the notoriously unstable weapon jerked out of control, not even hitting the mower. Sergeant Braden fired two rounds back, but the range was over ten yards, and the Chief's Special had only a two-inch barrel, which gave it an effective combat range measured in feet, not yards. With the instant and unexpected stress added to his poorly selected weapon, he managed to hit the van behind his target with only one round.

But machine-gun fire is a highly distinctive sound — not the least mistakable for firecrackers or any other normal noise — and the neighborhood immediately realized that something very unusual was happening. At a house across the street a fifteen-year-old boy was cleaning his rifle. It was a old Marlin .22 lever-action that had once belonged to his grandfather, and its proud owner had learned to play third base from Sergeant Braden, whom he thought to be a really neat guy. The young man in question, Erik Sanderson, set down his cleaning gear and walked to the window just in time to see his former coach shooting from behind his mower at somebody. In the clarity that comes in such moments, Erik Sanderson realized that people were trying to kill his coach, a police officer, that he had a rifle and cartridges ten feet away, and that it Would Be All Right for him to use the rifle to come to the aid of the policeman. The fact that he'd spent the morning plinking away at tin cans merely meant that he was ready. Erik Sanderson's main ambition in life was to become a U.S. Marine, and he seized the chance to get an early feel for what it was all about.

While the sound of gunfire continued to crackle around the wooded street, he grabbed the rifle and a handful of the small copper-colored rimfire cartridges and ran out to the front porch. First he twisted the spring-loaded rod that pushed rounds down the magazine tube which hung under the barrel. He pulled it out too far, dropping it, but the young man had the good sense to ignore that for the moment. He fed the .22 rounds into the loading slot one at a time, surprised that his hands were already sweaty. When he had fourteen rounds in, he bent down to get the rod, and two rounds fell out the front of the tube. He took the time to reload them, reinserted the rod, twisting it shut, then slammed his hand down and up on the lever, loading the gun and cocking the exposed hammer.

He was surprised to see that he didn't have a shot, and ran down the sidewalk to the street, taking a position across the hood of his father's pickup truck. From this point he could see two men, each firing a submachine gun from the hip. He looked just in time to see Sergeant Braden fire off his last round, which missed as badly as the first four had. The police officer turned to run for the safety of his house, but tripped over his own feet and had trouble getting up. Both gunmen advanced on Braden, loading new magazines into their weapons. Erik Sanderson's hands were trembling as he shouldered his rifle. It had old-fashioned iron sights, and he had to stop and remind himself how to line them up as he'd been taught in Boy Scouts, with the front-sight post centered in the notch of the rear-sight leaf, the top of the post even with the top of the leaf as he maneuvered it on a target.

He was horrified to be too late. Both men blew his little-league coach to shreds with extended bursts at point-blank range. Something snapped inside Erik's head at that moment. He sighted on the head of the nearer gunman and jerked off his round.

Like most young and inexperienced shooters, he immediately looked up to see what had happened. Nothing. He'd missed — with a rifle at a range of only thirty yards, he'd missed. Amazed, he sighted again and squeezed the trigger, but nothing happened. The hammer was down. He'd forgotten to cock the rifle. Swearing something his mother would have slapped him to hear, he reloaded the Marlin .22 and took exquisitely careful aim, squeezing off his next shot.

The murderers hadn't heard his first shot, and with their ears still ringing from their own shots, they didn't hear the second, but one man's head jerked to the side with the wasp's-sting impact of the round. The man knew what had happened, turned to his left, and fired off a long burst despite the crushing pain that seized his head in an instant. The other one saw Erik and fired as well.

But the young man was now jacking rounds into the breech of his rifle as fast as he could fire them. He watched in rage as he kept missing, unconsciously flinching as bullets came his way, trying to kill both men before they could get back into their car. He had the satisfaction of seeing them duck behind cover, and wasted his last three rounds trying to shoot through the car body to get them. But a .22 can't accomplish that, and the minivan pulled away.

Erik watched it pull away, wishing he'd loaded more rounds into his rifle, wishing that he could try a shot through the back window before the car turned right and disappeared.

The young man didn't have the courage to go over and see what had happened to Sergeant Braden. He just stayed there, leaning across the truck, cursing himself for letting them get away. He didn't know, and would never believe, that he had, in fact, done better than many trained police officers could have done.

In the minivan, one of the gunmen took more note of the bullet in his chest than the one in his head. But it was the head shot that would kill him. As the man bent down, a lacerated artery let go completely and showered the inside of the car with blood, much to the surprise of the dying man, who had but a few seconds to realize what had happ —

Another Air Force flight, as luck had it, also a C-141B, took Mr. Clark out of Panama, heading for Andrews, where rapid preparations were being made for the arrival ceremony. Before the funeral flight arrived, Clark was in Langley talking to his boss, Bob Ritter. For the first time in a generation, the Operations Directorate had been granted a presidential hunting license. John Clark, carried on the personnel rolls as a case-officer instructor, was the CIA chief hunter. He hadn't been asked to exercise that particular talent in a very long time, but he still knew how.

Ritter and Clark didn't watch the TV coverage of the arrival. All that was part of history now, and while both men had an interest in history, it was mainly in the sort that is never written down.

"We're going to take another look at the idea you handed me at St. Kitts," the Deputy Director (Operations) said.

"What's the objective?" Clark asked carefully. It wasn't hard to guess why this was happening, or the originator of the directive. That was the reason for his caution.

"The short version is revenge," Ritter answered.

"Retribution is a more acceptable word," Clark pointed out. Lacking in formal education though he was, he did read a good deal.

"The targets represent a clear and present danger to the security of the United States."

"The President said that?"

"His words," Ritter affirmed.

"Fine. That makes it all legal. Not any less dangerous, but legal."

"Can you do it?"

Clark smiled in a distant, smoky way. "I run my side of the op my way. Otherwise, forget it. I don't want to die from oversight. No interference from this end. You give me the target list and the assets I need. I do the rest, my way, my schedule."

"Agreed," Ritter nodded.

Clark was more than surprised by that. "Then I can do it. What about the kids we have running around in the jungle?"

480

"We're pulling them out tonight."

"To be reinserted where?" Clark asked.

Ritter told him.

"That's really dangerous," the case officer observed, though he was not surprised by the answer. It had probably been planned all along. But, if it had . . .

"We know that."

"I don't like it," Clark said after a moment's thought. "It complicates things."

"We don't pay you to like it."

Clark had to agree to that. He was honest enough with himself, though, to admit that part of it he did like. A job such as this, after all, had gotten him into the protective embrace of the Central Intelligence Agency in the first place, so many years before. But that job had been on a free-agent basis. This one was legal, but arguably. Once that would not have mattered to Mr. Clark, but with a wife and kids, it did now.

"Do I get to see the family for a couple of days?"

"Sure. It'll take awhile to get things in place. I'll have all the information you need messengered down to The Farm."

"What do we call this one?"

"RECIPROCITY."

"I guess that about covers it." Clark's face broke into a grin. He walked out of the room toward the elevator. The new DDI was there, Dr. Ryan, heading to Judge Moore's office.

They'd never quite met, Clark and Ryan, and this wasn't the time, though their lives had already touched on two occasions.

14.

Snatch and Grab

"I must thank your Director Jacobs," Juan said. "Perhaps we will meet someday." He'd taken his time with this one. Soon, he judged, he'd be able to extract any information he wanted from her with the same intimate confidence that might be expected of husband and wife — after all, true love did not allow for secrets, did it?

"Perhaps," Moira replied after a moment. Already part of her was thinking that the Director would come to her wedding. It wasn't too much to hope for, was it?

"What did he travel to Colombia for, anyway?" he asked while his fingertips did some more exploring over what was now very familiar ground.

"Well, it's public information now. They called it Operation TARPON." Moira explained on for several minutes during which Juan's caresses didn't miss a beat.

Which was only due to his experience as an

intelligence officer. He actually found himself smiling lazily at the ceiling. *The fool. I warned him. I warned him more than once in his own office, but no — he was too smart, too confident in his own cleverness to take my advice. Well, maybe the stupid bastard will heed my advice now.* . . . It took another few moments before he found himself asking how his employer would react. That was when the smiling and the caresses stopped.

"Something wrong, Juan?"

"Your director picked a dangerous time to visit Bogotá. They will be very angry. If they discover that he is there — "

"The trip is a secret. Their attorney general is an old friend — I think they went to school together, and they've known each other for forty years."

The trip was a secret. Cortez told himself that they couldn't be so foolish as to — but they could. He was amazed that Moira didn't feel the chill that swept over his body. But what could he do?

As was true of the families of military people and sales executives, Clark's family was accustomed to having him away at short notice and for irregular intervals. They were also used to having him reappear without much in the way of warning. It was almost a game, and one, strangely enough, to which his wife didn't object. In this case he took a car from the CIA pool and made the two-and-a-half-hour drive to Yorktown, Virginia, by himself to think over the operation he was about to undertake. By the time he turned off Interstate 64, he'd answered most of the procedural questions, though the exact details would wait until he'd had a chance to go over the intelligence package that Ritter had promised to send down.

Clark's house was that of a middle-level executive, a four-bedroom split-foyer brick dwelling set in an acre of the long-needled pines common to the American South. It was a ten-minute drive from The Farm, the CIA's training establishment whose post-office address is Williamsburg, Virginia, but which is actually closer to Yorktown, adjacent to an installation in which the Navy keeps both submarine-launched ballistic missiles and their nuclear warheads. The development in which he lived was mainly occupied by other CIA instructors, obviating the need for elaborate stories for the neighbors' benefit. His family, of course, had a pretty good idea what he did for a living. His two daughters, Maggie, seventeen, and Patricia, fourteen, occasionally called him "Secret Agent Man," which they'd picked up from the revival of the Patrick McGoohan TV series on one of the cable channels, but they knew not to discuss it with their schoolmates — though they would occasionally warn their boyfriends to behave as responsibly as possible around their father. It was an unnecessary warning. On instinct, most men watched their behavior around Mr. Clark. John Clark did not have horns and hooves, but it seldom took more than a single glance to know that he was not to be trifled with, either. His wife, Sandy, knew even more, including what he had done before joining the Agency. Sandy was a registered nurse who taught student nurses in the operating rooms of the local teaching hospital. As such she was accustomed to dealing with issues of life and death, and she took comfort from the fact that her husband was one of the few "laymen" who understood what that was all about, albeit from a reversed perspective. To his wife and children, John Terence Clark was a devoted husband and father, if somewhat overly protective at times. Maggie had once complained that he'd scared off one prospective "steady" with nothing more than a look. That the boy in question had later been arrested for drunken driving had only proved her father correct, rather to her chagrin. He was also a far easier touch than their mother on issues like privileges and had a ready shoulder to cry on, when he was home. At home, his counsel was invariably quiet and reasoned, his language mild, and his demeanor relaxed, but his family knew that away from home he was something else entirely. They didn't care about that.

He pulled into the driveway just before dinnertime, taking his soft two-suiter in through the kitchen to find the smells of a decent dinner. Sandy had been surprised too many times to overreact on the matter of how much food she'd prepared.

"Where have you been?" Sandy asked rhetorically, then went into her usual guessing game. "Not much work done on the tan. Someplace cold or cloudy?"

"Spent most of my time indoors," Clark replied honestly. *Stuck with a couple of clowns in a damned commo van on a hilltop surrounded by jungle. Just like the bad old days. Almost.* For all her intelligence, she almost never guessed where he'd been. But then, she wasn't supposed to.

"How long . . . ?"

"Only a couple of days, then I have to go out again. It's important."

"Anything to do with — " Her head jerked toward the kitchen TV.

Clark just smiled and shook his head.

"What do you think happened?"

"From what I see, the druggies got real lucky," he said lightly.

Sandy knew what her husband thought of druggies, and why. Everyone had a pet hate. That was his — and hers; she'd been a nurse too long, had too often seen the results of substance abuse, to think otherwise. It was the one thing he'd lectured the girls on, and though they were as rebellious as any pair of healthy adolescents, it was one line they didn't approach, much less cross.

"The President sounds angry."

"How would you feel? The FBI Director was his friend — as far as a politician has friends." Clark felt the need to qualify the statement. He

487

was wary of political figures, even the ones he'd voted for.

"What is he going to do about it?"

"I don't know, Sandy." *I haven't quite figured it out yet.* "Where are the kids?"

"They went to Busch Gardens with their friends. There's a new coaster, and they're probably screaming their brains out."

"Do I have time to shower? I've been traveling all day."

"Dinner in thirty minutes."

"Fine." He kissed her again and headed for the bedroom with his bag. Before entering the bathroom, he emptied his dirty laundry into the hamper. Clark would give himself one restful day with the family before starting on his mission planning. There wasn't that much of a hurry. For missions of this sort, haste made death. He hoped the politicians would understand that.

Of course, they wouldn't, he told himself on the way to the shower. They never did.

"Don't feel bad," Moira told him. "You're tired. I'm sorry I've worn you out." She cradled his face to her chest. A man was not a machine, after all, and five times in just over one day's time . . . what could she fairly expect of her lover? He had to sleep, had to rest. As did she, Moira realized, drifting off herself.

Within minutes, Cortez gently disengaged himself, watching her slow, steady breathing, a dreamy smile on her placid face while he wondered what the hell he could do. If anything. Place a phone call — risk everything for a brief conversation on a nonsecure line? The Colombian police or the Americans, or *somebody* had to have taps on all those phones. No, that was more dangerous than doing nothing at all.

His professionalism told him that the safest course of action was to do nothing. Cortez looked down at himself. Nothing was precisely what he had just accomplished. It was the first time that had happened in a very long time.

Team KNIFE, of course, was completely — if not blissfully — unaware of what had transpired the previous day. The jungle had no news service, and their radio was for official use only. That made the new message all the more surprising. Chavez and Vega were again on duty at the observation post, enduring the muggy heat that followed a violent thunderstorm. There had been two inches of rain in the previous hour, and their observation point was now a shallow puddle, and there would be more rain in the afternoon before things cleared off.

Captain Ramirez appeared, without much in the way of warning this time, even to Chavez, whose woodcraft skills were a matter of considerable pride. He rationalized to himself that the captain had learned from watching him.

"Hey, Cap'n," Vega greeted their officer.

"Anything going on?" Ramirez asked.

Chavez answered from behind his binoculars.

"Well, our two friends are enjoying their morning siesta." There would be another in the afternoon, of course. He was pulled away from the lenses by the captain's next statement.

"I hope they like it. It's their last one."

"Say again, Cap'n?" Vega asked.

"The chopper's coming in to pick us up tonight. That's the LZ right there, troops." Ramirez pointed to the airstrip. "We waste this place before we leave."

Chavez evaluated that statement briefly. He'd never liked druggies. Having to sit here and watch the lazy bastards go about their business as matter-of-factly as a man on a golf course hadn't mitigated his feelings a dot.

Ding nodded. "Okay, Cap'n. How we gonna do it, sir?"

"Soon as it's dark, you and me circle around the north side. Rest of the squad forms up in two fire teams to provide fire support in case we need it. Vega, you and your SAW stay here. The other one goes down about four hundred meters. After we do the two guards, we booby-trap the fuel drums in the shack, just as a farewell present. The chopper'll pick us up at the far end at twenty-three hundred. We bring the bodies out with us, probably dump 'em at sea."

Well, how about that, Chavez thought. "We'll need like thirty-forty minutes to get around to them, just to play it safe and all, but the way those two fuckers been actin', no sweat, sir." The sergeant knew that the killing would be his job.

He had the silenced weapon.

"You're supposed to ask me if this is for-real," Captain Ramirez pointed out. He had done just that over the satellite radio.

"Sir, you say do it, I figure it's for-real. It don't bother me none," Staff Sergeant Domingo Chavez assured his commander.

"Okay — we'll move out as soon as it's dark."

"Yes, sir."

The captain patted both men on the shoulder and withdrew to the rally point. Chavez watched him leave, then pulled out his canteen. He unscrewed the plastic top and took a long pull before looking over at Vega.

"*Fuck!*" the machine-gunner observed quietly.

"Whoever's runnin' this party musta grown a pair o' balls," Ding agreed.

"Be nice to get back to a place with showers and air conditioning," Vega said next. That two people would have to die to make that possible was, once it was decided, a matter of small consequence. It bemused both men somewhat that after years of uniformed service they were finally being told to do the very thing for which they'd trained endlessly. The moral issue never occurred to them. They were soldiers of their country. Their country had decided that those two dozing men a few hundred meters away were enemies worthy of death. That was that, though both men wondered what it would actually be like to do it.

"Let's plan this one out," Chavez said, getting

491

back to his binoculars. "I want you to be careful with that SAW, *Oso.*"

Vega considered the situation. "I won't fire to the left of the shack unless you call in."

"Yeah, okay. I'll come in from the direction of that big-ass tree. Shouldn't be no big deal," he thought aloud.

"Nah, shouldn't be."

Except that this time it was all real. Chavez stayed on the glasses, examining the men whom he would kill in a few hours.

Colonel Johns got his stand-to order at roughly the same time as all of the field teams, along with a whole new set of tactical maps that were for further study. He and Captain Willis went over the plan for this night in the privacy of their room. There was a snatch-and-grab tonight. The troops they'd inserted were coming back out far earlier than scheduled. PJ suspected that he knew why. Part of it, anyway.

"Right on the airfields?" the captain wondered.

"Yeah, well, either all four were dry holes, or our friends are going to have to secure them before we land for the snatch-and-grab."

"Oh." Captain Willis understood after a moment's thought.

"Get ahold of Buck and have him check the miniguns out again. He'll get the message from that. I want to take a look at the weather for tonight."

492

"Pickup order reverse from the drop-off?"

"Yeah — we'll tank fifty miles off the beach and then again after we make the pickup."

"Right." Willis walked out to find Sergeant Zimmer. PJ went in the opposite direction, heading for the base meteorological office. The weather for tonight was disappointing: light winds, clear skies, and a crescent moon. Perfect flying weather for everyone else, it was not what special-ops people hoped for. Well, there wasn't much you could do about that.

They checked out of The Hideaway at noon. Cortez thanked whatever fortune smiled down on him that it had been her idea to cut the weekend short, claiming that she had to get back to her children, though he suspected that she had made a conscious decision to go easy on her weary lover. No woman had ever felt the need to take pity on him before, and the insult of it was balanced against his need to find out what the hell was going on.

They drove up Interstate 81, in silence as usual. He'd rented a car with an ordinary bench seat, and she sat in the center, leaning against him with his right arm wrapped warmly around her shoulder. Like teenagers, almost, except for the silence, and again he found himself appreciating her for it. But it wasn't for the quiet passion now. His mind was racing far faster than the car, which he kept exactly at the posted limit. He could have turned on the car radio, but that would have been out of character. He couldn't risk that, could he? If his employer had only exercised intelligence — and he had plenty of that, Cortez compelled himself to admit — then he still had his arm draped over a supremely valuable source of strategic intelligence. Escobedo took an appropriately long view of his business operations. He understood — but Cortez remembered the man's arrogance, too. How easily he took offense — it wasn't enough for him to win, Escobedo also felt the need to humiliate, crush, utterly destroy those who offended him in the slightest way. He had power, and the sort of money normally associated only with governments, but he lacked perspective. For all his intelligence, he was a man ruled by childish emotions, and that thought merely grew in Cortez's mind as he turned onto I-66, heading east now, for Washington. It was so strange, he mused with a thin, bitter smile, that in a world replete with information, he was forced to speculate like a child when he could have all he needed merely from the twist of a radio knob, but he commanded himself to do without.

They reached the airport parking lot right on time. He pulled up to Moira's car and got out to unload her bags.

"Juan . . ."

"Yes?"

"Don't feel badly about last night. It was my fault," she said quietly.

He managed a grin. "I already told you that I

494

am no longer a young man. I have proved it true. I will rest for the next time so that I will do better."

"When — "

"I don't know. I will call you." He kissed her gently. She drove off a minute later, and he stood there in the parking lot watching her leave, as she would have expected. Then he got into his car. It was nearly four o'clock, and he flipped on the radio to get the hourly news broadcast. Two minutes after that he'd driven the car to the return lot, taken out his bags, and walked into the terminal, looking for the first plane anywhere. A United flight to Atlanta was the next available, and he knew that he could make the necessary connections at that busy terminal. He barely squeezed aboard at the last call.

Moira Wolfe drove home with a smile tinged with guilt. What had happened to Juan the previous night was one of the most humiliating things a man could experience, and it was all her fault. She'd demanded too much of him and he was, as he'd said himself, no longer young. She'd let her enthusiasm take charge of her own judgment, and hurt a man whom she — loved. She was certain now. Moira had thought she'd never know the emotion again, but there it was, with all the carefree splendor of her youth, and if Juan lacked the vigor of those years, he more than compensated with his patience and fantastic skill. She reached down and turned on her radio to an oldies FM channel, and for the remainder of her drive basked in the glow of the most pleasant of emotions, her memories of youthful happiness brought further to the fore by the sounds of the teenage ballads to which she'd danced thirty years before.

She was surprised to see what looked like a Bureau car parked across the street from her house, but it might just as easily have been a cheap rental or something else — except for the radio antenna, she realized. It was a Bureau car. That was odd, she thought. She parked against the curb and got out her bags, walking up the sidewalk, but when the door was opened, she saw Frank Weber, one of the Director's security detail.

"Hi, Frank." Special Agent Weber helped her with the bags, but his expression was serious. "Something wrong?"

There wasn't any easy way of telling her, though Weber felt guilty for spoiling what must have been a very special weekend for her.

"Emil was killed Friday evening. We've been trying to reach you since then."

"*What?*"

"They got him on the way to the embassy. The whole detail — everybody. Emil's funeral's tomorrow. The rest of 'em are Tuesday."

"Oh, my God." Moira sat on the nearest chair. "Eddie — Leo?" She thought of the young agents on Emil's protection detail as her own kids.

"All of them," Weber repeated.

496

"I didn't know," she said. "I haven't seen a paper or turned on a TV in — since Friday night. Where — ?"

"Your kids went out to the movies. We need you to come down to help us out with a few things. We'll have somebody here to look after them for you."

It was several minutes before she was able to go anywhere. The tears started as soon as the reality of Weber's words got past her newly made storehouse of other feelings.

Captain Ramirez didn't like the idea of accompanying Chavez. It wasn't cowardice, of course, but a question of what his part of the job actually was. His command responsibilities were muddled in some ways. As a captain who had recently commanded a company, he had learned that "commanding" isn't quite the same thing as "leading." A company commander is supposed to stay a short distance back from the front line and manage — the Army doesn't like that word — the combat action, maneuvering his units and keeping an overview of the battle underway so that he could control matters while his platoon leaders handled the actual fighting. Having learned to "lead from the front" as a lieutenant, he was supposed to apply his lessons at the next higher level, though there would be times when the captain was expected to take the lead. In this case he was commanding only a squad, and though the mission demanded circumspection and command judgment, the size of his unit demanded personal leadership. Besides, he could not very well send two men out on their first killing mission without being there himself, even though Chavez had far superior movement skills than Captain Ramirez ever expected to attain. The contradiction between his command and leadership responsibilities troubled the young officer, but he came down, as he had to, on the side of leading. He could not exercise command, after all, if his men didn't have confidence in his ability to lead. Somehow he knew that if this one went right, he'd never have the same problem again. Maybe that's how it always worked, he told himself.

After setting up his two fire teams, he and Chavez moved out, heading around the northern side of the airstrip with the sergeant in the lead. It went smoothly. The two targets were still lolling around, smoking their joints — or whatever they were — and talking loudly enough to be heard through a hundred meters of trees. Chavez had planned their approach carefully, drawing on previous nights' perimeter patrolling which Captain Ramirez had ordered. There were no surprises, and after twenty minutes they curved back in and again saw where the airstrip was. Now they moved more slowly.

Chavez kept the lead. The narrow trail that the trucks followed to get in here was a convenient guide. They stayed on the north side of it, which would keep them out of the fire lanes established for the squad's machine guns. Right on time, they sighted the shack. As planned, Chavez waited for his officer to close up from his approach interval of ten meters. They communicated with hand signals. Chavez would move straight in with the captain to his right front. The sergeant would do the shooting, but if anything went wrong, Ramirez would be in position to support him at once. The captain tapped out four dashes on the transmit key of his radio and got two signals back. The squad was in place on the far side of the strip, aware of what was about to happen and ready to play its part in the action if needed.

Ramirez waved Ding forward.

Chavez took a deep breath, surprised at how rapidly his heart was beating. After all, he'd done this a hundred times before. He jerked his arms around just to get loose, then adjusted the fit of his weapon's sling. His thumb went down on the selector switch, putting the MP-5 on the three-round-burst setting. The sights were painted with small amounts of tritium, and glowed just enough to be visible in the near-total darkness of the equatorial forest. His night-vision goggles were stowed in a pocket. They'd just get in the way if he tried to use them.

He moved very slowly now, moving around trees and bushes, finding firm, uncluttered places for his feet or pushing the leaves out of his way with his toe before setting his boot down for the next step. It was all business. The obvious tension in his body disappeared, though there was something like a buzz in his ear that told him that this was not an exercise.

There.

They were standing in the open, perhaps two meters apart, twenty meters from the tree against which Chavez leaned. They were still talking, and though he could understand their words easily enough, for some reason it was as foreign to him as the barking of dogs. Ding could have gotten closer, but didn't want to take the chance, and twenty meters was close enough — sixty-six feet. It was a clear shot past another tree to both of them.

Okay.

He brought the gun up slowly, centering the ringed forward sight in the aperture rear sight, making sure that he could see the white circle all around, and putting the center post right on the black, circular mass that represented the back of a human head that was no longer part of a human being — it was just a target, just a thing. His finger squeezed gently on the trigger.

The weapon jerked slightly in his grip, but the double-looped sling kept it firmly in place. The target dropped. He moved the gun right even as it fell. The next target was spinning around in surprise, giving him a dull white circle of reflected moonlight to aim at. Another burst. There had hardly been any noise at all. Chavez waited, moving his weapon back and forth across the two bodies, but there was no movement.

Chavez darted out of the trees. One of the bodies clutched an AK-47. He kicked it loose and pulled a penlight from his breast pocket, shining it on the targets. One had taken all three rounds in the back of the head. The other had only caught two, but both through the forehead. The second one's face showed surprise. The first one no longer had a face. The sergeant knelt by the bodies and looked around for further movement and activity. Chavez's only immediate emotion was one of elation. Everything he'd learned and practiced — it all worked! Not exactly easy, but it wasn't a big deal, really.

Ninja really does *own the night.*

Ramirez came over a moment later. There was only one thing he could say.

"Nice work, Sergeant. Check out the shack." He activated his radio. "This is Six. Targets down, move in."

The squad was over to the shack in a couple of minutes. As was the usual practice with armies, they clustered around the bodies of the dead guards, getting their first sample of what war was really all about. The intelligence specialist went through their pockets while the captain got the squad spread out in a defensive perimeter.

"Nothing much here," the intel sergeant told his boss.

"Let's go see the shack." Chavez had made sure that there was no additional guard whom they might have overlooked. Ramirez found four gasoline drums and a hand-crank pump. A carton of cigarettes was sitting on one of the gasoline drums, evoking a withering comment from the captain. There was some canned food on a few rough-cut shelves, and a two-roll pack of toilet paper. No books, documents, or maps. A well-thumbed deck of cards was the only other thing found.

"How you wanna booby-trap it?" the intelligence sergeant asked. He was also a former Green Beret, and an expert on setting booby traps.

"Three-way."

" 'Kay." It was easily done. He dug a small depression in the dirt floor with his hands, taking some wood scraps to firm up the sides. A one-pound block of C-4 plastic explosive — the whole world used it — went snugly into the hole. He inserted two electrical detonators and a pressure switch like the one used for a land mine. The control wires were run along the dirt floor to switches at the door and window, and were set as to be invisible to outside inspection. The sergeant buried the wires under an inch of dirt. Satisfied, he rocked the drum around, bringing it down gently on the pressure switch. If someone opened the door or the window, the C-4 would go off directly underneath a fifty-five-gallon drum of aviation gasoline, with predictable results. Better still, if someone were very clever indeed and defeated the electrical detonators on the door and window, he would then follow the wires to the oil drums in order to recover the explosives for his own later use . . . and that very clever person would be removed from the other team. Anyone could kill a dumb enemy. Killing the smart ones required artistry.

"All set up, sir. Let's make sure nobody goes near the shack from now on, sir," the intelligence sergeant told his captain.

"Roger that." The word went out at once. Two men dragged the bodies into the center of the field, and after that, they all settled down to wait for the helicopter. Ramirez redeployed his men to keep the area secured, but the main object of concern now was to have every man inventory his gear to make sure that nothing was left behind.

PJ handled the refueling. The good visibility helped, but would also help if there were anyone on the surface looking for them. The drogue played out from the wing tank of the MC-130E Combat Talon on the end of a reinforced rubber hose, and the Pave Low's refueling probe extended telescopically, stabbing into the center of it. Though it was often observed that having a helicopter refuel in this way seemed a madly unnatural act — the probe and drogue met twelve feet under the edge of the rotor arc, and contact between blade tips and hose meant certain death for the helicopter crew — the Pave Low crews always responded that it was a very natural act indeed, and one in which, of course, they had ample practice. That didn't alter the fact that Colonel Johns and Captain Willis concentrated to a remarkable degree for the whole procedure, and didn't utter a single unnecessary syllable until it was over:

"Breakaway, breakaway," PJ said as he backed off the drogue and withdrew his probe. He pulled up on the collective and eased back on the stick to pull his rotors up and away from the hose. On command, the MC-130E climbed to a comfortable cruising altitude, where it would circle until the helicopter returned for another fill-up. The Pave Low III turned for the beach, heading down to cross at an unpopulated point.

"Uh-oh," Chavez whispered to himself when he heard the noise. It was the laboring sound of a V-8 engine that needed service, and a new muffler. It was getting louder by the second.

"Six, this is Point, over," he called urgently.

"Six here. Go," Captain Ramirez replied.

"We got company coming in. Sounds like a truck, sir."

"KNIFE, this is Six," Ramirez reacted immediately. "Pull back to the west side. Take your covering positions. Point, fall back now!"

"On the way." Chavez left his listening post on the dirt road and raced back past the shack — he gave it a wide berth — and across the landing strip. There he found Ramirez and Guerra pulling the dead guards toward the far treeline. He helped the captain carry his burden into cover, then came back to assist the operations sergeant. They made the shelter of the trees with twenty seconds to spare.

The pickup traveled with lights ablaze. The glow snaked left and right along the trail, glowing through the underbrush before coming out just next to the shack. The truck stopped, and you could almost see the puzzlement even before the engine was switched off and the men dismounted. As soon as the lights were off, Chavez activated his night goggles. As before, there were four, two from the cab and two from the back. The driver was evidently the boss. He looked around in obvious anger. A moment later he shouted something, then pointed to one of the people who'd jumped out of the back of the truck. One of them walked straight to the shack —

— "Oh, shit!" Ramirez keyed his radio switch. "Everybody get down!" he ordered unnecessarily —

— and wrenched open the door.

A gasoline drum rocketed upward like a space launch, leaving a cone of white flame behind as it blasted through the top of the shack. Flames from the other drums spread laterally. The one who'd opened the door was a silhouette of black, as though he'd just opened the front door of hell, but only for an instant before he vanished in the spreading flames. Two of his companions vanished into the same white-yellow mass. The third was on the edge of the initial blast, and started running away, directly toward the soldiers, before the falling gasoline from the flying drum splashed on him and he became a stick figure made of fire who lasted only ten steps. The circle

505

of flames was forty yards wide, its center composed of four men whose high-pitched screams were distinct above the low-frequency roar of the blaze. Next the truck's fuel tank added its own punctuation to the explosion. There were perhaps two hundred gallons of gasoline afire, sending up a mushroom cloud illuminated by the flames below. In less than a minute the ammunition in various firearms cooked off, sounding like firecrackers within the roaring flames. Only the afternoon's heavy rain prevented the fire from spreading rapidly into the forest.

Chavez realized that he was lying next to the intelligence specialist.

"Nice work on the booby trap."

"Wish the fuckers coulda waited." The screaming was over by now.

"Yeah."

"Everybody check in," Ramirez ordered over the radio. They all did. Nobody was hurt.

The fire died down quickly. The aviation gasoline had been spread thinly over a wide area, and burned rapidly. Within three minutes all that was left was a wide scorched area defined by a perimeter of burning grass and bushes. The truck was a blackened skeleton, its loadbed still alight from the box of flares. They'd continue to burn for quite a while.

"What the hell was that?" Captain Willis wondered in the left seat of the helicopter. They'd just made their first pickup, and on climbing back to cruising altitude, the glow on the horizon looked like a sunrise on their infrared vision systems.

"Plane crash, maybe — that's right on the bearing to the last pickup," Colonel Johns realized belatedly.

"Super."

"Buck, be advised we have possible hostile activity at Pickup Four."

"Right, Colonel," Sergeant Zimmer replied curtly.

With that observation, Colonel Johns continued the mission. He'd find out what he needed to know soon enough. One thing at a time.

Thirty minutes after the explosion, the fire was down enough that the intelligence sergeant donned his gloves and moved in to try to recover his triggering devices. He found part of one, but the idea, though good, was hopeless. The bodies were left in place, and no attempt was made to search them. Though IDs might have been recovered — leather wallets resist fire reasonably well — their absence would have been noticed. Again the airfield guards were dragged to the center of the northern part of the runway, which was to have been the pickup point anyway. Ramirez redeployed his men to guard against the possibility that someone might have noticed the fire and reported it to someone else. The next concern was the courier flight that was probably heading in tonight. Their experience told them that it was still over two hours away — but they'd seen only one full cycle, and that was a thin basis for making any sort of prediction.

What if the airplane comes in? Ramirez asked himself. He'd already considered the possibility, but now it was an immediate threat.

The crew of that aircraft could not be allowed to report to anyone that they'd seen a large helicopter. On the other hand, leaving bullet holes in the airplane would be almost as clear a message of what had happened.

For that matter, Ramirez asked himself, *why the hell were we ordered to kill those two poor bastards and leave from here instead of the preplanned exfiltration point?*

So, what if an airplane comes in?

He didn't have an answer. Without the flares to mark the strip it wouldn't land. Moreover, one of the new arrivals had brought a small VHF radio. The druggies were smart enough that they'd have radio codes to assure the flight crew that the airfield was safe. So, what if the aircraft just orbited? Which it probably would do. Might the helicopter shoot it down? What if it tried and missed? What if? What if?

Before insertion, Ramirez had thought that the mission had been exquisitely planned, with every contingency thought out — as it had, but halfway through their planned stay they were being yanked out, and the plan had been trashed. What dickhead had decided to do that?

What the hell is going on? he demanded of himself. His men looked to him for information and knowledge and leadership and assurance. He had to pretend that everything was all right, that he was in control. It was all a lie, of course. His greater overall knowledge of the operation only increased his ignorance of the real situation. He was used to being moved around like a chess piece. That was the job of a junior officer — but this was *real*. There were six dead men to prove it.

"KNIFE, this is NIGHT HAWK, over," his high-frequency radio crackled.

"HAWK, this is KNIFE. LZ is the northern edge of RENO. Standing by for extraction, over."

"Bravo X-Ray, over."

Colonel Johns was interrogating for possible trouble. Juliet Zulu was the coded response indicating that they were in enemy hands and that a pickup was impossible. Charlie Foxtrot meant that there was active contact, but that they could still be gotten out. Lima Whiskey was the all-clear signal.

"Lima Whiskey, over."

"Say again, KNIFE, over."

"Lima Whiskey, over."

"Roger, copy. We are three minutes out."

"Hot guns," PJ ordered his flight crew. Sergeant Zimmer left his instruments to take the right-side gun position. He activated the power to his six-barreled minigun. The newest version of the Gatling gun of yore began spinning, ready to draw shells from the hopper to Zimmer's left.

"Ready right," he reported over the intercom.

"Ready left," Bean said on the other side.

Both men scanned the trees with their night-vision goggles, looking for anything that might be hostile.

"I got a strobe light at ten o'clock," Willis told PJ.

"I see it. Christ — what happened here?"

As the Sikorsky slowed, the four bodies were clearly visible around what had once been a simple wooden shack . . . and there was a truck, too. Team KNIFE was right where it was supposed to be, however. And they had two bodies as well.

"Looks clear, Buck."

"Roger, PJ." Zimmer left his gun on and headed aft. Sergeant Bean could jump to the opposite gun station if he had to, but it was Zimmer's job to get a count on the last pickup. He did his best to avoid stepping on people as he moved, but the soldiers understood when his feet landed on several of them. Soldiers are typically quite forgiving toward those who lift them out of hostile territory.

Chavez kept his strobe on until the helicopter touched down, then ran to join his squad. He found Captain Ramirez standing by the ramp, counting them off as they raced aboard. Ding waited his turn, then the captain's hand thumped down on his shoulder.

"Ten!" he heard as he leaped over several bodies on the ramp. He heard the number again from the big Air Force sergeant, then: "Eleven! Go-go-go!" as the captain came aboard.

The helicopter lifted off immediately. Chavez fell hard onto the steel deck, where Vega grabbed him. Ramirez came down next to him, then rose and followed Zimmer forward.

"What happened here?" PJ asked Ramirez a minute later. The infantry officer filled him in quickly. Colonel Johns increased power somewhat and kept low, which he would have done anyway. He ordered Zimmer to stay at the ramp for two minutes, watching for a possible aircraft, but it never appeared. Buck came forward, killed power to his gun, and resumed his vigil with the flight instruments. Within ten minutes they were "feet-wet," over the water, looking for their tanker to top off for the flight back to Panama. In the back, the infantrymen buckled into place and promptly began dropping off to sleep.

But not Chavez and Vega, who found themselves sitting next to six bodies, lying together on the ramp. Even for professional soldiers — one of whom had done some of the killing — it was a grisly sight. But not as bad as the explosions. Neither had ever seen pictures of people burning to death, and even for druggies, they agreed, it was a bad way out.

The helicopter ride became rough as the Pave Low entered the propwash from the tanker, but it was soon over. A few minutes after that, Sergeant Bean — the little one, as Chavez thought of him — came aft, walking carefully over the soldiers. He clipped his safety belt to a fitting on the deck, then spoke into his helmet microphone. Nodding, he went aft to the ramp. Bean motioned to Chavez for a hand. Ding grabbed the man's belt at the waist and watched him kick the bodies off the edge of the ramp. It seemed kind of cold, but then, the scout reflected, it no longer mattered to the druggies. He didn't look aft to see them hit the water, but instead settled back down for a nap.

A hundred miles behind them, a twin-engined private plane circled over where the landing strip — known to the flight crew simply as Number Six — was still marked by a vaguely circular array of flames. They could see where the clearing was, but the airstrip itself wasn't marked with flares, and without that visual reference a landing attempt would have been madness. Frustrated, yet also relieved because they knew what had happened to a number of flights over the previous two weeks, they turned back for their regular airfield. On landing they made a telephone call.

Cortez had risked a direct flight from Panama to Medellín, though he did place the charge on an as-yet unused credit card so that the name couldn't be tracked. He drove his personal car to his home and immediately tried to contact Escobedo, only to discover that he was at his hilltop hacienda. Félix didn't have the energy to drive that far this late on a long day, nor would he entrust a substantive conversation to a cellular phone, despite all the assurances about how safe those channels were. Tired, angry, and frustrated for a dozen reasons, he poured himself a stiff drink and went off to bed. All that effort wasted, he swore at the darkness. He'd never be able to use Moira again. Would never call her, never talk to her, never see her. And the fact that his last "performance" with her had ended in failure, caused by his fears at what he'd thought — correctly! — his boss had done, merely put more genuine emotion into his profanities.

Before dawn a half-dozen trucks visited a half-dozen different airfields. Two groups of men died fiery deaths. A third entered the airfield shack and found exactly what they'd expected to find: nothing. The other three found their airstrips entirely normal, the guards in place, content and bored with the monotony of their duties. When two of the trucks failed to return, others were sent out after them, and the necessary information quickly found its way to Medellín. Cortez was awakened by the phone and given new travel orders.

In Panama, all of the infantrymen were still asleep. They'd be allowed to stand down for a full day, and sleep in air-conditioned comfort — under heavy blankets — after hot showers and

513

meals which, if not especially tasty, were at least different from the MREs they'd had for the preceding week. The four officers, however, were awakened early and taken elsewhere for a new briefing. Operation SHOWBOAT, they learned, had taken a very serious turn. They also learned why, and the source of their new orders was as exhilarating as it was troubling.

The new S-3, operations officer, for the 3rd Battalion of the 17th Infantry, which formed part of the First Brigade, 7th Infantry Division (Light), checked out his office while his wife struggled with the movers. Already sitting on his desk was a Mark-2 Kevlar helmet, called a Fritz for its resemblance to the headgear of the old German Wehrmacht. For the 7th LID, the camouflage cloth cover was further decorated with knotted shreds of the same material used for their battle-dress uniform fatigues. Most of the wives referred to it as the Cabbage Patch Hat, and like a cabbage, it broke up the regular outline of the helmet, making it harder to spot. The battalion commander was off at a briefing, along with the XO, and the new S-3 decided to meet with the S-1, or personnel officer. It turned out that they'd served together in Germany five years before, and they caught up on personal histories over coffee.

"So how was Panama?"

"Hot, miserable, and I don't need to fill you in on the political side. Funny thing — just before I

514

left I ran into one of your Ninjas."

"Oh, yeah? Which one?"

"Chavez. Staff sergeant, I think. Bastard wasted me on an exercise."

"I remember him. He was a good one with, uh . . . Sergeant Bascomb?"

"Yes, Major?" A head appeared at the office door.

"Staff Sergeant Chavez — who was he with?"

"Bravo Company, sir. Lieutenant Jackson's platoon . . . second squad, I think. Yeah, Corporal Ozkanian took it over. Chavez transferred out to Fort Benning, he's a basic-training instructor now," Sergeant Bascomb remembered.

"You sure about that?" the new S-3 asked.

"Yes, sir. The paperwork got a little ruffled. He's one of the guys who had to check out in a hurry. Remember, Major?"

"Oh, yeah. That was a cluster-fuck, wasn't it?"

"Roge-o, Major," the NCO agreed.

"What the hell was he doing running an FTX in the Canal Zone?" the operations officer wondered.

"Lieutenant Jackson might know, sir," Bascomb offered.

"You'll meet him tomorrow," the S-1 told the new S-3.

"Any good?"

"For a new kid fresh from the Hudson, yeah, he's doing just fine. Good family. Preacher's kid, got a brother flies fighter planes for the Navy — squadron commander, I think. Bumped into him

515

at Monterey a while back. Anyway, Tim's got a good platoon sergeant to teach him the ropes."

"Well, that was one pretty good sergeant, that Chavez kid. I'm not used to having people sneak up on me!" The S-3 fingered the scab on his face. "Damn if he didn't, though."

"We got a bunch of good ones, Ed. You're gonna like it here. How 'bout lunch?"

"Sounds good to me. When do we start PT in the morning?"

"Zero-six-fifteen. The boss likes to run."

The new S-3 grunted on his way out the door. Welcome back to the real Army.

"Looks like our friends down there are a little pissed," Admiral Cutter observed. He held a telex form that had emanated from the CAPER side of the overall operation. "Who was it came up with the idea of tapping into their communications?"

"Mr. Clark," the DDO replied.

"The same one who — "

"The same."

"What can you tell me about him?"

"Ex-Navy SEAL, served nineteen months in Southeast Asia in one of those special operations groups that never officially existed. Got shot up a few times," Ritter explained. "Left the service as a chief bosun's mate, age twenty-eight. He was one of the best they ever had. He's the guy who went in and saved Dutch Maxwell's boy."

Cutter's eyes went active at that. "I knew

Dutch Maxwell, spent some time on his staff when I was a j.g. So, he's the guy who saved Sonny's ass? I never did hear the whole story on that."

"Admiral Maxwell made him a chief on the spot. That's when he was COMAIRPAC. Anyway, he left the service and got married, went into the commercial diving business — the demolitions side; he's an expert with explosives, too. But his wife got killed in a car accident down in Mississippi. That's when things started going bad for him. Met a new girl, but she was kidnapped and murdered by a local drug ring — seems she was a mule for them before they met. Our former SEAL decided to go big-game hunting on his own hook. Did pretty well, but the police got a line on him. Anyway, Admiral Maxwell was OP-03 by then. He caught a rumble, too. He knew James Greer from the old days, and one thing led to another. We decided that Mr. Clark had some talents we needed. So the Agency helped stage his 'death' in a boating accident. We changed his name — new identity, the whole thing, and now he works for us."

"How — "

"It's not hard. His service records are just gone. Same thing we did with the SHOWBOAT people. His fingerprints in the FBI file were changed — that was back when Hoover still ran things and, well, there were ways. He died and got himself reborn as John Clark."

"What's he done since?" Cutter asked, enjoy-

517

ing the conspiratorial aspects of this.

"Mainly he's an instructor down at The Farm. Every so often we have a special job that requires his special talents," Ritter explained. "He's the guy who went on the beach to get Gerasimov's wife and daughter, for example."

"Oh. And this all started because of a drug thing?"

"That's right. He has a special, dark place in his heart for druggies. Hates the bastards. It's about the only thing he's not professional about."

"Not pro — "

"I don't mean it that way. He'll enjoy doing this job. It won't affect how he does it, but he will enjoy it. I don't want you to misunderstand me. Clark is a very capable field officer. He's got great instincts, and he's got brains. He knows how to plan it, and he knows how to run it."

"So what's his plan?"

"You'll love it." Ritter opened his portfolio and started taking papers out. Most of them, Cutter saw, were "overhead imagery" — satellite photographs.

"Lieutenant Jackson?"

"Good morning, sir," Tim said to the new battalion operations officer after cracking off a book-perfect salute. The S-3 was walking the battalion area, getting himself introduced.

"I've heard some pretty good things about you." That was always something that a new second lieutenant wanted to hear. "And I met one of your squad leaders."

"Which one, sir?"

"Chavez, I think."

"Oh, you just in from Fort Benning, Major?"

"No, I was an instructor at the Jungle Warfare School, down in Panama."

"What was Chavez doing down there?" Lieutenant Jackson wondered.

"Killing me," the major replied with a grin. "All your people that good?"

"He was my best squad leader. That's funny, they were supposed to send him off to be a drill sergeant."

"That's the Army for you. I'm going out with Bravo Company tomorrow night for the exercise down at Hunter-Liggett. Just thought I'd let you know."

"Glad to have you along, sir," Tim Jackson told the Major. It wasn't strictly true, of course. He was still learning how to be a leader of men, and oversight made him uncomfortable, though he knew that it was something he'd have to learn to live with. He was also puzzled by the news on Chavez, and made a mental note to have Sergeant Mitchell check that out. After all, Ding was still one of "his" men.

"Clark." That was how he answered the phone. And this one came in on his "business" line.

"It's a Go. Be here at ten tomorrow morning."

"Right." Clark replaced the phone.

519

"When?" Sandy asked.

"Tomorrow."

"How long?"

"A couple of weeks. Not as long as a month." *Probably*, he didn't add.

"Is it — "

"Dangerous?" John Clark smiled at his wife. "Honey, if I do my job right, no, it's not dangerous."

"Why is it," Sandra Burns Clark wondered, "that I'm the one with gray hair?"

"That's because I can't go into the hair parlor and have it fixed. You can."

"It's about the drug people, isn't it?"

"You know I can't talk about that. It would just get you worried anyway, and there's no real reason to worry," he lied to his wife. Clark did a lot of that. She knew it, of course, and for the most part she wanted to be lied to. But not this time.

Clark returned his attention to the television. Inwardly he smiled. He hadn't gone after druggies for a long, long time, and he'd never tried to go this far up the ladder — back then he hadn't known how, hadn't had the right information. Now he had everything he needed for the job. Including presidential authorization. There were advantages to working for the Agency.

Cortez surveyed the airfield — what was left of it — with a mixture of satisfaction and anger. Neither the police nor the army had come to visit

520

yet, though eventually they would. Whoever had been here, he saw, had done a thorough, professional job.

So what am I supposed to think? he asked himself. Did the Americans send some of their Green Berets in? This was the last of five airstrips that he'd examined today, moved about by a helicopter. Though not a forensic detective by training, he had been thoroughly schooled in booby traps and knew exactly what to look for. Exactly what he would have done.

The two guards who'd been here, as at the other sites, were simply gone. That surely meant that they were dead, of course, but the only real knowledge he had was that they were gone. Perhaps he was supposed to think that they had set the explosives, but they were simple peasants in the pay of the Cartel, untrained ruffians who probably hadn't even patrolled around the area to make certain that . . .

"Follow me." He left the helicopter with one of his assistants in trail. This one was a former police officer who did have some rudimentary intelligence; at least he knew how to follow simple orders.

If I wanted to keep watch of a place like this . . . I'd think about cover, and I'd think about the wind, and I'd think about a quick escape. . . .

One thing about military people was that they were predictable.

They'd want a place from which they could watch the length of the airstrip, and also keep an

521

eye on the refueling shack. That meant one of two corners, Cortez judged, and he walked off toward the northwest one. He spent a half hour prowling the bushes in silence with a confused man behind him.

"Here is where they were," Félix said to himself. The dirt just behind the mound of dirt was smoothed down. Men had lain there. There was also the imprint from the bipod of a machine gun.

He couldn't tell how long they'd watched the strip, but he suspected that here was the explanation for the disappearing aircraft. Americans? If so, what agency did they work for? CIA? DEA? Some special-operations group from the military, perhaps?

And why were they pulled out?

And why had they made their departure so obvious?

What if the guards were not dead? What if the Americans had bought them off?

Cortez stood and brushed the mud off his trousers. They were sending a message. Of course. After the murder of their FBI Director — he hadn't had time to talk to *el jefe* about that act of lunacy yet — they wanted to send a message so that such things were not to be repeated.

That the Americans had done anything at all was unusual, of course. After all, kidnapping and/or killing American citizens was about the safest thing any international terrorist could do. The CIA had allowed one of their station chiefs to be tortured to death in Lebanon — and done nothing. All those Marines blown up — and the Americans had done nothing. Except for the occasional attempt at sending a message. The Americans were fools. They'd tried to send messages to the North Vietnamese for nearly ten years, and failed, and *still* they hadn't learned better. So this time, instead of doing nothing at all, they'd done something that was less useful than nothing. To have so much power and have so little appreciation of it, Cortez thought. Not like the Russians. When one of their people had been kidnapped in Lebanon, the KGB's First Directorate men had snatched their own hostages off the street and returned them — one version said headless, another with more intimate parts removed — immediately after which the missing Russians had been returned with something akin to an apology. For all their crudeness, the Russians understood how the game was played. They were predictable, and played by all the classic rules of clandestine behavior so that their enemies knew what would not be tolerated. They were serious. And they were taken seriously.

Unlike the Americans. As much as he warned his employer to be wary of them, Cortez was sure that they wouldn't answer even something as outrageous as the murder of senior officials of their government.

That was too bad, Cortez told himself. He could have made it work for him.

"Good evening, boss," Ryan said as he took his seat.

"Hi, Jack." Admiral Greer smiled as much as he could. "How do you like the new job?"

"Well, I'm keeping your chair warm."

"It's your chair now, son," the DDI pointed out. "Even if I do get out of here, I think it's time to retire."

Jack didn't like the way he pronounced the word *if*.

"I don't think I'm ready yet, sir."

"Nobody's ever ready. Hell, when I was still a naval officer, about the time I actually learned how to do the job, it was time to leave. That's the way life is, Jack."

Ryan thought that one over as he surveyed the room. Admiral Greer was getting his nourishment through clear plastic tubes. A blue-green gadget that looked like a splint kept the needles in his arm, but he could see where previous IV lines had "infiltrated" and left ugly bruises. That was always a bad sign. Next to the IV bottle was a smaller one, piggybacked with the D5W. That was the medication he was being given, the chemotherapy. It was a fancy name for poison, and poison was exactly what it was, a biocide that was supposed to kill the cancer a little faster than it killed the patient. He didn't know what this one was, some acronym or other that designated a compound developed at the National Institutes of Health instead of the Army's Chemical Warfare Center. Or maybe, Jack thought, they cooperated on such concoctions. Certainly Greer looked as though he were the victim of some dreadful, vicious experiment.

But that wasn't true. The best people in the field were doing everything they knew to keep him alive. And failing. Ryan had never seen his boss so thin. It seemed that every time he came — never less than three times per week — he'd lost additional weight. His eyes burned with defiant energy, but the light at the end of this painful tunnel was not recovery. He knew it. So did Jack. There was only one thing he could do to ease the pain. And this he did. Jack opened his briefcase and took out some documents.

"You want to look these over." Ryan handed them over.

They nearly tangled on the IV lines, and Greer grumbled his annoyance at the plastic spaghetti.

"You're leaving for Belgium tomorrow night, right?"

"Yes, sir."

"Give my regards to Rudi and Franz from the BND. And watch the local beer, son."

Ryan laughed. "Yes, sir."

Admiral Greer scanned through the first folder. "The Hungarians are still at it, I see."

"They got the word to cool it down, and they have, but the underlying problem isn't going to go away. I think it's in the interests of everyone concerned that they should cool it. Our friend Gerasimov has given us some tips on how to get word to a few people ourselves."

Greer nearly laughed at that. "It figures. How is the former KGB Director adapting to life in America?"

"Not as well as his daughter is. Turns out that she always wanted a nose job. Well, she got her wish." Jack grinned. "Last time I saw her she was working on a tan. She restarts college next fall. The wife is still a little antsy, and Gerasimov is still cooperating. We haven't figured out what to do with him when we're finished, though."

"Tell Arthur to show him my old place up in Maine. He'll like the climate, and it ought to be easy to guard."

"I'll pass that along."

"How do you like being let in on all the Operations stuff?" James Greer asked.

"Well, what I've seen is interesting enough, but there's still 'need-to-know' to worry about."

"Says who?" the DDI asked in surprise.

"Says the Judge," Jack replied. "They have a couple of things poppin' that they don't want me in on."

"Oh, really?" Greer was quiet for a moment. "Jack, in case nobody ever told you, the Director, the Deputy Director — they still haven't refilled that slot, have they? — and the directorate chiefs are cleared for everything. You are now a chief of directorate. There isn't anything you aren't supposed to know. You *have* to know. You brief Congress."

Ryan waved it off. It wasn't important, really. "Well, maybe the Judge doesn't see things that way and — "

The DDI tried to sit up in bed. "Listen up, son. What you just said is bullshit! You *have* to know, and you tell Arthur I said so. That 'need-to-know' crap stops at the door to my office."

"Yes, sir. I'll take care of that." Ryan didn't want his boss to get upset. He was only an acting chief of directorate, after all, and he was accustomed to being cut out of operational matters which, for the past six years, he'd been quite content to leave to others. Jack wasn't ready to challenge the DCI on something like this. His responsibility for the Intelligence Directorate's output to Congress, of course, was something he would make noise over.

"I'm not kidding, Jack."

"Yes, sir." Ryan pointed to another folder. He'd fight that battle after he got back from Europe. "Now, this development in South Africa is especially interesting and I want your opinion. . . ."

15.

Deliverymen

Clark walked off the United flight in San Diego and rented a car for the drive to the nearby naval base. It didn't take very long. He felt the usual pang of nostalgia when he saw the towering gray-blue hulls. He'd once been a part of this team and though he'd been young and foolish then, he remembered it fondly as a time in which things were simpler.

USS *Ranger* was a busy place. Clark parked his car at the far end of the area used by the enlisted crewmen and walked toward the quay, dodging around the trucks, cranes, and other items of mobile hardware that cycled in and out from their numerous tasks. The carrier was preparing to sail in another eight hours, and her thousands of sailors were on-loading all manner of supplies. Her flight deck was empty save for a single old F-4 Phantom fighter which no longer had any engines and was used for training new members of the flight-deck crew. The carrier's air wing was scattered among three different naval air stations and would fly out after the carrier sailed. That fact spared the pilots of the wing from the tumult normal to a carrier's departure. Except for one.

Clark walked up to the officer's brow, guarded by a Marine corporal who had his name written down on his clipboard list of official visitors. The Marine checked off the line on his list and lifted the dock phone to make the call that was mandated by his instructions. Clark just kept going up the steps, entering the carrier at the hangar-deck level, then looking around for a way topside. Finding one's way around a carrier is not easy for the uninitiated, but if you kept going up you generally found the flight deck soon enough. This he did, heading for the forward starboard-side elevator. Standing there was an officer whose khaki collar bore the silver leaf of a Commander, USN. There was also a gold star over one shirt pocket that denoted command at sea. Clark was looking for the CO of a squadron of Grumman A-6E Intruder medium attack bombers.

"Your name Jensen?" he asked. He'd flown down early to make this appointment.

"That's right, sir. Roy Jensen. And you are Mr. Carlson?"

Clark smiled. "Something like that." He motioned to the officer to follow him forward. The flight deck here was idle. Most of the loading activity was aft. They walked toward the bow across the black no-skid decking material, little different from the blacktop on any country road. Both men had to talk loudly to be heard. There was plenty of noise from the dock, plus a fifteen-knot onshore wind. Several people could see the two men talking, but with all the activity on the carrier's flight deck, there was little likelihood that anyone would notice. And you couldn't bug a flight deck. Clark handed over an envelope and let Jensen read its contents before taking it back. By this time they were nearly at the bow, standing between the two catapult tracks.

"This for-real?"

"That's right. Can you handle it?"

Jensen thought for a moment, staring off into the naval base.

"Sure. Who's going to be on the ground?"

"Not supposed to tell you — but it's going to be me."

"The battle group's not supposed to be going down there, you know — "

"That's already been changed."

"What about the weapons?"

"They're being loaded aboard *Shasta* tomorrow. They'll be painted blue, and they're light for — "

"I know. I did one of the drops a few weeks ago over at China Lake."

"Your CAG will get the orders three days from now. But he won't know what's happening. Neither will anybody else. We'll have a 'tech-rep' flown aboard with the weapons. He'll baby-sit the mission from this side. Your BDA cassettes go to him. Nobody else sees them. He's bringing his own set, and they're color-coded with orange-and-purple tape so they don't get mixed up with anything else. You got a B/N you can trust to keep his mouth shut?"

"With these orders?" Commander Jensen asked. "No sweat."

"Fair enough. The 'tech-rep' will have the details when he gets aboard. He reports to the CAG first, but he'll ask to see you. From there on it's eyes-only. The CAG'll know that it's a quiet project. If he asks about it, just tell him it's a Drop-Ex to evaluate a new weapon." Clark raised an eyebrow. "It really is a Drop-Ex, isn't it?"

"The people we're — "

"What people? You do not need to know. You do not want to know," Clark said. "If you have a problem with that, I want you to tell me right now."

"Hey, I told you we could do it. I was just curious."

"You're old enough to know better." Clark delivered the line gently. He didn't want to insult the man, though he did have to get the message across.

"Okay."

USS *Ranger* was about to deploy for an extended battle-group exercise whose objective was work-ups: battle practice to prepare the group for a deployment to the Indian Ocean. They were scheduled for three weeks of intensive operations that involved everything from carrier landing practice to underway-replenishment drills, with a mock attack from another carrier battle group returning from WestPac. The operations would be carried out, Commander Jensen had just learned, about three hundred miles from Panama instead of farther west. The squadron commander wondered who had the juice to reroute a total of thirty-one ships, some of them outrageous fuelhogs. That confirmed the source of the orders he'd just been given. Jensen was a careful man; though he'd gotten a very official telephone call, and the orders hand-delivered by Mr. Carlson said everything they needed to say, it was nice to have outside confirmation.

"That's it. You'll get notice when you need it. Figure eight hours or so of warning time. That enough?"

"No sweat. I'll make sure the ordies put the weapons in a convenient place. You be careful on the ground, Mr. Carlson."

"I'll try." Clark shook hands with the pilot and walked aft to find his way off the ship. He'd be catching another plane in two hours.

The Mobile cops were in a particularly foul mood. Bad enough that one of their own had been murdered in such an obvious, brutal way, Mrs. Braden had made the mistake of coming to the door to see what was wrong and caught two rounds herself. The surgeons had almost saved her, but after thirty-six hours that too was over, and all the police had to show for it was a kid not yet old enough to drive who claimed to have hit one of the killers with his granddad's Marlin '39, and some bloodstains that might or might not have supported the story. The police preferred to believe that Braden had scored for the points, of course, but the experienced homicide investigators knew that a two-inch belly gun was the next thing to useless unless the shoot-out were held inside a crowded elevator. Every cop in Mississippi, Alabama, Florida, and Louisiana was looking for a blue Plymouth Voyager minivan with two male Caucs, black hair, medium, medium, armed and dangerous, suspected cop-killers.

The van was found Monday afternoon by a concerned citizen — there really were some in Alabama — who called the local county sheriff's office, who in turn called the Mobile force.

"The kid was right," the lieutenant in charge of the case observed. The body on the back of the van was about as distasteful to behold as any cadaver would be after two days locked inside a car, in Alabama, in June, but for all that the hole near the base of the skull, just at the hairline, was definitely a .22. It was also clear that the killer had died in the right-front seat, hemorrhaging explosively from the head wound. There was one more thing.

"I've seen this guy. He's a druggie," another detective observed.

"So what was Ernie wrapped up with?"

"Christ knows. What about his kids?" the detective asked. "They lose their mom and dad — we gonna tell the whole fucking world that their dad was a dirty cop? Do that to a couple of orphaned kids?"

It merely required a single look for both men to agree that, no, you couldn't do something like that. They'd find a way to make Ernie a hero, and damned sure somebody'd give the Sanderson kid a pat on the head.

"Do you realize what you have done?" Cortez asked. He'd steeled himself going in to restrain his temper. In an organization of Latins, his would be — had to be — the only voice of reason. They would respect that in the same sense that the Romans valued chastity: a rare and admirable commodity best found in others.

"I have taught the *norteamericanos* a lesson," Escobedo replied with arrogant patience that nearly defeated Félix's self-discipline.

"And what did they do in reply?"

Escobedo made a grand gesture with his hand, a gesture of power and satisfaction. "The sting of an insect."

"You also know, of course, that after all the effort I made to establish a valuable information source, you have pissed it away like — "

"What source?"

"The secretary of the FBI Director," Cortez answered with his own self-satisfied smile.

"And you cannot use her again?" Escobedo was puzzled.

Fool! "Not unless you wish me to be arrested, *jefe*. Were that to happen, my services would cease to be useful to you. We could have used information from this woman, carefully, over years. We could have identified attempts to infiltrate the organization. We could have discovered what new ideas the *norteamericanos* have, and countered them, again carefully and thoughtfully, protecting our operations while allowing them enough successes to think that they were accomplishing something." Cortez almost said that he'd just figured out why all those aircraft had disappeared, but didn't. His anger wasn't under that much control. Félix was just beginning to realize that he really could supplant the man who sat behind the desk. But first he would have to demonstrate his value to the organization and gradually prove to all of the criminals that he was more useful than this buffoon. Better to let them stew in their own juice for a while, the better to appreciate the difference between a trained intelligence professional and a pack of self-taught and over-rich smugglers.

Ryan gazed down at the ocean, forty-two thousand feet below him. The VIP treatment wasn't hard to get used to. As a directorate chief he also rated a special flight from Andrews direct to a military airfield outside of the NATO headquarters at Mons, Belgium. He was representing the

Agency at a semiannual conference with his intelligence counterparts from the European Alliance. It would be a major performance. He had a speech to give, and favorable impressions to make. Though he knew many of the people who'd be there, he'd always been an upscale gofer for James Greer. Now he had to prove himself. But he'd succeed. Ryan was sure of that. He had three of his own department heads along, and a comfortable seat on a VC-20A to remind him how important he was. He didn't know that it was the same bird that had taken Emil Jacobs to Colombia. That was just as well. For all his education, Ryan remained superstitious.

As Executive Assistant Director (Investigations), Bill Shaw was the Bureau's senior official, and until a new Director was appointed by the President and confirmed by the Senate, he'd be acting Director. That might last for a while. It was a presidential election year, and with the coming of summer, people were thinking about conventions, not appointments. Perversely, Shaw didn't mind a bit. That meant that he'd be running things, and for a case of this magnitude, the Bureau needed an experienced cop at the helm. "Political realities" were not terribly important to William Shaw. Crime cases were something that agents solved, and to him the case was everything. His first act on learning of the death of Director Jacobs had been to recall his friend, Dan Murray. It would be Dan's job to oversee the case from his deputy assistant director's office, since there were at least two elements to it: the investigation in Colombia and the one in Washington. Murray's experience as legal attaché in London gave him the necessary political sensitivity to understand that the overseas aspect of the case might not be handled to the Bureau's satisfaction. Murray entered Shaw's office at seven that morning. Neither had gotten much sleep in the previous two days, but they'd sleep on the plane. Director Jacobs would be buried in Chicago today, and they'd be flying out on the plane with the body to attend the funeral.

"Well?"

Dan flipped open his folder. "I just talked to Morales in Bogotá. The shooter they bagged is a stringer for M-19, and he doesn't know shit. Name is Héctor Buente, age twenty, college dropout from the University of the Andes — bad marks. Evidently the locals leaned on him a little bit — Morales says they're pretty torqued about this — but the kid doesn't know much. The shooters got a heads-up for an important job several days ago, but they didn't know what or where until four hours before it actually took place. They didn't know who was in the car aside from the ambassador. There was another team of shooters, by the way, staked out on a different route. They have some names, and the local cops're taking the town apart looking for them. I think that's a dead end. It was a contract job, and the people who know anything are long gone."

"What about places they fired from?"

"Broke in both apartments. They undoubtedly had the places surveyed beforehand. When the time came, they got in, tied up — actually cuffed — the owners, and sat it out. A real professional job from beginning to end," Murray said.

"Four hours' warning?"

"Correct."

"That makes it after the time the plane lifted off Andrews," Shaw observed.

Murray nodded. "That makes it clear that the leak was on our side. The airplane's flight plan was filed for Grenada — where the bird actually ended up. That was changed two hours out from the destination. The Colombian Attorney General was the only guy who knew that Emil was going down, and he didn't spread the word until *three* hours before the landing. Other senior government members knew that something was up, and that could explain the alert order to our M-19 friends, but the timing just isn't right. The leak was here unless their AG himself blew the cover off. Morales says that's very unlikely. The man is supposed to be the local Oliver Cromwell, honest as God and the balls of a lion. No mistress to blab to or anything like that. The leak was on our end, Bill."

Shaw rubbed his eyes and thought about some more coffee, but he had enough caffeine in his system already to hyperactivate a statue. "Go on."

"We've interviewed everyone who knew about

the trip. Needless to say, nobody claims to have talked. I've ordered a subpoena to check phone records, but I don't expect anything there."

"What about — "

"The guys at Andrews?" Dan smiled. "They're on the list. Maybe forty people, tops, who could have known that the Director was taking a flight. That includes people who found out up to an hour *after* the bird lifted off."

"Physical evidence?"

"Well, we have one of the RPG launchers and assorted other weapons. The Colombian Army troops reacted damned well — Christ, running into a building where you *know* there's heavy weapons, that's real balls. The M-19ers were carrying Soviet-bloc light weapons also, probably from Cuba, but that's incidental. I'd like to ask the Sovs to help us identify the RPG lot and shipment."

"You think we'll get any cooperation?"

"The worst thing they can say is no, Bill. We'll see if this *glasnost* crap is for-real or not."

"Okay, ask."

"The rest of the physical side is pretty straightforward. It'll confirm what we already know, but that's about it. Maybe the Colombians will be able to work their way back through M-19, but I doubt it. They've been working on that group for quite a while, and it's a tough nut."

"Okay."

"You look a little punked out, Bill," Murray observed. "We got young agents to burn both ends of the candle. Us old farts are supposed to know about pacing ourselves."

"Yeah, well, I have all this other stuff to get current with." Shaw waved at his desk.

"When's the plane leave?"

"Ten-thirty."

"Well, I'm going to go back to my office and grab a piece of the couch. I suggest you do the same."

Shaw realized that it wasn't such a bad idea. Ten minutes later, he'd done the same, asleep despite all the coffee he'd drunk. An hour after that, Moira Wolfe came to his door minutes ahead of the time his own executive secretary showed up. She knocked but got no answer. She didn't want to open the door, didn't want to disturb Mr. Shaw, even though there was something important that she wanted to tell him. It could wait until they were all on the airplane.

"Hi, Moira," Shaw's secretary said, catching her on the way out. "Anything wrong?"

"I wanted to see Mr. Shaw, but I think he's asleep. He's been working straight through since —"

"I know. You look like you could use some rest, too."

"Tonight, maybe."

"Want me to tell him —"

"No, I'll see him on the airplane."

There was a mixup on the subpoena. The agent who'd made the arrangements had gotten the name of the wrong judge from the U.S. Attorney, and found himself sitting in the anteroom until 9:30 because the judge was also late coming in this Monday morning. Ten minutes after that, he had everything he needed. The good news was that it was but a short drive to the phone company, and that the local Bell office could access all the billing records it needed. The total list was nearly a hundred names, with over two hundred phone numbers and sixty-one credit cards, some of which were not AT&T. It took an hour to get a hard copy of all the records, and the agent rechecked the numbers he had written down to make sure that there hadn't been any garbles or overlooks. He was a new agent, only a few months out of the Academy, on his first assignment to the Washington Field Division, essentially running an important errand for his supervisor as he learned the ropes, and he hadn't paid all that much attention to the data he'd just received. He didn't know, for example, that a 58 prefix on a certain telephone number denoted an overseas call to Venezuela. But he was young, and he'd know that before lunch.

The aircraft was a VC-135, the military version of the old 707. It was windowless, which the passengers always enjoyed, but had a large cargo door that was necessary for loading Director Jacobs aboard for his last trip to Chicago. The President was in another aircraft, scheduled to arrive at O'Hare International a few minutes ahead of this one. He would speak both at the temple and the graveside.

Shaw, Murray, and several other senior FBI officials rode in the second aircraft, which was often used for similar missions, and had the appropriate hardware to keep the casket in place in the forward section of the cabin. It gave them a chance to stare at the polished oak box for the entire flight, without even a small window to distract them. Somehow that brought it home more than anything else might have done. It was a very quiet flight, only the whine of the turbofan engines to keep the living and the dead company.

But the aircraft was part of the President's own fleet, and had all of the communications gear needed for that duty. An Air Force lieutenant came aft, asking for Murray, then led him forward to the communications console.

Mrs. Wolfe was in an aisle seat thirty feet aft of the senior executives. There were tears streaming down her face, and while she remembered that there was something she ought to tell Mr. Shaw, this wasn't the time or place, was it? It didn't really matter anyway — just that she'd made a mistake when the agent had interviewed her the previous afternoon. It was the shock of the event, really. It was so — hard. Her life had known too many losses in the past few years, and the mental whiplash of the weekend had . . . what? Confused her? She didn't know. But this wasn't the right time. Today was a time to remember the best boss she'd ever had, a man who was every bit as thoughtful to her as he'd ever been to the agents who lionized him. She saw Mr. Murray walk forward for something or other, past the coffin that her hand had brushed on the way in, her last goodbye to the Director.

The call didn't take more than a minute. Murray emerged from the small radio compartment, his face as much under control as it ever was. He didn't look again at the casket, just looked aft, Moira saw, straight down the aisle before he took his place next to his wife.

"Oh, shit!" Dan muttered to himself after he was seated. His wife's head snapped around. It wasn't the sort of thing you say at a funeral. She touched his arm, but Murray shook his head. When he looked at his wife, the expression she saw was sadness, but not grief.

The flight lasted just over an hour. The honor guard came up from the rear of the aircraft to take charge of the Director, all polished and scrubbed in their dress uniforms. After they were out, the passengers exited to find the rest of the assembly waiting for them on the tarmac, watched by distant TV news cameras. The honor guard marched their burden behind two flags, that of their nation and the banner of the FBI, emblazoned with the "Fidelity — Bravery — Integrity" motto of the Bureau. Murray watched as the wind played with the flag, watched the words curl and flap in the breeze, and realized just how intangible such words really were. But he couldn't tell Bill just yet. It would be noticed.

"Well, now we know why we wasted the air-field." Chavez watched the ceremony in the squad bay of the barracks. It was all very clear to him now.

"But why'd they yank us out?" Vega asked.

"We're going back, *Oso*. An' the air's gonna be thin where we're goin' back to."

Larson didn't need to watch the TV coverage. He hovered over a map, plotting known and suspected processing sites southwest of Medellín. He knew the areas — who didn't? — but isolating individual locations . . . that was harder, but, again, it was a technological question. The United States had invented modern reconnaissance technology and spent almost thirty years perfecting it. He was in Florida, having flown to the States ostensibly to take delivery of a new aircraft, which had unaccountably developed engine problems.

"How long have we been doing this?"

"Only a couple of months," Ritter answered.

Even with so thin a data base, it wasn't all that hard. All of the towns and villages in the area were plotted, of course, even individual houses. Since nearly all had electricity, they were easy to spot, and once identified, the computer simply erased them electronically. That left energy sources that were not towns, villages, and individual farmsteads. Of these, some were regular or fairly so. It had been arbitrarily decided that anything that appeared more than twice in a week was too obvious to be of real interest, and these, too, were erased. That left sixty or so locations that appeared and disappeared in accordance with a chart next to the map and photographs. Each was a possible site where raw coca leaves began the refining process. They were not encampments for the Colombian Boy Scouts.

"You can't track in on them chemically," Ritter said. "I checked. The ether and acetone concentrations released into the air aren't much more than you'd expect from the spillage of nail-polish remover, not to mention the usual biochemical processes in this sort of environment. It's a jungle, right? Lots of stuff rots on the ground, and they give off all sorts of chemicals when they do. So all we have off the satellite is the usual infrared. They still do all their processing at night? I wonder why?"

Larson grunted agreement. "It's a carry-over from when the Army was actively hunting them. They still do it mainly from habit, I suppose."

"Well, it gives us something, doesn't it?"

"What are we going to do with it?"

Murray had never been to a Jewish funeral. It wasn't very different from a Catholic one. The prayers were in a language he couldn't understand, but the message wasn't very different. *Lord, we're sending a good man back to You. Thanks for letting us have him for a while.* The

545

President's eulogy was particularly impressive, having been drafted by the best White House speechwriter, quoting from the Torah, the Talmud, and the New Testament. Then he started talking about Justice, the secular god that Emil had served for all of his adult life. When, toward the end, he talked about how men should turn their hearts away from vengeance, however, Murray thought that . . . it wasn't the words. The speech was as poetically written as any he'd ever heard. It was just that the President started sounding like a politician at that point, Dan thought. *Is that my own cynicism talking?* the agent thought. He was a cop, and justice to him meant that the bastards who committed crimes had to pay. Evidently the President thought the same way, despite the statesmanlike stuff he was saying. That was fine with Murray.

The soldiers watched the TV coverage in relative silence. A few men worked knives across sharpening stones, but mainly they just sat there, listening to their President speak, knowing who had killed the man whose name few had heard until after he was dead. Chavez had been the first to make the correct observation, but it hadn't been all that great a leap of imagination, had it? They accepted the as-yet-unspoken news phlegmatically. Here was merely additional proof that their enemy had struck out directly against one of the most important symbols of their nation. There was their country's flag, draped across the coffin. There was the banner of the man's own agency, but this wasn't a job for cops, was it? So the soldiers traded looks in silence while their Commander-in-Chief had his say. When it was all over, the door to the squad bay opened, and there was their commander.

"We're going back in tonight. The good news is, it's going to be cooler where we're going," Captain Ramirez told his men. Chavez cocked an eyebrow at Vega.

USS *Ranger* sailed on the tide, assisted away from the dock by a flotilla of tugs while her escorts formed up, already out of the harbor and taking rolls from the broad Pacific swells. Within an hour she was clear of the harbor, doing twenty knots. Another hour, and it was time to begin flight operations. First to arrive were the helicopters, one of which refueled and took off again to take plane-guard station off the carrier's starboard quarter. The first fixed-wing aircraft aboard were the Intruder attack bombers, led, of course, by the skipper, Commander Jensen. On the way out he'd seen the ammunition ship, USS *Shasta*, just beginning to get up steam. She'd join the underway-replenishment group that was to sail two hours behind the battle group. *Shasta* had the weapons that he'd be dropping. He already knew the sort of targets. Not the exact places yet, but he had the rough idea, and that, he realized as he climbed down from his aircraft, was all the idea he wanted to have. Worrying about "Collateral Damage" wasn't strictly his concern, as somebody had told him earlier in the day. *What an odd term,* he thought. *Collateral Damage.* What an offhand way of condemning people whom fate had already selected to be in the wrong place. He felt sorry for them, but not all that sorry.

Clark arrived in Bogotá late that afternoon. No one met him, and he rented a car as he usually did. One hour out of the airport he stopped to park on a secondary road. He waited several annoying minutes for another car to pull up alongside. The driver, a CIA officer assigned to the local station, handed him a package and drove off without a word. Not a large package, it weighed about twenty pounds, half of which was a stout tripod. Clark set it gently on the floor of the passenger compartment and drove off. He'd been asked to "deliver" quite a few messages in his time, but never quite so emphatically as this. It was all his idea. Well, he thought, mostly his idea. That made it somewhat more palatable.

The VC-135 lifted off two hours after the funeral. It was too bad they didn't have a wake in Chicago. That was an Irish custom, not one for the children of Eastern European Jews, but Emil would have approved, Dan Murray was sure. He would have understood that many a beer or whiskey would be lifted to his memory tonight, and somewhere, in his quiet way he'd laugh in the knowledge of it. But not now. Dan had gotten his wife to maneuver Mrs. Shaw onto the other side of the airplane so that he could sit next to Bill. Shaw noticed that immediately, of course, but waited until the aircraft leveled off to make the obvious question.

"What is it?"

Murray handed over the sheet he pulled off the aircraft's facsimile printer a few hours earlier.

"Oh, shit!" Shaw swore quietly. "Not Moira. Not her."

16.

Target List

"I'm open to suggestions," Murray said. He regretted his tone at once.

"Christ's sake, Dan!" Shaw's face had gone gray for a moment, and his expression was now angry.

"Sorry, but — damn it, Bill, do we handle it straight or do we candy-ass our way around the issue?"

"Straight."

"One of the kids from WFO asked her the usual battery of questions, and she said that she didn't tell anybody . . . well, maybe so, but who the hell did she call in Venezuela? They rechecked going back a year, no such calls ever before. The boy I left behind to run things did some further checking — the number she called is an apartment, and the phone there rang someplace in Colombia within a few minutes of Moira's call."

"Oh, God." Shaw shook his head. From anyone else he would merely have felt anger, but Moira had worked with the Director since before he'd returned to D.C., from his command of the New York Field Division.

"Maybe it's an innocent thing. Maybe even a coincidence," Murray allowed, but that didn't improve Bill's demeanor very much.

"Care to do a probability assessment of that statement, Danny?"

"No."

"Well, we're all going back to the office after we land. I'll have her into my place an hour after we get back. You be there, too."

"Right." It was time for Murray to shake his head. She'd shed as many tears at the graveside as anyone else. He'd seen a lifetime's worth of duplicity in his law-enforcement career, but to think that of Moira was more than he could stomach. *It has to be a coincidence. Maybe one of her kids has a pen pal down there. Or something like that*, Dan told himself.

The detectives searching Sergeant Braden's home found what they were looking for. It wasn't much, just a camera case. But the case had a Nikon F-3 body and enough lenses that the entire package had to be worth eight or nine thousand dollars. More than a Mobile detective sergeant could afford. While the rest of the officers continued the search, the senior detective called Nikon's home office and checked the number on the camera to see if the owner had registered it for warranty purposes. He had. And with the name that was read off to him, the officer knew that he had to call the FBI office as well. It was part of a federal case, and he hoped that somehow they could protect the name of a man who had certainly been a dirty cop. Dirty or not, he did leave kids behind. Perhaps the FBI would understand that.

He was committing a federal crime to do this, but the attorney considered that he had a higher duty to his clients. It was one of those gray areas which decorate not so much legal textbooks, but rather the volumes of written court decisions. He was sure a crime had been committed, was sure that nothing was being done to investigate it, and was sure that its disclosure was important to the defense of his clients on a case of capital murder. He didn't expect to be caught, but if he were, he'd have something to take to the professional ethics panel of the state bar association. Edward Stuart's professional duty to his clients, added to his personal distaste for capital punishment, made the decision an inevitable one.

They didn't call it Happy Hour at the base NCO club anymore, but nothing had really changed. Stuart had served his time in the U.S. Navy as a legal officer aboard an aircraft carrier — even in the Navy, a mobile city of six thousand people needed a lawyer or two — and knew about sailors and suds. So he'd visited a uniform store and gotten the proper outfit of a Coast Guard chief yeoman complete with the appropriate ribbons and just walked onto the base, heading for the NCO club where, as long as he paid for his drinks in cash, nobody would take great note of his presence. He'd had a yeoman himself while aboard USS *Eisenhower*, and knew the lingo well enough to pass any casual test of authenticity. The next trick, of course, was finding a crewman from the cutter *Panache*.

The cutter was finishing up the maintenance period that always followed a deployment, preparatory to yet another cruise, and her crewmen would be hitting the club after working hours to enjoy their afternoon beers while they could. It was just a matter of finding the right ones. He knew the names, and had checked tape archives at the local TV stations to get a look at the faces. It was nothing more than good luck that the one he found was Bob Riley. He knew more about that man's career than the other chiefs.

The master chief boatswain's mate strolled in at 4:30 after ten hot hours supervising work on various topside gear. He'd had a light lunch and sweated off all of that and more, and now figured that a few mugs of beer would replace all the fluids and electrolytes that he'd lost under the hot Alabama sun. The barmaid saw him coming and had a tall one of Samuel Adams all ready by the time he selected a stool. Edward Stuart got there a minute and half a mug later.

"Ain't you Bob Riley?"

"That's right," the bosun said before turning. "Who're you?"

"Didn't think you'd remember me. Matt Stevens. You near tore my head off on the *Mellon* awhile back — said I'd never get my shit together."

"Looks like I was wrong," Riley noted, searching his memory for the face.

"No, you were right. I was a real punk back then, but you — well, I owe you one, Master Chief. I did get my shit together. Mainly 'causa what you said." Stuart stuck out his hand. "I figure I owe you a beer at least."

It wasn't all that unusual a thing for Riley to hear. "Hell, we all need straightenin' out. I got bounced off a coupla bulkheads when I was a kid, too, y'know?"

"Done a little of it myself." Stuart grinned. "You make chief an' you gotta be respectable and responsible, right? Otherwise who keeps the officers straightened out?"

Riley grunted agreement. "Who you workin' for?"

"Admiral Hally. He's at Buzzard's Point. Had to fly down with him to meet with the base commander. I think he's off playing golf right now. Never did get the hang of that game. You're on *Panache*, right?"

"You bet."

"Captain Wegener?"

"Yep." Riley finished off his beer and Stuart waved to the barmaid for refills.

"Is he as good as they say?"

"Red's a better seaman 'n I am," Riley replied honestly.

"Nobody's that good, Master Chief. Hey, I was there when you took the boat across — what was the name of that container boat that snapped in half . . . ?"

"*Arctic Star*." Riley smiled, remembering. "Jesus, if we didn't earn our pay that afternoon."

"I remember watching. Thought you were crazy. Well, shit. All I do now is drive a word processor for the Admiral, but I did a little stuff in a forty-one boat before I made chief, working outa Norfolk. Nothing like *Arctic Star*, of course."

"Don't knock it, Matt. One of those jobs's enough for a couple years of sea stories. I'll take an easy one any day. I'm gettin' a little old for that dramatic stuff."

"How's the food here?"

"Fair."

"Buy you dinner?"

"Matt, I don't even remember what I said to you."

"I remember," Stuart assured him. "God knows how I woulda turned out if you hadn't turned me around. No shit, man. I owe you one. Come on." He waved Riley over to a booth against the wall. They were quickly going through their third beer when Chief Quartermaster Oreza arrived.

"Hey, Portagee," Riley called to his fellow master chief.

"I see the beer's cold, Bob."

Riley waved to his companion. "This here's Matt Stevens. We were on the *Mellon* together. Did I ever tell you about the *Arctic Star* job?"

"Only about thirty times," Oreza noted.

"You wanna tell the story, Matt?" Riley asked.

"Hey, I didn't even see it all, you know — "

"Yeah, half the crew was puking their guts out. I'm talking a real gale blowing. No way the helo could take off, and this container boat — the after half of her, that is; the fo'ard part was already gone — look like she was gonna roll right there an' then . . . "

Within an hour, two more rounds had been consumed, and the three men were chomping their way through a disk of knockwurst and sauerkraut, which went well with beer. Stuart stuck with stories about his new Admiral, the Chief Counsel of the Coast Guard, in which legal officers are also line officers, expected to know how to drive ships and command men.

"Hey, what's with these stories I been hearing about you an' those two drug pukes?" the attorney finally asked.

"What d'ya mean?" Oreza asked. Portagee still had some remaining shreds of sobriety.

"Hey, the FBI guys went in to see Hally, right? I had to type up his reports on my Zenith, y'know?"

"What did them FBI guys say?"

"I'm not supposed — oh, fuck it! Look, you're all in the clear. The Bureau isn't doing a fuckin' thing. They told your skipper 'go forth and sin no more,' okay? The shit you got outa those pukes — didn't you hear? Operation TARPON. That whole sting operation came from you guys. Didn't you know that?"

"What?" Riley hadn't seen a paper or turned on a TV in days. Though he did know about the death of the FBI Director, he had no idea of the connection with his Hang-Ex, as he had taken to calling it in the goat locker.

Stuart explained what he knew, which was quite a lot.

"Half a billion dollars?" Oreza observed quietly. "That oughta build us a few new hulls."

"Christ knows we need 'em," Stuart agreed.

"You guys didn't really — I mean, you didn't really . . . hang one of the fuckers, did you?" Stuart extracted a Radio Shack mini-tape recorder from his pocket and thumbed the volume switch to the top.

"Actually it was Portagee's idea," Riley said.

"Couldn't have done it without you, Bob," Oreza said generously.

"Yeah, well, the trick was how to do the hangin'," Riley explained. "You see, we had to make it look real if we was gonna scare the piss outa the little one. Wasn't really all that hard once I thought it over. After we got him alone, the pharmacist mate gave him a shot of ether to knock him out for a few minutes, and I rigged a rope harness on his back. When we took him topside, the noose had a hook on the back, so when I

557

looped the noose around his neck, all I hadda do was attach the hook to an eye I put on the harness, so we was hoistin' him by the harness, not the neck. We didn't really wanna kill the fucker — well, I did," Riley said. "But Red didn't think it was a real good idea." The bosun grinned at the quartermaster.

"The other trick was baggin' him," Oreza said. "We put a black hood over his head. Well, there was a gauze pad inside soaked in ether. The bastard screamed bloody murder when he smelled it, but it had him knocked out as soon as we ran his ass up to the yardarm."

"The little one believed the whole thing. Fucker wet his pants, it was beautiful! Sang like a canary when they got him back to the wardroom. Soon as he was outa sight, of course, we lowered the other one and got him woke back up. They were both half in the bag from smokin' grass all day. I don't think they ever figured out what we did to them."

No, they didn't. "Grass?"

"That was Red's idea. They had their own pot stash — looked like real cigarettes. We just gave 'em back to 'em, and they got themselves looped. Throw in the ether and everything, and I bet they never figured out what really happened."

Almost right, Stuart thought, hoping that his tape recorder was getting this.

"I wish we really could have hung 'em," Riley said after a few seconds. "Matt, you ain't never seen anything like what that yacht looked like.

Four people, man — butchered 'em like cattle. Ever smell blood? I didn't know you could. You can," the bosun assured him. "They raped the wife and the little girl, then cut 'em up like they was — God! You know, I been having nightmares from that? Nightmares — me! Jesus, that's one sea story I wish I could forget. I got a little girl that age. Those fuckers raped her an' killed her, and cut her up an' fed her to the fuckin' sharks. Just a little girl, not even big enough to drive a car or go out on a date.

"We're supposed to be professional cops, right? We're supposed to be cool about it, don't get personally involved. All that shit?" Riley asked.

"That's what the book says," Stuart agreed.

"The book wasn't written for stuff like this," Portagee said. "People who do this sort of thing — they ain't really people. I don't know what the hell they are, but people they ain't. You can't do that kinda shit and be people, Matt."

"Hey, what d'you want me to say?" Stuart asked, suddenly defensive, and not acting a part this time. "We got laws to deal with people like that."

"Laws ain't doin' much good, are they?" Riley asked.

The difference between the people he was obliged to defend and the people he had to impeach, Stuart told himself through the fog of alcohol, was that the bad ones were his clients and the good ones were not. And now, by impersonating a Coast Guard chief, he too had broken a law, just as these men had done, and like them, he was doing it for some greater good, some higher moral cause. So he asked himself who was right. Not that it mattered, of course. Whatever was "right" was lost somewhere, not to be found in lawbooks or canons of ethics. Yet if you couldn't find it there, then where the hell was it? But Stuart was a lawyer, and his business was law, not right. Right was the province of judges and juries. Or something like that. Stuart told himself that he shouldn't drink so much. Drink made confused things clear, and the clear things confused.

The ride in was far rougher this time. Westerly winds off the Pacific Ocean hit the slopes of the Andes and boiled upward, looking for passes to go through. The resulting turbulence could be felt at thirty thousand feet, and here, only three hundred feet AGL — above ground level — the ride was a hard one, all the more so with the helicopter on its terrain-following autopilot. Johns and Willis were strapped in tight to reduce the effects of the rough ride, and both knew that the people in back were having a bad time indeed as the big Sikorsky jolted up and down in twenty-foot bounds at least ten times per minute. PJ's hand was on the stick, following the motions of the autopilot but ready to take instant command if the system showed the first sign of failure. This was real flying, as he liked to say. That generally meant the dangerous kind.

Skimming through this pass — it was more of a saddle, really — didn't make it any easier. A ninety-six-hundred-foot peak was to the south, and one of seventy-eight hundred feet to the north, and a lot of Pacific air was being funneled through as the Pave Low roared at two hundred knots. They were heavy, having tanked only a few minutes earlier just off Colombia's Pacific Coast.

"There's Mistrato," Colonel Johns said. The computer navigation system had already veered them north to pass well clear of the town and any roads. The two pilots were also alert for anything on the ground that hinted at a man or a car or a house. The route had been selected off satellite photographs, of course, both daylight and night-time infrared shots, but there was always the chance of a surprise.

"Buck, LZ One in four minutes," PJ called over the intercom.

"Roger."

They were flying over Risaralda Province, part of the great valley that lay between two enormous ridgelines of mountains flung into the sky by a subductal fault in the earth's crust. PJ's hobby was geology. He knew how much effort it took to bring his aircraft to this altitude, and he boggled at the forces that could push mountains to the same height.

"LZ One in sight," Captain Willis said.

"Got it." Colonel Johns took the stick. He

keyed his microphone. "One minute. Hot guns."

"Right." Sergeant Zimmer left his position to head aft. Sergeant Bean activated his minigun in case there was trouble. Zimmer slipped and nearly fell on a pool of vomit. That wasn't unusual. The ride smoothed out now that they were in the lee of the mountains, but there were some very sick kids in back who would be glad to get on firm, unmoving ground. Zimmer had trouble understanding that. It was dangerous on the ground.

The first squad was up as the helicopter flared to make its first landing, and as before, the moment it touched down, they ran out the back. Zimmer made his count, watched to be certain that everyone got off safely, and notified the pilot to lift off as soon as they were clear.

Next time, Chavez told himself, *next time I fucking walk in and out!* He had had some rough chopper rides in his time, but nothing like that one. He led off to the treeline and waited for the remainder of the squad to catch up.

"Glad to be on the ground?" Vega asked as soon as he got there.

"I didn't know I ate that much," Ding groaned. Everything he'd eaten in the last few hours was still aboard the helicopter. He opened a canteen and drank a pint of water just to wash away the vile taste.

"I usta love roller coasters," *Oso* said. "No more, *'mano!*"

"Fuckin' A!" Chavez remembered standing in line for the big ones at Knott's Berry Farm and other California theme parks. Never again!

"You okay, Ding?" Captain Ramirez asked.

"Sorry, sir. That never happened to me — ever! I'll be okay in a minute," he promised his commander.

"Take your time. We picked a nice, quiet spot to land." *I hope.*

Chavez shook his head to clear it. He didn't know that motion sickness started in the inner ear, had never known what motion sickness was until half an hour earlier. But he did the right thing, taking deep breaths and shaking his head to get his equilibrium back. The ground wasn't moving, he told himself, but part of his brain wasn't sure.

"Where to, Cap'n?"

"You're already heading in the right direction." Ramirez clapped him on the shoulder. "Move out."

Chavez put on his low-light goggles and started moving off through the forest. God, but that was embarrassing. He'd never do anything that dumb again, the sergeant promised himself. With his head still telling him that he was probably moving in a way that his legs couldn't possibly cause, he concentrated on his footing and the terrain, rapidly moving two hundred meters ahead of the main body of the squad. The first mission into the swampy lowlands had just been practice, hadn't really been serious, he thought now. But

563

this was the real thing. With that thought foremost in his mind, he batted away the last remnants of his nausea and got down to work.

Everyone worked late that night. There was the investigation to run, and routine office business had to be kept current as well. By the time Moira came into Mr. Shaw's office, she'd managed to organize everything he'd need to know, and it was also time to tell him what she'd forgotten. She wasn't surprised to see Mr. Murray there, too. She was surprised when he spoke first.

"Moira, were you interviewed about Emil's trip?" Dan asked.

She nodded. "Yes. I forgot something. I wanted to tell you this morning, Mr. Shaw, but when I came in early you were asleep. Connie saw me," she assured him.

"Go on," Bill said, wondering if he should feel a little better about that or not.

Mrs. Wolfe sat down, then turned to look at the open door. Murray walked over to close it. On the way back he placed his hand on her shoulder.

"It's okay, Moira."

"I have a friend. He lives in Venezuela. We met . . . well, we met a month and a half ago, and we — this is hard to explain." She hesitated, staring at the rug for a moment before looking up. "We fell in love. He comes up to the States on business every few weeks, and with the Director away, we wanted to spend a weekend — at The

564

Hideaway, in the mountains near Luray Caverns?"

"I know it," Shaw said. "Nice place to get away from it all."

"Well, when I knew that Mr. Jacobs was going to be away and we had a chance for a long weekend, I called him. He has a factory. He makes auto parts — two factories, actually, one in Venezuela and one in Costa Rica. Carburetors and things like that."

"Did you call him at his home?" Murray asked.

"No. He works such long hours that I called him at his factory. I have the number here." She handed over the scrap of Sheraton note paper that he'd written it down on. "Anyway, I got his secretary — her name's Consuela — because he was out on the shop floor, and he called me back, and I told him that we could get together, so he came up — we met at the airport Friday afternoon. I left early after Mr. Jacobs did."

"Which airport?"

"Dulles."

"What's his name?" Shaw asked.

"Díaz. Juan Díaz. You can call him there at the factory and — "

"That phone number goes to an apartment, not a factory, Moira," Murray said. And it was that clear, that fast.

"But — but he — " She stopped. "No. No. He isn't — "

"Moira, we need a complete physical description."

"Oh, no." Her mouth fell open and wouldn't close. She looked from Shaw to Murray and back again as the horror of it all closed in on her. She was dressed in black, of course, probably the same outfit she'd worn to bury her own husband. For a few weeks she'd been a bright, beautiful, happy woman again. No more. Both FBI executives felt her pain, hating themselves for having brought it to her. She was a victim, too. But she was also a lead, and they needed a lead.

Moira Wolfe summoned what little dignity she had left and gave them as complete a description as they had ever had of any man in a voice as brittle as crystal before she lost control entirely. Shaw had his personal assistant drive her home.

"Cortez," Murray said as soon as the door closed behind her.

"That's a pretty solid bet," the Executive Assistant Director (Investigations) agreed. "The book on him says that he's a real ace at compromising people. Jesus, did he ever prove that right." Shaw's head went from side to side as he reached for some coffee. "But he couldn't have known what they were doing, could he?"

"Doesn't make much sense to have come here if he did," Murray said. "But since when are criminals logical? Well, we start checking immigration control points, hotels, airlines. See if we can track this cocksucker. I'll get on it. What are we going to do about Moira?"

"She didn't break any laws, did she?" That was the really odd part. "Find a place where she doesn't have to see classified material, maybe in another agency. Dan, we can't destroy her, too."

"No."

Moira Wolfe got home just before eleven. Her kids were all still up waiting for her. They assumed that her tears were a delayed reaction from the funeral. They'd all met Emil Jacobs, too, and mourned his passing as much as anyone else who worked for the Bureau. She didn't say very much, heading upstairs for bed while they continued to sit before the television. Alone in the bathroom she stared in the mirror at the woman who'd allowed herself to be seduced and *used* like . . . like a fool, something worse than a fool, a stupid, vain, lonely old woman looking for her youth. So desperate to be loved again that . . . That she had condemned — how many? Seven people? She couldn't remember, staring at her empty face in the glass. The young agents on Emil's security detail had families. She'd knitted a sweater for Leo's firstborn son. He was still too young — he'd never remember what a nice, handsome young man his father had been.

It's all my fault.

I helped kill them.

She opened the mirrored door to the medicine cabinet. Like most people, the Wolfes never threw out old medicine, and there it was, a plastic container of Placidyls. There were still — she counted six of them. Surely that would be enough.

★

"What brings you out this time?" Timmy Jackson asked his big brother.

"I gotta go out on *Ranger* to observe a Fleet-Ex. We're trying out some new intercept tactics I helped work up. And a friend of mine just got command of *Enterprise*, so I came out a day early to watch the ceremony. I go down to D'ego tomorrow and catch the COD out to *Ranger*."

"COD?"

"The carrier's delivery truck," Robby explained. "Twin-engine prop bird. So how's life in the light infantry?"

"We're still humpin' hills. Got our clock cleaned on the last exercise. My new squad leader really fucked up. It isn't fair," Tim observed.

"What do you mean?"

Lieutenant Jackson tossed off the last of his drink. " 'A green lieutenant and a green squad leader is too much burden for any platoon to bear' — that's what the new S-3 said. He was out with us. Of course, the captain didn't exactly see it that way. Lost a little weight yesterday — he chewed off a piece of my ass for me. God, I wish I had Chavez back."

"Huh?"

"Squad leader I lost. He — that's the odd part. He was supposed to go to a basic-training center as an instructor, but seems he got lost. The S-3 says he was in Panama a few weeks ago. Had my platoon sergeant try to track him down, see what the hell was going on — he's still my man, you know?" Robby nodded. He understood. "Anyway, his paperwork is missing, and the clerks are runnin' in circles trying to find it. Fort Benning called to ask where the hell he was, 'cause they were still waiting for him. Nobody knows where the hell Ding got to. That sort of thing happen in the Navy?"

"When a guy goes missing, it generally means that he wants to be missing."

Tim shook his head. "Nah, not Ding. He's a lifer, I don't even think he'll stop at twenty. He'll retire as a command sergeant major. No, he's no bugout."

"Then maybe somebody dropped his file in the wrong drawer," Robby suggested.

"I suppose. I'm still new at this," Tim reminded himself. "Still, it is kind of funny, turning up down there in the jungle. Enough of that. How's Sis?"

About the only good thing to say was that it wasn't hot. In fact, it was pretty cool. Maybe there wasn't enough air to be hot, Ding told himself. The altitude was marginally less than they'd trained at in Colorado, but that was weeks behind them, and it would be a few days before the soldiers were reacclimated. That would slow them down some, but on the whole Chavez thought that heat was more debilitating than thin air, and harder to get used to.

The mountains — nobody called these mothers hills — were about as rugged as anything he'd ever seen, and though they were well forested, he was paying particularly close attention to his footing. The thick trees made for limited visibility, which was good news. His night scope, hanging on his head like a poorly designed cap, allowed him to see no more than a hundred meters, and usually less than that, but he could see something, while the overhead cover eliminated the light needed for the unaided eye to see. It was scary, and it was lonely, but it was home for Sergeant Chavez.

He did not move in a straight line to the night's objective, following instead the Army's approved procedure of constantly veering left and right of the direction in which he was actually traveling. Every half hour he'd stop, double back, and wait until the rest of the squad was in view. Then it was their turn to rest for a few minutes, checking their own back for people who might take an interest in the new visitors to the jungle highlands.

The sling on his MP-5 was double-looped so that he could carry it slung over his head, always in firing position. There was electrician's tape over the muzzle to keep it from being clogged, and more tape was wrapped around the sling swivels to minimize noise. Noise was their enemy. Chavez concentrated on that, and seeing, and a dozen other things. This one was for-real. The mission brief had told them all about that. Their job wasn't reconnaissance anymore.

After six hours, the RON — remain overnight — site was in view. Chavez radioed back — five taps on the transmit key answered by three — for the squad to remain in place while he checked it out. They'd picked a real eyrie — he knew the word for an eagle's nest — from which, in daylight, they could look down on miles of the main road that snaked its way from Manizales to Medellín, and off of which the refining sites were located. Six of them, supposedly, were within a night's march of the RON site. Chavez circled it carefully, looking for footprints, trash, anything that hinted at human activity. It was too good a site for someone not to have used it for something or other, he thought. Maybe a photographer for *National Geographic* who wanted to take shots of the valley. On the other hand, getting here was a real bitch. They were a good three thousand feet above the road, and this wasn't the sort of country that you could drive a tank across, much less a car. He spiraled in, and still found nothing. Maybe it was too far out of the way. After half an hour he keyed his radio again. The rest of the squad had had ample time to check its rear, and if anyone had been following them, there would have been contact by now. The sun outlined the eastern wall of the valley in red by the time Captain Ramirez appeared. It was just as well that the covert insertion had shortened the night. With only half a night's march behind them they were tired, but not too tired, and would have a day to get used to the altitude all over again. They'd come five linear miles from the LZ — more like seven miles actually walked, and two thousand feet up.

As before, Ramirez spread his men out in pairs. There was a nearby stream, but nobody was dehydrated this time. Chavez and Vega took position over one of the two most likely avenues of approach to their perch, a fairly gentle slope with not too many trees and a good field of fire. Ding hadn't come in this way, of course.

"How you feelin', *Oso?*"

"Why can't we ever go to a place with plenty of air and it's cool and flat?" Sergeant Vega slipped out of his web gear, setting it in a place where it would make a comfortable pillow. Chavez did the same.

"People don't fight wars there, man. That's where they build golf courses."

"Fuckin' A!" Vega set up his Squad Automatic Weapon next to a rocky outcropping. A camouflage cloth was set across the muzzle. He could have torn up a shrub to hide the gun behind, but they didn't want to disturb anything they didn't have to. Ding won the toss this time, and fell off to sleep without a word.

"Mom?" It was after seven o'clock, and she was always up by now, fixing breakfast for her family of early risers. Dave knocked at the door, but heard nothing. That was when he started being afraid. He'd already lost a father, and knew that even parents were not the immortal, unchanging beings that all children need at the center of their growing universe. It was the constant nightmare that each of Moira's children had but never spoke about, even among themselves, lest their talk somehow make it more likely to happen. *What if something happens to Mom?* Even before his hand felt for the doorknob, Dave's eyes filled with tears at the anticipation of what he might find.

"Mom?" His voice quavered now, and he was ashamed of it, fearful also that his siblings would hear. He turned the knob and opened the door slowly.

The shades were open, flooding the room with morning light. And there she was, lying on the bed, still wearing her black mourning dress. Not moving.

Dave just stood there, the tears streaming down his cheeks as the reality of his personal nightmare struck him with physical force.

" . . . Mom?"

Dave Wolfe was as courageous as any teenager, and he needed all of it this morning. He summoned what strength he had and walked to the bedside, taking his mother's hand. It was still warm. Next he felt for a pulse. It was there, weak and slow, but there. That galvanized him into action. He lifted the bedside phone and punched 911.

"Police emergency," a voice answered immediately.

"I need an ambulance. My mom won't wake up."

"What is your address?" the voice asked. Dave gave it. "Okay, now describe your mother's condition."

"She's asleep, and she won't wake up, and — "

"Is your mother a heavy drinker?"

"*No!*" he replied in outrage. "She works for the FBI. She went right to bed last night, right after she got home from work. She — " And there it was, right on the night table. "Oh, God. There's a pill bottle here . . . "

"Read the label to me!" the voice said.

"*P-l-a-c-i-d-y-l*. It's my dad's, and he — " That was all the operator needed to hear.

"Okay — we'll have an ambulance there in five minutes."

Actually, it was there in just over four minutes. The Wolfe house was only three blocks from a firehouse. The paramedics were in the living room before the rest of the family knew anything was wrong. They ran upstairs to find Dave still holding his mother's hand and shaking like a twig in a heavy wind. The leading fireman pushed him aside, checked the airway first, then her eyes, then the pulse.

"Forty and thready. Respiration is . . . eight and shallow. It's Placidyl," he reported.

"Not that shit!" The second one turned to Dave. "How many were in there?"

"I don't know. It was my dad's, and — "

"Let's go, Charlie." The first paramedic lifted her by the arms. "Move it, kid, we gotta roll." There wasn't time to fool around with the Stokes litter. He was a big, burly man and carried Moira Wolfe out of the room like a baby. "You can follow us to the hospital."

"How — "

"She's still breathin', kid. That's the best thing I can tell you right now," the second one said on the way out the door.

What the hell is going on? Murray wondered. He'd come by to pick Moira up — her car was still in the FBI garage — and maybe help ease the guilt she clearly felt. She'd violated security rules, she'd done something very foolish, but she was also a victim of a man who'd searched and selected her for her vulnerabilities, then exploited them as professionally as anyone could have done. Everybody had vulnerabilities. That was another lesson he'd picked up over his years in the Bureau.

He'd never met Moira's kids, though he did know about them, and it wasn't all that hard to figure out who would be there, following the paramedic out of the house. Murray double-parked his Bureau car and hopped out.

"What gives?" he asked the second paramedic. Murray held up his ID so that he'd get an answer.

"Suicide attempt. Pills. Anything else you need?" the paramedic asked on his way to the driver's seat.

"Get moving." Murray turned to make sure he wasn't in the ambulance's way.

When he turned back to look at the kids, it was plain that "suicide" hadn't yet been spoken aloud, and the ugliness of that word made them wilt before his eyes.

That fucker Cortez! You'd better hope that I never get my hands on you!

"Kids, I'm Dan Murray. I work with your mom. You want me to take you to the hospital?" The case could wait. The dead were dead, and they could afford to be patient. Emil would understand.

He let them off in front of the emergency entrance and went off to find a parking place and use his car phone. "Get me Shaw," he told the watch officer. It didn't take long.

"Dan, this is Bill. What gives?"

"Moira tried to kill herself last night. Pills."

"What are you going to do?"

"Somebody has to sit with the kids. Does she have any friends we can bring out?"

"I'll check."

"Until then I'm going to hang around, Bill. I mean — "

"I understand. Okay. Let me know what's happening."

"Right." Murray replaced the phone and walked over to the hospital. The kids were sitting together in the waiting room. Dan knew about emergency-room waiting. He also knew that the gold badge of an FBI agent could open nearly any door. It did this time, too.

"You just brought a woman in," he told the nearest doctor. "Moira Wolfe."

"Oh, she's the OD."

She's a person, *not a goddamned OD!* Murray didn't say. Instead he nodded. "Where?"

576

"You can't — "

Murray cut him off cold. "She's part of a major case. I want to see what's happening."

The doctor led him to a treatment cubicle. It wasn't pretty. Already there was a respirator tube down her throat, and IV lines in each arm — on second inspection, one of the tubes seemed to be taking her blood out and running it through something before returning it to the same arm. Her clothing was off, and EKG sensors were taped to her chest. Murray hated himself for looking at her. Hospitals robbed everyone of dignity, but life was more important than dignity, wasn't it?

Why didn't Moira know that?

Why didn't you catch the signal, Dan? Murray demanded of himself. *You should have thought to have somebody keep an eye on her. Hell, if you'd put her in custody, she couldn't have done this!*

Maybe we should have yelled at her instead of going so easy. Maybe she took it the wrong way. Maybe. Maybe. Maybe.

Cortez, you are fucking dead. I just haven't figured out when yet.

"Is she going to make it?" Murray asked.

"Who the hell are you?" a doctor asked without turning.

"FBI, and I need to know."

The doctor still didn't look around. "So do I, sport. She took Placidyl. That's a pretty potent sleeping pill, not too many docs prescribe it anymore, 'cause it's too easy to OD on. LD-50 is

577

anywhere from five to ten caps. LD-50 means the dose that'll kill half the people that take it. I don't know how much she took. At least she isn't completely gone, but her vitals are too goddamned low for comfort. We're dialyzing her blood to keep any more from getting into her, hope it's not a waste of time. We've put her on hundred-percent oxygen, then we'll zap her full of IV fluids and wait it out. She'll be out for at least another day. Maybe two, maybe three. Can't tell yet. I can't tell you what the odds are either. Now you know as much as I do. Get out of here, I got work to do."

"There are three kids in the waiting room, Doctor."

That turned his head around for about two seconds. "Tell 'em we got a pretty good chance, but it's going to be tough for a while. Hey, I'm sorry, but I just don't know. The good news is, if she comes back, she'll come all the way back. This stuff doesn't usually do permanent damage. Unless it kills you," the doctor added.

"Thanks."

Murray left to tell the kids what he could. Within an hour, some neighbors showed up to take their place with the Wolfe children. Dan left quietly after an agent arrived to keep his own vigil in the waiting room. Moira was probably their only link with Cortez, and that meant that her life was potentially in danger from hands other than her own. Murray got to the office just after nine, his mood still quiet and angry when he arrived. There were three agents waiting for him, and he waved them to follow.

"Okay, what have you found out?"

" 'Mr. Díaz' used an American Express card at The Hideaway. We've identified the number at two airline ticket counters — thank God for those credit-checking computers. Right after he dropped Mrs. Wolfe off, he caught a flight out of Dulles to Atlanta, and from there to Panama. That's where he disappeared. He must have paid cash for the next ticket, 'cause there's no record of a Juan Díaz on any flight that evening. The counter clerk at Dulles remembers him — he was in a hurry to catch the Atlanta flight. The description matches the one we already have. However he got into the country last week, it wasn't Dulles. We're running computer records now, ought to have an answer later this morning — call it an even-money chance to figure his route in. I'm betting on one of the big hubs, Dallas-Fort Worth, Kansas City, Chicago, one of them. But that's not the interesting thing we've discovered.

"American Express just discovered that it has a bunch of cards for Juan Díaz. Several have been generated recently, and they don't know how."

"Oh?" Murray poured some coffee. "How come they weren't noticed?"

"For one thing, the statements are paid on time and in full, so that dog didn't bark. The addresses are all slightly different, and the name itself isn't terribly unusual, so a casual look at the records won't tip anyone off. What it looks like is that somebody has a way to tap into their computer system — all the way into the executive programming, and that might be another lead for us to run down. He's probably been staying with the name in case Moira gets a look at the card. But what it has told us is that he's made five trips to the D.C. area in the past four months. Somebody is playing with the AmEx computer system, somebody good. Somebody," the agent went on, "good enough to tap into a lot of computers. This guy can generate complete credit lines for Cortez or anyone else. There ought to be a way to check that out, but I wouldn't be real hopeful about running him down fast."

There was a knock at the door, and another young agent came in. "Dallas-Fort Worth," he said handing over a fax sheet. "The signatures match. He came in there and took a late flight to New York-La Guardia, got in after midnight local time on Friday. Probably caught the Shuttle down to D.C. to meet Moira. They're still checking."

"Beautiful," Murray said. "He's got all the moves. Where'd he come in from?"

"Still checking, sir. He got the New York ticket at the counter. We're talking with Immigration to see when he passed through customs control."

"Okay, next?"

"We have prints on him now. We have what looks like a left forefinger on the note paper he left Mrs. Wolfe, and we've matched that with the

580

credit receipt from the airline counter at Dulles. It was tough, but the lab guys used their lasers to bring 'em out. We sent a team to The Hideaway, but nothing yet. The cleanup crew there is pretty good — too damned good for our purposes, but our guys are still working on it."

"Everything but a picture on the bastard. Everything but a picture," Murray repeated. "What about after Atlanta?"

"Oh, thought I said that. He caught a flight to Panama after a short layover."

"Where's the AmEx card addressed to?"

"It's in Caracas, probably just a letterdrop. They all are."

"How come Immigration doesn't — oh." Murray grimaced. "Of course his passport is under a different name or he has a collection of them to go with his cards."

"We're dealing with a real pro. We're lucky to have gotten this much so fast."

"What's new in Colombia?" he asked the next agent.

"Not much. The lab work is going nicely, but we're not developing anything we didn't already know. The Colombians now have names on about half of the subjects — the prisoner says he didn't know all of them, and that's probably the truth. They've launched a major operation to try an' find 'em, but Morales isn't real hopeful. They're all names of people the Colombian government's been after for quite a while. All M-19 types. It was a contract job, just as we thought."

Murray checked his watch. Today was the funeral for the two agents on Emil's protection detail. It would be held at the National Cathedral, and the President would be speaking there, too. His phone rang.

"Murray."

"This is Mark Bright down at Mobile. We have some additional developments."

"Okay."

"A cop got himself blown away Saturday. It was a contract job, Ingrams at close range, but a local kid popped a subject with his trusty .22, right in the back of the head. Killed him; they found the body and the vehicle yesterday. The shooter was positively ID'd as a druggie. The local cops searched the victim's — Detective Sergeant Braden — house and found a camera that belonged to the victim in the Pirates Case. The new victim is a burglary sergeant. I am speculating that he was working for the druggies and probably checked out the victim's place prior to the killings, looking for the records that we ultimately found."

Murray nodded thoughtfully. That added something to their knowledge. So they'd wanted to make sure that the victim hadn't left any records behind before they'd taken him and his family out, but their guy wasn't good enough, and they killed him for it. It was also part of the murder of Director Jacobs, additional fallout from Operation TARPON. *Those bastards are really flexing their muscles, aren't they?* "Anything else?"

"The local cops are in a pretty nasty mood about this. First time somebody's put a hit on a cop that way. It was a 'public' hit, and his wife got taken out by a stray round. Local cops are pretty pissed. A drug dealer got taken all the way out last night. It'll come out as a righteous shoot, but I don't think it was a coincidence. That's it for now."

"Thanks, Mark." Murray hung up. "The bastards have declared war on us, all right," he murmured.

"What's that, sir?"

"Nothing. Have you back-checked on the earlier trips Cortez made — hotels, car rentals?"

"We have twenty people out there on it. Ought to have some preliminary information in two hours."

"Keep me posted."

Stuart was the first morning appointment for the U.S. Attorney, and he looked unusually chipper this morning, the secretary thought. She couldn't see the hangover.

"Morning, Ed," Davidoff said without rising. His desk was a mass of papers. "What can I do for you?"

"No death penalty," Stuart said as he sat down. "I'll trade a guilty plea for twenty years, and that's the best deal you're going to get."

"See ya' in court, Ed," Davidoff replied, looking back down at his papers.

"You want to know what I've got?"

"If it's good, I'm sure you'll let me know at the proper time."

"May be enough to get my people off completely. You want 'em to walk on this?"

"Believe that when I see it," Davidoff said, but he was looking up now. Stuart was an overly zealous defense lawyer, the United States Attorney thought, but an honest one. He didn't lie, at least not in chambers.

Stuart habitually carried an old-fashioned briefcase, the wedge-shaped kind made of semistiff leather instead of the newer and trimmer attaché case that most lawyers toted now. From it he extracted a tape recorder. Davidoff watched in silence. Both men were trial lawyers and both were experts at concealing their feelings, able to say what they had to say, regardless of what they felt. But since both had this ability, like professional poker players they knew the more subtle signs that others couldn't spot. Stuart knew that he had his adversary worried when he punched the play button. The tape lasted several minutes. The sound quality was miserable, but it was audible, and with a little cleaning up in a sound laboratory — the defendants could afford it — it would be as clear as it needed to be.

Davidoff's ploy was the obvious one: "That has no relevance to the case we're trying. All of the information in the confession is excluded from the proceedings. We agreed on that."

Stuart eased his tone now that he had the upper hand. It was time for magnanimity. "You agreed. I didn't say anything. The government committed a gross violation of my clients' constitutional rights. A simulated execution constitutes mental torture at the very least. It's sure as hell illegal. You have to put these two guys on the stand to make your case, and I'll crucify those Coast Guard sailors when you do. It might be enough to impeach everything they say. You never know what a jury's going to think, do you?"

"They might just stand up and cheer, too," Davidoff answered warily.

"That's the chance, isn't it? One way to find out. We try the case." Stuart replaced the player in his briefcase. "Still want an early trial date? With this as background information I can attack your chain of evidence — after all, if they were crazy enough to pull this number, what if my clients claim that they were forced to masturbate to give you the semen samples that you told the papers about, or were forced to hold the murder weapons to make prints — I haven't yet discussed any of those details with them, by the way — and I link all that in with what I know about the victim? I think I have a fighting chance to send them home alive and free." Stuart leaned forward, resting his arms on Davidoff's desk. "On the other hand, as you say, it's hard to predict how a jury'll react. So what I'm offering you is, they plead guilty to twenty years' worth of whatever charge you want, with no unseemly recommendation from the judge about how they have to serve all twenty — so they're out in, say, eight years. You tell the press that there's problems with the evidence, and you're pretty mad about that, but there's nothing you can do. My clients are out of circulation for a fairly long time. You get your conviction but nobody else dies. Anyway, that's my deal. I'll give you a couple of days to think it over." Stuart rose to his feet, picked up his briefcase, and left without another word. Once outside, he looked for the men's room. He felt an urgent need to wash his hands, but he wasn't sure why. He was certain that he'd done the right thing. The criminals — they really were criminals — would be found guilty, but they wouldn't die in the electric chair — and who knows, he thought, maybe they'll straighten out. That was the sort of lie that lawyers tell themselves. He wouldn't have to destroy the careers of some Coast Guard types who had probably stepped over the line only once and would never do so again. That was something he was prepared to do, but didn't relish. This way, he thought, everybody won something, and for a lawyer that was as successful an exercise as you generally got. But he still felt a need to wash his hands.

For Edwin Davidoff, it was harder. It wasn't just a criminal case, was it? The same electric chair that would deliver those two pirates to hell would deliver him to a suite in the Dirksen Senate Office Building. Since he had read *Advise and Consent* as a freshman in high school, Davidoff had lusted for a place in the United States Senate. And he'd worked very hard to earn it: top of his class at Duke Law School, long hours for which he was grossly underpaid by the Department of Justice, speaking engagements all over the state that had nearly wrecked his family life. He had sacrificed his own life on the altar of justice . . . and ambition, he admitted to himself. And now when it was all within his grasp, when he could rightfully take the lives of two criminals who had forfeited their rights to them . . . this could blow it all, couldn't it? If he wimped out on the prosecution, plea-bargaining down to a trifling twenty years, all his work, all his speeches about Justice would be forgotten. Just like that.

On the other hand, what if he disregarded what Stuart had just told him and took the case to trial — and risked being remembered as the man who lost the case entirely. He might blame the Coast Guardsmen for what they had done — but then he would be sacrificing their careers and possibly their freedom on what altar? Justice? Ambition? How about revenge? he asked himself. Whether he won or lost the Pirates Case, those men would suffer even though what they had done had also given the government its strongest blow yet against the Cartel.

Drugs. It all came down to that. Their capacity to corrupt was like nothing he'd ever known. Drugs corrupted people, clouded their thoughts at the individual level, and ultimately ended their lives. Drugs generated the kinds of money to corrupt those who didn't partake. Drugs corrupted institutions at every level and in every way imaginable. Drugs corrupted whole governments. So what was the answer? Davidoff didn't have that answer, though he knew that if he ever ran for that Senate seat he'd prance about in front of the TV cameras and announce that he did — or at least part of it, if only the people of Alabama would trust him to represent them. . . .

Christ, he thought. *So now what do I do?*

Those two pirates deserve *to die for what they have done. What about my duty to the victims?* It wasn't all a lie — in fact none of it was. Davidoff did believe in Justice, did believe that law was what men had built to protect themselves from the predators, did believe that his mission in life was to be an instrument of that justice. Why else had he worked so hard for so little? *It wasn't entirely ambition, after all, was it?*

No.

One of the victims had been dirty, but what of the other three? What did the military call that? "Collateral damage." That was the term when an act against an individual target incidentally destroyed the other things that happened to be close by. Collateral damage. It was one thing when the State did it in time of war. In this case it was simply murder.

No, it wasn't simple murder, was it? Those bastards took their time. They enjoyed *themselves. Is eight years of time enough to pay for them?*

But what if you lose the case entirely? Even if you

win, can you sacrifice those Coasties to get justice? Is that "collateral damage," too?

There had to be a way out. There usually was, anyway, and he had a couple of days to figure that one out.

They'd slept well, and the thin mountain air didn't affect them as badly as they'd expected. By sundown the squad was up and eager. Chavez drank his instant coffee as he went over the map, wondering which of the marked targets they'd stake out tonight. Throughout the day, squad members had kept a close eye on the road below, knowing more or less what they were looking for. A truck with containers of acid. Some cheap local labor would off-load the jars and head into the hills, followed by people with backpacks of coca leaves and some other light equipment. Around sundown a truck stopped. Light failed before they could see all of what happened, and their low-light goggles had no telescopic features, but the truck moved off rather soon, and it was within three kilometers of HOTEL, one of the locations on the target list, four miles away.

Show time. Each man sprayed a goodly bit of insect repellent onto his hands, then rubbed it on face, neck, and ears. In addition to keeping the bugs off, it also softened the camouflage paint that went on next like some ghastly form of lipstick. The members of each pair assisted one another in putting it on. The darker shades went on forehead, nose, and cheekbones, while the lighter ones went to the normal shadow areas under the eyes and in the hollow of cheeks. It wasn't war paint, as one might think from watching movie representations of soldiers. The purpose was invisibility, not intimidation. With the naturally bright spots dulled, and the normally dark ones brightened, their faces no longer looked like faces at all.

It was time to earn their pay for real. Approach routes and rally points were preselected and made known to every member of the squad. Questions were asked and answered, contingencies examined, alternate plans made, and Ramirez had them up and moving while there was still light on the eastern wall of the valley, heading downhill toward their objective.

17.

Execution

The standard Army field order for a combat mission follows an acronym known as SMESSCS: Situation; Mission; Execution; Service and Support; Command and Signal.

Situation is the background information for the mission, what is going on that the soldiers need to know about.

Mission is a one-sentence description of the task at hand.

Execution is the methodology for *how* the mission is to be accomplished.

Service and Support covers the support functions that might aid the men in the performance of their job.

Command defines who gives the orders through every step of the chain, theoretically all the way back up to the Pentagon, and all the way down to the most junior member of the unit who in the final exigency would be commanding himself alone.

Signal is the general term for communications procedures to be followed.

The soldiers had already been briefed on the overall situation, which had hardly been necessary. Both that and their current mission had changed somewhat, but they already knew that, too. Captain Ramirez had briefed them on the execution of their current mission, also giving his men the other information they needed for this evening. There was no outside support; they were on their own. Ramirez was in tactical command, with subordinate leaders identified in case of his disablement, and he'd already issued radio codes. His last act before leading his men down from their perch was to radio his intentions to VARIABLE, whose location he didn't know, but whose approval he receipted.

As always Staff Sergeant Domingo Chavez had the point, now one hundred meters ahead of Julio Vega, again "walking slack" fifty meters ahead of the main body, whose men were spread out at ten-meter intervals for the approach. Going downhill made it tougher on the legs, but the men hardly noticed. They were too pumped up. Every few hundred meters Chavez angled for a clear spot from which they could look down at the objective — the place they were going to hit — and through his binoculars he could see the vague glow of gasoline lanterns. With the sun behind him he didn't have to worry about a reflection off the glasses. The spot was right where the map said it was — he wondered how

592

that information had been developed — and they were following exactly the procedure that he'd been briefed about. Somebody, he thought, had really done his homework on this job. They expected ten to fifteen people at HOTEL. He hoped they had that right, too.

The going wasn't so bad. The cover was not as dense as it had been in the lowlands, and there were fewer bugs. Maybe, he thought, the air was too thin for them, too. There were birds calling to one another, the usual forest chatter to mask the sounds of his unit's approach — but there was damned little of that. Chavez had heard one guy slip and fall a hundred meters back, but only a Ninja would have noticed. He was able to cover half the distance in under an hour, stopping at a preplanned rally point for the rest of the squad to catch up.

"So far, so good, *jefe*," he told Ramirez. "I ain't seen nothing, not even a llama," he added to show that he was at ease. "Little over three thousand more meters to go."

"Okay. Stop at the next checkpoint. Remember there might be folks out taking a stroll."

"Roger that, Cap'n." Chavez took off at once. The rest started moving two minutes later.

Ding moved more slowly now. The probability of contact increased with every step he took toward HOTEL. The druggies couldn't be all that dumb, he warned himself. They had to have a little brains, and the people they used would be locals, people who'd grown up in this valley and knew its ways. And lots of them would have weapons. He was surprised how different it felt from the last time, but then he'd watched and evaluated his targets over a period of days. He didn't even have a proper count on them, didn't know how they were armed, didn't know how good they were.

Christ, this is real combat. We don't know shit.

But that's what Ninja are for! he told himself, taking small comfort in his bravado.

Time started doing strange things. Each single step seemed to take forever, but when he got to the final rally point, it hadn't been all that long at all, had it? He could see the glow of the objective now, a vague green semicircle on the goggle display, but still there was no movement to be seen or heard on the woods. When he got to the last checkpoint, Chavez picked a tree and stood beside it, keeping his head up, swiveling left and right to gather as much information as possible. He thought he could hear things now. It came and went, but occasionally there was an odd, not-natural sound from the direction of the objective. It worried him that he didn't really see anything as yet. Just that glow, but nothing else.

"Anything?" Captain Ramirez asked in a whisper.

"Listen."

"Yeah," the captain said after a moment.

The squad members dropped off their rucksacks and divided according to plan. Chavez, Vega, and Ingeles would advance directly toward

594

HOTEL while the rest circled around to the left. Ingeles, the communications sergeant, had an M-203 grenade launcher slung under his rifle, Vega had the machine gun, and Chavez still had his silenced MP-5. Their job was overwatch. They would get in as close as possible to provide fire support for the actual assault. If anyone was in the way, it was Chavez's job to drop him quietly. Ding led his group off first, while Captain Ramirez moved off a minute later. In the case of both groups, the interval between the men was tightened up to five meters. Another real danger now was confusion. If any of the soldiers lost contact with his comrades, or if an enemy sentry somehow got mixed up with their group, the results could be lethal to the mission and the men.

The last five hundred meters took over half an hour. Ding's over-watch position was clear on the map, but not so clear in the woods at night. Things always looked different at night, and even with the low-light goggles, things were just . . . different. In a distant sort of way, Chavez knew that he was having an attack of the jitters. It wasn't so much that he was afraid, just that he felt much less certain now. He told himself every two or three minutes that he knew exactly what he was doing, and each time it worked — but only for a few minutes before the uncertainty hit him again. Logic told him that he was having what the manuals called a normal anxiety reaction. Chavez didn't like it, but found that he could live with it. Just like the manuals said.

He saw movement and froze. His left hand swung around his back, palm perpendicular to warn the two behind him to stop also. Again he kept his head up, trusting to his training. The human eye sees only movement at night, the manuals and his experience told him. Unless the opposition had goggles. . . .

And this one didn't. The man-shape was almost a hundred meters away, moving slowly and casually through the trees between Chavez and the place where Chavez wanted to be. So simple a thing as that gave the man an early death sentence. Ding waved for Ingeles and Vega to stay put while he moved right, opposite his target's current path to get behind him. Perversely, he moved quickly now. He had to be in place in another fifteen minutes. Using his goggles to select clear places, he set his feet as lightly as he could, moving almost at a normal walking speed. Pride surged past the anxiety now that he could see what he had to do. He made no sound at all, moving alone, crouched down, swiveling his head from his path to his target and back again. Within a minute he was in a good place. There was a worn path there. This was a path for the guard. The idiot stuck to a path, Chavez recognized. You didn't do things like that and expect to live.

He was coming back now, moving with slow, almost childish steps, his legs snapping out from the knees — but he moved quietly enough by walking on the worn path, Ding noticed belatedly. Maybe he wasn't a total fool. His head was looking uphill. But his rifle was slung over his shoulder. Chavez let him approach, taking off his goggles when the man was looking away. The sudden loss of the display made him lose his target for a few seconds, and the edges of panic appeared in his consciousness, but Ding commanded them to be still. The man would reappear presently as he walked back to the south.

He did, first as a spectral outline, then as a black mass walking down the worn corridor in the jungle. Ding crouched at the base of a tree, his weapon aimed at the man's head, and let him come closer. Better to wait and get a sure kill. His selector switch was on the single-shot position. The man was ten meters away. Chavez wasn't even breathing now. He aimed for the center of the man's head and squeezed off a single round.

The metallic sound of the H&K's action cycling back and forth seemed incredibly loud, but the target dropped at once, just a muted clack from his own rifle as it hit the ground alongside the body. Chavez leaped forward, his submachine gun fixed on the target, but the man — it had been a man, after all — didn't move. With his goggles back on, he could see the single hole right in the center of the nose, and the bullet had angled upward, ripping through the bottom of the brain for an instant, noiseless kill.

Ninja! his mind exulted.

He stood beside the body and looked uphill,

holding his weapon high. *All clear.* A moment later the shapes of Vega and Ingeles appeared on the green image display, heading downhill. He turned, found a spot from which to observe the objective, and waited for them.

There it was, seventy meters away. The glow from the gasoline lanterns blazed on his goggles, and he realized that he could take them off once and for all. There were more voices now. He could even catch the odd word. It was the bored, day-to-day talk of people doing a job. There was a splashing sound, almost like . . . what? Ding didn't know, and it didn't matter for the present. Their fire-support position was in view. There was just one little problem.

It was oriented the wrong way. The trees that should have provided cover to their right flank instead prevented them from covering the objective. They'd planned the overwatch position in the wrong place, he decided. Chavez grimaced and made other plans, knowing that the captain would do the same. They found a spot almost as good fifteen meters away and oriented in the proper direction. He checked his watch. Nearly time. It was time to make his final, vital inspection of the objective.

He counted twelve men. The center of the site was . . . what looked like a portable bathtub. Two men were walking in it, crushing or stirring up or doing something to the curious-looking soup of coca leaves and . . . *what was it they told us?* he asked himself. *Water and sulfuric acid?*

Something like that. *Christ*, he thought. *Walking in fucking acid!* The men doing that distasteful task took turns. He watched one change, and those who got out poured fresh water over their feet and calves. It must have hurt or burned or something, Ding realized. But their banter was good-natured enough, thirty meters away. One was talking about his girlfriend in rather crude terms, boasting of what she did for him and what he did to her.

There were six men with rifles, all AKs. *Christ, the whole world carries those goddamned things*. They stood at the perimeter of the site, watching inward, however, rather than outward. One was smoking. There was a backpack by the lantern. One of the walkers said something to one of the gunmen and pulled a beer bottle out of it for himself, and another for the one who'd given him permission.

Idiots! Ding told himself. The radio earpiece made three rasping dashes of static. Ramirez was in place and asking if Ding was ready. He keyed his radio two times in reply, then looked left and right. Vega had his SAW up on the bipod, and the canvas ammo pouch unzipped. Two hundred rounds were all ready, and a second pouch lay next to the first.

Chavez again nestled himself as close to a thick tree as he could and selected the farthest target. He figured the range to him at about eighty meters, a touch long for his weapon, too long for a head shot, he decided. He thumbed the selector to the burst setting, tucked the weapon in tight, and took careful aim through the diopter sight.

Three rounds were ejected from the side of his weapon. The man's face was surprised when two of them struck his chest. His breath came out in a rasping scream that caused heads to turn in his direction. Chavez shifted aim to another rifleman, whose gun was already coming off his shoulder. This one also took two or three hits, but that didn't stop him from trying to get his weapon around.

As soon as it appeared that fire might be returned, Vega opened up, transfixing that man with tracers from his machine gun, then shifting fire to two more armed men. One of them got a couple of rounds off, but they went high. The other, unarmed men reacted more slowly than the guards. Two started to run but were cut down by Vega's stream of fire. The others fell to the ground and crawled. Two more armed men appeared — or their weapons did. The flaming signatures of automatic weapons appeared in the trees on the far side of the site, aimed up at the fire-support team. Exactly as planned.

The assault element, led by Captain Ramirez, opened up from their right flank. The distinctive chatter of M-16 fire tore through the trees as Chavez, Vega, and Ingeles continued to pour fire into the objective and away from the incoming assault element. One of the people firing from the trees must have been hit. The muzzle flash from his weapon changed direction, blazing straight up. But two others turned and fired into the assault element before they went down. The soldiers were shooting at anything that moved now. One of the men who'd been walking in the tub tried to pick up a discarded rifle and didn't make it. One stood and might have been trying to surrender, but his hands never got high enough before the squad's other SAW lanced a line of tracers through his chest.

Chavez and his team ceased fire to allow the assault element to enter the objective safely. Two of them finished off people who were still moving despite their wounds. Then everything stopped for a moment. The lantern still hissed and illuminated the area, but there was no other sound but the echoes of the shooting and the calls of outraged birds.

Four soldiers checked out the dead. The rest of the assault element would now have formed a perimeter around the objective. Chavez, Vega, and Ingeles safed their weapons, collected their things, and moved in.

What Chavez saw was thoroughly horrible. Two of the enemy were still alive, but wouldn't be for long. One had fallen victim to Vega's machine gun, and his abdomen was torn open. Both of the other's legs had been nearly shot off and were bleeding rapidly onto the beaten dirt. The squad medic looked on without pity. Both died within a minute. The squad's orders were a little vague on the issue of prisoners. No one could lawfully order American soldiers not to take prisoners, and the circumlocutions had been a problem for Captain Ramirez, but the message had gotten through. It was too fucking bad. But these people were involved in killing American kids with drugs, and that wasn't exactly under the Rules of Land Warfare either, was it? It was too fucking bad. Besides, there were other things to worry about.

Chavez had barely gotten into the site when he heard something. Everyone did. Someone was running away, straight downhill. Ramirez pointed to Ding, who immediately ran after him.

He reached for his goggles and tried to hold them in his hand as he ran, then realized that running was probably a stupid thing to do. He stopped, held the goggles to his eyes, and spotted both a path and the running man. There were times for caution, and times for boldness. Instinct told him that this was one of the latter. Chavez raced down the path, trusting to his skills to keep his footing and rapidly catching up with the sound that was trying to get away. Inside three minutes he could hear the man's thrashing and falling through the cover. Ding stopped and used his goggles again. Only a hundred meters ahead. He started running again, the blood hot in his veins. Fifty meters now. The man fell again. Ding slowed his approach. More attention to noise now, he told himself. This guy wasn't going to get away. He left the path, moving at a tangent to his left, his movements looking like an elaborate dance step as he picked his way as quickly as he could. Every fifty yards he stopped and used his night scope. Whoever the man was, he'd tired and was moving more slowly. Chavez got ahead of him, curving back to his right and waiting on the path.

Ding had nearly miscalculated. He'd just gotten his weapon up when the shape appeared, and the sergeant fired on instinct from a range of ten feet into his chest. The man fell against Chavez with a despairing groan. Ding threw the body off and fired another burst into his chest. There was no other sound.

"Jesus," the sergeant said. He knelt to catch his breath. Whom had he killed? He put the scope back on his head and looked down.

The man was barefoot. He wore the simple cotton shirt and pants of . . . Chavez had just killed a peasant, one of those poor dumb bastards who danced in the coca soup. Wasn't that something to be proud of?

The exhilaration that often follows a successful combat operation left him like the air released from a toy balloon. Some poor bastard — didn't even have shoes on. The druggies hired 'em to hump their shit up the hills, paid 'em half of nothing to do the dirty, nasty work of pre-refining the leaves.

His belt was unbuckled. He'd been off in the bushes taking a dump when the shooting started, and only wanted to get away, but his half-mast pants had made it a futile effort. He was about Ding's age, smaller and more lightly built, but puffy around the face from the starchy diet of the local peasant farmers. An ordinary face, it still bore the signs of the fear and panic and pain with which his death had come. He hadn't been armed. He'd been part of the casual labor. He'd died because he'd been in the wrong place, at the wrong time.

It was not something for Chavez to be proud of. He keyed his radio.

"Six, this is Point. I got him. Just one."

"Need help?"

"Negative. I can handle it." Chavez hoisted the body on his shoulder for the climb back to the objective. It took ten exhausting minutes, but that was part of the job. Ding felt the man's blood oozing from the six holes in his chest, staining the back of his khaki shirt. Maybe staining more than that.

By the time he got back, the bodies had all been laid side by side and searched. There were many sacks of coca leaves, several additional jars of acid, and a total of fourteen dead men when Chavez dumped his at the end of the line.

"You look a little punked out," Vega observed.

"Ain't as big as you, *Oso*," Ding gasped out in reply.

There were two small radios, and various other personal things to catalog, but nothing of real military value. A few men cast eyes on the pack full of beers, but no one made the expected "Miller Time!" joke. If there had been radio codes, they were in the head of whoever had been the boss here. There was no way of telling who he might have been; in death all men look alike. The bodies were all dressed more or less the same, except for the webbed pistol belts of the armed men. All in all, it was rather a sad thing to see. Some people who had been alive half an hour earlier were no longer so. Beyond that, there wasn't much to be said about the mission.

Most importantly, there were no casualties to the squad, though Sergeant Guerra had gotten a scare from a close burst. Ramirez completed his inspection of the site, then got his men ready to leave. Chavez again took the lead.

It was a tough uphill climb, and it gave Captain Ramirez time to think. It was, he realized, something that he ought to have thought about a hell of a lot sooner:

What is this mission all about? To Ramirez, *Mission* now meant the purpose for their being here in the Colombian highlands, not just the job of taking this place out.

He understood that watching the airfields had the direct effect of stopping flights of drugs into the United States. They'd performed covert reconnaissance, and people were making tactical use of the intelligence information which they'd developed. Not only was it simple — but it also made sense. But what the hell were they doing now? His squad had just executed a picture-perfect small-unit raid. The men could not have done better — aided by the inept performance of the enemy, of course.

That was going to change. The enemy was going to learn damned fast from this. Their security would be better. They would learn that much even before they figured out what was going on. A blown-away processing site was all the information they needed to learn that they had to improve their physical security arrangements.

What had the attack actually accomplished? A few hundred pounds of coca leaves would not be processed tonight. He didn't have instructions to cart the leaves away, and even if he had, there was no ready means of destroying them except by fire, and he wasn't stupid enough to light a fire on a mountainside at night, orders or not. What they had accomplished tonight was . . . nothing. Nothing at all, really. There were tons of coca leaves, and scores — perhaps hundreds — of refining sites. They hadn't made a dent in the trade tonight, not even a dimple.

So what the hell are we risking our lives for? he asked himself. He ought to have asked that question in Panama, but like his three fellow officers, he'd been caught up in the institutional rage accompanying the assassination of the FBI Director and the others. Besides, he was only a captain, and he was more an order-follower than an order-giver. As a professional officer, he was used to being given orders from battalion or brigade commanders, forty-or-so-year-old professional soldiers who knew what the hell they were doing, most of the time. But his orders now were coming from someplace else — where? Now he wasn't so sure — and he'd allowed himself to be lulled in the complacency that assumed whoever generated the orders knew what the hell *he* was doing.

Why didn't you ask more questions!

Ramirez had seen success in his mission tonight. Prior to it his thought had been directed toward a fixed goal. But he'd achieved that goal, and seen nothing beyond it. He ought to have realized that earlier. Ramirez knew that now. But it was too late now.

The other part of the trap was even more troubling. He had to tell his men that everything was all right. They'd done as well as any commander could have asked. But —

What the hell are we doing here? He didn't know, because no one had ever told him, that he was not the first young captain to ask that question all too late, that it was almost a tradition of American arms for bright young officers to wonder why the hell they were sent out to do things. But almost always they asked the question too late.

He had no choice, of course. He had to assume, as his training and experience told him to assume, that the mission really did make sense. Even though his reason — Ramirez was far from being a stupid man — told him otherwise, he commanded himself to have faith in his command leadership. His men had faith in him. He had to have the same faith in those above himself.

An army could work no other way.

Two hundred meters ahead, Chavez felt the stickiness on the back of his shirt and asked himself other questions. It had never occurred to him that he'd have to carry the dead, bleeding body of an enemy halfway up a mountain. He'd not anticipated how this physical reminder of what he had done would wear on his conscience. He'd killed a peasant. Not an armed man, not a real enemy, but some poor bastard who had just taken a job with the wrong side, probably just to feed his family, if he had one. But what else could Chavez have done? Let him get away?

It was simpler for the sergeant. He had an officer who told him what to do. Captain Ramirez knew what he was doing. He was an officer, and that was his job: to know what was going on and give the orders. That made it a little easier as he climbed back up the mountain to the RON site, but his bloodied shirt continued to cling to his back like the questions of a nagging conscience.

Tim Jackson arrived back at his office at 2230 hours after a short squad-training exercise right on the grounds of Fort Ord. He'd just sat down in his cheap swivel chair when the phone rang. The exercise hadn't gone well. Ozkanian was a little slow catching on in his leadership of second squad. This was the second time in a row that he'd screwed up and made his lieutenant look bad. That offended Sergeant Mitchell, who had hopes for the young officer. Both knew that you didn't make a good squad sergeant in less than four years, and only then if you had a man as sharp as Chavez had been. But it was Ozkanian's job to lead the squad, and Mitchell was now explaining a few things to him. He was doing so in the way of platoon sergeants, with vigor, enthusiasm, and a few speculative observations about Ozkanian's ancestry. If any.

"Lieutenant Jackson," Tim answered after the second ring.

"Lieutenant, this is Colonel O'Mara at Special Ops Command."

"Yes, sir!"

"I hear you've been making some noise about a staff sergeant named Chavez. Is that correct?" Jackson looked up to see Mitchell walk in, his cabbage-patch helmet tucked under his sweaty arm and a whimsical smile on his lips. Ozkanian had gotten the message this time.

"Yes, sir. He didn't show up where he's supposed to be. He's one of mine, and — "

"Wrong, Lieutenant! He's one of mine now. He's doing something that you do not need to know about, and you will not, repeat *not* burn up any more phone lines *fucking around into something that does not concern you. IS THAT CLEAR, LIEUTENANT?*"

"But, sir, excuse me, but I — "

"You got bad ears or something, son?" The voice was quieter now, and that was really frightening to a lieutenant who'd already had a bad day.

"No, sir. It's just that I got a call from — "

"I know about that. I took care of that. Sergeant Chavez is doing something that you do not need to know about. Period. End. Is that clear?"

"Yes, sir."

The line clicked off.

"Shit," Lieutenant Jackson observed.

Sergeant Mitchell hadn't caught any words from the conversation, but the buzz from the phone line had made it to the doorway he was standing in.

"Chavez?"

"Yeah. Some colonel at Special Ops — Fort MacDill, I guess — says that they have him and he's off doing something. And I don't need to know about that. Says he took care of Fort Benning for us."

"Oh, horseshit," Mitchell observed, taking his place in the seat opposite the lieutenant's desk, after which he asked: "Mind if I sit down, sir?"

"What do you suppose is going on?"

"Beats the hell outa me, sir. But I know a guy at MacDill. Think I'll make a phone call tomorrow. I don't like one of my guys getting lost like that. It's not supposed to work like that. He didn't have no place chewing your ass either, sir. You're just doin' your job, looking after your people that way, and you don't come down on people for doing their job. In case nobody ever told you, sir," Mitchell explained, "you don't chew some poor lieutenant's ass over something like this. You make a quiet call to the battalion commander, or maybe the S-1, and have him settle things nice 'n quiet. Lieutenants get picked on enough by their own colonels without needin' to get chewed on by strange ones. That's why things go through channels, so you know who's chewing' ya'."

"Thank you, Sergeant," Jackson said with a smile. "I needed that."

"I told Ozkanian that he ought to concentrate a little more on leadin' his squad instead of trying to be Sergeant Rock. I think this time he'll listen. He's a pretty good kid, really. Just needs a little seasoning." Mitchell stood. "See you at PT tomorrow, sir. Good night."

"Right. 'Night, Sergeant." Tim Jackson decided that sleep made more sense than paperwork and headed off to his car. On the drive to the BOQ he was still pondering the call he'd gotten from Colonel O'Mara, whoever the hell he was. Lieutenants didn't interact with bird-colonels very much — he'd made his (required) New Year's Day appearance at the brigade commander's home, but that was it. New lieutenants were supposed to maintain a low profile. On the other hand, one of the many lessons remembered from West Point was that he was responsible for his men. The fact that Chavez hadn't arrived at Fort Benning, that his departure from Ord had been so . . . irregular, and that his natural and responsible inquiry into his man's situation had earned him nothing more than a chewing only made the young officer all the more curious. He'd

611

let Mitchell make his calls, but he'd stay out of it for the moment, not wanting to draw additional attention to himself until he knew what the hell he was doing. In this Tim Jackson was fortunate. He had a big brother on Pentagon duty who knew how things were supposed to work and was pushing hard for O-6 — captain's or colonel's — rank, even if he was a squid. Robby could give him some good advice, and advice was what he needed.

It was a nice, smooth flight in the COD. Even so, Robby Jackson didn't like it much. He didn't like sitting in an aft-facing seat, but mainly he didn't like being in an airplane unless he had the stick. A fighter pilot, test pilot, and most recently commander of one of the Navy's elite Tomcat squadrons, he knew that he was about the best flyer in the world, and didn't like trusting his life to the lesser skills of another aviator. Besides, on Navy aircraft the stewardesses weren't worth a damn. In this case it was a pimply-faced kid from New York, judging by his accent, who'd managed to spill coffee on the guy next to him.

"I hate these things," the man said.

"Yeah, well, it ain't Delta, is it?" Jackson noted as he tucked the folder back in his bag. He had the new tactical scheme committed to memory. As well he might. It was mainly his idea.

The man wore khaki uniform clothing, with a "U.S." insignia on his collar. That made him a tech-rep, a civilian who was doing something or other for the Navy. There were always some aboard a carrier — electronics specialists or various sorts of engineers who either provided special service to a new piece of gear or helped train the Navy personnel who did. They were given the simulated rank of warrant officer, but treated more or less as commissioned officers, eating in the officers' mess and quartered in relative luxury — a very relative term on a U.S. Navy ship unless you were a captain or an admiral, and tech-reps did not rate that sort of treatment.

"What are you going out for?" Robby asked.

"Checking out performance on a new piece of ordnance. I'm afraid I can't say any more than that."

"One of them, eh?"

" 'Fraid so," the man said, examining the coffee stain on his knee.

"Do this a lot?"

"First time," the man said. "You?"

"I fly off boats for a living, but I'm serving time in the Pentagon now. OP-05's office, fighter-tactics desk."

"Never made a carrier landing," the man added nervously.

"Not so bad," Robby assured him. "Except at night."

"Oh?" The man wasn't too scared to know that it was dark outside.

"Yeah, well, carrier landings aren't all that bad in daylight. Flying into a regular airfield, you look ahead and pick the spot you're gonna touch on. Same thing on a carrier, just the runway's smaller. But at night you can't really see where you're gonna touch. So that makes it a little twitchy. Don't sweat it. The gal we got driving — "

"A girl?"

"Yeah, a lot of the COD drivers are girls. The one up front is pretty good, instructor pilot, they tell me." It always made people safer to think that the pilot was an instructor, except: "She's breaking in a new ensign tonight," Jackson added maliciously. He loved to needle people who didn't like flying. It was always something he bothered his friend Jack Ryan about.

"New ensign?"

"You know, a kid out of P-cola. Guess he wasn't good enough for fighters or attack bombers, so he flies the delivery truck. They gotta learn, right? Everybody makes a first night carrier landing. I did. No big deal," Jackson said comfortably. Then he checked to make sure his safety belts were nice and tight. Over the years he'd found that one sure way of alleviating fear was to hand it over to someone else.

"Thanks."

"You part of the Shoot-Ex?"

"Huh?"

"The exercise we're running. We get to shoot some real missiles at target drones. 'Shoot-Ex.' Missile-Firing Exercise."

"I don't think so."

"Oh, I was hoping you were a guy from Hughes.

614

We want to see if the fix on the Phoenix guidance package really works or not."

"Oh, sorry — no. I work with something else."

"Okay." Robby pulled a paperback from his pocket and started reading. Now that he was sure there was somebody on the COD more uncomfortable than he was, he could concentrate on the book. He wasn't really frightened, of course. He just hoped that the new nugget sitting in the copilot's right seat wouldn't splatter the COD and its passengers all over the ramp. But there wasn't much that he could do about that.

The squad was tired when they got back to the RON site. They took their positions while the captain made his radio call. One of each pair immediately stripped his weapon down for cleaning, even those few who hadn't gotten a shot off.

"Well, *Oso* and his SAW got on the scoreboard tonight," Vega observed as he pulled a patch through the twenty-one-inch barrel. "Nice work, Ding," he added.

"They weren't very good."

"Hey, *'mano*, we do our thing right, they don't have the chance to be very good."

"It's been awful easy so far, man. Might change."

Vega looked up for a moment. "Yeah. That's right."

At geosynchronous height over Brazil, a weather satellite of the National Oceanic and Atmospheric Administration had its low-resolution camera pointed forever downward at the planet it had left eleven months before and to which it would never return. It seemed to hover almost in a fixed position, twenty-two thousand six hundred miles over the emerald-green jungles of the Amazon valley, but in fact it was moving at a speed of about seven thousand miles per hour, its easterly orbital path exactly matching the rotation speed of the earth below. The satellite had other instruments, of course, but this particular color-TV camera had the simplest of jobs. It watched clouds that floated in the air like distant balls of cotton. That so prosaic a function could be important was so obvious as to be hard to recognize. This satellite and its antecedents had saved thousands of lives and were arguably the most useful and efficient segment of America's space program. The lives saved were those of sailors for the most part, sailors whose ships might otherwise stray into the path of an undetected storm. From its perch, the satellite could see from the great Southern Ocean girdling Antarctica to beyond the North Cape of Norway, and no storm escaped its notice.

Almost directly below the satellite, conditions still not fully understood gave birth to cyclonic storms in the broad, warm Atlantic waters off the West Coast of Africa, from which they were carried westward toward the New World, where they were known by the West Indian name, hurricane. Data from the satellite was downlinked to

NOAA's National Hurricane Center at Coral Gables, Florida, where meteorologists and computer scientists were working as part of a multi-year project to determine how the storms began and why they moved as they did. The busy season for these scientists was just beginning. Fully a hundred people, some with their doctor's degrees years behind them, others summer interns from a score of universities, examined the photographs for the first storm of the season. Some hoped for many, that they might study and learn from them. The more experienced scientists knew that feeling, but also knew that those massive oceanic storms were the most destructive and deadly force of nature, and regularly killed thousands who lived too close to the sea. They also knew that the storms would come in their own good time, for no one had a provable model for explaining exactly why they formed. All man could do was see them, track them, measure their intensity, and warn those in their path. The scientists also named them. The names were chosen years in advance, always starting at the top of the alphabet and proceeding downward. The first name on the list for the current year was *Adele*.

As the camera watched, clouds grew skyward five hundred miles from the Cape Verde islands, cradle of hurricanes. Whether it would become an organized tropical cyclone or simply be just another large rainstorm, no one could say. It was still early in the season. But it had all the makings of a big season. The West African desert was unusually hot for the spring, and heat there had a demonstrable connection with birth of hurricanes.

The truck driver appeared at the proper time to collect the men and the paste processed from the coca leaves, but they weren't there as expected. He waited an hour, and still they weren't there. There were two men with him, of course, and these he sent up to the processing site. The driver was the "senior" man of the group and didn't want to be bothered climbing those cursed mountains anymore. So while he smoked his cigarettes, they climbed. He waited another hour. There was quite a bit of traffic on the highway, especially big diesel trucks whose mufflers and pollution controls were less well attended to than was the case in other, more prosperous regions — besides, their removal made for improved fuel economy in addition to the greater noise and smoke. Many of the big tractor-trailer combinations roared past, vibrating the roadbed and rocking his own truck in the rush of air. That was why he missed the sound. After waiting a total of ninety minutes, it was clear that he'd have to go up himself. He locked the truck, lit yet another cigarette, and began his way up the path.

The driver found it hard going. Though he'd grown up in these hills, and could remember a boyhood in which a thousand-foot climb was just another footrace with his playmates, he'd been driving the truck for some time, and his leg muscles were more accustomed to pushing down pedals than this sort of thing. What would once have taken forty minutes now took over an hour, and with the place almost in sight he was venomously angry, too angry and too tired to pay attention to things that ought to have been obvious by now. He could still hear the traffic sounds on the road below, could hear the birds twittering in the trees around him, but nothing else when he should have been hearing something. He paused, bending over to catch his breath when he got his first warning. It was a dark spot on the trail. Something had turned the brown earth to black, but that could have been anything, and he was in a hurry to see what the problem was up the hill and didn't ponder it. After all, there hadn't been any problem lately with the army or the police, and he wondered why the refining work was done so far up the mountainside in any case. It was no longer necessary.

Five minutes more and he could see the little clearing, and only now he noticed that there were no sounds coming from it, though there was an odd, acrid smell. Doubtless the acid used in the pre-refining process, he was sure. Then he made the last turn and saw.

The truck driver was not a man unaccustomed to violence. He'd been involved in the pre-Cartel fighting and had also killed a few M-19 sympathizers in the wars because of which the Cartel had actually been formed. He'd seen blood, therefore, and had spilled some himself.

But not like this. All fourteen of the men he'd driven in the previous night were lined up shoulder to shoulder in a neat little row on the ground. The bodies were already bloated, and animals had been picking at several of the open wounds. The two men he'd dispatched up the mountainside were more freshly dead. Though the driver didn't fathom it, they'd been killed by a claymore mine triggered when they'd examined the bodies, and their bodies were newly shredded, with major sections missing where the ball-bearing-sized fragments had struck, and with the blood still trickling out. One's face showed the surprise and shock. The other man was facedown, with a section about the size of a shoe box messily removed from his back.

The driver stood still for a minute or so, afraid to move in any direction, his quivering hands reaching for another cigarette, then dropping two which he was too terrified to reach for. Before he could get a third, he turned and moved carefully down the path. A hundred meters after that, he was running for his life as every bird call and every breeze through the trees sounded to him like an approaching soldier. They had to be soldiers. He was sure of that. Only soldiers killed with that sort of precision.

"That was a splendid paper you delivered this afternoon. We hadn't considered the Soviet 'nationalities' question as thoroughly as you have. Your analytical skills are as sharp as ever." Sir

Basil Charleston raised his glass in salute. "Your promotion was well earned. Congratulations, Sir John."

"Thanks, Bas'. I just wish it could have happened another way," Ryan said.

"That bad?"

Jack nodded. "I'm afraid so."

"And Emil Jacobs, too. Bloody bad time for your chaps."

Ryan smiled rather grimly. "You might say that."

"So, what are you going to do about it?"

"I'm afraid there's not much I can say about that," Jack replied carefully. *I don't know, but I can't exactly say* that, *can I?*

"Quite so." The head of Her Majesty's Secret Intelligence Service nodded sagely. "Whatever your response is, I'm sure it will be appropriate."

At that moment he knew that Greer had been right. He had to know such things or risk being taken for a fool by his counterparts here and everywhere else in the world. He'd get home in a few more days and talk things over with Judge Moore. Ryan was supposed to have some bureaucratic muscle now. Might as well flex it a little to see if it worked.

Commander Jackson woke after six hours' sleep. He, too, enjoyed that greatest of luxuries aboard a warship, privacy. His rank and former station as a squadron commander put him high on the list of VIPs, and there happened to be a spare one-man stateroom in this floating city. His was just under the flight deck foreward. Close to the bow catapults by the sound of things, which explained why one of *Ranger*'s own squadron commanders didn't want it. On arrival, he'd made the necessary courtesy calls, and he didn't have any official duties to attend to for another . . . three hours. After washing and shaving and morning coffee, he decided to do a few things on his own. Robby headed below for the carrier's magazine.

This was a large compartment with a relatively low ceiling where the bombs and missiles were kept. Several rooms, really, with nearby shops so that the "smart" weapons could be tested and repaired by ordnance technicians. Jackson's personal concern was with the AIM-54C Phoenix air-to-air missiles. There had been problems with the guidance systems, and one purpose of the battle-group exercise was to see if the contractor's fix really worked or not.

Entry into the space was restricted, for obvious reasons. Robby identified himself to a senior chief petty officer, and it turned out that they'd both served on the *Kennedy* a few years before. Together they entered a work space where some "ordies" were playing with the missiles, with an odd-looking box hanging on the pointed nose of one.

"What d'ya think?" one asked.

"Reads out okay to me, Duke," the one on the oscilloscope replied. "Let me try some simulated jamming."

"That's the bunch we're prepping for the Shoot-Ex, sir," the senior chief explained. "So far they seem to be working all right, but . . . "

"But wasn't it you who found the problem in the first place?" Robby asked.

"Me and my old boss, Lieutenant Frederickson." The chief nodded. The discovery had resulted in several million dollars in penalties to the contractor. And all the AIM-54C missiles in the fleet had been decertified for several months, taking away what should have been the most capable air-to-air missile in the Navy. He led Jackson to the rack of test equipment. "How many we supposed to shoot?"

"Enough to tell whether the fix works or not," Robby replied. The chief grunted.

"That could be quite a Shoot-Ex, sir."

"Drones are cheap!" Robby pointed out in a most outrageous lie. But the chief knew what he meant. It was cheaper than going to the Indian Ocean and maybe having a shoot-out with *Iranian* F-14A Tomcats (they had them, too) and then finding out that the goddamned missiles didn't work properly. That was a most efficient way of killing off pilots whose training went for a million dollars a pop. The good news was that the fix was working, at least as far as the test equipment could tell. To make sure, Robby told the chief, between ten and twenty of the Phoenix-Cs would be shot off, plus a larger number of Sparrows and Sidewinders. Jackson started to leave.

He'd seen what he needed to see, and the ordies all had work to do.

"Looks like we're really going to be emptying this here locker out, sir. You know about the new bombs we're checking out?"

"No. I met with a tech-rep on the COD flight in. He didn't talk a hell of a lot. So what the hell is new? Just a bomb, right?"

The senior chief laughed. "Come on, I'll show you the Hush-A-Bomb."

"What?"

"Didn't you ever watch Rocky and Bullwinkle, sir?"

"Chief, you have really lost me."

"Well, when I was a kid I used to watch Rocky the Flying Squirrel and Bullwinkle the Moose, and one of the stories was about how Boris and Natasha — they were the bad guys, Commander — were trying to steal something called Hush-A-Boom. That was an explosive that blew stuff up without making any noise. Looks like the guys at China Lake came up with the next-best thing!"

The chief opened a door to the bomb-storage area. The stream-lined shapes — they didn't have any fins or fuses attached until they were taken topside — sat on storage pallets securely chained down to the steel deck. On a pallet close to the rectangular elevator that delivered them topside was a group of blue-painted bombs. The blue color made them exercise units, but from the tag on the pallet it was clear that they were also loaded with the customary explosive filler.

Robby Jackson was a fighter pilot, and hadn't dropped very many bombs, but that was just another side of his profession. The weapons he looked at appeared to be standard two-thousand-pound low-drag cases, which translated to nine hundred eighty-five pounds of high explosives, and just over a thousand pounds of steel bomb-case. The only difference between a "dumb" or "iron" bomb and a guided "smart" bomb was the attachment of a couple of hardware items: a seeker head on the nose, and movable fins on the tail. Both units attached to the normal fusing points, and in fact the fuses were part of the guid-ance-package attachments. For obvious reasons these were kept in a different compartment. On the whole, however, the blue bombcases ap-peared grossly ordinary.

"So?" he asked.

The chief tapped the nearest bombcase with his knuckle. There was an odd sound. Odd enough that Robby did the same.

"That's not steel."

"Cellulose, sir. They made the friggin' things outa paper! How you like that?"

"Oh." Robby understood. "Stealth."

"These babies gotta be guided, though. They ain't gonna make fragments worth a damn." The purpose of the steel bombcase, of course, is to transform itself into thousands of high-speed razors, ripping into whatever lay within their bal-listic range after detonation. It wasn't the explo-sion that killed people — which was, after all, the reason to build bombs — but rather the fragments they generated. "That's why we call it the Hush-A-Bomb. Fucker's gonna be right loud, sir, but after the smoke clears you're gonna wonder what the hell it was."

"New wonders from China Lake," Robby observed. What the hell good was a bomb that — but then, it was probably something for the new Stealth tactical bomber. He didn't know all that much about Stealth yet. It wasn't part of his brief in the Pentagon. Fighter tactics were, and Robby went off to go over his notes with the air-group commander. The first part of the battle-group exercise would begin in just over twenty-four hours.

The word got to Medellín fairly quickly, of course. By noon it was known that two refining operations had been eliminated and a total of thirty-one people killed. The loss of manpower was incidental. In each case more than half had been local peasants who did the coolie work, and the rest had been scarcely more important permanent employees whose guns kept the curious away, generally by example rather than persuasion. What was troubling was the fact that if word of these events got out, there might be some difficulties in recruiting new people to do the refining.

But most troubling of all was the simple fact that nobody knew what was going on. Was the Colombian Army going back into the hills? Was it M-19, breaking its word, or FARC, doing the same thing? Or something else? No one knew. That was most annoying, since they paid a good deal of money to get information. But the Cartel was a group of people, and action was taken only after consensus was reached. It was agreed that there must be a meeting. But then people began to worry if that might be dangerous. After all, clearly there were armed people about, people with little regard for human life, and that was also troubling for the senior Cartel officials. Most of all, these people had heavy weapons and the skill to use them. It was decided, therefore, that the meeting should be held at the most secure location possible.

FLASH
TOP SECRET ***** CAPER
1914Z
SIGINT REPORT
Intercept 1993 INIT 1904Z FRQ 887.020 MHZ

INIT: SUBJECT FOXTROT

RECIP: SUBJECT UNIFORM

F: IT IS AGREED. WE'LL MEET AT YOUR HOUSE TOMORROW NIGHT AT [2000L].

U: WHO WILL COME?

F: [SUBJECT ECHO] CANNOT ATTEND, BUT PRODUCTION IS NOT HIS CONCERN ANYWAY. [SUBJECT ALPHA], [SUBJECT GOLF], AND [SUBJECT WHISKEY] WILL COME WITH ME. HOW IS YOUR SECURITY?

U: AT MY [EMPHASIS] CASTLE? [LAUGHTER.] FRIEND, WE COULD HOLD OFF A REGIMENT THERE, AND MY HELICOPTER IS ALWAYS READY. HOW ARE YOU COMING?

F: HAVE YOU SEEN MY NEW TRUCK?

U: YOUR GREAT FEET [MEANING UNKNOWN]? NO I HAVE NOT SEEN YOUR MARVELOUS NEW TOY.

F: I GOT IT BECAUSE OF YOU, PABLO. WHY DON'T YOU EVER REPAIR THE ROAD TO YOUR CASTLE?

U: THE RAIN KEEPS DESTROYING IT. YES, I SHOULD PAVE IT, BUT I USE A HELICOPTER TO GET HERE.

F: AND YOU COMPLAIN ABOUT MY TOYS! [LAUGHTER.] SEE YOU TOMORROW NIGHT, FRIEND.

U: GOODBYE.

END CALL. DISCONNECT SIGNAL. END INTERCEPT.

The intercept was delivered to Bob Ritter's office within minutes of its receipt. So here was the chance, the whole purpose of the exercise. He got his own signals out at once, without checking with Cutter or the President. After all, he was the one with the hunting license.

Aboard *Ranger*, the "tech-rep" got the encrypted message less than an hour later. He immediately placed a telephone call to the office of Commander Jensen, then headed off to see him personally. It wasn't all that hard. He was an experienced field officer and particularly good with maps. That was very useful on a carrier where even experienced sailors got lost in the gray-painted maze all the time. Commander Jensen was surprised he got there so quickly, but already had his personal bombardier-navigator in his office for the mission briefing.

Clark got his signal about the same time. He linked up with Larson and immediately arranged a flight down the valley south of Medellín to make a final reconnaissance of the objective.

Whatever problems his conscience gave Ding Chavez washed out when he did his shirt. There was a nice little creek a hundred meters from their patrol base, and one by one the squad members washed their things out and cleaned themselves up as best they could without soap. After all, he reasoned, poor, dumb peasant or not, he was doing something that he shouldn't have been doing. To Chavez the main concern was that he'd used up a magazine and a half of ammo, and the squad was short one claymore mine which, they'd heard a few hours earlier, went off exactly as planned. Their intel specialist was a real whiz with booby traps. Finished with his abbreviated personal hygiene routine, Ding returned to the unit perimeter. They'd lay up tonight, putting a listening post out a few hundred meters and running a routine patrol to make sure that there was nobody hunting them, but this would be a night of rest. Captain Ramirez had explained that they didn't want to be too active in this area. It might spook the game sooner than they wanted.

18.

Force Majeure

The easiest thing for Sergeant Mitchell to do was to call his friend at Fort MacDill. He'd served with Ernie Davis in the 101st Air Assault Division, lived right next to him in a duplex, and crumpled many an empty beer can after charcoaled franks and burgers in the backyard. They were both E-7s, well schooled in the ways of the Army, which was really run by the sergeants, after all. The officers got more money and all of the worries while the long-service NCOs kept things on an even keel. He had an Army-wide phone directory at his desk and called the proper AUTOVON number.

"Ernie? Mitch."

"Yo, how's life out in wine country?"

"Humpin' the hills, boy. How's the family?"

"Doing fine, Mitch. And yours?"

"Annie's turning into quite a little lady. Hey, the reason I called, I wanted to check up to make

631

sure one of our people got out to you. Staff Sergeant named Domingo Chavez. You'd like him, Ernie, he's a real good kid. Anyway, the paperwork got fucked up on this end, and I just wanted to make sure that he showed up in the right place."

"No problem," Ernie said. "Chavez, you said?"

"Right." Mitchell spelled it.

"Don't ring a bell. Wait a minute. I gotta switch phones." A moment later Ernie's voice came back, accompanied by the clicking sound that denoted a computer keyboard. What was the world coming to? Mitchell wondered. Even infantry sergeants had to know how to use the goddamned things. "Run that name past me again?"

"Chavez, first name Domingo, E-6." Mitchell read off his service number, which was the same as his Social Security number.

"He ain't here, Mitch."

"Huh? We got a call from this Colonel O'Mara of yours — "

"Who?"

"Some bird named O'Mara. My ell-tee took the call and got a little flustered. New kid, still got a lot to learn," Mitchell explained.

"I never heard of no Colonel O'Mara. I think maybe you got the wrong post, Mitch."

"No shit?" Mitchell was genuinely puzzled. "My ell-tee must have really booted this one. Okay, Ernie, I'll take it from here. You give my love to Hazel now."

"Roge-o, Mitch. You have a good one, son. 'Bye."

"Hmph." Mitchell stared at the phone for a moment. What the hell was going on? Ding wasn't at Benning, and wasn't at MacDill. So where the fuck was he? The platoon sergeant flipped to the number for the Military Personnel Center, located in Alexandria, Virginia. The sergeants' club is a tight one, and the community of E-7s was especially so. His next call was to Sergeant First Class Peter Stankowski. It took two tries to get him.

"Hey, Stan! Mitch here."

"You looking for a new job?" Stankowski was a detailer. His job was to assign his fellow sergeants to new jobs. As such, he was a man with considerable power.

"Nah, I just love being a light-fighter. What's this I hear about you turning track-toad on us?" Stankowski's next job, Mitchell had recently learned, was in the 1st Cavalry Division at Fort Hood, where he'd lead his squad from inside an M-2 Bradley Fighting Vehicle.

"Hey, Mitch, my knees are goin'. Ever think it might be nice to fight sittin' down once in a while? Besides, that twenty-five-millimeter chain gun makes for a nice equalizer. What can I do for you?"

"Trying to track somebody down. One of my E-6s checked out a couple of weeks back, and we have to ship some shit to him, and he ain't where we thought he was."

"Oooo-kay. Wait while I punch up my magic

machine and we'll find the lad for you. What's his name?" Stankowski asked. Mitchell gave him the information.

"Eleven-Bravo, right?" 11-B was Chavez's Military Occupation Specialty, or MOS. That designated Chavez as a light infantryman. Mechanized infantry was Eleven-Mike.

"Yep." Mitchell heard some more tapping.

"C-h-a-v-e-z, you said?"

"Right."

"Okay, he was supposed to go to Benning and wear the Smokey Bear hat — "

"That's the guy!" Mitchell said, somewhat relieved.

" — but they changed his orders an' sent him down to MacDill."

But he ain't at MacDill! Mitchell managed not to say.

"That's a spooky bunch down there. You know Ernie Davis, don't you? He's there. Why don't you give him a call?"

"Okay," Mitchell said, really surprised by that one. *I just did!* "When you going to Hood?"

"September."

"Okay, I'll, uh, call Ernie. You take it easy, Stan."

"Stay in touch, Mitch. Say hi to the family. 'Bye."

"Shit," Mitchell observed after he hung up. He'd just proved that Chavez didn't exist anymore. That was decidedly strange. The Army wasn't supposed to lose people, at least not like this. The sergeant didn't know what to do next, except maybe talk to his lieutenant about it.

"We had another hit last night," Ritter told Admiral Cutter. "Our luck's holding. One of our people got scratched, but nothing serious, and that's three sites taken out, forty-four enemy KIAs — "

"And?"

"And tonight, four senior Cartel members are going to have a sit-down, right here." Ritter handed over a satellite photograph, along with the text of the intercept. "All people on the production end: Fernández, d'Alejandro, Wagner, and Untiveros. Their ass is ours."

"Fine. Do it," Cutter said.

Clark was examining the same photo at that moment, along with a few obliques that he'd shot himself and a set of blueprints for the house.

"You figure this room, right here?"

"I've never been in this one, but that sure looks like a conference room to me," Larson said. "How close you have to be?"

"I'd prefer under four thousand meters, but the GLD is good to six."

"How about this hilltop right here? We've got a clear line of sight into the compound."

"How long to get there?"

"Three hours. Two to drive, one to walk. You know, you could almost do this from an airplane. . . ."

"Yours?" Clark asked with a sly grin.

"Not on a bet!" They'd use a four-wheel-drive Subaru for the drive. Larson had several different sets of plates, and the car didn't belong to him anyway. "I got the phone number and I got a cellular phone."

Clark nodded. He was really looking forward to this. He'd done jobs against people like this before, but never with official sanction, and never this high up the line. "Okay, I gotta get final approval. Pick me up at three."

Murray hustled over from his office as soon as he got the news. Hospitals never made people look glamorous, but Moira appeared to have aged ten years in the past sixty hours. Hospitals weren't especially big on dignity, either. Her hands were in restraints. She was on suicide watch. Murray knew that it was necessary — could scarcely be more so — but her personality had taken enough battering already, and this didn't make things any better.

The room was already bedecked with flowers. Only a handful of FBI agents knew what had transpired, and the natural assumption at the office was that she'd taken Emil's death too hard. Which wasn't far off, after all.

"You gave us quite a scare, kiddo," he observed.

"It's all my fault." She couldn't bring her eyes to look at him for more than a few seconds at a time.

"You're a victim, Moira. You got taken in by one of the best in the business. It happens, even to the smarties. Trust me, I know."

"I let him *use* me. I acted like a whore — "

"I don't want to hear that. You made a mistake. That happens. You didn't mean to hurt anybody, and you didn't break any laws. It's not worth dying for. It's damned sure not worth dying over when you got kids to worry about."

"What'll they think? What'll they think when they find out. . . . "

"You've already given them all the scare they need. They love you, Moira. Can anything erase that?" Murray shook his head. "I don't think so."

"They're ashamed of me."

"They're scared. They're ashamed of themselves. They think it's partly their fault." That struck a nerve.

"But it's not! It's all my fault — "

"I just told you it isn't. Moira, you got in the way of a truck named Félix Cortez."

"Is that his real name?"

"He used to be a colonel in the DGI. Trained at the KGB Academy, and he's very, very good at what he does. He picked you because you're a widow, a young, pretty one. He scouted you, figured out that you're lonely, like most widows, and he turned on the charm. He probably has a lot of inborn talent, and he was educated by experts. You never had a chance. You got hit by a truck you never saw coming. We're going to have a shrink come down, Dr. Lodge from Temple University. And he's going to tell you the same thing I am, but he's going to charge a lot more. Don't worry, though. It comes under Workers Comp."

"I can't stay with the Bureau."

"That's true. You're going to have to give up your security clearance," Dan told her. "That's no great loss, is it? You're going to get a job at the Department of Agriculture, right down the street, same pay grade and everything," Murray said gently. "Bill set it all up for you."

"Mr. Shaw? But — why?"

" 'Cause you're a good guy, Moira, not a bad guy. Okay?"

"So what exactly are we going to do?" Larson asked.

"Wait and see," Clark replied, looking at the road map. There was a place called Don Diego not too far from where they were going. He wondered if somebody named Zorro lived there. "What's your cover story in case somebody sees us together?"

"You're a geologist, and I've been flying you around looking for new gold deposits."

"Fine." It was one of the stock cover-stories Clark used. Geology was one of his hobbies, and he could discuss the subject well enough to fool a professor in the subject. In fact, that's exactly what he'd done a few times. That cover would also explain some of the gear in the back of the four-wheel-drive station wagon, at least to the casual or unschooled observer. The GLD, they'd explain, was a surveying instrument, which was pretty close.

The drive was not terribly unusual. The local roads lacked the quality of paving common in America, and there weren't all that many guard rails, but the main hazard was the way the locals drove, which was a little on the passionate side, Clark thought. He liked it. He liked South America. For all the social problems, the people down here had a zest for life and an openness that he found refreshing. Perhaps the United States had been this way a century before. The old West probably had. There was much to admire. It was a pity that the economy hadn't developed along proper lines, but Clark wasn't a social theorist. He, too, was a child of his country's working class, and in the important things working people are the same everywhere. Certainly the ordinary folk down here had no more love for the druggies than he did. Nobody likes criminals, especially the sort that flaunt their power, and they were probably angry that their police and army couldn't do anything about it. Angry and helpless. The only "popular" group that had tried to deal with them was M-19, a Marxist guerrilla group — actually more an elitist collection of city-bred and university-educated intellectuals. After kidnapping the sister of a major cocaine trafficker, the others in the business had banded together to get her back, killing over two hundred M-19 members and actually forming the Medellín Cartel in the process. That allowed Clark to admire the Cartel. Bad guys or not, they had made a Marxist revolutionary group back off by playing the urban guerrilla game by M-19's own rules. Their mistake — aside from being in a business which Clark abhorred — had been in assuming that they had the ability to play against another, larger enemy by the same set of rules, and that their new enemy wouldn't respond in kind. Turnabout was fair play, Clark thought. He settled back in his seat to catch a nap. Surely they'd understand.

Three hundred miles off the Colombian coast, USS *Ranger* turned into the wind to commence flight operations. The battle group was composed of the carrier, the Aegis-class cruiser *Thomas S. Gates*, another missile cruiser, four missile-armed destroyers and frigates, and two dedicated antisubmarine destroyers. The underway replenishment group, with a fleet oiler, the ammunition ship *Shasta*, and three escorts, was fifty miles closer to the South American coast. Five hundred miles to seaward was another similar group returning from a lengthy deployment at "Camel Station" in the Indian Ocean. The returning fleet simulated an oncoming enemy formation — pretending to be Russians, though nobody said that anymore in the age of *glasnost*.

The first aircraft off, as Robby Jackson watched from Pri-Fly, the control position high up on the carrier's island structure, were F-14 Tomcat interceptors, loaded out to maximum takeoff weight, squatting at the catapults with cones of fire trailing from each engine. As always, it was exciting to watch. Like a ballet of tanks, the massive, heavily loaded aircraft were choreographed about the four acres of flight deck by teenaged kids in filthy, color-coded shirts who gave instructions in pantomime while keeping out of the way of the jet intakes and exhausts. It was for them a game more dangerous than racing across city streets at rush hour, and more stimulating. Crewmen in purple shirts fueled the aircraft, and were called "grapes." Other kids, red-shirted ordnancemen called "ordies," were loading blue-painted exercise weapons aboard aircraft. The actually shooting part of the Shoot-Ex didn't start for another day. Tonight they'd practice interception tactics against fellow Navy aviators. Tomorrow night, Air Force C-130s would lift out of Panama to rendezvous with the returning battle group and launch a series of target drones which, everyone hoped, the Tomcats would blast from the sky with their newly repaired AIM-54C Phoenix missiles. It was not to be a contractor's test. The drones would be under the control of Air Force NCOs whose job it was to evade fire as though their lives depended on it, for whom every successful evasion involved a stiff penalty to be paid in beer or some other medium of exchange by the flight crew who missed.

Robby watched twelve aircraft launch before heading down to the flight deck. Already dressed in his olive-green flight suit, he carried his personal flight helmet. He'd ride tonight in one of the E-2C Hawkeye airborne-early-warning aircraft, the Navy's own diminutive version of the larger E-3A AWACS, from which he'd see if his new tactical arrangement worked any better than current fleet procedures. It had in all the computer simulations, but computers weren't reality, a fact often lost upon people who worked in the Pentagon.

The E-2C crew met him at the door to the flight deck. A moment later the Hawkeye's plane captain, a First-Class Petty Officer who wore a brown shirt, arrived to take them to the aircraft. The flight deck was too dangerous a place for pilots to walk unattended, hence the twenty-five-year-old guide who knew these parts. On the way aft Robby noticed an A-6E Intruder being loaded with a single blue bombcase to which guidance equipment had been attached, converting it into a GBU-15 laser-guided weapon. It was, he saw, the squadron-skipper's personal bird. That, he thought, must be part of the system-validation test, called a Drop-Ex. It wasn't that often you got to drop a real bomb, and squadron commanders like to have their fair share of fun. Robby wondered for a moment what the target was — probably a raft, he decided — but he had other things to worry about. The plane captain had them at their aircraft a minute later. He said a few things to the pilot, then saluted him smartly and moved off to perform his next set of duties. Robby strapped into the jump seat in the radar compartment, again disliking the fact that he was in an airplane as a passenger rather than a driver.

After the normal preflight ritual, Commander Jackson felt vibration as the turboprop engines fired up. Then the Hawkeye started moving slowly and jerkily toward one of the waist catapults. The engines were run up to full power after the nosewheel attachment was fixed to the catapult shuttle and the pilot spoke over the intercom to warn his crew that it was time. In three stunning seconds, the Grumman-built aircraft went from a standing start to one hundred forty knots. The tail sank as it left the ship, then the aircraft leveled out and tipped up again for its climb to twenty thousand feet. Almost immediately, the radar controllers in back started their systems checks, and in twenty minutes the E-2C was on station, eighty miles from the carrier, its rotodome turning, sending radar beams through the sky to start the exercise. Jackson was seated so as to observe the entire "battle" on the radar screens, his helmet plugged into the command circuit so that he could see how well the *Ranger*'s air wing executed his plan, while the Hawkeye flew a racetrack pattern in the sky.

From their position they could also see the battle group, of course. Half an hour after taking off, Robby noted a double launch from the carrier. The radar-computer system tracked both new contacts as a matter of course. They climbed to thirty thousand feet and rendezvoused. A tanker exercise, he realized at once. One of the aircraft immediately returned to the carrier, while the other flew east-southeast. The intercept exercise began in earnest right about then, but every few seconds Robby noted the course of the new contact, until it disappeared off the screen, still heading toward the South American mainland.

"Yes, yes, I will go," Cortez said. "I am not ready yet, but I will go." He hung up his phone with a curse and reached for his car keys. Félix hadn't even had the chance to visit one of the smashed refining sites yet and they wanted him to address the — "The Production Committee," *el jefe* called it. That was amusing. The fools were so bent on taking over the national government that they were starting to use quasi-official terminology. He swore again on the way out the door. Drive all the way down to that fat, pompous lunatic's castle on the hill. He checked his watch. It would take two hours. And he would get there late. And he would not be able to tell them anything because he hadn't had time to learn anything. And they would be angry. And he would have to be humble again. Cortez was getting tired of abasing himself to these people. The money they paid him was incredible, but no amount of money was worth his self-respect. That was something he should have thought about before he signed up, Cortez reminded himself as he started his car. Then he swore again.

The newest CAPER intercept was number 2091 and was an intercept from a mobile phone to the home of Subject ECHO. The text came up on Ritter's personal computer printer. Then came 2092, not thirty seconds later. He handed both to his special assistant.

"Cortez . . . going right there? Christmas in June."

"How do we get the word to Clark?" Ritter wondered.

The man thought for a moment. "We can't."

"Why not?"

"We don't have a secure voice channel we can use. Unless — we can get a secure VOX circuit to the carrier, and from there to the A-6, and from the A-6 to Clark."

It was Ritter's turn to swear. No, they couldn't do that. The weak link was the carrier. The case officer they had aboard to oversee that end of the mission would have to approach the carrier's commanding officer — it might not start there, but it would sure as hell end there — and ask for a cleared radio compartment to handle the messages by himself on an ears-only basis. That would risk too much, even assuming that the CO went along. Too many questions would be asked, too many new people in the information loop. He swore again, then recovered his senses. Maybe Cortez would get there in time. Lord, wouldn't it be nice to tell the Bureau that they'd nailed the bastard! Or, more properly, that someone had, plausibly deniably. Or maybe not. He didn't know Bill Shaw very well, and didn't know how he might react.

Larson had parked the Subaru a hundred yards off the main road in a preselected spot that made detection unlikely. The climb to their perch was not a difficult one, and they arrived well before sundown. The photos had identified a perfect place, right on the crest of a ridge, with a direct line of sight toward a house that took their breath away. Twenty thousand square feet it was — a hundred-foot square, two stories, no basement — set within a fenced six-acre perimeter four kilometers away, perhaps three hundred feet lower than their position. Clark had a pair of seven-power binoculars and took note of the guard force while light permitted. He counted twenty men, all armed with automatic weapons. Two crew-served heavy machine guns were sited in built-for-the-purpose strongpoints on the wall. Bob Ritter had called it right on St. Kitts, he thought: *Frank Lloyd Wright meets Ludwig the Mad.* It was a beautiful house, if you went for the neoclassical-Spanish-modern style, fortified in hi-tech fashion to keep the unruly peasants away. There was also the *de rigueur* helicopter pad with a new Sikorsky S-76 sitting on it.

"Anything else I need to know about the house?" Clark asked.

"Pretty massive construction, as you can see.

I'd worry about that. This is earthquake country, you know. Personally, I'd prefer something lighter, wood-post and beam, but they like concrete construction — to stop bullets and mortar rounds, I suppose."

"Better and better," Clark observed. He reached into his backpack. First he removed the heavy tripod, setting it up quickly and expertly on solid ground. Then came the GLD, which he attached and sighted in. Finally, he removed a Varo Noctron-V night-sighting device. The GLD had the same capability, of course, but once it was set up he didn't want to fool with it. The Noctron had only five-power magnification — Clark preferred the binocular lens arrangement — but was small, light, and handy. It also amplified ambient light about fifty thousand times. This technology had come a long way since his time in Southeast Asia, but it still struck him as a black art. He remembered being out in the boonies with nothing better than a Mark-1 eyeball. Larson would handle the radio traffic, and had his unit all set up. Then there was nothing left to do but wait. Larson produced some junk food and both men settled down.

"Well, now you know what 'Great Feet' means," Clark chuckled an hour later. The cryppies should have known. He handed the Noctron over.

"Gawd! Only difference between a man and a boy . . ."

It was a Ford three-quarter-ton pickup with optional four-wheel drive. Or at least that was how it had left the factory. Since then it had visited a custom-car shop where four-foot-diameter tires had been attached. It wasn't quite grotesque enough to be called "Big Foot," after the monster trucks so popular at auto shows, but it had the same effect. It was also quite practical, and that was the really strange part. The road up to the *casa* did need some serious help, but this truck didn't notice — though the chieftain's security pukes did, struggling to keep up with their boss's new and wonderful toy.

"I bet the mileage sucks," Larson observed as it came through the gate. He handed the night-sight back.

"He can afford it." Clark watched it maneuver around the house. It was too much to hope for, but it happened. The dickhead parked the truck right next to the house, right next to the windows to the conference room. Perhaps he didn't want to take his eyes off his new toy.

Two men alighted from the vehicle. They were greeted at the veranda — Clark couldn't remember the Spanish name for that — by their host with handshakes and hugs while armed men stood about as nervously as the President's Secret Service detail. He could see them relax when their charges went inside, spreading out, mixing with their counterparts — after all, the Cartel was one big, happy family, wasn't it?

For now, anyway, Clark told himself. He shook

his head in amazement at the placement of the truck.

"Here comes the last one." Larson pointed to headlights struggling up the gravel road.

This car was a Mercedes, a stretch job, doubtless armored like a tank — *Just like the ambassador's car,* Clark thought. How poetic. This VIP was also met with pomp and circumstance. There were now at least fifty guards visible. The wall perimeter was fully manned, with other teams constantly patrolling the grounds. The odd thing, he thought, was that there were no guards outside the wall. There had to be a few, but he couldn't spot them. It didn't matter. Lights went on in the room behind the truck. That did matter.

"Looks like you guessed right, boy."

"That's what they pay me for," Larson pointed out. "How close do you think that truck — "

Clark had already checked, keying the laser in on both the house and the truck. "Three meters from the wall. Close enough."

Commander Jensen finished tanking his aircraft, disconnecting from the KA-6 as soon as his fuel gauges pegged. He recovered the refueling probe and maneuvered downward to allow the tanker to clear the area. The mission profile could hardly have been easier. He eased the stick to the right, taking a heading of one-one-five and leveling off at thirty thousand feet. His IFF transponder was switched off at the moment, and he was able to relax and enjoy the ride, something he almost always did. The pilot's seat in the Intruder is set rather high for good visibility during a bomb run — it did make you feel a little exposed when you were being shot at, he remembered. Jensen had done a few missions before the end of the Vietnam War, and he could vividly recall the 100-mm flak over Haiphong, like black cotton balls with evil red hearts. But not tonight. The seat placement now was like a throne in the sky. The stars were bright. The waning moon would soon rise. And all was right with the world. Added to that was his mission. It didn't get any better than this.

With only starlight to see by they could pick out the coast from over two hundred miles away. The Intruder was cruising along at just under five hundred knots. Jensen brought the stick to the right as soon as he was beyond the radar coverage from the E-2C, taking a more southerly heading toward Ecuador. On crossing the coast he turned left to trace along the spine of the Andes. At this point he flipped on his IFF transponder. Neither Ecuador nor Colombia had an air-defense radar network. It was an extravagance that neither country needed. As a result, the only radars that were now showing up on the Intruder's ESM monitors were the usual air-traffic-control type. They were quite modern. A little-known paradox of radar technology was that these new, modern radars didn't really detect aircraft at all. Instead they detected radar transponders. Every commercial aircraft in the world carried a small "black box" — as aircraft electronic equipment is invariably known — that noted receipt of a radar signal and replied with its own signal, giving aircraft identification and other relevant information which was then "painted" on the control scopes at the radar station — most often an airport down here — for the controllers to use. It was cheaper and more reliable than the older radars that did "skin-paints," detecting the aircraft merely as nameless blips whose identity, course, and speed then had to be established by the chronically overworked people on the ground. It was an odd footnote in the history of technology that the new scheme was a step both forward and backward.

The Intruder soon entered the air-control zone belonging to El Dorado International Airport outside Bogotá. A radar controller there called the Intruder as soon as its alphanumeric code appeared on his scope.

"Roger, El Dorado," Commander Jensen replied at once. "This is Four-Three Kilo. We are Inter-America Cargo Flight Six out of Quito, bound for LAX. Altitude three-zero-zero, course three-five-zero, speed four-nine-five. Over."

The controller verified the track with his radar data and replied in English, which is the language of international air travel. "Four-Three Kilo, roger, copy. Be advised no traffic in your area. Weather CAVU. Maintain course and altitude. Over."

"Roger, thank you, and good night, sir." Jensen killed the radio and spoke over his intercom to his bombardier-navigator. "That was easy enough, wasn't it? Let's get to work."

In the right seat, set slightly below and behind the pilot's, the naval flight officer got on his own radio after he activated the TRAM pod that hung on the Intruder's center-line hardpoint.

At T minus fifteen minutes, Larson lifted his cellular phone and dialed the proper number. *"Señor Wagner, por favor."*

"Momento," the voice replied. Larson wondered who it was.

"Wagner," another voice replied a moment later. "Who is this?"

Larson took the cellophane from off a pack of cigarettes and crumpled it over the receiver while he spoke garbled fragments of words, then finally: "I can't hear you, Carlos. I will call back in a few minutes." Larson pressed the kill button on the phone. This location was at the far edge of the cellular system anyway.

"Nice touch," Clark said approvingly. "Wagner?"

"His dad was a sergeant in the *Allgemeine-SS* — worked at Sobibor — came over in forty-six, married a local girl and went into the smuggling business, died before anyone caught up with him. Breeding tells," Larson said. "Carlos is a real prick, likes his women with bruises on them. His colleagues aren't all that wild about him, but he's good at what he does."

"Christmas," Mr. Clark observed. The radio made the next sound, five minutes later.

"Bravo Whiskey, this is Zulu X-Ray, over."

"Zulu X-Ray, this is Bravo Whiskey. I read you five-by-five. Over," Larson answered at once. His radio was the sort used by forward air controllers, encrypted UHF.

"Status report, over."

"We are in place. Mission is go. Say again, mision is go."

"Roger, copy, we are go-mission. We are ten minutes out. Start the music."

Larson turned to Clark. "Light her up."

The GLD was already powered up. Mr. Clark flipped the switch from standby to active. The GLD was more fully known as the Ground Laser Designator. Designed for use by soldiers on the battlefield, it projected a focused infrared (hence invisible) laser beam through a complex but rugged series of lenses. Bore-sighted with the laser system was a separate infrared sensor that told the operator where he was aiming — essentially a telescopic sight. "Great Feet" had a fiberglass cargo box over its load area, and Clark trained the crosshairs on one of its small windows, using the fine-adjustment knobs on the tripod with some delicacy. The laser spot appeared as desired, but then he rethought his aiming point and took advantage of the fact that they were slightly higher than their target, respotting his aim on the center of the vehicle's roof. Finally he turned on the videotape recorder that took its feed from the GLD. The big boys in D.C. wanted to count coup on this one.

"Okay," he said quietly. "The target is lit."

"The music is playing, and it sounds just fine," Larson said over the radio.

Cortez was driving up the hill, having already passed a security checkpoint manned by two people drinking beer, he noted disgustedly. The road was about on a par with what he'd grown up with in Cuba, and the going was slow. They'd still blame him for being late, of course.

It was too easy, Jensen thought as he heard the reply. Tooling along at thirty thousand feet, clear night, no flak or missiles to evade. Even a contractor's validation test wasn't this easy.

"I got it," the B/N noted, staring down at his own scope. You can see a very, very long way at thirty thousand feet on a clear night, especially with a multimillion-dollar system doing the looking. Underneath the Intruder, the Target Recognition and Attack Multisensor pod noted the laser dot that was still sixty miles away. It was a modulated beam, of course, and its carrier signal was known to the TRAM. They now had positive identification of the target.

"Zulu X-Ray confirms music sounds just fine," Jensen said over the radio. Over intercom: "Next step."

On the port inboard weapon station, the bomb's

seeker head was powered up. It immediately noted the laser dot as well. Inside the aircraft, a computer was keeping track of the aircraft's position, altitude, course, and speed, and the bombardier-navigator programmed in the position of the target to an accuracy of two hundred meters. He could have dialed it in even closer, of course, but didn't need to. The bomb release would be completely automatic, and at this altitude the laser "basket" into which the bomb had to be dropped was miles wide. The computer took note of all these facts and decided to make an optimum drop, right in the most favorable portion of the basket.

Clark's eyes were now fixed to the GLD. He was perched on his elbows, and no part of his body was touching the instrument except for his eyebrow on the rubber cup that protected the eyepiece.

"Any second now," the B/N said.

Jensen kept the Intruder straight and level, heading straight down the electronic path defined by various computer systems aboard. The entire exercise was now out of human hands. On the ejector rack, a signal was received from the computer. Several shotgun shells — that's precisely what was used — fired, driving down the "ejector feet" onto small steel plates on the upper side of the bombcase. The bomb separated cleanly from the aircraft.

The aircraft jerked upward a bit at the loss of just over eleven hundred pounds of weight.

"Breakaway, breakaway," Jensen reported.

There, finally. Cortez saw the wall. His car — he'd have to buy a jeep if he were going to come here very often — was still losing its grip on the gravel, but he'd be through the gate in a moment, and if he remembered right, the road inside the perimeter was paved decently — probably left-over materials from the helipad, he thought.

"On the way," Larson told Clark.

The bomb was still traveling at five hundred knots. Once clear of the aircraft, gravity took over, arcing it down toward the ground. It actually accelerated somewhat in the rarefied air as the seeker head moved fractionally to correct for wind drift. The seeker head was made of fiberglass and looked like a round-nose bullet with some small fins attached. When the laser dot on which it tracked moved out of the center of its field of view, the entire seeker body moved itself and the plastic tail fins in the appropriate direction to bring the dot back where it belonged. It had to fall exactly twenty-two thousand feet, and the microchip brain in the guidance package was trying to hit the target exactly. It had plenty of time to correct for mistakes.

Clark didn't know what to expect, exactly. It

had been too long a time since he'd called air strikes in, and he'd forgotten some of the details — when you had to call in air support, you generally didn't have time to notice the small stuff. He found himself wondering if there'd be the whistle — something he never remembered from his war service. He kept his eye on the target, still careful not to touch the GLD lest he screw things up. There were several men standing close to the truck. One lit a cigarette, and it appeared that several were talking about something or other. On the whole, it seemed like this was taking an awfully long time. When it happened, there was not the least warning. Not a whistle, not anything at all.

Cortez felt his front wheels bump upward as they got on solid pavement.

The GBU-15 laser-guided bomb had a "guaranteed" accuracy of under three meters, but that was under combat conditions, and this was a far easier test of the system. It landed within inches of its target point, striking the top of the truck. Unlike the first test shot, this bomb was impact-fused. Two detonators, one in the nose and one in the tail, were triggered by a computer chip within a microsecond of the instant when the seeker head struck the fiberglass top of the truck. There were mechanical backups to the electronic triggers. Neither proved necessary, but even explosives take time, and the bomb fell an additional thirty inches while the detonation process got underway. The bombcase had barely penetrated the cargo cover when the bomb filler was ignited by both detonators. Things happened more quickly now. The explosive filler was Octol, a very expensive chemical explosive also used to trigger nuclear weapons, with a detonation rate of over eight thousand meters per second. The combustible bombcase vaporized in a few microseconds. Then expanding gas from the explosion hurled fragments of the truck body in all directions — except up — immediately behind which was the rock-hard shock wave. Both the fragments and the shock wave struck the concrete-block walls of the house in well under a thousandth of a second. The effects were predictable. The wall disintegrated, transformed into millions of tiny fragments traveling at bullet speed, with the remainder of the shock wave still behind to attack other parts of the house. The human nervous system simply doesn't work quickly enough for such events, and the people in the conference room never had the first hint that their deaths were underway.

The low-light sensor on the GLD went white (with a touch of green). Clark cringed on instinct and looked away from the eyepiece to see an even whiter flash in the target area. They were too far away to hear the noise at once. It wasn't often that you could *see* sound, but large bombs make that possible. The compressed air of the shock wave was a ghostly white wall that expanded radially from where the truck had been, at a speed over a thousand feet per second. It took about twelve seconds for the noise to reach Clark and Larson. Everyone who had been in the conference room was dead by that time, of course, and the *crump* of the pressure wave sounded like the outraged cry of lost souls.

"Christ," Larson said, awed by the event.

"Think you used enough dynamite there, Butch?" Clark asked. It was all he could do not to laugh. That was a first. He'd killed his share of enemies, and never taken joy from it. But the nature of the target combined with the method of the attack made the whole thing seem like a glorious prank. *Son of a BITCH!* The sober pause followed a moment later. His "prank" had just ended the lives of over twenty people, only four of whom were listed targets, and that was no joke. The urge to laugh died. He was a professional, not a psychopath.

Cortez had been less than two hundred meters from the explosion, but being downhill from it saved his life since most of the fragments sailed well over his head. The blast wave was bad enough, hurling his windshield backward into his face, where it fractured but didn't shatter, held together by the polymer filler of the safety-glass sandwich. His car was flipped on its back, but he managed to crawl free even before his mind had decided what his eyes had just witnessed. It was fully six seconds before the word "explosion" occurred to him. At that his reactions were far more rapid than that of the security guards, half of whom were dead or dying in any case. His first considered action was to draw his pistol and advance toward the house.

Except that there wasn't a house there anymore. He was too deafened to hear the scream of the injured. Several guards wandered aimlessly about with their guns held ready — for what, they didn't know. The ones from the far corner of the perimeter wall were the least affected. The body of the house had absorbed most of the blast, protecting them from everything but the projectiles, which had been quite lethal enough.

"Bravo Whiskey, this is Zulu X-Ray requesting BDA, over." BDA was bomb-damage assessment. Larson keyed his microphone one last time.

"I evaluate CEP as zero, I repeat, zero, with high-order detonation. Score this one-four-point-oh. Over."

"Roger that. Out." Jensen switched his radio off again. "You know," he said over the intercom, "I can remember back when I was a lieutenant I made a Med cruise on *Kennedy* and us officers were afraid to go into some spaces because the troops were fuckin' around with drugs."

"Yeah," the bombardier/navigator answered.

"Fuckin' drugs. Don't worry, skipper. I ain't likely to have a conscience attack. Hey, the White House says it's okay, that means that it's really okay."

"Yep." Jensen lapsed back into silence. He'd proceed on his current heading until he was out of El Dorado's radar coverage, then turn southwest for the *Ranger*. It really was a pretty night. He wondered how the air-defense exercise was going. . . .

Cortez had little experience with explosions, and the vagaries of such events were new to him. For example, the fountain in front of the house was still running. The electrical power cables to the *casa* were buried and unharmed, and the breaker box inside hadn't been totally destroyed. He lowered his face into the water to clear it. When he came back up, he felt almost normal except for the ache in his head.

There had been a dozen or so vehicles inside the wall when the explosion happened. About half of them were shredded, and their gas tanks had ruptured, illuminating the area with isolated fires. Untiveros' new helicopter was a smashed wreck against the fractured wall. There were other people rushing about. Cortez stood still and started thinking.

He remembered seeing a truck, one with huge wheels, parked right next to . . . He walked over that way. Though the entire three-hectare area around the house was littered with rubble, here it was clear, he saw as he approached. Then he saw the crater, fully two meters deep and six meters wide.

Car bomb.

A big one. Perhaps a thousand kilos, he thought, looking away from the hole while his brain went to work.

"I think that's all we really need to see," Clark observed. He made a last look through the eyepiece of the GLD and switched it off. Repacking took less than three minutes.

"Who do you suppose that is?" Larson asked while he put his backpack on. He handed the Noctron over to Clark.

"Must be the guy who showed up late in the BMW. Suppose he's important or something?"

"Don't know. Maybe next time."

"Right." Clark led the way down the hill.

It was the Americans, of course. CIA, without doubt. They'd made some financial arrangements and somehow managed to place a ton of explosives in the back of that monstrous truck. Cortez admired the touch. It was Fernández's truck — he'd heard about it but never seen it. *Now I never will*, he thought. Fernández had loved his new truck and had kept it parked right in front of . . . That had to be it. The Americans had gotten lucky. Okay, he thought, how did they do it? They wouldn't have gotten their own hands involved, of course. So they must have arranged for someone else . . . who? Somebody — no, more than one, at least four or five from M-19 or FARC . . . ? Again, that made sense. Might it have been indirect? Have the Cubans or KGB arrange it. With all the changes between East and West, might CIA have managed to get such cooperation? Unlikely, Félix thought, but possible. A direct attack on high government officials such as the Cartel had executed was the sort of thing to generate the most unlikely of bedfellows.

Was the bomb placement here an accident? Might the Americans have learned of the meeting?

There were voices from inside the rubble pile that had once been a castle. Security people were nosing around, and Cortez joined them. Untiveros' family had been here. His wife and two children, and a staff of eight or more people. Probably treated them like serfs, Cortez thought. The Cartel chieftains all did. Perhaps he'd offended one greatly — gone after a daughter, maybe. They all did that. *Droit du seigneur.* A French term, but one which the chieftains understood. The fools, Cortez told himself. Was there no perversion beneath them?

Security guards were already scrambling through the rubble. It was amazing that anyone could be alive in there. His hearing was coming back now. He caught the shrill screams of some poor bastard. He wondered what the body count would be. Perhaps. Yes. He turned and walked back to his overturned BMW. It was leaking gasoline out the filler cap, but Cortez reached in and got his cellular phone. He walked twenty meters from the car before switching it on.

"*Jefe*, this is Cortez. There has been an explosion here."

It was ironic, Ritter thought, that his first notification of the mission's success should come from another CAPER intercept. The really good news, the NSA guys reported, was that they now had a voiceprint on Cortez. That greatly improved their chances of locating him. It was better than nothing, the DDO thought as his visitor arrived for the second time today.

"We missed Cortez," he told Admiral Cutter. "But we got d'Alejandro, Fernández, Wagner, and Untiveros, plus the usual collateral damage."

"What do you mean?"

Ritter looked again at the satellite photo of the house. He'd have to get a new one to quantify the damage. "I mean there were a bunch of security guards around, and we probably got a bunch of them. Unfortunately there was also Untiveros's family — wife, a couple of kids, and various domestic servants."

Cutter snapped erect in his chair. "You didn't tell me anything about that! This was supposed to be a surgical strike."

Ritter looked up in considerable annoyance. "*Well, for Christ's sake, Jimmy!* What the hell do you expect? You are still a naval officer, aren't you? Didn't anybody ever tell you that there are *always* extraneous people standing around? We used a *bomb*, remember? You don't do surgery with bombs, despite what all the 'experts' say. Grow up!" Ritter himself took no pleasure from the extraneous deaths, but it was a cost of doing business — as the Cartel's own members well understood.

"But I told the President — "

"The President told *me* that I had a hunting license, and no bag limit. This is my op to run, remember?"

"It wasn't supposed to be this way! What if the papers get hold of it? This is cold-blooded murder!"

"As opposed to taking out the druggies and their shooters? That's murder, too, isn't it? Or it would be, if the President hadn't said that the gloves were off. You said it's a war. The President told us to treat it as a war. Okay, we are. I'm sorry there were extraneous people around, but, damn it, there always are. If there were a way to bag these jokers without hurting innocent people, we'd use it — but there isn't." To say that Ritter was amazed didn't begin to explain matters. This guy was supposed to be a professional military officer. The taking of human life was part of his job description. Of course, Ritter told himself, Cutter'd spent most of his career driving a desk in the Pentagon — he probably hadn't seen much blood since he learned how to shave. A pussycat hiding in tiger's stripes. No, Ritter corrected himself. Just a pussy. Thirty years in uniform and he'd allowed himself to forget that real weapons killed people somewhat less precisely than in the movies. Some professional officer. And he was advising the President on issues of national security. Great.

"Tell you what, Admiral. If you don't tell the newsies, neither will I. Here's the intercept. Cortez says it was a car bomb. Clark must have rigged it just the way we hoped."

"But what if the local police do an investigation?"

"First of all, we don't know if the local cops will even be allowed there. Second, what makes you think they have the resources to figure it out? I worked pretty hard setting this up to look like a car-bombing, and it looks like Cortez got faked out. Third, what makes you think that the local cops'll give a flying fuck one way or another?"

"But the media!"

"You've got media on the brain. You're the one who's been arguing for turning us loose on these characters. So now you're changing your mind? It's a little late for that," Ritter said disgustedly. This was the best op his Directorate had run in years, and the guy whose idea it had been was now wetting his pants.

Admiral Cutter wasn't paying enough attention to Ritter's invective to be angry. He'd promised the President a surgical removal of the people who had killed Jacobs and the rest. He hadn't bargained for the deaths of "innocent" people. More importantly, neither had WRAN-GLER.

Chavez was too far south to have heard the explosion. The squad was staked out on another processing site. Evidently the sites were set up in relays. As he watched, two men were erecting the portable bathtub under the supervision of several armed men, and he could hear the grunts and gripes of others who were climbing up the mountainside. Four peasants appeared, their backpacks containing jars of acid. They were accompanied by two more riflemen.

Probably the word hadn't gotten out yet, Ding thought. He'd been certain that what the squad had done the other night would discourage people from supplementing their income this way. The sergeant didn't consider the possibility that they had to run such risks to feed their families.

Ten minutes later the third relay of six brought the coca leaves, and five more armed men. The laborers all had collapsible canvas buckets. They went off to a nearby stream for water. The boss guard ordered two of his people to walk into the woods to stand sentry, and that's where things went wrong. One of them walked straight toward the assault element, fifty meters away.

"Uh-oh," Vega observed quietly.

Chavez tapped four dashes on his radio button, the danger signal.

I see it, the captain replied with two dashes. Then three dashes. *Get ready.*

Oso got his machine gun up and flipped off the safety.

Maybe they'll drop him quietly, Chavez hoped.

The guys with the buckets were just coming back when Chavez heard a scream over to his left. The riflemen below him reacted at once. Vega started firing then.

The sudden shooting from another direction confused the guards, but they reacted as people with automatic weapons invariably reacted to surprise — they started shooting in all directions.

"Shit!" Ingeles snarled, and fired his grenade into the objective. It landed among the jars and exploded, showering everyone in the area with sulfuric acid. Tracers flew everywhere, and people dropped, but it was too confused, too unplanned for the soldiers to keep track of what was happening. The shooting stopped in a few seconds. Everyone in view was down. The assault group appeared soon thereafter, and Chavez ran down to join them. He counted bodies and came up three short.

"Guerra, Chavez, find 'em!" Captain Ramirez ordered. He didn't have to say *Kill 'em!*

But they didn't. Guerra stumbled across one and killed him on the spot. Chavez came up dry, neither seeing nor hearing anything. He found the stream and one bucket, three hundred meters from the objective. If they'd been right there when the shooting started, that meant they had four or five minutes head start in the country they'd grown up in. Both soldiers spent half an hour rushing and stopping, looking and listening, but two men were away clean.

When they got back to the objective they learned that this was the good news. One of their men was dead. Rocha, one of their riflemen, had taken a burst full in the chest from one of the guards and died instantly. The squad was very quiet.

Jackson was also in an angry mood. The aggressor force had beaten him. *Ranger*'s fighters hadn't gotten it right. His tactical scheme had come apart when one of the squadrons turned the wrong way, and what should have been a masterful trap had turned into a clear avenue for the "Russians" to blaze in and get close enough to the carrier to launch missiles. That was embarrassing, if not completely unexpected. New ideas took time to work out, and maybe he had to rethink some of his arrangements. Just because it had all worked on the computer simulation didn't mean that the plan was perfect, Jackson reminded himself. He continued to stare at the radar screen, trying to remember the patterns and how they had moved. While he watched, a single blip reappeared on the screen, heading southwest toward the carrier. He wondered who that was as the Hawkeye prepared for landing.

The E-2C made a perfect trap, catching the number-three wire and rolling forward to clear the deck for the next aircraft. Robby dismounted in time to see the next one land. It was an Intruder, the same one he'd noticed before boarding the Hawkeye a few hours earlier. The squadron commander's personal bird, he noticed. The one that had flown toward the beach. But that wasn't important. Commander Jackson immediately headed for the CAG's office to start the debrief.

Commander Jensen also taxied clear of the landing area. The Intruder's wings folded up to minimize its deck space as it took its parking place forward. By the time he and his B/N dismounted, his plane captain was there waiting for them. He'd already pulled the videotape from its compartment in the nose instrument bay. This he handed to the skipper — squadron commanders are given that title — before leading them into the island and safety. The "tech-rep" was there to meet them, and Jensen handed the tape over to him.

"Four-oh, the man said," the pilot reported. Jensen just kept walking.

The "tech-rep" carried the tape cassette to his cabin, where he put it in a metal container with a lock. He sealed it further with multicolored tape and affixed a Top Secret label to both sides. It was then placed in yet another shipping box, which the man carried to a compartment on the O-3 level. There was a COD flight scheduled out in thirty minutes. The box would go on it in a courier's pocket and get flown to Panama, where an Agency field officer would take custody of it and fly to Andrews Air Force Base for final delivery to Langley.

19.

Fallout

Intelligence services pride themselves on getting information from Point A to Points B, C, D, and so forth with great speed. In the case of highly sensitive information, or data that can be gathered only by covert means, they are highly effective. But for data that is open for all the world to see, they generally fall well short of the commercial news media, hence the fascination of the American intelligence community — and probably many others — with Ted Turner's Cable News Network.

As a result, Ryan was not overly surprised to see that his first notice of the explosion south of Medellín was captioned as having been copied from CNN and other news services. It was breakfast time in Mons. His quarters were in the American VIP section of the NATO complex and had access to CNN's satellite service. He switched the set on halfway through his first cup of coffee to see a TV shot obviously taken from a helicopter with a low-light rig. The caption underneath said, MEDELLÍN, COLOMBIA.

"Lord," Jack breathed, setting his cup down. The chopper didn't get very close, probably worried about being shot at by the people milling about on the ground, but it didn't need to be all that clear. What had been a massive house was now a disordered array of rubble set next to a hole in the ground. The ground signature was unmistakable. Ryan had said *car bomb* to himself even before the voice-over of the reporter gave the same evaluation. That meant the Agency wasn't involved, Jack was sure. Car bombs were not the American way. Americans believed in single aimed bullets. Precision firepower was an American invention.

His feelings changed on reflection, however. First, the Agency had to have the Cartel leadership under some sort of surveillance by now, and surveillance was something that CIA was exceedingly good at. Second, if a surveillance operation was underway, he ought to have heard of the explosion through Agency channels, not as a copy of a news report. Something did not compute.

What was it Sir Basil had said? Our response would surely be appropriate. And what does that mean? The intelligence game had become rather civilized over the past decade. In the 1950s, toppling governments had been a standard exercise in the furtherance of national policy. Assassinations had been a rare but real alternative to more complex exercises of diplomatic muscle. In the case of CIA, the Bay of Pigs fiasco and bad press over some operations in Vietnam — which had been a war after all, and wars were violent enterprises at best — had largely terminated such things for everyone. It was odd but true. Even the KGB rarely involved itself in "wet work" any longer — a Russian phrase from the thirties, denoting the fact that blood made one's hands wet — instead leaving it to surrogates like the Bulgarians, or more commonly to terrorist groups who performed such irregular services as a *quid pro quo* for arms and training assistance. And remarkably enough, that, too, was dying out. The funny part was that Ryan believed such vigorous action was occasionally necessary — and likely to become all the more so now that the world was turning away from open warfare and drifting to a twilight contest of state-sponsored terrorism and low-intensity conflict. "Special-operations" forces offered a real and semicivilized alternative to the more organized and destructive forms of violence associated with conventional armed forces. *If war is nothing more or less than sanctioned murder on an industrial scale, then was it not more humane to apply violence in a much more focused and discrete way?*

That was an ethical question that didn't need contemplation over breakfast.

But what *was* right and what was wrong at this level? Ryan asked himself. It was accepted in law, ethics, and religion that a soldier who killed in war was not a criminal. That only begged the question: What is war? A generation earlier that question had been an easy one. Nation-states would assemble their armies and navies and send them off to do battle over some damned-fool issue or other — afterward it would usually appear that there had been a peaceful alternative — and that was morally acceptable. But war itself was changing, wasn't it? And who decided what war was? Nation-states. So, could a nation-state determine what its vital interests were and act accordingly? How did terrorism enter into the equation? Years earlier, when he'd been a target himself, Ryan had determined that terrorism could be seen as the modern manifestation of piracy, whose practitioners had always been seen as the common enemies of mankind. So, historically, there was a not-quite-war situation in which military forces could be used directly.

And where did that put international drug traffickers? Was it a civil crime, to be dealt with as such? What if the traffickers could subvert a nation to their own commercial will? Did that nation then become mankind's common enemy, like the Barbary Pirates of old?

"Damn," Ryan observed. He didn't know what the law said. An historian by training, his degrees didn't help. The only previous experience with such trafficking had been at the hands of a powerful nation-state, fighting a "real" war to enforce its "right" to sell opium to people whose government objected — but who had lost

675

the war and with it the right to protect its own citizens against illegal drug use.

That was a troubling precedent, wasn't it?

Jack's education compelled him to look for justification. He was a man who believed that Right and Wrong really existed as discrete and identifiable values, but since law books didn't always have the answers, he sometimes had to find his answers elsewhere. As a parent, he regarded drug dealers with loathing. Who could guarantee that his own children might not someday be tempted to use the goddamned stuff? Did he not have a duty to protect his own children? As a representative of his country's intelligence community, what about extending that protective duty to all his nation's children? And what if the enemy started challenging his country directly? Did that change the rules? In the case of terrorism, he had already reached that answer: Challenge a nation-state in that way, and you run a major risk. Nation-states, like the United States, had capabilities that are almost impossible to comprehend. They had people in uniform who did nothing but practice the fine art of visiting death on their fellowman. They had the ability to deliver fearsome tools of that art. Everything from drilling a bullet into one particular man's chest from a thousand yards away to putting a two-thousand-pound smart-bomb right through somebody's bedroom window. . . .

"Christ."

There was a knock at his door. Ryan found one

of Sir Basil's aides standing there. He handed over an envelope and left.

When you get home, do tell Bob that the job was nicely done. Bas.

Jack folded the note back into the envelope and slid it into his coat pocket. He was correct, of course. Ryan was sure of it. Now he had to decide if it was *right* or not. He soon learned that it was much easier to second-guess such decisions when they were made by others.

They had to move, of course. Ramirez had them all doing something. The more work to be done, the fewer things had to be thought about. They had to erase any trace of their presence. They had to bury Rocha. When the time came, if it did, his family, if any, would get a sealed metal casket with one hundred fifty pounds of ballast inside to simulate the body that wasn't there. Chavez and Vega got the job of digging the grave. They went down the customary six feet, not liking the fact that they were going to leave one of their own behind like this. There was the hope that someone might come back to recover their comrade, but somehow neither expected that the effort would ever be made. Even coming from a peacetime army, neither was a stranger to death. Chavez remembered the two kids in Korea, and others killed in training accidents, helicopter crashes and the like. The life of the soldier is dangerous, even when there are no wars to fight. So they tried to rationalize it along the lines of an accidental death. But Rocha had not died by accident. He'd lost his life doing his job, soldiering at the behest of the country which he had volunteered to serve, whose uniform he'd worn with pride. He'd known what the hazards were, taken his chances like a man, and now he was being planted in the ground of a foreign land.

Chavez knew that he'd been irrational to assume that something like this would never happen. The surprise came from the fact that Rocha, like the rest of the squad members, had been a real pro, smart, tough, good with his weapons, quiet in the bush, an intense and very serious soldier who really liked the idea of going after druggies — for reasons he'd never explained to anyone. Oddly, that helped. Rocha had died doing his job. Ding figured that was a good enough epitaph for anyone. When the hole was finished, they lowered the body as gently as they could. Captain Ramirez said a few words, and the hole was filled in partway. As always, Olivero sprinkled his CS tear-gas powder to keep animals from digging it up, and the sod was replaced to erase any trace of what had been done. Ramirez made a point of recording the position, however, in case anyone ever did come back for his man. Then it was time to move.

They kept moving past dawn, heading for an alternate patrol base five miles from the one that Rocha now guarded alone. Ramirez planned to rest his men, then lead them on another mission as soon as possible. Better to have them working than thinking too much. That's what the manuals said.

An aircraft carrier is as much a community as a warship, home for over six thousand men, with its own hospital and shopping center, church and synagogue, police force and videoclub, even its own newspaper and TV network. The men work long hours, and the services they enjoyed while off duty were nothing more than they deserved — and more to the point, the Navy had found that the sailors worked far better when they received them.

Robby Jackson rose and showered as he always did, then found his way to the wardroom for coffee. He'd be having breakfast with the captain today, but wanted to be fully awake before he did so. There was a television set mounted on brackets in the corner, and the officers watched it just as they did at home, and for the same reason. Most Americans start off the day with TV news. In this case the announcer wasn't paid half a million dollars per year, and didn't have to wear makeup. He did have to write his own copy, however.

"At about nine o'clock last night — twenty-one hundred hours to us on the *Ranger* — an explosion ripped through the home of one Esteban Untiveros. *Señor* Untiveros was a major figure in the Medellín Cartel. Looks like one of his friends wasn't quite as friendly as he thought. News reports indicate that a car bomb totally destroyed his expensive hilltop residence, along with everyone in it.

"At home, the first of the summer's political conventions kicks off in Chicago next week. Governor J. Robert Fowler, the leading candidate for his party's nomination, is still a hundred votes short of a majority and is meeting today with representatives from . . ."

Jackson turned to look around. Commander Jensen was thirty feet away, motioning to the TV and chuckling with one of his people, who grinned into his cup and said nothing.

Something in Robby's mind simply went *click*.

A Drop-Ex.

A tech-rep who didn't want to talk very much.

An A-6E that headed to the beach on a heading of one-one-five toward Ecuador and returned to *Ranger* on a heading of two-zero-five. The other side of that triangle must — might — have taken the bird over . . . Colombia.

A report of a car bomb.

A bomb with a combustible case. A *smart*-bomb with a combustible case, Commander Jackson corrected himself.

Well, son of a bitch . . . .

It was amusing in more than one way. Taking out a drug dealer didn't trouble his conscience very much. Hell, he wondered why they didn't just shoot those drug-courier flights down. All that loose politician talk about threats to national security and people conducting chemical warfare against the United States — well, shit, he

680

thought, why not have a for-real Shoot-Ex? You wouldn't even have to spend money for target drones. There was not a man in the service who wouldn't mind taking a few druggies out. Enemies are where you find them — where National Command Authority said they were, that is — and dealing with his country's enemies was what Commander Robert Jefferson Jackson, USN, did for a living. Doing them with a smart-bomb, and making it look like something else, well, that was just sheer artistry.

More amusing was the fact that Robby thought he knew what had happened. That was the trouble with secrets. They were impossible to keep. One way or another, they always got out. He wouldn't tell anyone, of course. And that really was too bad, wasn't it?

But why bother keeping it a secret? Robby wondered. The way the druggies killed the FBI Director — that was a declaration of war. Why not just go public and say, *We're coming for you!* In a political year, too. When had the American people *ever* failed to support their President when he declared the necessity to go after people?

But Jackson's job was not political. It was time to see the skipper. Two minutes later he arrived at the CO's stateroom. The Marine standing guard opened the door for him, and Robby found the captain reading dispatches.

"You're out of uniform!" the man said sternly.

"What — excuse me, Cap'n?" Robby stopped cold, looking to see that his fly was zipped.

"Here." *Ranger*'s CO rose and handed over the message flimsy. "You just got frocked, Robby — excuse *me*, Captain Jackson. Congratulations, Rob. Sure beats coffee for startin' off the day, doesn't it?"

"Thank you, sir."

"Now if we can just get those charlie-fox fighter tactics of yours to work. . . . "

"Yes, sir."

"Ritchie."

"Okay, Ritchie."

"You can still call me 'sir' on the bridge and in public, though," the captain pointed out. Newly promoted officers always got razzed. They also had to pay for the "wetting down" parties.

The TV news crews arrived in the early morning. They, too, had difficulty with the road up to the Untiveros house. The police were already there, and it didn't occur to any of the crews to wonder if these police officers might be of the "tame" variety. They wore uniforms and pistol belts and seemed to be acting like real cops. Under Cortez's supervision, the real search for survivors had been completed already, and the two people found taken off, along with most of the surviving security guards and almost all of the firearms. Security guards per se were not terribly unusual in Colombia, though fully automatic weapons and crew-served machine guns were. Of course, Cortez was also gone before the news crews arrived, and by the time they started taping, the police search was fully underway. Several of the crews had direct satellite feeds, though one of the heavy ground-station trucks had failed to make the hill.

The easiest part of the search, lovingly recorded for posterity by the portacams, began in what had been the conference room, now a three-foot pile of gravel. The largest piece of a Production Committee member found (that title was also not revealed to the newsies) was a surprisingly intact lower leg, from just below the knee to a shoe still laced on the right foot. It would later be established that this "remain" belonged to Carlos Wagner. Untiveros's wife and two young children had been in the opposite side of the house on the second floor, watching a taped movie. The VCR, still plugged in and on play, was found right before the bodies. Yet another TV camera followed the man — a security guard temporarily without his AK-47 — who carried the limp, bloody body of a dead child to an ambulance.

"Oh, my God," the President said, watching one of the several televisions in the Oval Office. "If anybody figures this out . . . "

"Mr. President, we've dealt with this sort of thing before," Cutter pointed out. "The Libyan bombing under Reagan, the air strikes into Lebanon and — "

"And we caught hell for it every time! Nobody cares why we did it, all they care about is that we killed the wrong people. Christ, Jim, that was a kid! What are we going to say? 'Oh, that's too bad, but he was in the wrong place'?"

"It is alleged," the TV reporter was saying, "that the owner of this house was a member of the Medellín Cartel, but local police sources tell us that he was never officially charged with any crime, and, well . . . " The reporter paused in front of the camera. "You saw what this car bomb did to his wife and children."

"Great," the President growled. He lifted the controller and punched off the TV set. "Those bastards can do whatever the hell they want to our kids, but if we go after them on their turf, all of a sudden *they're* the goddamned victims! Has Moore told Congress about this yet?"

"No, Mr. President. CIA doesn't have to tell them until forty-eight hours after such an operation begins, and, for administrative purposes, the operation didn't actually begin until yesterday afternoon."

"They don't find out," the President said. "If we tell 'em, then it'll leak sure as hell. You tell Moore and Ritter that."

"Mr. President, I can't — "

"The hell you can't! I just gave you an order, mister." The President walked to the windows. "It wasn't supposed to be this way," he muttered.

Cutter knew what the real issue was, of course. The opposition's political convention would begin shortly. Their candidate, Governor Bob Fow-

684

ler of Missouri, was leading the President in the polls. That was normal, of course. The incumbent had run through the primaries without serious opposition, resulting in a dull, predetermined result, while Fowler had fought a tooth-and-nail campaign for his party's nomination and was still an eyelash short of certain nomination. Voters always responded to the lively candidates, and while Fowler was personally about as lively as a dishrag, his contest had been the interesting one. And like every candidate since Nixon and the first war on drugs, he was saying that the President hadn't made good on his promise to restrict drug traffic. That sounded familiar to the current occupant of the Oval Office. He'd said the same thing four years earlier, and ridden that issue, and others, into the house on Pennsylvania Avenue. So now he'd actually tried something radical. And this had happened. The government of the United States had just used its most sophisticated military weapons to murder a couple of kids and their mother. That's what Fowler would say. After all, it was an election year.

"Mr. President, it would be unsound to terminate the operations we have running at this point. If you are serious about avenging the deaths of Director Jacobs and the rest, and serious about putting a dent in drug trafficking, you cannot stop things now. We're just about to show results. Drug flights into the country are down twenty percent," Cutter pointed out. "Add that to the money-laundering bust and we can say that we've achieved a real victory."

"How do we explain the bombing?"

"I've been thinking about that, sir. What if we say that we don't know, but it could be one of two things. First, it might be an attack by M-19. That group's political rhetoric lately has been critical of the drug lords. Second, we could say that it results from an internecine dispute within the Cartel itself."

"How so?" he asked without turning around. It was a bad sign when WRANGLER didn't look you in the eye, Cutter knew. He was really worried about this. Politics were such a pain in the ass, the Admiral thought, but they were also the most interesting game in town.

"Killing Jacobs and the rest was an irresponsible action on their part. Everyone knows that. We can leak the argument that some parts of the Cartel are punishing their own peers for doing something so radical as to endanger their whole operation." Cutter was rather proud of that argument. It had come from Ritter, but the President didn't know that. "We know that the druggies aren't all that reticent about killing off family members — it's practically their trademark. This way we can explain what 'they' are doing. We can have our cake and eat it, too," he concluded, smiling at the President's back.

The President turned away from the windows. His mien was skeptical, but ... "You really think you can bring that off?"

"Yes, sir, I do. It also allows us at least one

more RECIPROCITY attack."

"I have to show that we're doing *something*," the President said quietly. "What about those soldiers we have running around in the jungle?"

"They have eliminated a total of five processing sites. We've lost two people killed, and have two more wounded, but not seriously. That's a cost of doing business, sir. These people are professional soldiers. They knew what the risks were going in. They are proud of what they are doing. You won't have any problems on that score, sir. Pretty soon the word's going to get out that the local peasants ought not to work for the druggies. That will put a serious dent in the processing operations. It'll be temporary — only a few months, but it'll be real. It'll be something you can point to. The street price of cocaine is going to go up soon. You can point to that, too. That's how we gauge success or failure in our interdiction operations. The papers will run that bit of news before we have to announce it."

"So much the better," the President observed with his first smile of the day. "Okay — let's just be more careful."

"Of course, Mr. President."

Morning PT for the 7th Division commenced at 0615 hours. It was one explanation for the puritanical virtue of the unit. Though soldiers, especially young soldiers, like to drink as much as any other segment of American society, doing physical training exercises with a hangover is one step down from lingering death. It was already warm at Fort Ord, and by seven o'clock, at the finish of the daily three-mile run, every member of the platoon had worked up a good sweat. Then it was time for breakfast.

The officers ate together this morning and table talk was on the same subject being contemplated all over the country.

"About fucking time," one captain noted.

"They said it was a car bomb," another pointed out.

"I'm sure the Agency knows how to arrange it. All the experience from Lebanon an' all," a company XO offered.

"Not as easy as you think," the battalion S-2, intelligence officer, observed. A former company commander in the Rangers, he knew a thing or two about bombs and booby traps. "But whoever did it, it was a pretty slick job."

"Shame we can't go down there," a lieutenant said. The junior officers grunted agreement. The senior ones were quiet. Plans for that contingency had been the subject of division and corps staff discussion for some years. Deploying units for war — and that's exactly what it was — was not to be discussed lightly, though the general consensus was that it could be done . . . if the local governments approved. Which they would not, of course. That, the officers thought, was understandable but most unfortunate. It was difficult to overstate the level of loathing in the Army for drugs. The senior battalion officers, major and above, could remember the drug problems of the seventies, when the Army had been every bit as hollow as critics had said it was, and it hadn't been unknown for officers to travel in certain places only with armed guards. Conquering that particular enemy had required years of effort. Even today every member of the American military was liable to random drug testing. For senior NCOs and all officers, there was no forgiveness. One positive test and you were gone. For E-5s and below, there was more leeway: one positive test resulted in an Article 15 and a very stern talking to; a second positive, and out they went. The official slogan was a simple one: NOT IN MY ARMY! Then there was the other dimension. Most of the men around this table were married, with children whom some drug dealer might approach sooner or later as a potential client. The general agreement was that if anyone sold drugs to the child of a professional soldier, that dealer's life was in mortal danger. Such events rarely took place because soldiers are above all disciplined people, but the desire was there. As was the ability.

And the odd dealer had disappeared from time to time, his death invariably ascribed to turf wars. Many of those murders went forever unsolved.

And that's where Chavez is, Tim Jackson realized. There were just too many coincidences. He and Muñoz and León. All Spanish-speakers. All checked out the same day. So they were doing a covert operation, probably at CIA bequest. It was dangerous work in all likelihood, but they were soldiers and that was their business. Lieutenant Jackson breathed easier now that he "knew" what he didn't need to know. Whatever Chavez was doing, it was okay. He wouldn't have to follow that up anymore. Tim Jackson hoped that he'd be all right. Chavez was damned good, he remembered. If anyone could do it, he could.

The TV crews soon got bored, leaving to write their copy and do their voice-overs. Cortez returned as soon as the last of their vehicles went up the road toward Medellín. This time he drove a jeep up the hill. He was tired and irritable, but more than that he was curious. Something very odd had happened and he wasn't sure what it was. He wouldn't be satisfied until he did. The two survivors from the house had been taken to Medellín, where they would be treated privately by a trusted physician. Cortez would be talking to them, but there was one more thing he had to do here. The police contingent at the house was commanded by a captain who had long since come to terms with the Cartel. Félix was certain that he'd shed no tears over the deaths of Untiveros and the rest, but that was beside the point, wasn't it? The Cuban parked his jeep and walked over to where the police commander was talking with two of his men.

"Good morning, *Capitán*. Have you determined what sort of bomb it was?"

"Definitely a car bomb," the man replied seriously.

"Yes, I suspected that myself," Cortez said patiently. "The explosive agent?"

The man shrugged. "I have no idea."

"Perhaps you might find out," Félix suggested. "As a routine part of your investigation."

"Fine. I can do that."

"Thank you." He walked back to his jeep for the ride north. A locally fabricated bomb might use dynamite — there was plenty of that available from local mining operations — or a commercial plastic explosive, or even something made from nitrated fertilizer. If made by M-19, however, Cortez would expect Semtex, a Czech-made variant of RDX currently favored by Marxist terrorists all over the world for its power and ready, cheap supply. Determining what had actually been used would tell him something, and it amused Cortez to have the police run that information down. It was one thing to smile about as he drove down the mountainside.

And there were others. The elimination of four senior Cartel chieftains did not sadden him any more than it had the policeman. After all, they were just businessmen, not a class of individual for which Cortez had great regard. He took their money, that was all. Whoever had done the bombing had done a marvelous, professional job. That started him thinking that it could not have been CIA. They didn't know very much about killing people. Cortez was less offended than one

691

might imagine that he'd come so close to being killed. Covert operations were his business, after all, and he understood the risks. Besides, if he had been the primary target of so elegant a plan, clearly he'd not be trying to analyze it now. In any case, the removal of Untiveros, Fernández, Wagner, and d'Alejandro meant that there were four openings at the top of the Cartel, four fewer people with the power and prestige to stand in his way if . . . If, he told himself. Well, why not? A seat at the table, certainly. Perhaps more than that. But there was work to do, and a "crime" to solve.

By the time he reached Medellín, the two survivors from Untiveros' hilltop house had been treated and were ready for questioning, along with a half-dozen servants from the dead lord's Medellín condominium. They were in a top-floor room of a sturdy, fire-resistive high-rise building, which was also quite soundproof. Cortez walked into the room to find the eight trusted servants all sitting, handcuffed to straight-back chairs.

"Which of you knew about the meeting last night?" he asked pleasantly.

There were nods. They all did, of course. Untiveros was a talker, and servants were invariably listeners.

"Very well. Which of you told, and whom did you tell?" he asked in a formal, literate way. "No one will leave this room until I know the answer to that," he promised them.

The immediate response was a confused flood of denials. He'd expected that. Most of them were true. Cortez was sure of that, too.

It was too bad.

Félix looked to the head guard and pointed to the one in the left-most chair.

"We'll start with her."

Governor Fowler emerged from the hotel suite in the knowledge that the goal to which he had dedicated the last three years of his life was now in his grasp. *Almost,* he told himself, remembering that in politics there are no certainties. But a congressman from Kentucky who'd run a surprisingly strong campaign had just traded his pledged delegates for a cabinet post, and that put Fowler over the top, with a safety margin of several hundred votes. He couldn't say that, of course. He had to let the man from Kentucky make his own announcement, scheduled for the second day of the convention to give him one last day in the sun — or more properly the klieg lights. It would be leaked by people in both camps, but the congressman would smile in his aw-shucks way and tell people to speculate all they wanted — but that he was the only one who knew. Politics, Fowler thought, could be so goddamned phony. This was especially odd since above all things Fowler was a very sincere man, which did not, however, allow him to violate the rules of the game.

And he played by those rules now, standing

before the bright TV lights and saying nothing at all for about six minutes of continuous talking. There had been "interesting discussions" of "the great issues facing our country." The Governor and the congressman were "united in their desire to see new leadership" for a country which, both were sure, though they couldn't say it, would prosper whichever man won in November, because petty political differences of presidents and parties generally got lost in the noise of the Capitol Building, and because American parties were so disorganized that every presidential campaign was increasingly a beauty contest. Perhaps that was just as well, Fowler thought, though it was frustrating to see that the power for which he lusted might really be an illusion, after all. Then it was time for questions.

He was surprised by the first one. Fowler didn't see who asked it. He was dazzled by the lights and the flashing strobes — after so many months of it, he wondered if his vision would ever recover — but it was a male voice who asked, from one of the big papers, he thought.

"Governor, there is a report from Colombia that a car bomb destroyed the home of a major figure in the Medellín Cartel, along with his family. Coming so soon after the assassination of the FBI Director and our ambassador to Colombia, would you care to comment?"

"I'm afraid I didn't get a chance to catch the news this morning because of my breakfast with the congressman. What are you suggesting?"

Fowler asked. His demeanor had changed from optimistic candidate to careful politician who hoped to become a statesman — whatever the hell that was, he thought. It had seemed so clear once, too.

"There is speculation, sir, that America might have been involved," the reporter amplified.

"Oh? You know the President and I have many differences, and some of them are very serious differences, but I can't remember when we've had a President who was willing to commit cold-blooded murder, and I certainly will not accuse our President of that," Fowler said in his best statesman's voice. He'd meant to say nothing at all — that's what statesmen's voices are for, after all, either nothing or the obvious. He'd kept a fairly high road for most of his presidential campaign. Even Fowler's bitterest enemies — he had several in his own party, not to mention the opposition's — said that he was an honorable, thoughtful man who concentrated on issues and not invective. His statement reflected that. He hadn't meant to change United States government policy, hadn't meant to trap his prospective opponent. But he had, without knowing it, done both.

The President had scheduled the trip well in advance. It was a customary courtesy for the chief executive to maintain a low profile during the opposition's convention. It was just as easy to work at Camp David — easier in fact since it was far easier to shoo reporters away. But you had to run the gauntlet to get there. With the Marine VH-3 helicopter sitting and waiting on the White House lawn, the President emerged from the ground-level door with the First Lady and two other functionaries in tow, and there they were again, a solid phalanx of reporters and cameras. He wondered if the Russians with their *glasnost* knew what they were in for.

"*Mister President!*" called a senior TV reporter. "*Governor Fowler says that he hopes we weren't involved in the bombing in COLOMBIA! Do you have any comment?*"

Even as he walked over to the roped enclosure of journalists, the President knew that it was a mistake, but he was drawn to them and the question as a lemming is drawn to the sea. He couldn't *not* do it. The way the question was shouted, everyone would know that he'd heard it, and no answer would itself be seen as an answer of sorts. *The President ducked the question of . . .* And he couldn't leave Washington for a week of low-profile existence, leaving the limelight to the other side — not with that question lying unanswered behind him on the White House lawn, could he?

"The United States," the President said, "does not kill innocent women and children. The United States fights *against* people who do that. We do not sink down to their bestial level. Is that a clear enough answer?" It was delivered in a quiet, reasoned voice, but the look the President gave the reporter made that experienced journalist wilt before his eyes. It was good, the President thought, to see that his power occasionally reached the bastards.

It was the second major political lie of the day — a slow news day to be sure. Governor Fowler well remembered that John and Robert Kennedy had plotted the deaths of Castro and others with a kind of elitist glee born of Ian Fleming's novels, only to learn the hard way that assassination was a messy business. Very messy indeed, for there were usually people about whom you didn't especially want to kill. The current President knew all about "collateral damage," a term which he found distasteful but indicative of something both necessary and impossible to explain to people who didn't understand how the world really worked: terrorists, criminals, and all manner of cowards — brutal people are most often cowards, after all — regularly hid behind or among the innocent, daring the mighty to act, using the altruism of their enemies as a weapon against those enemies. *You cannot touch me. We are the "evil" ones. You are the "good" ones. You cannot attack us without casting away your self-image.* It was the most hateful attribute of those most hateful of people, and sometimes — rarely, but sometimes — they had to be shown that it didn't work. And that was messy, wasn't it? Like some sort of international auto accident.

But how the hell do I explain that to the American people? In an election year? *Vote to re-elect the President who just killed a wife, two kids, and vari-*

ous domestic servants to protect your children from drugs . . . ? The President wondered if Governor Fowler understood just how illusory presidential power was — and about the awful noise generated when one principle crashed hard up against another. That was even worse than the noise of the reporters, the President thought. It was something to shake his head about as he walked to his helicopter. The Marine sergeant saluted at the steps. The President returned it — a tradition despite the fact that no sitting President had ever worn a uniform. He strapped in and looked back at the assembled mob. The cameras were still on him, taping the takeoff. The networks wouldn't run that particular shot, but just in case the chopper blew up or crashed, they wanted the cameras rolling.

The word got to the Mobile police a little late. The clerk of the court handled the paperwork, and when information leaks from a courthouse, that is usually the hole. In this case the clerk was outraged. He saw the cases come and go. A man in his middle fifties, he'd gotten his children educated and through college, managing to avoid the drug epidemic. But that had not been true of every child in the clerk's neighborhood. Right next door to his house, the family's youngest had bought a "rock" of crack cocaine and promptly driven his car into a bridge abutment at over a hundred miles per hour. The clerk had watched the child grow up, had driven him to school once or twice, and paid the child to mow his lawn. The coffin had been sealed for the funeral at Cypress Hill Baptist Church, and he'd heard that the mother was still on medications after having had to identify what was left of the body. The minister talked about the scourge of drugs like the scourging of Christ's own passion. He was a fine minister, a gifted orator in the Southern Baptist tradition, and while he led them in prayer for the dead boy's soul his personal and wholly genuine fury over the drug problem merely amplified the outrage already felt by his congregation. . . .

The clerk couldn't understand it. Davidoff was a superb prosecuting attorney. Jew or not, this man was one of God's elect, a true hero in a profession of charlatans. How could this be? *Those two* scum *were going to get off!* the clerk thought. It was *wrong!*

The clerk was unaccustomed to bars. A Baptist serious about his religious beliefs, he had never tasted spiritous liquors, had tried beer only once as a boy on a dare, and was forever guilt-ridden for that. That was one of only two narrow aspects to this otherwise decent and honorable citizen. The other was justice. He believed in justice as he believed in God, a faith that had somehow survived his thirty years of clerking in the federal courts. Justice, he thought, came from God, not from man. Laws came from God, not from man. Were not all Western laws based on Holy Scripture in one way or another? He revered his country's Constitution as a divinely inspired document, for freedom was surely the way in which God intended man to live, that man could learn to know and serve his God not as a slave, but as a positive choice for Right. That was the way things were supposed to be. The problem was that the Right did not always prevail. Over the years he'd gotten used to that idea. Frustrating though it was, he also knew that the Lord was the ultimate Judge, and His justice would always prevail. But there were times when the Lord's Justice needed help, and it was well known that God chose His Instruments though Faith. And so it was this hot, sultry Alabama afternoon. The clerk had his Faith, and God had His Instrument.

The clerk was in a cop bar, half a block from police headquarters, drinking club soda so that he could fit in. The police knew who he was, of course. He appeared at all the cop funerals. He headed a civic committee that looked after the families of cops and firemen who died in the line of duty. Never asked for anything in return, either. Never even asked to fix a ticket — he'd never gotten one in his life, but no one had ever thought to check.

"Hi, Bill," he said to a homicide cop.

"How's life with the feds?" the detective lieutenant asked. He thought the clerk slightly peculiar, but far less so than most. All he really needed to know was that the clerk of the court took care of cops. That was enough.

"I heard something that you ought to know about."

"Oh?" The lieutenant looked up from his beer. He, too, was a Baptist, but wasn't *that* Baptist. Few cops were, even in Alabama, and like most he felt guilty about it.

"The 'pirates' are getting a plea-bargain," the clerk told him.

"What?" It wasn't his case, but it was a symbol of all that was going wrong. And the pirates were in the same jail in which his prisoners were guests.

The clerk explained what he knew, which wasn't much. Something was wrong with the case. Some technicality or other. The judge hadn't explained it very well. Davidoff was enraged by it all, but there was nothing he could do. That was too bad, they both agreed. Davidoff was one of the Good Guys. That's when the clerk told his lie. He didn't like to tell lies, but sometimes Justice required it. He'd learned that much in the federal court system. It was just a practical application of what his minister said: "God moves in mysterious ways, His wonders to perform."

The funny part was that it wasn't entirely a lie: "The guys who killed Sergeant Braden were connected with the pirates. The feds think that the pirates may have ordered his murder — and his wife's."

"How sure are you of that?" the detective asked.

"Sure as I can be." The clerk emptied his glass and set it down.

"Okay," the cop said. "Thanks. We never

heard it from you. Thanks for what you guys did for the Braden kids, too."

The clerk was embarrassed by that. What he did for the families of cops and firemen wasn't done for thanks. It was Duty, pure and simple. His Reward would come from Him who assigned that Duty.

The clerk left, and the lieutenant walked to a corner booth to join a few of his colleagues. It was soon agreed that the pirates would not — could not — be allowed to cop a plea on this one. Federal case or not, they were guilty of multiple rape and murder — and, it would seem, guilty of another double murder in which the Mobile police had direct interest. The word was already on the street: the lives of druggies were at risk. It was another case of sending a message. The advantage that police officers had over more senior government officials was that they spoke in a language that criminals fully understood.

But who, another detective asked, would deliver the message?

"How about the Patterson boys?" the lieutenant answered.

"Ahh," the captain said. He considered the question for a moment, then: "Okay." It was, on the whole, a decision far more easily arrived at than the great and weighty decisions reached by governments. And far more easily implemented.

The two peasants arrived in Medellín around sundown. Cortez was thoroughly frustrated by this time. Eight bodies to be disposed of — not all that difficult a thing to do in Medellín — for no good reason. He was sure of that now. As sure as he'd been of the opposite thing six hours earlier. So where was the information leak? Three women and five men had just died proving that they weren't it. The last two had just been shot in the head, uselessly catatonic after watching the first six die under less merciful circumstances. The room was a mess, and Cortez felt soiled by it. All that effort wasted. Killing people for no good reason. He was too angry to be ashamed.

He met with the peasants in another room on another floor after washing his hands and changing his clothes. They were frightened, but not of Cortez, which surprised Félix greatly. It took several minutes to understand why. They told their stories in an overly rapid and disjointed manner, which he allowed, memorizing the details — some of them conflicting, but that was not unexpected since there were two of them — before he began asking his own, directed questions.

"The rifles were not AK-47s," one said positively. "I know the sound. It was not that one." The other shrugged. He didn't know one weapon from another.

"Did you see anyone?"

"No, señor. We heard the noise and the shouting, and we ran."

Very sensible of you, Cortez noted. "Shouting, you say? In what language?"

"Why, in our language. We heard them chasing after us, but we ran. They didn't catch us. We know the mountains," the weapons expert explained.

"You saw and heard nothing else?"

"The shooting, the explosions, lights — flashes from the guns, that is all."

"The place where it happened — how many times had you been there?"

"Many times, señor, it is where we make the paste."

"Many times," the other confirmed. "For over a year we have gone there."

"You will tell no one that you came here. You will tell no one anything that you know," Félix told them.

"But the families of —"

"You will tell no one," Cortez repeated in a quiet, serious voice. Both men knew danger when they saw it. "You will be well rewarded for what you have done, and the families of the others will be compensated."

Cortez deemed himself a fair man. These two mountain folk had served his purposes well, and they would be properly rewarded. He still didn't know where the leak was, but if he could get ahold of one of those — what? M-19 bands? Somehow he didn't think so.

Then who?

Americans?

If anything, the death of Rocha had only increased their resolve, Chavez knew. Captain Ramirez had taken it pretty hard, but that was to be expected from a good officer. Their new patrol base was only two miles from one of the many coffee plantations in the area, and two miles in a different direction from yet another processing site. The men were in their normal daytime routine. Half asleep, half standing guard.

Ramirez sat alone. Chavez was correct. He had taken it hard. In an intellectual sense, the captain knew that he should accept the death of one of his men as a simple cost of doing business. But emotions are not the same as intellect. It was also true, though Ramirez didn't think along these precise lines, that historically there is no way to predict which officers are suited for combat operations and which are not. Ramirez had committed a typical mistake for combat leaders. He had grown too close to his men. He was unable to think of them as expendable assets. His failure had nothing to do with courage. The captain had enough of that; risking his own life was a part of the job he readily accepted. Where he failed was in understanding that risking the lives of his men — which he also knew to be part of the job — inevitably meant that some would die. Somehow he'd forgotten that. As a company commander he'd led his men on countless field exercises, training them, showing them how to do their jobs, chiding them when their laser-sensing Miles gear went off to denote a simulated casualty. But Rocha hadn't been a simulation, had he? And it wasn't as though Rocha had been a slick-sleeved new kid. He'd been a skilled pro. That meant that he'd somehow failed his men, Ramirez told himself, knowing that it was wrong even as he thought it. If he'd deployed better, if he'd paid more attention, if, if, if. The young captain tried to shake it off but couldn't. But he couldn't quit either. So he'd be more careful next time.

The tape cassettes arrived together just after lunch. The COD flight from *Ranger,* unbeknownst to anyone involved, had been coordinated with a courier flight from Bogotá. Larson had handled part of it, flying the tape from the GLD to El Dorado where he handed it off to another CIA officer. Both cassettes were tucked in the satchel of an Agency courier who rode in the front cabin of the Air Force C-5A transport, catching a few hours' sleep in one of the cramped bunks on the right side of the aircraft, a few feet behind the flight deck. The flight came directly into Andrews, and, after its landing, the forty-foot ladder was let down into the cavernous cargo area and the courier walked out the opened cargo door to a waiting Agency car which sped directly to Langley.

Ritter had a pair of television sets in his office, each with its own VCR. He watched them alone, cueing the tapes until they were roughly synchronized. The one from the aircraft didn't show very much. You could see the laser dot and the rough outline of the house, but little else until the flash of the detonation. Clark's tape was far better. There was the house, its lighted windows flaring in the light-amplified picture, and the guards wandering about — those with cigarettes looked like lightning bugs; each time they took a drag their faces were lit brightly by the glow. Then the bomb. It was very much like watching a Hitchcock movie, Ritter thought. He knew what was happening, but those on the screen did not. They wandered around aimlessly, unaware of the part they played in a drama written in the office of the Deputy Director (Operations) of the Central Intelligence Agency. But —

"That's funny . . . " Ritter said to himself. He used his remote control to back up the tape. Seconds before the bomb went off, a new car appeared at the gate. "Who might you be?" he asked the screen. Then he fast-forwarded the tape past the explosion. The car he'd been driving — a BMW — had been flipped over by the shock wave, but seconds later the driver got out and pulled a pistol.

"Cortez . . . " He froze the frame. The picture didn't tell him much. It was a man of medium dimensions. While everyone else around the wrecked house raced about without much in the way of purpose, this man just stood there for a little while, then revived himself at the fountain — wasn't it odd that it still worked! Ritter thought — and next went to where the bomb had gone off. He couldn't have been a retainer of one of the Cartel members. They were all plowing through the rubble by this time. No, this one was already trying to figure out what had happened. It was right before the tape changed over to blank noise that he got the best picture. That had to be Félix Cortez. Looking around, already thinking, already trying to figure things out. That was a real pro.

"Damn, that was close," Ritter breathed. "One more minute and you would have parked your car over with the others. One more damned minute!" Ritter pulled both tapes and tucked them in his office safe along with all of the EAGLE EYE, SHOWBOAT, and RECIPROCITY material. *Next time*, he promised the tape cassette. Then he started thinking. Was Cortez really involved in the assassination?

"Gawd," Ritter said aloud in his office. He'd assumed that, but . . . Would he have set up the crime and then come to America . . . ? Why do such a thing? According to the statement that secretary had made, he'd not even pumped her very hard for information. Instead it had been a basic get-away-with-your-lover weekend. The technique was a classic one. First, seduce the target. Second, determine if you can get information from her (usually *him* the way Western intelligence services handled sexual recruitments, but the other way around for the Eastern bloc). Third, firm up the relationship — and then use it. If Ritter understood the evidence properly, Cortez hadn't yet gotten to the point . . .

It wasn't Cortez at all, was it? He'd probably

forwarded what information he had as a matter of course, not knowing about the FBI operation against the Cartel's money operations. He hadn't been there when the decision to whack the Director had been made. And he would have recommended against it. Why lash out when you have just developed a good intel source? No, that wasn't professional at all.

So, Félix, how do you feel about all this? Ritter would have traded much for the ability to ask that question, though the answer was plain enough. Intelligence officers were regularly betrayed by their political superiors. It wouldn't be the first time for him, but he'd be angry just the same. Just as angry as Ritter was with Admiral Cutter.

For the first time, Ritter found himself wondering what Cortez was really doing. Probably he had simply defected away from Cuba and made a mercenary of himself. The Cartel had hired him on for his training and experience, thinking that they were buying just another mercenary — a very good one to be sure, but a mercenary nonetheless. Just like they bought local cops — hell, American cops — and politicians. But a police officer wasn't the same thing as a professional spook educated at Moscow Center. He was giving them his advice, and he'd think they had betrayed him — well, acted very stupidly, because killing Emil Jacobs had been an act of emotion, not of reason.

Why didn't I see that before! Ritter growled at himself. The answer: because not seeing had given him an excuse to do something he'd always wanted to do. He hadn't thought because somehow he'd known that thinking would have prevented him from taking action.

Cortez wasn't a terrorist, was he? He was an intelligence officer. He'd worked with the Macheteros because he'd been assigned to the job. Before that his experience had been straight espionage, and merely because he'd worked with that loony Puerto Rican group, they'd just assumed . . . That was probably one reason why he'd defected.

It was clearer now. The Cartel had hired Cortez for his expertise and experience. But in doing so they had adopted a pet wolf. And wolves made for dangerous pets, didn't they?

For the moment there was one thing he could do. Ritter summoned an aide and instructed him to take the best frame they had of Cortez, run it through the photo-enhancing computer, and forward it to the FBI. That was something worth doing, so long as they isolated the figure from the background, but that was just another task for the imaging computer.

Admiral Cutter remained at his White House office while the President was away in the western Maryland hills. He'd fly up every day for his usual morning briefing — delivered at a somewhat later hour while the President was on his "vacation" regime — but for the most part he'd stay here. He had his own duties, one of which was being "a senior administration official." ASAO, as he thought of the title, was his name when he gave off-the-record press briefings. Such information was a vital part of presidential policymaking, all part of an elaborate game played by the government and the press: Official Leaking. Cutter would send up "trial balloons," what people in the consumer-products business called test-marketing. When the President had a new idea that he was not too sure about, Cutter — or the appropriate cabinet secretary, each of whom was also an ASAO — would speak on background, and a story would be written in the major papers, allowing Congress and others to react to the idea before it was given an official presidential *imprimatur*. It was a way for elected officials and other players in the Washington scene to dance and posture without the need for anyone to lose face — an Oriental concept that translated well inside the confines of the Capital Beltway.

Bob Holtzman, the senior White House correspondent for one of the Washington papers, settled into his chair opposite Cutter for the deep-background revelations. The rules were fully understood by both sides. Cutter could say anything he wished without fear that his name, title, or the location of his office would be used. Holtzman would feel free to write the story any way he wished, within reason, so long as he did not compromise his source to anyone except his editor. Neither man especially liked the other.

Cutter's distaste for journalists was about the only thing he still had in common with his fellow military officers, though he was certain that he concealed it. He thought them all, especially the one before him now, to be lazy, stupid people who couldn't write and didn't think. Holtzman felt that Cutter was the wrong man in the wrong place — the reporter didn't like the idea of having a military officer giving such intimate advice to the President; more importantly, he thought Cutter was a shallow, self-serving apple-polisher with delusions of grandeur, not to mention an arrogant son of a bitch who looked upon reporters as a semiuseful form of domesticated vulture. As a result of such thoughts, they got along rather well.

"You going to be watching the convention next week?" Holtzman asked.

"I try not to concern myself with politics," Cutter replied. "Coffee?"

Right! the reporter told himself. "No, thanks. What the hell's going on down in coca land?"

"Your guess is as good as — well, that's not true. We've had the bastards under surveillance for some time. My guess is that Emil was killed by one faction of the Cartel — no surprise — but without their having made a really official decision. The bombing last night might be indicative of a faction fight inside the organization."

"Well, somebody's pretty pissed," Holtzman observed, scribbling notes on his pad under his personal heading for Cutter. "A Senior Adminis-

712

tration Official" was transcribed as *ASO'l*. "The word is that the Cartel contracted M-19 to do the assassination, and that the Colombians really worked over the one they caught."

"Maybe they did."

"How'd they know that Director Jacobs was going down?"

"I don't know," Cutter replied.

"Really? You know that his secretary tried to commit suicide. The Bureau isn't talking at all, but I find that a remarkable coincidence."

"Who's running the case over there? Believe it or not, I don't know."

"Dan Murray, a deputy assistant director. He's not actually doing the field work, but he's the guy reporting to Shaw."

"Well, that's not my turf. I'm looking at the overseas aspects of the case, but the domestic stuff is in another office," Cutter pointed out, erecting a stone wall that Holtzman couldn't breach.

"So the Cartel was pretty worked up about Operation TARPON, and some senior people acted without the approval of the whole outfit to take Jacobs out. Other members, you say, think that their action was precipitous and decided to eliminate those who put out the contract?"

"That's the way it looks now. You have to understand, our intel on this is pretty thin."

"Our intel is always pretty thin," Holtzman pointed out.

"You can talk to Bob Ritter about that." Cutter set his coffee mug down.

"Right." Holtzman smiled. If there were two people in Washington whom you could trust never to leak anything, it was Bob Ritter and Arthur Moore. "What about Jack Ryan?"

"He's just settling in. He's been in Belgium all week anyway, at the NATO intel conference."

"There are rumbles on The Hill that somebody ought to do something about the Cartel, that the attack on Jacobs was a direct attack on — "

"I watch C-SPAN, too, Bob. Talk is cheap."

"And what Governor Fowler said this morning . . . ?"

"I'll leave politics to the politicians."

"You know that the price of coke is up on the street?"

"Oh? I'm not in that market. Is it?" Cutter hadn't heard that yet. *Already* . . .

"Not much, but some. There's word on the street that incoming shipments are off a little."

"Glad to hear it."

"But no comment?" Holtzman asked. "You're the one who's been saying that this is a for-real war and we ought to treat it as such."

Cutter's smile froze on his face for a moment. "The President decides about things like war."

"What about Congress?"

"Well, that, too, but since I've been in government service there hasn't been a congressional declaration along those lines."

"How would you feel personally if we were involved in that bombing?"

"I don't know. We weren't involved." The interview wasn't going as planned. What did Holtzman know?

"That was a hypothetical," the reporter pointed out.

"Okay. We go off the record — completely — at this point. Hypothetically, we could kill all the bastards and I wouldn't shed many tears. How about you?"

Holtzman snorted. "Off the record, I agree with you. I grew up here. I can remember when it was safe to walk the streets. Now I look at the body count every morning and wonder if I'm in D.C. or Beirut. So it wasn't us, then?"

"Nope. Looks more like the Cartel is shaking itself out. That's speculation, but it's the best we have at the moment."

"Fair enough. I suppose I can make a story out of that."

20.

Discoveries

It was amazing. But it was also true. Cortez had been there for over an hour. There were six armed men with him, and a dog that sniffed around for signs of the people who had assaulted this processing site. The empty cartridge cases were mostly of the 5.56mm round now used by most of the NATO countries and their surrogates all over the world, but which had begun as the .223 Remington sporting cartridge. In America. There were also a number of 9mm cases, and a single empty hull from a 40mm grenade launcher. One of the attackers had been wounded, perhaps severely. The method of the attack was classic, a fire unit uphill and an assault group on the same level, to the north. They'd left hastily, not booby-trapping the bodies as had happened in two other cases. Probably because of the injured man, Cortez judged. Also because they knew — suspected? No, they probably knew — that two men had gotten away to summon help.

Definitely more than one team was roaming the mountains. Maybe three or four, judging by the number and location of sites that had so far been attacked. That eliminated M-19. There weren't enough trained men in that organization to do something like this — not without his hearing of it, he corrected himself. The Cartel had done more than suborn the local guerrilla factions. It also had paid informants in each unit, something the Colombian government had signally failed to do.

So, he told himself, *now you have probable American covert-action teams working in the hills. Who and what are they? Probably soldiers, or very high-guality mercenaries. More likely the former.* The international mercenary community wasn't what it had once been — and truthfully had never been especially effective. Cortez had been to Angola and seen what African troops were like. Mercenaries hadn't had to be all that effective to defeat them, though that was now changing along with everything else in the world.

Whoever they were, they'd be far away — far enough that he didn't feel uncomfortable at the moment, though he'd leave the hunting to others. Cortez was an intelligence officer, and had no illusions about being a soldier. For now, he gathered his evidence almost like a policeman. The rifle and machine-gun cartridges, he saw, came from a single manufacturer. He didn't have such information committed to memory, but he noted that the 9mm cases had the same lot codes — stamped on the case heads — as those he'd gotten from one of the airfields on Colombia's northern coast. The odds against that being a coincidence were pretty high, he thought. So whoever had been watching the airfields had moved here . . . ? How would that have been done? The simple way would be by truck or bus, but that was a little too simple; that's how M-19 would have done it. Too great a risk for Americans, however. The *yanquis* would use helicopters. Staging from where? A ship, perhaps, or more likely one of their bases in Panama. He knew of no American naval exercises within helicopter range of the coast. Therefore a large aircraft capable of midair refueling. Only the Americans did that. And it would have to be based in Panama. And he had assets in Panama. Cortez pocketed the cartridges and started walking down the hill. Now he had a starting place, and that was all someone with his training needed.

Ryan's VC-20A — thinking of it as his airplane still required a stretch of the imagination — lifted off from the airfield outside Mons in the early afternoon. His first official foray into the big leagues of the international intelligence business had gone well. His paper on the Soviets and their activities in Eastern Europe had met with general approval and agreement, and he'd been gratified to learn that the analysis chiefs of all the NATO intelligence agencies held exactly the same opinion of the changes in their enemy's policies as he did: nobody knew what the hell was going on. There were theories ranging all the way from the peace-is-breaking-out-and-now-what-do-we-do? view to the equally unlikely it's-all-a-trick opinion, but when it came down to doing a formal intelligence estimate, people who'd been in the business since before Jack was born just shook their heads and muttered into their beer — exactly what Ryan did some of the time. The really good news for the year, of course, was the signal success that the counterintelligence groups had had turning KGB operations throughout Europe, and while CIA had not told anyone (except Sir Basil, who'd been there when the plan had been hatched) exactly how that had come about, the Agency enjoyed considerable prestige for its work in that area. The bottom line that Jack had often cited in the investment business was fairly clear: militarily NATO was in its best-ever condition, its security services were riding higher than anyone thought possible — it was just that the alliance's overall mission was now in doubt politically. To Ryan that looked like success, so long as politicians didn't let things go to their heads, which was enough of a caveat for anyone.

So there was a lot to smile about as the Belgian countryside fell farther and farther below him until it looked like a particularly attractive quilt from Pennsylvania Dutch country. At least on the actual NATO side.

Possibly the truest testimony to NATO's

present happy condition, however, was that talk around the banquet tables and over coffee in the break periods between the plenary sessions was not on "business" as most of the conference attendees normally viewed it. Intelligence analysts from Germany and Italy, Britain and Norway, Denmark and Portugal, all of them expressed their concern at the growing problems of drugs in their countries. The Cartel's activities were expanding eastward, no longer content with marketing their wares to America alone. The intelligence professionals had noted the assassination of Emil Jacobs and the rest and wondered aloud if international narcoterrorism had taken a wholly new and dangerous turn — and what had to be done about it. The French, with their history of vigorous action to protect their land, were especially approving of the bomb blast outside Medellín, and nonplussed by Ryan's puzzled and somewhat exasperating response: *No comment. I don't know anything.* Their reaction to that was predictable, of course. Had an equivalent French official been so publicly murdered, DGSE would have mounted an immediate operation. It was something the French were especially good at. It was something that the French media and, more to the point, the French people understood and approved. And so the DGSE representatives had expected Ryan to respond with a knowing smile to accompany his lack of comment, not blank embarrassment. That wasn't part of the game as it was played in Europe, and just another odd thing about the Americans for their Old World allies to ponder. *Must they be so unpredictable?* they would ask themselves. Being that way to the Russians had strategic value, but not to one's allies.

And not to its own government officials, Ryan thought. *What the hell is going on?*

Being three thousand miles from home had given Jack a properly detached perspective to the affair. In the absence of a viable legal mechanism to deal with such crimes, maybe direct action was the right thing to do. Challenge directly the power of a nation-state and you risked a direct response from that nation-state. If we could bomb a foreign country for sponsoring action against American soldiers in a Berlin disco, then why not —

— kill people on the territory of a fellow American democracy?

What about that *political dimension?*

That was the rub, wasn't it? Colombia had its own laws. It wasn't Libya, ruled by a comic-opera figure of dubious stability. It wasn't Iran, a vicious theocracy ruled by a bitter testimonial to the skill of gerontologists. Colombia was a country with real democratic traditions, one that had put its own institutions at risk, fighting to protect the citizens of another land from — themselves.

What the hell are we doing?

Right and wrong assumed different values at this level of statecraft, didn't they? Or did they? What were the rules? What was the law? Were there any of either? Before he could answer those questions, Ryan knew that he'd have to learn the facts. That would be hard enough. Jack settled back into his comfortable seat and looked down at the English Channel, widening out like a funnel as the aircraft headed west toward Land's End. Beyond that lonely point of ship-killing rocks lay the North Atlantic, and beyond that lay home. He had seven hours to decide what he should do once he got there. *Seven whole hours,* Jack thought, wondering how many times he could ask himself the same questions, and how many times he'd only come up with new questions instead of answers.

Law was a trap, Murray told himself. It was a goddess to worship, a lovely bronze lady who held up her lantern in the darkness to show one the way. But what if the way led nowhere? They now had a dead-bang case against the one "suspect" in the assassination of the Director. The Colombians had gotten the confession and its thirty single-spaced pages of text were lying on his desk. There was ample physical evidence, which had been duly processed through the Bureau's legendary forensic laboratories. There was just one little problem. The extradition treaty the United States had with Colombia was not operative at the moment. Colombia's Supreme Court — more precisely, those justices who remained alive after twelve of their colleagues had been murdered by M-19 raiders not so long ago; all of whom, coincidentally, had been supporters of the extradition treaty before their violent deaths — had decided that the treaty was somehow in opposition to their country's constitution. No treaty. No extradition. The assassin would be tried locally and doubtless sent away for a lengthy prison term, but at the very least Murray and the Bureau wanted him caged in Marion, Illinois — the maximum-security federal prison for really troublesome offenders; Alcatraz without the ambience — and the Justice Department thought it could make a case for invoking the death statute that related to drug-related murders. But — the confession the Colombians had gotten hadn't exactly followed with American rules of evidence, and, the lawyers admitted, might be thrown out by an American judge; which would eliminate the death penalty. And the guy who took out the Director of the FBI might actually become something of a celebrity at Marion, Illinois, most of whose prisoners did not regard the FBI with the same degree of affection accorded by most U.S. citizens. The same thing, he'd learned the day before, was true of the Pirates Case. Some tricky bastard of a defense lawyer had uncovered what the Coast Guard had pulled, blowing that death case away also. And the only good news around was that Murray was sure his government had struck back in a way that was highly satisfying, but fell under the general legal category of cold-blooded murder.

It worried Dan Murray that he did view that development as good news. It wasn't the sort of thing that they'd lectured him — and he had later lectured others — about during his stint as a student and later an instructor at the FBI Academy, was it? What happened when governments broke the law? The textbook answer was anarchy — at least that's what happened when it became known that the government was breaking its own laws. But that was the really operative definition of a criminal, wasn't it — one who got caught breaking the law.

"No," Murray told himself quietly. He'd spent his life following that light because on dark nights that one beacon of sanity was all society had. His mission and the Bureau's was to enforce the laws of his country faithfully and honestly. There was leeway — there had to be, because the written words couldn't anticipate everything — but when the letter of the law was insufficient one was guided by the principle upon which the law was based. Maybe the situation wasn't always a satisfying one, but it beat the alternative, didn't it? But what did you do when the law didn't work? Was that just part of the game, too? Was it, after all was said and done, just a game?

Clark held a somewhat different view. Law had never been his concern — at least not his immediate concern. To him "legal" meant that something was "okay," not that some legislators had drafted a set of rules, and that some President or other had signed it. To him it meant that the sitting President had decided that the continued existence of someone or something was contrary to the best interests of his country. His government service had begun in the United States Navy as part of the SEALs, the Navy's elite, secretive commandos. In that tight, quiet community he'd made himself a name that was still spoken with respect: *Snake,* they'd called him, because you couldn't hear his footsteps. To the best of his knowledge, no enemy had ever seen him and lived to tell the tale. His name had been different then, of course, but only because after leaving the Navy he'd made the mistake — he truly thought of it as a mistake, but only in the technical sense — of applying his skills on a free-agent basis. And done quite well, of course, until the police had discovered his identity. The lesson from that adventure was that while people didn't really investigate happenings on the battlefield, they did elsewhere, requiring far greater circumspection on his part. A foolish error in retrospect, one result of his almost-discovery by a local police force was that he'd come to the attention of CIA, which occasionally needed people with his unique skills. It was even something of a joke: "When there's killing to be done, get someone who kills for a living." At least it had been funny back then, almost twenty years earlier.

Others decided who needed to die. Those others were the properly selected representatives of the American people, whom he'd served in one way or another for most of his adult life. The law, as he'd once bothered to find out, was that there was no law. If the President said "kill," then Clark was merely the instrument of properly defined government policy, all the more so now, since selected members of Congress had to agree with the executive branch. The rules which from time to time prohibited such acts were Executive Orders from the President's office, which orders the President could freely violate — or more precisely, redefine to suit the situation. Of course, Clark did very little of that. Mainly his jobs for the Agency involved his other skills — getting in and out of places without being detected, for example, at which he was the best guy around. But killing was the reason he'd been hired in the first place, and for Clark, who'd been baptized John Terrence Kelly at St. Ignatius Parish in Indianapolis, Indiana, it was simply an act of war sanctioned both by his country and also by his religion, about which he was moderately serious. Vietnam had never been granted the legal sanction of a declared war, after all, and if killing his country's enemies back then had been all right, why not now? Murder to the renamed John T. Clark was killing people without just cause. Law he left to lawyers, in the knowledge that his definition of just cause was far more practical, and far more effective.

His immediate concern was his next target. He had two more days of availability on the carrier battle group, and he wanted to stage another stealth-bombing if he could.

Clark was domiciled in a frame house in the outskirts of Bogotá, a safe house the CIA had set up a decade earlier, officially owned by a corporate front and generally rented out commercially to visiting American businessmen. It had no obvious special features. The telephone was ordinary until he attached a portable encrypting device — a simple one that wouldn't have passed muster in Eastern Europe, but sufficient for the relatively low-intercept threat down here — and he also had a satellite dish that operated just fine through a not very obvious hole in the roof and also ran through an encrypting system that looked much the same as a portable cassette player.

So what to do next? he asked himself. The Untiveros bombing had been carefully executed to look like a car bomb. Why not another, a real one? The trick was setting it up to scare hell out of the intended targets, flushing them into a better target area. To accomplish that it had to appear an earnest attempt, but at the same time it couldn't be earnest enough to injure innocent people. That was the problem with car bombs.

Low-order detonation? he thought. That was an idea. Make the bomb look like an earnest attempt that fizzled. *Too hard to do*, he decided.

Best of all would be a simple assassination with a rifle, but that was too hard to set up. Just getting a perch overlooking the proper place would be difficult and dangerous. The Cartel overlords kept tabs on every window with a line of sight to their own domiciles. If an American rented one, and soon thereafter a shot was fired from it — well, that wouldn't exactly be covert, would it? The whole point was for them not to know exactly what was happening.

Clark's operational concept was an elegantly simple one. So elegant and so simple that it hadn't occurred to the supposed experts in "black" operations at Langley. What Clark wanted to do, simply, was to kill enough of the people on his list to increase the paranoia within his targeted community. Killing them all, desirable though it might be, was a practical impossibility. What he wanted to do was merely to kill enough of them, and to do so in such a way as to spark another reaction entirely.

The Cartel was composed of a number of very ruthless people whose intelligence was manifested in the sort of cunning most often associated with a skilled enemy on the battlefield. Like good soldiers they were always alert to danger, but unlike soldiers they looked for danger from within in addition to from without. Despite the success of their collaborative enterprise, these men were rivals. Flushed with money and power, they didn't and would never have enough. There was never enough of either for men like this, but power most of all. It seemed to Clark and others that their ultimate goal was to assume political control of their country, but countries are not run by committees, at least not by large ones. All

Clark needed to accomplish was to make the Cartel chieftains think that there was a power grab underway within their own hierarchy, at which point they would merrily start killing one another off in a new version of the Mafia wars of the 1930s.

Maybe, he admitted to himself. He gave the plan about a 30 percent chance of total success. But even if it failed, some major players would be removed from the field, and that, too, counted as a tactical success if not a strategic one. Weakening the Cartel might increase Colombia's chances of dealing with it, which was another possible strategic outcome, but not the only one. There was also the chance that the war he was hoping to start could have the same result as the final act of the Castellammare Wars, remembered as the Night of the Italian Vespers, in which scores of mafiosi had been killed by their own colleagues. What had grown out of that bloody night was a stronger, better-organized, and more dangerous organized-crime network under the far more sophisticated leadership of Carlo Luchiano and Vito Genovese. That was a real danger, Clark thought. But things couldn't get much worse than they already were. Or so Washington had decided. It was a gamble worth the taking.

Larson arrived at the house. He'd come here only once before, and while it was in keeping with Clark's cover as a visiting prospector of sorts — there were several boxes of rocks lying around the house — it was one aspect of the mission that bothered him.

"Catch the news?"

"Everyone says car bomb," Larson replied with a sly smile. "We won't be that lucky next time."

"Probably not. The next one has to be really spectacular."

"Don't look at me! You don't expect that *I'm* going to find out when the next meet is, do you?"

It would be nice, Clark told himself, but he didn't expect it, and would have disapproved any order requiring it. "No, we have to pray for another intercept. They have to meet. They have to get together and discuss what's happened."

"Agreed. But it might not be up in the mountains."

"Oh?"

"They all have places in the lowlands, too."

Clark had forgotten about that. It would make targeting very difficult. "Can we spot in the laser from an aircraft?"

"I don't see why not. But then I land, refuel, and fly the hell out of this country forever."

Henry and Harvey Patterson were twin brothers, twenty-seven years of age, and were proof of whatever social theory a criminologist might hold. Their father had been a professional, if not especially proficient, criminal for all of his abbreviated life — which had ended at age thirty-two when a liquor-store owner had shot him with a 12-gauge double at the range of eleven feet. That was important to adherents of the behavioral school, generally populated by political conservatives. They were also products of a one-parent household, poor schooling, adverse peer-group pressure, and an economically depressed neighborhood. Those factors were important to the environmental school of behavior, whose adherents are generally political liberals.

Whatever the reason for their behavior, they were career criminals who enjoyed their life-style and didn't give much of a damn whether their brains were preprogrammed into it or they had actually learned it in childhood. They were not stupid. Had intelligence tests not been biased toward the literate, their IQs would have tested slightly above average. They had animal cunning sufficient to make their apprehension by police a demanding enterprise, and a street-smart knowledge of law that had allowed them to manipulate the legal system with remarkable success. They also had principles. The Patterson brothers were drinkers — each was already a borderline alcoholic — but not drug users. This marked them as a little odd, but since neither brother cared a great deal for law, the discontinuity with normal criminal profiles didn't trouble them either.

Together, they had robbed, burglarized, and assaulted their way across southern Alabama since their mid-teens. They were treated by their peers with considerable respect. Several people had crossed one or both — since they were identical twins, crossing one inevitably meant crossing both — and turned up dead. Dead by blunt trauma (a club), or dead by penetrating trauma (knife or gun). The police suspected them of five murders. The problem was, which one of them? The fact that they were identical twins was a technical complication to every case which their lawyer — a good one they had identified quite early in their careers — had used to great effect. Whenever the victim of a Patterson was killed, the police could bet their salaries on the fact that one of the brothers — generally the one who had the motive to kill the victim — would be ostentatiously present somewhere miles away. In addition, their victims were never honest citizens, but members of their own criminal community, which fact invariably cooled the ardor of the police.

But not this time.

It had taken fourteen years since their first officially recorded brush with the law, but Henry and Harvey had finally fucked up big-time, cops all over the state learned from their watch commanders: the police had finally gotten them on a major felony rap and, they noted with no small degree of pleasure, it was because of another pair of identical twins. Two whores, lovely ones of eighteen years, had smitten the hearts of the Patterson brothers. For the past five weeks Henry and Harvey had not been able to get enough of Noreen and Doreen Grayson, and as the patrol officers in the neighborhood had watched the romance blossom, the general speculation in the station was how the hell they kept one another straight — the behavioralist cops pronounced that it wouldn't actually matter, which observation was dismissed by the environmentalist cops as pseudoscientific bullshit, not to mention sexually perverse, but both sides of the argument found it roundly entertaining speculation. In either case, true love had been the downfall of the Patterson brothers.

Henry and Harvey had decided to liberate the Grayson sisters from their drug-dealing pimp, a very disreputable but even more formidable man with a long history of violence, and a suspect in the disappearance of several of his girls. What had brought it to a head was a savage beating to the sisters for not turning over some presents — jewelry — given them by the Pattersons as one-month anniversary presents. Noreen's jaw had been broken, and Doreen had lost six teeth, plus other indignities that had enraged the Pattersons and put both girls in the University of South Alabama Medical Center. The twin brothers were not people to bear offense lightly, and one week later, from the unlit shadows of an alley, the two of them had used identical Smith & Wesson revolvers to end the life of Elrod McIlvane. It was their misfortune that a police radio car had been half a block away at the time. Even the cops thought that, in this case, the Pattersons had rendered a public service to the city of Mobile.

The police lieutenant had both of them in an interrogation room. Their customary defiance was a wilted flower. The guns had been recovered less than fifty yards from the crime scene. Though there had been no usable fingerprints on either — firearms do not always lend themselves to this purpose — the four rounds recovered from McIlvane's body did match up with both; the Pattersons had been apprehended four blocks away; their hands bore powder signatures from having fired guns of some sort; and their motive for eliminating the pimp was well known. Criminal cases didn't get much better than that. The only thing the police didn't have was a confession. The twins' luck had finally run out. Even their lawyer had told them that. There was no hope of a plea-bargain — the local prosecutor hated them even more than the police did — and while they stood to do hard time for murder, the good news was that they probably wouldn't get the chair, since the jurors probably would not want to execute people for killing a drug-dealing pimp who'd put two of his whores in the hospital and probably killed a few more. This was arguably a crime of passion, and under American law such motives are generally seen as mitigating circumstances.

In identical prison garb, the Pattersons sat across the table from the senior police officer. The lieutenant couldn't even tell them apart, and didn't bother asking which was which, because they would probably have lied about it out of pure spite.

"Where's our lawyer?" Henry or Harvey asked.

"Yeah," Harvey or Henry emphasized.

"We don't really need him here for this. How'd you boys like to do a little favor for us?" the lieutenant asked. "You do us a little favor and maybe we can do you a little favor." That settled the problem of legal counsel.

"Bullshit!" one of the twins observed, just as a bargaining position, of course. They were at the straw-grasping stage. Prison beckoned, and while neither had ever served a serious stretch, they'd done enough county time to know that it wouldn't be fun.

"How do you like the idea of life imprisonment?" the lieutenant asked, unmoved by the show of strength. "You know how it works, seven or eight years before you're rehabilitated and they let you out. If you're lucky, that is. Awful long time, eight years. Like that idea, boys?"

"We're not fools. Watchu here for?" the other Patterson asked, indicating that he was ready to discuss terms.

"You do a job for us, and, well, something nice might happen."

"What job's that?" Already both brothers were amenable to the arrangement.

"You seen Ramón and Jesús?"

"The pirates?" one asked. "Shit." In the criminal community as with any other, there is a hierarchy of status. The abusers of women and children are at the bottom. The Pattersons were violent criminals, but had never abused women.

735

They only assaulted men — men much smaller than themselves for the most part, but men nonetheless. That was important to their collective self-image.

"Yeah, we seen the fucks," the other said to emphasize his brother's more succinct observation. "Actin' like king shit last cupla days. Fuckin' spics. Hey, man, we bad dudes, but we ain't never raped no little girl, ain't never killed no little girl neither — and they be gettin' off, they say? Shit! We waste a fuckin' pimp likes to beat on his ladies, and we lookin' at life. What kinda justice you call that, mister po-liceman? Shit!"

"If something were to happen to Ramón and Jesús, something really serious," the lieutenant said quietly, "maybe something else might happen. Something beneficial to you boys."

"Like what?"

"Like you get to see Noreen and Doreen on a very regular basis. Maybe even settle down."

"Shit!" Henry or Harvey said.

"That's the best deal in town, boys," the lieutenant told them.

"You want us to kill the motherfuckers?" It was Harvey who asked this question, disappointing his brother, who thought of himself as the smart one.

The lieutenant just stared at them.

"We hear you," Henry said. "How we know you keep your word?"

"What word is that?" The captain paused.

"Ramón and Jesús killed a family of four, raped the wife and the little girl first, of course, and they probably had a hand in the murder of a Mobile police officer and his wife. But something went wrong with the case against them, and the most they'll get is twenty years, walk in seven or eight, max. For killing six people. Hardly seems fair, does it?"

By this time both twins had gotten the message. The lieutenant could see the recognition, an identical expression in both pairs of eyes. Then came the decision. The two pairs of eyes were guarded for a moment as they considered how to do it. Then they became serene. Both Pattersons nodded, and that was that.

"You boys be careful now. Jail can be a very dangerous place." The lieutenant rose to summon the jailer. If asked, he'd say that — after getting their permission to talk to them without a lawyer present, of course — he'd wanted to ask them about a robbery in which the Pattersons had not been involved, but about which they might have some knowledge, and that he had offered them some help with the DA in return for their assistance. Alas, they'd professed no knowledge of the robbery in question, and after less than five minutes of conversation, he'd sent them back to their cell. Should they ever refer to the actual content of the conversation, it would be the word of two career criminals with an open-and-shut murder charge hanging over their heads against the word of a police lieutenant. At most that would result in a page-five story in the *Mobile Register*, which took rather a stern line on violent crime. And they could scarcely confess to a double murder whether done at police behest or not, could they?

The lieutenant was an honorable man, and immediately went to work to hold up his end of the bargain in anticipation of the fact that the Pattersons would do the same. Of the four bullets removed from the body of Elrod McIlvane, one was unusable for ballistic-matching purposes due to its distortion — unjacketed lead bullets are very easily damaged — and the others, though good enough for the criminal case, were borderline. The lieutenant ordered the bullets removed from evidence storage for re-examination, along with the examiner's notes and the photographs. He had to sign for them, of course, to maintain "chain of evidence." This legal requirement was written to ensure that evidence used in a trial, once taken from the crime scene or elsewhere and identified as significant, was always in a known location and under proper custody. It was a safeguard against the illicit manufacture of incriminating evidence. When a piece of evidence got lost, even if it were later recovered, it could never be used in a criminal case, since it was then tainted. He walked down to the laboratory area, but found the technicians leaving to go home. He asked the ballistics expert if he could recheck the Patterson Case bullets first thing Monday morning, and the man replied, sure, one of the matches was a little shaky, but, he thought, close enough for trial purposes. He didn't mind doing a recheck, though.

The policeman walked back to his office with the bullets. The manila envelope which held them was labeled with the case number, and since it was still in proper custody, duly signed for by the lieutenant, chain of evidence had not yet been violated. He made a note on his desk blotter that he didn't want to leave them in his desk over the weekend, and would take them home, keeping the whole package locked in his combination-locked briefcase. The lieutenant was fifty-three years old, and within four months of retirement with full benefits. Thirty years of service was enough, he thought, looking forward to getting full use from his fishing boat. He could scarcely retire in good conscience leaving two cop-killers with eight years of soft time.

The influx of drug money to Colombia has produced all manner of side effects and one of them, in a stunningly ironic twist, is that the Colombian police had obtained a new and very sophisticated crime lab. Residue from the Untiveros house was run through the usual series of chemical tests, and within a few hours it had been determined that the explosive agent had been a mixture of cyclotetramethylenetetranitramine and trinitrotoluene. Known more colloquially as HMX and TNT, when combined in a 70-30 mixture, the chemist wrote, they formed an ex-

739

plosive compound called Octol, which, he wrote on, was a rather expensive, very stable, and extremely violent high explosive made principally in the United States, but available commercially from American, European, and one Asian chemical company. And that ended his work for the day. He handed over his report to his secretary, who faxed it to Medellín, where another secretary made a Xerox copy, which found its way twenty minutes later to Félix Cortez.

The report was yet another piece in the puzzle for the former intelligence officer. No local mining operation used Octol. It was too expensive, and simple nitrate-based explosive gels were all that commercial applications required. If you needed a larger explosive punch to loosen rocks, you simply drilled a wider hole and crammed in more explosives. The same option did not exist, however, for military forces. The size of an artillery shell was limited by the diameter of the gun barrel, and the size of a bomb was limited by the aerodynamic drag it imposed on the aircraft that carried it. Therefore, military organizations were always looking for more powerful explosives to get better performance from their size-limited weapons. Cortez lifted a reference book from his library shelf and confirmed the fact that Octol was almost exclusively a military explosive . . . and was used as a triggering agent for nuclear devices. That evoked a short bark of a laugh.

It also explained a few things. His initial reaction to the explosion was that a ton of dynamite had been used. The same result could be explained by less than five hundred kilos of this Octol. He pulled out another reference book and learned that the actual explosive weight in a two-thousand-pound bomb was under one thousand pounds.

But why were there no fragments? More than half the weight of a bomb was in the steel case. Cortez set that aside for the moment.

An aircraft bomb explained much. He remembered his training in Cuba, when North Vietnamese officers had briefed his class on "smart-bombs" that had been the bane of their country's bridges and electrical generating plants during the brief but violent Linebacker-II bombing campaign in 1972. After years of costly failures, the American fighter-bombers had destroyed scores of heavily defended targets in a matter of days, using their new precision-guided munitions.

If targeted on a truck, such a bomb would give every appearance of a car bomb, wouldn't it?

But why were there no fragments? He reread the lab report. There had also been cellulose residue which the lab tech explained away as the cardboard containers in which the explosives had been packed.

Cellulose? That meant paper or wood fibers, didn't it? Make a bomb out of paper? Cortez lifted one of his reference books — *Jane's Weapons Systems*. It was a heavy book with a hard, stiff cover . . . cardboard, covered with cloth. It really was that simple, wasn't it? If you could make paper that strong for so prosaic a purpose as a book binding . . .

Cortez leaned back in his chair and lit a cigarette to congratulate himself — and the *norteamericanos*. It was brilliant. They'd sent a bomber armed with a special smart-bomb, targeted it on that absurd truck, and left nothing behind that could remotely be called evidence. He wondered who had come up with this plan, amazed that the Americans had done something so intelligent. The KGB would have assembled a company of *Spetznaz* commandos and fought a conventional infantry battle, leaving all manner of evidence behind and "delivering the message" in a typically Russian way, which was effective but lacking in subtlety. The Americans for once had managed the sort of subtlety worthy of a Spaniard — of a Cortez, Félix chuckled. That was remarkable.

Now he had the "How." Next he had to figure out the "What For." But of course! There had been that American newspaper story about a possible gang war. There had been fourteen senior Cartel lords. Now there were ten. The Americans would try to reduce that number further by . . . what? Might they assume that the single bombing incident would ignite a savage war of infighting? No, Cortez decided. One such incident wasn't enough. Two might be, but not one.

So the Americans had commando teams prowling the mountains south of Medellín, had dropped one bomb, and were doing something else to curtail the drug flights. That became clear as well. They were shooting the airplanes down, of course. They had people watching airfields and forwarding their intelligence information elsewhere for action. It was a fully integrated operation. The most incredible thing of all was that it was actually working. The Americans had decided to do something that worked. Now, *that* was miraculous. For all the time he had been an intelligence officer, CIA had been reasonably effective at gathering information, but not for actually doing something.

Félix rose from his desk and walked over to his office bar. This called for serious contemplation, and that meant a good brandy. He poured a triple portion into a balloon glass, swirling it around, letting his hand warm the liquid so that the aromatic vapors would caress his senses even before he took the first sip.

The Chinese language was ideographic — Cortez had met his share of Chinese intelligence types as well — and its symbol for "crisis" was a combination of the symbols denoting "danger" and "opportunity." The dualism had struck him the first time he'd heard it, and he'd never forgotten it. Opportunities like this one were exceedingly rare, and equally dangerous. The principal danger, he knew, was the simple fact that he didn't know how the Americans were developing their intelligence information. Everything he

743

knew pointed to a penetration agent within the organization. Someone high up, but not as high as he wished to be. The Americans had compromised someone just as he had so often done. Standard intelligence procedure, and that was something CIA excelled at. Someone. Who? Someone who had been deeply offended, and wanted to get even while at the same time acquiring a seat around the table of chieftains. Quite a few people fell into that category. Including Félix Cortez. And instead of having to initiate his own operation to achieve that goal, he could now depend on the Americans to do it for him. It struck him as very odd indeed that he was trusting the Americans to do his work, but it was also hugely amusing. It was, in fact, almost the definition of the perfect covert operation. All he had to do was let the Americans carry out their own plan, and stand by the sidelines to watch it work. It would require patience and confidence in his enemy — not to mention the degree of danger involved — but Cortez felt that it was worth the effort.

In the absence of knowing how to get the information to the Americans, he decided, he'd just have to trust to luck. No, not luck. They seemed to be getting the word somehow, and they'd probably get it this time, too. He lifted his phone and made a call, something very uncharacteristic for him. Then, on reflection, he made one other arrangement. After all, he couldn't expect that the Americans would do exactly what he wanted exactly when he wanted. Some things he had to do for himself.

Ryan's plane landed at Andrews just after seven in the evening. One of his assistants — it was so nice having assistants — took custody of the classified documents and drove them back to Langley while Jack tossed his bags in the back of his XJS and drove home. He'd get a decent night's sleep to slough off the effects of jet lag, and tomorrow he'd be back at his desk. First order of business, he told himself as he took the car onto Route 50, was to find out what the Agency was up to in South America.

Ritter shook his head in wonder and thanksgiving. CAPER had come through for them again. Cortez himself this time, too. They just hadn't twigged to the fact that their communications were vulnerable. It wasn't a new phenomenon, of course. The same thing had happened to the Germans and Japanese in World War II, and had been repeated time and again. It was just something that Americans were good at. And the timing could hardly have been better. The carrier was available for only thirty more hours, barely time enough to get the message to their man on *Ranger*. Ritter typed up the orders and mission requirements on his personal computer. They were printed, sealed in an envelope, and handed to one of his senior subordinates, who caught an Air Force supply flight to Panama.

★

Captain Robby Jackson was feeling a little better. If nothing else, he thought he could just barely feel the added weight of the fourth stripe on the shoulders of his undress-white shirt, and the silver eagle that had replaced the oak leaf on the collar of his khakis was so much nicer a symbol for a pilot, wasn't it? The below-the-zone promotion meant that he was seriously in the running for CAG, command of his own carrier air wing — that would be his last real flying job, Jackson knew, but it was the grandest of all. He'd have to check out in several different types of aircraft, and would be responsible for over eighty birds, their flight crews, and the maintenance personnel, without which the aircraft were merely attractive ornaments for a carrier's flight deck.

The bad news was that his tactical ideas hadn't worked out as well as planned, but he consoled himself with the knowledge that all new ideas take time. He'd seen that a few of his original ideas were flawed, and the fixes suggested by one of *Ranger*'s squadron commanders had almost worked — had actually improved the idea markedly. And that, too, was normal. The same could also be said of the Phoenix missiles, whose guidance-package fixes had performed fairly well; not quite as well as the contractor had promised, but that wasn't unusual either, was it?

Robby was in the carrier's Combat Information Center. No flight operations were underway at the moment. The battle group was in some heavy weather that would clear in a few hours, and while the maintenance people were tinkering with their airplanes, Robby and the senior air-defense people were reviewing tapes of the fighter engagements for the sixth time. The "enemy" force had performed remarkably well, diagnosing *Ranger*'s defense plans and reacting to them quickly and effectively to get its missile-shooters within range. That *Ranger*'s fighters had clobbered them on the way out was irrelevant. The whole point of the Outer Air Battle was to clobber the Backfires on the way in.

The tape recording had been made from the radar coverage of the E-2C Hawkeye which Robby had ridden for the first engagement, but six times really were enough. He'd learned all he could learn, and his mind was wandering now. There was the Intruder again, mating up with the tanker, then heading off toward Ecuador and disappearing off the screen just before it made the coast. Captain Jackson settled back in his chair while the discussion went on around him. They fast-forwarded the tape for the approach phase, spent over an hour replaying the actual battle — what there had been of it, Jackson noted with a frown — then fast-forwarded it again. *Ranger*'s CAG was particularly annoyed with the lackadaisical manner in which his squadrons had reformed for the return to the carrier. The poor organization of the fighters elicited some scathing comments from the captain who had the title that

Robby now looked forward to. Listening to his remarks was a good education, though it was a touch profane. The ensuing discussion kept the tape running until — there, again, the A-6 reappeared, heading into the carrier after having done whatever the hell it had done. Robby knew that he was making an assumption, and for professional officers assumptions were dangerous things. But there it was.

"Cap'n Jackson, sir?"

Robby turned to see a yeoman with a clipboard. It was an action message for which he had to sign, which he did before accepting the form and reading it.

"What gives, Rob?" the carrier's operations officer asked.

"Admiral Painter is flying out to the PG School. He wants me to meet him there instead of flying back to D.C. I s'pose he wants an early reading on how my wonderful new tactics worked out," Jackson replied.

"Don't sweat it. They ain't going to take the shoulder boards back."

"I didn't think this all the way through," Robby replied, gesturing at the screen.

"Nobody ever does."

Ranger cleared the bad weather an hour later. The first plane off was the COD, which headed off to Panama to drop off mail and pick up various things. It returned in four hours. The "tech-rep" was waiting for it, already prepped by an innocuous signal over a clear channel. When he'd finished reading the message, he called Commander Jensen's stateroom.

Copies of the photo were being taken to The Hideaway, but the closest witness was in Alexandria, and he took it there himself.

Murray knew better than to ask where the photo had come from. That is, he knew that it came from CIA, and that it was some sort of surveillance photo, but the circumstances that surrounded it were things he didn't need to know — or so he would have been told had he asked, which he hadn't. It was just as well, since he might not have accepted the "need-to-know" explanation in this case.

Moira was improving. The restraints were off, but she was still being treated for some side effects of the sleeping pills she'd taken. Something to do with her liver function, he'd heard, but she was responding well to treatment. He found her sitting up, the motorized bed elevated at the command of a button. Visiting hours were over — her kids had been in tonight, and that, Murray figured, was the best treatment she could possibly get. The official story was an accidental OD. The hospital knew different, and that had leaked, but the Bureau took the public position that it had been an accident since she hadn't quite taken a lethal dose of the drug. The Bureau's own psychiatrist saw her twice a day, and his report was optimistic. The suicide attempt, while real, had been based on impulse, not prolonged contemplation. With care and counseling, she'd come around and would probably fully recover. The psychiatrist also thought that what Murray was about to do would help.

"You look a hell of a lot better," he told her. "How are the kids?"

"I'll never do this to them again," Moira Wolfe replied. "What a stupid, selfish thing to do."

"I keep telling you, you got hit by the truck." Murray took the chair by her bedside and opened the manila envelope he'd carried in. "Is this the truck?"

She took the photo from his hand and stared at it for a moment. It wasn't a very good photograph. Taken at a distance of over two miles, even with the high-power lens and computer enhancement of the image, it didn't show anything approaching the detail of an amateur photographer's action shot of his child. But there is more to a picture than the expression on a person's face. The shape of the head, the style of the hair, the posture, the way he held his hands, the tilt of the head. . . .

"It's him," she said. "That's Juan Díaz. Where did you get it?"

"It came from another government agency," Murray replied, his choice of words telling her nothing — the exact nothing that meant CIA. "They had a discreet surveillance of some place or other — I don't know where — and got this. They thought it might be our boy. For your information, this is the first confirmed shot we have of Colonel Félix Cortez, late of the DGI. At least now we know what the bastard looks like."

"Get him," Moira said.

"Oh, we'll get him," Murray promised her.

"I know what I'll have to do — testify and all that. I know what the lawyers will do to me. I can handle it. I can, Mr. Murray."

She isn't kidding, Dan realized. It wasn't the first time that revenge had been part of saving a life, and Murray was glad to see it. It was one more purpose, one more thing Moira had to live for. His job was to see that she and the Bureau got their revenge. The approved term at the FBI was retribution, but the hundreds of agents on the case weren't using that word now.

Jack arrived at his office early the next morning to find the expected pile of work, on top of which was a note from Judge Moore.

"The convention closes tonight," it read. "You're booked on the last flight to Chicago. Tomorrow morning you will brief Gov. Fowler. This is a normal procedure for presidential candidates. Guidelines for your briefing are attached, along with a copy of the national-security brief done in the 1984 presidential campaign. 'Restricted' and 'Confidential' information may be discussed, but nothing 'Secret' or higher. I need to see your written presentation before five."

And that completely blew the day away. Ryan called home to let his family know that he'd be gone yet another night. Then he got to work.

Now he wouldn't be able to quiz Ritter and Moore until the following Monday. And Ritter, he learned, would be spending most of the day over at the White House anyway. Jack's next call was to Bethesda, to check in with Admiral Greer and get some guidance. He was surprised to learn that Greer had done the last such briefing personally. He wasn't surprised that the old man's voice was measurably weaker than the last time they'd talked. The good cheer was still there, but, welcome sound that it was, the image in Jack's mind was of an Olympic skater giving a medal-winning performance on thin, brittle ice.

21.

Explanations

He'd never thought of the COD as the busiest aircraft in the carrier's air wing. It was, of course, and he'd always known it, but the machinations of the ugly, slow, prop-driven aircraft had hardly been a matter of interest to a pilot who'd been "born" in an F-4N Phantom-II and soon thereafter moved up in class to the F-14A Tomcat. He hadn't flown a fighter in weeks, and as he walked out toward the COD — officially the C-2A Greyhound, which was almost appropriate since it did indeed fly like a dog — he resolved that he'd sneak down to Pax River for a few hours of turnin' and burnin' in a proper airplane just as soon as he could. "I feel the need," he whispered to himself with a smile. "The need for speed." The COD was spotted for a shot off the starboard bow catapult, and as Robby headed toward it he again saw an A-6E Intruder, again the squadron commander's personal aircraft, parked next to the island. Outboard from the structure was a narrow area called the Bomb Farm, used for ordnance storage and preparation. It was a convenient spot, too small an area for airplanes to be parked and agreeably close to the edge of the deck so that bombs could easily be jettisoned over the side if the need arose. The bombs were moved about on small, low-slung carts, and just as he boarded the COD, he saw one, carrying a blue "practice" bomb toward the Intruder. On the bomb were the odd attachments for laser guidance.

So, another Drop-Ex tonight, eh? It was something else to smile about. *You put that one right down the pickle barrel, too, Jensen,* Robby thought. Ten minutes later he was off, heading for Panama, where he'd hop a ride with the Air Force for California.

Ryan was over West Virginia on a commercial flight, sitting in coach on an American Airlines DC-9. It was quite a comedown from the Air Force VIP group, but there hadn't been sufficient cause for that sort of treatment this time. He was accompanied by a security guard, which Jack was gradually getting used to. This one was a case officer who'd been injured on duty — he'd fallen off something and badly injured his hip. After recovering, he'd probably rotate back to Operations. His name was Roger Harris. He was thirty or so and, Jack thought, pretty smart.

"What did you do before you joined up?" he asked Harris.

"Well, sir, I — "

"Name's Jack. They don't issue a halo along with the job title."

"Would you believe? A street cop in Newark. I decided that I wanted to try something safer, so I came here. And then look what happened," he chuckled.

The flight was only half booked. Ryan looked around and saw that no one was close, and listening devices invariably had trouble with the whine of the engines.

"Where'd it happen?"

"Poland. A meet went down bad — I mean, something just felt bad and I blew it off. My guy got away clean and I boogied the other way. Two blocks from the embassy I hopped over a wall. Tried to. There was a cat, just a plain old alley cat. I stepped on it, and it screeched, and I tripped and broke my fucking hip like some little old lady falling in the bathtub." A rueful smile. "This spy stuff ain't like the movies, is it?"

Jack nodded. "Sometime I'll tell you about a time when the same sort of thing happened to me."

"In the field?" Harris asked. He knew that Jack was Intelligence, not Operations.

"Hell of a good story. Shame I can't tell it to anyone."

"So what are you gonna tell J. Robert Fowler?"

"That's the funny part. It's all stuff he can get

755

in the papers, but it isn't official unless it comes from one of us."

The stewardess came by. It was too short a flight for a meal, but Ryan ordered a couple of beers.

"Sir, I'm not supposed to drink on duty."

"You just got a dispensation," Ryan told him. "I don't like drinking alone, and I always drink when I fly."

"They told me you don't like it up here," Harris observed.

"I got over that," Jack replied, almost truthfully.

"So what is going on?" Escobedo asked.

"Several things," Cortez answered slowly, carefully, speculatively, to show *el jefe* that he was still somewhat in the dark, but working hard to use his impressive analytical talents to find the correct answer. "I believe the Americans have two or perhaps three teams of mercenaries in the mountains. They are, as you know, attacking some of the processing sites. The objective here would appear to be psychological. Already the local peasants have shown reluctance to assist us. It is not hard to frighten such people. Do it enough and we have problems producing our product."

"Mercenaries?"

"A technical term, *jefe*. A mercenary, as you know, is anyone who performs services for money, but the term most often denotes paramilitary services. Exactly who are they? We know that they speak Spanish. They could be Colombian citizens, disaffected Argentines — you know that the *norteamericanos* used people from the Argentine Army to train the *contras*, correct? Dangerous ones from the time of the Junta. Perhaps with all the turmoil in their home country, they have decided to enter American employ on a semipermanent basis. That is only one of many possibilities. You must understand, *jefe*, that operations such as this must be plausibly deniable. Wherever they come from, they may not even know that they are working for the Americans."

"Whoever they may be, what do you propose to do about them?"

"We will hunt them down and kill them, of course," Cortez said matter-of-factly. "We need about two hundred armed men, but certainly we can assemble such a force. I have people scouting the area already. I need your permission to gather the necessary forces together to sweep the hills properly."

"You'll get it. And what of the Untiveros bombing?"

"Someone loaded four hundred kilos of a very high-grade explosive into the back of his truck. Very cleverly done, *jefe*. In any other vehicle it would have been impossible, but that truck . . . "

"*Sí*. The tires each weighed more than that. Who did it?"

"Not the Americans, nor any of their hirelings," Cortez replied positively.

"But — "

"*Jefe*, think for a moment," Félix suggested. "Who could possibly have had access to the truck?"

Escobedo chewed on that one for a while. They were in the back of his stretch Mercedes. It was an old 600, lovingly maintained and in new-car condition. Mercedes-Benz is the type of car favored by people who need to worry about violent enemies. Already heavy, and with a powerful engine, it easily carried over a thousand pounds of Kevlar armor embedded in vital areas, and thick polycarbonate windows that would stop a .30-caliber machine-gun round. Its tires were filled with foam, not air, so that a puncture wouldn't flatten them — at least not very quickly. The fuel tank was filled with a honeycombed metal lattice that could not prevent a fire, but would prevent a more dangerous explosion. Fifty meters ahead and behind were BMW M3s, fast, powerful cars filled with armed men, much in the way that chiefs of state had lead- and chase-cars for security purposes.

"One of us, you think?" Escobedo asked after a minute's contemplation.

"It is possible, *jefe*." Cortez's tone of voice said that it was more than merely possible. He was pacing his disclosures carefully, keeping an eye on the roadside signs.

"But who?"

"That is a question for you to answer, is it not?

I am an intelligence officer, not a detective." That Cortez got away with his outrageous lie was testimony to Escobedo's paranoia.

"And the missing aircraft?"

"Also unknown," Cortez reported. "Someone was watching the airfields, perhaps American paramilitary teams, but more likely the same mercenaries who are now in the mountains. They probably sabotaged aircraft somehow, possibly with the connivance of the airport guards. I speculate that when they left, they killed off the guards so that no one could prove what they had been doing, then booby-trapped the fuel dumps to make it appear to be something else entirely. A very clever operation, but one to which we could have adapted except for the assassinations in Bogotá." Cortez took a deep breath before going on.

"The attack on the Americans in Bogotá was a mistake, *jefe*. It forced the Americans to change what had been a nuisance operation to one which threatens our activities directly. They have suborned someone in the organization, executing their own wish for revenge through the ambition or anger of one of your own senior colleagues." Cortez spoke throughout in the same quiet, reasoned voice that he'd used to brief his seniors in Havana, like a tutor to an especially bright student: His method of delivery reminded people of a doctor, and was an exceedingly effective way of persuading people, particularly Latins, who are given to polemics but conversely respect those who control their passions. By reproaching Escobedo for the death of the Americans — Escobedo did not like to be reproached; Cortez knew it; Escobedo knew that Cortez knew it — Félix merely added to his own credibility. "The Americans have foolishly said so themselves, perhaps in a clumsy attempt to mislead us, speaking of a 'gang war' within the organization. That is a trick the Americans invented, by the way, to use the truth to deny the truth. It is clever, but they have used it too often. Perhaps they feel that the organization is not aware of this trick, but anyone in the intelligence community knows of it." Cortez was winging it, and had just made that up — but, he thought, it certainly sounded good. And it had the proper effect. Escobedo was looking out through the thick windows of the car, his mind churning over the new thought.

"Who, I wonder . . ."

"That is something I cannot answer. Perhaps you and Señor Fuentes can make some progress on that tonight." The hardest part for Cortez was to keep a straight face. For all his cleverness, for all his ruthlessness, *el jefe* was a child to be manipulated once you knew the right buttons to push.

The road traced down the floor of a valley. There was also a rail line, and both followed a path carved into the rock by a mountain-fed river. From a strictly tactical point of view, it was not something to be comfortable with, Cortez knew. Though he had never been a soldier —

aside from the usual paramilitary classes in the Cuban school system — he recognized the disadvantage of low ground. You could be seen a long way off from people on the heights. The highway signs assumed a new and ominous significance now. Félix knew everything he needed to know about the car. It had been modified by the world's leading provider of armored transport, and was regularly checked by technicians from that firm. The windows were replaced twice annually, because sunlight altered the crystalline structure of the polycarbonate — all the faster near the equator and at high altitude. The windows *would* stop a 7.62 NATO machine-gun bullet, and the Kevlar sheets in the doors and around the engines could, under favorable circumstances, stop larger rounds than that. He was still nervous, but through force of will did not allow himself to react visibly to the danger.

"Who might it be . . . ?" Escobedo asked as the car came around a sweeping turn.

There were five teams of two men each, gunners and loaders. They were armed with West German MG3 squad machine guns, which the Colombian Army had just adopted because it used the same 7.62mm round as their standard infantry weapon, the G3, also of German manufacture. These five had recently been "stolen" — actually purchased from a greedy supply sergeant — out of an army depot. Based on the earlier German MG-42 of World War II fame, the MG3 retained the older weapon's 1,200-

round-per-minute cyclic rate of fire — twenty rounds per second. The gun positions were spaced thirty meters apart, with two guns tasked to engage the chase car, two on the lead car, but only one on the Mercedes. Cortez didn't trust the car's armor quite that much. He looked at the digital clock. They were exactly on time. Escobedo had a fine set of drivers. But then, Untiveros had had a fine set of servants, too.

On the muzzle of each gun was a cone-shaped extension called a flash-hider. Often misunderstood by the layman, its purpose was to shield the flash from the gunner — to prevent him from being blinded by his own shots. Hiding the flash from anyone else is a physical impossibility.

The gunners began firing at the same instant, and five separate yard-long cylinders of pure white flame appeared on the right side of the road. From each muzzle flash sprang a line of tracers, allowing the gunners to walk their fire right into their targets without the need to use the metal sights on their weapons.

None of the occupants of the cars heard the sound of the guns, but all did hear the sound of the impacts — at least those who lived long enough.

Escobedo's body went as rigid as a bar of steel when he saw the yellow line of tracers attach itself to the leading M-3. That car was not as heavily armored as his. The taillights wavered left, then right, and then the car left the road at an angle, rolling over like one of his son's toys. Before that had happened, both he and Cortez felt the impacts of twenty rounds on their own car. It sounded like hail on a tin roof. But it was 150-grain bullets, not hail, impacting steel and Kevlar, not tin. His driver, well trained and always nervously alert, fishtailed the long Mercedes for a moment to avoid the BMW ahead, at the same time flooring the accelerator. The six-liter Mercedes engine responded at once — it, too, was protected by armor — doubling both horsepower and torque in a second and hurling all of the passengers back in their seats. By this time Escobedo's head had turned to see the threat, and it seemed that the tracers were aimed straight at his face, stopped by some apparent miracle by the thick windows — which, he saw, were breaking under the impact.

Cortez hurled his own body against Escobedo's, knocking him down to the floor. Neither man had time to speak a word. The car had been doing seventy miles per hour when the first round was fired. It was already approaching ninety, escaping from the kill zone more rapidly than the gunners could adjust fire as the car body absorbed a total of over forty hits. In two minutes, Cortez looked up.

He was surprised to see that two rounds had hit the left-side windows from the inside. The gunners had been a little too good; had managed to drive repeated rounds through the armored windows. There was no sign of either the lead- or the chase-car. Félix took a very deep breath. He had just won the most daring gamble of his life.

"Take the next turn anywhere!" he shouted at the driver.

"No!" Escobedo said an instant later. "Straight to —"

"Fool!" Cortez turned *el jefe* over. "Do you wish to find another ambush ahead of us! How do you suppose they knew to kill us! *Take the next turn!*" he shouted at the driver again.

The driver, who had a good appreciation of ambush tactics, stood on the brakes and took the next turn. It was a right, leading to a small network of side roads serving local coffee farms.

"Find a quiet place to stop," Cortez ordered next.

"But —"

"They will expect us to run, not to think. They will expect us to do what all the antiterrorist manuals say to do. Only a fool is predictable," Cortez said as he brushed polycarbonate fragments from his hair. His pistol was out now, and he ostentatiously replaced it in his shoulder holster. "José, your driving was magnificent!"

"Both cars are gone," the driver reported.

"I'm not surprised," Cortez replied. Quite honestly. "*Jesús María* — that was close."

Whatever Escobedo might have been, coward was not among them. He too saw the damage to the window that had been inches from his head. Two bullets had come through the car — they were half-buried in the glass. *El jefe* pried one loose and rattled it around in his hand. It was still warm.

"We must speak to the people who make the windows," Escobedo observed coolly. Cortez had saved his life, he realized.

The odd part was that he was right. But Cortez was more impressed with the fact that his reflexes — even forewarned, he had reacted with commendable speed — had saved his own life. It had been a long time since he'd had to pass the physical fitness test required by the DGI. It was moments like this that can make the most circumspect of men feel invincible.

"Who knew that we were going to see Fuentes?" he asked.

"I must — " Escobedo lifted the phone receiver and started to punch in a number. Cortez gently took it away from him and replaced it in the holder.

"Perhaps that would be a serious mistake, *jefe*." he said quietly. "With all respect, señor, please let me handle this. This is a professional matter."

Escobedo had never been so impressed with Cortez than at that moment.

"You will be rewarded," he told his faithful vassal. Escobedo reproached himself for having occasionally mistreated him, and worse, for having occasionally disregarded Cortez's wise counsel. "What should we do?"

"José," Cortez told the driver, "find a high spot from which we can see the Fuentes house."

Within a minute, the driver found a switchback overlooking the valley. He pulled the car off the road and all three got out. José inspected the damage to the car. Fortunately neither the tires nor the engine had been damaged. Though the car's body would have to be totally reworked, its ability to move and maneuver was unimpaired. José truly loved this car, and though he mourned for its defacement, he nearly burst with pride that it and his own skill had saved all their lives.

In the trunk were several rifles — German G3s like those the Army carried, but legally purchased — and a pair of binoculars. Cortez let the others have the rifles. He took the field glasses and trained them in on the well-lit home of Luis Fuentes, about six miles away.

"What are you looking for?" Escobedo asked.

"*Jefe*, if he had part in the ambush, he will know by now that it might have failed, and there will be activity. If he had no such knowledge, we will see no activity at all."

"What of those who fired on us?"

"You think they know that we escaped?" Cortez shook his head. "No, they will not be sure, and first they will try to prove that they succeeded, that our car struggled on for a short while — so they will first of all try to find us. José, how many turns did you take to get us here?"

"Six, señor, and there are many roads," the driver answered. He looked quite formidable with his rifle.

"Do you see the problem, *jefe*? Unless they

have a great number of men, there are too many roads to check. We are not dealing with a police or military force. If we were, we'd still be moving. Ambushes like this one — no, *jefe*, once they fail, they fail completely. Here." He handed the glasses over. It was time for a little machismo. He opened the car door and pulled out a few bottles of Perrier — Escobedo liked the stuff. He opened them by inserting the bottlecaps into bullet holes in the trunk lid and snapping down. Even José grunted with amusement at that, and Escobedo was one who admired such panache.

"Danger makes me thirsty," Cortez explained, passing the other bottles around.

"It has been an exciting night," Escobedo agreed, taking a long pull on his bottle.

But not for Commander Jensen and his bombardier/navigator. The first one, as with the first time for anything, had been a special occasion, but already it was routine. The problem was simply that things were too damned easy. Jensen had faced surface-to-air missiles and radar-directed flak in his early twenties, testing his courage and skill against that of North Vietnamese gunners with their own experience and cunning. This mission was about as exciting as a trip to the mailbox, but, he reminded himself, important things often go through the mail. The mission went exactly according to plan. The computer ejected the bomb right on schedule, and the B/N tracked his TRAM sight around to keep an eye on the target. This time Jensen let his right eye wander down to the TV screen.

"I wonder what held Escobedo up?" Larson asked.

"Maybe he got here early?" Clark thought aloud, his eye on the GLD.

"Maybe," the other field officer allowed. "Notice how no cars are parked near the house this time?"

"Yeah, well, this one is fused for one-hundredth-of-a-second delay," Clark told him. "Should go off just about the time it gets to the conference table."

It was even more impressive from this distance, Cortez thought. He didn't see the bomb fall, didn't hear the aircraft that had dropped it — which, he told himself, was rather strange — and he saw the flash long before the sound reached him. *The Americans and their toys*, he thought. *They can be dangerous.* Most dangerous of all, whatever their intelligence source, it was a very, very good one, and Félix didn't have a clue what it might be. That was a continuing source of concern.

"It would seem that Fuentes was not involved," Cortez noted even before the sound reached them.

"That could have been us in there!"

"Yes, but it was not. I think we should leave, *jefe.*"

768

★

"What's that?" Larson asked. Two automobile headlights appeared on a hillside three miles away. Neither man had noticed the Mercedes pull into the overlook. They'd been concentrating on the target then, but Clark reproached himself for not remembering to check around further. That sort of mistake was often fatal, and he'd allowed himself to forget just how serious it was.

Clark put his Noctron on it as soon as the lights had turned away. It was a big —

"What kind of car does Escobedo have?"

"Take your pick," Larson replied. "It's like the horse collection at Churchill Downs. Porsches, Rolls, Benzes . . ."

"Well, that looked like a stretch limo, maybe a big Mercedes. Kinda odd place for one, too. Let's get the hell out of here. I think two trips to this particular well is enough. We're out of the bomb business."

Eighty minutes later their Subaru had to slow down. A collection of ambulances and police cars was parked on the shoulder while uniformed men appeared and disappeared in the pinkish light from hazard flares. A pair of black BMWs were lying on their sides just off the road. Whoever owned them, somebody didn't like them, Clark saw. There wasn't much traffic, but here as with every other place in the world where people drove cars, the drivers slowed down to give it all a look.

"Somebody blew the shit out of them," Larson

noted. Clark's evaluation was more professional.

"Thirty-cal fire. Heavy machine guns at close range. Pretty slick ambush. Those are M3 BMWs."

"The big, fast one? Somebody with big-time money, then. You don't suppose . . . ?"

"You don't 'suppose' very often in this business. How fast can you get a line on what happened here?"

"Two hours after we get back."

"Okay." The police were looking at the passing cars, but not searching them. One shined his flashlight into the back of the Subaru. There were some curious things there, but not the right size and shape to be machine guns. He waved them on. Clark took that in and did some supposing. Had the gang war he'd hoped to start already begun?

Robby Jackson had a two-hour layover before boarding the Air Force C-141B, which with its refueling housing looked rather like a green, swept-wing snake. Also aboard were sixty or so soldiers with full gear. The fighter pilot looked at them with some amusement. This was what his little brother did for a living. A major sat down next to him after asking permission — Robby was two grades higher.

"What outfit?"

"Seventh Light." The major leaned back, trying to get as much comfort as he could. His helmet rested on his lap. Robby lifted it. Shaped much like the German helmet of World War II, it was made of Kevlar, with a cloth camouflage cover around it, and around that, held in place by a green elasticized cloth band, was a medusa-like collection of knotted cloth strips.

"You know, my brother wears one of these things. Heavy enough. What the hell good is it?"

"The Cabbage Patch Hat?" The major smiled, his eyes closed. "Well, the Kevlar's supposed to stop stuff from tearing your skull apart, and the mop we wrap around it breaks up your outline — makes you harder to see in the bush, sir. Your brother's with us, you said?"

"He's a new nugget — second lieutenant I guess you call him — in the, uh, they call it Ninja-something . . . "

"Three-Seventeen. First Brigade. I'm brigade intel, Second Brigade. What do you do?"

"Serving two-to-three in the Pentagon at the moment. I fly fighter planes when I'm not driving a desk."

"Must be nice to do all your work sitting down," the major observed.

"No." Robby chuckled. "The best part is I can get the hell outa Dodge right quick if I got to."

"Roger that, Captain. What brings you to Panama?"

"We got a carrier group operating offshore. I was down to watch. You?"

"Regular training rotation for one of our battalions. Jungle and tight country is where we work. We hide a lot," the major explained.

771

"Guerrilla stuff?"

"Roughly similar tactics. This was mainly a reconnaissance exercise, trying to get inside to gather information, conduct a few raids, that sort of thing."

"How'd it go?"

The major grunted. "Not as well as we hoped. We lost some good people out of some important slots — same with you, right? People rotate in, rotate out, and it takes awhile to get the new ones up to speed. Anyway, the reconnaissance units in particular lost some good ones, and it cost us some. That's why we train," the major concluded. "Never stops."

"It's different with us. We deploy as a unit and usually don't lose anybody that way until we come back home."

"Always figured the Navy was smart, sir."

"Is it that bad? My brother told me he lost a really good — squad leader? Anyway, is it that big a deal?"

"Can be. I had a guy named Muñoz, really good man for going in the bushes and finding stuff out. Just disappeared one day, off doing some special-ops shit, they told me. The guy who's in his slot now just isn't that good. It happens. You live with it."

Jackson remembered the name Muñoz, but couldn't remember where from. "How do I arrange transport down to Monterey?"

"Hell, it's right next door. You want to catch a ride with us, Captain? We don't have all the amenities of the Navy, of course."

"We do occasionally rough it, Major. Hell, once I didn't even get my bedsheets changed for three whole days. Same week, they made us eat hot dogs for dinner — never forget that cruise. Real bitch that one was. I presume your jeeps have air conditioning?" The two men looked at each other and laughed.

Ryan was given a suite of rooms one floor up from the Governor's entourage, actually paid for by the campaign, which was quite a surprise. That made security easier. Fowler now had a full Secret Service detail, and would keep it until November, and if he were successful, for four years after that. It was a very nice, modern hotel with thick concrete floors, but the sound of the parties down below made its way through.

There came a knock on Jack's door just as he got out of the shower. The hotel had a monogrammed robe hanging there. Ryan put it on to answer the door. It was a fortyish woman dressed to kill — in red, again the current "power" color. No expert on women's fashions, he wondered how the color of one's clothing imparted anything other than visibility.

"Are you Dr. Ryan?" she asked. It was the way she asked that Jack immediately disliked, rather as though he were a disease carrier.

"Yes. Who might you be?"

"I'm Elizabeth Elliot," she replied.

"Ms. Elliot," Jack said. She looked like a

Mizz. "You have me at a disadvantage. I don't know who you are."

"I'm the assistant adviser for foreign policy."

"Oh. Okay. Come on in, then." Ryan pulled the door all the way open and waved her in. He should have remembered. This was "E.E.," professor of political science at Bennington, whose geopolitical views, Ryan thought, made Lenin look like Theodore Roosevelt. He'd walked several feet before he realized that she hadn't followed. "You coming in or aren't you?"

"Like *this?*" She just stood there for another ten seconds before speaking again. Jack continued to towel off his hair without saying anything, more curious than anything else.

"I know who you are," she said defiantly. What the hell she was defying, Jack didn't know. In any case, Ryan had had a long day and was still suffering jetlag from his European trip, added to which was one more hour of Central Time Zone. That partly explained his reply.

"Look, doc, you're the one who caught me coming out of the shower. I have two children, and a wife, who also graduated Bennington, by the way. I'm not James Bond and I don't fool around. If you want to say something to me, just be nice enough to say it. I've been on the go for the past week, and I'm tired, and I need my sleep."

"Are you always this impolite?"

Jesus! "Dr. Elliot, if you want to play with the big kids in D.C., Lesson Number One is, Business is Business. You want to tell me something, tell. You want to ask me something, ask."

"What the hell are you doing in Colombia?" she snapped at him.

"What are you talking about?" Jack asked in a more moderate tone.

"You know what I'm talking about. I know that you know."

"In that case would you please refresh my memory?"

"Another drug lord just got blown up," she said, casting a nervous glance up and down the corridor as though a passerby might wonder if she was negotiating price with someone. There is a lot of that at political conventions, and E.E. was not physically unattractive.

"I have no knowledge of any such operation being conducted by the American government or any other. That is to say, I have zero information on the subject of your inquiry. I am not omniscient. Believe it or not, even when you are sanctified by employment in the Central Intelligence Agency, you do not automatically know everything that happens on every rock, puddle, and hilltop in the world. What does the news say?"

"But you're supposed to know," Elizabeth Elliot protested. Now she was puzzled.

"Dr. Elliot, two years ago you wrote a book about how pervasive we are. It reminded me of an old Jewish story. Some old guy on the *shtetl* in Czarist Russia who owned two chickens and a broken-down horse was reading the hate rag of the antisemites — you know, the Jews are doing *this*, the Jews are doing *that*. So a neighbor asked him why he got it, and the old guy answered that it was nice to see how powerful he was. That's what your book was, if you'll pardon me: about one percent fact and ninety-nine percent invective. If you really want to know what we can and cannot do, I can tell you a few things, within the limits of classification. I promise that you'll be as disappointed as I regularly am. I wish we were half as powerful as you think."

"But you've *killed* people."

"You mean me personally?"

"Yes!"

Maybe that explained her attitude, Jack thought. "Yes, I have killed people. Someday I'll tell you about the nightmares, too." Ryan paused. "Am I proud of it? No. Am I glad that I did it? Yes, I am. Why? you ask. My life, the lives of my wife and daughter, or the lives of other innocent people were at risk at the times in question, and I did what I had to do to protect my life and those other lives. You do remember the circumstances, don't you?"

Elliot wasn't interested in those. "The Governor wants to see you at eight-fifteen."

Six hours' sleep was what that meant to Ryan. "I'll be there."

"He is going to ask you about Colombia."

"Then you can make points with your boss by giving him the answer early: I do not know."

"If he wins, Dr. Ryan, you're — "

"Out?" Jack smiled benignly at her. "You know, this is like something from a bad movie, Dr. Elliot. If your man wins, maybe you will have the power to fire me. Let me explain to you what that means to me.

"You will then have the power to deny me a total of two and a half hours in a car every working day; the power to fire me from a difficult, stressful job that keeps me away from my family much more than I would like; and the power to compel me to live a life commensurate with the money that I earned ten or so years ago; the power to force me to go back to writing my history books, or maybe to teach again, which is why I got my doctorate in the first place. Dr. Elliot, I've seen loaded machine guns pointed at my wife and daughter, and I managed to deal with *that* threat. If you want to threaten me in a serious way, you'll need something better than taking my job away. I'll see you in the morning, I suppose, but you should know that my briefing is only for Governor Fowler. My orders are that no one else can be in the room." Jack closed, bolted, and chained the door. He'd had too many beers on the airplane, and knew it, but nobody had ever pushed Ryan's buttons that hard before.

Dr. Elliot took the stairs down instead of the elevator. Unlike most of the people in the entourage, Governor Fowler's chief aide was cold sober — he rarely drank in any case — and already at work planning a campaign that would start in a week instead of the customary wait until

Labor Day. "Well?" he asked E.E.

"He says he doesn't know. I think he's lying."

"What else?" Arnold van Damm asked.

"He's arrogant, offensive, and insulting."

"So are you, Beth." They both laughed. They didn't really like each other, but political campaigns make for the strangest of bedfellows. The campaign manager was reading over a briefing paper about Ryan from Congressman Alan Trent, new chairman of the House Select Committee for Intelligence Oversight. E.E. hadn't seen it. She had told him, though he already knew (though neither of them knew what it had really all been about), that Ryan had confronted Trent in a Washington social gathering and called him a queer in public. Trent had never forgiven or forgotten an insult in his life. Nor was he one to give gratuitous praise. But Trent's report on Ryan used words like *bright*, *courageous*, and *honest*. Now what the hell, van Damm wondered, did *that* mean?

It was going to be their third no-hit night, Chavez was sure. They'd been out since sundown and had just passed through the second suspected processing site — the signs had been there. The discoloration of the soil from acid spills, the beaten earth, discarded trash, everything to show that men had been there and probably went there regularly — but not tonight, and not for the two preceding nights. Ding knew that he ought to have expected it. All the manuals, all the lectures of his career, had emphasized the fact that combat operations were some crazy mixture of boredom and terror, boredom because for the most part nothing happened, terror because "it" could happen at any second. Now he understood how men got sloppy out in the field. On exercises you always knew what — well, you knew that something would happen. The Army rarely wasted time on no-contact exercises. Training time cost too much. And so he was faced with the irksome fact that real combat operations were less *exciting* than training, but infinitely more dangerous. The dualism was enough to give the young man a headache.

Aches were something he already had enough of. He was now gobbling a couple of his Tylenol caplets every four hours because of muscle aches and low-order sprains — and simple tension and stress. A young man, he was learning that the combination of strenuous exercise and real mental stress made you old in a hurry. In fact he was no more tired than an office worker after a slightly long day at his desk, but the mission and the environment combined to amplify everything he felt. Joy or sadness, elation or depression, fear or invincibility were all much greater down here. In a word, combat operations were not fun. But then, why did he — not like it, not that, really, but . . . what? Chavez shook the thought away. It was affecting his concentration.

And though he didn't know it, that was the answer. Ding Chavez was a born combat soldier.

Just as a trauma surgeon took no pleasure from seeing the broken bodies of accident victims, Chavez would easily have preferred sitting on a barstool next to a pretty girl or watching a football game with his friends. But the surgeon knew that his skills at the table were crucial to the lives of his patients, and Chavez knew that his skills on point were crucial to the mission. This was his place. On the mission, everything was so wonderfully clear — except when he was confused, and even *that* was clear in a different, very strange way. His senses searched out through the trees like radar, filtering out the twitters of birds and the rustle of animals — except when there was a special message in that sort of noise. His mind was a perfect balance of paranoia and confidence. He was a weapon of his country. That much he understood, and fearful though he was, fighting off boredom, struggling to keep alert, concerned for his comrades, Chavez was now a breathing, thinking machine whose single purpose was the destruction of his nation's enemies. The job was hard, but he was the man for it.

But there was still nothing out here to be found this night. The trails were cold. The processing sites unoccupied. Chavez stopped at a preplanned rally point and waited for the rest of the squad to catch up. He switched off his night goggles — you only used them about a third of the time in any case — and had himself a drink of water. At least the water was good here, coming off clear mountain streams.

"Whole lot of nothin', Captain," he told Ramirez when the officer arrived at his side. "Ain't seen nothing, ain't heard nothing."

"Tracks, trails?"

"Nothing less'n two, maybe three days old."

Ramirez knew how to determine the age of a trail, but couldn't do it as well as Sergeant Chavez. He breathed in a way that almost seemed relieved.

"Okay, we start heading back. Take a couple more minutes to relax, then lead off."

"Right. Sir?"

"Yeah, Ding?"

"This area's dryin' up on us."

"You may be right, but we'll wait a few more days to be sure," Ramirez said. Part of him was glad that there had been no contact since the death of Rocha, and that part was blanking out warning signals that he ought to have been getting. Emotion was telling him that something was good, while intelligence and analysis should have told him that something was bad.

Chavez didn't quite catch that one either. There was a distant rumble at the edge of his consciousness, like the strangely noticeable quiet that precedes an earthquake, or the first hint of clouds on a clear horizon. Ding was too young and inexperienced to notice. He had the talents. He was the right man in the right place, but he hadn't been there long enough. He didn't know that, either.

But there was work to do. He led off five min-

781

utes later, climbing back up the mountainside, avoiding all trails, taking a path different from any path they had taken to this point, alert to any present danger but oblivious to a danger that was distant but just as clear.

The C-141B touched down hard, Robby thought, though the soldiers didn't seem to notice. In fact, most of them were asleep and had to be roused. Jackson rarely slept on airplanes. It was, he thought, a bad habit for a pilot to acquire. The transport slowed and taxied around every bit as awkwardly as a fighter on the tight confines of a carrier's deck until finally the clamshell cargo doors opened at the tail.

"You come along with me, Captain," the major said. He stood and hefted his rucksack. It looked heavy. "I had the wife bring my personal car here."

"How'd she get home?"

"Car pool," the major explained. "This way the battalion commander and I can discuss the exercise some more on the way down to Ord. We'll drop you off at Monterey."

"Can you take me right into the Fort? I'll kick my little brother's door down."

"Might be out in the field."

"Friday night? I'll take the chance." Robby's real reason was that his conversation with the major had been his first talk with an Army officer in years. Now that he was a captain, the next step was making flag. If he wanted to make that —

Robby was as confident as any other fighter pilot, but the step from captain to rear admiral (lower half) is the most treacherous in the Navy — having a somewhat broader field of knowledge wouldn't hurt. It would make him a better staff officer, and after his CAG job, if he got it, he'd go back to being a staff puke again.

"Okay."

The two-hour drive down from Travis Air Force Base to Fort Ord — Ord has only a small airfield, not large enough for transports — was an interesting one, and Robby was in luck. After two hours of swapping sea stories for war stories and learning things that he'd never known about, he found that Tim was just arriving home from a long night on the town. The elder brother found that the couch was all he needed. It wasn't what he was used to, of course, but he figured he could rough it.

Jack and his bodyguard arrived at the Governor's suite right on time. He didn't know any of the Secret Service detail, but they'd been told to expect him, and he still had his CIA security pass. A laminated plastic ID about the size of a playing card with a picture and a number, but no name, it ordinarily hung around his neck on a chain like some sort of religious talisman. This time he showed it to the agents and tucked it back into his coat pocket.

The briefing was set up as that most cherished of political institutions, the working breakfast.

Not as socially important as a lunch, much less a dinner, breakfasts were for some reason or other perceived to be matters of great import. Breakfasts were serious.

The Honorable J. (for Jonathan, which he didn't like) Robert (call me Bob) Fowler, Governor of Ohio, was a man in his middle fifties. Like the current President, Fowler was a former state's attorney with an impressive record of law enforcement behind him. He'd ridden the reputation of the man who'd cleaned up Cleveland into six terms in the U.S. House of Representatives, but you didn't go from that House to the White House, and the Senate seats in his state were too secure. So he'd become Governor six years before, and by all reports an effective one. His ultimate political goal had been formed over twenty years before, and now he'd made it to the finals.

He was a trim five-eleven, with brown eyes and hair showing the first signs of gray over the ears. And he was weary. America demands much of her presidential candidates. Marine Corps boot camp was a tryst by comparison. Ryan looked at a man almost twenty years his senior who for the past six months had lived on too much coffee and bad political-dinner food, yet somehow managed to smile at all the bad jokes told by people he didn't like and, most remarkably of all, to make a speech given no less than four times per day sound new and fresh and exciting to everyone who heard it. He also had about as much appreciation of foreign policy, Ryan thought, as Jack did of Einstein's General Theory of Relativity, which wasn't a hell of a lot.

"You're Dr. John Ryan, I take it." Fowler looked up from his morning paper.

"Yes, sir."

"Excuse me for not getting up. I sprained my ankle last week, and it hurts like a son of a bitch." Fowler waved to the cane beside him. Jack hadn't seen that on the morning news broadcasts. He'd given his acceptance speech, danced around the stage . . . on a bum ankle. The man had sand. Jack walked over to shake hands with him.

"They tell me that you are the acting Deputy Director of Intelligence."

"Excuse me, Governor, but the title is Deputy Director (Intelligence). That means I currently head one of the Agency's principal directorates. The others are Operations, Science and Technology, and Administration. Admin is what it sounds like. The Ops guys gather data the old-fashioned way; they're the real field spooks. The S and T guys run the satellite programs and other scientific stuff. The Intel guys try to figure out what Ops and S and T deliver to us. That's what I try to do. The real DDI is Admiral James Greer, and he's — "

"I've heard. Too bad. I hear he is a fine man. Even his enemies say he's honest. That's probably the best compliment any man can have. How about some breakfast?" Fowler fulfilled the first requirement of political life. He was pleasant. He was charming.

"Sounds okay to me, sir. Can I give you a hand?"

"No, I can manage." Fowler used the cane to rise. "You are an ex-Marine, ex-broker, ex-history teacher. I know about the business with the terrorists a few years back. My people — my informants, I should say," he added with a grin as he sat back down, "tell me that you've moved up the ladder at CIA very quickly, but they will not tell me why. It's not in the press either. I find that puzzling."

"We do keep some secrets, sir. I am not at liberty to discuss all the things you might like to know, and in any case you'd have to depend on others to tell you about me. I'm not objective."

The Governor nodded pleasantly. "You and Al Trent had one pisser of a fight awhile back, but he says things about you that ought to make you blush. How come?"

"You'll have to ask Mr. Trent that, sir."

"I did. He won't say. He doesn't actually like you very much, either."

"I am not at liberty to discuss that at all. Sorry, sir. If you win in November, you can find that out." How to explain that Al Trent had helped CIA arrange the defection of the head of KGB — to get even with the people who had put a very close Russian friend of his in a labor camp. Even if he could tell the story, who would ever believe it?

"And you really pissed Beth Elliot off last night."

"Sir, do you want me to talk like a politician, which I am not, or like what I am?"

"Tell it straight, son. That's one of the rarest pleasures a man in my position has." Ryan missed that signal entirely.

"I found Dr. Elliot arrogant and abusive. I'm not used to being jacked around. I may owe her an apology, but maybe she owes me one, too."

"She wants your ass, and the campaign hasn't even started yet." This observation was delivered with a laugh.

"It belongs to someone else, Governor. Maybe she can kick it, but she can't *have* it."

"Don't ever run for public office, Dr. Ryan."

"Don't get me wrong, sir, but there is no way in hell that I would ever subject myself to what people like you have to put up with."

"How do you like being a government employee? That's a question, not a threat," Fowler explained.

"Sir, I do what I do because I think it's important, and because I think I'm good at it."

"The country needs you?" the presidential candidate asked lightly. That one rocked the acting DDI back in his chair. "That's a tough answer to have to make, isn't it? If you say no, then you ought not to have the job because somebody can do it better. If you say yes, then you're an arrogant son of a bitch who thinks he's better than everybody else. Learn something from that, Dr. Ryan. That's my lesson for the day. Now let me hear yours. Tell me about the world — your version of it, that is."

Jack took out his notes and talked for just under an hour and just over two cups of coffee. Fowler was a good listener. The questions he asked were pointed ones.

"If I read you right, you say you do not know what the Soviets are up to. You've met the General Secretary, haven't you?"

"Well —" Ryan stopped cold. "Sir, I cannot — that is, I shook hands with him twice at diplomatic receptions."

"You've met him for more than a handshake, but you can't talk about it? That is most interesting. You're no politician, Dr. Ryan. You tell the truth before you think to lie. It would appear that you think the world is in pretty good shape at the moment."

"I can remember when it was in far worse shape, Governor," Jack said, grateful for having been let off the hook.

"So why not ease back, cut arms, like I propose?"

"I think it's too soon for that."

"I don't."

"Then we disagree, Governor."

"What is going on in South America?"

"I don't know."

"Does that mean that you do not know what we are doing, or that you do not know if we are doing anything, or that you do know and have been ordered not to discuss it?"

He sure talks like a lawyer. "As I told Ms. Elliot

last night, I have no knowledge on that subject. That is the truth. I have already indicated areas in which I do have knowledge which I am not allowed to discuss."

"I find that very strange, given your position."

"I was in Europe for a NATO intelligence meeting when all this started, and I'm a European and Soviet specialist."

"What do you think we ought to do about the killing of Director Jacobs?"

"In the abstract, we should react forcefully to the murder of any of our citizens, even more so in a case like this. But I'm Intelligence, not Operations."

"Including cold-blooded murder?" Fowler pressed.

"If the government decides that killing people is the correct course of action in the pursuit of our national interests, then such killing falls outside the legal definition of murder, doesn't it?"

"That's an interesting position. Go on."

"Because of the way our government works, such decisions have to be made . . . have to reflect the way the American people want things to be, or would want them to be, if they had the knowledge available to the people who make the decisions. That's why we have congressional oversight of covert operations, both to ensure that the operations are appropriate, and to depoliticize them."

"So you're saying that that sort of decision depends upon reasonable men making a reasoned decision — to commit murder."

"That's overly simplified, but, yes."

"I disagree. The American people support capital punishment; that's wrong, too. We demean ourselves and we betray the ideals of our country when we do things like that. What do you think of that?"

"I think you are wrong, Governor, but I don't make government policy. I provide information to those who do."

Bob Fowler's voice changed to something Jack had not yet heard this morning. "Just so we know where we stand. You've lived up to your billing, Dr. Ryan. You are indeed honest, but despite your youth I think that your views reflect times past. People like you *do* make government policy, by casting your analysis in directions of your own choosing — hold it!" Fowler held up his hand. "I'm not questioning your integrity. I do not doubt that you do the best job you can, but to tell me that people like you do not make government policy is arrant nonsense."

Ryan flushed red at that, feeling it, trying to control it, but failing miserably. Fowler wasn't questioning Jack's integrity, just the second-brightest star in his personal constellation, his intelligence. He wanted to snarl back what he thought, but couldn't.

"Now you're going to tell me that if I knew what you knew, I'd think differently, right?" Fowler asked.

"No, sir. I don't use that argument. It sounds

and smells like bullshit. Either you believe me or you do not. All I can do is persuade, not convince. Maybe I am wrong sometimes," Jack allowed as he cooled off. "All I can do is give you the best I have. May I pass along a lesson, too, sir?"

"Go on."

"The world is not always what we wish it to be, but wishes don't change it."

Fowler was amused. "So I should listen to you even when you're wrong? What if I know you're wrong?"

A marvelous philosophical discussion might have followed, but Ryan knew when he was beaten. He'd just wasted ninety minutes. Perhaps one final try.

"Governor, there are tigers in the world. Once I saw my daughter lying near death in a hospital because somebody who hated me tried to kill her. I didn't like it, and I tried to wish it away, but it didn't work. Maybe I just learned a harder lesson. I hope you never have to."

"Thank you. Good morning, Dr. Ryan."

Ryan collected his papers and left. It was like something dimly remembered from the Bible. He'd been measured and found wanting by the man who might be his country's next President. He was even more disturbed by his reaction to it: *Fuck him.* He'd fulfilled Fowler's own observation. It was a very dumb thing to think.

"Kick it loose, big brother!" Tim Jackson

said. Robby cracked open one eye to see Timmy clad in his multicolored uniform and boots. "It's time for our morning run."

"I remember changing your diapers."

"You gotta catch me first. Come on, you got five minutes to get ready."

Captain Jackson grinned up at his little brother. He was in pretty good shape, and a kendo master. "I'm gonna run your ass right into the ground."

Pride goeth before the fall, Captain Jackson told himself fifteen minutes later. He would have settled for a fall. If he fell down, he might rest for a few seconds. When he started staggering, Tim backed the pace off.

"You win," Robby gasped. "I ain't gonna change your diapers again."

"Hey, we've barely done two miles."

"A carrier's only a thousand feet long!"

"Yeah, and I bet the steel deck's bad on the knees, too. Go on, head back and get breakfast ready, sir. I got two more miles to do."

"Aye aye, sir." *Where are my kendo sticks?* Robby thought, *I can still whip his ass at that!*

It took Robby five minutes to find his way back to the right BOQ building. He passed a number of officers heading to or from their runs, and for the first time in his life, Robby Jackson felt old. It was hardly fair. He was one of the youngest captains in the Navy, and still one hell of a fighter pilot. He also knew how to fix breakfast. It was all on the table when Timmy got back.

"Don't feel too bad, Rob. This is what I do for a living. I can't fly airplanes."

"Shut up and drink your juice."

"Where the hell did you say you were?"

"Aboard *Ranger* — that's a carrier, boy. Observing ops off Panama. My boss gets into Monterey this afternoon and I'm s'posed to meet him there."

"Down where the bombs are going off," Tim observed as he buttered his toast.

"Another one last night?" Robby asked. Well, that made sense, didn't it?

"Looks like we bagged us another druggie. Nice to see the CIA, or somebody, grew hisself a pair of balls for a change. Love to know how the guys are getting the bombs in."

"What do you mean?" Robby asked. Something wasn't right.

"Rob, I *know* what's going down. It's some of our people down there doin' it."

"Tim, you've lost me."

Second Lieutenant Timothy Jackson, Infantry, leaned across the breakfast table in the conspiratorial way of junior officers. "Look, I know it's a secret and all, but, hell, how smart do you have to be? One of my people is down there right now. Figure it out, man. One of my best people disappears, don't show up where he's supposed to be — where the Army thinks he is, for Christ's sake. He's a Spanish speaker. So are some others who checked out funny, Muñoz out of recon, León, two others I heard about. All Spanish

793

speakers, okay? Then all of a sudden there's some serious ass-kickin' going on down in banana land. Hey, how smart you gotta be?"

"Have you told anyone about this?"

"Why tell anybody? I'm a little worried about Chavez — he's one of my people, and I worry a little about him, but he's one good fucking soldier. Far as I'm concerned, he can kill all the druggies he wants. I just want to know how they did the bombs. That might come in handy someday. I'm thinking about going special-ops."

The Navy did the bombs, Timmy, Robby thought very loudly indeed.

"How much talk is there about this?"

"About the first bombing, everybody thought that was pretty good, but talk about our people bein' involved? Uh-uh. Maybe some folks're thinking the same way I am, but you don't talk about shit like that. Security, right?"

"That's right, Tim."

"You know a senior Agency guy, right?"

"Sort of. Godfather for Jack Junior."

"Tell him for us, kill all you want."

"I'll do that," Robby said quietly. It had to be an Agency operation. A very "black" Agency operation, but it wasn't nearly as black as they wanted it to be. If some nugget a year out of the academy could figure it out. . . . The ordies on *Ranger*, personnel officers and NCOs all over the Army — lots of people must have put it together by now. Not all of those who heard the talk would be on the good side.

"Let me give you a tip. You hear talk about this, you tell people to clam up. You get talk started about an operation like this, people start disappearing."

"Hey, Rob, anybody wants to mess with Chavez and Muñoz and — "

"Listen to me, boy! I've *been* there. I've been shot at by machine guns, and my Tomcat ate a missile once, damned near killed the best RIO I ever had. It's dangerous out there, and talk gets people dead. You remember that. This isn't college anymore, Tim."

Tim considered that for a moment. His brother was right. His brother was also wondering what, if anything, he should do about it. Rob considered just sitting on it, but he was a Tomcat driver, a man of action, not the sort to do nothing at all. If nothing else, he decided, he'd have to warn Jack that the security on the operation wasn't as secure as it ought to be.

22.

Disclosures

Unlike Air Force and Army generals, most Navy admirals do not have personal aircraft to chauffeur them around, and for the most part they fly commercial. A coterie of aides and drivers waiting at the gates helps ease the pain, of course, and Robby Jackson was not above making points with his boss by appearing at San José Airport just as the 727 pulled up to the jetway that evening. He had to wait for the first-class passengers to deplane, of course, since even flag officers fly coach.

Vice Admiral Joshua Painter was the current Assistant Chief of Naval Operations for Air Warfare, known to insiders by his "designator," OP-05, or just "oh-five." His three-star rank was a miracle. Painter was first of all an honest man; second, an outspoken one; third, someone who thought the real Navy was at sea, not alongside the Potomac River; finally and most damagingly, he was that rarest of naval officers, the author of a book. The Navy does not encourage its officers to commit their thoughts to paper, except for the odd piece on thermodynamics or the behavior of neutrons within a reactor vessel. An intellectual, a maverick, and a warrior in a service that was increasingly anti-intellectual, conformist, and bureaucratized, he thought of himself as the token exception in what was turning into The Corporate Navy. Painter was a crusty, acerbic Vermont native, short and slight of build, with pale, almost colorless blue eyes and a tongue sharp enough to chip stone. He was also the living god of the aviation community. He'd flown more than four hundred missions over North Vietnam in several different models of the F-4 Phantom, and had two MiGs to his credit — the side panel from his jet, with two red stars painted on it, hung in his Pentagon office, along with the caption, SIDEWINDER MEANS NOT HAVING TO SAY YOU'RE SORRY. Though a perfectionist and a very demanding boss, he deemed nothing too good for his pilots or his enlisted crews, especially the latter.

"I see you got the message," Josh Painter observed, reaching a finger out to tap Robby's bright new shoulder boards.

"Yes, sir."

"I also hear your new tactics were a disaster."

"They could have worked out a little better," Captain Jackson admitted.

"Yeah, it does help if the carrier survives.

Maybe a CAG slot will reinforce that in your mind. I just approved you for one," OP-05 announced. "You get Wing Six. It chops to *Abe Lincoln* when *Indy* goes in for overhaul. Congratulations, Robby. Try not to screw up too badly in the next eighteen months. Now, what went wrong with the Fleet-Ex?" he asked as they walked off toward the waiting car.

"The 'Russians' cheated," Robby answered. "They were smart." That earned him a laugh from his boss. Though crusty, Painter did have a lively sense of humor. The discussion took care of the drive to flag quarters at the Naval Post-Graduate School on the California coast at Monterey.

"Any more on the news about those drug bastards?" Painter asked while his aide carried his bags in.

"We're sure giving them a hard time, aren't we?" Jackson observed.

The Admiral stopped dead in his tracks. "What the hell do you mean?"

"I know that I'm not supposed to know, sir, but I mean, I was there, and I did see what was going on."

Painter waved Jackson inside. "Check the fridge. See if you can put a martini together while I pump bilges. Fix whatever you want for yourself."

Robby made the proper arrangements. Whoever set up flag quarters for them knew what Painter liked to drink. Jackson opened a Miller

Lite for himself.

Painter reappeared without his uniform shirt and took a sip from his glass. Then he dismissed his aide and gave Jackson a very close look.

"I want you to repeat what you said on the way in, Captain."

"Admiral, I know I'm not cleared for this, but I'm not blind. I watched the A-6 head for the beach on radar, and I don't figure it was a coincidence. Whoever set up security on the op could have done a better job, sir."

"Jackson, you're going to have to forgive me, but I just spent five and a half hours sitting too close to the engines on a beat-up old 727. You're telling me that those two bombs that took druggies out fell off one of *my* A-6s?"

"Yes, sir. You didn't know?"

"No, Robby, I didn't." Painter knocked off the rest of his drink and set the glass down. "Jesus Christ. What lunatic set up this abortion?"

"But that new bomb, it had to — I mean, the orders and everything — shit, for this sort of thing, the orders have to chop through -05."

"*What* new bomb?" Painter nearly shouted that out, but managed to control himself.

"Some kind of plastic, fiberglass, whatever, some kind of new bombcase. It looks like a stock, low-drag two-thousand-pounder with the usual attachment points for the smart-bomb gear, but it's not made out of steel or any other kind of metal, and it's painted blue like an exercise bomb."

"Oh, okay. There has been a little work on a low-observable bomb for the ATA" — Painter referred to the new Stealth attack plane the Navy was working on — "but, hell, we've just done a little preliminary testing, maybe a dozen drops. Whole program's experimental. They don't even use the regular bomb filler, and I'm probably going to shit-can the program, 'cause I don't think it's worth the money. They haven't even taken those things off China Lake yet."

"Sir, there were several in *Ranger*'s bomb locker. I saw 'em, Admiral, I touched 'em. I saw one attached to an A-6. I watched that A-6 on radar while I was up in the E-2 for the Fleet-Ex. It flew off to the beach and came back from a different direction. The timing might be a coincidence, but I'd be careful putting money down on that. The night I flew back, I saw another one attached to the same aircraft. Next day I hear that another druggie got his house knocked flat. It stands to reason that half a ton of HE'll do just fine for that, and a combustible bombcase won't leave shit behind for evidence."

"Nine hundred eighty-five pounds of Octol — that's what they use in those things." Painter snorted. "It'll do a house, all right. You know who flew the mission?"

"Roy Jensen, he's skipper of — "

"I know him. We were shipmates on — Robby, what the hell is going on here? I want you to start over from the beginning and tell me everything you saw."

Captain Jackson did just that. It took ten uninterrupted minutes.

"Who was the 'tech-rep' from?" Painter asked.

"I didn't ask, sir."

"How much you want to bet he isn't even aboard anymore? Son, we've been had. *I've* been had. Goddammit! Those orders should have come through my office. Somebody's been using my fucking airplanes and not telling me."

It wasn't about the bombings, Robby understood, it was about propriety. And it was about security. Had the Navy planned the job, it would have been done better. Painter and his senior A-6 expert would have set it up so that there would have been no awkward evidence for other people — like Robby in the E-2C — to notice. What Painter feared was the simple fact that now his people could be left holding the bag for an operation imposed from above, bypassing the regular chain of command.

"Get Jensen up here?" Robby wondered.

"I thought of that. Too obvious. Might get Jensen in too much trouble. But I've got to find out where the hell his orders came from. *Ranger*'s out for another ten days or so, right?"

"I believe so, sir."

"Has to be an Agency job," Josh Painter observed quietly. "Authorized higher up than that, but it has to be Agency."

"For what it's worth, sir, I got a good friend who's pretty senior there. I'm godfather for one of his kids."

"Who's that?"

"Jack Ryan."

"Oh, yeah, I've met him. He was with me on *Kennedy* for a day or two back when — you're sure to remember that cruise, Rob." Painter smiled. "Right before you took that missile hit. By that time he was off on HMS *Invincible.*"

"*What?* Jack was aboard then? But — why the hell didn't he come down to see me?"

"You never did find out what that op was all about, did you?" Painter shook his head, thinking of the *Red October* affair. "Maybe he can tell you about it. I can't."

Robby accepted it without questioning and turned back to the matter at hand. "There's a land side to this operation, too, Admiral," he said, and explained on for another couple of minutes.

"Charlie-Fox," Painter said when he was done. That was the Navy's shorthand and sanitized version of an expression that had begun in the Marine Corps to denote a confused and self-destructive military operation: Cluster-Fuck. "Robert, you get your ass on the first plane back to D.C. and tell your friend that his operation is going to hell in a basket. Jesus, don't those Agency clowns ever learn? If this gets out, and from what you're telling me, it's sure as hell going to, it's going to hurt us. It's going to hurt the whole country. We don't need this kind of shit, not in an election year with that asshole Fowler running. Also tell him that the next time the Agency decides to play soldier, it *might help* if they asked somebody who knows something about it ahead of time."

The Cartel had an ample supply of people who were accustomed to carrying guns, and assembling them took only a few hours. Cortez was detailed to run the operation. He'd coordinate it from the village of Anserma, which was in the center of the area in which the "mercenary" teams seemed to be operating. He hadn't told his boss everything he knew, of course, nor did he reveal his full objective. The Cartel was a cooperative enterprise. Nearly three hundred men had been brought in by cars, trucks, and buses, personal retainers from all of the Cartel chieftains, all of them reasonably fit and accustomed to violence. Their presence here reduced the security details of the remaining drug lords. That would allow Escobedo a sizable advantage as he tried to discover which of his colleagues was making the "power play," while Cortez dealt with the "mercenaries." He had every intention of running the American soldiers to ground and killing them all, of course, but there was no special hurry in that. Félix had every reason to suspect that he was up against elite troops, perhaps even American Green Berets, formidable opponents for whom he had due respect. Casualties among his force, therefore, were to be expected. Félix wondered how many he'd have to kill off in order to alter the overall balance of power within the

Cartel to his personal advantage.

There was no point in telling the assembled multitude, of course. These harsh, brutal men were used to brandishing their weapons like the Japanese samurai warriors of all those bad movies that they liked to watch, and like those actors playing at killers, these men were accustomed to having people cower before them, the omnipotent, invincible warriors of the Cartel, armed with their AK-47s, swaggering down village streets. *Comical scum*, Cortez thought.

It was all rather comical, really. Cortez would not mind a bit. It was to be a diverting and entertaining exercise, something from half a millennium before, when brutal men would tether a bear in a pit and let dogs at it. Eventually the bear died, and though it was frequently rather hard on the dogs, you could always get new ones. Those new dogs would be trained differently, to be loyal to a new master. . . . It was marvelous, Cortez realized after a moment. He'd be playing a game, with men instead of bears and dogs, a game that hadn't been played since the time of the Caesars. He understood now why some of the drug lords had gotten the way they were. This sort of God-like power was destructive to one's soul. He'd have to remember that. But first there was work to do.

The chain of command was established. There were five groups of fifty or so men. They were assigned operating areas. Communications would be by radio, coordinated through Cortez, in the safety of a house outside the village. About the only complication was the possible interference of the Colombian Army. Escobedo was taking care of that. M-19 and FARC would start making trouble elsewhere. That would keep the Army occupied.

The "soldiers," as they immediately took to calling themselves, moved off into the hills in trucks. *Buena suerte,* Cortez told their leaders: Good luck. Of course, he wished them nothing of the kind. Luck was no longer a factor in the operation, which suited the former colonel of the DGI. In a properly planned operation, it never was.

It was a quiet day in the mountains. Chavez heard the pealing of church bells echoing up and down the valley, calling the faithful to Sunday liturgy. Was it Sunday? Chavez wondered. He'd lost track. Whichever day it was, traffic sounds were less than normal. Except for the loss of Rocha, things were in rather good shape. They hadn't even expended much of their ammunition, though in another few days they were due for a resupply drop from the helicopter supporting the operation. You could never have too much ammunition. That was one truth Chavez had learned. Happiness is a full bandolier. And a full canteen. And hot food.

The topography of the valley allowed them to hear things especially well. Sound carried up the slopes with a minimum of attenuation, and the air, though thin, seemed to give every noise a special bell-like clarity. Chavez heard the trucks well off and put his binoculars on a bend in the road, several miles away, to see what it was. He wasn't the least concerned. Trucks were targets, not things to worry about. He adjusted the focus on the binoculars to get the sharpest possible image, and the sergeant had a good pair of eyes. After a minute or so he spotted three of them, flatbed trucks like farmers used, with removable wooden sides. But they were filled with men, and the men appeared to be carrying rifles. The trucks stopped, and the men jumped out. Chavez punched his sleeping companion.

"*Oso*, get the captain here right now!"

Ramirez was there in less than a minute, with his own pair of binoculars.

"You're standing up, sir!" Chavez growled. "Get the fuck down!"

"Sorry, Ding."

"You see 'em?"

"Yeah."

They were just milling around, but it was impossible to miss their rifles, slung over their shoulders. As both men watched, they divided into four groups and started moving off the road. A moment later, they were lost in the trees.

"It'll take 'em about three hours to get here, Cap'n," Ding estimated.

"By that time we'll be six miles north. Get ready to move."

Ramirez set up his satellite radio.

"VARIABLE, this is KNIFE, over." He got a reply on the first call.

"KNIFE, this is VARIABLE. We read you loud and clear. Over."

"KNIFE reports armed men entering the woods five miles east-southeast our position. Estimate reinforced platoon in strength, and heading our way."

"Are they soldiers, over."

"Negative — say again, negative. Weapons in evidence, but no uniforms. I repeat, they do not appear to be wearing uniforms. We are getting ready to move."

"Roger that, KNIFE. Move immediately, check in when you can. We'll try to find out what's going on."

"Roger. KNIFE out.

"What's that all about?" one of the case officers asked.

"I don't know. I wish Clark was here," the other said. "Let's check in with Langley."

Jackson managed to catch a United red-eye flight out of San Francisco direct to Dulles International Airport. Admiral Painter had called ahead, and a Navy sedan took him to Washington National, where his Corvette had been parked, and remarkably enough, not stolen. Robby had played it all back and forth in his mind during the entire flight. In the abstract, CIA operations were fun things to think about: spies skulking about and doing whatever the hell it was that they did. He didn't especially mind what this one was doing, but, damn it, the Navy was being used, and you didn't do that without letting people know. His first stop was at his home to change clothes. Then he made a phone call.

Ryan was home, and enjoying it. He'd managed to get home Friday evening a few minutes ahead of his wife's return from Hopkins and slept in late Saturday to shake off the lingering effects of travel shock. The remainder of the day had been devoted to playing with his kids and taking them to Saturday-night mass so that he could get another long night's sleep, plus reacquainting himself with his wife. Now he was sitting on his John Deere lawn tractor. He might be one of the top people in CIA, but he still cut his own grass. Others seeded and fertilized, but for Jack the pastoral act of cutting was therapy. It was a three-hour ritual done every two weeks — somewhat more often in the spring, but by now the growth rate was down to a reasonable level. He enjoyed the smell of the cut grass. For that matter, he enjoyed the greasy smell of the tractor and the vibration of the motor. He couldn't entirely escape reality, of course. Clipped to his belt was a portable telephone whose electronic chiming was noticeable over the rumble of the tractor. Jack switched off as he hit the activation button on the phone.

"Hello."

"Jack? Rob."

"How you doing, Robby?"

"Just got myself frocked."

"Congratulations, *Captain* Jackson! Aren't you a little young for that?"

"Call it affirmative action, lettin' the aviators catch up with the bubbleheads. Hey, Sissy and I are heading over to Annapolis. Any problem we stop by on the way?"

"Hell, no. How about lunch?"

"Sure it's no trouble?" Jackson asked.

"Robby, give me a break," Ryan replied. "Since when did you get humble on me?"

"Ever since you got important and all."

Ryan violated an FCC rule with his retort.

"Little over an hour okay?"

"Yeah, I'll be finished with the grass by then. See ya', bud." Ryan terminated the call and placed one to his house, which had three lines. It was, perversely, a long-distance call. He needed a D.C. line for his work. Cathy needed a Baltimore connection for hers, plus a local line for other matters.

"Hello?" Cathy answered.

"Rob and Sis are coming over for lunch," Jack told his wife. "How about hot dogs on the grill?"

"My hair's a mess!" Caroline Ryan announced.

"Okay, I'll grill that, too. Can you set up the charcoal for me? I ought to be finished out here in twenty minutes or so."

In fact, it took just over thirty. Ryan parked the mower in the garage next to his Jaguar and went into the house to wash up. He had to shave, too, which he barely finished doing when Robby pulled into the driveway.

"How the hell did you make it this fast?" Jack demanded. He was still wearing his dingy cut-offs.

"You prefer I should be late, Dr. Ryan?" Robby asked as he and his wife got out of the car. Cathy appeared at the door. Handshakes and kisses were exchanged as everyone caught up on what they'd been doing since the last time they'd gotten together. Cathy and Sissy went into the living room while Jack and Robby got the hot dogs and walked out to the deck. The charcoal wasn't quite ready yet.

"So how do you like being a captain?"

"Be even better when they pay me what I am most clearly worth." Being frocked meant that Robby could wear the four stripes of a captain, but still drew the pay of a mere commander. "I'm getting a CAG slot, too. Admiral Painter told me last night."

"Shit hot!" Jack clapped Robby on the shoulder. "That's the next big step, isn't it?"

"So long as I don't step on my weenie. The Navy giveth, and the Navy taketh away. I don't get it for a year and a half, which means giving up part of my delightful tour in the Pentagon, sob." Robby stopped for a moment and got serious. "That's not why I came."

"Oh?"

"Jack, what the hell have you guys got going in Colombia?"

"Rob, I don't know."

"Look, Jack, this is cool, okay? I fucking know! Your security on the op sucks. Hey, I know you got need-to-know rules, but my admiral is kinda pissed that you're using his assets without telling him about it."

"Who's that?"

"Josh Painter," Jackson answered. "You met him on *Kennedy*, remember?"

"Who told you that!"

"A reliable source. I've been thinking about it. The story back then was that Ivan lost a sub and we were out to help 'em find it, but things got a little rough for a while, explaining why my RIO had to have brain surgery and my Tomcat needed three weeks before it could fly again. I guess there was more to that than met the eye, and it never made the papers. Shame I can't hear the story. Anyway, we'll set that one aside for a while. This is why I'm here:

"Those two druggie houses that got blown up — the bombs came off of an A-6E Intruder medium attack bomber belonging to the United States Navy. I'm not the only one who knows. Whoever set up this operation, well, the security's for shit, Jack. You also got a bunch of light-infantry soldiers running around. Doing what, I don't know, but people also know that they're down there. Maybe you can't tell me what's happening. Okay, it's compartmented and all that, and you can't tell me anything, but I'm telling *you*, Jack, the word's leaking out, and some folks in the Pentagon are going to be big-league angry when this sucker hits the networks. Whatever dickhead set this thing up is in way the hell over his head, and the word from on high is that us guys in blue and green suits will not repeat *not* get left holding the bag this time."

"Cool off, Rob." Ryan popped open a can of beer for Robby and one for himself.

"Jack, we're friends, and ain't nothing gonna change that. I know you'd never do anything this dumb, but — "

"I don't know what you're talking about. I don't fucking know, okay? I was in Belgium last week and I told them I didn't know. I was in Chicago Friday morning with that Fowler guy, and I told him and his aide that I don't know. And I'm telling *you* that I don't know."

Jackson was quiet for a moment. "You know, anybody else, I'd call him a liar. I know what your new job is, Jack. You're telling me that you're serious? Honest to God, Jack, this here is important."

"Word of honor, Captain, I don't know dick."

Robby drained his beer and crushed the can flat. "Ain't that the way it always is?" he said. "We got people out there killing, maybe getting hurt, too, and nobody knows anything. God, I love being a fucking pawn. You know, I don't mind taking my chances, but it's nice to know why."

"I'll do my best to find out."

"Good idea. They really haven't told you what's happening, eh?"

"They haven't told me shit, but I'm going to damned well find out. You might want to drop a hint on your boss," Jack added.

"What's that?"

"Tell him to keep a low profile until I get back to you."

Whatever doubt the Patterson brothers had about what they should do ended that Sunday afternoon. The Grayson sisters came for visitors' day, sitting across from their men — neither pair had trouble distinguishing who was who — and proclaiming their undying love for the men who'd liberated them from their pimp. It was no longer just a question of getting out of jail. The final decision was made on the way back to their cell.

Henry and Harvey were in the same cell, mainly for security reasons. Had they been separated, then by the simple expedient of changing shirts, they could have swapped cells and somehow — the jailers knew that the Pattersons were clever bastards — done something to screw things up for everybody. The additional advantage was that the brothers didn't fight each other, as was hardly uncommon with the rest of the jail population, and the fact that they were quiet and untroublesome allowed them to work in undisturbed peace.

Jails are necessarily buildings designed to take abuse. The floors are of bare reinforced concrete, since carpets or tile would just be ripped up to start a fire or some other mischief. The resulting hard, smooth concrete floor made a good grinding surface. Each brother had a simple length of heavy metal wire taken from the bedstead. No one has yet designed a prison bed that doesn't require metal, and metal makes good weapons. In prison such weapons are called shanks, an ugly word completely suitable to their ugly purpose. Law requires that jails and prisons cannot be mere cages for housing prisoners like animals in a zoo, and this jail, like others, had a crafts shop. An idle mind, judges have ruled for decades, is the devil's workshop. The fact that the devil is already a resident in the criminal mind simply means that the craft shops provide tools and material for making shanks more effective. In this case, each brother had a small, grooved piece of wood doweling and some electrician's tape. Henry and Harvey took turns, one rubbing his shank on the concrete to get a needle-like point while the other stood guard for an approaching uniform. It was high-quality wire, and the sharpening process took some hours, but people in jail have lots of idle time. Finished, each wire was inserted in the groove in the dowel — miraculously enough, the groove, cut by a craft-shop router, was exactly the right size and length. The electrician's tape secured the wire in place, and now each brother had a six-inch shank, capable of inflicting a deep, penetrating trauma upon a human body.

They hid their weapons — prison inmates are

very effective at it — and discussed tactics. Any graduate of a guerrilla or terrorist school would have been impressed. Though the language was coarse and the discussion lacking in the technical jargon preferred by trained professionals in the field of urban warfare, the Patterson brothers had a clear understanding of the idea of *Mission*. They understood covert approach, the importance of maneuver and diversion, and they knew about clearing the area after the mission was successfully executed. In this they expected the tacit assistance of their cellmates, but jails and prisons, though violent and evil places, remain communities of men, and the pirates were decidedly unpopular, whereas the Pattersons were fairly high in the hierarchical chain as tough, "honest" hoods. Besides, everyone knew that they were not people to cross, which encouraged cooperation and discouraged informants.

Jails are also places with hygienic rules. Since criminals are frequently the type to defer bathing, and brushing and flossing their teeth, and since such behavior lends itself to epidemic, showers are part of an unbending routine. The Patterson brothers were counting on it.

"What do you mean?" the man with a Spanish accent asked Mr. Stuart.

"I mean they'll be out in eight years. Considering they murdered a family of four and got caught red-handed with a large supply of cocaine, it's one hell of a good deal," the attorney replied. He didn't like doing business on Sunday, and especially didn't like doing business with this man in the den of his home with his family in the backyard, but he had chosen to do business with drug types. He told himself at least ten times with every single case that he'd been a fool to have taken the first one — and gotten him off, of course, because the DEA agents had screwed up their warrant, tainting all the evidence and tossing the case on a classic "legal technicality." That success, which had earned him fifty thousand dollars for four days' work, had given him a "name" within the drug community, which had money to burn — or to hire good criminal lawyers. You couldn't easily say no to such people. They were genuinely frightening. They had *killed* lawyers who displeased them. And they paid so well, well enough that he could take time to apply his considerable talents to indigent clients who couldn't pay. At least that was one of the arguments he used on sleepless nights to justify dealing with the animals. "Look, these guys were looking at a seat in the electric chair — life at minimum — and I knocked that down to twenty years and out in eight. For Christ's sake, that's a goddamned good deal."

"I think you could do better," the man replied with a blank look and in a voice so devoid of emotion as to be mechanistic. And decidedly frightening to a lawyer who had never owned or shot a gun.

That was the other side of the equation. They

didn't merely hire him. Somewhere else was another lawyer, one who gave advice without getting directly involved. It was a simple security provision. It also made perfect professional sense, of course, to get a second opinion of anything. It also meant that in special cases the drug community could make sure that its own attorney wasn't making some sort of arrangement with the state, as was not entirely unknown in the countries from which they came. And as was the case here, some might say. Stuart could have played his information from the Coasties for all it was worth, gambling to have the whole case thrown out. He estimated a fifty-fifty chance of that. Stuart was good, even brilliant in a courtroom, but so was Davidoff, and there is not a trial lawyer in the world who would have predicted the reaction of a jury — a south Alabama, law-and-order jury — to a case like this one. Whoever was in the shadows giving advice to the man in his den, he was not as good as Stuart in a courtroom. Probably an academic, the trial lawyer thought, maybe a professor supplementing his teaching income with some informal consulting. Whoever he — she? — was, Stuart hated him on instinct.

"If I do what you want me to do, we run the risk of blowing the whole case. They really could end up in the chair." It also would mean wrecking the careers of Coast Guard sailors who had done wrong, but not nearly so wrong as Stuart's clients had most certainly done. His ethical duty as a lawyer was to give his clients the best possible defense within the law, within the Standards of Professional Conduct, but most of all, within the scope of his knowledge and experience — instinct, which was as real and important as it was impossible to quantify. Exactly how a lawyer balanced his duty on that three-cornered scale was the subject of endless class hours in law school, but the answers arrived at in the theater-like lecture halls were always clearer than in the real legal world found beyond the green campus lawns.

"They could also go free."

The man's thinking reversal on appeal, Stuart realized. It *was* an academic lawyer giving advice.

"My professional advice to my clients is to accept the deal that I have negotiated."

"Your clients will decline that advice. Your clients will tell you tomorrow morning to — what is the phrase? Go for broke?" The man smiled like a dangerous machine. "Those are your instructions. Good day, Mr. Stuart. I can find the door." The machine left.

Stuart stared at his bookcases for a few minutes before making his telephone call. He might as well do it now. No sense making Davidoff wait. No public announcement had yet been made, though the rumors were out on the street. He wondered how the U.S. Attorney would take it. It was easier to predict what he'd say. The outraged *I thought we had a deal!* would be followed by a resolute *Okay, we'll see what the jury says!* Davidoff would muster his considerable talents, and the battle in Federal District Court would be an epic duel. But that was what courts were all about, wasn't it? It would be a fascinating and exciting technical exercise in the theory of the law, but like most such exercises, it would have little to do with right and wrong, less to do with what had actually happened aboard the good ship *Empire Builder,* and nothing at all to do with justice.

Murray was in his office. Moving into their townhouse had been a formality. He slept there — most of the time — but he saw far less of it than he'd seen of his official apartment in the Kensington section of London while legal attaché to the embassy on Grosvenor Square. It was hardly fair. For what it had cost him to move back to the D.C. area — the city that provided a home for the United States government denied decent housing to those on government salaries — one would have thought that he'd have gotten some real use from it.

His secretary was not in on Sunday, of course, and that meant Murray had to answer his own phone. This one came in on his direct, private line.

"Yeah, Murray here."

"Mark Bright. There's been a development on the Pirates Case that you need to know about. The lawyer for the subjects just called the U.S.

Attorney. He's tossing the deal they made. He's going to fight it out; he's going to put those Coasties on the stand and try to blow away the whole case on the basis of that stunt they pulled. Davidoff's worried."

"What do you think?" Murray asked.

"Well, he'll reinstate the whole case: drug-related capital murder. If it means clobbering the Coast Guard, well, that's the price of justice. His words, not mine," Bright pointed out. Like many FBI agents, the agent was also a member of the bar. "Going on my experience, not his, I'd say it's real gray, Dan. Davidoff's good — I mean, he's really good in front of a jury — but so's the defense guy, Stuart. The local DEA hates his guts, but he's an effective son of a bitch. The law is pretty muddled. What'll the judge say? Depends on the judge. What'll the jury say — depends on what the judge says and does. It's like putting a bet down on the next Super Bowl right now, before the season starts, and that doesn't even take into account what'll happen in the U.S. Court of Appeals after the trial's over in District Court. Whatever happens, the Coasties are going to get raped. Too bad. No matter what, Davidoff is going to tear each of 'em a new asshole for getting him into this mess."

"Warn 'em," Murray said. He told himself that it was an impulsive statement, but it wasn't. Murray believed in law, but he believed in justice more.

"You want to repeat that, sir?"

"They gave us TARPON."

"Mr. Murray" — he wasn't "Dan" now — "I might have to arrest them. Davidoff just might set up a grand jury on this and — "

"Warn them. That is an order, Mr. Bright. I presume the local cops have a good attorney who represents them. Recommend that attorney to Captain Wegener and his men."

Bright hesitated before replying. "Sir, what you just told me to do might be seen as — "

"Mark, I've been in the Bureau a long time. Maybe too damned long," Murray's fatigue — and some other things — said. "But I won't stand by and watch these men get ambushed for doing something that helped us. They'll have to take their chances with the law — but by God, they'll have the same advantages that those fucking pirates have! We owe them that much. Log that one in as my order and carry it out."

"Yes, sir." Murray could hear Bright thinking the rest of the answer: *Damn!*

"On the case, anything else you need from our end that you need help with?"

"No, sir. The forensics are all in. From that side the case is tight as hell. DNA matches on both semen samples to the subjects, DNA blood matches to two of the victims. The wife was a blood donor, and we found a quart of her stuff in a Red Cross freezer; the other one's to the daughter. Davidoff might just bring this one off on that basis alone." The new DNA-match technology was rapidly becoming one of the Bureau's deadliest forensic weapons. Two California men who'd thought themselves to have committed the perfect rape-murder were now contemplating the gas chamber due to the work of two Bureau biochemists and a relatively inexpensive laboratory test.

"Anything else you need, you call me direct. This one is directly tied in with Emil's murder, and I've got all the horsepower I need."

"Yes, sir. Sorry to bother you on a Sunday."

"Right." It was one small thing to chuckle about as he hung up. Murray turned in his swivel chair to stare out the windows onto Pennsylvania Avenue. A pleasant Sunday afternoon, and people were walking up the street of presidents like pilgrims, stopping along the way to purchase ice-creams and T-shirts from vendors. Farther down the street, beyond the Capitol, in the areas that tourists were careful to avoid, there were other places that people entered, also like pilgrims, also stopping to buy things.

"Fucking drugs," he observed quietly. Just how much more damage would they do?

The Deputy Director (Operations) was also in his office. Three signals from VARIABLE had come in within the space of two hours. Well, it was not entirely unexpected that the opposition would react. They were acting more rapidly and in a more organized way — it appeared — than he had expected, but it wasn't something that he'd neglected to consider beforehand. The whole point of using the troops he was using, after all, was for their field skills . . . and their anonymity. Had he selected Green Berets from the John F. Kennedy Special Warfare Center at Fort Bragg, North Carolina, or Rangers from Fort Stewart, Georgia, or people from the new Special Operations Command at MacDill — it would have been too many people from too small a community. That would have been noticed. But light-fighters had four nearly complete and widely separated divisions, over forty thousand men spread from New York to Hawaii, with the same field skills as soldiers in higher-profile units; and taking forty people out of forty thousand was a far more concealable exercise. Some would be lost. He'd known that going in and so, he was sure, did the soldiers themselves. They were assets, and assets sometimes get expended. That was harsh, but it was reality. If the infantrymen had wanted a safe life, they would not have chosen to be infantrymen, to have re-enlisted at least once each, and to volunteer for a job that was advertised as being potentially dangerous. These weren't government clerks tossed into the jungle and told to fend for themselves. They were professional soldiers who knew what the score was.

At least, that's what Ritter told himself. *But,* his mind asked him, *if you don't know what the score is, how can they?*

The craziest part of all was that the operation was working out exactly as planned — in the field. Clark's brilliant idea, using a few disconnected violent acts to instigate a gang war within the Cartel, appeared to be happening. How else to explain the attempted ambush of Escobedo? He found himself glad that Cortez and his boss had escaped. Now there would be revenge and confusion and turmoil from which the Agency could step back and cover its tracks.

Who, us? the Agency would ask by way of answer to reporters' questions, which would start the following day, Ritter was certain. He was, in fact, surprised that they hadn't started already. But the pieces of the puzzle were coming apart now instead of together. The *Ranger* battle group would sail back north, continuing its Fleet-Ex during the slow trip back to San Diego. The CIA representative was already off the ship and on his way home with the second and final tape cassette. The rest of the "exercise" bombs would be dropped at sea, targeted on discarded life-rafts as normal Drop-Ex's. The fact that they'd never been officially released from the Navy weapons-testing base in California would never be noticed. If it were? Some paperwork screwup — they happened all the time. No, the only tricky part was with those troops in the field. He could have made immediate arrangements to lift them out. Better to leave them there for a few more days. There might be more work for them to do, and as long as they were careful, they'd be all right. The opposition would not be all that good.

"So?" Colonel Johns asked Zimmer.

"Gotta change engines. This one's shot. The burner cans are all right, but the compressor failed big-time. Maybe the boys back home can rebuild it. No way we can fix it with what we've got here, sir."

"How long?"

"Six hours, if we start now, Colonel."

"Okay, Buck."

They'd brought two spare engines, of course. The hangar that held the Pave Low III helicopter wasn't big enough for both it and the MC-130 which provided aerial tanking and spare parts, however, and Zimmer waved to another NCO to punch the button to open the door. They needed a special cart and hoist to handle the T-64 turboshaft engines in any case.

The hangar doors rolled on their metal tracks just as a roach wagon drove onto the flight line. Immediately men descended on the truck. It was a hot day at the Canal Zone — a place where snow is something one sees on television — and it was time for cold drinks. Everyone knew the truck driver, a Panamanian who'd been doing this since God knew when and made a pretty good living at it.

He was also a serious airplane buff. From his own years of observations, plus casual conversations with the enlisted men who serviced them, he'd acquired a familiarity with everything in the inventory of the United States Air Force, and would have been a useful intelligence asset had anyone bothered trying to recruit him. He would never have done anything to hurt them in any case. Though often overbearing, more than once he'd had trouble with his truck and had it fixed on the spot for free by a green-clad mechanic, and around Christmas — everyone knew he had children — there would be presents for him and his sons. He'd even managed a few helicopter rides for them, showing them what the family house outside the base looked like. It was not every father who could do that for his children! The *norteamericanos* were not perfect, he knew, but they were fair and they were generous if you dealt with them honestly, since honesty wasn't something they expected from "natives." That was all the more true now that they were having trouble with the pineapple-faced buffoon who was running his country's government.

As he passed out his Cokes and munchies, he noticed that there was a Pave Low III in the hangar across the way, a large, formidable and in its peculiar way, a very beautiful helicopter. Well, that explained the Combat Talon transport/tanker, and the armed guards who kept him from taking his normal route. He knew much about both aircraft, and while he would never reveal what he knew of their capabilities, telling someone the simple fact that they were here, that was no crime, was it?

But next time, after the money was passed, he'd be asked to take note of the times they came and went.

826

They'd moved very rapidly for the first hour, then slowed to their normal slow, careful, and very alert pace. Even so, moving in daylight wasn't something they preferred to do. While the Ninja might well own the night, day was something for all, a far easier time to teach people to hunt than in the dark. While the soldiers still had practical advantages over anyone who might come hunting them — even other soldiers — those advantages were minimized by daytime operations. Like gamblers, the light-fighters preferred to use every card in the deck. Doing so, they consciously avoided what some sportsman might call a "fair" fight, but combat had stopped being a sport when a gladiator named Spartacus decided to kill on a free-agent basis, though it had taken the Romans a few more generations to catch on.

Everyone had his war paint on. They wore gloves despite the fact that it was warm. They knew that the nearest other SHOWBOAT team was fifteen klicks to the south, and anyone they saw was either an innocent or a hostile, not a friendly, and to soldiers trying to stay covert, "innocent" was rather a thin concept. They were to avoid contact with anything and anyone, and if contact were made, it would be an on-the-spot call.

The other rules were also different now. They didn't move in single file. Too many people following a single path made for tracks. Though Chavez was at point, with *Oso* twenty meters behind, the rest of the squad was advancing in line abreast, with frequent changes of direction, shifting almost like a football backfield, but over a much larger area. Soon they'd start looping their path, waiting to see if someone might be following. If so, that someone was in for a surprise. For the moment, the mission was to move to a preselected location and evaluate the opposition. And wait for orders.

The police lieutenant didn't often go to evening services at Grace Baptist Church, but he did this time. He was late, but the lieutenant had a reputation for being late, even though he customarily drove his unmarked radio car wherever he went. He parked on the periphery of the well-filled parking lot, walked in, and sat in the back, where he made sure his miserable singing would be noticed.

Fifteen minutes later, another plain-looking car stopped right next to his. A man got out with a tire iron, smashed the window on the right-side front door, and proceeded to remove the police radio, the shotgun clipped under the dash — and the locked, evidence-filled attaché case on the floor. In less than a minute he was back in his car and gone. The case would be found again only if the Patterson brothers didn't keep their word. Cops are honest folk.

23.

The Games Begin

The morning routine was exactly the same despite the fact that Ryan had been away from it for a week. His driver awoke early and drove his own car to Langley, where he switched over to the official Buick and also picked up some papers for his passenger. These were in a metal case with a cipher lock and a self-destruct device. No one had ever tried to interfere with the car or its occupants, but that wasn't to say that it would never happen. The driver, one of the official CIA security detail, carried his own 9mm Beretta 92-F pistol, and there was an Uzi submachine gun under the dash. He had trained with the Secret Service and was an expert on protecting his "principal," as he thought of the acting DDI. He also wished that the guy lived closer to D.C., or that he was entitled to mileage pay for all the driving he did. He drove around the inner loop of the Capital Beltway, then took the cloverleaf east on Maryland Route 50.

Jack Ryan rose at 6:15, an hour that seemed increasingly early as he marched toward forty, and followed the same kind of morning routine as most other working people, though his being married to a physician guaranteed that his breakfast was composed of healthy foods, as opposed to those he liked. What was wrong with grease, sugar, and preservatives, anyway?

By 6:55 he was finished with breakfast, dressed, and about halfway through his paper. It was Cathy's job to get the children off to school. Jack kissed his daughter on his way to the door, but Jack Jr. thought himself too old for that baby stuff. The Agency Buick was just arriving, as regular and reliable as airlines and railroads tried to be.

"Good morning, Dr. Ryan."

"Good morning, Phil." Jack preferred to open his own doors, and slid into the right-rear seat. First he would finish his *Washington Post*, ending, as always, with the comics, and saving Gary Larson for last. If there was anything an Agency person needed it was his daily dose of *The Far Side*, far and away the most popular cartoon at Langley. It wasn't hard to understand why. By that time the car was back on Route 50, in the heavy Washington-bound traffic. Ryan worked the lock on the letter case. After opening it he used his Agency ID card to disarm the destruct device. The papers within were important, but anyone who attacked the car now would be more interested in him than in any written material, and no one at the Agency had illusions about Ryan's — or any other person's — ability to resist attempts to extract information. He now had forty minutes to catch up on developments that had taken place overnight — in this case over the weekend — so that he'd be able to ask intelligent questions of the section chiefs and night watch officers who'd brief him when he got in.

Reading the newspaper first always put a decent spin on the official CIA reports. Ryan had his doubts about journalists — their analysis was often faulty — but the fact of the matter was that they were in the same basic job as the Agency: information-gathering and -dissemination, and except for some very technical fields — which were, however, vitally important in matters like arms control — their performance was often as good as and sometimes better than the trained government employees who reported to Langley. Of course, a good foreign correspondent was generally paid better than a GS-12-equivalent case officer, and talent often went where the money was. Besides, reporters were allowed to write books, too, and that's where you could make real money, as many Moscow correspondents had done over the years. All a security clearance really meant, Ryan had learned over the years, was sources. Even at his level in the Agency, he often had access to information little different in substance than any competent newspaper reported. The difference was that Jack knew the sources for that information, which was important in gauging its reliability. It was a subtle but often crucial difference.

The briefing folders began with the Soviet Union. All sorts of interesting things were happening there, but still no one knew what it meant or where it was leading. Fine. Ryan and CIA had been reporting that analysis for longer than he cared to remember. People expected better. Like that Elliot woman, Jack thought, who hated the Agency for what it did — actually, for things it never did anymore — but conversely expected it to know everything. When would they wake up and realize that predicting the future was no easier for intelligence analysts than for a good sportswriter to determine who'd be playing in the Series? Even after the All-Star break, the American League East had three teams within a few percentage points of the lead. That was a question for bookmakers. It was a pity, Ryan grunted to himself, that Vegas didn't set up a betting line on the Soviet Politburo membership, or *glasnost,* or how the "nationalities question" was going to turn out. It would have given him some guidance. By the time they got to the beltway, he was reading through reports from Latin and South America. Sure enough, some drug lord named Fuentes had gotten himself blown up by a bomb.

Well, isn't that too bad? was Jack's initial observation. He was thinking abstractly, but came down to earth. No, it wasn't all that bad that he was dead. It was very worrisome that he'd been killed by an American aircraft bomb. That was the sort of thing that Beth Elliot hated CIA for, Jack reminded himself. All that judge-jury-and-executioner stuff. It had nothing to do with right or wrong. The question, to her, was political expediency and maybe aesthetics. Politicians are more concerned with "issues" than "principles," but talked as though the two nouns had the same meaning.

Jesus, you're really into Monday-morning cynicism, aren't you?

How the hell did Robby Jackson tumble to this? Who set up the operation? What will happen if the word really does get out?

Better yet: *Am I supposed to care about that? If yes, why? If not, why not?*

It's political, Jack. How do politics enter into your job? Are politics even supposed to enter into your job?

As with many things, this would have been a superb topic for a philosophical discussion, something for which Ryan's Jesuit education had both prepared him and given him a taste. But the case at hand wasn't an abstract examination of principles and hypotheticals. He was supposed to have answers. What if a member of the Select Committee asked him a question that he *had* to answer? That could happen at any time. He could defer such a question only for as long as it took to drive from Langley to The Hill.

And if Ryan lied, he'd go to jail. That was the downside of his promotion.

For that matter, if he honestly said that he didn't know, he might not be believed, probably not by the committee members, maybe not by a jury. Even honesty might not be real protection. Wasn't that a fun thought?

Jack looked out the window as they passed the Mormon temple, just outside the beltway near Connecticut Avenue. A decidedly odd-looking building, it had grandeur with its marble columns and gilt spires. The beliefs represented by that impressive structure seemed curious to Ryan, a lifelong Catholic, but the people who held them were honest and hardworking, and fiercely loyal to their country, because they believed in what America stood for. And that was what it all came down to, wasn't it? Either you stand *for* something, or you don't, Ryan told himself. Any jackass could be against things, like a petulant child claiming to hate an untasted vegetable. You could tell what these people stood for. The Mormons tithed their income, which allowed their church to construct this monument to faith, just as medieval peasants had taken from their need to build the cathedrals of their age, for precisely the same purpose. The peasants were forgotten by all but the God in Whom they believed. The cathedrals — testimony to those beliefs — remained in their glory, still used for their intended purpose. Who remembered the political issues of that age? The nobles and their castles had crumbled away, the royal bloodlines had mostly ended, and all that age had left behind were memorials to faith, belief in something more important than man's corporeal existence, expressed in stonework crafted by the hands of men. What better proof could there be of what really mattered? Jack knew he wasn't the first to wonder at the fact, not by a very long shot indeed, but it wasn't often that anyone perceived Truth so clearly as Ryan did on this Monday morning. It made expediency seem a shallow, ephemeral, and ultimately useless commodity. He still had to figure out what he would do, and knew that his action would possibly be decided by others, but he knew what sort of guide, what sort of measure he would use to determine his action. That was enough for now, he told himself.

The car pulled through the gate fifteen minutes later, then around the front of the building and into the garage. Ryan tucked all of his material back into the case and took the elevator to the seventh floor. Nancy already had his coffee machine perking as he walked in. His people would arrive in five minutes to complete his morning brief. Ryan had a few more moments for thought.

What had been enough on the beltway faded in the confines of his office. Now he had to *do* something, and while his guide would be principle, his actions would be tactically drawn. And Jack didn't have a clue.

His department chiefs arrived on schedule and began their briefings. They found the acting

DDI curiously withdrawn and quiet this morning. Normally he asked questions and had a humorous remark or two. This time he nodded and grunted, hardly saying anything. Maybe he'd had a tough weekend.

For others, Monday morning meant going to court, seeing lawyers, and facing juries. Since the defendant in a criminal trial had the right to put his best face before a jury, it was shower time for the residents of the Mobile jail.

As with all aspects of prison life, security was the foremost consideration. The cell doors were opened, and the prisoners, wearing towels and sandals, trooped toward the end of the corridor under the watchful eyes of three experienced guards. The morning banter among the prisoners was normal: grumbling, jokes, and the odd curse. On their own or during their exercise or eating periods, the prisoners tended to form racially polarized groups, but jail policy forbade such segregation in the blocks — the guards knew it merely guaranteed violence, but the judges who'd made the rules were guided by principle, not reality. Besides, if somebody got killed, it was the guards' fault, wasn't it? The guards were the most cynical of all law-enforcement people, shunned by street cops as mere custodians, hated by the inmates, and not terribly well regarded by the community. It was hard for them to care greatly about their jobs, and their foremost concern was personal survival.

The danger involved in working here was very real. The death of an inmate was no small matter to be sure — a serious criminal investigation was conducted both by the guards and the police, or in some cases, federal officers — but the life of a criminal was a smaller concern than the life of a guard — to the guards themselves.

For all that, they did their best. They were mostly experienced men and they knew what to look for. The same was true of the inmates, of course, and what went on here was no different in principle from what happened on a battlefield or in the shadow wars between intelligence agencies. Tactics evolved as measures and countermeasures changed over time. Some prisoners were craftier than others. Some were goddamned geniuses. Others, especially the young, were frightened, meek people whose only objective was exactly the same as the guards': personal survival in a dangerous environment. Each class of prisoner required a slightly different form of scrutiny, and the demands on the guards were severe. It was inevitable that some mistakes would be made.

Towels were hung on numbered hooks. Each prisoner had his own personal bar of soap, and a guard watched them parade naked into the shower enclosure, which had twenty shower heads. He made sure that no weapons were visible. But he was a young guard, and he'd not yet learned that a really determined man always has one place in which he can hide something.

Henry and Harvey Patterson picked neighboring shower heads directly across from the pirates, who had foolishly selected places that could not be seen from the guard's position at the door. The brothers traded a happy look. The bastards might be king shit, but they weren't real swift in the head. Neither brother was particularly comfortable at the moment. The electrician's tape on the three-quarter-inch wood dowels was smooth, but had edges, and walking to the shower in a normal manner had required all their determination. It hurt. The hot water started all at once, and the enclosure started filling up with steam. The Patterson brothers applied their soap bars in the obvious place to facilitate getting their shanks, part of which were visible to a careful onlooker in any case, but they knew that the guard was new. Harvey nodded to a couple of people at the end of the enclosure. The act began with rather an uninspired bit of extemporaneous dialogue.

"Give me my fuckin' soap back, motherfucker!"

"Yo' *momma*," the other replied casually. He'd thought about his line.

A blow was delivered, and returned.

"Knock it the fuck off — get the fuck out here!" the guard shouted. That's when two more people entered the fray, one knowing why, the other a young first-timer who only knew that he was scared and fighting back to protect himself. The chain reaction expanded almost at once to include the entire shower area. Outside, the guard backed off, calling for help.

Henry and Harvey turned, their shanks concealed in their hands. Ramón and Jesús were watching the fighting, looking the wrong way, fairly certain that they'd stay out of it; not knowing that it had been staged.

Harvey took Jesús, and Henry took Ramón.

Jesús never saw it coming, just a brown shape approaching him like a shadow and a punch in the chest, followed by another. He looked down to see blood spouting from a hole that went all the way into his heart — with each beat the holes tore further open — then a brown hand struck again, and a third red arc of blood joined the first two. He panicked, trying to hold his hand over the wounds to stop the bleeding, not knowing that most of the blood went into the pericardial sac, where it was already causing his death by congestive heart failure. He fell back against the wall and slid to the floor. Jesús died without knowing why.

Henry, who knew that he was the smart one, went for a faster kill. Ramón only made it easier, seeing the danger coming and turning away. Henry drove him against the tiled wall and smashed his shank into the side of the man's head, at the temple, where he knew the bone was eggshell-thin. Once in, he wiggled it left-right, up-down twice. Ramón wriggled like a caught fish for a few seconds, then went limp as a rag doll.

Each Patterson put his weapon in the hand of his brother's victim — they didn't have to worry about fingerprints in the shower — pushed the two bodies together, and stepped back to their own shower streams, where both washed down vigorously and cooperatively to remove any blood that might have splattered on them. By this time things had quieted down. The two men who'd disagreed over ownership of a bar of Dial had shaken hands, apologized to the guard, and were completing their morning ablutions. The steam continued to cloud the enclosure, and the Pattersons continued their thorough washdown. Cleanliness was especially next to godliness where evidence was concerned. After five minutes the water stopped and the men trooped out.

The guard did his count — if there is anything a jail guard knows how to do, it is count — and came up two short while the other eighteen started drying off and playing grab-ass in the way of prisoners in an all-male environment. He stuck his head into the shower, ready to shout something in high-school Spanish, but saw at the bottom of the steam cloud what looked like a body.

"Oh, fuck!" He turned and screamed for the other guards to return. "Nobody fucking move!" he screamed at the prisoners.

"What's the problem?" an anonymous voice asked.

"Hey, man, I gotta be in court in an hour," another pointed out.

The Patterson brothers dried themselves off,

put their sandals back on, and stood quietly. Other conspirators might have exchanged a satisfied look — they had just committed a perfect double murder with a cop standing fifteen feet away — but the twins didn't need to. Each knew exactly what the other was thinking: Freedom. They'd just dodged one murder by doing two more. They knew that the cops would play ball. That lieutenant was a righteous cop, and righteous cops kept their word.

Word of the pirates' deaths spread with speed that would have done any news organization proud. The lieutenant was sitting at his desk filling out an incident report when it reached him. He nodded at the news and went back to the embarrassing task of explaining how his personal police radio car had been violated, and an expensive radio, his briefcase, and, worst of all, a shotgun removed. That last item required all kinds of paperwork.

"Maybe that's God's way of telling you to stay home and watch TV," another lieutenant observed.

"You agnostic bastard, you know I finally decided to — oh, shit!"

"Problem?"

"The Patterson Case. I had all the bullets in my briefcase, forgot to take them out. They're gone. Duane, the bullets are gone! The examiner's notes, the photos, everything!"

"The DA's gonna love you, boy. You just put

the Patterson boys back on the street."

It was worth it, the police lieutenant didn't say.

At his office four blocks away, Stuart took the call and breathed a sigh of relief. He ought to have been ashamed, of course, and knew it, but this time he just couldn't bring himself to mourn for his clients. For the system that had failed them, yes, but not for their lives, which had manifestly benefited no one. Besides, he'd gotten his fee paid up-front, as any smart attorney did with druggies.

Fifteen minutes later, the U.S. Attorney had a statement out saying that he was outraged that federal prisoners had died in such a way, and that their deaths would be investigated by the appropriate federal authorities. He added that he'd hoped to arrange their deaths within the law, but death under law was a far different thing from death at the unknown hand of a murderer. All in all, it was an excellent statement which would make the noon and evening news broadcasts, which delighted Edward Davidoff even more than the deaths. Losing that case might have ended his chance for a Senate seat. Now people would say that justice had in fact been done, and they'd associate his statement and his face with it. It was almost as good as a conviction.

The Pattersons' lawyer was in the room, of course. They never spoke to a police officer without their attorney present — or so he thought, anyway.

"Hey," Harvey said. "Nobody fuck with me, I don't fuck with nobody. I heard a scuffle, like. That was it, man. You hear something like that in a place like this, smart move is you don't even look, y'know? You be better off not knowin'."

"It would appear that my clients have nothing to contribute to your investigation," the lawyer told the detectives. "Is it possible that the two men killed each other?"

"We don't know. We are just interviewing those who were present when it happened."

"I understand, then, that you do not contemplate charging my clients with anything having to do with this regrettable incident?"

"Not at this time, counselor," the senior detective said.

"Very well, I want that on the record. Also, for the record, my clients have no knowledge that is pertinent to your investigation. Finally, and this, too, is for the record, you will not question my clients except in my presence."

"Yes, sir."

"Thank you. Now, if you will excuse me, I would like to confer with my clients in private."

That conference lasted for about fifteen minutes, after which the attorney knew what had taken place. Which is to say that he didn't "know" in the metaphysical or legal sense, or in any way that had anything to do with legal ethics — but he knew. Under the Canons of Ethics, of course, he could not act on his speculation without betraying his oath as an officer of the court. And so he did what he could do. He filed a new discovery motion on his clients' murder case. By the end of the day he would have added proof of what he did not know.

"Good morning, Judge," Ryan said.

" 'Morning, Jack. This'll have to be fast. I'm going out of town in a few minutes."

"Sir, if somebody asks me what the hell's going on in Colombia, what do I tell 'em?"

"We have kept you out of this one, haven't we?" Moore said.

"Yes, sir, you have."

"I have orders to do that. You can guess where the orders come from. What I can tell you is, the Agency hasn't blown anybody up, okay? We do have an op running down there, but we haven't planted any car bombs."

"That's good to know, Judge. I really didn't think that we were in the car-bomb business," Ryan said as casually as he could. *Oh, shit! The Judge, too?* "So, if I get a call from The Hill, I tell them that, right?"

Moore smiled as he rose. "You're going to have to get used to dealing with them, Jack. It's not easy, and it's often not fun, but I think you'll find that they do business — better than Fowler and his people do, from what I heard this morning."

"It could have gone better, sir," Ryan admitted. "I understand the Admiral handled the last one. I suppose I ought to have spoken more with him before I flew out."

"We don't expect you to be perfect, Jack."

"Thank you, sir."

"And I have to catch a flight out to California."

"Safe trip, Judge," Ryan said as he walked out of the room. Jack entered his office and closed the door before he let his face slip out of neutral.

"Oh, my God," he breathed to himself. If it had been a simple, straight lie from Judge Moore, it would have been easier to take. But it hadn't been. The lie had been carefully crafted, and must have been planned, must have been rehearsed. *We haven't planted any car bombs.*

No, you let the Navy drop them for you.

Okay, Jack. Now what the hell do you do?

He didn't know, but he had all day to worry about it.

Whatever lingering doubts they might have had were eliminated by Monday's dawn. The people who'd come into the hills hadn't left. They had spent all night at a base camp of their own, just a few klicks to the south, and Chavez could hear them blundering around now. He'd even heard a single shot, but whatever it had been aimed at wasn't a member of his squad. Maybe a deer, or whatever, maybe a guy slipped and let one go by mistake. It was ominous enough all by itself.

The squad was tucked into a tight defensive

position. The cover and concealment were good, as were the fire lanes, but best of all their position was unobvious. They'd refilled their canteens on the way and were far from a water source; anyone hunting soldiers would look for the reverse. They'd also look for a spot on higher ground, but this one was almost as good. The uphill side was dense with trees and could not be approached quietly. The reverse slope was treacherous, and other paths to the overlook point could be seen from the squad's position, allowing them to wait for their chance and move out of the way if necessary. Ramirez had a good eye for terrain. Their current mission was to avoid contact if possible; and if not, to sting and move. That also meant that Chavez and his comrades were no longer the only hunters in the woods. None of them would admit to being afraid, but the wariness factor had just doubled.

Chavez was outside the perimeter at a listening/observation post which gave him a good view of the most likely avenue of approach to the rest of the squad, and a covert path back to it, should he have to move. Guerra, the operations sergeant, was with him. Ramirez wanted both SAWs in close.

"Maybe they'll just go away," Ding thought aloud — in a whisper, really.

Guerra snorted. "I think maybe we yanked their tail one time too many, man. What we need right now's a deep hole."

"Sounds like they stopped off for lunch. Wonder how long?"

"Also sounds like they're sweeping up and down like they think they're a fucking broom. If I guess right, we'll see them over on that point, then they'll come down that little draw and head back up right in front of us."

"You may be right, Paco."

"We oughta be movin'."

"Better to do it at night," Ding replied. "Now we know what they're doing, we can keep out of their way."

"Maybe. Looks like rain, Ding. You suppose maybe they'll go home 'steada gettin' wet like us fools?"

"We'll know in an hour or two."

"It's going to blow visibility to shit, too."

"Roger that."

"There!" Guerra pointed.

"Got 'em." Chavez put his glasses on the distant treeline. He saw two of them at once, joined by six more in less than a minute. Even from a few miles away it was obvious that they were huffing and puffing. One man stopped and took a drink from a bottle — beer? Ding wondered — right out in the open, standing up like he wanted to be a target. Who were these scum? They wore ordinary clothing with no thought of camouflage, but had web gear just like Chavez. The rifles were demonstrably AK-47s, mainly folding-stock.

"Six, this is Point, over."

"Six here."

"I got eight — no, ten people carrying AKs,

half a klick east and downhill of the top of hill two-zero-one. They're not doin' much of anything at the moment, just standing there, over."

"Where are they looking, over."

"Just jerkin' off, sir. Over."

"Keep me posted," Captain Ramirez ordered.

"Roger. Out." Chavez went back to his glasses. One of them waved toward the top. Three others headed that way with a marked lack of enthusiasm.

"Wassa matta, wittle baby don wanna cwime da widdle fucking hill?" Ding asked. Though Guerra didn't know it, he was quoting his first platoon sergeant from Korea. "I think they're gettin' tired, Paco."

"Good. Maybe they'll go home."

They were tired, all right. The three took their own sweet time going up. Once there, they shouted down that they hadn't seen anyone. Below them, the others stood mostly in the clearing, just stood there like fools, Ding noted in some surprise. Confidence was a good thing in a soldier, but that wasn't confidence, and those weren't soldiers. About the time the three climbers were halfway down, clouds blotted out the sun. Almost immediately thereafter rain started to fall. A major tropical thunderstorm had built up on the western side of the mountain. Two minutes behind the rain came lightning. One bolt struck the summit, right where the climbers had been. It hung there for a surprisingly long fraction of a second like the finger of an angry god. Then others started hitting everywhere, and the rain started falling in earnest. What had been unrestricted visibility was now a radius of four hundred meters at most, expanding and contracting with the march of the opaque, wet curtains. Chavez and Guerra traded a concerned look. Their mission was look-and-listen, but now they couldn't see very far and could hear less. Worse, even after the storm passed, the ground around them would be wet. Leaves and twigs wouldn't crackle when people stepped on them. Humidity in the air would absorb sound. The inept clowns they'd been watching could therefore approach much closer to the outpost without notice. On the other hand, if the squad had to move, it could move faster with a lower risk of detection, for the same reasons. As always, the environment was neutral, giving advantage only to those who knew how to take it, and sometimes imposing the same handicaps on both sides.

The storm lasted all afternoon, dropping several inches of rain. Lightning touched down within a hundred yards of the sergeants, an experience new to both and as frightening as an artillery barrage, with its sudden burst of light and noise. After that it was just wet, cold, and miserable as the temperature dropped into the upper fifties.

"Ding, look left front," Guerra whispered urgently.

"Oh, fuck!" Chavez didn't have to ask aloud

how they'd gotten this close. With their hearing still affected by the thunder, and the whole mountain sodden, there were two men, not two hundred meters away.

"Six, this is Point, we got a pair of gomers two hundred meters southeast of us," Guerra reported to his captain. "Stand by. Over."

"Roger, standing by," Ramirez answered. "Be cool, Paco."

Guerra keyed his transmit switch by way of reply.

Chavez moved very slowly, bringing his weapon closer to a firing position, making sure the safety was on but leaving his thumb on the lever. He knew that they were the nearest thing to invisible, well concealed in ground cover and sapling trees. Each man had his war paint on, and even from fifty feet away they would look like part of the environment. They had to keep still, since the human eye is very effective at detecting movement, but as long as they did, they were invisible. This was a very practical demonstration of why the Army trained people to be disciplined. Both sergeants wished they had their camouflage fatigues, but it was a little late to worry about that, and the khaki cloth was brown with rain and mud anyway. By unspoken agreement, each man watched a discrete sector so that they wouldn't have to turn their heads very much. They knew that they could speak if they did so in whispers, but they would do so only for really important information.

"I hear something behind us," Chavez said ten minutes later.

"Better look," Guerra answered.

Ding had to take his time, over thirty seconds to rotate his body and head.

"Uh-oh." There were several men putting bedrolls down on the ground. "Stayin' for the night."

It was clear what had happened. The people they'd been watching had continued their patrol routine and ended up straddling the observation post with their night camp. They could now see or hear over twenty men.

"This is gonna be a fun night," Guerra whispered.

"Yeah, and I gotta take a leak, too." It was a feeble attempt at a joke. Ding looked up at the sky. The rainfall was down to sprinkles now, but the clouds were just as thick. It would be dark a little early, maybe in two hours.

The enemy was spread out in three groups, which wasn't entirely stupid, but each group built fires for cooking, which was. They were also noisy, talking as though they were sitting down for a meal in some village *cantina*. That was good news for Chavez and Guerra. It allowed them to use their radio again.

"Six, this is Point, over."

"Six here."

"Six, uh . . . " Chavez hesitated. "The bad guys have set up their camp all around us. They don't know we're here."

"Tell me what you want to do."

"Nothin' right now. I think maybe we can walk on out when it gets dark. We'll let you know when."

"Roger. Out."

"Walk on out?" Guerra whispered.

"No sense gettin' him all worried, Paco."

"Hey, 'mano, I'm fucking worried."

"Bein' worried don't help."

There were still no answers. Ryan left his office after what appeared to have been a normal day's work of catching up on correspondence and reports. Not much work had actually been accomplished, however. There were too many distractions that simply hadn't gone away.

He told his driver to head for Bethesda. He hadn't called ahead, but going there would not seem to be too much out of the ordinary. The security watch on the VIP suite was as strong as ever, but they all knew Ryan. The one by the door gave him a sorrowful shake of the head as he reached for the door. Ryan caught that signal clearly enough. He stopped and composed himself before going in. Greer didn't need to see shock on the faces of his visitors. But shock was what Jack felt.

He was barely a hundred pounds now, a scarecrow that had once been a man, a professional naval officer who'd commanded ships and led men in the service of their country. Fifty years of government service lay wasting away on the hospital bed. It was more than the death of a man. It was the death of an age, of a standard of behavior. Fifty years of experience and wisdom and judgment were slipping away. Jack took his seat next to the bed and waved the security officer out of the room.

"Hey, boss."

His eyes opened.

Now what do I say? How are you feeling? There's something to say to a dying man!

"How was the trip, Jack?" the voice was weak.

"Belgium was okay. Everybody sends regards. Friday I got to brief Fowler, like you did the last time."

"What do you think of him?"

"I think he needs some help on foreign policy."

A smile: "So do I. Gives a nice speech, though."

"I didn't exactly hit it off with one of his aides, Elliot, the gal from Bennington. Obnoxious as hell. If her man wins, she says, I retire." That was really the wrong thing to say. Greer tried to move but couldn't.

"Then you find her, and kiss and make up. If you have to kiss her ass at noon on the Bennington quad, you do that. When are you going to learn to bend that stiff Irish neck of yours? Ask Basil sometime how much he likes the people he has to work for. Your duty is to serve the *country*, Jack, not just the people you happen to like." A blow from a professional boxer could not have stung worse.

"Yes, sir. You're right. I still have a lot to learn."

"Learn fast, boy. I haven't got many lessons left."

"Don't say that, Admiral." The line was delivered like the plea of a child.

"It's my time, Jack. Some men I served with died off Savo Island fifty years ago, or at Leyte, or lots of other parts of ocean. I've been a lot luckier than they were, but it's my time. And it's your turn to take over for me. I want you to take my place, Jack."

"I do need some advice, Admiral."

"Colombia?"

"I could ask how you know, but I won't."

"When a man like Arthur Moore won't look you in the eye, you know that something is wrong. He was in here Saturday and he wouldn't look me in the eye."

"He lied to me today." Ryan explained on for five minutes, outlining what he knew, what he suspected, and what he feared.

"And you want to know what to do?" Greer asked.

"I could sure use a little guidance, Admiral."

"You don't need guidance, Jack. You're smart enough. You have all the contacts you need. And you know what's right."

"But what about — "

"Politics? All that shit?" Greer almost laughed. "Jack, you know, when you lay here like this, you know what you think about? You think

854

about all the things you'd like another chance at, all the mistakes, all the people you might have treated better, and you thank God that it wasn't worse. Jack, you will never regret honesty, even if it hurts people. When they made you a Marine lieutenant you swore an oath before God. I understand why we do that now. It's a help, not a threat. It's something to remind you how important words are. Ideas are important. Principles are important. Words are important. Your word is the most important of all. Your word is who you are. That's the last lesson, Jack. You have to carry on from here." He paused, and Jack could see the pain coming through the heavy medications. "You have a family, Jack. Go home to them. Give 'em my love and tell them that I think their daddy is a pretty good guy, and they ought to be proud of him. Good night, Jack." Greer drifted off to sleep.

Jack didn't get up for several minutes. It took that long for him to regain control of himself. He dried his eyes and walked out of the room. The doctor was on his way in. Jack stopped him and identified himself.

"Not much longer. Less than a week. I'm sorry, but there never was much hope."

"Keep him comfortable," Ryan said quietly. Another plea.

"We are," the oncologist replied. "That's why he's out most of the time. He's still quite lucid when he's awake. I've had some nice talks with him. I like him, too." The doctor was used to losing patients, but had never grown to enjoy it. "In a few years, we might have saved him. Progress isn't fast enough."

"Never is. Thanks for trying, doc. Thanks for caring." Ryan took the elevator back down to ground level and told the driver to take him home. On the way they passed the Mormon temple again, the marble lit with floodlights. Jack still didn't know exactly what he'd do, but now he was certain of what he had to accomplish. He'd made his silent promise to a dying man, and no promise could be more important than that.

The clouds were breaking up and there would be moonlight soon. It was time. The enemy had sentries out. They paced around the same as the ones who'd guarded the processing sites. The fires were still burning, but conversation had died off as weary men fell asleep.

"Just walk out together," Chavez said. "They see us creep or crawl, they know we're bad guys. They see us walkin', we're some of them."

"Makes sense," Guerra agreed.

Both men slung their weapons across their chests. The profile of each would be distinctively wrong to the enemy, but close up against their bodies the outlines would be obscured and the weapons could still be ready for immediate use. Ding could depend on his MP5 SD2 to kill quietly if the necessity arose. Guerra took out his machete. The metal blade was black-anodized, of course, and the only shiny part was the razor-sharp edge itself. Guerra was especially good with edged weapons, and was ever sharpening his steel. He was also ambidextrous, and held it loosely in his left hand while his right was on the pistol grip of his M-16.

The squad had already moved to a line roughly a hundred meters from the camp past which they'd be walking, ready to provide support if it were needed. It would be a tricky exercise at best, and everyone hoped that it wouldn't be necessary.

" 'kay, Ding, you lead off." Guerra actually ranked Chavez, but this was a situation where expertise counted for more than seniority.

Chavez headed down the hill, keeping to cover as long as he could, then angling left and north toward safety. His low-light goggles were in his rucksack, back at the squad's hideout because he was supposed to have been relieved before nightfall. Ding missed the night scope. A lot.

The two men moved as quietly as they could, and the soaked ground helped, but the cover got very thick along the path they took. It was only three or four hundred meters to safety, but this time it was too far.

They didn't use paths, of course, but they couldn't entirely avoid them, and one of the paths twisted around. Just as Chavez and Guerra crossed it, two men appeared a mere ten feet away.

"What are you doing out?" one asked. Chavez just waved in a friendly sort of way, hoping that the gesture would stop him, but he approached, trying to see who it was, his companion at his side. About the time he noticed that Ding was carrying the wrong sort of weapon it was too late for everyone.

Chavez had both hands back on his submachine gun, and swiveled it around on the double-looped sling, delivering a single round under the man's chin that exploded out the top of his head. Guerra turned and brought his machete around, and just like in the movies, the whole head came off. Both he and Chavez leaped to catch both victims before they made too much noise.

Shit! Ding thought. Now they'd know that somebody was here. There wasn't time to remove the bodies to a hiding place — they might bump into someone else. If that was true, he reasoned, better to get full value from the kills. He found the loose head and set it on the chest of Guerra's victim, held in both lifeless hands. The message was a clear one: *Don't fuck with us!*

Guerra nodded approval and Ding led off again. It took ten more minutes before they heard a spitting sound just to the right.

"I been watchin' ya' half of forever," *Oso* said.

"You okay?" Ramirez whispered.

"Met two guys. They're dead," Guerra said.

"Let's get moving before they find 'em."

That was not to be. A moment later they heard the thud of a falling body, followed by a shout, followed by a scream, followed by a wild burst of AK-47 fire. It went in the wrong direction, but it

858

sufficed to awaken any sleeping soul within a couple of klicks. The squad members activated their low-light gear, the better to pick their way through the cover as quickly as possible while the camp behind them exploded with noise and shouts and curses aimed in all directions. They didn't stop for two hours. It was as official as orders off their satellite net: they were now the hunted.

It had happened with unaccustomed rapidity, one hundred miles from the Cape Verde Islands. The satellite cameras had been watching for some days now, scanning the storm on several different light frequencies. The photos were downlinked to anyone with the right equipment, and already ships were altering course to get clear of it. Very hot, dry air had spilled off the West African desert in what was already a near-record summer and, driven by the easterly trade winds, combined with moist ocean air to form towering thunderheads, hundreds of them that had begun to merge. The clouds reached down into the warm surface water, drawing additional heat upward into the air to add that energy to what the clouds already contained. When some critical mass of heat and rain and cloud was reached, the storm began to organize itself. The people at the National Hurricane Center still didn't understand why it happened — or why, given the circumstances, it happened so seldom — but it was happening now. The chief scientist manipulated his computer controls to fast-forward the satellite photos, rewind, and fast-forward again. He could see it clearly. The clouds had begun their counter-clockwise orbit around a single point in space. It was becoming an organized storm, using its circular motion to increase its own coherence and power as though it knew that such activity would give it life. It wasn't the earliest that such a storm had begun, but conditions were unusually "good" this year for their formation. How lovely they appeared on the satellite photographs, like some kind of modern art, feathery pinwheels of gossamer cloud. *Or*, the chief scientist thought, *that's how they would look if they didn't kill so many people.* When you got down to it, the reason they gave the storms names was that it was unseemly for hundreds or thousands of human lives to be ended by a number. This one would be such a storm, the meteorologist thought. For the moment they'd call it a tropical depression, but if it kept growing in size and power, it would change to a tropical storm. At that point they'd start calling it *Adele*.

About the only thing that the movies got right, Clark thought, was that they often had spies meeting in bars. Bars were useful things in civilized countries. They were places for men to go and have a few, and meet other men, and strike up casual conversations in dimly lit, anonymous rooms, usually with the din of bad music to mute out their words beyond a certain, small radius.

Larson arrived a minute late, sliding up to Clark's spot. This *cantina* didn't have stools, just a real brass bar on which to rest one's foot. Larson ordered a beer, a local one, which was something the Colombians were good at. They were good at a lot of things, Clark thought. Except for the drug problem this country could really be going places. This country was suffering — as much as? No, more than his own. Colombia's government was having to face the fact that it had fought a war against the druggies and was losing . . . unlike America? the CIA officer wondered. Unlike America, the Colombian government was threatened? Yeah, sure, he told himself, we're *so* much better off than this place.

"Well?" he asked when the owner moved to the other end of the bar.

Larson spoke quietly, in Spanish. "It's definite. The number of troops the big shots have out on the street has dropped way the hell off."

"Gone where?"

"A guy told me southwest. They were talking about a hunting expedition in the hills."

"Oh, Christ," Clark muttered in English.

"What gives?"

"Well, there's about forty light-infantry soldiers . . ." he explained on for several minutes.

"We've *invaded?*" Larson looked down at the bar. "Jesus Christ, what lunatic came up with that idea?"

"We both work for him — for them, I suppose."

"Goddammit, there is one thing we cannot do to these people, and that's *fucking* it!"

"Fine. You fly back to D.C. and tell the DDO. If Ritter still has a brain, he'll pull them out quick, before anybody really gets hurt." Clark turned. He was thinking very hard at the moment, and didn't like some of the ideas he was getting. He remembered a mission in "Eye" Corps, when . . . "How about you and me take a look down that way tomorrow?"

"You really want me to blow my cover, don't you?" Larson observed.

"You got a bolt-hole?" Clark meant what every field officer sets up when he goes covert, a safe place to run to and hide in if it becomes necessary.

Larson snorted. "Is the Pope Polish?"

"What about your lady friend?"

"We don't take care of her, too, and I'm history with this outfit." The Agency encouraged loyalty to one's agents, even when one didn't sleep with them, and Larson was a man with the normal affection for his year-long lovers.

"We'll try to cover it like a prospecting trip, but after this one, on my authorization, your cover is officially blown, and you will return to D.C. for reassignment. Her, too. That's an official order."

"I didn't know you had — "

Clark smiled. "Officially I don't, but you'll soon discover that Mr. Ritter and I have an understanding. I do the field work and he doesn't

862

second-guess me."

"Nobody has that much juice." All Larson got for a reply was a raised eyebrow and a look into eyes that appeared far more dangerous than he had ever appreciated.

Cortez sat in the one decent room in the house. It was the kitchen, a large one by local standards, and he had a table on which to set his radios and his maps, and a ledger sheet on which he kept a running tally. So far he had lost eleven men in short, violent, and for the most part noiseless encounters — and gotten nothing in return. The "soldiers" he had in the field were still too angry to be afraid, but that wholly suited his purpose. There was a clear acetate cover on the main tactical map, and he used a red grease pencil to mark areas of activity. He had made contact with two — maybe three — of the American teams. He determined contact, of course, by the fact that he had lost eleven men. He chose to believe that he'd lost eleven stupid ones. That was a relative measure, of course, since luck was always a factor on the battlefield, but by and large history taught that the dumb ones die off first, that there was a Darwinian selection process on the field of combat. He planned to lose another fifty or so men before doing anything different. At that point he'd call for reinforcements, further stripping the lords of their retainers. Then he would call his boss and say that he'd identified two or three fellow lords whose men were behaving rather oddly in the field — he already knew whom he would accuse, of course — and the next day he would warn one of those — also preselected — that his own boss was behaving rather oddly, and that his — Cortez's — loyalty was to the organization as a whole which paid him, not to single personalities. His plan was for Escobedo to be killed off. It was necessary, and not especially regrettable. The Americans had already killed off two of the really smart members, and he would help to eliminate the remaining two intellects. The surviving lords would need Cortez, and would know that they needed him. His position as chief of security and intelligence would be upgraded to a seat around the table while the rest of the Cartel was restructured in accordance with his ideas for a streamlined and more secure organization. Within a year he'd be first among equals; another year and he'd merely be first. He wouldn't even have to kill the rest off. Escobedo was one of the smart ones, and he'd proven so easy to manipulate. The rest would be as children, more interested in their money and their expensive toys than with what the organization could really accomplish. His ideas in that area were vague. Cortez was not one to think ten steps ahead. Four or five were enough.

He reexamined the maps. Soon the Americans would become alert to the danger of his operation and would react. He opened his briefcase and compared aerial photographs with the maps. He now knew that the Americans had been brought in and were supported probably by a single helicopter. That was so daring as to be foolish. Hadn't the Americans learned about helicopters on the plains of Iran? He had to identify likely landing zones . . . or did he?

Cortez closed his eyes and commanded himself to return to first principles. That was the real danger in operations like this. One got so caught up in what was going on that one lost sight of the overall situation. Perhaps there was another way. The Americans had already helped him. Perhaps they might help him again. How might he bring that about? What could he do to and for them? What might they do for him? It gave him something to ponder for the rest of the sleepless night.

Bad weather had prevented them from testing out the new engine the previous night, and for the same reason they had to wait until 0300 local time to try this night. The Pave Low was not allowed to show itself by day under any circumstances, without a direct order from on high.

A cart pulled the chopper out of the hangar, and the rotor was unfolded and locked into place before the engines were started. PJ and Captain Willis applied power, with Sergeant Zimmer at his engineer's console. They taxied normally to the runway and started their takeoff in the way of helicopters, with an uneven lurch as the reluctant tons of metal and fuel climbed into the air like a child on his first ladder.

It was hard to say what happened first. A terrible screech reached the pilot's ears, coming through the protective foam of his Darth Vader helmet. At the same time, perhaps a millisecond earlier, Zimmer shouted a warning too loudly over the intercom circuit. Whatever happened first, Colonel Johns' eyes flicked down to his instrument panel and saw that his Number One engine dials were all wrong. Willis and Zimmer both killed the engine while PJ slewed the chopper around, thankful that he was only fifty feet off the pavement. In less than three seconds, he was back on the ground, powering his single working engine down to idle.

"Well?"

"The new engine, sir. It just came apart on us — looks like a total compressor failure. Sounds worse. I'm going to have to give it a look to see if it damaged anything else," Zimmer reported.

"Did you have any problem putting it in?"

"Negative. It went just like the book says, sir. That's the second time with this lot of engines, sir. The contractor's fucking up somewhere with those new composite turbine blades. That's going to down-check the whole engine run until we identify the problem, ground every bird that's using them, us, the Navy, Army, everybody." The new engine design used turbine-compressor blades made from ceramic instead of steel. It was lighter — you could carry a little more gas — and cheaper — you could buy a few more engines — than the old way, and contractor tests had shown the new version to be just as reliable — until they

866

had reached line service, that is. The first failure had been blamed on an ingested bird, but two Navy choppers using this engine had gone down at sea without a trace. Zimmer was right. Every aircraft with this engine installed would be grounded until the problem was understood and fixed.

"Oh, that's just great, Buck," Johns said. "The other spare we brought down?"

"Take a guess, sir," Zimmer suggested. "I can have 'em send us an old rebuilt one down."

"Tell me what you think."

"I think we go for a rebuilt, or maybe yank one from another bird back at Hurlburt."

"Get on the horn as soon as I cool her down," the colonel ordered. "I want *two* good engines down here ASAP."

"Yes, sir." The crewmen shared looks on the other issue. What about the people they were supposed to support?

His name was Esteves, and he, too, was a staff sergeant, Eleven-Bravo, U.S. Army. Before all this had started, he'd also been part of the recon unit of the 5th Battalion, 14th Infantry Regiment, First Brigade of the 25th "Tropical Lightning" Infantry Division (Light), based at Schofield Barracks, Hawaii. Young, tough, and proud like every other SHOWBOAT soldier, he was also tired and frustrated. And at the moment, sick. Something he'd eaten, or maybe drunk. When the time came, he'd check in with the squad medic and get some pills to handle it, but right now his bowels rumbled and his arms felt weaker than he would have liked. They'd been in the field exactly twenty-seven minutes less than Team KNIFE, but they hadn't made any contact at all since trashing that little airfield. They'd found six processing sites, four of them very recently used, but all of them devoid of people. Esteves wanted to get on the scoreboard, as he was sure the other squads were doing. Like Chavez he'd grown up in a gang area, and unlike him had been deeply involved with one until fate had shaken him loose long enough to join the Army. Also unlike Chavez, he'd once used drugs, until his sister had OD'd on a needle of overrich heroin. He'd been there, seen her life just stop as though someone had pulled the plug from a wall socket. He'd found that dealer the next night, and joined the Army to escape the murder rap, not ever thinking that he'd become a professional soldier, never dreaming that there were opportunities in life beyond car washes and family-assistance checks. He'd leapt at this chance to get even with the scum who had killed his sister and enslaved his people. But he hadn't yet killed one, hadn't yet gotten on the scoreboard. Fatigue and frustration were a deadly combination in the face of the enemy.

Finally, he thought. He saw the glow of the fire from half a klick away. He did what he was supposed to do, calling his sighting into his captain, waiting for the squad to form up in two teams, then moving in to take out the ten or so men who were doing their idiot dance in acid. Tired and eager though he was, discipline was still the central fact of his life. He led his section of two other men to a good fire-support position while the captain took charge of the assault element. The very moment he was certain that tonight would be different, it became so.

There was no bathtub, no backpacks full of leaves, but there were fifteen men with weapons. He tapped the danger signal on his radio but got no reply. Though he didn't know it, a branch had broken the antenna off his radio ten minutes earlier. He stood, trying to decide what to do, looking around for some sign, some clue, while the two soldiers at his side wondered what the hell was the matter. Then his stomach cramped up on him again. Esteves doubled over, tripped on a root, and dropped his weapon. It didn't go off, but the buttstock hit the ground hard enough that the bolt jerked back and forth one time with a metallic *clack*. That was when he discovered that twenty feet away was another man whose presence he hadn't yet detected.

This man was awake, massaging his aching calves so that he could get some sleep. He was startled by the noise. A man who liked to hunt, his first reaction was disbelief. How could anyone be out there? He'd made sure that none of his fellows had gone beyond his lookout position, but that sound was man-made and could have come only from a weapon of some sort. His team had already been warned of some brushes with — whoever the hell they were, they had killed the people who were supposed to kill them, which surprised and worried this one. The sudden noise had startled him at first, but that emotion was immediately followed by fright. He moved his rifle to his left and fired off a whole magazine. Four rounds hit Esteves, who died slowly enough to scream a curse at destiny. His two teammates hosed down the area from which the fire had come, killing the man loudly and messily, but by that time the others around the fire were up and running, and the assault element wasn't yet in place. The captain's reaction to the noise was the logical one. His support team had been ambushed, and he had to get in to the objective to take the heat off of them. The fire-support element shifted fire to the encampment, and soon learned that there were other men about. Most of them ran away from the fire and blundered into the assault element, which was racing in the opposite direction.

Had there been a proper after-action report, the first comment would have been that control was lost on both sides. The captain leading the squad had reacted precipitously, and, leading from the front instead of laying back to think about it, he was one of the first men killed. The rest of the squad was now leaderless but didn't know it. The prowess of the individual soldiers was undiminished, of course, but soldiers are first, last, always, members of teams, each a living, thinking organism whose total strength is far greater than the sum of its parts. Without leadership to direct them, they fell back on training, but that was confused by the sound and the dark. Both groups of men were now intermixed, and the Colombians' lack of training and leadership was less important now as the battle was fought by individuals on one side, and by mutually supporting pairs on the other. It lasted under five confused and bloody minutes. The pairs "won." They killed with abandon and efficiency, then crawled away, eventually rising to race to their rally point while those enemies left alive continued to shoot, mostly at each other. Only five made it to the rally point, three from the assault element and Esteves' two from the support element. Half of the squad was dead, including the captain, the medic, and the radioman. The soldiers still didn't know what they'd run into — through a communications foul-up they hadn't been warned of the Cartel's operations against them. What they did know was bad enough. They headed back to their base camp, collected their packs, and moved out.

The Colombians knew less and more. They knew that they had killed five Americans — they hadn't found Esteves yet — and that they had lost twenty-six, some of them probably to their own fire. They didn't know if any had gotten away, didn't know the strength of the unit that had attacked them, didn't even know that they had in fact been attacked by Americans at all — the weapons they recovered were mainly American, but the M-16 was popular throughout South America. They, like the men they'd chased away, knew that something terrible had happened. Mainly they grouped together and sat down and threw up and experienced postcombat shock, having learned for the first time that the mere possession of an automatic weapon didn't make one into a god. Shock was gradually replaced by rage as they collected their dead.

Team BANNER — what was left of it — didn't have that luxury. They didn't have time to think about who had won and who had lost. Each of them had learned a shocking lesson about combat. Someone with a better education might have pointed out that the world was not deterministic, but each of the five men from BANNER consoled himself with the bleakest of soldierly observations: Shit happens.

24.

Ground Rules

Clark and Larson started off well before dawn, heading south again in their borrowed Subaru four-wheel-drive wagon. In the front was a briefcase. In the back were a few boxes of rocks, under which were two Beretta automatics whose muzzles were threaded for silencers. It was a pity to abuse the guns by placing all those rocks in the same box, but neither man figured to take the weapons home after the job was completed, and both fervently hoped that they wouldn't be needed in any way.

"What exactly are we looking for?" Larson asked after an hour or so of silence.

"I was kind of hoping that you'd know. Something unusual."

"Seeing people walk around with guns down here isn't terribly unusual, in case you haven't noticed."

"Organized activity?"

"That, too, but it does give us something to think about. We won't be seeing much military activity," Larson said.

"Why?"

"Guerrillas raided a small army post again last night — heard it on the radio this morning. Either M-19 or FARC is getting frisky."

"Cortez," Clark said at once.

"Yeah, that makes sense. Pull all the official heat in a different direction."

"I'm going to have to meet that boy," Mr. Clark told the passing scenery.

"And?" Larson asked.

"And what do you think? The bastard was part of a plot to kill one of our ambassadors, the Director of the FBI, and the Administrator of DEA, plus a driver and assorted bodyguards. He's a terrorist."

"Take him back?"

"Do I look like a cop?" Clark responded.

"Look, man, we don't —"

"I do. By the way, have you forgotten those two bombs? I believe you were there."

"That was —"

"Different?" Clark chuckled. "That's what they always say, 'But that's different.' Larson, I didn't go to Dartmouth like you did, and maybe the difference is lost on me."

"This isn't the fucking movies!" Larson said angrily.

"Carlos, if this was the movies, you'd be a blond with big tits and a loose blouse. You know,

I've been in this business since you were driving cars made by Matchbox, and I've never got laid on the job. Never. Not once. Hardly seems fair." He might have added that he was married and took it seriously, but why confuse the lad? He had accomplished what he'd intended. Larson smiled. The tension was broken.

"I guess maybe I got you there, Mr. Clark."

"Where is she?"

"Gone till the end of the week — European run. I left a message in three places — I mean, *the* message for her to bug out. Soon as she gets back, she hops the next bird for Miami."

"Good. This one is complicated enough. When it's all over, marry the girl, settle down, raise a family."

"I've thought about that. What about — I mean, is it fair to — "

"The job you're in is less dangerous statistically than running a liquor store in a big city. They all raise families. What holds you together on a big job in a faraway place is the knowledge that there is somebody to come back to. You can trust me on that one, son."

"But for the moment we're in the area you want to look at. Now what do we do?"

"Start prowling the side roads. Don't go too fast." Clark cranked down his window and started smelling the air. Next he opened his briefcase and pulled out a topographical map. He grew quiet for several minutes, getting his brain in synch with the situation. There were soldiers up there, trained men in Indian country, being hunted and trying to evade contact. He had to get himself in the proper frame of mind, alternately looking at the terrain and the map. "God, I'd kill for the right kind of radio right now." *Your fault, Johnny*, Clark told himself. *You should have demanded it. You should have told Ritter that there had to be someone on the ground to liaise with the soldiers instead of trying to run it through a satellite link like it was a goddamned staff study.*

"Just to talk to them?"

"Look, kid, how much security you seen so far?"

"Why, none."

"Right. With a radio I could call them down out of the hills and we could pick them up, clean them up, and drive 'em to the fucking airport for the flight home," Clark said, the frustration manifest in his voice.

"That's craz — Jesus, you're right. This situation really is crazy." The realization dawned on Larson, and he was amazed that he'd misinterpreted the situation so completely.

"Make a note — this is what happens when you run an op out of D.C. instead of running it from the field. Remember that. You might be a supervisor someday. Ritter thinks like a spymaster instead of a line-animal like me, and he's been out of the field too long. That's the biggest problem at Langley: the guys who run the show have forgotten what it's like out here, and the rules have changed a lot since they serviced all their dead-drops in Budapest. Moreover, this is a very different situation from what they think it is. This isn't intelligence-gathering. It's low-intensity warfare. You gotta know when not to be covert, too. This sort of thing is a whole new ball game."

"They didn't cover this sort of thing at The Farm."

"That's no surprise. Most of the instructors there are a bunch of old — " Clark stopped. "Slow down some."

"What is it?"

"Stop the car."

Larson did as he was told, pulling off the gravel surface. Clark jumped out with his briefcase, which seemed very strange indeed, and took the ignition keys as he did so. His next move was open the back, then to toss the keys back to Larson. Clark dug into one of the boxes, past the samples of gold-bearing rock, and came out with his Beretta and silencer. He was wearing a bush jacket, and the gun disappeared nicely in the small of his back, silencer and all. Then he waved to Larson to stay put and follow him slowly in the car. Clark started walking with his map and a photograph in his hands. There was a bend in the road; just around it was a truck. Near the truck were some armed men. He was looking at his map when they shouted, and his head came up in obvious surprise. A man jerked his AK in a way that required no words: *Come here at once or be shot.*

Larson was overcome with the urge to wet his pants, but Clark waved for him to follow and walked confidently to the truck. Its loadbed was covered with a tarp, but Clark already knew what was under it. He'd smelled it. That was why he'd stopped around the bend.

"Good day," he said to the nearest one with a rifle.

"You have picked a bad day to be on the road, my friend."

"He told me you would be out here. I have permission," Clark replied.

"What? Permission? Whose permission?"

"Señor Escobedo, of course," Larson heard him say.

Jesus, this isn't happening, please tell me this isn't happening!

"Who are you?" the man said with a mixture of anger and wariness.

"I am a prospector. I am looking for gold. Here," Clark said, turning his photo around. "This area I have marked, I think there is gold here. Of course I would not come here without permission of Señor Escobedo, and he told me to tell those I met that I am here under his protection."

"Gold — you look for gold?" another man said as he came up. The first one deferred to him, and Clark figured he was talking to the boss now.

"*Sí.* Come, I will show you." Clark led them to the back of the Subaru and pulled two rocks from the cardboard box. "My driver there is Señor

Larson. He introduced me to Señor Escobedo. If you know Señor Escobedo — you must know him, no?"

The man clearly didn't know what to do or think. Clark was speaking in good Spanish, with a trace of accent, and talking as normally as though he were asking directions from a policeman.

"Here, you see this?" Clark said, pointing to the rock. "That is gold. This may be the biggest find since Pizarro. I think Señor Escobedo and his friends will buy all of this land."

"They did not tell me of this," the man temporized.

"Of course. It is a secret. And I must warn you, señor, not to speak of it to anyone or you will surely speak to Señor Escobedo!"

Bladder control was a major problem for Larson now.

"When are we leaving?" someone called from the truck.

Clark looked around while the two gunmen tried to decide what to do. A driver and perhaps one other in the truck. He didn't hear or see anyone else. He started walking toward it. Two more steps and he saw what he'd needed and feared to see. Sticking out from under the edge of the tarp was the front sight assembly of an M-16A2 rifle. What he had to do was decided in less than a second. Even to Clark it was amazing how the old habits kept coming back.

"Stop!" the leader said.

"Can I load my samples on your truck?" Clark asked without turning. "To take to Señor Escobedo? He will be very pleased to see what I have found, I promise you," Clark added.

The two men ran to catch up with him, their rifles dangling from their hands as they did so. They'd gotten within ten feet when he turned. As he did so, his right hand remained fixed in space, and took the Beretta from his waistband while his left hand fluttered the map and photo. Neither one saw it coming, Larson realized. He was so smooth. . . .

"Not this truck, señor, I — "

It was just one more thing to surprise him, but it would be the last. Clark's hand came up and fired into the man's forehead at a range of five feet. Before the leader had even started to fall, the second was also dead from the same cause. Without pause he moved around the right side of the truck. He hopped up on the running board and saw that there was just a driver. He, too, took a silenced round in the head. By this time Larson was out of the car. Approaching Clark from the rear, he came close to getting a round for his trouble.

"Don't do that!" Clark said as he safed his pistol.

"Christ, I just — "

"You announce your presence in a situation like this. You almost died 'cause you didn't. Remember that. Come on." Clark hopped onto the back of the truck and pulled back the tarp.

Most of the dead were locals, judging by their clothes, but there were two faces that Clark vaguely recognized. It took a moment for him to remember. . . .

"Captain Rojas. Sorry, kid," he said quietly to the body.

"Who?"

"He had command of Team BANNER. One of ours. These fuckers killed some of our people." His voice seemed quite tired.

"Looks like our guys did all right, too — "

"Let me explain something to you about combat, kid. There are two kinds of people in the field: your people and other people. The second category can include noncombatants, and you try to avoid hurting them if you have the time, but the only ones who really matter are your own people. You got a handkerchief?"

"Two."

"Give 'em to me, then load those two in the truck."

Clark pulled the cap of the gas tank that hung under the cab. He tied the handkerchiefs together and fed them in. The tank was full and the cloth was immediately saturated with gasoline.

"Come on, back to the car." Clark disassembled his pistol and put it back in the rock box, then closed the back hatch and got back into the front seat. He punched the cigarette lighter. "Pull up close."

Larson did so, getting there about the time the lighter popped out. Clark took it out and touched

881

it to the soaked handkerchiefs. They ignited at once. Larson didn't have to be told to take off. They were around the next bend before the fire started in earnest.

"Back to the city, fast as you can," Clark ordered next. "What's the fastest way to get to Panama?"

"I can have you there in a couple of hours, but it means — "

"Do you have the radio codes to get onto an Air Force base?"

"Yes, but — "

"You are now out of country. Your cover is completely blown," Mr. Clark said. "Get a message to your girl before she gets back. Have her desert, or jump ship, or whatever you call it with an airline so that she doesn't have to come back here. She's blown, too. Both your lives are in danger — no-shit danger. There might have been somebody watching us. Somebody might have noticed that you drove me down here. Somebody might have noticed that you borrowed this car twice. Probably not, but you don't get old in this business by taking unnecessary chances. You have nothing more to contribute to this operation, so get your asses clear."

"Yes, sir." They reached the highway before Larson spoke again. "What you did . . . "

"What about it?"

"You were right. We can't let people do that and — "

"You're wrong. You don't know why I did

that, do you?" Clark asked. He spoke like a man teaching a class, but gave only one of the reasons. "You're thinking like a spy, and this is no longer an intelligence operation. We have people, soldiers, running and hiding up in those hills. What I did was to create a *diversion*. If they think our guys came down to avenge their dead, it may pull some of the bad guys down off the mountain, get them to look in the wrong place, take some of the heat off our guys. Not much, but it's the best I could do." He paused for a moment. "I won't say it didn't feel good. I don't like seeing our people killed, and I fucking well don't like not being allowed to do anything about it. That's been happening for too many years — Middle East, everywhere — we lose people and don't do a goddamned thing about it. This time I just had an excuse. It's been a long time. And you know something — it *did* feel good," Clark admitted coldly. "Now shut up and drive. I have some thinking to do."

Ryan was in his office, still quiet, still thinking. Judge Moore was finding all sorts of excuses to be away. Ritter was spending a lot of time out of the office. Jack couldn't ask questions and demand answers if they weren't here. That also made Ryan the senior executive present, and gave him all sorts of extraneous paper to shuffle and telephone calls to return. Maybe he could make that work for him. Of one thing he was certain. He had to find out what the hell was happening. It was also plain that Moore and Ritter had made two mistakes of their own. First, they thought that Ryan didn't know anything. They ought to have known better. He'd only gotten this far in the Agency because he was good at figuring things out. Their second mistake was in their likely assumption that his inexperience would prevent him from pressing too hard even if he did start figuring things out. Fundamentally they were both thinking like bureaucrats. People who spent their lives in bureaucracies were typically afraid of breaking rules. That was a sure way to get fired, and it cowed people to think of tossing their careers away. But that was an issue Jack had decided on long before. He didn't know what his profession was. He'd been a Marine, a stockbroker, an assistant professor of history, and then joined CIA. He could always go back to teaching. The University of Virginia had already talked to Cathy about becoming a full professor at their medical school, and even Jeff Pelt wanted Ryan to come and liven up the history department as a visiting lecturer. It would be nice to teach again, Jack thought. It would certainly be easier than what he was doing here. Whatever he saw in his future, he didn't feel trapped by his job. And James Greer had given him all the guidance he needed: *Do what you think is right.*

"Nancy." Jack keyed his intercom. "When is Mr. Ritter going to be back?"

"Tomorrow morning. He had to meet with somebody down at The Farm."

"Okay, thanks. Could you call my wife and leave a message that I'm going to be pretty late tonight?"

"Surely, Doctor."

"Thanks. I need the file on INF verification, the OSWR preliminary report."

"Dr. Molina is out at Sunnyvale with the Judge," Nancy said. Tom Molina was the head of the Office of Strategic Weapons Research, which was back-checking two other departments on the Intermediate Nuclear Forces Treaty verification procedures.

"I know. I just want to look the report over so I can discuss it with him when he gets back."

"Take about fifteen minutes to get it."

"No rush," Jack replied and killed the intercom. That document could tie up King Solomon himself for three days, and it gave him a wholly plausible excuse for staying late. Congress had gotten antsy about some technical issues as both sides worked to destroy the last of their launchers. Ryan and Molina would have to testify there in the next week. Jack pulled the writing panel out from the side of his desk, knowing what he'd do after Nancy and the other clerical people left.

Cortez was a very sophisticated political observer. That was one reason he'd made colonel so young in an organization as bureaucratized as the DGI. Based on the Soviet KGB model, it had already grown a collection of clerks and inspectors and security officers to make the American

CIA look like a mom-and-pop operation — which made the relative efficiencies of the agencies all the more surprising. For all their advantages, the Americans lacked political will, always fighting over issues that ought to have been quite clear. At the KGB Academy, one instructor had compared them to the Polish parliament of old, a collection of over five hundred barons, *all* of whom had had to agree before anything happened — and because of which nothing ever happened, allowing Poland to be raped by anyone with the ability to make a simple decision.

The Americans had acted in this case, however, acted decisively and well. What had changed?

What had changed — what had to have changed in this case — was that the Americans were breaking their own laws. They had responded emotionally . . . no, that wasn't fair, Félix told himself. They had responded forcefully to a direct and arrogant challenge, just as the Soviets would have reacted, though with minor tactical differences. The emotional aspect to the reaction was that they had done the proper thing only by violating their incredible intelligence-oversight laws. And it was an election year in America. . . .

"Ah," Cortez said aloud. It really was that simple, wasn't it? The Americans, who had already helped him, would do so again. He just had to identify the proper target. That took only ten minutes more. So fitting, he thought, that his military rank had been that of colonel. For a century of Latin American history, it was always the colonels who did this sort of thing.

What would Fidel say? Cortez nearly laughed out loud at the thought. For as long as that bearded ideologue had breathed, he'd hated the *norteamericanos* as an evangelist hated sin, enjoyed every small sting he'd been able to inflict on them, dumped his criminals and lunatics on the unsuspecting Carter — *Anyone could have taken advantage of that fool,* Cortez thought with amusement — played every possible gambit of guerrilla diplomacy against them. He really would have enjoyed this one. Now Félix just had to figure a way to pass the message along. It was a high-risk play on his part, but he'd won every toss to this point, and the dice were hot in his hand.

Perhaps it had been a mistake, Chavez reflected. Perhaps leaving the head on the man's chest had merely enraged them. Whatever the cause, the Colombians were prowling the woods with gusto now. They hadn't caught Team KNIFE's trail, and the soldiers were working very hard not to leave one, but one thing was clear to him: there would be a knock-down, drag-out firefight, and it wouldn't be long in coming.

But that wasn't clear to Captain Ramirez. His orders were still to evade and avoid, and he was following them. Most of the men didn't question that, but Chavez did — or more precisely, wanted to. But sergeants don't question captains, at least not very often, and then only if you were a first sergeant and had the opportunity to take the man aside. If there was going to be a fight, and it sure as hell looked that way, why not set it up on favorable terms? Ten good men, armed with automatic weapons and grenades, plus two SAWs, made for one hell of an ambush. Give them a trail to follow, lead them right into the killzone. They were still carrying a couple of claymores. With luck, they'd drop ten or fifteen men in the first three seconds. Then the other side — those few who ran away fast enough — wouldn't be pissed. They'd be pissing in their pants. Nobody would be crazy about hot pursuit then. Why didn't Ramirez see that? Instead he was keeping everyone on the move, wearing them out, not looking for a good place to rest up, prepare a major ambush, duke it out, and *then* take off again. There was a time for caution. There was a time to fight. What that most favored word in any military lexicon, "initiative," meant was who did the deciding on which time was which. Chavez knew it on instinct. Ramirez, he suspected, was thinking too much. About what, Chavez didn't know, but the captain's thinking was starting to worry the sergeant.

Larson returned the car and drove Clark to the airport in his own BMW. He'd miss the car, he realized, as they walked to his aircraft. Clark was carrying all of his classified or sensitive equipment out with him, and nothing else. He hadn't stopped to pack, not even his razor, though his

Beretta 92-F, with silencer, was again tucked into the small of his back. He walked coolly and normally, but Larson now knew what tension looked like in Mr. Clark. He appeared even more relaxed than usual, even more offhand, even more absentminded, all the more to appear harmless to the people around him. This, Larson told himself, was one very dangerous cat. The pilot played back the shooting at the truck, the way he'd put the two gunmen at ease, confused them, asked for their help. He'd never known that the Agency had people like this, not after the Church Committee hearings.

Clark climbed up into the aircraft, tossing his gear in the back, and managed to look a little impatient as Larson ran through his preflight procedures. He didn't return to normal until the wheels were retracted.

"How long to Panama?"

"Two hours."

"Take us out over the water as soon as you can."

"You're nervous?"

"Now — only about your flying," Clark said over his headset. He looked over and smiled. "What I'm worried about is thirty or so kids who may just be hung out to dry."

Forty minutes later they left Colombian airspace. Once over the Bay of Panama, Clark reached back for his gear, then forced open the door and dumped it into the sea.

"You mind if I ask . . . ?"

"Let's assume for the moment that this whole operation is coming apart. Just how much evidence do you want to be carrying into the Senate hearing room?" Clark paused. "Not much danger of that, of course, but what if people see us carrying stuff and wonder what it is and why we're carrying it?"

"Oh. Okay."

"Keep thinking, Larson. Henry Kissinger said it: Even paranoids have enemies. If they're willing to hang those soldiers out, what about us?"

"But . . . Mr. Ritter — "

"I've known Bob Ritter for quite a while. I have a few questions for him. I want to see if he has good enough answers. It's for goddamned sure he didn't keep us informed of things we needed to know. Maybe that's just another example of D.C. perspective. Then again, maybe it's not."

"You don't really think — "

"I don't know what to think. Call in," Clark ordered. There was no sense getting Larson thinking about it. He hadn't been in the Agency long enough to understand the issues.

The pilot nodded and did what he was told. He switched his radio over to a seldom-used frequency and began transmitting. "Howard Approach, this is special flight X-Ray Golf Whiskey Delta, requesting permission to land, over."

"Whiskey Delta, this is Howard Approach, stand by," replied some faceless tower controller, who then checked his radio codes. He didn't know who XGWD was, but those letters were on his "hot" list. CIA, he thought, or some other agency that put people where they didn't belong, which was all he needed to know. "Whiskey Delta, squawk one-three-one-seven. You are cleared for a direct visual approach. Winds are one-nine-five at ten knots."

"Roger, thank you. Out." At least one thing had gone well today, Larson thought. Ten minutes later he put the Beech on the ground and followed a jeep to a parking place on the ramp. Air Force Security Police were waiting for them there, and whisked both officers over to Base Operations. The base was on security-alert drill; everyone was wearing green and most had sidearms. This included the operations staff, most of whom were in flight suits to look militant.

"Next flight stateside?" Clark asked a young female captain. Her uniform "poopy suit" bore the silver wings of a pilot, and Clark wondered what she flew.

"We have a -141 inbound to Charleston," she replied. "But if you want to get on it — "

"Young lady, check your ops orders for this." Clark handed over his "J. T. Williams" passport. "In the SI section," he added helpfully.

The captain rose from her seat and pulled open the top drawer of her classified file cabinet, the one with the double combination lock. She extracted a red-bordered ring binder and flipped to the last divider. This was the "Special Intelligence" section, which identified certain things and people that were more closely guarded than mere "top" secrets. It took only a couple of seconds before she returned.

"Thank you, Colonel Williams. The flight leaves in twenty minutes. Is there anything that you and your aide require, sir?"

"Have Charleston arrange to have a puddle-jumper standing by to take us to D.C., if you would, please, Captain. Sorry to have to drop in on you so unexpectedly. Thank you for your assistance."

"Any time, sir," she replied, smiling at this polite colonel.

"Colonel?" Larson asked on the way out the door.

"Special Ops, no less. Pretty good for a beat-up old chief bosun's mate, isn't it?" A jeep had them to the Lockheed Starlifter in five minutes. The tunnel-like cargo compartment was empty. This was an Air Force Reserve flight, the load-master explained. They dropped some cargo off but were deadheading back home. That was fine with Clark, who stretched out as soon as the bird lifted off. It was amazing, he thought as he dozed off, all the things his countrymen did well. You could transition from being in mortal danger to being totally safe in a matter of hours. The same country that put people into the field and failed to support them properly treated them like VIPs — so long as they had the right ID notification in the right book, as though that could make it all better. It was crazy, the things we could do, and the things we couldn't. A moment later he was snoring next to an amazed Carlos Larson. He didn't wake until just before the landing, five hours later.

As with any other government agency, CIA had regular business hours. By 3:30, those who came in early on "flex-time" were already filing out to beat the traffic, and by 5:30 even the seventh floor was quiet. Outside Jack's office, Nancy Cummings put the cover over her IBM typewriter — she used a word processor, too, but Nancy still liked typewriters — and hit a button on her intercom.

"Anything else you need me for, Dr. Ryan?"

"No, thank you. See you in the morning."

"Okay, Good night, Dr. Ryan."

Jack turned in his chair, back to staring out at the trees that walled the complex off from outside view. He was trying to think, but his mind was a blank void. He didn't know what he'd find. Part of him hoped that he'd find nothing. He knew that what he would do was going to cost him his career at the Agency, but he didn't really give much of a damn anymore. If this was what his job required, then the job wasn't really worth having, was it?

But what would the Admiral say about that?

Jack didn't have that answer. He pulled a paperback out of his desk drawer and started reading. A few hundred pages later it was seven o'clock.

Time. Ryan lifted his phone and called the floor security desk. When the secretaries were gone home, it was the security guys who ran errands.

"This is Dr. Ryan. I need some documents from central files." He read off three numbers. "They're big ones," he warned the desk man. "Better take somebody else to help."

"Yes, sir. We'll head down in a minute."

"Not that much of a hurry," Ryan said as he hung up. He already had a reputation as an easygoing boss. As soon as the phone was back in its cradle, he jumped to his feet and switched on his personal Xerox machine. Then he walked out his door to Nancy's outer office space, listening for the diminishing sound of the two security officers walking out to the main corridor.

They didn't lock office doors up here. There was no point. You had to pass through about ten security zones to get here, each guarded by armed officers, each supervised by a separate central security office on the first floor. There were also roving patrols. Security at CIA was tighter than at a federal prison, and about as oppressive. But it didn't really apply to the senior executives, and all Jack had to do was walk across the corridor and open the door to Bob Ritter's office.

The DDO's office safe — vault was a better term — was set up the same way as Ryan's, behind a false panel in the wall. It was less for secrecy — any competent burglar would find it in under a minute — than for aesthetics. Jack opened the panel and dialed the combination for the safe. He wondered if Ritter knew that Greer had the combination. Perhaps he did, but certainly he didn't know that the Admiral had written it down. It was so odd a thing for the Agency, so odd that no one had ever considered the possibility. The smartest people in the world still had blind spots.

The safe doors were all alarmed, of course. The alarm systems were foolproof, and worked the same way as the safety locks on nuclear weapons — and they were the best kind available, weren't they? You dialed in the right combination or the alarm went off. If you goofed doing it the first time, a light would go on above the dial, indicating that you had ten seconds to get it right or another light would go on at two separate security desks. A second goof would set off more alarms. A third would put the safe in lock-down for two hours. Several CIA executives had learned to curse the system and become the subject of jokes in the security department. But not Ryan, who was not intimidated by combination locks. The computer that kept track of such things decided that, well, it must be Mr. Ritter, and that was that.

Jack's heart beat faster now. There were over twenty files in here, and his time was measured in minutes. But again Agency procedures came to his rescue. Inside the front cover of each file was a summary sheet telling what "Operation

WHATEVER" was all about. He didn't really pay attention to what they said, but used the summary sheets only to identify items of interest. In less than two minutes, Jack had files labeled EAGLE EYE, SHOWBOAT-I and SHOWBOAT-II, CAPER, and RECIPROCITY. The total stack was nearly eighteen inches high. Jack made careful note of where the folders went, then closed the safe door without locking it. Next he returned to his office, setting the papers on the floor behind his desk. He started reading EAGLE EYE first of all.

"Holy Christ!" "Detection and interdiction of incoming drug flight," he saw, meant . . . shooting them down. Someone knocked on his door.

"Come on in." It was the security guys with the files he'd requested. Ryan had them set the files on a chair and dismissed them. Jack figured he had an hour, two at most, to do what he had to do. That meant he had time to scan, not to read. Each operation had a more detailed summary of objectives and methods plus an event log and daily progress report. Jack's personal Xerox machine was a big, sophisticated one that organized and collated sheets, and most importantly, zipped them through very rapidly. He started feeding sheets into the hopper. The automatic feed allowed him to read and copy at the same time. Ninety minutes later he had copied over six hundred sheets, maybe a quarter of what he'd taken. It wasn't enough, but it would have to do. He summoned the security guards to return the files they'd brought up — he took the time to ruffle them up first. As soon as they were gone, he assembled the files he'd . . .

. . . stolen? Jack asked himself. It suddenly dawned on him that he'd just violated the law. He hadn't thought of that. He really hadn't. As he loaded the files back in the safe, Ryan told himself that really he hadn't violated anything. As a senior executive, he was entitled to know these things, and the rules didn't *really* apply to him . . . but that, he remembered, was a dangerous way to think. He was serving a higher cause. He was doing What Was Right. He was —

"Shit!" Ryan said aloud when he closed the safe door. "You don't know what the hell you're doing." He was back in his office a minute later.

It was time to leave. First he made a notation on the Xerox count sheet. You didn't make Xerox copies anywhere in this building without signing off for them, but he'd thought ahead on that. Roughly the right number of sheets were assembled in a pile and placed in his safe, ostensibly a copy of the OSWR report that Nancy had retrieved. Making such copies was something that directorate chiefs were allowed to do fairly freely. Inside his safe, he found, was the manual for its operation. The copies he'd made went into his briefcase. The last thing Ryan did before leaving was to change his combination to something nobody would ever guess. He nodded to the security officer at the desk next to the elevator on his way out. The Agency Buick was waiting when he got to the basement garage.

"Sorry to make you stay in so late, Fred," Jack said as he got in. Fred was his evening driver.

"No problem, sir. Home?"

"Right." It required all of his discipline not to start reading on the way. Instead he leaned back and commanded himself to take a nap. It would be the only sleep he would get tonight, he was sure.

Clark got into Andrews just after eight. His first call was to Ritter's office, but it was short-stopped elsewhere and he learned that the DDO was unavailable until morning. With nothing better to do, Clark and Larson checked into a motel near the Pentagon. After picking up shaving gear and a toothbrush from the Marriott's gift shop, Clark again went to sleep, again surprising the younger officer, who was far too keyed up to do so.

"How bad is it?" the President asked.

"We've lost nine people," Cutter replied. "It was inevitable, sir. We knew going in that this was a dangerous operation. So did they. What we can do —"

"What we can do is shut this operation down, and do it at once. And keep a nice tight lid on it forever. This one never happened. I didn't bargain for any of this, not for the civilian casualties, and sure as hell not for losing nine of our own people. Damn it, Admiral, you told me that these kids were so good — "

"Mr. President, I never — "

"The hell you didn't!" the President said loudly enough to startle the Secret Service agent outside his upstairs office. "How the hell did you get me into this mess?"

Cutter's patrician face went pale as a corpse. Everything he'd worked for, the action he'd been proposing for three years. . . . Ritter was proclaiming success. That was the maddest part of all.

"Sir, our objective was to hurt the Cartel. We have accomplished that. The CIA officer who's running RECIPROCITY, in Colombia, right now, said that he could start a gang war within the Cartel — and we have done just that! They just tried to assassinate one of their own people — Escobedo. Drug shipments coming in are down. We haven't announced it yet, but the papers are already talking about how prices are going up on the street. We're winning."

"Fine. You tell Fowler that!" The President slammed a file folder down on his desk. His own private polls showed Fowler ahead by fourteen points.

"Sir, after the convention, the opposition candidate always — "

"Now you're giving me political advice? Mister, you haven't shown me a hell of a lot of competence in your supposed area of expertise."

"Mr. President, I — "

"I want this whole thing shut down. I want it

kept quiet. I want you to do it, and I want you to do it fast. This is your mess and you will clean it up."

Cutter hesitated. "Sir, how do you want me to go about it?"

"I don't want to know. I just want to know when it's done."

"Sir, that may mean that I'll have to disappear for a while."

"Then *disappear!*"

"People might notice."

"Then you are on a special, classified mission for the President. Admiral, I want this thing closed out. I don't care what you have to do. Just do it!"

Cutter came to attention. He still remembered how to do that. "Yes, Mr. President."

"Reverse your rudder," Wegener said. USCGC *Panache* pivoted with the change of rudder and engine settings, pointing herself down the channel.

"Midships."

"Rudder amidships, aye. Sir, my rudder is amidships," the young helmsman announced under the watchful eye of Master Chief Quartermaster Oreza.

"Very well. All ahead one-third, steady up on course one-nine-five." Wegener looked at the junior officer of the deck. "You have the conn. Take her out."

"Aye aye, sir, I have the conn," the ensign

acknowledged in some surprise. "Take her out" generally means that you start from the dock, but the skipper was unusually cautious today. The kid on the wheel could handle it from here. Wegener lit his pipe and headed out for the bridge wing. Portagee followed him there.

"That's about as happy as I've ever been to head out to sea," Wegener said.

"I know what you mean, Cap'n."

It had been one scary day. Only one, but that had been enough. The FBI agent's warning had come as quite a shock. Wegener had grilled his people one by one — something that he'd found as distasteful as it had been unfruitful — to find out who had spilled the beans. Oreza thought he knew but wasn't sure. He was thankful that he'd never have to be. That danger had died with the pirates in Mobile jail. But both men had learned their lesson. From now on they'd abide by the rules.

"Skipper, why d'ya suppose that FBI guy warned us?"

"That's a good question, Portagee. It figures that what we choked out of the bastards turned that money seizure they pulled off. I guess they figured they owed us some. Besides, the local guy says that it was his boss in Washington who ordered him to warn us."

"I think we owe him one," Oreza said.

"I think you're right." Both men stayed out to savor yet another sunset at sea, and *Panache* took a heading of one-eight-one, heading for her patrol station in the Yucatan Channel.

Chavez was down to his last set of batteries. The situation, if anything, had gotten worse. There was a group somewhere behind them, necessitating a rear guard. It was something that he, on point, couldn't concern himself about, but it was there, a nagging concern as real as the sore muscles that had him popping Tylenol every few hours. Maybe they were being followed. Maybe it was just accidental — or maybe Ramirez had gotten predictable in his evasion tactics. Chavez didn't think so, but he was becoming too tired to think coherently, and knew it. Maybe the captain had the same problem, he realized. That was especially worrisome. Sergeants were paid to fight. Captains were paid to think. But if Ramirez was too tired to do that, then they might as well not have him.

Noise. A whisper from a branch swishing through the air. But there was no wind blowing at the moment. Maybe an animal. Maybe not.

Chavez stopped. He held his hand straight up. Vega, walking slack fifty meters back, relayed the signal. Ding moved alongside a tree and stayed standing for the best possible visibility. He started to lean against it and found himself drifting. The sergeant shook his head to clear it. Fatigue was really getting to him now.

There. Movement. It was a man. Just a spectral green shape, barely more than a stick figure on the goggle display, nearly two hundred meters to Ding's right front. He was moving uphill and — another one, about twenty meters behind. They were moving like . . . soldiers, with the elaborate footwork that looked so damned crazy when somebody else was doing it. . . .

There was one way to check. On the bottom side of his PVS-7 goggles was a small infrared light for use in reading maps. Invisible to the human eye, it would show up like a beacon to anyone wearing another PVS-7. He didn't even have to make a noise. They'd be looking around constantly.

It was still a risk, of course.

Chavez stepped away from the tree. It was too far to see if they were wearing their headsets, if they were. . . .

Yes. The lead figure was turning his head left and right. It stopped dead on where Chavez was standing. Ding tipped his goggles up to expose the IR light and blinked it three times. He dropped his night scope back into place just in time to see the other one do the same.

"I think they're our guys," Chavez whispered into his radio mike.

"Then they're pretty lost," Ramirez replied through his earpiece. "Be careful, Sergeant."

Click-Click. Okay.

Chavez waited for *Oso* to set his SAW up in a convenient place, then walked toward the other man, careful to keep where Vega could cover him. It seemed an awfully long way to walk, farther still without being able to put his weapon on the target, but he couldn't exactly do that, could he? He spotted one more, and there would be others out there also, watching him over the sights of their weapons. If that wasn't a friendly, his chances of seeing the sunrise were somewhere between zero and not much.

"Ding, is that you?" a whisper called the remaining ten meters. "It's León."

Chavez nodded. Both men took very deep breaths as they walked together and hugged. Somehow a handshake just wasn't enough under the circumstances.

"You're lost, 'Berto."

"No shit, man. I know where the fuck we are, but we're fucking lost all right."

"Where's Cap'n Rojas?"

"Dead. Esteves, Delgado, half the team."

"Okay. Hold it." Ding punched his radio button. "Six, this is Point. We just made contact with BANNER. They've had a little trouble, sir. You better get up here."

Click-click.

León waved for his men to come in. Chavez didn't even think to count. It was enough to see that half weren't there. Both men sat on a fallen tree.

"What happened?"

"We walked right into it, man. Thought it was a processing site. It wasn't. Musta been thirty-forty guys there. I think Esteves fucked up and it all came apart. Like a bar fight with guns, man. Then Captain Rojas went down, and — it was pretty bad, *'mano*. Been on the run ever since."

"We got people chasing us, too."

"What's the good news?" León asked.

"I ain't heard any lately, 'Berto," Ding said. "I think it's time for us to get our asses outa this place."

"Roge-o," Sergeant León said just as Ramirez appeared. He made his report to the captain.

"Cap'n," Chavez said when he was finished, "we're all pretty beat. We need a place to belly up."

"The man's right," Guerra agreed.

"What about behind us?"

"They ain't heard nothin' in two hours, sir," Guerra reminded him. "That knoll over there looks like a good spot to me." That was about as hard as he could press his officer, but finally it was enough.

"Take the men up. Set up the perimeter and two outposts. We'll try to rest up till sundown, and maybe I can call in and get us some help."

"Sounds good to me, Cap'n." Guerra took off to get things organized. Chavez left at once to sweep the area while the rest of the squad moved to its new RON site — except, Chavez thought, this was an ROD — remain-over-day — site. It was a bleak attempt at humor, but it was all he could manage under the circumstances.

"My God," Ryan breathed. It was four in the morning, and he was awake only because of coffee and apprehension. Ryan had uncovered his

905

share of things with the Agency. But never anything like this. The first thing he had to do was . . . what?

Get some sleep, even a few hours, he told himself. Jack lifted the phone and called the office. There was always a watch officer on duty.

"This is Dr. Ryan. I'm going to be late. Something I ate. I've been throwing up all night . . . no, I think it's over now, but I need a few hours of sleep. I'll drive myself in tomorr — today," he corrected himself. "Yeah, that's right. Thanks. 'Bye."

He left a note on the refrigerator door for his wife and crawled into a spare bed to avoid disturbing her.

Passing the message was the easiest part for Cortez. It would have been hard for anyone else, but one of the first things he'd done after joining the Cartel was to get a list of certain telephone numbers in the Washington, D.C., area. It hadn't been hard. As with any task, it was just a matter of finding someone who knew what you needed to know. That was something Cortez excelled at. Once he had the list of numbers — it had cost him $10,000, the best sort of money well spent, that is to say, someone's else's well-spent money — it was merely a matter of knowing schedules. That was tricky, of course. The person might not be there, which risked disclosure, but the right sort of eyes-only prefix would probably serve to warn off the casual viewer. The secretaries of such people typically were disciplined people who risked their jobs when they showed too much curiosity.

But what really made it easy was a new bit of technology, the facsimile printer. It was a brand-new status symbol. Everyone had to have one, just as everyone, especially the important, had to have a direct private telephone line that bypassed his secretary. That and the fax went together. Cortez had driven to Medellín to his private office and typed the message himself. He knew what official U.S. government messages looked like, of course, and did his best to reproduce it here. EYES-ONLY NIMBUS was the header, and the name in the FROM slot was bogus, but that in the TO place was quite genuine, which ought to have been sufficient to get the attention of the addressee. The body of the message was brief and to the point, and indicated a coded reply-address. How would the addressee react? Well, there was no telling, was there? But this, too, Cortez felt was a good gamble. He inserted the single sheet in his fax, dialed the proper number, and waited. The machine did the rest. As soon as it heard the warbling electronic love-call of another fax machine, it transmitted the message form. Cortez removed the original and folded it away into his wallet.

The addressee turned in surprise when he heard the whir of his fax printing out a message. It had to be official, because only half a dozen people knew that private line. (It never occurred to him that the telephone company's computer knew about it, too.) He finished what he was doing before reaching over for the message.

What the hell is NIMBUS? he wondered. Whatever it was, it was eyes-only to him, and therefore he started to read the message. He was sipping his third cup of morning coffee while he did so, and was fortunate that his cough deposited some of it onto his desk and not his trousers.

Cathy Ryan was nothing if not punctual. The phone in the guest room rang at precisely 8:30. Jack's head jerked off the pillow as though from an electric shock, and his hand reached out to grab the offensive instrument.

"Hello?"

"Good morning, Jack," his wife said brightly. "What's the problem with you?"

"I had to stay up late with some work. Did you take the other thing with you?"

"Yes, what's the — "

Jack cut her off. "I know what it says, babe. Could you just make the call? It's important." Dr. Caroline Ryan was also bright enough to catch the meaning of what he said.

"Okay, Jack. How do you feel?"

"Awful. But I have work to do."

"So do I, honey. 'Bye."

"Yeah." Jack hung up and commanded himself to get out of the bed. First a shower, he told himself.

Cathy was on her way to Surgery, and had to hurry. She lifted her office phone and called the proper number on the hospital's D.C. line. It rang only once.

"Dan Murray."

"Dan, this is Cathy Ryan."

"Morning! What can I do for you this fine day, Doctor?"

"Jack said to tell you that he'd be in to see you just after ten. He wants you to let him park in the drive-through, and he said to tell you that the folks down the hall aren't supposed to know. I don't know what that means, but that's what he told me to say." Cathy didn't know whether to be amused or not. Jack did like to play funny little games — she thought they were pretty dumb little games — with people who shared his clearances, and wondered if this was some sort of joke or not. Jack especially liked to play games with his FBI friend.

"Okay, Cath', I'll take care of that."

"I have to run off to fix somebody's eyeball. Say hi to Liz for me."

"Will do. Have a good one."

Murray hung up with a puzzled look on his face. *Folks down the hall aren't supposed to know.* "The folks down the hall" was a phrase Murray had used the first time they'd met, in St. Thomas's Hospital in London when Dan had been the legal attaché at the U.S. Embassy on

Grosvenor Square. The folks down the hall were CIA.

But Ryan was one of the top six people at Langley, arguably one of the top three.

What the hell did that mean?

"Hmph." He called his secretary and had her notify the security guards to allow Ryan into the driveway that passed under the main entrance to the Hoover Building. Whatever it meant, he could wait.

Clark arrived at Langley at nine that morning. He didn't have a security pass — not the sort of thing you carry into the field — and had to use a code-word to get through the main gate, which seemed very conspiratorial indeed. He parked in the visitors' lot — CIA has one of those — and walked in the main entrance, heading immediately to the left where he quickly got what looked like a visitor's badge which, however, worked just fine in the electronically controlled gates. Now he angled off to the right, past the wall murals that looked as though some enormous child had daubed mud all over the place. The decorator for this place, Clark was sure, had to have been a KGB plant. Or maybe they'd just picked the lowest bidder. An elevator took him to the seventh floor, and he walked around the corridor to the executive offices that have their own separate corridor on the face of the building. He ended up in front of the DDO's secretary.

"Mr. Clark to see Mr. Ritter," he said.

"Do you have an appointment?" the secretary asked.

"No, I don't, but I think he wants to see me," Clark said politely. There was no sense in abusing her. Besides, Clark had been raised to show deference to women. She lifted her phone and passed the message. "You can go right in, Mr. Clark."

"Thank you." He closed the door behind him. The door, of course, was heavy and soundproof. That was just as well.

"What the hell are you doing here?" the DDO demanded.

"You're going to have to shut SHOWBOAT down," Clark said without preamble. "It's coming apart. The bad guys are hunting those kids down and —"

"I know. I heard late last night. Look, I never figured this would be a no-loss operation. One of the teams got clobbered pretty good thirty-six hours ago, but based on intercepts, looks like they gave better than they took, and then they got even with some others who —"

"That was me," Clark said.

"What?" Ritter asked in surprise.

"Larson and I took a little drive about this time yesterday, and I found three of those — whatevers. They were just finished loading up the bodies into the back of a truck. I didn't see any point in letting them live," Mr. Clark said in a normal tone of voice. It had been a very long time since anyone at CIA had said something like that.

911

"Christ, John!" Ritter was even too surprised to blast Clark for violating his own security by stepping into a separate operation.

"I recognized one of the bodies," Clark went on. "Captain Emilio Rojas, United States Army. He was a hell of a nice kid, by the way."

"I'm sorry about that. Nobody ever said this was safe."

"I'm sure his family, if any, will appreciate that. This operation is blown. It's time to cut our losses. What are we doing to get them out?" Clark asked.

"I'm looking at that. I have to coordinate with somebody. I'm not sure that he'll agree."

"In that case, sir," Clark told his boss, "I suggest that you make your case rather forcefully."

"Are you threatening me?" Ritter asked quietly.

"No, sir, I would prefer not to have you read me that way. I am telling you, on the basis of my experience, that this operation must be terminated ASAP. It is your job to make that necessity plain to the people who authorized the operation. Failing to get such permission, I would advise you to terminate the operation anyway."

"I could lose my job for that," the DDO pointed out.

"After I identified the body of Captain Rojas, I set fire to the truck. Couple reasons. I wanted to divert the enemy somewhat, and, of course, I also wanted to render the bodies unrecognizable. I've never burned the body of a friendly before. I did not like doing that. Larson still doesn't know why I did it. He's too young to understand. You're not, sir. You sent those people into the field and you are responsible for them. If you are telling me that your job is more important than that, I am here to tell you that you are wrong, sir." Clark hadn't yet raised his voice above the level of a reasonable man discussing ordinary business, but for the first time in a very long time, Bob Ritter feared for his personal safety.

"Your diversion attempt was successful, by the way. The opposition has forty people looking in the wrong place now."

"Good. That will make the extraction effort all the easier to accomplish."

"John, you can't give me orders like this."

"Sir, I am not giving you orders. I am telling you what has to be done. You told me that the operation was mine to run."

"That was RECIPROCITY, not SHOW-BOAT."

"This is not a time for semantics, sir. If you do not pull those people out, more — possibly all of them — will be killed. That, sir, is your responsibility. You can't put people in the field and not support them. You know that."

"You're right, of course," Ritter said after a moment. "I can't do it on my own. I have to inform — well, you know. I'll take care of that. We'll pull them out as quickly as we can."

"Good." Clark relaxed. Ritter was a sharp operator, often too sharp in his dealings with subordinates, but he was a man of his word. Besides, the DDO was too smart to cross him on a matter like this. Clark was sure of that. He had made his own position pretty damned clear, and Ritter had caught the signal five-by-five.

"What about Larson and his courier?"

"I've pulled them both out. His plane's at Panama, and he's at the Marriott down the road. He's pretty good, by the way, but he's probably blown as far as Colombia is concerned. I'd say they could both use a few weeks off."

"Fair enough. What about you?"

"I can head back tomorrow if you want. You might want me to help with the extraction."

"We may have a line on Cortez."

"Really?"

"And you're the guy who got the first picture of him."

"Oh. Where — the guy at the Untiveros house, the guy we just barely missed?"

"The same. Positive ID from the lady he seduced. He's running the people they have in the field from a little house near Anserma."

"I'd have to take Larson back for that."

"Think it's worth the risk?"

"Getting Cortez?" Clark thought for a moment. "Depends. It's worth a look. What do we know about his security?"

"Nothing," Ritter admitted, "just a rough idea where the house is. We got that from an intercept. Be nice to get him alive. He knows a lot of things we want to find out. We bring him back here and we can hang a murder rap over his head. Death-penalty kind."

Clark nodded thoughtfully. Another element of spy fiction was the canard about how people in the intelligence business were willing to take their cyanide capsules or face a firing squad with a song in their hearts. The facts were to the contrary. Men faced certain death courageously only when there was no attractive alternative. The trick was to give them such an alternative, which didn't require the mind of a rocket scientist, as the current aphorism went. If they got Cortez, the normal form would be take him all the way through a trial, sentence him to death — just a matter of picking the right judge, and in national-security matters, there was always lots of leeway — and take it from there. Cortez would crack in due course, probably even before the trial started. Cortez was no fool, after all, and would know when and how to strike a bargain. He'd already sold out on his own country. Selling out on the Cartel was trivial beside that.

Clark nodded. "Give me a few hours to think about it."

Ryan turned left off 10th Street, Northwest, into the drive-through. There were uniformed and plainclothes guards, one of whom held a clipboard. He approached the car.

"Jack Ryan to see Dan Murray."

"Could I see some ID, please?"

Jack pulled out his CIA pass. The guard recognized it for what it was and waved to another guard. This one punched the button to lower the steel barrier that was supposed to prevent people with car bombs from driving under the headquarters of the FBI. He pulled over it and found a place to park the car. A young FBI agent met him in the lobby and handed him a pass that would work the Bureau's electronic gate. If someone invented the right sort of computer virus, Jack thought, half of the government would be prevented from going to work. And maybe the country would be safe until the problem was fixed.

The Hoover Building has a decidedly unusual layout, a maze of diagonal corridors intersecting with squared-off corridors. It is even worse than the Pentagon for the uninitiated to find their way about. In this case, Ryan was well and truly disoriented by the time they found the right office. Dan was waiting for him and led him into his private office. Jack closed the door behind him.

"What gives?" Murray asked.

Ryan set his briefcase on Murray's desk and opened it.

"I need some guidance."

"About what?"

"About what is probably an illegal operation — several of them, as a matter of fact."

"How illegal?"

"Murder," Jack said as undramatically as he could manage.

"The car bombs in Colombia?" Murray asked

from his swivel chair.

"Not bad, Dan. Except they weren't car bombs."

Oh? Dan sat down and thought for a few seconds before speaking. He remembered that whatever was being done was retribution for the murder of Emil and the rest. "Whatever they were, the law on this is fairly muddled, you know. The prohibition against killing people in intelligence operations is an Executive Order, promulgated by the President. If he writes *except in this case* on the bottom of the order, then it's legal — sort of. The law on this issue is really strange. More than anything else, it's a constitutional matter, and the Constitution is nice and vague where it has to be."

"Yeah, I know about that. What makes it illegal is that I've been told to give incorrect information to Congress. If the oversight people were in on it, it wouldn't be murder. It would be properly formulated government policy. In fact, as I understand the law, it would not be murder even if we did it first and then told Congress, because we have a lead time to start a covert op if the oversight folks are out of town. But if the DCI tells me to give false information to Congress, then we're committing murder, because we're not following the law. That's the good news, Dan."

"Go on."

"The bad news is that too many people know what's going on, and if the story gets out, some people we have out in the field are in a world of hurt. I'll set the political dimension aside for the moment except to say that there's more than one. Dan, I don't know what the hell I'm supposed to do." Ryan's analysis, as usual, was very accurate. He'd made only a single mistake. He didn't know what the real bad news was.

Murray smiled, not because he wanted to, but because his friend needed it. "What makes you think I do?"

Ryan's tension eased a bit. "Well, I could go to a priest for guidance, but they ain't cleared SI. You are, and the FBI's the next best thing to the priesthood, isn't it?" It was an inside joke between the two. Both were Boston College graduates.

"Where's the operation being run out of?"

"Guess. It isn't Langley, not really. It's being run out of a place exactly six blocks up the street."

"That means I can't even go to the AG."

"Yeah, he just might tell his boss, mightn't he?"

"So I get in trouble with my bureaucracy," Murray observed lightly.

"Is government service really worth the hassle?" Jack asked bleakly, his depression returning. "Hell, maybe we can retire together. Who can you trust?"

That answer came easily. "Bill Shaw." Murray rose. "Let's go see him."

"Loop" is one of those computer words that

has gained currency in society. It identifies things that happen and the people who make them happen, an action- or decision-cycle that exists independently of the things around it. Any government has a virtually infinite collection of such loops, each defined by its own special set of ground rules, understood by the players. Within the next few hours a new loop had been established. It included selected members of the FBI, but not the U.S. Attorney General, who had authority over the Bureau. It would also include members of the Secret Service, but not their boss, the Secretary of the Treasury. Investigations of this sort were mainly exercises in paper-chasing and analysis, and Murray — who was also tasked to head this one up — was surprised to see that one of his "subjects" was soon on the move. It didn't help him at all to learn that he was driving to Andrews Air Force Base.

By that time, Ryan was back at his desk, looking slightly wan, everyone thought, but everyone had heard that he'd been sick the night before. Something he ate. He now knew what to do: nothing. Ritter was gone, and the Judge still wasn't back. It wasn't easy to do nothing. It was harder still to do things that didn't matter a damn right now. He did feel better, however. Now the problem wasn't his alone. He didn't know that this was nothing to feel better about.

25.

The ODYSSEY File

Murray had a senior agent drive to Andrews immediately, of course, and he got there just in time to watch the small jet taxi off to the end of runway One-Left. The agent used his ID to get himself into the office of the colonel who commanded the 89th Military Airlift Wing. That got the agent the flight plan for the aircraft that had just taken off. He used the colonel's phone to call Murray, then admonished the colonel that he, the agent, had never been there, had never made an official inquiry; that this was part of a major criminal investigation and was code-word material. The code-word for the case was ODYSSEY.

Murray and Shaw were together within a minute of taking the call. Shaw had found that he could handle the duties of acting Director. He was sure that it was not a permanent job, and after the proper political figurehead was found, he'd revert to Executive Assistant Director (Investigations). Part of him thought that too bad. What was wrong with having a career cop running the Bureau? Of course, that was politics, not police work, and in over thirty years of police work he'd discovered that politics was not his cup of tea.

"We gotta get somebody there," Shaw observed. "But *how*, for God's sake?"

"Why not the Panama legal attaché?" Murray asked. "I know him. Solid guy."

"He's out doing something with DEA. Won't be back in the office for a couple of days. His number-two's not up to it. Too inexperienced to run this himself."

"Morales is available in Bogotá — but somebody'd notice. . . . We're playing catch-up again, Bill, and that guy is flying down there at five hundred miles per hour. . . . How about Mark Bright? Maybe he can steal a jet from the Air Guard."

"Do it!"

"Special Agent Bright," he said as he picked up the phone.

"Mark, this is Dan Murray. I need you to do something. Start taking notes, Mark." Murray kept talking. Two minutes later Bright muttered a mild obscenity and pulled out his phone book. The first call went to Eglin Air Force Base, the second to the local Coast Guard, and the third to his home. He sure as hell wouldn't be home for dinner. Bright grabbed a few items on his way out the door and had another agent drive him to the Coast Guard yard, where a helicopter was already waiting. It took off a minute after he got aboard and headed east to Eglin Air Force Base.

The Air Force had only three F-15E Strike-Eagles, all prototypes for a ground-attack version of the big, twin-engined fighter, and two of those were at Eglin for technical tests while Congress decided if the service would actually put the aircraft into serial production. Aside from some training birds located elsewhere, this was the only two-seat version of the Air Force's prime air-superiority fighter. The major who'd be flying him was standing at the side of the aircraft when Bright stepped out of the helicopter. A couple of NCOs assisted the agent into his flight suit, parachute harness, and life vest. The helmet was sitting on the top of the rear ejection seat. In ten minutes the aircraft was ready to roll.

"What gives?" the pilot asked.

"I need to be at Panama, just as fast as you can arrange it."

"Gee, you mean you're going to make me fly fast?" the major responded, then laughed. "Then there's no rush."

"Say again?"

"The tanker took off three minutes ago. We'll let him get up to thirty thousand before we lift off. He'll top us off up there, and we go balls to the wall. Another tanker is taking off from Panama to meet us — so we'll have enough fuel to land, sir. That way we can go supersonic most of the flight. You did say you were in a hurry?"

"Uh-huh." Bright was struggling to adjust his helmet. It didn't fit very well. It was also quite warm in the cockpit, and the air-conditioning system hadn't taken hold yet. "What if the other tanker doesn't show up?"

"The Eagle is a very good glider," the major assured him. "We won't have to swim *too* far."

A radio message crackled in Bright's ears. The major answered it, then spoke to his passenger. "Grab your balls, sir. It is now post time." The Eagle taxied to the end of the runway, where it sat still for a moment while the pilot brought the engines to full, screaming, vibrating power, and then slipped his brakes. Ten seconds later Bright wondered if a catapult shot off a carrier could be more exciting than this. The F-15E held a forty-degree angle of climb and just kept accelerating, leaving Florida's gulf coast far behind. They tanked a hundred miles offshore — Bright was too fascinated to be frightened, though the buffet was noticeable — and after separating, the Eagle climbed to forty thousand feet and the pilot punched burners. The aft cockpit was mainly concerned with delivering bombs and missiles on target, but did have a few instruments. One of them told the agent that they had just topped a thousand miles per hour.

"What's the hurry?" the pilot asked.

"I want to get to Panama ahead of somebody."

"Can you give me some details? Might help, you know."

"One of those business jets — G-Three, I think. Left Andrews eighty-five minutes ago."

The pilot laughed. "Is that all? Hell, you can check into a hotel 'fore he gets down. We're already ahead of him. We're wasting fuel going this fast."

"So waste it," Bright said.

"Fine with me, sir. Mach-2 or sittin' still, they pay me the same. Okay, figure we'll get in ninety minutes ahead of your guy. How do you like the ride?"

"Where's the drink cart?"

"Should be a bottle down by your right knee. A nice domestic vintage, good nose, but not the least pretentious."

Bright got it and had a drink out of sheer curiosity.

"Salt and electrolytes, to keep you alert," the pilot explained a few seconds later. "You're FBI, right?"

"Correct."

"What gives?"

"Can't say. What's that?" He heard a beeping sound in his headphones.

"SAM radar," the major said.

"What?"

"That's Cuba over there. There's a SAM battery on that point that doesn't like American military aircraft. I can't imagine why. We're out of range anyway. Don't sweat it. It's normal. We

924

use them to calibrate our systems, too. Part of the game."

Murray and Shaw were reading over the material Jack had dropped off. Their immediate problems were, first, to determine what was supposed to be going on; next, to determine what was actually going on; next, to determine if it was legal or not; next, if not, then to take appropriate action, once they could figure what appropriate action was. This wasn't a mere can of worms. It was a can of poisonous snakes that Ryan had spilled over Murray's desk.

"You know how this might end up?"

Shaw turned away from the desk. "The country doesn't need another one." *Not by my hands,* he didn't say.

"We got one whether we need it or not," Murray said. "I admit, part of me says, 'Right on!' about why they're doing it, but from what Jack tells me, we have at the very least a technical violation of the oversight laws, and definitely a violation of the Executive Order."

"Unless there's a classified codicil that we don't know about. What if the AG knows?"

"What if he's part of it? The day Emil got hit, the AG flew to Camp David along with the rest of 'em, remember?"

"What I want to know is, what the hell our friend is going to Panama for?"

"Maybe we'll find out. He's going down alone. No security troops, everybody sworn to secrecy.

Who'd you send over to Andrews to choke it out of 'em?"

"Pat O'Day," Murray answered. That explained matters. "I want him to handle the liaison with the Secret Service guys, too. He's done a lot of work with them. When the time comes, that is. We're a mile away from being ready for that."

"Agreed. We have eighteen people working ODYSSEY. That's not enough."

"We have to keep it tight for the moment, Bill. I think the next step is getting somebody over from Justice to cover our asses for us. Who?"

"Christ, I don't know," Shaw replied in exasperation. "It's one thing to run an investigation that the AG knows about but is kept out of, but I can't remember ever running one completely unknown to him."

"Let's take our time, then. The main thing right now is to figure out what the plan was, then branch out from there." It was a logical observation from Murray. It was also wrong. It was to be a day of errors.

The F-15E touched down at Howard Field right on time, eighty minutes before the scheduled arrival of the flight from Andrews. Bright thanked the pilot, who refueled and took off at once for a more leisurely return to Eglin. The base intelligence officer met Bright, along with the most senior agent from the legal attaché's office in Panama City, who was young, sharp, but too new in his post for a case of this sensitivity. The arriving agent briefed his two colleagues on what little he knew and swore both to secrecy. It was enough to get things going. His first stop was the post exchange, where he got some nondescript clothing. The intelligence officer supplied a very plain automobile with local tags that they left outside the gate. On base they'd use an anonymous blue Air Force sedan. The Plymouth sat near the flight line when the VC-20A landed. Bright pulled his Nikon out of the bag and attached a 1000mm telephoto lens. The aircraft taxied to a stop at one of the hangars, and the stairs folded down with the hatch. Bright snugged his camera in and started shooting close-ups from several hundred yards away as the single passenger stepped out of the plane and into a waiting car.

"Jesus, it's really him." Bright rewound and removed the film cassette. He handed it to the other FBI agent and reloaded another thirty-six-frame spool.

The car they followed was a twin to their Air Force sedan. It drove straight off post. Bright and the rest barely had time to switch cars, but the Air Force colonel driving had ambitions to race the NASCAR circuit and took up a surveillance position a hundred yards behind it.

"Why no security?" he asked.

"He generally doesn't bother, they told me," Bright told him. "Sounds odd, doesn't it?"

"Hell, yes, given who he is, what he knows, and

927

where the hell he happens to be at the moment."

The trip into town was unremarkable. The Air Force sedan dropped Cutter off at a luxury hotel on the outskirts of Panama City. Bright hopped out and watched him check in, just like a man on a business trip. The other agent came in a few minutes later while the colonel stayed with the car.

"Now what?"

"Anybody you can trust on the local PD?" Bright asked.

"Nope. I know a few, some of them pretty good guys. But trust? Not down here, man."

"Well, there's always the old-fashioned way," Bright observed.

" 'kay." The assistant legal attaché reached for his wallet and walked to the registration desk. He came back two minutes later. "The Bureau owes me twenty bucks. He's registered as Robert Fisher. Here's the American Express number." He handed over a crumpled carbon sheet that also had the scrawled signature.

"Call the office and run it. We need to keep an eye on his room. We need — Christ, how many assets do we have?" Bright waved him outside.

"Not enough for this."

Bright's face twisted into an ugly shape for a moment. This was no easy call to make. OD-YSSEY was a code-word case, and one thing that Murray had impressed on him was the need for security, but — there was always a "but," wasn't there? — this was something that needed doing.

So he was the senior man on the scene and he had to make the call. Of such things, he knew, careers were made and broken. It was murderously hot and humid, but that wasn't the only reason Mark Bright was sweating.

"Okay, tell him we need a half-dozen good people to help us with the surveillance."

"You sure — "

"I'm not sure of anything right now! The man we're supposed to be shadowing — if we suspect him — Christ Almighty, *if* we suspect him — " Bright stopped talking. There wasn't much else to say, was there?

"Yeah."

"I'll hang out here. Tell the colonel to get things organized."

It turned out that they needn't have hurried. The subject — that's what he was now, Bright told himself — appeared in the lobby three hours later, looking fresh and scrubbed in his tropical-weight suit. Four cars waited outside for him, but Cutter only knew about the small, white Mercedes into which he climbed and which drove off to the north. The other three kept it in visual contact.

It was getting dark. Bright had shot only three frames on his second roll of film. He ejected that one and replaced it with some super-high-speed black and white film. He shot a few pictures of the car just to make sure that he got the license number. The driver at this point wasn't the colonel, but a sergeant from the criminal-investigation detachment who knew the area and was impressed as hell to be working a code-word case with the Bureau. He identified the house the Mercedes pulled into. They ought to have guessed it.

The sergeant knew a place that overlooked the house, not a thousand yards away, but they were too late getting there and the car couldn't stay on the highway. Bright and the local FBI representative jumped out and found a wet, smelly place to lie down and wait. The sergeant left them a radio with which to summon him and wished them luck.

The owner of the house was away attending to matters of state, of course, but he had been kind enough to give them free use of it. That included a small but discreet staff which served light snacks and drinks, then withdrew, leaving the tape recorders, both men were sure, to record events. Well, that didn't matter, did it?

The hell it doesn't! Both men realized the sensitivity of the conversation that was about to take place, and it was Cortez who surprised his guest by graciously suggesting that they speak outside, despite the weather. Both men dropped off their suitcoats and went through the French doors to the garden. About the only good news was the impressive collection of blue bug-lights which crackled and sparkled as they attracted and electrocuted thousands of insects. The noise would make hash out of most recording attempts, and who would have expected either of them to es-

930

chew the house's air conditioning?

"Thank you for responding to my message," Cortez said pleasantly. It was not a time for bluster or posturing. It was time for business, and he'd have to appear appropriately humble before this man. It didn't bother him. Dealing with people of his rank required it, and it was something he'd have to get used to, Félix expected. They needed deference. It made surrendering all the easier.

"What do you want to talk about?" Admiral Cutter asked.

"Your operations against the Cartel, of course." Cortez waved toward a cane chair. He disappeared for a moment, then returned with the tray of drinks and glasses. For tonight, Perrier was the drink of choice. Both men left the alcohol untouched. For Félix, that was the first good sign.

"What operations are you talking about?"

"You should know that I had nothing personally to do with the death of Mr. Jacobs. It was an act of madness."

"Why should I believe that?"

"I was in America at the time. Didn't they tell you?" Cortez filled in some details. "An information source like Mrs. Wolfe," he concluded, "is worth far more than stupid, emotional revenge. It is more foolish still to challenge a powerful nation in so obvious a way. Your response was quite well done. In fact, the operations you are running are most impressive. I didn't even suspect your airport-surveillance operations until after they were terminated, and the way you simulated the car bomb — a work of *art*, if I may say so. Can you tell me what the strategic objective of your operation is?"

"Come now, Colonel."

"Admiral, I have the power to expose the totality of your activities to the press," Félix said almost sadly. "Either you tell me or you tell the members of your own Congress. You will find me far more accommodating. We are, after all, men of the same profession."

Cutter thought for a moment, and told him. He was greatly irritated to see his interlocutor start laughing.

"Brilliant!" Cortez said when he was able to. "One day I would wish to meet this man, the one who proposed this idea. Truly he is a professional!"

Cutter nodded as though accepting the compliment. For a moment Félix wondered if that might be true . . . it was easy enough to find out.

"You must forgive me, Admiral Cutter. You think I am making light of your operation. I say to you honestly that I am not. You have, in fact, accomplished your goal."

"We know. We know that somebody tried to kill you and Escobedo."

"Yes," Félix replied. "Of course. I would also like to know how you are developing such fine intelligence on us, but I know that you will not tell me."

Cutter played the card for all he thought it was

worth. "We have more assets than you think, Colonel." It wasn't worth that much.

"I am sure," Cortez allowed. "I think we have an area of agreement."

"What might that be?"

"You wish to initiate a war within the Cartel. So do I."

Cutter betrayed himself by the way he stopped breathing. "Oh? How so?"

Already Cortez knew that he had won. And this fool was advising the American President?

"Why, I will become a *de facto* part of your operation and restructure the Cartel. That means eliminating some of the more offensive members, of course."

Cutter wasn't a total fool, but made the further mistake of stating the obvious as a question: "With yourself as the new head?"

"Do you know what sort of people these 'drug lords' are? Vicious peasants. Barbarians without education, drunk with power, yet they complain like spoiled children that they are not *respected*." Cortez smiled up at the stars. "They are not people to be taken seriously by men such as ourselves. Can we agree that the world will be better when they have left it?"

"The same thought has occurred to me, as you have already pointed out."

"Then we are in agreement."

"Agreement on what?"

"Your 'car bombs' have already eliminated five of the chieftains. I will further reduce the num-

933

ber. Those eliminated will include all who approved the murder of your ambassador and the others, of course. Such actions cannot go unpunished or the world is plunged into chaos. Also, to show good faith, I will unilaterally reduce cocaine shipments to your country by half. The drug trade is disordered and overly violent," the former DGI colonel said judiciously. "It needs restructuring."

"We want it stopped!" Even as he said it, Cutter knew that it was a foolish thing to say.

Cortez sipped at his Perrier and continued to speak reasonably. "It will never be stopped. So long as your citizens wish to destroy their brains, someone will make this possible. The question, then, is how do we make the process more orderly? Your education efforts will eventually reduce the demand for drugs to tolerable levels. Until then, I can regularize the trade to minimize the dislocation of your society. I will reduce exports. I can even give you some major arrests so that your police can take credit for the reductions. This is an election year, is it not?"

Cutter's breathing took another hiatus. They were playing highstakes poker, and Cortez had just announced that the deck was marked.

"Go on," was all he managed to say.

"Was this not the objective of your operations in Colombia? To sting the Cartel and reduce drug trafficking? I offer you success, the sort of success to which your President can point. Reduction in exports, some dramatic seizures and arrests, an intermural war within the Cartel for which you will not be blamed, yet for which you will also take credit. I give you victory," Cortez said.

"In return for . . . ?"

"I, too, must have a small victory to establish my position with the chieftains, yes? You will withdraw support for the Green Berets you have climbing those horrible mountains. You know — the men you are supporting with that large black helicopter in Hangar Three at Howard Air Force Base. You see, those chieftains whom I wish to displace have large groups of retainers, and the best way for me to reduce their numbers is to have your men kill them for me. At the same time, unfortunately, in order to gain standing with my *superiors*" — this word was delivered with Richter-scale irony — "my bloody and costly operation must ultimately be successful. It is a regrettable necessity, but from your point of view it also eliminates a potential security problem, does it not?"

My God. Cutter looked away from Cortez, out past the bug lights into the jungle.

"What do you suppose they're talking about?"

"Beats the hell out of me," Bright replied. He was on his last roll of film. Even with the high-speed setting, to get a good shot he had to bring the shutter speed way down, and that meant holding the camera as still as a hunting rifle on a distant pronghorn.

★

What was it the President said? Close the operation out, and I don't care how. . . .

But I can't do that.

"Sorry," Cutter said. "Impossible."

Cortez made a helpless, shrugging gesture with both hands. "In that case we will inform the world that your government has invaded Colombia and has committed murder on a particularly epic scale. You are aware, of course, of what will probably happen to you, your President, and many senior members of your government. It took so long for you to get over all those other scandals. It must be very troubling to serve a government that has so many problems with its own laws and then uses them against its own servants."

"You can't blackmail the United States government."

"Why not, Admiral? Our mutual profession carries risks, does it not? You nearly killed me with your first 'car bomb,' and yet I have taken no personal offense. Your risk is exposure. Untiveros's family was there, you know, his wife and two little ones, eleven domestic servants, I believe. All dead from your bomb. I will not count those who were carrying guns, of course. A soldier must take a soldier's chance. As did I. As must you, Admiral, except that yours is not a soldier's chance. Your chance will be before your courts and television reporters, and congressional committees." *What was the old soldier's code?* Cortez asked himself. *Death before dishonor.* He knew that his guest had no stomach for either.

"I need time to — "

"Think? Excuse me, Admiral, but I must be back in four hours, which means I must leave here in fifteen minutes. My superiors do not know that I am gone. I have no time. Neither do you. I offer you the victory for which you and your President hoped. I require something in return. If we cannot agree, then the consequences will be unpleasant for both of us. It is that simple. Yes or no, Admiral?"

"What do you suppose they just shook hands about?"

"Cutter doesn't look real happy about it. Call the car! Looks like they're buggin' out."

"Who the hell was he meeting with, anyway? I don't recognize him. If he's a player, he's not a local one."

"I don't know." The car was late getting back, but the backup followed Cutter right back to his hotel. By the time Bright got back to the airfield, he learned that the subject was planning a good night's sleep for himself. The VC-20A was scheduled for a noon departure right back to Andrews. Bright planned to beat it there by taking an early commercial flight to Miami and connecting into Washington National. He'd arrive half dead from fatigue, but he'd get there.

Ryan took the call for the Director — Judge

937

Moore was finally on his way back, but was still three hours out of Dulles. Jack's driver was ready as the executive elevator opened onto the garage, and they immediately left for Bethesda. They got there too late. Jack opened the door to see the bed covered with a sheet. The doctors had already left.

"I was there at the end. He went out easy," one of the CIA people told him. Jack didn't recognize him, though he gave the impression that he'd been waiting for Jack to appear. "You're Dr. Ryan, right?"

"Yes," Jack said quietly.

"About an hour before he faded out, he said something about — to remember what you two talked about. I don't know what he meant, sir."

"I don't know you."

"John Clark." The man came over to shake Ryan's hand. "I'm Operations, but Admiral Greer recruited me, too, long time ago." Clark let out a breath. "Like losing a father. Twice."

"Yeah," Ryan said huskily. He was too tired, too wrung out to hide his emotions.

"Come on, I'll buy you a cup of coffee and tell you a few stories about the old guy." Clark was sad, but he was a man accustomed to death. Clearly Ryan was not, which was his good luck.

The cafeteria was closed, and they got coffee from a waiting-room pot. It was reheated and full of acid, but Ryan didn't want to go home just yet, and was late remembering that he'd driven his own car in. He'd have to drive himself home tonight. He was too tired for that. He decided to call home and tell Cathy that he'd be staying over in town. CIA had an arrangement with one of the local Marriotts. Clark offered to drive him down, and Jack dismissed his driver. By this time both men decided that a drink wasn't a bad idea.

Larson was gone from the room. He'd left a note saying that Maria would be coming in later that night, and he was going to pick her up. Clark had a small bottle of bourbon, and this Marriott had real glasses. He mixed two and handed one over to Jack Ryan.

"James Greer, the last of the good guys," Clark said as he raised his glass.

Jack took a sip. Clark had mixed it a little strong, and he nearly coughed.

"If he recruited you, how come — "

"Operations?" Clark smiled. "Well, sir, I never went to college, but Greer spotted me through some of his Navy contacts. It's a long story, and parts of it I'm not supposed to tell, but our paths have crossed three times."

"Oh?"

"When the French went in to bag those *Action Directe* folks you found on the satellite photos, I was the liaison officer in Chad. The second time they went in, after the ULA people who took that dislike to you, I was on the chopper. And I'm the fool who went on the beach to bring Mrs. Gerasimov and her daughter out. And that, sir, was all your fault. I do the crazy stuff," Clark explained. "All the field work that the espionage boys wet their pants over. Of course, maybe they're just smarter than I am."

"I didn't know."

"You weren't supposed to know. Sorry we missed on bagging those ULA pukes. I've always wanted to apologize to you for that. The French were really good about it. They were so happy with us for fingering *Action Directe* that they wanted to give us the ULA heads on plaques. But there was this damned Libyan unit out on maneuvers, and the chopper just stumbled on them — that's a problem when you go zooming in low — and it turned out that the camp was probably empty anyway. Everybody was real sorry it didn't work out as planned. Might have saved you a little grief. We tried, Dr. Ryan. We surely tried."

"Jack." Ryan held out his glass for a refill.

"Fine. Call me John." Clark topped both drinks off. "The Admiral said I could tell you all that. He also said that you tumbled to what was happening down south. I was down there," Clark said. "What do you want to know?"

"You sure you can tell me that?"

"The Admiral said so. He's — excuse me, he *was* a deputy director, and I figure that means I can do what he told me to do. This bureaucratic stuff is a little confusing to a humble line-animal, but I figure you can never go far wrong by telling the truth. Besides, Ritter told me that everything we did was legal, that he had all the permission he needed for this hunting expedition. That permission had to come from one place. Somebody decided that this drug stuff was a 'clear and present danger' — that's a quote — to the security of the United States. Only one man has the power to say that for-real, and if he does, he has the authority to do something about it. Maybe I never went to college, but I do read a lot. Where do you want me to start?"

"At the beginning," Jack replied. He listened for over an hour.

"You're going back?" Ryan asked when he was finished.

"I think a chance at bagging Cortez is worth it, and I might be able to help with the extraction of those kids up in the mountains. I don't really like the idea, but it is what I do for a living. I don't suppose your wife likes all the things she has to do as a doc."

"One thing I gotta ask. How did you feel about guiding those bombs in?"

"How did you feel about shooting people, back when you did it?"

Jack nodded. "Sorry — I had that coming."

"I joined up as a Navy SEAL. Lot of time in Southeast Asia. I got orders to go and kill people, and I went and killed 'em. That wasn't a declared war either, was it? You don't go around braggin' about it, but it's the job. Since I joined the Agency I haven't done very much of that — there have been times when I wished I could have done more of it, 'cause it might have saved a few lives in the long run. I had the head of Abu Nidal in my gunsights, but I never got permission to take the fucker out. Same story with two other people just as bad. It would have been deniable, clean, everything you want, but the lace-panty section at Langley couldn't make up their minds. They told me to see if it was possible, and it's just as dangerous to do that as it is to pull the trigger, but I never got the green light to complete the mission. From where I sit, it's a good mission. Those bastards are the enemies of our country, they kill our citizens — taken out a couple Agency people, too, and not real pretty how they did it — but we don't do anything about it. Tell me that makes sense. But I follow orders like I'm supposed to. Never violated one since I joined up."

"How do you feel about talking to the FBI?"

"You gotta be kidding. Even if I felt like it, which I don't, my main concern is those kids up in the hills. You hold me up on that, Jack, and some of them might get killed. Ritter called me earlier this evening and asked if I was willing to go back. I leave eight-forty tomorrow morning for Panama, and I stage from there back into Colombia."

"You know how to get in touch with me?"

"That might be a good idea," Clark agreed.

The rest had done everyone good. Aches had eased, and all hoped that the remaining stiffness would be worked out by the first few hours of movement. Captain Ramirez assembled his men and explained the new situation to them. He'd called in via his satellite link and requested extraction. The announcement was met with general approval. Unfortunately, he went on, the request had to be booted upstairs — with a favorable endorsement, VARIABLE had told him — and in any case the helicopter was down for an engine change. They'd be in-country at least one more night, possibly two. Until then, their mission was to evade contact and head for a suitable extraction point. These were already identified, and Ramirez had indicated the one he was heading for. It was fifteen kilometers away to the south. So the job for tonight was to skirt past the group that had been hunting for them. That would be tricky, but once past them it should be clear sailing through an area already swept. They'd try to cover eight or nine klicks tonight and the rest the following night. In any case the mission was over and they were pulling out. The recent arrivals from Team BANNER would form a third fire-team, augmenting KNIFE's already formidable firepower. Everyone still had at least two-thirds of his original ammo load-out. Food was running short, but they had enough for two days if nobody minded a few stomach rumbles. Ramirez ended his briefing on a confident note. It hadn't been cheap, and it hadn't been easy, but they had accomplished their mission and put a real hurtin' on the druggies. Now everybody had to keep it together for the trip out. The squad members exchanged nods and prepared to leave.

Chavez led off twenty minutes later. The idea was to keep as high on the mountain as they could. The opposition had shown a tendency to camp out lower down, and this way they stood the best chance of keeping clear. As always he was to avoid anything that looked like habitation. That meant giving a wide berth to the coffee plantations and associated villages, but that was what they had been doing anyway. They also had to move as fast as caution allowed, which meant that caution was downgraded. It was something often done in exercises, always with confidence. Ding's confidence in that sort of thing had also been downgraded by his experience in the field. The good news, as far as he was concerned, was that Ramirez was acting like an officer again. Probably he'd just been tired, too.

One nice thing about being close to the coffee plantations was that the cover wasn't so thick. People went into the woods to get fuel for their fires, and that thinned things out quite a bit. What effects it had on erosion wasn't Chavez's concern. That helped him to go faster, and he was covering nearly two kilometers per hour, which was far faster than he'd expected. By midnight his legs were telling him about every meter. Fatigue, he was learning again, was a cumulative factor. It took more than one day's rest to slough off all of its effects, no matter what sort of shape you were in. He wondered if the altitude wasn't also to blame. In any case he was still fighting to keep up the pace, to keep alert, to remember the path he was supposed to follow. Infantry operations are far more demanding intellectually than most people realize, and intellect is ever the first victim of fatigue.

He remembered a small village on the map, about half a klick from where he was at the moment, downhill. He'd taken the right turn at a landmark a klick back — he'd rechecked it at the rally point where they'd rested forty minutes earlier. He could hear noise from that direction. It seemed odd. The local peasants worked hard on the coffee plantations, he'd been told. They should have been asleep by now. Ding missed the obvious signal. He didn't miss the scream — more of a pant, really, the sort of sound made when —

He switched on his night scope and saw a figure running toward him. He couldn't tell — then he could. It was a girl, moving with considerable skill through the cover. Behind her was the noise of someone running after her with less skill. Chavez tapped the danger signal on his radio. Behind him everyone stopped and waited for his all-clear.

There wouldn't be one. The girl tripped and changed directions. A few seconds later she tripped again and landed right at Chavez's feet.

The sergeant clamped his left hand across her mouth. His other hand put a finger to his lips in the universal sign to be quiet. Her eyes went wide and white as she saw him — or more properly, didn't see him, just a melange of camouflage paint that looked like something from a horror movie.

"Señorita, you have nothing to fear from me. I am a soldier. I do not molest women. Who is chasing you?" He removed his hand and hoped that she wouldn't scream.

But she couldn't even if she had wanted to, instead gasping out her reply. She'd run too far too fast. "One of their 'soldiers,' the men with guns. I —"

His hand went back on her mouth as the crashing sound came closer.

"Where are you?" the voice crooned.

Shit!

"Run that way," Chavez told her, pointing. "Do not stop and do not look back. Go!"

The girl took off and the man made for the noise. He ran right past Ding Chavez and precisely one foot farther. The sergeant clasped his hand across the man's face and took him down, pulling the head back as he did so. Just as both men hit the ground, Ding's combat knife made a single lateral cut. He was surprised by the noise. Escaping air from the windpipe combined with the spurting blood to make a gurgling sound that made him cringe. The man struggled for a few futile seconds, then went limp. The victim had a knife of his own, and Chavez set it in the wound. He hoped the girl wouldn't be blamed for it, but he'd done all that he could as far as she was concerned. Captain Ramirez showed up a minute later and was not very pleased.

"Didn't have much choice, sir," Chavez said in his own defense. Actually he felt rather proud of himself. After all, protecting the weak was the job of the soldier, wasn't it?

"Move your ass outa here!"

The squad moved especially fast to clear the area, but if anyone came looking for the amorous sleepwalker, no one heard anything to suggest it. It was the last incident of the night. They arrived at the preplanned stopover point just before dawn. Ramirez set up his radio and called in.

"Roger, KNIFE, we copy your position and your objective. We do not as yet have confirmation for the extraction. Please call back around eighteen hundred Lima. We ought to have things set up by then. Over."

"Roger, will call back at eighteen hundred. KNIFE out."

"Shame about BANNER," one communicator said to the other.

"These things do happen."

"Your name Johns?"

"That's right," the colonel said without turning at once. He'd just come back from a test flight. The new — actually rebuilt five-year-old — engine worked just fine. The Pave Low III was back in business. Colonel Johns turned to see to whom he was talking.

"Do you recognize me?" Admiral Cutter asked curtly. He was wearing his full uniform for a change. He hadn't done that in months, but the three stars on each braided shoulder board gleamed in the morning sun, along with his ribbons and surface-warfare officer's badge. In fact, the general effect of the undress-white uniform was quite overpowering, right down to the white buck shoes. Just as he had planned.

"Yes, sir, I do. Please excuse me, sir."

"Your orders have been changed, Colonel. You are to return to your stateside base as soon as possible. That means today," Cutter emphasized.

"But what about — "

"That will be taken care of through other means. Do I have to tell you whose authority I speak with?"

"No, sir, you do not."

"You will not discuss this matter with anyone. That means nobody, anywhere, ever. Do you require any further instructions, Colonel?"

"No, sir, your orders are quite clear."

"Very well." Cutter turned and walked back to the staff car, which drove off at once. His next stop was a hilltop near the Gaillard Cut. There was a communications van there. Cutter walked right past the armed guard — he wore a Marine uniform but was a civilian — and into the van, where he made a similar speech. Cutter was surprised to learn that moving the van would be difficult and would require a helicopter, since the van was too large to be pulled down the little service road. He was, however, able to order them to shut down, and he'd see about getting a helicopter to lift the van out. Until then they would stay put and not do anything. Their security was blown, he explained, and further transmissions would only further endanger the people with whom they communicated. He got agreement on that, too, and left. He boarded his aircraft at eleven in the morning. He'd be home in Washington for supper.

Mark Bright was there just after lunch. He handed his film cassettes over to a lab expert and proceeded to Dan Murray's busy office, where he reported what he had seen.

"I don't know who he met with, but maybe you'll recognize the face. How about the Amex number?"

"It's a CIA account that he's had access to for the past two years. This is the first time he's used it, though. The local guy faxed us a copy so we could run the signature. Forensics has already given us a handwriting match," Murray said. "You look a little tuckered."

"I don't know why — hell, I must have slept three hours in the past day and a half. I've done my D.C. time. Mobile was supposed to be a nice vacation."

Murray grinned. "Welcome back to the unreal world of Washington."

"I had to get some help to pull this off," Bright said next.

"Like what?" Murray wasn't smiling anymore.

"Air Force personnel, intel and CID types. I told 'em this was code-word material, and, hell, even if I had told them everything I know, which I didn't, I don't know what the story is myself. I take responsibility, of course, but if I hadn't done it, I probably wouldn't have gotten the shots."

"Sounds to me like you did the right thing," Murray said. "I don't suppose you had much choice in the matter. It happens like that sometimes."

Bright acknowledged the official forgiveness. "Thanks."

They had to wait five more minutes for the photographs. Decks had been cleared for this case, but even priority cases took time, much to the annoyance of everyone. The technician — actually a section chief — arrived with the moist prints.

"I figured you'd want these babies in a hurry."

"You figured right, Marv — Holy Christ!" Murray exclaimed. "Marv, this is code-word."

"You already told me, Dan. Lips are zipped. We can enhance them some, but that'll take another hour. Want me to get that started?"

"Fast as you can." Murray nodded, and the technician left. "Christ," Murray said again when he reexamined the photos. "Mark, you take a mean picture."

"So who the hell is it?"

"Félix Cortez."

"Who's that?"

"Used to be a DGI colonel. We missed him by a whisker when we bagged Filiberto Ojeda."

"The Macheteros case?" That didn't make any sense.

"No, not exactly." Murray shook his head. He spoke almost reverently, thought for a minute, and called for Bill Shaw to come down. The acting Director was there within a minute. Agent Bright was still in the dark when Murray pointed his boss to the photographs. "Bill, you ain't going to believe this one."

"So who the hell is Félix Cortez?" Bright asked.

Shaw answered the question. "After he skipped out of Puerto Rico, he went to work for the Cartel. He had a piece of Emil's murder, how much we don't know, but he sure as hell was involved. And here he is, sitting with the President's National Security Adviser. Now what do you suppose they had to talk about?"

"It's not with this batch, but I got a picture of them shaking hands," the junior agent announced.

Shaw and Murray just stared at him when he said that. Then at each other. *The President's head national-security guy shook hands with somebody who works for the drug Cartel . . . ?*

"Dan," Shaw said, "what the hell is going on? Has the whole world just gone crazy?"

"Sure looks that way, doesn't it?"

"Put a call in to your friend Ryan. Tell him . . . Tell his secretary that there's a terrorism thing — no, we can't risk that. Pick him up on the way home?"

"He's got a driver."

"That's a big help."

"I got it." Murray lifted his phone and dialed a Baltimore number. "Cathy? Dan Murray. Yeah, we're fine, thanks. What time does Jack's driver usually get him home? Oh, he didn't? Okay, I need you to do something, and it's important, Cathy. Tell Jack to stop off at Danny's on the way home to, uh, to pick the books up. Just like that, Cathy. This isn't a joke. Can you do that? Thanks, doc." He replaced the phone. "Isn't that conspiratorial?"

"Who's Ryan — isn't he CIA?"

"That's right," Shaw answered. "He's also the guy who dumped this case in our laps. Unfortunately, Mark, you are not cleared for it."

"I understand, sir."

"Why don't you see how quick you can fly home and find out how much that new baby's grown. Damned nice work you did here. I won't forget," the acting Director promised him.

Pat O'Day, a newly promoted inspector working out of FBI Headquarters, watched from the parking lot as a subordinate stood on the flight line in the soiled uniform of an Air Force technical sergeant. It was a clear, hot day at Andrews Air Force Base, and a D.C. Air National Guard F-4C landed right ahead of the VC-20A. The converted executive jet taxied to the 89th's terminal on the west side of the complex. The stairs dropped and Cutter walked out wearing civilian

952

clothes. By this time — through Air Force intelligence personnel — the Bureau knew that he'd visited a helicopter crew and a communications van in the morning. So far no one had approached either of them to find out why, because headquarters was still trying to figure things out, and, O'Day thought, failing miserably — but that was headquarters for you. He wanted to go back out to the field where the real cops were, though this case did have its special charm. Cutter walked across to where his personal car was parked, tossed his bag in the back seat, and drove off, with O'Day and his driver in visual pursuit. The National Security Adviser got onto Suitland Parkway heading toward D.C., then, after entering the city, onto I-395. They expected him to get off at the Maine Avenue exit, possibly heading toward the White House, but instead the man just kept going to his official residence at Fort Myer, Virginia. A discreet surveillance didn't get more routine than that.

"Cortez? I know that name. Cutter met with a former DGI guy?" Ryan asked.

"Here's the photo." Murray handed it over. The lab troops had run it through their computerized enhancement process. One of the blackest of the Bureau's many forensic arts, it had converted a grainy photographic frame to glossy perfection. Moira Wolfe had again verified Cortez's identity, just to make everyone sure. "Here's another." The second one showed them shaking hands.

"This'll look good in court," Ryan observed as he handed the frames back.

"It's not evidence," Murray replied.

"Huh?"

Shaw explained. "High government officials meet with . . . with strange people all the time. Remember the time when Kissinger made the secret flight to China?"

"But that was — " Ryan stopped when he realized how dumb his objection sounded. He remembered a clandestine meeting with the Soviet Party chairman that he couldn't tell the FBI about. How would *that* look to some people?

"It isn't evidence of a crime, or even a conspiracy, unless we know that what they talked about was illegal," Murray told Jack. "His lawyer will argue, probably successfully, that his meeting with Cortez, while appearing to be irregular, was aimed at the execution of sensitive but proper government policy."

"Bullshit," Jack observed.

"The attorney would object to your choice of words, and the judge would have it stricken from the record, instruct the jury to disregard it, and admonish you about your language in court, Dr. Ryan," Shaw pointed out. "What we have here is a piece of interesting information, but it is not evidence of a crime until we know that a crime is being committed. Of course, it is bullshit."

"Well, I met with the guy who guided the 'car bombs' into the targets."

"Where is he?" Murray asked at once.

"Probably back in Colombia by now." Ryan explained on for a few minutes.

"Christ, who is this guy?" Murray asked.

"Let's leave his name out of it for a while, okay?"

"I really think we should talk to him," Shaw said.

"He's not interested in talking to you. He doesn't want to go to jail."

"He won't." Shaw rose and paced around the room. "In case I never told you, I'm a lawyer, too. In fact, I have a J.D. If we were to attempt to try him, his lawyer would throw Martinez-Barker at us. You know what that is? A little-known result of the Watergate case. Martinez and Barker were Watergate conspirators, right? Their defense, probably an honest one, was that they thought the burglary was sanctioned by properly constituted authority as part of a national-security investigation. In a rather wordy majority opinion, the appeals court ruled that there had been no criminal intent, the defendants had acted in good faith throughout, and therefore no actual crime had been committed. Your friend will say on the stand that once he'd heard the 'clear and present danger' pronouncement from his superiors, and been told that authorization came from way up the chain of command, he was merely following orders given by people who had sufficient constitutional authority to do so. I suppose Dan already told you, there really isn't any law in a case like this. Hell,

955

the majority of my agents would probably like to buy your guy a beer for avenging Emil's death."

"What I can tell you about this guy is that he's a serious combat vet, and as far as I could tell, he's a very straight guy."

"I don't doubt it. As far as the killing is concerned — we've had lawyers say that the actions of police snipers come awfully close to cold-blooded murder. Drawing a distinction between police work and combat action isn't always as easy as we would like. In this case, how do you draw the line between murder and a legitimate counter-terrorist operation? What it'll come down to — hell, it will mainly reflect the political beliefs of the judges who try the case, and the appeal, and every other part of the proceeding. Politics. You know," Shaw said, "it was a hell of a lot easier chasing bank robbers. At least then you knew what the score was."

"There's the key to it right there," Ryan said. "How much you want to bet that this whole thing started because it was an election year?"

Murray's phone rang. "Yeah? Okay, thanks." He hung up. "Cutter just got in his car. He's heading up the G.W. Parkway. Anybody want to guess where he's going?"

26.

Instruments of State

Inspector O'Day thanked his lucky stars — he was an Irishman and believed in such things — that Cutter was such an idiot. Like previous National Security Advisers he'd opted against having a Secret Service detail, and the man clearly didn't know the first thing about counter-surveillance techniques. The subject drove right onto the George Washington Parkway and headed north in the firm belief that nobody would notice. No doubling back, no diversion into a one-way street, nothing that one could learn from watching a TV cop show or better yet, reading a Philip Marlowe mystery, which was how Patrick O'Day amused himself. Even on surveillances, he'd play Chandler tapes. He had more problems figuring those cases out than the real ones, but that was merely proof that Marlowe would have made one hell of a G-Man. This sort of case didn't require that much talent. Cutter might have been a Navy three-star, but he was a babe in the woods as far as conspiracy went. His personal car didn't even change lanes, and took the exit for CIA unless, O'Day thought, he had an unusual interest in the Federal Highway Administration's Fairbanks Highway Research Station, which was probably closed in any case. About the only bad news was that picking Cutter up when he left would be tough to do. There wasn't a good place to hide a car here — CIA security was pretty good. O'Day dropped his companion off to keep watch in the woods by the side of the road and whistled up another car to assist. He fully expected that Cutter would reappear shortly and drive right home.

The National Security Adviser never noticed the tail and parked in a VIP slot. As usual, someone held open the door and escorted him to Ritter's office on the seventh floor. The Admiral took his seat without a friendly word.

"Your operation is really coming apart," he told the DDO harshly.

"What do you mean?"

"I mean I met with Félix Cortez last night. He knows about the troops. He knows about the recon on the airfields. He knows about the bombs, and he knows about the helicopter we've been using to support SHOWBOAT. I'm shutting everything down. I've already had the helicopter fly back to Eglin, and I ordered the communications people at VARIABLE to terminate operations."

"The hell you have!" Ritter shouted.

"The hell I haven't. You're taking your orders from me, Ritter. Is that clear?"

"What about our people?" the DDO demanded.

"I've taken care of that. You don't need to know how. It's all going to quiet down," Cutter said. "You got your wish. There is a gang war underway. Drug exports are going to be cut by half. We can let the press report that the drug war is being won."

"And Cortez takes over, right? Has it occurred to you that as soon as he's settled in, things change back?"

"Has it occurred to you that he can blow the operation wide open? What do you suppose will happen to you and the Judge if he does that?"

"The same thing that'll happen to you," Ritter snarled back.

"Not to me. I was there, so was the Attorney General. The President never authorized you to kill anybody. He never said anything about invading a foreign country."

"This whole operation was your idea, Cutter."

"Says who? Do you have my signature on a single memo?" the Admiral asked. "If this gets blown, the *best* thing you can hope for is that we'll be on the same cellblock. If that Fowler guy wins, we're both fucked. That means we can't let it get blown, can we?"

"I do have your name on a memo."

"That operation is already terminated, and there's no evidence left behind, either. So what can you do to expose me without exposing yourself and the Agency to far worse accusations?" Cutter was rather proud of himself. On the flight back from Panama he'd figured the whole thing out. "In any case, I'm the guy giving the orders. The CIA's involvement in this thing is over. You're the only guy with records. I suggest that you do away with them. All the traffic from SHOWBOAT, VARIABLE, RECIPROCITY, and EAGLE EYE gets destroyed. We can hold on to CAPER. That's one part of the op that the other side hasn't cottoned to. Convert that into a straight covert operation and we can still use it. You have your orders. Carry them out."

"There will be loose ends."

"Where? You think people are going to volunteer for a stretch in federal prison? Will your Mr. Clark announce the fact that he killed over thirty people? Will that Navy flight crew write a book about dropping two smart-bombs on private homes in a friendly country? Your radio people at VARIABLE never actually saw anything. The fighter pilot splashed some airplanes, but who's he going to tell? The radar plane that guided him in never saw him do it, because they always switched off first. The special-ops people who handled the land side of the operation at Pensacola won't talk. And there are only a few people from the flight crews we captured. I'm sure we can work something out with them."

"You forgot the kids we have in the mountains," Ritter said quietly. He knew that part of the story already.

"I need information on where they are so that I can arrange for a pickup. I'm going to handle that through my own channels, if you don't mind. Give me the information."

"No."

"That wasn't a request. You know, I just could be the guy who exposes you. Then your attempts to tie me in with all this would merely look like a feeble effort at exculpating yourself."

"It would still wreck the election."

"And guarantee your imprisonment. Hell, Fowler doesn't even believe in putting serial killers in the chair. How do you think he'll react to dropping bombs on people who haven't even been indicted — and what about that 'collateral damage' you were so cavalier about? This is the only way, Ritter."

"Clark is back in Colombia. I'm sending him after Cortez. That would also tie things up." It was Ritter's last play, and it wasn't good enough.

Cutter jerked in his chair. "And what if he blows it? It is not worth the risk. Call off your dog. That, too, is an order. Now give me that information — and shred your files."

Ritter didn't want to. But he didn't see an alternative. The DDO walked to his wall safe — the panel was open at the moment — and pulled out the files. In SHOWBOAT-II was a tactical map showing the programmed exfiltration sites.

He gave it to Cutter.

"I want it all done tonight."

Ritter let out a breath. "It will be."

"Fine." Cutter folded the map into his coat pocket. He left the office without another word.

It all came down to this, Ritter told himself. Thirty years of government service, running agents all over the world, doing things that his country needed to have done, and now he had to follow an outrageous order or face Congress, and courts, and prison. And the best alternative would be to take others there with him. It wasn't worth it. Bob Ritter worried about those kids in the mountains, but Cutter said that he'd take care of it. The Deputy Director (Operations) of the Central Intelligence Agency told himself that he could trust the man to keep his word, knowing that he wouldn't, knowing that it was cowardice to pretend that he would.

He lifted the files off the steel shelves himself, taking them to his desk. Against the wall was a paper shredder, one of the more important instruments of contemporary government. These were the only copies of the documents in question. The communications people on that hilltop in Panama shredded everything as soon as they uplinked copies to Ritter's office. CAPER went through NSA, but there was no operational traffic there, and those files would be lost in the mass of data in the basement of the Fort Meade complex.

The machine was a big one, with a self-feeding

hopper. It was entirely normal for senior government officials to destroy records. Extra copies of sensitive files were liabilities, not assets. No notice would be taken of the fact that the clear plastic bag that had been empty was now filled with paper pasta that had once been important intelligence documents. CIA burned tons of the stuff every day, and used some of the heat that was generated to make hot water for the washrooms. Ritter set the papers in the hopper in half-inch lots, watching the entire history of his field operations turn to rubbish.

"There he is," the junior agent said into his portable radio. "Southbound."

O'Day picked the man up three minutes later. The backup car was already on Cutter, and by the time O'Day had caught up, it was clear that he was merely returning to Fort Myer, the VIP section off Sherman Road, east of the officers' club. Cutter lived in a red brick house with a screen porch overlooking Arlington National Cemetery, the garden of heroes. To Inspector O'Day, who'd served in Vietnam, what little he knew of the man and the case made it seem blasphemous that he should live here. The FBI agent told himself that he might be jumping to an inaccurate conclusion, but his instincts told him otherwise as he watched the man lock his car and walk into the house.

One benefit of being part of the President's

staff was that he had excellent personal security when he wanted it, and the best technical security services as a matter of course. The Secret Service and other government agencies worked very hard and very regularly to make sure that his phone lines were secure. The FBI would have to clear any tap with them, and would also have to get a court order first, neither of which had been done. Cutter called a WATS line number — with a toll-free 800 prefix — and spoke a few words. Had anyone recorded the conversation he would have had a problem explaining it, but then so would the listener. Each word he spoke was the first word on a dictionary page, and the number of each page had three digits. The old paperback dictionary had been given him before he left the house in Panama, and he would soon discard it. The code was as simple and easy to use as it was effective, and the few words he spoke indicated pages whose numbers combined to indicate map coordinates for a few locations in Colombia. The man on the other end of the line repeated them back and hung up. The WATS-line call would not show up on Cutter's phone bill as a long-distance call. The WATS account would be terminated the next day. His final move was to take the small computer disk from his pocket. Like many people he had magnets holding messages to his refrigerator door. Now he waved one of them over the disk a few times to destroy the data on it. The disk itself was the last existing record of the soldiers of Operation SHOWBOAT. It was also the last means of reopening the satellite radio link to them. It went into the trash. SHOWBOAT had never happened.

Or that's what Vice Admiral James A. Cutter, USN, told himself. He mixed himself a drink and walked out onto his porch, looking down across the green carpet to the countless headstones. Many times he'd walked over to the Tomb of the Unknown Soldier, watching the soldiers of the President's Guard go through their mechanistic routine before the resting places of men who had served their country to the utmost. It occurred to him now that there would be more unknown soldiers, fallen on some nameless field. The original unknown soldier had died in France in World War I, and had known what he fought for — or thought he did, Cutter corrected himself. Most often they never really understood what it was all about. What they were told wasn't always the truth, but their country called, and off they went to do their duty. But you really needed a perspective to understand what it was all about, how the game was played. And that didn't always — ever? — jibe with what the soldiers were told. He remembered his own service off the coast of Vietnam, a junior officer on a destroyer, watching five-inch-gun rounds pound the beach, and wondering what it was like to be a soldier, living in the mud. But still they went to serve their country, not knowing that the country herself didn't know what service she needed or wanted. An army was composed of young kids who did

965

their job without understanding, serving with their lives, and in this case, with their deaths.

"Poor bastards," he whispered to himself. It really was too bad, wasn't it? But it couldn't be helped.

It surprised everyone that they couldn't get the radio link working. The communications sergeant said that his transmitter was working just fine, but there was no answer from VARIABLE at six o'clock local time. Captain Ramirez didn't like it, but decided to press on to the extraction point. There had been no fallout from Chavez's little adventure with the would-be rapist, and the young sergeant led off for what he expected would be the last time. The enemy forces had swept this area, stupidly and oafishly, and wouldn't be back soon. The night went easily. They moved south in one-hour segments, stopping off at rally points, looping their path of advance to check for trailers, and detecting none. By four the following morning, they were at the extraction site. It was a clearing just downhill from a peak of eight thousand feet, lower than the really big crests, and conducive to a covert approach. The chopper could have picked them up nearly anywhere, of course, but their main consideration was still stealth. They'd be picked up, and no one would ever be the wiser. It was a shame about the men they'd lost, but no one would ever really know what they'd been here for, and the mission, though a costly one, had been a success. Captain Ramirez had said so.

He set his men in a wide perimeter to cover all approaches, with fallback defensive positions in case something untoward and unexpected happened. When that task was completed, he again set up his satellite radio and started transmitting. But again, there was no reply from VARIABLE. He didn't know what the problem was, but to this point there had been no hint of trouble, and communications foul-ups were hardly unknown to any infantry officer. He wasn't very worried about this one. Not yet, anyway.

Clark was caught rather short by the message. He and Larson were just planning their flight back to Colombia when it arrived. Just a message form with a few code-words, it was enough to ignite Clark's temper, so vile a thing that he labored hard to control it in the knowledge that it was his most dangerous enemy. He wanted to call Langley, but decided against it, fearing that the order might be restated in a way difficult to ignore. As he cooled off, his brain started working again. That was the danger of his temper, Clark reminded himself, it stopped him from thinking. He sure as hell needed to think now. In a minute he decided that it was time for a little initiative.

"Come on, Larson, we're going to take a little ride." That was easily accomplished. He was still "Colonel Williams" to the Air Force, and got himself a car. Next came a map, and Clark picked his brain to remember the path to that hilltop. . . .

It took an hour, and the last few hundred yards were a potholed nightmare of a twisted, half-paved road. The van was still there, as was the single armed guard, who came forward to give them a less than eager greeting.

"Stand down, mister, I was here before."

"Oh, it's you — but, sir, I'm under orders to —"

Clark cut him off. "Don't argue with me. I know about your orders. Why the hell do you think I'm here? Now be a good boy and safe that weapon before you hurt yourself." Clark walked right past him, again amazing Larson, who was far more impressed with loaded and pointed guns.

"What gives?" Clark asked as soon as he was inside. He looked around. All the gear was turned off. The only noise was from the air-conditioning units.

"They shut us down," the senior communicator answered.

"Who shut you down?"

"Look, I can't say, all right, I got orders that we're shut down. That's it. You want answers, go see Mr. Ritter."

Clark walked right up to the man. "He's too far away."

"I got my orders."

"What orders?"

"To shut down, damn it! We haven't transmitted or received anything since lunchtime yesterday," the man said.

"Who gave you the orders?"

"I can't say!"

"Who's looking after the field teams?"

"I don't know. Somebody else. He said our security was blown and it was being handed over to somebody else."

"Who — you can tell me this time," Clark said in an eerily calm voice.

"No, I can't."

"Can you call up the field teams?"

"No."

"Why not?"

"Their satellite radios are encoded. The algorithm is on computer disk. We downloaded all three copies of the encryption keys and erased two of 'em. He watched us do it and took the third disk himself."

"How do you reestablish the link?"

"You can't. It's a unique algorithm that's based on the time transmissions from NAVSTAR satellites. Secure as hell, and just about impossible to duplicate."

"In other words those kids are completely cut off?"

"Well, no, he took the third disk, and there's somebody else who's — "

"Do you really believe that?" Clark asked. The man's hesitation answered the question. When the field officer spoke again, it was in a voice that didn't brook resistance. "You just told me that the commo link was unbreakable, but you accepted a statement from somebody you never saw before that it had been compromised. We got thirty kids down there, and it sounds like they've been abandoned. Now, who gave the orders to do it?"

"Cutter."

"He was *here?*"

"Yesterday."

"Jesus." Clark looked around. The other officer couldn't bring himself to look up. Both men had speculated over what was really happening, and had come to the same conclusion that he had. "Who set up the commo plan for this mission?"

"I did."

"What about their tactical radios?"

"Basically they're commercial sets, a little customized. They have a choice of ten SSB frequencies."

"You have the freqs?"

"Well, yeah, but — "

"Give them to me right now."

The man thought to say that he couldn't do that, but decided against it. He'd just say that Clark threatened him, and it didn't seem like the right time to start a little war in the van. That was accurate enough. He was very much afraid of Mr. Clark at this moment. He pulled the sheet of frequencies from a drawer. It hadn't occurred to Cutter to destroy that, too, but he had the radio channels memorized anyway.

"If anybody asks . . . "

"You were never here, sir."

"Very good." Clark walked out into the darkness. "Back to the air base," Clark told Larson.

"We're looking for a helicopter."

Cortez had made it back to Anserma without note having been taken of his seven-hour absence, and had left behind a communications link that knew how to find him, and now, rested and bathed, he waited for the phone to ring. He congratulated himself, first, on having set up a communications net in America as soon as he'd taken the job with the Cartel; next on his performance with Cutter, though not as much for this. He could scarcely have lost, though the American had made it easier through his own stupidity, not unlike Carter and the *marielitos*, though at least the former President had been motivated by humanitarian aims, not political advantage. Now it was just a matter of waiting. The amusing part was the book code that he was using. It was backwards from the usual thing. Normally a book code was transmitted in numbers to identify words, but this time words indicated numbers. Cortez already had the American tactical maps — anyone could buy American military maps from their Defense Mapping Agency, and he'd been using them himself to run his operation against the Green Berets. The book-code system was always a secure method of passing information; now it was even more so.

Waiting was no easier for Cortez than for anyone else, but he amused himself with further planning. He knew what his next two moves were, but what about after that? For one thing, Cortez

971

thought, the Cartel had neglected the European and Japanese markets. Both regions were flush with hard currency, and while Japan might be hard to crack — it was hard to import things legally into that market — Europe would soon get much easier. With the EEC beginning its integration of the continent into a single political entity, trade barriers would soon start to come down. That meant opportunity for Cortez. It was just a matter of finding ports of entry where security was either lax or negotiable, and then setting up a distribution network. Reducing exports to America could not be allowed to interfere with Cartel income, after all. Europe was a market barely tapped, and there he would begin to expand the Cartel horizons with his surplus product. In America, reduced demand would merely increase price. In fact, he expected that his promise to Cutter — a temporary one to be sure — would have a small but positive effect on Cartel income. At the same time, the disorderly American distribution networks would sort themselves out rapidly after the supply was reduced. The strong and efficient would survive, and once firmly established, would conduct business in a more orderly way. Violent crime was more troublesome to the *yanquis* than the actual drug addiction that caused it. Once the violence abated, drug addiction itself would lose some of the priority in the pantheon of American social problems. The Cartel wouldn't suffer. It would grow in riches and power so long as people desired its product.

While that was happening, Colombia itself would be further subverted, but more subtly. That was one more area in which Cortez had been given professional training. The current lords used a brute-force approach, offering money while at the same time threatening death. No, that would also have to stop. The lust in the developed countries for cocaine was a temporary thing, was it not? Sooner or later it would become unfashionable, and demand would gradually diminish. That was one thing that the lords didn't see. When it began to happen, the Cartel had to have a solid political base and a diversified economic foundation if it wished to survive the diminution of its power. That demanded a more accommodating stance with its parent country. Cortez was prepared to establish that, too. Eliminating some of the more obnoxious lords would be a major first step toward that goal. History taught that you could reach a *modus vivendi* with almost anybody. And Cortez had just proven it to be true.

The phone rang. He answered it. He wrote down the words given him and after hanging up, picked up the dictionary. Within a minute he was making marks on his tactical map. The American Green Berets were not fools, he saw. Their encampments were all set on places difficult to approach. Attacking and destroying them would be very costly. Too bad, but all things had their price. He summoned his staff and started getting radio messages out. Within an hour, the hunter groups were coming down off the mountains to redeploy. He'd hit them one at a time, he decided. That would guarantee sufficient strength to overwhelm each detachment, and also guarantee sufficient losses that he'd have to draw further on the retainers of the lords. He would not accompany the teams up the mountains, of course, but that was also too bad. It might have been amusing to watch.

Ryan hadn't slept at all well. A conspiracy was one thing when aimed at an external enemy. His career at CIA had been nothing more than that, an effort to bring advantage to his own country, often by inflicting disadvantage, or harm, upon another. That was his job as a servant of his country's government. But now he was in a conspiracy that was arguably against the government itself. The fact denied him sleep.

Jack was sitting in his library, a single reading lamp illuminating his desk. Next to him were two phones, one secure, one not. It was the latter which rang.

"Hello?"

"This is John," the voice said.

"What's the problem?"

"Somebody cut off support for the field teams."

"But why?"

"Maybe somebody wants them to disappear."

Ryan felt a chill at the back of his neck. "Where are you?"

"Panama. Communications have been shut down and the helicopter is gone. We have thirty kids on hilltops waiting for help that ain't gonna come."

"How can I reach you?" Clark gave him a number. "Okay, I'll be back to you in a few hours."

"Let's not screw around." The line clicked off.

"Jesus." Jack looked into the shadows of his library. He called his office to say that he'd drive himself into work. Then he called Dan Murray.

Ryan was back in the FBI building underpass sixty minutes later. Murray was waiting for him and took him back upstairs. Shaw was there, too, and much-needed coffee was passed out.

"Our field guy called me at home. VARIABLE has been shut down, and the helicopter crew that was supposed to bring them out has been pulled. He thinks they're going to be — hell, he thinks — "

"Yeah," Shaw observed. "If so, we now have a probable violation of the law. Conspiracy to commit murder. Proving it might be a little tough, though."

"Stuff your law — what about those soldiers?"

"How do we get them out?" Murray asked. "Get help from — no, we can't get the Colombians involved, can we?"

"How do you think they'd react to an invasion from a foreign army?" Shaw noted. "About the same way we would."

"What about confronting Cutter?" Jack asked. Shaw answered.

"Confront him with what? What do we have? Zip. Oh, sure, we can get those communications guys and the helicopter crews and talk to them, but they'll stonewall for a while, and then what? By the time we have a case, those soldiers are dead."

"And if we can bring them out, then what case do we have?" Murray asked. "Everybody runs for cover, papers get shredded. . . . "

"If I may make a suggestion, gentlemen, why don't we forget about courtrooms for the moment and try to concentrate on getting those grunts the hell out of Indian country?"

"Getting them out is fine, but — "

"You think your case will get better with thirty or forty new victims?" Ryan snapped. "What is the objective here?"

"That was a cheap shot, Jack," Murray said.

"Where's your case? What if the President authorized the operation, with Cutter as his go-between, and there's no written orders? CIA acted in accordance with verbal orders, and the orders are arguably legal, except that I got told to mislead Congress if they ask, *which they haven't done yet!* There's also that little kink in the law that says we can start a covert operation without telling them, no matter what it is — the limits on our covert ops come from a White House Executive Order, remember — as long as we do get around to telling them. Therefore a killing authorized by the guy who puts out the Executive Order can only become a murder *retroactively* if something extraneous to the murder itself does *not* happen! What bonehead ever set these statutes up? Have they ever really been tested in court?"

"You left something out," Murray observed.

"Yeah, the most obvious reply from Cutter is that this isn't a covert operation at all, but a paramilitary counterterrorist op. That evades the whole issue of intelligence-oversight. Now we come under the War Powers Resolution, which has another lead-time factor. Have any of these laws ever been tested in court?"

"Not really," Shaw answered. "There's been a lot of dancing around, but nothing actually on point. War-Powers especially is a constitutional question that both sides are afraid to put in front of a judge. Where are you coming from, Ryan?"

"I got an agency to protect, don't I? If this adventure goes public, the CIA reverts back to what it was in the seventies. For example, what happens to your counterterrorist programs if the info we feed you dries up?" That one scored points, Jack saw. CIA was the silent partner in the war on terrorism, feeding most of its data to the Bureau, as Shaw had every reason to know. "On the other hand, from what we've talked about the last couple of days, what real case do you have?"

"If by withdrawing support for SHOWBOAT, Cutter made it easier for Cortez to kill them, we have a violation of the District of Columbia law against conspiracy to commit murder. In the absence of a federal law, a crime committed on federal property can be handled by the municipal law that applies to the violation. Some part of what he did was accomplished here or on other federal property, and that's where the jurisdiction comes from. That's how we investigated the cases back in the seventies."

"What cases were they?" Jack asked Shaw.

"It spun out of the Church Committee hearings. We investigated assassination plots by CIA against Castro and some others — they never came to trial. The law we would have used was the conspiracy statute, but the constitutional issues were so murky that the investigation died a natural death, much to everyone's relief."

"Same thing here, isn't it? Except while we fiddle . . ."

"You've made your point," the acting Director said. "Number one priority is getting them out, any way we can. Is there a way to do it covertly?"

"I don't know yet."

"Look, for starters let's get in touch with your field officer," Murray suggested.

"He doesn't —"

"He gets immunity, anything he wants," Shaw said at once. "My word on it. Hell, far as I can tell he hasn't really broken any laws anyway — because of Martinez-Barker — but you have my word, Ryan, no harm comes to him."

"Okay." Jack pulled the slip of paper from his

shirt pocket. The number Clark had given him wasn't a real number, of course, but by adding and subtracting to the digits in a prearranged way, the call went through.

"This is Ryan. I'm calling from FBI Headquarters. Hold on and listen." Jack handed the phone over.

"This is Bill Shaw. I'm acting Director. Number one, I just told Ryan that you are in the clear. My word: no action goes against you. Will you trust me on that? Good." Shaw smiled in no small surprise. "Okay, this is a secure line, and I presume that your end is the same way. I need to know what you think is going on, and what you think we can do about it. We know about the kids, and we're looking for a way to get them out. From what Jack tells us, you might have some ideas. Let's hear them." Shaw punched the speaker button on his phone, and everyone started taking notes.

"How fast do you think we can have the radios set up?" Ryan wondered when Clark had finished.

"The technicians start getting in around seven-thirty, figure by lunch. What about transport?"

"I think I can handle that," Jack said. "If you want covert, I can arrange covert. It means letting somebody else in, but it's somebody we can trust."

"No way we can talk to them?" Shaw asked Clark, whose name he didn't yet know.

"Negative," the speaker said. "You sure you

can pull it off on your end?"

"No, but we can give it a pretty good try," Shaw replied.

"See you tonight, then." The line clicked off.

"Now all we have to do is steal some airplanes," Murray thought aloud. "Maybe a ship, too? So much the better if we bring it off covertly, right?"

"Huh?" That one threw Ryan. Murray explained.

Admiral Cutter emerged from his house at 6:15 for his daily jog. He headed downhill toward the river and chugged along the path paralleling the George Washington Parkway. Inspector O'Day followed. A reformed smoker, the inspector had no problems keeping up, and watched for anything unusual, but nothing appeared. No messages passed, no dead-drops laid, just a middle-aged man trying to keep fit. Another agent picked him up as Cutter turned for home. O'Day would change and be ready to follow Cutter into work, wondering if he'd spot some unusual behavior there.

Jack showed up for work at the usual hour, looking as tired as he felt. The morning conference in Judge Moore's office began at 8:30, and for once there was a full crew, though there might as well not have been. The DCI and DDO, he saw, were quiet, nodding but not taking very many notes.

These were — well, not friends, Ryan thought.

Admiral Greer had been a friend and mentor. But Judge Moore had been a good boss, and though he and Ritter had never really gotten along, the DDO had never treated him unfairly. He had to give them one more chance, Jack told himself impulsively. When the conference ended, he was slow picking up his things while the others left. Moore caught the cue, as did Ritter.

"Jack, you want to say something?"

"I'm not sure I'm right for DDI," Ryan opened.

"Why do you say that?" Judge Moore asked.

"Something's happening that you aren't telling me about. If you don't trust me, I shouldn't have the job."

"Orders," Ritter said. He was unable to hide his discomfort.

"Then you look me straight in the eye and tell me it's all legitimate. I'm supposed to know. I have a right to know." Ritter looked to Judge Moore.

"I wish we were able to let you in on this, Dr. Ryan," the DCI said. He tried to bring his eyes up to meet Jack's, but they wavered and fixed on a spot of wall. "But I have to follow orders, too."

"Okay. I've got some leave coming. I want to think a few things over. My work is all caught up. I'm out of here for a few days, starting in an hour."

"The funeral's tomorrow, Jack."

"I know. I'll be there, Judge," Ryan lied. Then he left the room.

"He knows," Moore said after the door closed.

"No way."

"He knows and he wants to be out of the office."

"So what do we do about it if you're right?"

The Director of Central Intelligence looked up this time. "Nothing. That's the best thing we can do right now."

That was clear. Cutter had done better than he knew. In destroying the radio encryption codes needed to communicate with the four teams, KNIFE, BANNER, FEATURE, and OMEN, he'd eliminated the Agency's ability to affect the turn of events. Neither Ritter nor Moore really expected the National Security Adviser to get the men out, but they had no alternative that would not damage themselves, the Agency, and their President — and, incidentally, their country. If Ryan wanted out of the way if things came apart — well, Moore thought, maybe he had sensed something. The DCI didn't blame him for wanting to stay clear.

There were still things he had to tie up, of course. Ryan left the building just after eleven that morning. He had a car phone in his Jaguar and placed a call to a Pentagon number. "Captain Jackson, please," he said when it was picked up. "Jack Ryan calling." Robby picked up a few seconds later.

"Hey, Jack!"

"How's lunch grab you?"

"Fine with me. My place or yours, boy?"

"You know Artie's Deli?"

"K Street at the river. Yeah."

"Be there in half an hour."

"Right."

Robby spotted his friend at a corner table and came right over. There was already a place set for him, and another man was at the table.

"I hope you like corned beef," Jack said. He waved to the other man. "This is Dan Murray."

"The Bureau guy?" Robby asked as they shook hands.

"Correct, Captain. I'm a deputy assistant director."

"Doing what?"

"Well, I'm supposed to be in the Criminal Division, but ever since I got back I've been stuck supervising two major cases. You ought to be able to guess which ones they are."

"Oh." Robby started working on his sandwich.

"We need some help, Rob," Jack said.

"Like what?"

"Like we need you to get us somewhere quietly."

"Where?"

"Hurlburt Field. That's part of — "

"Eglin, I know. Hurlburt's where the Special Operations Wing works out of; it's right next to P-cola. Whole lot of people been borrowing Navy airplanes lately. The boss doesn't like it."

"You can tell him about this," Murray said. "Just so it doesn't leave his office. We're trying to clean something up."

"What?"

"I can't say, Rob," Jack replied. "But part of it is what you brought to me. It's a worse mess than you think. We have to move real fast, and nobody can know about it. We just need a discreet taxi service for the moment."

"I can do that, but I want to clear it with Admiral Painter."

"Then what?"

"Meet me at Pax River at two o'clock, down the hill at Strike. Hell, I've wanted to do a little proficiency flying anyway."

"Might as well finish your lunch."

Jackson left them five minutes later. Ryan and Murray did the same, driving to the latter's house. Here Jack made a phone call to his wife, telling her that he had to be out of town for a few days and not to worry. They drove away in Ryan's car.

Patuxent River Naval Air Test Center is located about an hour's drive from Washington, on the western shore of the Chesapeake Bay. Formerly one of the nicer plantations of antebellum Maryland, it was now the Navy's primary flight-test and evaluation center, fulfilling most of the functions of the better-known Edwards Air Force Base in California. It is the home of the Navy's Test Pilot School, where Robby had been an instructor, and houses various test directorates, one of which, located a mile or two downhill from the main flight line, is called Strike. The Strike Directorate is concerned with fighter and attack planes, the sexy fast-movers. Murray's FBI identification was sufficient to get them on base, and after checking in with the Strike security shack, they found a place to wait, listening to the bellow of afterburning jet engines. Robby's Corvette arrived twenty minutes later. The new captain led them into the hangar.

"You're in luck," he told them. "We're taking a couple of Tomcats down to Pensacola. The Admiral called ahead, and they're preflighting the birds already. I, uh —"

Another officer came into the room. "Cap'n Jackson? I'm Joe Bramer," the lieutenant said. "I hear we're heading down south, sir."

"Correct, Mr. Bramer. These gents are going with us. Jack Murphy and Dan Tomlinson. They're government employees who need some familiarization with Navy flight procedures. Think you can rustle up some poopy suits and hard hats?"

"No problem, sir. Be back in a minute."

"You wanted covert. You got covert," Jackson chuckled. He pulled his flight suit and helmet from a bag. "What gear you guys bringing along?"

"Shaving kits," Murray replied. "And one bag."

"We can handle that."

Fifteen minutes later, everyone climbed up

ladders to board the aircraft. Jack got to fly with his friend. Five minutes after that, the Tomcats were taxiing to the end of the runway.

"Go easy, Rob," Ryan said as they awaited clearance for takeoff.

"Like an airliner," Jackson promised. It wasn't quite that way. The fighters leapt off the ground and streaked to cruising altitude about twice as fast as a 727, but Jackson kept the ride smooth and level once he got there.

"What gives, Jack?" he asked over the intercom.

"Robby, I can't —"

"Did I ever tell you all the things I can make this baby do for me? Jack, my boy, I can make this baby sing. I can turn inside a virgin quail."

"Robby, what we're trying to do is rescue some people who may be cut off. And if you tell that to anyone, even your Admiral, you might just screw things up for us. You ought to be able to figure it out from there."

"Okay. What about your car?"

"Just leave it there."

"I'll get somebody to put the right sticker on it."

"Good idea."

"You're getting better about flying, Jack. You haven't whimpered once."

"Yeah, well, I got one more flight today, and that one's in a fucking helicopter. I haven't ridden one of those since the day my back got broken on Crete." It felt good to tell him that. The real question, of course, was whether or not they'd get the chopper. But that was Murray's job. Jack turned his head to look around and was stunned to see the other Tomcat only a few feet off their right wingtip. Murray waved at him. "Christ, Robby!"

"Huh?"

"The other plane!"

"Hell, I told him to ease it off some, must be twenty feet away. We always fly in formation."

"Congratulations, you just got your whimper."

The flight lasted just over an hour. The Gulf of Mexico appeared first as a blue ribbon on the horizon, then grew into an oceanic mass of water as the two fighters headed down to land. Pensacola's strips were visible to the east, then got lost in the haze. It struck Ryan as odd that he feared flying less when he rode in a military aircraft. You could see better, and somehow that made a difference. But the fighters even landed in formation, which seemed madly dangerous, though nothing happened. The wingman touched first, and then Robby's a second or two later. Both Tomcats rolled out and turned at the end of the runway, stopping near a pair of automobiles. Some groundcrew men had ladders.

"Good luck, Jack," Robby said as the canopy came up.

"Thanks for the ride, man." Jack managed to detach himself from the airplane without help and climbed down. Murray was beside him a minute later. Both entered the waiting cars, and behind them the Tomcats taxied away to complete their flight to nearby Pensacola Naval Air Station.

Murray had called ahead. The officer who met them was the intelligence chief for the 1st Special Operations Wing.

"We need to see Colonel Johns," Murray said after identifying himself. That was the only conversation needed for the moment. The car took them past the biggest helicopters Ryan had ever seen, then to a low block building with cheap windows. The wing intelligence officer took them in. He handled the introduction of the visitors, thinking erroneously that Ryan was also FBI, then left the three alone in the room.

"What can I do for you?" PJ asked warily.

"We want to talk about trips you made to Panama and Colombia," Murray replied.

"Sorry, we don't discuss what we do here very freely. That's what special ops are all about."

"A couple of days ago you were given some orders by Vice Admiral Cutter. You were in Panama then," Murray said. "Before that you had flown armed troops into Colombia. First you took them into the coastal lowlands, then you pulled them out and reinserted them into the hill country, correct?"

"Sir, I cannot comment on that, and whatever inference you draw is yours, not mine."

"I'm a cop, not a reporter. You've been given illegal orders. If you carry them out, you may be an accessory to a major felony charge." Best to get things immediately on the table, Murray thought. It had the desired effect. Hearing from a senior FBI official that his orders might be illegal forced Johns to respond, though only a little bit.

"Sir, you're asking me something I don't know how to respond to."

Murray reached into his bag and pulled out a manila envelope. He removed a photograph and handed it to Colonel Johns. "The man who gave you those orders, of course, was the President's National Security Adviser. Before he met with you, he met with this guy. That is Colonel Félix Cortez. He used to be with the DGI, but now he's working for the Drug Cartel as chief of security. He was instrumental in the Bogotá murders. Exactly what they agreed on we do not know, but I can tell you what we do know. There is a communications van over the Gaillard Cut that had been the radio link with the four teams on the ground. Cutter visited it and shut it down. Then he came to see you and ordered you to fly home and never talk about the mission. Now, you put all three of those things together and tell me if what you do come up with sounds like something you want to be part of."

"I don't know, sir." Johns' response was automatic, but his face had gone pink.

"Colonel, those teams have already taken casualties. It appears likely that the orders you were given might have been aimed at getting them all killed. People are out hunting them right now,"

Ryan said. "We need your help to go get them out."

"Who exactly are you, anyway?"

"CIA."

"But it's your goddamned operation!"

"No, it isn't, but I won't bore you with the details," Jack said. "We need your help. Without it, those soldiers aren't going to make it home. It's that simple."

"So you're sending us back to clean up your mess. That's the way it always is with you people, you send us out — "

"Actually," Murray said, "we were planning to go with you. Part of the way anyway. How soon can you be in the air?"

"Tell me exactly what you want." Murray did just that. Colonel Johns nodded and checked his watch.

"Ninety minutes."

The MH-53J was far larger than the CH-46 that had nearly ended Ryan's life at twenty-three, but no less frightening to him. He looked at the single rotor and remembered that they were making a long, over-water flight. The flight crew was businesslike and professional, hooking both civilians up to the intercom and telling them where to sit and what to do. Ryan was especially attentive to the ditching instructions. Murray kept looking at the miniguns, the impressive six-barrel gatlings set next to enormous hoppers of live shells. There were three for this flight. The helicopter lifted off just after four and headed southwest. As soon as they were airborne, Murray had a crewman attach him to the floor with a twenty-foot safety line so that he could walk around. The hatch at the rear of the aircraft was half open, and he walked back to watch the ocean pass beneath them. Ryan stayed put. The ride was better than the Marine Corps helicopters he remembered, but it still felt like sitting on a chandelier during an earthquake as the aircraft vibrated and oscillated beneath its enormous six-bladed rotor. He could look forward and see one of the pilots, just sitting there as comfortably as though at the wheel of a car. But, Ryan told himself, it wasn't a car.

What he hadn't anticipated was the midair refueling. He felt the aircraft increase power and take a slightly nose-up attitude. Then through the front window he saw the wing of another aircraft. Murray hastened forward to watch, standing behind the crew chief, Sergeant Zimmer. He and Ryan were both hooked into the intercom.

"What happens if you tangle with the hose?" Murray asked as they neared the drogue.

"I don't know," Colonel Johns answered coolly. "It's never happened to me yet. You want to keep it quiet now, sir?"

Ryan looked around for "facilities." He saw what looked like a camper's john, but getting to it meant taking his seat belt off. Jack decided against it. The refueling ended without incident, entirely due, Jack was sure, to his prayers.

Panache was cruising on her station in the Yucatan Channel, between Cuba and the Mexican Coast, following a racetrack pattern. There hadn't been much in the way of activity since the cutter had gotten here, but the crew took comfort from the fact that they were back at sea. The great adventure at the moment was observing the new female crewmen. They had a new female ensign fresh from the Coast Guard Academy in Connecticut, and a half dozen others, mainly unrated seamen, but two petty officers, both electronics types, who, their peers grudgingly admitted, knew their jobs. Captain Wegener was watching the new ensign stand watch as junior officer of the deck. Like all new ensigns she was nervous and eager and a little scared, especially with the skipper on the bridge. She was also cute as a button, and that was something Wegener had never thought of an ensign before.

"Commanding officer, commanding officer," the bulkhead speaker called. Wegener picked up the phone next to his bridge chair.

"Captain here. What is it?"

"Need you in the radio room, sir."

"On the way." Red Wegener rose from his chair. "Carry on," he said on his way aft.

"Sir," the petty officer told him in the radio shack, "we just got a transmission from an Air Force helo, says he's got a person he has to drop off here. Says it's secret, sir. I don't have anything on my board about it, and . . . well, sir, I

992

didn't know what to do, sir. So I called you."

"Oh?" The woman handed him the microphone. Wegener depressed the transmit button. "This is *Panache*. Commanding officer speaking. Who am I talking to?"

"*Panache*, this is CAESAR. Helicopter inbound your position on a Sierra-Oscar. I have a drop-off for you, over."

Sierra-Oscar meant some sort of special operation. Wegener thought for a moment, then decided that there wasn't all that much to think about.

"Roger, CAESAR, say your ETA."

"ETA one-zero minutes."

"Roger, one-zero minutes. We'll be waiting. Out." Wegener handed the microphone back and returned to the bridge.

"Flight quarters," he told the OOD. "Miss Walters, bring us to Hotel Corpin."

"Aye aye, sir."

Things started happening quickly and smoothly. The bosun's mate of the watch keyed the 1-MC: "Flight quarters, flight quarters, all hands man your flight-quarter stations. Smoking lamp is out topside." Cigarettes sailed into the water and hands removed their caps, lest they be sucked into somebody's engines. Ensign Walters looked to see where the wind was, and altered course accordingly, also increasing the cutter's speed to fifteen knots, thus bringing the ship to Hotel Corpin, the proper course for flight operations. And all, she told herself proudly, without having to be told. Wegener turned away and grinned. It was one of many first steps in the career of a new officer. She'd actually known what to do and done it without help. For the captain it was like watching his child take a first step. Eager and smart.

"Christ, it's a big one," Riley said on the bridge wing. Wegener went out to watch.

The helicopter, he saw, was an Air Force -53, far larger than anything the Coast Guard had. The pilot brought it in from aft, then pivoted to fly sideways. Someone was attached to the rescue cable and lowered down to the waiting arms of four deck crewmen. The instant he was detached from the harness, the helicopter lowered its nose and moved off to the south. Quick and smooth, Red noted.

"Didn't know we were getting company, sir," Riley observed as he pulled out a cigar.

"We're still at flight quarters, Chief!" Ensign Walters snapped from the wheelhouse.

"Yes, ma'am, beg pardon, I forgot," the bosun responded with a crafty look at Wegener. Another test passed. She wasn't afraid to yell at the master chief, even if he was older than her father.

"You can secure from flight quarters," the CO told her. "I didn't know either," Wegener told Riley. "I'm going aft to see who it is." He heard Ensign Walters give her orders, under the supervision of a lieutenant and a couple of chiefs.

The visitor, he saw as he approached the helo deck door, was stripping off a green flight suit, but didn't appear to be carrying anything, which seemed odd. Then the man turned around, and it just got stranger.

"Howdy, Captain," Murray said.

"What gives?"

"You got a nice quiet place to talk?"

"Come along." They were in Wegener's cabin shortly thereafter.

"I figure I owe you for a couple of favors," he said. "You could have given me a bad time over that dumb stunt we pulled. Thanks for the tip on the lawyer, too. What he told me was pretty scary — but it turns out that I didn't talk to him until after the two bastards were killed. Last time I ever do something that dumb," Wegener promised. "You're here to collect, right?"

"Good guess."

"So what's going on? You don't just borrow one of those special-ops helos for a personal favor."

"I need you to be someplace tomorrow night."

"Where?"

Murray pulled an envelope from his pocket. "These coordinates. I have the radio plan, too." Murray gave him a few more details.

"You did this yourself, didn't you?" the captain said.

"Yeah, why?"

"Because you ought to have checked the weather."

27.

The Battle of Ninja Hill

Armies have habits. These often appear strange or even downright crazy to outsiders, but for all of them there is an underlying purpose, learned over the four millennia in which men have fought one another in an organized fashion. Mainly the lessons learned are negative ones. Whenever men are killed for no good purpose, it is the business of armies to learn from the mistake and ensure that it will never happen again. Of course, such mistakes are repeated as often in the profession of arms as in any other, but also as in all professions, the really good practitioners are those who never forget fundamentals. Captain Ramirez was one of these. Though the captain had learned that he had too much sentiment, that the loss of life which was part and parcel of his chosen way of life was too difficult a burden to bear, he still remembered the other lessons, one of which was reinforced by the most recent and unpleasant discovery. He still expected to be picked up tonight by the Air Force helicopter, and felt reasonably sure that he had evaded the teams set out to hunt Team KNIFE, but he remembered all the lessons of the past when soldiers died because the unexpected happened, because they took things for granted, because they forgot the fundamentals.

The fundamental rule here was that a unit in a fixed location was always vulnerable, and to reduce that vulnerability, the intelligent commander prepared a defense plan. Ramirez remembered that, and hadn't lost a keen eye for terrain. He didn't think that anyone would come to trouble his men that night, but he had already prepared for that eventuality.

His deployments reflected the threat, which he evaluated as a very large but relatively untrained force, and his two special advantages: first, that all of his men had radios, and second, that there were three silenced weapons at his disposal. Ramirez hoped that they wouldn't come calling, but if they did, he planned to give them a whole series of nasty surprises.

Each of his men was part of a two-man team for mutual support — there is nothing so fearful as to be alone in a combat action, and the effectiveness of any soldier is multiplied many times over merely by having a single comrade at his side. Each pair had dug three holes — called Primary, Alternate, and Supplementary — as part of three separate defensive networks, all of them camouflaged and carefully sited to be mutually supporting. Where possible, fire lanes were cleared, but always on oblique lines so that the fire would take the attacker from the side, not the front, and part of the plan was to force the attacker to move in a direction anticipated by the Team. Finally, if everything broke down, there were three preplanned escape routes and corresponding rally points. His men kept busy all day, digging their holes, preparing their positions, siting their remaining claymore mines, until their rest periods were occupied only with sleep and not conversation. But he couldn't keep himself quite that busy, and couldn't keep himself from thinking.

Through the day things kept getting worse. The radio link was never reestablished, and every time Ramirez came up at a scheduled time and heard nothing, the thinner became his explanations for it. He could no longer wave it off as an equipment or power failure at the downlink. Throughout the afternoon he told himself that it was impossible they were cut off, and he never even considered the possibility that they had *been* cut off, but the nagging thought grew louder in the back of his mind that he and his men were alone, far from home, facing a potential threat with only what they had carried in on their own backs.

The helicopter landed back at the same facility

it had only left two days before, taxiing into the hangar whose door was immediately closed. The MC-130 that had accompanied them down was similarly hidden. Ryan was exhausted by the flight and walked off with wobbly legs to find Clark waiting. The one really good piece of news was that Cutter had neglected to take the simple expedient of meeting with the base commander, never thinking that his orders would be disregarded. As a result, the reappearance of the special-operations aircraft was just another odd occurrence, and one green helicopter — in shadows they looked black — was pretty much the same as another.

Jack returned to the aircraft after making a trip to the rest room and drinking about a quart of water from the cooler. Introductions had already been explained, and he saw that Colonel Johns had hit it off with Mr. Clark.

"Third SOG, eh?"

"That's right, Colonel," Clark said. "I never made it into Laos myself, but you guys saved a few of our asses. I've been with the Agency ever since — well, almost," Clark corrected himself.

"I don't even know where to go. That Navy prick had us destroy all our maps. Zimmer remembers some of the radio freqs, but — "

"I got the freqs," Clark said.

"Fine, but we still have to find 'em. Even with tanker support, I don't have the legs to do a real search. There's a lot of country down there, and the altitude murders our fuel consumption.

What's the opposition like?"

"Lots of people with AKs. Oughta sound familiar."

PJ grimaced. "It does. I got three minis. Without any air support . . . "

"You guessed right: you are the air support. I'd hold on to the miniguns. Okay, the exfiltration sites were agreed upon beforehand?" Clark asked.

"Yeah — a primary and two backups for each team, total of twelve."

"We have to assume that they are known to the enemy. The job for tonight is finding 'em and getting them somewhere else that we know about and they don't. Then tomorrow night you can fly in for the pickup."

"And from there out. . . . The FBI guy wants us to land on that little boat. I'm worried about *Adele*. The last weather report I saw at noon had it heading north towards Cuba. I want to update that."

"I just did," Larson said as he rejoined the group. "*Adele* is heading west again, and she made hurricane an hour ago. Core winds are now seventy-five."

"Oh, shit," Colonel Johns observed. "How fast is she moving?"

"It's going to be close for tomorrow night, but no problem for our flight this evening."

"What flight is that, now?"

"Larson and I are going to hop down to locate the teams." Clark pulled a radio out of what had been Murray's bag. "We fly up and down the valley, talking on these. With luck we'll get contact."

"You must really believe in luck, son," Johns said.

O'Day reflected that the life of an FBI agent wasn't always as glamorous as people thought. There was also the little problem that with less than twenty agents on the case he couldn't assign this distasteful task to a junior agent. But the case had enough of those problems. They hadn't even considered getting a search warrant yet, and sneaking into Cutter's quarters without legal authorization — something that the Bureau seldom did anymore — was impossible. Cutter's wife had just gotten back and was bossing her staff of stewards around like a woman to the manor born. On the other hand, the Supreme Court had ruled a few years before that trash-searching didn't require the sanction of a court. That fact enabled Pat O'Day to get the best upper-body workout he'd had in years. Now he could barely raise his arms after having loaded a few tons of malodorous garbage bags into the back of a white-painted trash truck. It might have been one of several cans. The VIP section of Fort Myer was still a military post; even the trash cans had to be set up just so, and in this case, two homes shared each stopping place for the equally well organized trash contractor. O'Day had marked the bags before loading them into the back of the truck, and as a result, fifteen garbage bags were now sitting in one of the Bureau's many laboratories, though not one that was part of the tourist route, since the FBI shows only its best face to those who tour the Hoover Building, the nice, clean, antiseptic labs. The only good news was that the ventilation system was good, and there were several cans of air freshener around to disguise the smells that got past the technicians' surgical masks. O'Day himself felt as though a squadron of bluebottle flies would follow him for the rest of his life. The search took an hour as the garbage was processed across a white tabletop of imitation marble, about four days' worth of coffee grinds and half-eaten croissants, decomposing merengue, and several diapers — those were from the wrong house: the officer next door to the Cutters had his new granddaughter visiting.

"Bingo," a technician said. His gloved hand held up a computer disk. Even with the gloves, he held it on opposite corners and dropped it into an extended plastic baggie. O'Day took the bag and walked upstairs to latent prints.

Two senior technicians were working overtime tonight. They'd cheated somewhat, of course. They already had a copy of Admiral Cutter's fingerprints from the central print index — all military personnel are printed as a matter of course upon their enlistment — along with their entire bag of tricks, which included a laser.

"What was it in?" one of them asked.

"On top of some newspapers," O'Day replied.

"Aha! No extraneous grease, and good insulation against the heat. There may be a chance." The technician removed the disk from the clear bag and went to work. It took ten minutes, while O'Day paced the room.

"I got a thumbprint with eight points on the front side, and what is probably a smudged ring finger on the back side with one good point and one very marginal one. There is one completely different set, but it's too smudged to identify. It's a different pattern, though, has to be a different person."

O'Day figured that that was more than he'd had the right to expect under the circumstances. A fingerprint identification ordinarily required ten individual points — the irregularities that constituted the art of fingerprint identification — but that number had always been arbitrary. The inspector was certain that Cutter had handled this computer disk, even if a jury might not be completely sure, if that time ever came. Now it was time to see what was on it, and for that he headed to a different lab.

Since personal computers had entered the marketplace, it was only a matter of time until they were used in criminal enterprises. To investigate such use, the Bureau had its own department, but the most useful people of all were private consultants whose real business was "hacking," and for whom computers were marvelous toys and their use the most entertaining of games. To have an important government agency pay them for playing the game was their equivalent of a pro-football career. The one O'Day found waiting for him was one of the champs. He was twenty-five, and still a student at a local community college despite over two hundred hours of credits, the lowest grade for which had been a B+. He had longish red hair and a beard, both of which needed washing. O'Day handed it over.

"This is a code-word case," he said.

"That's nice," the consultant said. "This is a Sony MFD-2DD microfloppy, double-sided, double-density, 135TPI, probably formatted for 800K. What's supposed to be on it?"

"We're not sure, but probably an encipherment algorithm."

"Ah! Russian communications systems? The Sovs getting sophisticated on us?"

"You don't need to know that," O'Day pointed out.

"You guys are no fun at all," the man said as he slid the disk into the drive. The computer to which it was attached was a new Apple Macintosh IIx, each of whose expander slots was occupied by a special circuit board, two of which the technician had personally designed. O'Day had heard that he'd work on an IBM only if someone put a gun to his head.

The programs he used for this task had been designed by other hackers to recover data from damaged disks. The first one was called Rescue-data. The operation was a delicate one. First the read heads mapped each magnetic zone on the disk, copying the data over to the eight-megabyte memory of the IIx and making a permanent copy on the hard drive, plus a floppy-disk copy. That allowed him to eject the original, which O'Day immediately reinserted in the baggie.

"It's been wiped," the man said next.

"What?"

"It's been wiped, not erased or initialized, but wiped. Probably with a little toy magnet."

"Shit," O'Day observed. He knew enough about computers to realize that the magnetically stored data was destroyed by magnetic interference.

"Don't get excited."

"Huh?"

"If this guy had initialized the disk, we'd be screwed, but he just swiped a magnet around. Some of the data is gone, but some probably isn't. Give me a couple of hours and maybe I can get some of this data back for you — there's a smidge right there. It's in machine language, but I don't recognize the format . . . looks like a transposition algorithm. I don't know any of that cryppie stuff, sir. Looks fairly complex." He looked around. "This is going to take some time."

"How long?"

"How long to paint the Mona Lisa? How long to build a cathedral, How long . . . " O'Day was out of the room before he heard the third one. He dropped the disk off in the secure file in his office, then headed for the gym for a shower and a half hour in the Jacuzzi. The shower removed the stink, and while the whirlpool went to work on the aches, O'Day reflected that the case against the son of a bitch was shaping up rather nicely.

"Sir, they just ain't there."

Ramirez handed the headset back and nodded. There was no denying it now. He looked over to Guerra, his operations sergeant.

"I think somebody forgot about us."

"Well, that's good news, Cap'n. What are we gonna do about it?"

"Our next check-in time is zero-one-hundred. We give 'em one more chance. If nothing by then, I guess we move out."

"Where to, sir?"

"Head down off the mountain, see if we can borrow some transport and — Christ, I don't know. We probably have enough cash we can use to fly out of here — "

"No passports, no ID."

"Yeah. Make it to the Embassy in Bogotá?"

"That violates about a dozen different orders, sir," Guerra pointed out.

"First time for everything," Captain Ramirez observed. "Have everybody eat their last rations, rest up as best they can. We stand-to in two hours, and stay alert all night. I want Chavez and León to patrol down the hill, say two klicks' worth." Ramirez didn't have to say what he was worried about. As unlikely as intellect told them it had to be, he and Guerra were on the same wavelength.

"It's cool, Cap'n," the sergeant assured him. "We're going to be all right, just as soon as those REMFs get their shit together."

The mission briefing took fifteen minutes. The men were angry and restive at the losses they had taken, not fully appreciative of the danger that lay ahead, only of their rage at what had already happened to their numbers. Such bravado, Cortez thought, such machismo. *The fools.*

The first target was only thirty kilometers away — for the obvious reasons he wanted to deal with the nearest one first — and twenty-two of them could be covered by truck. They had to wait for darkness, of course, but sixteen trucks rolled out, each with fifteen or so men aboard. Cortez watched them depart, muttering to one another as they pulled out of sight. His own people stayed behind, of course. He had so far recruited ten men, and their loyalty was to him alone. He'd recruited well, of course. No nonsense about who their parents were or how faithfully they had killed. He'd selected them for their skills. Most were dropouts from M-19 and FARC, men for whom five years of playing at guerrilla warfare had been enough. Some had received training in Cuba or Nicaragua and had basic soldier skills — actually terrorist skills, but that put them ahead of the "soldiers" of the Cartel, most of whom had never received formal training at all. They were mercenaries. Their only interest in Cortez was in the money he'd paid them, but he'd also promised them more. More to the point, there was nowhere else for them to go. The Colombian government had no use for them. The Cartel would not have trusted them. And they had forsworn their loyalty to the two Marxist groups which were so politically bankrupt that they allowed themselves to be hired out by the Cartel. That left Cortez. He was the man they would kill for. He hadn't confided in them, since he didn't yet trust them to do any more than that, but all great movements began with small groups of people whose methods were as murky as their objectives, who knew only loyalty to a single man. At least that's what Cortez had been taught. He didn't fully believe that himself, but it was enough for the moment. He had no illusions about leading a revolution. He was merely executing — what was it called? A hostile takeover. Yes, that was right. Cortez chuckled to himself as he walked back inside and started looking at his maps.

"Good thing neither one of us is a smoker," Larson said as the wheels came up. In the cabin behind them was an auxiliary fuel tank. They had a two-hour flight down to their patrol area, and two hours back, with three hours of loiter time on station. "You suppose this is going to work?"

"If it doesn't, somebody's going to pay," Clark replied. "What about the weather?"

"We'll sneak back in ahead of it. Don't make any bets on tomorrow, though."

Chavez and León were two kilometers away from the team's farthest listening post. Both carried silenced weapons. León hadn't been the point scout for BANNER, but had woodcraft skills that Chavez liked. The best news of all was that they found nothing. Captain Ramirez had briefed them on what he was worried about. So far they hadn't detected it, which was fine with the two sergeants. They'd gone down to the north initially, then gradually come south while covering an arc of several kilometers, looking for signs, listening for noise. They were just turning for the climb back to the LZ when Chavez stopped and turned.

It was a metallic sound. He waved for León to freeze and pivoted his head around, hoping — what? he asked himself. Hoping that he'd really heard something? Hoping that he'd imagined it? He switched his goggles and scanned downhill. There was a road down there somewhere. If somebody came calling, it would be from that direction.

It was hard to tell at first. There was thick overhead cover here, and the relative absence of light forced him to turn the brightness control to the maximum. That made the picture fuzzy, like a precable TV signal from a distant city, and what he was looking for was far off — at least five hundred meters, which was as far as he could see down a thinned-out area of the forest. The tension only made him more alert, but that made his imagination work all the harder, and he had to guard against seeing things that weren't there.

But something was there. He could feel it even before the noise returned. There were no more metallic sounds, but there was . . . there was the over-loud whisper of leaves, and then it was a calm night again in the lee of the mountain. Chavez looked over to León, who also had his goggles on, was also looking that way, a green image on the tube. The goggled face turned toward Chavez and nodded. There was no emotion in the gesture, just the professional communication of an unpleasant thought. Chavez knelt to activate his radio.

"Six, this is Point," Ding called.

"Six here."

"We're at the turn-back point. We got movement down here, about half a klick below us. We're gonna wait to see what it is."

"Roger. Be careful, Sergeant," Ramirez said.

"Will do. Out." León came over to join him.

"How d'you want to play this?" 'Berto asked.

"Let's stay close, try not to move too much till we see what they're up to."

"You got it. Better cover about fifty meters uphill."

"Go ahead, I'll be right behind you." Chavez took one more look downhill before following his comrade up to a stand of thick trees. Still nothing he could really identify on the speckled screen. Two minutes later he was at the new perch.

'Berto saw it first and pointed down a trail. The moving specks were larger than the noise generated by the viewing system. Heads. Four or five hundred meters off. Coming straight up the hill.

Okay, Chavez said to himself. *Let's get a count.* He felt himself relaxing. This was business. He'd done it all before. The great unknown was now behind him. There would be a fight. He knew how to do that.

"Six, this is Point, estimate company strength, heading right up to you."

"Anything else?"

"They're moving kinda slow. Careful, like."

"How long can you stay there?"

"Maybe a couple minutes."

"Stay as long as it's safe, then move. Try to pace them for another klick or so. We want to get as many as possible into the sack."

"Roger."

"These numbers suck, man," León whispered.

"We sure as hell want to whittle 'em down some 'fore we run, don't we?" Chavez returned his eyes to the advancing enemy. He saw no obvious organization. They were taking their time, moving slowly up the hill, though he could easily hear them now. They moved in little bands of three or four, probably groups of friends, he thought, like street gangs did. You wanted a friend at your back.

Street gang, he thought. They didn't bother

with colors down here like in his barrio, just those damned AK-47s. No real plan, no fire and maneuver teams. He wondered if they had radios to coordinate with. Probably not. He realized, a little late, that they did know where they were going. He didn't understand how they knew, but it only meant that they were heading into one hell of an ambush. But there were still a lot of 'em. An awful lot.

"Time to move," Ding told 'Berto.

They raced uphill, or went as fast as their training allowed, choosing one good observation point after another and keeping their commander posted on their position and the enemy's. Ahead of them, up the hill, the squad had nearly two hours to reorient itself and prepare its ambush. Chavez and León copied his radio message on their own sets. The squad was moving forward to meet the attackers well in front of the primary defensive line. It was set between two particularly steep sections, anchored at those points with the SAWs, covering an approach route less than three hundred meters wide. If the enemy was dumb enough to come through there, well, that was their problem, wasn't it? So far they had taken a direct route to the LZ. Maybe they'd been told that KNIFE probably was there, not certainly, Chavez thought, as he and León picked their spot, just below one of the SAWs.

"Six, this is Point, we are in position. Enemy is three hundred meters below us."

Click-click.

"I see 'em," another voice called over the radio net. "Grenade One sees 'em."

"Medic has 'em."

"SAW One has 'em."

"Grenade Two. We got 'em."

"Knife, this is Six. Let's everybody be cool," Ramirez said calmly. "Looks like they're coming right in the front door. Remember the signal, people. . . ."

It took another ten minutes. Chavez switched off his scope both to save batteries and to get his eyes back to normal. His mind played and re-played the squad fire-plan. He and León had specific areas of responsibility. Each soldier was supposed to limit his fire to an individual arc. All the arcs interlocked and overlapped somewhat, but they were supposed to hunt in their own little patch and not hose down the entire area. Even the SAWs on line were so limited. The third was well behind the firing line with the small reserve force, ready to support the squad as it pulled back or to react to something unexpected.

They were within a hundred meters of the line now. The front rank of the advancing enemy was perhaps eighteen or twenty men, with others struggling behind to keep up. They moved slowly, careful of their footing, weapons held at port across their chests. Chavez counted three in his area of responsibility. León kept watch downhill as he brought his weapon up.

In the old days it was done with volley fire. Napoleonic infantry formed up shoulder-to-shoulder in ranks of two or four, leveling their muskets on command and firing on one another in one dreadful blast of power and ball. The purpose was shock. The purpose still is. Shock to unsettle those enemies fortunate enough to escape instant death, shock to tell them that this was not a place they wanted to be, shock to interfere with their performance, to stop them, to confuse them. It is no longer done with massed columns of muskets. Today it is done by letting them get very, very close, but the impact remains as much psychological as physical.

Click-click-click. Get ready, Ramirez ordered. Across the line, the riflemen snugged their weapons into their shoulders. The machine guns came up on their bipods. Safeties went off. In the center of the line, the captain wrapped his hand around a length of communications wire. It was fifty yards long, and attached to its other end was a tin can containing a few pebbles. Slowly, carefully, he pulled the wire taut. Then he yanked it hard.

The sudden sound froze the moment in time. It was as if everything stopped for an instant that seemed to last for hours. The men in front of the light-fighters turned instinctively toward the sound in their midst, away from the unknown threat that lay to their front and their flanks, away from the fingers that had just begun to press down.

The moment ended with the white muzzle flashes of the squad. The leading fifteen attackers dropped in an instant. Behind them five more died or were wounded before fire was returned. Then the firing from above stopped. The attackers responded late. Many of them emptied whole magazines in the general direction of uphill, but the soldiers were down in their holes, denying the attackers targets.

"Who fired? Who fired? What is going on here?" It was the voice of Sergeant Olivero, whose accent was perfect.

Confusion is the ally of the prepared. More men rushed forward into the killing zone to see what was happening, wondering who had shot at whom. Chavez and all the others counted to ten before coming back up. Ding had two men within thirty meters of his position. On "Ten!" he dropped one with a three-round burst and wounded the other. Maybe a dozen more enemies were down now.

Click-click-click-click-click. "Everybody move out," Ramirez called over the radios.

The drill was the same across the line. One man from each pair took off at once, racing fifty meters uphill before stopping at a preselected spot. The SAWs, which had thus far fired only short bursts as though they were mere rifles, now fired long ones to cover the disengagement. Within a minute, KNIFE had moved away from the area now being beaten with late and inaccurate fire. One man was grazed by a stray round, but ignored it. As usual, Chavez was the last to leave and the slowest to move, picking his way from one thick tree to another as the returning fire became heavier. He reactivated his goggles to get a view of things. Perhaps thirty men were down in the kill zone, only half of them moving. Too late, the enemy was looping around the south side, trying to envelop a position already deserted. He watched them come into the position he and León had occupied only minutes before, and they just stood there in confusion, still wondering what had happened. There were screams from the wounded now, and then the curses started, obscene, powerful curses of enraged men who were accustomed to inflicting death, not receiving it. New voices became clear over the din of sporadic rifle fire and curses and screams. Those would be the leaders, giving orders loudly and in a language all of the soldiers understood. Chavez had just started believing that this battle would be easily won when he took his final look.

"Oh, shit." He keyed his radio. "Six, this is Point. This is greater than company strength, sir. Say again, more than company strength. I estimate three-zero enemy casualties at this time. They just started moving up again. I got thirty or so moving south. Somebody's telling 'em to try 'n surround us."

"Roger, Ding. Get moving uphill."

"On the way." Chavez ran hard, leapfrogging past León's position.

"Mr. Clark, you've got me believing in miracles," Larson said at the wheel of his Beechcraft.

They'd made contact with Team OMEN on the third try, and ordered them to move five klicks to a clearing barely large enough for the Pave Low. The next attempt took longer, nearly forty minutes. Now they were looking for BANNER. What was left of it, Clark reminded himself. He didn't know that its survivors had linked up with KNIFE, which was the last team on his list.

The second defense position was of necessity more dispersed than the first, and Ramirez was starting to worry. His men had handled the first ambush so perfectly that someone at the Infantry School might one day write a paper about it, but one immutable law of military operations was that successful tricks can rarely be repeated. There was nothing like death to teach someone a lesson. The enemy would maneuver now, would spread out, trying to coordinate or at least to make better use of his larger numbers. And the enemy was doing something smart. He was moving faster. Now that they knew that they had a real enemy with real teeth, they knew on instinct that the best thing to do was to push, to take the initiative and force the pace of the combat action. That was the one thing that Ramirez could not really prevent. But he, too, had cards to play.

His flank scouts kept him posted on enemy movements. There were now three groups of about forty men each. Ramirez couldn't deal with all three, but he could hurt them one at a time. He also had three fire teams of five men each.

One — the remains of BANNER — he left in the center, with a scout on the left to keep track of the third enemy group while he slid the bulk of his force south and deployed on an oblique uphill-downhill line, almost an L-shaped ambush line anchored at the uphill side with both SAWs.

They didn't have to wait very long. The enemy was moving faster than Ramirez hoped, and there was barely time for his men to select good firing positions, but the attackers were still moving predictably over the terrain, which was again to be their misfortune. Chavez was at the bottom end and gave warning as they approached. Again, they allowed the enemy to close to fifty meters' distance. Chavez and León were several meters apart, looking for leaders. Their job was to fire first, silently, to remove anyone who might try to coordinate and lead the attackers. There was one, Ding thought, someone gesturing to others. He leveled his MP-5 and squeezed off a burst which missed. Despite the silenced weapon, its cycling made enough noise to draw a shot, and the whole squad opened up. Five more attackers fell. The rest returned fire accurately this time and formed up to assault the defenders' position, but when their muzzle flashes revealed their position, both SAW machine guns raked up and down their line.

The theater of combat was horrible and fascinating to watch. As soon as people started firing, night vision fell away. Chavez tried to protect his by keeping one eye shut as he'd been drilled, but found that it didn't work. The forest was alive with bright cylindrical tongues of flame, some of which became small globes of light that illuminated the moving men like a series of strobe lights. Tracers from the machine guns walked fire into living men. Tracers from the riflemen meant something else. The last three rounds in every magazine were lit to tell them that it was time to load new magazines. The noise was unlike anything Chavez had ever heard, the chatter of the M-16s, and the lower, slower rattle of the AK-47s. The shouted orders, the screams of rage and pain and despairing death.

"Run!" It was Captain Ramirez's voice, shouting in Spanish. Again they disengaged by pairs. Or tried to. Two squad members had been hit in this exchange. Chavez tripped on one, who was trying to crawl away. He lifted the man on his shoulders and ran up the hill while he tried to ignore the pain in his legs. The man — it was Ingeles — died at the rally point. There was no time for grief; his unused magazines were passed out among the other riflemen. While Captain Ramirez tried to get things organized again, all of them heard the mixed notes of gunfire down the hill, more shouts, more curses. Only one more man made it to the rally point. Team KNIFE now had two more dead and one seriously wounded. Olivero took charge of that, leading the injured man up the hill to the casualty collection point near the LZ. It had taken fifteen minutes to inflict a further twenty casualties on the enemy, at the cost of 30 percent of their strength. If Captain Ramirez had had time to think, he would have realized that for all his cleverness he was in a losing game. But there wasn't time for thinking.

The BANNER men discouraged another group of the enemy with a few bursts of fire, but lost one of their number withdrawing up the hill. The next defense line was four hundred meters away. Tighter than the second, it was disagreeably close to their final defensive position. It was time to play their last card.

The enemy again closed in on empty terrain, and still didn't know what casualties they had inflicted on the evil spirits that appeared and killed and disappeared like something from a nightmare. Two of the men who occupied something akin to leadership positions were gone, one dead, the other gravely wounded, and now they stopped to regroup while the surviving leaders conferred.

For the soldiers, the situation was much the same. As soon as the casualties were identified, Ramirez rearranged his deployment to compensate, distantly thankful that he didn't have time to mourn his dead, that his training really did force him to focus on the problem at hand. The helicopter wasn't going to come in time. Or was it? Or did it matter? What did matter?

What he had to do was further reduce the enemy numbers so that an escape attempt had a decent chance at success. They had to run away, but they had to do some more killing first. Ramirez had been keeping his explosives in reserve. None of his men had yet fired or thrown a grenade, and this position was the one protected by their remaining claymore mines, each of them set to protect a rifleman's hole.

"Why are you waiting, eh?" Ramirez called downhill. "Come on, we are not finished with you yet! First we kill you, then we fuck your women!"

"They don't have women," Vega shouted. "They do it to each other. Come fairies, it is time to die!"

And so they came. Like a puncher remorselessly closing on a boxer, cutting off the ring, still driven by anger, scarcely noting their losses, drawn to the voices and cursing them as they did so. But more carefully now, the enemy troops had learned. Moving from tree to tree, covering one another as they did so. Firing ahead to keep heads down.

"Something's happening down to the south, there. See the flashes?" Larson said. "Over at two o'clock on the mountainside."

"I see it." They'd spent over an hour trying to raise BANNER by flying and transmitting over all three exfiltration sites, and gotten nothing. Clark didn't like leaving the area, but had little choice. If that was what it might be, they had to get closer. Even with a clear line of sight, these little radios were good for less than ten miles.

"*Buster,*" he told the pilot. *Get there as fast as you can.*

Larson retracted his flaps and pushed the throttles forward.

★

It was called a fire-sack, a term borrowed from the Soviet Army, and perfectly descriptive of its function. The squad was spread out in a wide arc, every man in his hole, though four of the holes were occupied by one instead of two, and another was not occupied at all. In front of each hole were one or two claymores, faced convex side toward the enemy. The position was just inside a stand of trees and faced down across what must have been a rockfall or small landslide, an open space perhaps seventy meters wide, looking down on some fallen trees, and a few new ones. The noise and muzzle flashes of the enemy approached that line and stopped moving, though the firing did not abate at all.

"Okay, people," Ramirez said. "On command we get the hell out of here, back to the LZ, and from there down X-route two. But we gotta thin them down some more first."

The other side was talking, too, and finally doing so intelligently. They used names instead of places, just enough encoding to mask what they wanted to do, though they had again allowed themselves to follow terrain features instead of crossing them. Certainly they had courage, Ramirez thought; whatever sort of men they were, they didn't shrink from danger. If they'd had just a little training and one or two competent leaders, the fight would already have been over.

Chavez had other things on his mind. His weapon was flashless in addition to being noiseless and the Ninja was using his goggles to pick out individual targets and then dropping them without a shred of remorse. He got one possible leader. It was almost too easy. The rattle of fire from the enemy line masked the sound of his own weapon. But he checked his ammo bag and realized that he had only two magazines and sixty rounds beyond what were in his weapon already. Captain Ramirez was playing it smart, but he was also playing it close.

Another head appeared from behind a tree, then an arm gesturing to someone else. Ding tracked in on it and loosed a single round. It caught the man in the throat, but didn't prevent a gurgling scream. Though Chavez didn't know it, that was the main leader of the enemy, and his scream galvanized them to action. All across the treeline fire lanced out at the light-fighters, and with a shout, the enemy attacked.

Ramirez let them get halfway across, then fired a grenade from his launcher. It was a phosphorus round, which created an intense, spidery white fountain of light. Instantly, every man triggered his claymore mines.

— "Oh, shit, there's KNIFE. Willie Pete and claymores." Clark shoved his antenna out the aircraft's window.

"KNIFE, this is VARIABLE; KNIFE, this is VARIABLE. Come in, over!" His attempt at help could not have come at a worse moment.

Thirty more men fell dead, and ten wounded under the scything fragments from the mines. Next, grenades were launched into the treeline, including all of the WP rounds, to start fires. Far enough away to avoid instant death, but too close to be untouched by the showering bits of burning phosphorus, some men caught fire, adding their screams to the cacophony of the night. Hand-thrown grenades were added to the field, killing yet more of the attackers. Then Ramirez keyed his radio again.

"Move out, move out now!" But he'd done the right thing once too often.

When the KNIFE team moved out from their positions, they were swept with automatic-weapons fire from men shooting on reflex. Those soldiers who had them tossed smoke and CS tear-gas grenades to conceal their departure, but the sparkling of the pyrotechnics merely gave the other side a point of aim, and each drew the fire from a dozen weapons. Two were killed, and another two wounded as a direct result of doing what they'd been taught to do. Ramirez had done a stellar job of maintaining control of his unit to this point, but it was here that he lost it. The radio earpiece started crackling with an unfamiliar voice.

"This is KNIFE," he said, standing erect. "VARIABLE, where the hell are you?"

"Overhead, we are overhead. What is your situation, over?"

"We're in deep shit, falling back to the LZ

now, get down here, *get down here right now!*"
Ramirez shouted for his men. "Get to the LZ,
they're coming to get us!"

"Negative, negative. Knife, we cannot come
in now. You must get clear, you must get clear.
Acknowledge!" Clark told the radio. No reply.
He repeated the instructions and again there was
nothing.

And now there were only eight left of what had
once been twenty-two men. Ramirez was carrying a wounded man, and his earpiece had fallen
out as he ran for the LZ, two hundred meters up
the hill, through one last stand of trees into the
clearing where the helicopter would come.

But it didn't. Ramirez set his burden down,
looking up at the sky with his eyes, then with his
goggles, but there was no helicopter, no flash of
strobe lights, no heat from turboshaft engines to
light up the night sky. The captain yanked the
earpiece out of the radio and screamed into it.

"VARIABLE, where the hell are you?"

"Knife, this is VARIABLE. We are orbiting
your position in a fixed-wing aircraft. We cannot
execute a pickup until tomorrow night. You must
get clear, you must get clear. Acknowledge!"

"There's only eight of us left, there's only — "
Ramirez stopped, and his humanity returned
one last, lethal time. "Oh, my God." He hesitated, realizing that most of his men were gone,
and he had been their commander, and he was

1025

responsible. That he wasn't, really, was something he would never learn.

The enemy was approaching now, approaching from three sides. There was only one way to escape. It was a preplanned route, but Ramirez looked down at the man he'd carried to the LZ and watched him die. He looked up again, looked round at his men, and didn't know what to do next. There wasn't time for training to work. A hundred meters away, the first of the enemy force emerged from the last line of trees and fired. His men returned it, but there were too many and the infantrymen were down to their last magazines.

Chavez saw it happening. He'd linked back up with Vega and León, to help a man whose leg was badly wounded. As he watched, a line of men swept across the LZ. He saw Ramirez drop prone, firing his weapon at the oncoming enemy, but there was nothing Ding and his friends could do, and they headed west, down the escape route. They didn't look back. They didn't need to. The sound told them enough. The chattering of the M-16s was answered by the louder fire of the AKs. A few more grenades went off. Men screamed and cursed, all of them in Spanish. And then all the fire was from AKs. The battle for this hill had ended.

"Does that mean what I think it means?" Larson asked.

"It means that some stateside REMF is going to die," Clark said quietly. There were tears in

1026

his eyes. He'd seen this happen once before, when his helicopter had gotten off in time and the other hadn't, and he'd been ashamed at the time and long thereafter that he had survived while others had not. *"Shit!"* He shook his head and got control of himself.

"KNIFE, this is VARIABLE. Do you read me, over? Reply by name. Say again, reply by name."

"Wait a minute," Chavez said. "This is Chavez. Who's on this net?"

"Listen fast, kid, 'cause your net is compromised. This is Clark. We met awhile back. Head in the same direction you did on the practice night. Do you remember that?"

"Roger. I remember the way we headed then. We can do that."

"I'll be back for you tomorrow. Hang in there, kid. It ain't over yet. Repeat: I will be back for you. Now haul your ass out of there. Out."

"What was that all about?" Vega asked.

"We loop around east, down the hill to the north, then around east."

"And then what?" *Oso* demanded.

"How the fuck should I know?"

"Head back north," Clark ordered.

"What's an REMF?" Larson asked as he started the turn.

Clark's reply was so low as to be inaudible. "An REMF is a rear-echelon motherfucker, one of those useless, order-generating bastards who gets us line-animals killed. And one of them is going to pay for this, Larson. Now shut up and fly."

For another hour they continued their futile search for Team BANNER, then they headed back to Panama. That flight took two hours and fifteen minutes, during which Clark didn't say a word and Larson was afraid to. The pilot taxied the aircraft right into the hangar with the Pave Low, and the doors closed behind him. Ryan and Johns were waiting for them.

"Well?" Jack asked.

"We made contact with OMEN and FEATURE," Clark said. "Come on." He led them into an office with a table. There he spread out his map.

"What about the others?" Jack asked. Colonel Johns didn't have to. He already knew part of it from the look on Clark's face.

"OMEN will be right here tomorrow night. FEATURE will be here," Clark said, indicating two places marked on the map.

"Okay, we can handle that," Johns said.

"Goddammit!" Ryan growled. "What about the others?"

"We never made contact with BANNER. We watched the bad guys overrun KNIFE. Most of it," Clark corrected himself. "At least one man got away. I'm going in after him, on the ground." Clark turned to the pilot. "Larson, you'd better get a few hours. I need you bright-eyed and bushy-tailed in six hours."

"What about the weather?" he asked PJ.

"That fucking storm's jinking around like a Weasel on a SAM hunt. Nobody knows where the hell it's going, but it ain't there yet, and I've flown in weather before," Colonel Johns replied.

"Okay." The pilot walked off. There were some cots set in the next room. He landed on one and was asleep in a minute.

"Going in on the ground?" Ryan asked.

"What do you expect me to do — leave them there? Ain't we done enough of that?" Clark looked away. His eyes were red, and only PJ knew that it wasn't from strain and lack of sleep. "Sorry, Jack. There's some of our people there. I have to try. They'd try for me. It's cool, man. I know how to do it."

"How?" PJ asked.

"Larson and I'll fly in around noon, get a car and drive down. I told Chavez — that's the kid I talked to — to get around them and head east, down the mountain. We'll try to pick them up, drive 'em to the airport, and just fly them out."

"Just like that?" Ryan asked incredulously.

"Sure. Why not?"

"There's a difference between being brave and being an idiot," Ryan said.

"Who gives a fuck about being brave? It's my job." Clark walked off to get some sleep.

"You know what you're really afraid of?" Johns said when he'd left. "You're afraid of remembering the times that you could have done it and didn't. I can give you a play-by-play of every failure I've had in twenty-some years." The colonel was wearing his blue shirt with command wings and all the ribbons. He had quite a few.

Jack's eyes fixed on one, pale blue with five white stars. "But you . . . "

"It's a nice thing to wear, and it's nice to have four-stars salute me first and treat me like I'm something special. But you know what matters? Those two guys I got out. One's a general now. The other one flies for Delta. They're both alive. They both have families. That's what matters, Mr. Ryan. The ones I didn't get out, they matter, too. Some of them are still there, because I wasn't good enough or fast enough or lucky enough. Or they weren't. Or something. I should have gotten them out. That's the job," Johns said quietly. "That's what I do."

We sent them in there, Jack told himself. *My agency sent them in there. And some of them are dead now, and we let somebody tell us not to do anything about it. And I'm supposed to be . . .*

"Might be dangerous going in tonight."

"Possible. Looks that way."

"You have three minis aboard your chopper," Ryan said after a moment. "You only have two gunners."

"I couldn't whistle another one up this fast and — "

"I'm a pretty fair shot," Jack told him.

1030

28.

Accounting

Cortez sat at the table, doing his sums. The Americans had done marvelously well. Nearly two hundred Cartel men had gone up the mountain. Ninety-six had returned alive, sixteen of those wounded. They'd even brought a live American down with them. He was badly hurt, still bleeding from four wounds, and he hadn't been well handled by the Colombian gunmen. The man was young and brave, biting off his screams, shaking with the effort to control himself. Such a courageous young man, this Green Beret. Cortez would not insult his bravery with questions. Besides, he was incoherent, and Cortez had other things to do.

There was a medical team here to treat "friendly" casualties. Cortez walked out to it and picked up a disposable syringe, filling it with morphine. He returned and stabbed the needle into a vein on the soldier's uninjured arm, pushing down on the plunger after it was in. The soldier relaxed at once, his pain extinguished by a wonderful, brief sensation of well-being. Then his breathing just stopped, and his life, too, was extinguished. Most unfortunate. Cortez could really have used men like this one, but they rarely worked for anything other than a flag. He walked over to his phone and called the proper number.

"*Jefe*, we eliminated one of the enemy forces last night. . . . Yes, *jefe*, there were ten of them as I suspected, and we got them all. We go after another team tonight. . . . There is one problem, *jefe*. The enemy fought well, and we took many casualties. I need more men for tonight's mission. *Sí*, thank you, *jefe*. That will do nicely. Send the men to Ríosucio, and have the leaders report to me this afternoon. I will brief them here. Oh? Yes, that will be excellent. We'll be waiting for you."

With luck, Cortez thought, the next American team would fight equally as well. With luck he could eliminate two-thirds of the Cartel's stable of gunmen in a single week. Along with their bosses, also tonight. He was on the downslope now, Cortez thought. He'd gambled dangerously and hard, but the tricky ones were behind him.

It was an early funeral. Greer had been a widower, and estranged from his wife long before that. The reason for the estrangement was next to the rectangular hole in Arlington, the simple white headstone of First Lieutenant Robert

White Greer, USMC, his only son, who'd graduated from the Naval Academy and gone to Vietnam to die. Neither Moore nor Ritter had ever met the young man, and James had never kept a photo of him around the office. The former DDI had been a sentimental man but never a maudlin one. Yet he had long ago requested burial next to the grave of his son, and because of his rank and station an exception had been made and the place kept available for an event that for all men was as inevitable as it was untimely. He'd indeed been a sentimental man, but only in ways that mattered. Ritter thought that there were many explanations before his eyes. The way James had adopted several bright young people and brought them into the Agency, the interest he'd taken in their careers, the training and consideration he'd given them.

It was a small, quiet ceremony. James' few close friends were there, along with a much larger number of people from the government. Among the latter were the President — and, much to Bob Ritter's rage, Vice Admiral James A. Cutter, Jr. The President himself had spoken at the chapel service, noting the death of a man who had served his country continuously for more than fifty years, having enlisted in the U.S. Navy at seventeen, then entered the Academy, then reached two-star rank, achieving a third star for his flag after assuming his position at CIA. "A standard of professionalism, integrity, and devotion to his country that few have equaled and none have excelled" was how the President summarized the career of Vice Admiral James Greer.

And that bastard *Cutter sat right there in the front row as he said it, too,* Ritter told himself. He found it especially sickening as he watched the honor guard from the 3rd Infantry Regiment fold the flag that had been draped over the casket. There was no one to hand it to. Ritter had expected it to go to —

But where was Ryan? He moved his head, trying to look around. He hadn't noticed before because Jack hadn't come from Langley with the rest of the CIA delegation. The flag went to Judge Moore by default. Hands were shaken, words exchanged. Yes, it really was a mercy that he'd gone so rapidly at the end. Yes, men like this didn't appear every day. Yes, this was the end of the Greer line, and that was too bad, wasn't it? No, I never met his son, but I heard. . . . Ritter and Moore were in the Agency Cadillac ten minutes later, heading back up the George Washington Parkway.

"Where the hell was Ryan?" the DCI asked.

"I don't know. I figured he'd drive himself in."

Moore was not so much angered as upset by the impropriety. He still had the flag in his lap, holding it as gently as a newborn baby without knowing why — until he realized that if there really was a God, as the Baptist preachers of his youth had assured him, and if James had really had a soul, he held its best legacy in his hands. It felt warm to the touch, and though he knew that it was merely his imagination or at most the residual heat absorbed from the morning sun, the energy radiating from the flag that James had served from his teens seemed to accuse him of treachery. They had just watched a funeral this morning, but two thousand miles away there were other people whom the Agency had sent to do a job and who would not receive even the empty reward of a grave amidst others of their kind.

"Bob, what the hell have we done?" Moore asked. "How did we ever get into this?"

"I don't know, Arthur. I just don't know."

"James really was lucky," the Director of Central Intelligence murmured. "At least he went out — "

"With a clear conscience?" Ritter looked out the window, unable to bring himself to face his boss. "Look, Arthur — " He stopped, not knowing what to say next. Ritter had been with the Agency since the fifties, had worked as a case officer, a supervisor, station chief, then head of section at Langley. He had lost case officers, had lost agents, but he'd never betrayed them. There was a first time for everything, he told himself. It had just come home to him in a very immediate way, however, that for every man there was also a first time for death, and that to meet that final accounting improperly was the ultimate cowardice, the ultimate failure of life. But what else could they do?

It was a short drive to Langley, and the car

stopped before that question could be answered. They rode the elevator up. Moore walked to his office. Ritter walked to his. The secretaries hadn't returned yet. They were in a van. Ritter paced around his office until they arrived, then walked over to see Mrs. Cummings.

"Did Ryan call in or anything?"

"No, and I didn't see him at all. Do you know where he is?" Nancy asked.

"Sorry, I don't." Ritter walked back and on impulse called Ryan's home, where all he got was an answering machine. He checked his card file for Cathy's work number and got past the secretary to her.

"This is Bob Ritter. I need to know where Jack is."

"I don't know," Dr. Caroline Ryan replied guardedly. "He told me yesterday that he had to go out of town. He didn't say where."

A chill went across Ritter's face. "Cathy, I have to know. This is very important — I can't tell you how important. Please trust me. I have to know where he is."

"I *don't* know. You mean you don't, either?" There was alarm in her voice.

Ryan knows, Ritter realized.

"Look, Cathy, I'll track him down. Don't worry or anything, okay?" The effort to calm her down was wasted, but Ritter hung up as soon as he could. The DDO walked to Judge Moore's office. The flag was centered on the DCI's desk, still folded into its triangular section, called a cocked-hat. Judge Arthur Moore, Director of Central Intelligence, was sitting quietly, staring at it.

"Jack's gone. His wife says she doesn't know where. He knows, Arthur. He knows and he's off doing something."

"How could he have found out?"

"How the hell should I know?" Ritter thought for a moment, then waved at his boss. "Come on."

They walked into Ryan's office. Ritter opened the panel for Jack's wall safe and dialed in the proper combination, and nothing happened other than the fact that the warning light went on over the dial.

"Damn," Ritter said. "I thought that was it."

"James's combination?"

"Yeah. You know how he was, never did like the damned things, and he probably . . . " Ritter looked around. He got it on the third try, pulling out the writing panel from the desk, and there it was.

"I thought I did dial the right one." He turned and tried again. This time the light was accompanied by the goddamned beeper. Ritter turned back and checked the number again. There was some more writing on the sheet. Ritter pulled the panel farther out.

"Oh, my God."

Moore nodded and walked to the door. "Nancy, tell security that it's us trying to work the safe. Looks like Jack changed the combination without telling us like he was supposed to." The DCI closed the door and turned back.

"He knows, Arthur."

"Maybe. How do we check it out?"

A minute later they were in Ritter's office. He'd shredded all of his documents, but not his memory. You didn't forget the name of someone with the Medal of Honor. Then it was just a matter of flipping open his AUTOVON phone directory and calling the 1st Special Operations Wing at Eglin AFB.

"I need to talk to Colonel Paul Johns," Ritter told the sergeant who'd picked up the phone.

"Colonel Johns is off TDY somewhere, sir. I don't know where."

"Who does?"

"The wing operations officer might, sir. This is a nonsecure line, sir," the sergeant reminded him.

"Give me his number." The sergeant did so, and Ritter's next call went out on, and to, a secure line.

"I need to find Colonel Johns," Ritter said after identifying himself.

"Sir, I have orders not to give that information out to anybody. That means nobody, sir."

"Major, if he's down in Panama again, I need to know it. His life may depend on it. Something is happening that he needs to know about."

"Sir, I have orders — "

"Stuff your orders, sonny. If you don't tell me, and that flight crew dies, it will be your fault!

Now you make the call, Major, yes or no?"

The officer had never seen combat, and life-death decisions were theoretical matters to him — or had been until now.

"Sir, they're back where they were before. Same place, same crew. That's as far as I go, sir."

"Thank you, Major. You did the right thing. You really did. Now I suggest that you make written note of this call and its content." Ritter hung up. The phone had been on speaker.

"Has to be Ryan," the DCI agreed. "Now what do we do?"

"You tell me, Arthur."

"How many more people are we going to kill, Bob?" Moore asked. His greatest fear now was of mirrors, looking into them and seeing something less than the image he wanted to be there.

"You do understand the consequences?"

"Fuck the consequences," snorted the former chief judge of the Texas Court of Appeals.

Ritter nodded and punched a button on his phone. When he spoke, it was in his accustomed, decisive voice of command. "I need everything CAPER has developed in the last two days." Another button. "I want chief of Station Panama to call me in thirty minutes. Tell him to clear decks for the day — he's going to be busy." Ritter replaced the phone receiver in its cradle. They'd have to wait for a few minutes, but it wasn't the sort of occasion to wait in silence.

"Thank God," Ritter said after a moment.

Moore smiled for the first time this day. "Me,

too, Robert. Nice to be a man again, isn't it?"

The security police brought him in at gunpoint, the man in the tan suit. He said his name was Luna, and the briefcase he carried had already been searched for weapons. Clark recognized him.

"What the hell are you doing here, Tony?"

"Who's this?" Ryan asked.

"Station chief for Panama," Clark answered. "Tony, I hope you have a *very* good reason."

"I have a telex for Dr. Ryan from Judge Moore."

"What?"

Clark took Luna's arm and guided him into the office. He didn't have much time. He and Larson were to take off within minutes.

"This better not be some fucking joke," Clark announced.

"Hey, I'm delivering the mail, okay?" Luna said. "Now stop playing the macho game. I'm the spic here, remember?" He handed Jack the first sheet.

TOP SECRET — EYES ONLY DDI

IMPOSSIBLE TO REESTABLISH UPLINK TO SHOWBOAT TEAMS. TAKE WHATEVER ACTION YOU DEEM APPROPRIATE TO RETRIEVE ASSETS IN COUNTRY. TELL CLARK TO BE CAREFUL. THE ENCLOSED MIGHT BE OF HELP. C DOESN'T KNOW. GOOD LUCK. M/R.

"Nobody ever said they were stupid," Jack breathed as he handed the sheet to Clark. The heading was meant as a separate message in and of itself, one that had nothing to do with distribution or security. "But does this mean what I think it does?"

"One less REMF to worry about. Make that two," Clark observed. He started flipping through the faxes. "Holy shit!" He set the pile down on the desk and paced a bit, staring out of the windows at the aircraft sitting in the hangar. "Okay," he said to himself. Clark had never been one to dally over making plans. He spoke to Ryan for several minutes. Then, to Larson: "Let's move ass, kid. We got a job to do."

"Spare radios?" Colonel Johns asked him as he left.

"Two spares, new batteries in all of 'em, and extra batteries," Clark replied.

"Nice to work with somebody's been around the block," PJ said. "Check-six, Mr. Clark."

"Always, Colonel Johns," Clark said as he headed to the door. "See you in a few hours."

The hangar doors opened. A small cart pulled the Beechcraft out into the sun, and the hangar doors closed. Ryan listened to the engines start up, and the sound diminished as the aircraft taxied away.

"What about us?" he asked Colonel Johns.

Captain Frances Montaigne came in. She looked as French as her ancestry, short, with raven-black hair. Not especially pretty, but Ryan's first impression was that she was a handful in bed — which stopped his thought processes cold as he wondered why that had occurred to him. It seemed odder still that she was a command pilot in a special-ops outfit.

"Weather's going dogshit on us, Colonel," she announced at once. *"Adele* is heading west again, doing twenty-five knots."

"Can't help the weather. Getting down and doing the snatch oughtn't to be too bad."

"Getting back might be kinda exciting, PJ," Montaigne observed darkly.

"One thing at a time, Francie. And we do have that alternate place to land."

"Colonel, even you aren't that crazy."

PJ turned to Ryan and shook his head. "Junior officers aren't what they used to be."

They stayed over water for most of the way down. Larson was as steady and confident as ever at the controls, but his eyes kept turning northeast. There was no mistaking it, the high, thin clouds that were the perennial harbinger of an approaching hurricane. Behind them was *Adele*, and she had already made another chapter in history. Born off the Cape Verdes, she'd streaked across the Atlantic at an average speed of seventeen knots, then stopped as soon as she'd entered the eastern Caribbean, lost power, gained it back, jinked north, west, even east once. There hadn't been one this crazy since *Joan*, years before. Small as hurricanes went, and nowhere near the brutal power of a *Camille, Adele* was still a dangerous storm with seventy-five-knot winds. The only people who flew near tropical cyclones were dedicated hurricane-hunter aircraft flown by people for whom merely mortal danger was boring. It was not a place for a twin-engine Beechcraft, even with Chuck Yeager at the controls. Larson was already making plans. In case the mission didn't go right, or the storm changed course yet again, he started picking fields to put down on, to refuel and head southeast around the gray maelstrom that was marching toward them. The air was smooth and still, deceptively so. The pilot wondered how many hours until it changed to something very different. And that was only one of the dangers he'd face.

Clark sat quietly in the right seat, staring forward, his face composed and inhumanly serene while his mind turned over faster than the Beech's twin props. In front of the windshield he kept seeing faces, some living, some dead. He remembered past combat actions, past dangers, past fears, past escapes in which those faces had played their parts. Most of all he remembered the lessons, some learned in classrooms and lectures, but the important ones had come from his own experience. John Terence Clark was not a man who forgot things. Gradually he refreshed his memory on all the important lessons for this day, the ones about being alone in unfriendly territory. Then came the faces who'd play their part today. He looked at them, a few feet before his eyes, saw the expressions he expected them to wear, measuring the faces to understand the people who wore them. Finally came the plan of the day. He contemplated what he wanted to do and balanced that against the probable objectives of the opposition. He considered alternative plans and things that might go awry. When all that was done, he made himself stop. You could quickly get to the point that imagination became an enemy. Each segment of the operation was locked into its own little box which he'd open one at a time. He'd trust to his experience and instinct. But part of him wondered if — when — those qualities would fail him.

Sooner or later, Clark admitted to himself. *But not today.*

He always told himself that.

PJ's mission briefing took two hours. He, Captain Willis, and Captain Montaigne worked out every detail — where they'd refuel, where the aircraft would orbit if something went wrong. Which routes to take if things went badly. Each crew member got full information. It was more than necessary; it was a moral obligation to the crew. They were risking their lives tonight. They had to know why. As always, Sergeant Zimmer had a few questions, and one important suggestion that was immediately incorporated in the plan. Then it was time to preflight the aircraft. Every system aboard each aircraft was fully checked out in a procedure that would last hours.

Part of that was training for the new crewmen.

"What do you know about guns?" Zimmer asked Ryan.

"Never fired one of these babies." Ryan's hand stroked the handles of the minigun. A scaled-down version of the 20mm Vulcan cannon, it had a gang of six .30-caliber barrels that rotated clockwise under the power of an electrical motor, drawing shells from an enormous hopper to the left of the mount. It had two speed settings, 4,000 and 6,000 rounds per minute — 66 or 100 rounds *per second*. The bullets were almost half tracers. The reason for that was psychological. The fire from the weapon looked like a laser beam from a science-fiction movie, the very embodiment of death. It also made a fine way to aim the weapon, since Zimmer assured him that the muzzle blast would be the most blinding thing short of staring into a noon sun. He checked Ryan out on the whole system: where the switches were, how to stand, how to aim.

"What do you know about combat, sir?"

"Depends on what you mean," Ryan replied.

"Combat is when people with guns are trying to kill you," Zimmer explained patiently. "It's dangerous."

"I know. I've been there a few times. Let's not dwell on that, okay? I'm already scared." Ryan looked over his gun, out the door of the aircraft, wondering why he'd been such a damned fool to volunteer for this. But what choice did he have? Could he just send these men off to danger? If he did, how did that make him different from Cutter? Jack looked around the interior of the aircraft. It seemed so large and strong and safe, sitting here on the concrete floor of the hangar. But it was an aircraft designed for life in the troubled air of an unfriendly sky. It was a helicopter: Ryan especially hated helicopters.

"The funny thing is, probably no sweat on the mission," Zimmer said after a moment. "Sir, we do our job right, it's just a flight in and a flight back out."

"That's what I'm scared of, Sarge," Ryan said, laughing mostly at himself.

They landed at Santagueda. Larson knew the man who ran the local flying service and talked him out of his Volkswagen Microvan. The two CIA officers drove north, and an hour later passed through the village of Anserma. They dallied here for half an hour, driving around until they found what they wanted to find: a few trucks heading in and out of a private dirt road and one expensive-looking car. CAPER had called it right, Clark saw, and it was the place he thought it was from the flight in. Having confirmed that, they moved out, heading north again for another hour and taking a side road into the mountains just outside of Vegas del Río. Clark had his nose buried in a map, and Larson found a hilltop switchback at which to stop. That's where the radio came out.

"KNIFE, this is VARIABLE, over." Nothing,

despite five minutes of trying. Larson drove farther west, horsing the Microvan around cow paths as he struggled to find another high spot for Clark to try again. It was three in the afternoon, and their fifth attempt until they got a reply.

"KNIFE here. Over."

"Chavez, this is Clark. Where the hell are you?" Clark asked, in Spanish, of course.

"Let's talk awhile first."

"You're good, kid. We really could have used you in 3rd SOG."

"Why should I trust you? Somebody cut us off, man. Somebody decided to leave us here."

"It wasn't me."

"Glad to hear it," came the skeptical, bitter reply.

"Chavez, you're talking over a radio net that might be compromised. If you got a map, we're at the following set of coordinates," Clark told him. "There's two of us in a blue Volkswagen van. Check us out, take all the time you want."

"I already have!" the radio told him.

Clark's head spun around to see a man with an AK-47 twenty feet away.

"Let's be real cool, people," Sergeant Vega said. Three more men emerged from the treeline. One of them had a bloody bandage on his thigh. Chavez, too, had an AK slung over his shoulder, but he had held on to his silenced MP-5. He walked straight up to the van.

"Not bad, kid," Clark told him. "How'd you know?"

"UHF radio. You had to transmit from a high spot, right? The map says there's six of them. I heard you one other time, too, and I spotted you heading this way half an hour ago. Now what the fuck is going on?"

"First thing, let's get that casualty treated." Clark stepped out and handed Chavez his pistol, butt first. "I got a first-aid kit in the back."

The wounded man was Sergeant Juardo, a rifleman from the 10th Mountain at Fort Drum. Clark opened the back of the van and helped load him aboard, then uncovered the wound.

"You know what you're doing?" Vega asked.

"I used to be a SEAL," Clark replied, holding up his arm so that they could see the tattoo. "Third Special Operations Group. Spent a lot of time in 'Nam, doing stuff that never made the TV news."

"What were you?"

"Came out a chief bosun's mate, E-7 to you." Clark examined the wound. It was bad to look at, but not life-threatening as long as the man didn't bleed out, which he'd managed not to do yet. So far it seemed that the infantrymen had done most of the right things. Clark ripped open an envelope and redusted the wound with sulfa. "You have any blood-expanders?"

"Here," Sergeant León passed over an IV bag. "None of us knows how to start one."

"It's not hard. Watch how I do it." Clark grabbed Juardo's upper arm hard and told him to make a fist. Then he stabbed the IV needle into the big vein inside the elbow. "See? Okay, I cheat. My wife's a nurse, and sometimes I get to practice at her hospital," Clark admitted. "How's it feel, kid?" he asked the patient.

"Nice to be sitting down," Juardo admitted.

"I don't want to give you a pain shot. We might need you awake. Think you can hack it?"

"You say so, man. Hey, Ding, you got any candy?"

Chavez tossed over his Tylenol bottle. "Last ones, Pablo. Make 'em last, man."

"Thanks, Ding."

"We have some sandwiches in the front," Larson said.

"Food!" Vega darted that way at once. A minute later the four soldiers were wolfing it down, along with a six-pack of Cokes that Larson had picked up on the way.

"Where'd you pick up the weapons?"

"Bad guys. We were just about out of ammo for our -16s, and I figured we might as well try to fit in, like."

"You're thinking good, kid," Clark told him.

"Okay, what's the plan?" Chavez asked.

"It's your call," Clark replied. "One of two things. We can drive you back to the airport and fly you out, take about three hours to get there, another three hours in the airplane, and it's over, you're back on U.S. territory."

"What else?"

"Chavez, how'd you like to get the fucker who did this to you?" Clark knew the answer before

1049

he'd asked the question.

Admiral Cutter was leaning back in his chair when the phone buzzed. He knew who it was from the line that was blinking. "Yes, Mr. President?"

"Come in here."

"On the way, sir."

Summer is as slow a season for the White House as for most government agencies. The President's calendar was fuller than usual with the ceremonial stuff that the politician in him loved and the executive in him abhorred. Shaking hands with "Miss Whole Milk," as he referred to the steady stream of visitors — though, he occasionally wondered to himself if he'd ever meet a Miss Condom, what with the way sexual mores were changing of late. The burden was larger than most imagine. For each such visitor there was a sheet of paper, a few paragraphs of information so that the person would leave thinking that, gee, the President really knows what I'm all about. He's really *interested!* Pressing flesh and talking to ordinary people was an important and usually pleasurable part of the job, but not now, a week short of the convention, still behind in the goddamned polls, as every news network announced at least twice a week.

"What about Colombia?" the President asked as soon as the door was closed.

"Sir, you told me to shut it down. It's being shut down."

"Any problems with the Agency?"

"No, Mr. President."

"How exactly — "

"Sir, you told me you didn't want to know that."

"You're telling me it's something I shouldn't know?"

"I'm telling you, sir, that I am carrying out your instructions. The orders were given, and the orders are being complied with. I don't think you will object to the consequences."

"Really?"

Cutter relaxed a bit. "Sir, in a very real sense, the operation was a success. Drug shipments are down and will drop further in the next few months. I would suggest, sir, that you let the press talk about that for the moment. You can always point to it later. We've hurt them. With Operation TARPON we have something we can point to all we wish. With CAPER we have a way of continuing to gather intelligence information. We will have some dramatic arrests in a few months as well."

"And how do you know that?"

"I've made those arrangements myself, sir."

"And just how did you do that?" the President asked, and stopped. "Something else I don't want to know?"

Cutter nodded.

"I assume that everything you've done is within the law," the President said for the benefit of the tape recorder he had running.

"You may make that assumption, sir." It was an artful reply in that it could mean anything, or nothing, depending on one's point of view. Cutter also knew about the tape recorder.

"And you're sure that your instructions are being carried out?"

"Of course, Mr. President."

"Make sure again."

It had taken far longer than the bearded consultant expected. Inspector O'Day held the printout in his hands, and it might as well have been Kurdish. The sheet was half covered with paragraphs entirely composed of ones and zeroes.

"Machine language," the consultant explained. "Whoever programmed this baby was a real pro. I recovered about forty percent of it. It's a transposition algorithm, just like I thought."

"You told me that last night."

"It ain't Russian. It takes in a message and enciphers it. No big deal, anybody can do that. What's really clever is that the system is based on an independent input signal that's unique to the individual transmission — over and above the encipherment algorithm that's already built into the system."

"You want to explain that?"

"It means a very good computer lash-up — somewhere — governs how this baby operates. It can't be Russian. They don't have the hardware yet, unless they stole a really sexy one from us. Also, the input that adds the variable into the system probably comes from the NAVSTAR satellites. I'm guessing here, but I think it uses a very precise time mark to set the encryption key, one that's unique to each up-and-down transmission. Clever shit. That means NSA. The NAVSTAR satellites use atomic clocks to measure time with great precision, and the really sexy part of the system is also encrypted. Anyway, what we have here is a clever way of scrambling a signal in a way that you can't break or duplicate even if you know how it was done. Whoever set this baby up has access to everything we got. I used to consult with NSA, and never even heard of this puppy."

"Okay, and when the disk is destroyed . . . ?"

"The link is gone, man. I mean, *gone.* If this is what it seems to be, you have an uplink facility that controls the algorithm, and ground stations that copy it down. You wipe this algorithm off, like somebody did, and the guys you used to be talking to can't communicate with you anymore, and nobody else can communicate with them either. Systems don't get any more secure than that."

"You can tell all that? What else?"

"Half of what I just told you is informed speculation. I can't rebuild the algorithm. I can just tell you how it probably worked. The bit on the NAVSTAR is supposition, but good supposition. The transposition processing is partly recovered, and it has NSA written all over it. Whoever did it really knows how to write computer code. It's definitely ours. It's probably the most sophisticated machine code we have. Whoever got to use it must have some serious juice. And whoever it is, he scrubbed it. It can never be used again. Whatever operation it was used for must be over."

"Yeah," O'Day said, chilled by what he had just learned. "Good work."

"Now all you have to do is write a note to my prof and tell him why I missed an exam this morning."

"I'll have somebody do that," O'Day promised him on the way out the door. He headed for Dan Murray's office, and was surprised to see that he was out. The next stop was with Bill Shaw.

Half an hour later it was clear that a crime had probably been committed. The next question was what to do about it.

The helicopter took off light. Mission requirements were fairly complex — more so than in the previous insertions — and speed was important this time. As soon as the Pave Low got to cruising altitude, it tanked from the MC-130E. There was no banter this time.

Ryan sat in back, strapped into his place while the MH-53J bounced and buffeted in the wash of the tanker. He wore a green flight suit and a similarly green helmet. There was also a flak jacket. Zimmer had explained to him that it would stop a pistol round, probably, secondary fragments almost certainly, but that he shouldn't depend on it to stop a rifle bullet. One more thing to worry about. Once clear of the tanker for the first time — they'd have to tank again before making landfall — Jack turned around to look out the door. The clouds were nearly overhead now, the outlying reaches from *Adele*.

Juardo's wound complicated matters and changed plans somewhat. They loaded him into Clark's seat on the Beech, leaving him with a radio and spare batteries. Then Clark and the rest drove back toward Anserma. Larson was still checking the weather, which was changing on an hour-to-hour basis. He was due to take off in ninety minutes for his part of the mission.

"How you fixed for rounds?" Clark asked in the Microvan.

"All we need for the AKs," Chavez replied. "About sixty each for the subs. I never knew how useful a silenced gun was."

"They are nice. Grenades?"

"All of us?" Vega asked. "Five frags and two CS."

"What are we going into?" Ding asked next.

"It's a farmhouse outside Anserma."

"What's the security there like?"

"I don't know squat yet."

"Hey, wait a minute, what are you getting us into?" Vega demanded.

"Relax, Sarge. If it's too heavy to handle, we back off and leave. All I know is we're going in for a close look. Chavez and I can handle that. By the way, there's spare batteries in the bag down there. Need 'em?"

"Fuckin' A!" Chavez pulled out his night scope and replaced the batteries at once. "Who's in the house?"

"Two people we especially want. Number One is Félix Cortez," Clark said, giving some background. "He's the guy running the operation against the SHOWBOAT teams — that's the code name for this operation, in case nobody bothered to tell you. He also had a hand in the murder of the ambassador. I want his ass and I want it alive. Number Two is one Señor Escobedo. He's one of the big shots in the Cartel. A lot of people want his ass."

"Yeah," León said. "We ain't got no big shots yet."

"So far we've gotten five or six of the bastards. That was my end of the operation." Clark turned to look at Chavez. He had to say that to establish his credibility.

"But how, when — "

"We're not supposed to talk all that much, children," Clark told them. "You don't go around advertising about killing folks no matter who told you it was okay."

"Are you really that good?"

Clark just shook his head. "Sometimes. Sometimes not. If you guys weren't damned good, you wouldn't be here. And there are times when it's just pure dumb luck."

"We just walked into one," León said. "I don't

1056

even know what went wrong, but Captain Rojas just — "

"I know. I saw some pricks load his body into the back of a truck — "

León went rigid. "And what — "

"Did I do?" Clark asked. "There were three of them. I put them in the truck, too. Then I torched the truck. I'm not real proud of that, but I think I took some of the heat off you BANNER guys when I did. Wasn't much, but it was all I could do at the time."

"So who pulled the chopper back on us?"

"Same guy who chopped off the radio. I know who it is. After this is all over, I want his ass, too. You don't send people out in the field and then pull this crap on 'em."

"So what are you going to do?" Vega wanted to know.

"I'll slap him firmly on both wrists. Now listen, people, you worry about tonight. One job at a time. You're soldiers, not a bunch of teenage broads. Less talkin' and more thinkin'."

Chavez, Vega, and León took the cue. They started checking their gear. There was enough room in the van to strip and clean weapons. Clark pulled into Anserma at sundown. He found a quiet spot about a mile from the house and left the van. Clark took Vega's night goggles, and then he and Chavez went out to take a walk.

There had been farming here recently. Clark wondered what it had been, but that and the fact that it was close to the village meant that the trees had been thinned out for cooking fires. They were able to move fast. Half an hour later they could see the house, separated from the woods by two hundred meters of open ground.

"Not good," Clark observed from his place on the ground.

"I count six, all with AKs."

"Company," the CIA officer said, turning to see where the noise was coming from. It was a Mercedes, and therefore could have belonged to anyone in the Cartel. Two more cars came with it, one ahead and one behind. A total of six guards got out to check the area.

"Escobedo and LaTorre," Clark said from behind the binoculars. "Two big shots to see Colonel Cortez. I wonder why . . ."

"Too many, man," Chavez said.

"You notice there wasn't any password or anything?"

"So?"

"It's possible, if we play it right."

"But how . . ."

"Think creatively," Clark told him. "Back to the car." That took another twenty minutes. When they got there, Clark adjusted one of his radios.

"CAESAR, this is SNAKE, over."

The second refueling was accomplished within sight of the beach. They'd have to tank at least once more before heading back to Panama. The other alternative didn't seem especially likely at the moment. The good news was that Francie Montaigne was driving her Combat Talon with her usual aplomb, its four big propellers turning in a steady rhythm. Its radio operators were already talking to the surviving ground teams, taking that strain off the helicopter crew. For the first time in the mission, the air team was allowed to function as it had been trained. The MC-130E would coordinate the various pieces, coaching the Pave Low into the proper areas and away from possible threats in addition to keeping PJ's chopper filled up with gas.

In back, the ride had settled down. Ryan was up and walking around. Fear became boring after a while, and he even managed to use the Port-A-Pot without missing. The flight crew had accepted him at least as an approved interloper, and for some reason that meant a lot to him.

"Ryan, you hear me?" Johns asked.

Jack reached down to the mike button. "Yeah, Colonel."

"Your guy on the ground wants us to do something different."

"Like what?"

PJ told him. "It means another tanking, but otherwise we can hack it. Your call."

"You sure?"

"Special ops is what they pay us for."

"Okay, then. We want that bastard."

"Roger. Sergeant Zimmer, we'll be feet-dry in one minute. Systems check."

The flight engineer looked down his panel.

"Roger that, PJ. Everything looks pretty solid to me, sir. Everything's green."

"Okay. First stop is Team OMEN. ETA is two-zero minutes. Ryan, you'd better grab hold of something. We're going to start nap-of-the-earth. I have to talk to our backup."

Jack didn't know what that meant. He found out as soon as they crossed the first range of coastal mountains. The Pave Low leapt up like a mad elevator, then the bottom dropped out as it cleared the summit. The helicopter was on computer-assisted-flight mode, taking a six-degree slope — it felt much worse than that — up and down the terrain features, and skimmed over the ground with bare feet of clearance. The aircraft was made to be safe, not comfortable. Ryan didn't feel much of either.

"First LZ in three minutes," Colonel Johns announced half an eternity later. "Let's go hot, Buck."

"Roger." Zimmer reached down on his console and flipped a toggle switch. "Switches hot. Guns are hot."

"Gunners, stand to. That means you, Ryan," PJ added.

"Thanks." Jack gasped without toggling his mike. He took position on the left side of the aircraft and hit the activation switch for the mini-gun, which started turning at once.

"ETA one minute," the copilot said. "I got a good strobe at eleven o'clock. Okay. OMEN, this is CAESAR, do you copy, over?"

Jack heard only one side of the conversation, but mentally thanked the flight crew for letting the guys in back know something.

"Roger, OMEN, say again your situation. . . . Roger that, we're coming in. Good strobe light. Thirty seconds. Get ready in back," Captain Willis told Ryan and the rest. "Safe guns, safe guns."

Jack held his thumbs clear of the switch and elevated the minigun at the sky. The helicopter took a big nose-up attitude as it came down. It stopped and hovered a foot off the ground, not quite touching.

"Buck, tell the captain to come forward immediately."

"Roger, PJ." Behind him, Ryan heard Zimmer run aft, then, through the soles of his feet, felt the troops race aboard. He kept his eyes outboard, looking over the rotating barrels of his gun until the helicopter took off, and even then he trained the mini down at the ground.

"Well, that wasn't so bad, was it?" Colonel Johns observed as he brought the aircraft back to a southerly heading. "Hell, I don't even know why they pay us for this. Where's that groundpounder?"

"Hooking him up now, sir," Zimmer replied. "Got 'em all aboard. All clean, no casualties."

"Captain . . . ?"

"Yes, Colonel?"

"We got a job for your team if you think you're up to it."

"Let's hear it, sir."

★

The MC-130E Combat Talon was orbiting over Colombian territory, which made the crew a little nervous, since they didn't have permission. The main job now was to relay communications, and even with the sophisticated gear aboard the four-engine support aircraft, they couldn't handle it from over the ocean.

What they really needed was a good radar. The Pave Low/Combat Talon team was supposed to operate under supervision of an AWACS which, however, they hadn't brought along. Instead a lieutenant and a few NCOs were writing on maps and talking over secure radio circuits at the same time.

"CAESAR, say your fuel state," Captain Montaigne called.

"Looking good, CLAW. We're staying down in the valleys. Estimate we'll tank again in eight-zero minutes."

"Roger eight-zero minutes. Be advised negative hostile radio traffic at this time."

"Acknowledged." That was one possible problem. What if the Cartel had somebody in the Colombian Air Force? Sophisticated as both American aircraft were, a P-51 left over from the Second World War could easily kill both of them.

Clark was waiting for them. With two vehicles. Vega had stolen a farm truck big enough for their needs. It turned out that he was quite adept at rewiring ignition systems, a skill about whose acquisition he was vague. The helicopter touched down and the men ran out toward the strobe light that Chavez still had. Clark got their officer and briefed him quickly. The helicopter took off and headed north, helped by the twenty-knot wind blowing down the valley. Then it looped west, heading for the MC-130 and another mid-air refueling.

The Microvan and the truck drove back toward the farmhouse. Clark's mind was still racing. A really smart guy would have run the operation from inside the village, which would have been far tougher to approach. Cortez wanted to be far from anyone's view, but failed to consider his physical security requirements in military terms. Cortez was thinking like a spy, for whom security was secrecy, and not a line-animal, for whom security was a lot of guns and a clear field of fire. Everyone, he figured, had his limitations. Clark rode the back of the farm truck with the OMEN team group around him and his hand-drawn diagram of the objective. It was just like the old days, Clark thought, running missions on zero-minute notice. He hoped that these young light-fighters were as good as the animals in 3rd SOG. Even Clark, however, had limitations. The animals of 3rd SOG had been young then, too.

"Ten minutes, then," he concluded.

"All right," the captain agreed. "We haven't had much contact. We have all the weapons and ammo we need."

"So?" Escobedo asked.

"So we killed ten *norteamericanos* last night and we will kill ten more tonight."

"But the losses!" LaTorre objected.

"We are fighting highly skilled professional soldiers. Our men wiped them out, but the enemy fought bravely and well. Only one survived," Cortez said. "I have his body in the next room. He died here soon after they brought him in."

"How do you know that they are not close by?" Escobedo demanded. The idea of physical danger was something he'd allowed himself to forget.

"I know the location of every enemy group. They are waiting to be extracted by their helicopter support. They do not know that their helicopter has been withdrawn."

"How did you manage that?" LaTorre wondered aloud.

"Please permit me my methods. You hired me for my expertise. You should not be surprised when I demonstrate it."

"And now?"

"Our assault group — nearly two hundred men this time — should now be approaching the second American group. This one's code name is Team FEATURE," Félix added. "Our next question, of course, is which elements of the Cartel leadership are taking advantage of this — or perhaps I should say, which members are working with the Americans, using them for their own ends. As is often the case in such operations, both sides appear to be using the other."

"Oh?" it was Escobedo this time.

"*Sí, jefe.* And it should not surprise either of you that I have been able to identify those who have betrayed their comrades." He looked at both men, a thin smile on his lips.

There were only two road guards. Clark was back in the VW Microvan while OMEN raced through the woods to get to the objective. Vega and León had removed a side window, and now Vega, also in back, held it in place with his hand.

"Everybody ready?" Clark asked.

"Go!" Chavez replied.

"Here we go." Clark took the last turn in the road and slowed, taking the car right up to the two guards. They took their weapons off sling and assumed a more aggressive stance as he slowed the vehicle. "Excuse me, I am lost."

That was Vega's cue to let go of the glass. As it dropped, Chavez and León came up to their knees and aimed their MP-5s at the guards. Both took bursts in the head without warning, and both fell without a sound. Strangely, the submachine guns sounded awfully loud within the confines of the vehicle.

"Nicely done," Clark said. Before proceeding, he lifted his radio.

"This is SNAKE. OMEN, report in."

"SNAKE, this is OMEN Six. In position. Say

again, we are in position."

"Roger, stand by. CAESAR, this is SNAKE."

"SNAKE, this is CAESAR, ready to copy."

"Position check."

"We are holding at five miles out."

"Roger that, CAESAR, continue to hold at five miles. Be advised we are moving in."

Clark killed the lights and drove the van a hundred yards down the driveway. He selected a spot where the road twisted. Here he stopped the van and maneuvered it to block the road.

"Give me one of your frags," he said, stepping out and leaving the keys in the ignition. First he loosened the cotter pin on the grenade. Next he wired the body of the grenade to the door handle and ran another wire from the pin to the accelerator pedal. It took under a minute. The next person who opened that door was in for a nasty surprise. "Okay, come on."

"Tricky, Mr. Clark," Chavez observed.

"Kid, I was a Ninja before it became fashionable. Now shut up and do your jobs." No smile now, no time for banter. It was like the return of his youth, but while that feeling was a welcome one, it would have been more so if his youth had not been spent doing things best unremembered. The pure exhilaration of leading men into battle, however, was something that his memory had not lied about. It was terrible. It was dangerous. It was also something at which he excelled, and knew it. For the moment he was not Mr. Clark. He was, again, The Snake, the man whose footsteps no one had ever heard. It took five minutes to get to their jump-off point.

The NVA were smarter opponents than these. All the security troops were near the house. He took Vega's night scope and counted them, sweeping the grounds to check for strays, but there were none.

"OMEN Six, this is SNAKE. Say your position."

"We are in the treeline north of the objective."

"Toss your strobe to mark your position."

"Okay, done."

Clark turned his head and the goggles showed the infrared strobe blinking on the open ground, thirty feet from the treeline. Chavez, listening on the same radio circuit, did the same.

"Okay, stand by. CAESAR, this is SNAKE. We are in position on the east side of the objective where the driveway comes through the trees. OMEN is on the north side. We have two good strobes to mark friendly positions. Acknowledge."

"Roger, copy, you are in the treeline at the road, east side of the objective. Say again, east of the objective, with OMEN to the north. Copy strobes to mark friendly positions. We are standing by at five miles," PJ replied in his best computer voice.

"Roger, come on in. It's show time. I repeat, come on in."

"Roger, copy, CAESAR is turning in with hot guns."

"OMEN, this is SNAKE. Commence firing, commence firing."

Cortez had them both at a disadvantage, though neither knew the whole reason for it. LaTorre, after all, had talked to Félix the previous day and been told that Escobedo was the traitor in their midst. Because of that, he had his pistol out first.

"What is this?" Escobedo demanded.

"The ambush was very clever, *jefe*, but I saw through your ploy," Cortez said.

"What are you talking about?"

Before Cortez could give his preplanned answer, several rifles started firing north of the house. Félix wasn't a total fool. His first reaction was to extinguish the lights in the house. LaTorre still had his gun aimed at Escobedo, and Cortez dashed to the window, a pistol in his hand, to see what was happening. Just as he got there, he realized that he was being foolish, and dropped to his knees, peering around the frame. The house was of block construction and should stop a bullet, he told himself, though the windows certainly would not.

The fire was light and sporadic, just a few people, just an annoyance, and he had people to deal with that. Cortez's own men, assisted by the bodyguards for Escobedo and LaTorre, returned fire at once. Félix watched his men move like soldiers, spreading out into two fire teams, dropping at once into the usual infantry drill of fire and movement. Whatever annoyance this was, they'd soon take care of things. The Cartel bodyguards, as usual, were brave but oafish. Two of them were already down.

Yes, he saw, it was already working. The gun-fire from the trees was diminishing. Some bandits, perhaps, who'd been late realizing that they'd bitten off more than —

The sound was like nothing he'd ever heard.

"Target in sight," Jack heard over the inter-com phones. Ryan was looking the wrong way, of course. Though he was standing at a gun, Colonel Johns had not mistaken him for a gunner, not a real one. Sergeant Zimmer was on the right-side gun, the one that corresponded to the pi-lot's seat. They'd come skimming in so low that Ryan felt — *knew* that he could reach out and touch some treetops. Then the aircraft pivoted. The sound and vibration assaulted Jack through all the protective gear, and the flash that accom-panied the sound cast a shadow of the aircraft before Jack's eyes as he looked for other targets.

It looked like a huge, curving tube of yellow neon, Cortez's mind told him. Wherever it touched the ground, dust rose in a great cloud. It swept up and down the field between the house and the trees. Then it stopped after what could have been only a few seconds. Cortez couldn't see anything in the dust, and it took a second to real-ize that he should have been able to see some-thing, the flashes of his men's rifles at the very least. Then there were flashes, but those were from farther away, in the treeline, and there were more now.

"CAESAR: Check fire, check fire!"

"Roger," the radio replied. Overhead, the horrible noise stopped. Clark hadn't heard it in a very long time. Another sound from his youth, it was as fearful now as it had been then.

"Heads up, OMEN, we're moving now, SNAKE is moving. Acknowledge."

"OMEN, this is Six, cease fire, cease fire!" The shooting from the treeline stopped. "SNAKE: Go!"

"Come on!" It was stupid to lead them with only a silenced pistol in his hand, Clark knew, but he was in command, and the good commanders led from the front. They covered the two hundred yards to the house in thirty seconds.

"Door!" Clark said to Vega, who used his AK to blast off the hinges, then kicked it down. Clark dove through low, rolling when he hit, looking and seeing one man in the room. He had an AK, and fired it, but shot high. Clark dropped him with a silenced round in the face, then another as he fell. There was a doorway but no door to the next room. He gestured to Chavez, who tossed a CS grenade into it. They waited for it to go off, then both rushed the room, again diving in low.

There were three men. One, holding a pistol, took a step toward them. Clark and Chavez hit him in the chest and head. The other armed man, kneeling by the window, tried to turn about, but couldn't do it on his knees, and fell onto his side. Chavez was there in an instant, smashing his buttstock onto his forehead. Clark rushed the third man, slamming him against the block wall. León and Vega came in next, leapfrogging to the final door. That room was empty.

"Building is clear!" Vega shouted. "Hey, I —"

"Come on!" Clark dragged his man out the front. Chavez did the same, covered by León. Vega was slow in moving. They didn't know why until they were all outside.

Clark was already on his radio. "CAESAR, this is SNAKE. We got 'em. Let's get the fuck outa here."

"León," Vega said. "Look here."

"Tony," the sergeant said. The only other survivor from Ninja Hill had been a BANNER man. León walked over to Escobedo, who was still conscious. *"Motherfucker! You're fuckin' dead!"* León screamed, bringing his gun down.

"Stop!" Clark yelled at him. That almost didn't work, but Clark knocked him down, which did. "You're a soldier, goddammit, act like one! You and Vega — carry your friend on the chopper."

Team OMEN worked its way across the field. Several men, remarkably enough, weren't quite dead yet. That aberration was corrected with single rifle shots. The captain got his men together and counted them off with his finger.

1071

"Good work," Clark told him. "You got everybody?"

"Yes!"

"Okay, here's comes our ride."

The Pave Low swept in from the west this time, and again didn't quite touch the ground. *Just like the old days, Clark.* A helicopter that touched the ground could set off a mine. Not likely here, but PJ hadn't gotten old enough to be a colonel by overlooking any chances at all. He grabbed Escobedo — he'd gotten a good enough look by now to identify him — by the arm and propelled him to the ramp. One of the chopper crew met them there, did his count, and before Clark was sitting down with his charge, the MH-53J was moving up and north. He assigned a soldier to look after Señor Escobedo and went forward.

Sweet Jesus, Ryan thought. He'd counted eight bodies, and they'd just been the ones close to the helicopter. Jack switched off his gun motor and relaxed — and really did this time. Relaxation was a relative thing, he'd just learned. Being shot at really was worse than flying in the back of a goddamned helicopter. Amazing, he thought. A hand grabbed his shoulder.

"We got Cortez and Escobedo alive!" Clark shouted at him.

"Escobedo? What the hell was he — "

"You complaining?"

"What the hell can we do with him?" Jack asked.

"Well, I sure as shit couldn't just leave him there, could I?"

"But what — "

"If you want, I can give the bastard a flying lesson." Clark gestured toward the stern ramp. *If he learns to fly before he hits the ground, fine. . . .*

"No, goddammit, that's fucking murder!"

Clark grinned at him. "That gun next to you is not a negotiating tool, doc."

"Okay, people," PJ's voice came over the intercom before that conversation went any further. "One more stop and we call this one a day."

29.

Fill-ups

It had started with the President's warning. Admiral Cutter wasn't used to having to make sure his orders had been carried out. In his naval career orders were things that you gave and that other people did, or that you did after being told to do so by others. He placed a call to the Agency and got Ritter and asked the question, the one that had to be an unnecessarily insulting one. Cutter knew that he'd already humiliated the man, and that to do so further was not a smart move — but what if the President had been right? That risk called for further action. Ritter's reaction was a troubling one. The irritation that should have been in his voice, wasn't. Instead he'd spoken like any other government bureaucrat saying that yes, the orders were being carried out, of course. Ritter was a cold, effective son of a bitch, but even that sort had its limits, beyond which emotion comes to the fore; Cutter knew that he'd reached and passed that point with the DDO. The anger just hadn't been there, and it ought to have been.

Something is wrong. The National Security Adviser told himself to relax. *Something might be wrong.* Maybe Ritter was playing mind games. Maybe even he'd seen that his course of action was the only proper one, Cutter speculated, and resigned himself to the inevitable. After all, Ritter liked being Deputy Director (Operations). That was his rice bowl, as the government saying went. Even the most important government officials had those. Even they were often uncomfortable with the idea of leaving behind the office and the secretary and the driver and most of all the title that designated them as Important People despite their meager salaries. Like the line from some movie or other, leaving the government meant entering the real world, and in the real world, people expected results to back up position papers and National Intelligence Estimates. How many people stayed in government service because of the security, the benefits, and the insulation from that "real" world? There were more of those, Cutter was sure, than of the ones who saw themselves as the honest servants of the people.

But even if that were likely, Cutter considered, it was not certain, and some further checking was in order. And so he placed his own call to Hurlburt Field and asked for Wing Operations.

"I need to talk to Colonel Johns."

"Colonel Johns is off post, sir, and cannot be reached."

"I need to know where he is."

"I do not have that information, sir."

"What do you mean, you don't have that information, Captain?" The real wing operations officer was off duty by now, and one of the helicopter pilots had drawn the duty for this evening.

"I mean I don't know, sir," the captain replied. He wanted to be a little more insolent in his answer to so stupid a question, but the call had come in on a secure line, and there was no telling who the hell was on the other end.

"Who does know?"

"I don't know that, sir, but I can try to find out."

Was this just some command fuck-up? Cutter asked himself. What if it wasn't?

"Are all your MC-130s in place, Captain?" Cutter asked.

"Three birds are off TDY somewhere or other, sir. Where they are is classified — I mean, sir, that where our aircraft happen to be is almost always classified. Besides, what with that hurricane chasing around south of here, we're getting ready to move a lot of our birds in case it heads this way."

Cutter could have demanded the information right then and there. But that would have meant identifying himself, and even then, he was talking to some twenty-something-year-old junior officer who might just say no because nobody

1076

had told him otherwise, and such a junior officer knew that he'd never be seriously punished for not taking initiative and doing something he'd been told not to do — at least not over a telephone line, secure or not. Such a demand would also have called attention to something in a way that he didn't want. . . .

"Very well," Cutter said finally and hung up. Then he called Andrews.

The first hint of trouble came from Larson, whose Beech was circling the FEATURE LZ. Juardo, still fighting the pain of his leg wound, was scanning out the side of the aircraft with his low-light goggles.

"Hey, man, I got some trucks on the ground down there at three o'clock. Like fifteen of 'em."

"Oh, that's just great," the pilot observed, and keyed his microphone.

"CLAW, this is LITTLE EYES, over."

"LITTLE EYES, this is CLAW," the Combat Talon answered.

"Be advised we have possible activity on the ground six klicks southeast of FEATURE. Say again we have trucks on the ground. No personnel are visible at this time. Recommend you warn FEATURE and CAESAR of possible intruders."

"Roger, copy."

"Christ, I hope they're slow tonight," Larson said over the intercom. "We're going down to take a look."

"You say so, man."

Larson extended his flaps and reduced power as much as he dared. There was precious little light, and flying low over mountains at night was not his idea of fun. Juardo looked down with his goggles, but the tree canopy was too heavy.

"I don't see anything."

"I wonder how long those trucks have been there. . . ."

There was a bright flash on the ground, perhaps five hundred meters below the summit. Then there were several more, small ones, like sparklers on the ground. Larson made another call:

"CLAW, this is LITTLE EYES. We have a possible firefight underway below FEATURE LZ."

"Roger."

"Roger, copy," PJ said to the MC-130. "Aircraft commander to crew: we have a possible firefight at the next LZ. We may have a hot pickup." At that moment something changed. The aircraft settled a touch and slowed. "Buck, what is that?"

"Uh-oh," the flight engineer said. "I think we have a P3 leak here. Possible pressure bleed leak, maybe a bad valve, number-two engine. I'm losing some N_f speed and some N_g, sir. T_5 is coming up a little." Ten feet over the flight engineer's head, a spring had broken, opening a valve wider than it was supposed to be. It released bleed air supposed to recirculate within the turboshaft engine. That reduced combustion in the engine,

1078

and was manifested in reduced N_f or free-power turbine speed, also in N_g power from the gas-producer turbine, and finally the loss of air volume resulted in increased tailpipe temperature, called T_5. Johns and Willis could see all this from their instruments, but they really depended on Sergeant Zimmer to tell them what the problem was. The engines belonged to him.

"Talk to me, Buck," Johns ordered.

"We just lost twenty-six-percent power in Number Two, sir. Can't fix it. Bad valve, shouldn't get much worse, though. Tailpipe temp ought to stabilize short of max-sustainable . . . maybe. Ain't an emergency yet, PJ. I'll keep an eye on it."

"Fine," the pilot growled. At the valve, not at Zimmer. This was not good news. Things had gone well tonight, too well. Like most combat veterans, Paul Johns was a suspicious man. What his mind went over now were power and weight considerations. He had to climb over those goddamned mountains in order to tank and fly back to Panama. . . .

But first he had a pickup to make.

"Give me a time."

"Four minutes," Captain Willis answered. "We'll be able to see it over that next ridge. Starting to mush on us, sir."

"Yeah, I can tell." Johns looked at his instruments. Number One was at 104 percent rated power. Number Two was just over 73 percent. Since they could accomplish their next segment of the mission despite the problem, it went onto the back burner for now. PJ dialed some more altitude into his autopilot. Climbing ridges would be getting harder now with greater weight on the airframe and less power to drag it around.

"It's a real fight, all right," Johns said a minute later. His night-vision systems showed lots of activity on the ground. Johns keyed his radio. "FEATURE, this is CAESAR, over." No answer.

"FEATURE, this is CAESAR, over." It took two more tries.

"CAESAR, this is FEATURE, we are under attack."

"Roger, FEATURE, I can see that, son. I make your position about three hundred meters down from the LZ. Get up the hill, we can cover. Say again, we can cover."

"We have close contact, CAESAR."

"Run for it. I repeat, run for it, we can cover you," PJ told him calmly. *Come on, kid. I've been here before. I know the drill.* . . . "Break contact now!"

"Roger. FEATURE, this is Six, head for the LZ. I repeat, head for the LZ now!" they heard him say. PJ keyed his intercom.

"Buck, let's go hot. Gunners to stations, we have a hot LZ here. There are friendlies on the ground. I say again: *there are friendlies on the ground, people.* So let's be goddamned careful with those fucking guns!"

Johns had wished a hundred times that he'd had one of these over Laos. The Pave Low carried over a thousand pounds of titanium armor which went, of course, over the engines, fuel cells, and transmission. The flight crew was protected by less effective Kevlar. The rest of the aircraft was less fortunate — a child could push a screwdriver through the aluminum skin — but those were the breaks. He orbited the LZ, a thousand feet higher and two thousand yards out, traveling in a clockwise circle to get a feel for things. Things didn't feel good.

"I don't like this, PJ," Zimmer told him over intercom. Sergeant Bean on the ramp gun felt the same way but didn't say anything. Ryan, who hadn't seen anything at any of the landing zones, also kept his mouth shut.

"They're moving, Buck."

"Looks like it."

"Okay, I'm spiraling in. AC to crew, we're heading in for a closer look. You may return fire directed at us, but nothing else until I say otherwise. I want to hear acknowledgments."

"Zimmer, acknowledge."

"Bean, acknowledge."

"Ryan, okay." *I can't see anything to shoot at anyway.*

It was worse than it looked. The attackers from the Cartel had chosen to approach the primary LZ from an unexpected direction. This took them right through the alternate extraction site selected by FEATURE, and the team had not had the time needed to prepare a full defensive network. Worst of all, some of the attackers were those who had survived the fight against KNIFE, and had learned a few things, like the way in which caution was sometimes improved by a speedy advance, not diminished by it. They also knew of the helicopter, but not enough. Had they known of its armament, the battle might have ended then and there, but they expected the rescue chopper to be unarmed because they had never really encountered any other sort. As usual in battle, the contest was defined by purpose and error, knowledge and ignorance. FEATURE was pulling back rapidly, leaving behind hastily arranged booby traps and claymores, but, as before, the casualties were less a warning to the attackers than a goad, and the Cartel's veterans of Ninja Hill were learning. Now they split into three distinct groups and began to envelop the hilltop LZ.

"I got a strobe," Willis said.

"FEATURE, this is CAESAR, confirm your LZ."

"CAESAR, FEATURE, do you have our strobe?"

"That's affirm. Coming in now. Get all your people in the open. I say again, get all your people where we can see them."

"We have three down we're bringing in. We're doing our best."

"Thirty seconds out," PJ told him.

"We'll be ready."

As before, the gunners heard half of the conversation, followed by their instructions: "AC to crew, I've ordered all friendlies into the open.

Once we get a good count, I want you to hose down the area. Anything you can see is probably friendly. I want everything else suppressed hard. Ryan, that means beat the shit out of it."

"Roger," Jack replied.

"Fifteen seconds. Let's look sharp, people."

It came without warning. No one saw where it originated. The Pave Low was spiraling in steeply, but it could not wholly avoid flying over enemy troops. Six of them heard it approach and saw the black mass moving against the background of clouds. Simultaneously they aimed at the sky and let loose. The 7.62mm rounds lanced right through the floor of the helicopter. The sound was distinctive, like hail on a tin roof, and everyone who heard it knew immediately what it was. A scream confirmed it for the slow. Someone had been hit.

"PJ, we're taking fire," Zimmer said over the intercom circuit. As he said so, he trained his gun down and loosed a brief burst. Again the airframe vibrated. The line of tracers told the whole world what and where the Pave Low was, and more fire came in.

"Jesus!" Rounds hit the armored windshield. They didn't penetrate, but they left nicks, and their impacts sparked like fireflies. On instinct, Johns jinked to the right, away from the fire. That unmasked the left side of the aircraft.

Ryan was as scared as he had ever been. It seemed that there were a hundred, two hundred, a thousand muzzle flashes down there, all aimed straight at him. He wanted to cringe, but knew that his safest place was behind the thousand-plus-pound gun mount. The gun didn't really have much of a sight. He looked down the rotating barrels toward a particularly tight knot of flashes and depressed the trigger switch.

It felt like he was holding a jackhammer in his hands and sounded like a giant was ripping a canvas sail to bits. A gout of flame six feet long and three across erupted before his eyes, so bright that he could barely see through it, but the tight cylinder of tracers was impossible to miss, and it walked right into the flashes that were still sparkling on the ground. But not for long. He waved the gun around, assisted in the effort by the gyrations of the helicopter and the incredible vibration of the gun. The line of tracers wiggled and wavered over the target area for several seconds. By the time his thumbs came up, the sparkling of muzzle flashes had stopped.

"Son of a bitch," he said to himself, so surprised that he momentarily forgot about the danger. That wasn't the only incoming fire. Ryan selected another area and went to work, this time holding to short bursts, only a few hundred rounds each. Then the chopper turned fully away and he had no more targets.

On the flight deck, Willis and Johns scanned their instruments. They'd allowed themselves to be surprised. There was no critical damage to the aircraft. The flight controls, also protected by armor, engines, transmission, and fuel cells were impervious to rifle fire. Or supposed to be.

"We got some people hurt back here," Zimmer reported. "Let's get it over with, PJ."

"Okay, Buck, I hear you." PJ brought the chopper back around, looping to the left now. "FEATURE, this is CAESAR, we're going to try that again." Even his voice had lost its icy calm. Combat hadn't changed very much, but he'd grown older.

"They're closing in. Move your ass, mister! We're all here, we're all here."

"Twenty seconds, son. AC to crew, we're going back in. Twenty seconds."

The helicopter stopped and pivoted in the air, not continuing its majestic sweep, and Johns hoped that those who were watching would be unprepared for that. He twisted the throttle control to max power and lowered his nose to dive in hard on the LZ. Two hundred meters out he brought the nose up and yanked the collective to slow down. It was his usual perfect maneuver. The Pave Low lost forward airspeed exactly at the right place — and dropped hard on the ground because of the reduced power from Number Two. Johns cringed when he felt it, half expecting it to set off a booby trap, but that didn't happen and he left it there.

It seemed to take forever. Minds and bodies pumped up with adrenaline have their own time, the sort that stops the ticking of watches. Ryan thought that he could see the rotor blades spinning individually at the top of his peripheral vision. He wanted to look aft, wanted to see if the team had gotten aboard yet, but his area of responsibility was out the left-side gunner's door. He realized at once that he wasn't being paid to bring ammunition home. As soon as he was sure that there were no friendlies in front of him, he punched the gun switch and hosed down the treeline, sweeping his fire about a foot off the ground in a wide arc. On the other side, Zimmer was doing the same.

Aft, Clark was looking out the back door. Bean was on his minigun, and he couldn't shoot. This was where the friendlies were, and they moved toward the chopper, their legs pumping in what had to be a run, but seeming to be slow-motion. That was when the fire started from the trees.

Forward, Ryan was amazed that anyone could be alive in the area that he'd just hosed, but there it was. He saw a spark on the doorframe and knew it had to have been a bullet aimed right at him. Jack didn't cringe. There was no place to hide, and he knew that the side of the aircraft was getting hit far worse. He took an instant to look and see where the shooting was coming from, then trained on it and fired again. It seemed that the blast from the gun must push the aircraft sideways. The exhaust flames from the gun bored a hole through the dust kicked up by the spinning rotor, but still there were flashes of fire from the treeline.

Clark heard the screams inside and out over the low howl of the miniguns. He could feel the rounds hitting the side of the aircraft, and then saw two men fall just at the tail rotor of the helicopter while others were racing aboard.

"Shit!" He leapt to his feet and ran out the door, joined by Chavez and Vega. Clark lifted one of the fallen soldiers and dragged him toward the ramp. Chavez and Vega got the other. There was dust kicking up at their feet from the fire. Vega fell five feet from the ramp, taking his burden down with him. Clark tossed his soldier into the waiting hands of his team members and turned to assist. First he took the team member. When he turned, Chavez was struggling with Vega. Clark grabbed the man's shoulders and pushed backward, landing on the edge of the ramp. Ding grabbed *Oso*'s feet and swung them around, leaping over them to grab the base of the minigun as the helicopter started lifting off. Fire came straight through the door, but Bean now had a clear field for his weapon and swept it across the area.

It was slow getting off. The helicopter had several tons of new weight, was at over five thousand feet of altitude, and trying to fly with reduced power. Forward, PJ cursed the balky machine. The Pave Low struggled up a few feet, still taking fire.

On the ground around them the attackers were enraged that the men whom they wanted to kill were escaping, and ran for one last attempt to prevent it. They saw the helicopter as a trophy, some horrible apparition that had robbed them of success and their comrades of their lives, and each of them determined that this should not be. Over a hundred rifles were trained on the aircraft as it wavered, halfway between ground and flight.

Ryan felt the passage of several rounds — they were coming right through his door, going he knew not where, aiming for him and his gun. He was past fear. The flashes of rifle fire were places to aim, and that he did. One at a time he selected a target and touched his trigger, shifting rapidly from one to another. Safety, what there was of it, lay in eliminating the danger. There was no place to run, and he knew that the ability to respond was a luxury that everyone aboard the aircraft wanted, but only three of them had. He couldn't let them down. He moved the gun left to right and back again in a series of seconds that stretched out into hours, and he thought that he could hear each individual round the minigun spat out. His head jerked back when something hit his helmet, but he yanked it back and held the trigger down, spraying the area in one continuous blast of fire that changed as he realized that he had to bring his hands up and the muzzles down because the targets were dropping away. For one brief contradictory instant it seemed as if they and not he were getting away. Then it was over. For a moment, his hands wouldn't come off the gun. He tried to take a step back, but his hands wouldn't let go until he willed them to. Then they dropped to his side. Ryan shook his head to clear it. He was deafened by the noise from the minigun, and it took a few seconds before he started hearing the higher-frequency screams of wounded men. He looked around to see that the body of the aircraft was filled with the acidic smoke of the guns, but the rapidly increasing slipstream from forward flight was clearing it out. His eyes were still suffering from the gun flashes, and his legs were wobbly from the sudden fatigue that comes after violent action. He wanted to sit down, to go to sleep, to wake up in another place.

One of the screams was close by. It was Zimmer, only a few feet away, lying on his back and rolling around with his arms across his chest. Ryan went to see what the problem was.

Zimmer had taken three rounds in the chest. He was aspirating blood. It sprayed in a pink cloud from his mouth and nose. One round had shattered his right shoulder, but the serious ones were through the lungs. The man was bleeding to death before his eyes, Ryan knew at once. Was there a medic here? Might he do something?

"This is Ryan," he said over the intercom line. "Sergeant Zimmer is down. He's hit pretty bad."

"Buck!" PJ responded at once. "Buck, are you all right?"

Zimmer tried to answer but couldn't. His intercom line had been shot away. He shouted something Ryan couldn't understand, and Jack turned and screamed as loudly as he could at the rest of them, the others who didn't seem to care or know what the problem here was.

"*Medic! Corpsman!*" he added, not knowing what it was that Army troops said. Clark heard him and started heading that way.

"Come on, Zimmer, you're going to be all right," Jack told him. He remembered that much from his brief few months in the Marine Corps. Give them a reason to live. "We're going to fix this up and you're going to be all right. Hang in there, Sarge — it hurts, but you're going to be all right."

Clark was there a moment later. He stripped off the flight engineer's flak jacket, oblivious to the screech of pain that it caused from the wrecked shoulder. For Clark, too, it was too much a return to years past and things half-remembered. Somehow he'd forgotten just how scary, how awful this sort of thing was, and while he was recovering his senses more rapidly than most, the horror of having been helpless under fire and helpless with its aftermath had nearly overpowered him. And he was helpless now. He could see that from the placement of the wounds. Clark looked up at Ryan and shook his head.

"My kids!" Zimmer screamed. The sergeant had a reason to live, but the reason wasn't enough.

"Tell me about your kids," Ryan said. "Talk to me about your kids."

"Seven — I got seven kids — I gotta, I can't *die!* My kids — my kids need me."

"Hang in there, Sarge, we're going to get you

out of here. You're going to make it," Ryan told him, tears clouding in his eyes at the shame of lying to a dying man.

"They need me!" His voice was weaker now as the blood was filling his throat and lungs.

Ryan looked up at Clark, hoping that there was something to be said. Some hope. Something. Clark just stared into Jack's face. He looked back down at Zimmer and took his hand, the uninjured one.

"Seven kids?" Jack asked.

"They need me," Zimmer whimpered, knowing now that he wouldn't be there, wouldn't see them grow and marry and have their own children, wouldn't be there to guide them, to protect them. He had failed to do what a father must do.

"I'll tell you something about your kids that you don't know, Zimmer," Ryan said to the dying man.

"Huh? What?" He looked confused, looked to Ryan for the answer to the great question of life. Jack didn't have that one, but told him what he could.

"They're all going to college, man." Ryan squeezed the hand as hard as he could. "You got my word, Zimmer, all your kids'll go to college. I will take care of that for you. Swear to God, man, I'll do it."

The sergeant's face changed a bit at that, but before Ryan could decide what emotion he beheld, the face changed again, and there was no emotion left. Ryan hit the intercom switch. "Zimmer's dead, Colonel."

"Roger." Ryan was offended by the coldness of the acknowledgment. He didn't hear what Johns was thinking: *God, oh God, what do I tell Carol and the kids?*

Ryan had Zimmer's head cradled on his lap. He disengaged himself slowly, resting the head down on the metal floor of the helicopter. Clark wrapped his burly arms around the younger man.

"I'm going to do it," Jack told him in a choking voice. "That wasn't a fucking lie. I am going to do it!"

"I know. He knew it too. He really did."

"You sure?" The tears had started, and it was hard for Jack to repeat the most important question of his life. "Are you really sure?"

"He knew what you said, Jack, and he believed you. What you did, doc, that was pretty good." Clark embraced Ryan in the way that men do only with their wives, their children, and those with whom they had faced death.

In the right-front seat, Colonel Johns put his grief away into a locked compartment that he would later open and experience to the full. But for now he had a mission to fly. Buck would surely understand that.

Cutter's jet arrived at Hurlburt Field well after dark. He was met by a car which took him to Wing Operations. He'd arrived entirely without warning, and strode into the Operations office

1092

like an evil spirit.

"Who the hell's in charge here?"

The sergeant at the desk recognized the President's National Security Adviser immediately from seeing him on television. "Right through that door, sir."

Cutter found a young captain dozing in his swivel chair. His eyes had cracked open just as the door did, and the twenty-nine-year-old officer jumped to his feet quite unsteadily.

"I want to know where Colonel Johns is," Vice Admiral Cutter told him quietly.

"Sir, that is information which I am not able to — "

"You know who the hell I am?"

"Yes, sir."

"Are you trying to say no to me, Captain?"

"Sir, I have my orders."

"Captain, I am countermanding all of your orders. Now, you answer my question and you do it right now." Cutter's voice was a few decibels higher now.

"Sir, I don't know where the — "

"Then you find somebody who does, and you get him here."

The captain was frightened enough that he took the route of least resistance. He called a major, who lived on post and was in the office in under eight minutes.

"What the hell is this?" the major said on the way through the door.

"Major, I am what's going on here," Cutter

told him. "I want to know where Colonel Johns is. He's the goddamned CO of this outfit isn't he?"

"Yessir!" *What the hell is this . . . ?*

"Are you telling me that the people of this unit don't know where their CO is?" Cutter was sufficiently amazed that his authority hadn't generated immediate compliance with his orders that he allowed himself to bluster off on a tangent.

"Sir, in Special Operations, we — "

"Is this a fucking Boy Scout camp or a military organization?" the Admiral shouted.

"Sir, this is a military organization," the major replied. "Colonel Johns is off TDY. I am under orders, sir, not to discuss his mission or his location with anyone without proper authority, and you are not on the list, sir. Those are my orders, Admiral."

Cutter was amazed and only got angrier. "Do you know what my job is and who I work for?" He hadn't had a junior officer talk to him like this in over a decade. And he'd broken that one's career like a matchstick.

"Sir, I have written orders on this matter. The President ain't on the list either, sir," the major said from the position of attention. *Fucking squid, calling the United States Air Force a Boy Scout camp! Well, fuck you and the horse you rode in on —* Admiral, sir, his face managed to communicate quite clearly.

Cutter had to soften his voice, had to regain control of his emotions. He could take care of this insolent punk at leisure. But for now he needed that information. He started, therefore, with an apology, man to man, as it were. "Major, you'll have to excuse me. This is a most important matter, and I can't explain to you why it is important or the issues involved here. I can say that this is a real life-or-death situation. Your Colonel Johns may be in a place where he needs help. The operation may be coming apart around him, and I really need to know. Your loyalty to your commander is laudable, and your devotion to duty is exemplary, but officers are supposed to exercise judgment. You have to do that now, Major. I am telling you that I need that information — and I need it now."

Reason succeeded where bluster had failed. "Admiral, the colonel went back down to Panama along with one of our MC-130s. I do not know why, and I don't know what they're doing. That is normal in a special-ops wing, sir. Practically everything we do is compartmented, and this one is tighter than most. What I just told you is everything I know, sir."

"Exactly where?"

"Howard, sir."

"Very well. How can I get in touch with them?"

"Sir, they're out of the net. I do not have that information. They can contact us but we can't contact them."

"That's crazy," Cutter objected.

"Not so, Admiral. We do that sort of thing all

the time. With the MC-130 along, they're a self-contained unit. The Herky-bird takes maintenance and support personnel to sustain the operation, and unless they call us for something, they're completely independent of this base. In the event of a family emergency or something like that, we can try to contact them through Howard's base ops office, but we haven't had to do so in this case. I can try to open that channel now for you, if you wish, sir, but it might take a few hours."

"Thanks, but I can *be* there in a few hours."

"Weather's breaking down around that area, sir," the major warned him.

"That's okay." Cutter left the room and walked back to his car. His plane had already been refueled, and ten minutes later it was lifting off for Panama.

Johns was on an easier flight profile now, heading northeast down the great Andean valley that forms the spine of Colombia. The flight was smooth, but he had three concerns. First, he didn't have the necessary power to climb over the mountains to his west at his present aircraft weight. Second, he'd have to refuel in less than an hour. Third, the weather ahead was getting worse by the minute.

"CAESAR, this is CLAW, over."

"Roger, CLAW."

"When are we going to tank, sir?" Captain Montaigne asked.

"I want to get closer to the coast first, and maybe if we burn some more off I can head west some more to do it."

"Roger, but be advised that we're starting to get radar emissions, and somebody might just detect us. They're air-traffic radars, but this Herky-bird is big enough to give one a skin-paint, sir."

Damn! Somehow Johns had allowed himself to forget that.

"We got a problem here," PJ told Willis.

"Yeah. There's a pass about twenty minutes ahead that we might be able to climb over."

"How much?"

"Says eighty-one hundred on the charts. Drops down a lot lower farther up, but with the detection problem . . . and the weather. I don't know, Colonel."

"Let's find out how high we can take her," Johns said. He'd tried to go easy on the engines for the last half hour. Not now. He had to find out what he could do. PJ twisted the throttle control on the collective arm to full power, watching the gauge for Number Two as he did so. The needle didn't even reach 70 percent this time.

"The P3 leak is getting worse, boss," Willis told him.

"I see it." They worked to get maximum lift off the rotor, but though they didn't know it, that, too, had taken damage and was not delivering as much lift as it was supposed to. The Pave Low labored upward, reaching seventy-seven hundred feet, but that was where it stopped, and then it started descending, fighting every foot but gradually losing altitude.

"As we burn off more gas . . . " Willis said hopefully.

"Don't bet on it." PJ keyed his radio. "CLAW, CAESAR, we can't make it over the hills."

"Then we'll come to you."

"Negative, too soon. We have to tank closer to the coast."

"CAESAR, this is LITTLE EYES. I copy your problem. What sort of fuel you need for that monster?" Larson asked. He'd been pacing the helicopter since the pickup, in accordance with the plan.

"Son, right now I'd burn piss if I had enough."

"Can you make the coast?"

"That's affirmative. Close, but we ought to be able to make it."

"I can pick you an airfield one-zero-zero miles short of the coast that has all the avgas you need. I am also carrying a casualty who's bleeding and needs some medical help."

Johns and Willis looked at each other. "Where is it?"

"At current speed, about forty minutes. El Pindo. It's a little place for private birds. Ought to be deserted this time of night. They have ten-kay gallons of underground storage. It's a Shell concession and I've been in and out of there a bunch of times."

"Altitude?"

"Under five hundred. Nice, thick air for that rotor, Colonel."

"Let's do it," Willis said.

"CLAW, did you copy that?" Johns asked.

"That's affirm."

"That's what we're going to try. Break west. Stay close enough to maintain radio contact, but you are free to evade radar coverage."

"Roger, heading west," Montaigne replied.

In back, Ryan was sitting by his gun. There were eight wounded men in the helicopter, but two medics were working on them and Ryan was unable to offer any help better than that. Clark rejoined him.

"Okay, what are we going to do with Cortez and Escobedo?"

"Cortez we want, the other one, hell, I don't know. How do we explain kidnapping him?"

"What do you think we're going to do, put him on trial?" Clark asked over the din of the engines and the wind.

"Anything else is cold-blooded murder. He's a prisoner now, and killing prisoners is murder, remember?"

You're getting legal on me, Clark thought, but he knew that Ryan was right. Killing prisoners was contrary to the code.

"So we take him back?"

"That blows the operation," Ryan said. He knew he was talking too loudly for the subject. He was supposed to be quiet and thoughtful now, but the environment and the events of the evening defeated that. "Christ, I don't know what to do."

"Where are we going — I mean, where's this chopper going?"

"I don't know." Ryan keyed his intercom to ask. He was surprised by the answer and communicated it to Clark.

"Look, let me handle it. I got an idea. I'll take him out of here when we land. Larson and I will tidy that part of it up. I think I know what'll work."

"But — "

"You don't really want to know, do you?"

"You can't murder him!" Jack insisted.

"I won't," Clark said. Ryan didn't know how to read that answer. But it did offer a way out, and he took it.

Larson got there first. The airfield was poorly lit, only a few glow lights showing under the low ceiling, but he managed to get his aircraft down, and with his anticollision lights blinking, he guided the way to the fuel-service area. He'd barely stopped when the helicopter landed fifty yards away.

Larson was amazed. In the dim blue lights he could see numerous holes in the aircraft. A man in a flight suit ran out toward him. Larson met him and led him to the fuel hose. It was a long one, about an inch in diameter, used to fuel private aircraft. The power to the pumps was off, but Larson knew where the switch was, and he shot the door lock. He'd never done that before, but just like in the movies, five rounds removed the brass mechanism from the wooden frame of the door. A minute later, Sergeant Bean had the nozzle into one of the outrigger tanks. That was when Clark and Escobedo appeared. A soldier held a rifle to the latter's head while the CIA officers conferred.

"We're going back," Clark told the pilot.

"What?" Larson turned to see two soldiers taking Juardo out of the Beech and toward the helicopter.

"We're taking our friend here back home to Medellín. Couple of things we have to do first, though . . ."

"Oh, great." Larson walked back to his aircraft and climbed up on the wing to open his fuel caps. He had to wait fifteen minutes. The helicopter usually drank fuel through a far larger hose. When the crewman took the hose back, the chopper's rotor started turning again. Soon after that, it lifted off into the night. There was lightning ahead to the north, and Larson was just as happy that he wasn't flying there. He let Clark handle the fueling while he went inside to make a telephone call. The funny part was that he'd even make money off the deal. Except that there was nothing funny about anything that had happened during the preceding month.

"Okay," PJ said into the intercom. "That's the last pit stop, and we're heading for home."

"Engine temps aren't all that great," Willis said. The T-64-GE-7 engines were designed to burn aviation kerosene, not the more volatile and dangerous high-octane gas used by private planes. The manufacturer's warranty said that you could use that fuel for thirty hours before the burner cans were crisped down to ashes, but the warranty didn't say anything about bad valve springs and P3 loss.

"Looks like we're going to cool 'em down just fine," the colonel said, nodding at the weather ahead.

"Thinking positive again, are we, Colonel?" Willis said as coolly as he could manage. It wasn't just a thunderstorm there, it was a hurricane that stood between them and Panama. On the whole, it was something scarier than being shot at. You couldn't shoot *back* at a storm.

"CLAW, this is CAESAR, over," Johns called on his radio.

"I read you, CAESAR."

"How's the weather ahead look?"

"Bad, sir. Recommend that you head west, find a spot to climb over, and try to approach from the Pacific side."

Willis scanned the navigational display. "Uh-uh."

"CLAW, we just gained about five-kay pounds in weight. We, uh, looks like we need another way."

"Sir, the storm is moving west at fifteen knots, and your course to Panama takes you into the lower-right quadrant."

Headwinds all the way, PJ told himself.

"Give me a number."

"Estimated peak winds on your course home are seven-zero knots."

"Great!" Willis observed. "That makes us marginal for Panama, sir. Very damned marginal."

Johns nodded. The winds were bad enough. The rain that came with them would greatly reduce engine efficiency. His flight range might be less than half of what it should be . . . no way he could tank in the storm . . . the smart move would be to find a place to land and stay there, but he couldn't do that either. . . . Johns keyed his radio yet again.

"CLAW, this is CAESAR. We are heading for Alternate One."

"Are you out of your skull?" Francie Montaigne replied.

"I don't like it, sir," Willis said.

"Fine. You can testify to that effect someday. It's only a hundred miles off the coast, and if it doesn't work, we'll use the winds to slingshot us around. CLAW, I need a position check on Alternate One."

"You crazy fucker," Montaigne breathed. To her communications people: "Call up Alternate One. I need a position check and I need it now."

Murray was not having any fun at all. Though

Adele wasn't really a major hurricane, Wegener had told him, it was more than he had ever expected to see. The seas had been forty feet, and though once *Panache* had looked like a white steel cliff alongside the dock, she now rode like a child's toy in a bathtub. The FBI agent had a sco- polamine patch stuck to his head below and behind his ear to combat motion-sickness, but it wasn't fighting hard enough at the moment. But Wegener was just sitting in his bridge chair, smoking his pipe like the Old Man of the Sea while Murray held on to the grab-bar over his head, feeling like the man on the flying trapeze.

They were not in their programmed position. Wegener had explained to his visitor that there was only one place they could be. It moved, but that's where they had to be, and Murray was dis- tantly thankful that the seas weren't quite as bad as they had been. He worked his way over to the door and looked out at the towering cylinder of cloud.

"*Panache*, this is CLAW, over," the speaker said. Wegener rose to take the mike.

"CLAW, this is *Panache*. Your signal is weak but readable, over."

"Position check, over."

Wegener gave it to the pilot, who sounded like a girl, he thought. Christ, they were everywhere now.

"CAESAR is inbound yours."

"Roger. Please advise CAESAR that conditions are below margins. I say again, it is not good

1104

down here at the moment."

"Roger, copy. Stand by." The voice came back two minutes later. "*Panache*, this is CLAW. CAESAR says he wants to try it. If he can't do it, he plans to HIFR. Can you handle that, over."

"That's affirmative, we can sure as hell try. Give me an ETA, over."

"Estimate six-zero minutes."

"Roger, we'll be ready. Keep us posted. Out." Wegener looked across his bridge. "Miss Walters, I have the conn. I want chiefs Oreza and Riley on the bridge, now."

"Captain has the conn," Ensign Walters said. She was disappointed. Here she was in the middle of a goddamned tropical storm and having the time of her young life. She wasn't even ill from it, though many of the crew were. So why couldn't the skipper let her keep the goddamned conn?

"Left standard rudder," Wegener ordered. "Come to new course three-three-five. All ahead two-thirds."

"Left standard rudder, aye, coming to new course three-three-five." The helmsman turned the wheel, then reached for the throttle controls. "Two thirds, sir."

"Very well. How you feel, Obrecki?" the skipper asked.

"Hell of a coaster, but I'm wondering when the ride is going to stop, sir." The youngster grinned, but didn't take his eyes off the compass.

"You're doing just fine. Let me know if you get tired, though."

"Aye aye, sir."

Oreza and Riley appeared a minute later. "What gives?" the former asked.

"We go to flight quarters in thirty minutes," the captain told them.

"Oh, fuck!" Riley observed. "Excuse me, Red, but . . . shit!"

"Okay, Master Chief, now that we've gotten that behind us, I'm depending on you to get it done," Wegener said sternly. Riley accepted the rebuke like the pro he was.

"Beg pardon, Cap'n, you'll get my best shot. Put the XO in the tower?"

Wegener nodded. The executive officer was the best man to command the evolution from the flight-control station. "Go get him." Riley left and Wegener turned to his quartermaster. "Portagee, I want you on the wheel when we go Hotel Corpin. I'll have the conn."

"Sir, there ain't no Hotel Corpin."

"That's why you're on the wheel. Relieve Obrecki in half an hour and get a feel for her. We gotta give him the best target we can."

"Jesus." Oreza looked out the windows. "You got it, Red."

Johns held the aircraft down, staying a scant five hundred feet above ground level. He disengaged the automatic flight controls, trusting more to his skill and instinct now, leaving the throttle to Willis and concentrating on his instruments as much as he could. It started in an instant. One moment they were flying in clear air, the next there was rain pelting the aircraft.

"This isn't so bad," Johns lied outrageously over the intercom.

"They even pay us to do it," Willis agreed with no small irony.

PJ checked the navigation display. The winds were from the northwest at the moment, slowing the helicopter somewhat, but that would change. His eyes flickered from the airspeed indicator to another one that worked off a Doppler-radar aimed at the ground. Satellite and inertial navigation systems told a computer display where he was and where he wanted to go, a red dot. Another screen held the display of a radar system that interrogated the storm ahead, showing the worst sections in red. He'd try to avoid those, but the yellow areas he had to fly through were bad enough.

"Shit!" Willis shouted. Both pilots yanked up on the collective and twisted to maximum power. They'd caught a downdraft. Both pairs of eyes locked onto the dial that gave them vertical velocity in feet per minute. For an instant they were headed down at over a thousand, less than thirty seconds of life for an aircraft at five hundred feet. But microbursts like that are localized phenomena. The helicopter bottomed out at two hundred and clawed its way back up. PJ decided that seven hundred feet was a safer cruise altitude at the moment. He said one word:

"Close."

Willis grunted by way of reply.

In back, men were strapped down to the floor. Ryan had already done that, and was holding onto his minigun mount as though it would make a difference. He could see out the open door — at nothing, really. Just a mass of gray darkness occasionally lit by lightning. The helicopter was jolting up and down, tossed like a child's kite by the moving masses of air, except that the helicopter weighed forty thousand pounds. But there was nothing he could do. His fate was in the hands of others, and nothing he knew or did mattered now. Even vomiting didn't make him feel any better, though he and others were doing that. He just wanted it to be over, and only intellect told him that he really did care how it ended — didn't he?

The buffeting continued, but the winds shifted as the helicopter penetrated the storm. They had started off from the northeast, but shifted with measurable speed counterclockwise, and were soon on the port quarter of the aircraft. That increased their ground speed. With an airspeed of one-fifty, they now had a ground speed of one-ninety and increasing.

"This is doing wonders for our fuel economy," Johns noted.

"Fifty miles," Willis replied.

"CAESAR, this is CLAW, over."

"Roger, CLAW, we are five-zero miles from Alternate One, and it's a little bumpy —" *A little bumpy, my ass,* Captain Montaigne thought, roller-coastering through lighter weather a hundred miles away " — otherwise okay," Johns reported. "If we cannot make the landing, I think we can try to slingshot out the other side and make for the Panamanian coast." Johns frowned as more water struck the windshield. Some was ingested into the engines at the same time.

"Flameout! We've lost Number Two."

"Restart it," Johns said, still trying to be cool. He lowered the nose and traded altitude for speed to get out of the heavy rain. That, too, was supposed to be a local phenomenon. Supposed to be.

"Working on it," Willis rasped.

"Losing power in Number One,"Johns said. He twisted the throttle all the way and managed to get some of it back. His two-engine aircraft was now operating on one of its engines at 80 percent power. "Let's get Two back, Captain. We have a hundred foot per minute of 'down' right now."

"Working," Willis repeated. The rain eased a little, and Number Two started turning and burning again, but delivered only 40 percent. "I think the P3 loss just got worse. We got a shit sandwich here, Colonel. Forty miles. We're committed to Alternate One now."

"At least we have an option. I never could swim worth a damn." PJ's hands were sweaty now. He could feel them loose inside the handmade gloves. Intercom time: "AC to crew, we're

1109

about fifteen minutes out," he told them. "One-five minutes out."

Riley had assembled a group of ten, all experienced crewmen. Each had a safety line around his waist, and Riley checked every knot and buckle personally. Though all had life preservers on, finding a man overboard in these conditions would require a miracle from an especially loving God who had lots of things to keep Him busy tonight, Riley thought. Tie-down chains and more two-inch line was assembled and set in place, already secured to the deck wherever possible. He took the deck crew forward, standing them against the aft-facing wall of the superstructure. "All ready here," he said over the phone to the XO in flight control. To his people: "If any of you fuck up and go over the side, I'll fucking jump overboard an' strangle you myself!"

They were in a whirlpool of wind. According to the navigational display, they were now north of their target, traveling at nearly two hundred fifty knots. The buffet now was the worst it had been. One downburst hurled them down at the black waves until Johns stopped at a bare hundred feet. It was now to the point that the pilot wanted to throw up. He'd never flown in conditions like this, and it was worse than the manuals said it was. "How far?"

"We should be there right now, sir!" Willis said. "Dead south."

"Okay." Johns pushed the stick to the left. The sudden change of direction relative to the wind threatened to snap the helicopter over, but he held it and crabbed onto the new course. Two minutes later, they were in the clear.

"*Panache*, this is CAESAR, where the hell are you?"

"Lights on, everything, now!" Wegener shouted when he heard the call. In a moment *Panache* was lit up like a Christmas tree.

"Goddamn if you don't look pretty down there!" the voice said a few seconds later.

Adele was a small, weak, disorganized hurricane, now turning back into a tropical storm due to confused local weather conditions. That made her winds weaker than everyone had feared, but the eye was also small and disorganized, and the eye was what they needed now.

It is a common misconception that the eye of a hurricane is calm. It is not, though after experiencing the powerful winds in the innermost wall of clouds, the fifteen knots of breeze there seem like less than nothing to an observer. But the wind is unsteady and shifting, and the seas in the eye, though not as tall as those in the storm proper, are confused. Wegener had stationed his ship within a mile of the northwest edge of the eye, which was barely four miles across. The storm was moving at about fifteen knots. They had fifteen minutes to recover the helicopter. About the only good news was that the air was clear. No rain was falling, and the crew in the pilothouse could see the waves and allow for them.

Aft at flight control, the executive officer donned his headset and started talking.

"CAESAR, this is *Panache*. I am the flight-operations officer, and I will guide your approach. We have fifteen knots of wind, and the direction is variable. The ship is pitching and rolling in what looks like about fifteen-foot seas. We have about ten or fifteen minutes to do this, so there's not that much of a rush." That last sentence was merely aimed at making the helicopter's crew feel better. He wondered if anyone could bring this off.

"Skipper, a few more knots and I can hold her a little steadier," Portagee reported at the wheel.

"We can't run out of the eye."

"I know that, sir, but I need a little more way on."

Wegener went outside to look. The helicopter was visible now, its strobes blinking in the darkness as it circled the ship to allow the pilot to size things up. *If anything screws this up, it's going to be the roll*, Wegener realized. Portagee was right about the speed. "Two-thirds," he called back inside.

"Christ, that's a little boat," Johns heard Willis breathe.

"Just so the oars ain't in the way." PJ took the helicopter down, circling one last time and com-

1112

ing to a straight course dead aft of the cutter. He leveled out at one hundred feet and found that he couldn't hover very well. He lacked the power, and the aircraft wavered left and right when he tried.

"Hold that damned boat steady!" he said over the radio circuit.

"We are trying, sir," the XO replied. "We have the wind off the port bow at the moment. I recommend you come in from the portside and stay at an angle to the deck all the way in."

"Roger, I can see why." Johns adjusted power one more time and moved in.

"Okay, let's move!" Riley told his men. They divided into three teams, one for each of the helicopter's wheel assemblies.

The deck, Johns saw, was not quite large enough for a fore-and-aft landing, but by angling his approach he could plant all six wheels on the black surface. He came in slowly, fifteen knots faster than the ship to start, and sloughing that off as he closed, but the wind shifted and turned the helicopter. Johns swore and turned fully away to try again.

"Sorry about that," he said. "I have some power problems here."

"Roger, take your time, sir," the XO replied.

PJ started again, a thousand yards out. The approach this time went well. He flared the aircraft a hundred yards aft to drop off excess speed, then flattened out and eased forward. His main gear touched just where he wanted, but the ship rolled hard and threw the aircraft to starboard. Instinctively PJ hit power and collective to lift free of the deck. He shouldn't have, and knew it even as he did so.

"This is hard," he said over the radio, managing not to curse as he brought the chopper back around.

"Shame we don't have more time to practice," the Coast Guard officer agreed. "That was a good, smooth approach. The ship just took a bad roll on us. Do that one more time, you'll be just fine."

"Okay, one more time." PJ came in again. The ship was rolling twenty degrees left and right despite her stabilizers and bilge keels, but Johns fixed his eyes on the center of the target area, which wasn't rolling at all, just a fixed point in space. That had to be the trick, he told himself, pick the spot that isn't moving. Again he flared out to kill off speed and inched forward. Just as he approached the deck, his eyes shifted to where the nosewheels had to hit, and slammed the collective down. It felt almost as bad as a crash, but the collective held the chopper in place.

Riley was first up and rolled under the aircraft at the nosewheels. Another boatswain's mate followed with the tie-down chains. The master chief found a likely spot and hooked them in place, then shot his arm out and made a fist. Two men on the other end of the chains pulled them taut, and the chief rolled free and went down the port-side to get to work on the main gear. It took several minutes. The Pave Low shifted twice before they had it secured, but soon they had two-inch line to back up the chains. By the time Riley was finished, it would have taken explosives to lift it from the deck. The deck crew entered the helicopter at the stern ramp and guided the passengers out. Riley counted fifteen people. He'd been told to expect more than that. Then he saw the bodies, and the men who were struggling with them.

Forward, Johns and Willis shut down their engines.

"CLAW, CAESAR is down. Return to base." Johns took off his helmet too soon to catch the reply, though Willis caught it.

"Roger. Out."

Johns looked around. He didn't feel like a pilot now. His aircraft was down. He was safe. It was time to get out and do something else. He couldn't get out his door without risking a fall overboard and . . . he'd allowed himself to forget Buck Zimmer. That door in his mind opened itself now. Well, he told himself, Buck would understand. The colonel stepped over the flight-engineer console. Ryan was still there, his flight suit speckled from his nausea. Johns knelt by the side of his sergeant. They'd served together on and off for over twenty years.

"He told me he has seven kids," Ryan said.

Johns' voice was too tired for any overt emotions. He spoke like a man a thousand years old, tired of life, tired of flying, tired of everything. "Yeah, cute ones. His wife is from Laos. Carol, her name is. Oh, God, Buck — why now?"

"Let me help," Jack said. Johns took the arms. Ryan got the legs. They had to wait in line. There were other bodies to be carried out, some dead, some only wounded, and they got the understandable priority. The soldiers, Jack saw, carried their own, helped by Sergeant Bean. The Coasties offered help, but it was declined — not unkindly, and the sailors understood the reason. Ryan and Johns also declined the assistance, the colonel because of the years with his friend, and the CIA officer because of a duty self-imposed. Riley and his men stayed behind briefly to collect packs and weapons. Then they, too, went below.

The bodies were set in a passageway for the time being. The wounded went to the crew's mess. Ryan and the Air Force officers were guided to the wardroom. There they found the man who'd started it all, months before, though none of them would ever understand how it had all happened. There was one more face, one which Jack recognized.

"Hi, Dan."

"Bad?" the FBI agent asked.

Jack didn't respond to that. "We got Cortez. I think he was wounded. He's probably in sick bay with a couple of soldiers keeping an eye on him."

"What got you?" Murray asked. He pointed

to Jack's helmet.

Ryan took it off and saw a gouge where a 7.62 bullet had scraped away a quarter inch or so of fiberglass. Jack knew that he should have reacted to it, but that part of his life was four hundred miles behind him. Instead he sat down and stared at the deck and didn't say anything for a while. Two minutes later, Murray moved him onto a cot and covered him with a blanket.

Captain Montaigne had to fight the last two miles through high winds, but she was a particularly fine pilot and the Lockheed Hercules was a particularly fine aircraft. She touched down a little hard, but not too badly, and followed the guide jeep to her hangar. A man in civilian clothes was waiting there, along with some officers. As soon as she'd shut down, she walked out to meet them. She made them wait while she headed for the rest room, smiling through her fatigue that there was not a man in America who'd deny a lady a trip to the john. Her flight suit smelled horrible and her hair was a wreck, she saw in the mirror before she returned. They were waiting for her right outside the door.

"Captain, I want to know what you did tonight," the civilian asked — but he wasn't a civilian, she realized after a moment, though the prick certainly didn't deserve to be anything else. Montaigne didn't know everything that was behind all this, but she did know that much.

"I just flew a very long mission, sir. My crew

and I are beat to hell."

"I want to talk to all of you about what you did."

"Sir, that is *my* crew. If there's any talking to be done, you'll talk to me!" she snapped back.

"What did you do?" Cutter demanded. He tried pretending it wasn't a girl. He didn't know that she was not pretending that he wasn't a man.

"Colonel Johns went in to rescue some special-ops troopers." She rubbed both hands across the back of her neck. "We got 'em — he got 'em, most of 'em, I suppose."

"Then where is he?"

Montaigne looked him right in the eye. "Sir, he had engine trouble. He couldn't climb out to us — couldn't get over the mountains. He flew right into the storm. He didn't fly out of it, sir. Anything else you want to know? I want to get showered, get some coffee down, and start thinking about search and rescue."

"The field's closed," the base commander said. "Nobody gets out for another ten hours. I think you need some rest, Captain."

"I think you're right, sir. Excuse me, I have to see to my crew. I'll have you the SAR coordinates in a few minutes. Somebody's gotta try," she added.

"Look, General, I want —" Cutter started to say.

"Mister, you leave that crew alone," said an Air Force one-star who was retiring soon anyway.

1118

Larson landed at Medellín's city airport about the same time the MC-130 approached Panama. It had been a profane flight, Clark in the back with Escobedo, the latter's hands tied behind his back and a gun in his ribs. There had been many promises of death in the flight. Death to Clark, death to Larson and his girlfriend who worked for Avianca, death to many people. Clark just smiled through it all.

"So what do you do with me, eh? You kill me now?" he asked as the wheels locked in the down position. Finally, Clark responded.

"I suggested that we could give you a flying lesson out the back of the helicopter, but they wouldn't let me. So looks like we're going to have to let you go."

Escobedo didn't know how to answer. His bluster wasn't able to cope with the fact that they might not want to kill him. They just didn't have the courage to, Clark decided.

"I had Larson call ahead," he said.

"Larson, you motherless traitor, you think you will survive?"

Clark dug the pistol in Escobedo's ribs. "You don't bother the guy who's flying the goddamned airplane. If I were you, señor, I'd be very pleased to be coming home. We're even having you met at the airport."

"Met by whom?"

"By some of your friends," Clark said as the wheel squeaked down on the tarmac. Larson reversed his props to brake the aircraft. "Some of your fellow board members."

That's when he saw the real danger coming. "What did you tell them?"

"The truth," Larson answered. "That you were taking a flight out of the country under very strange circumstances, what with the storm and all. And, gee, what with all the odd happenings of the past few weeks, I thought that it was kind of a coincidence . . ."

"But I will tell them — "

"What?" Clark asked. "That we put our own lives at risk by delivering you back home? That it's all a trick? Sure, you tell them that."

The aircraft stopped but the engines didn't. Clark gagged the chieftain. Then he unbuckled Escobedo's seat belt and pulled him toward the door. A car was already there. Clark stepped down, his silenced automatic in Escobedo's back.

"You are not Larson," the man with the sub-machine gun said.

"I am his friend. He is flying. Here is your man. You should have something for us."

"You do not need to leave," said the man with the briefcase.

"This one has too many friends. It is best, I think, that we should leave."

"As you wish," the second one said. "But you have nothing to fear from us." He handed over the briefcase.

"*Gracias, jefe*," Clark said. They loved to be called that. He pushed Escobedo toward them.

"You should know better than to betray your

1120

friends," said the second one as Clark reentered the aircraft. The comment was aimed at the bound and gagged chieftain, whose eyes were very, very wide, staring back at Clark as he closed the door.

"Get us the hell out of here."

"Next stop, Venezuela," Larson said as he goosed the throttles.

"Then Gitmo. Think you can hack it?"

"I'll need some coffee, but they make it good down here." The aircraft lifted off and Larson thought, *Jesus, it's good to have this one behind us.* That was true for him, but not for everyone.

30.

The Good
of the Service

By the time Ryan awoke on his cot in the wardroom, they were out of the worst of it. The cutter managed to make a steady ten knots east, and with the storm heading northwest at fifteen, they were in moderate seas in six hours. Course was made northeast, and *Panache* increased to her best continuous speed of about twenty knots.

The soldiers were quartered with the cutter's enlisted crew, who treated them like visiting kings. By some miracle some liquor bottles were discovered — probably from the chiefs' quarters, but no one hazarded to ask — and swiftly emptied. Their uniforms was discarded and new clothing issued from ship's stores. The dead were placed in cold storage, which everyone understood was the only possible thing. There were five of them; two of them, including Zimmer,

1122

had died during the rescue. Eight men were wounded, one of them seriously, but the two Army medics, plus the cutter's independent-duty corpsman, were able to stabilize him. Mainly the soldiers slept and ate and slept some more during their brief cruise.

Cortez, who'd been wounded in the arm, was in the brig. Murray looked after him. After Ryan awoke, both men went below with a TV camera which was set up on a tripod, and the senior FBI executive started to ask some questions. It was soon apparent that Cortez had had nothing to do with the murder of Emil Jacobs, which was as surprising to Murray as it was reasonable on examination of the information. It was a complication that neither man had actually expected, but one that might work in their favor, Ryan thought. He was the one who started asking the questions about Cortez's experience with the DGI. Cortez was wholly cooperative throughout. He'd betrayed one allegiance, and doing so to another came easily, especially with Jack's promise that he wouldn't be prosecuted if he cooperated. It was a promise that would be kept to the letter.

Cutter remained in Panama for another day. The search-and-rescue operation aimed at locating the downed helicopter was delayed by weather, and it was hardly surprising to him that nothing was found. The storm kept heading northwest and blew itself out on the Yucatan

Peninsula, ending as a series of line squalls that caused half a dozen tornados in Texas several days later. Cutter didn't stay long enough for that. As soon as the weather permitted, he flew straight back to D.C. just hours after Captain Montaigne returned to Eglin Air Force Base, her crew sworn to secrecy that their commander had every reason to enforce.

Panache arrived at Guantánamo Naval Base thirty-six hours after taking the helicopter aboard. Captain Wegener had radioed for permission, claiming a machinery problem and wanting to get out of Hurricane *Adele*'s path. Several miles off, Colonel Johns started up their helicopter and flew it onto the base, where it was immediately rolled into a hangar. The cutter came alongside an hour later, showing moderate storm damage, some of which was quite real.

Clark and Larson met the ship at the dock. Their aircraft was also hidden away. Ryan and Murray joined them, and a squad of Marines went aboard the cutter to retrieve Félix Cortez. Some telephone calls were placed, and then it was time to decide what had to be done. There were no easy solutions, nothing that would be entirely legal. The soldiers were treated at the base hospital and flown the next day to Fort MacDill in Florida. The same day, Clark and Larson returned the aircraft to Washington, having stopped to refuel in the Bahamas. In Washington it was turned over to a small corporation that belongs to CIA. Larson went on leave, wondering if he should really marry the girl and raise a family. Of one thing he was certain: he would leave the Agency.

Predictably, one of the things that happened was quite unexpected, and would forever be a mystery to all but one.

Admiral Cutter had returned two days earlier, and was back in his regular routine. The President was off on a political trip, trying to reestablish himself in the polls before the convention started two weeks hence. That made easier what had been a very hectic few weeks for his National Security Adviser. One way or another, he decided, he'd had enough of this. He'd served this President well, done things that needed to be done, and was entitled to a reward. He thought a fleet command would be appropriate, preferably Commander-in-Chief Atlantic Fleet. Vice Admiral Painter, the current Assistant Chief of Naval Operations (Air Warfare), had been told to expect it, but it was the President's call to make, after all, and Cutter figured that he could have just about anything he wanted. After that, if the President was re-elected, maybe Chairman of the Joint Chiefs. . . . It was something to think about over breakfast, which was at a civilized hour for a change. He'd even have time for a jog after his morning briefing from CIA. The doorbell rang at 7:15. Cutter answered it himself.

"Who are you?"

"Your regular briefing officer was taken ill, sir. I have the duty today," the man said. Forties, looked like one tough old field officer.

"Okay, come on." Cutter waved him into the study. The man sat down, glad to see that the Admiral had a TV and VCR in here.

"Okay, where do we start today?" Cutter asked after the door was closed.

"Gitmo, sir," the man said.

"What's happening in Cuba?"

"Actually, I have it on videotape, sir." The field officer inserted it in the unit and punched "play."

"What is this . . . ?" *Jesus Christ!* The tape played on for several minutes before the CIA officer stopped it.

"So what? That's the word of a traitor to his own country," Cutter said to answer the man's expectant smile.

"There's this, too." He held up a photograph of the two of them. "Personally, I'd love to see you in federal prison. That's what the FBI wants. They're going to arrest you later today. You can imagine the charges. Assistant Deputy Director Murray is running the case. He's probably meeting with a U.S. Magistrate right now — whatever the mechanics are. Personally I don't care about that."

"Then why — ?"

"I'm a bit of a movie buff. Used to be in the Navy, too. In the movies at times like this, they always give a guy a chance to handle things himself — 'for the good of the service,' they usually say. I wouldn't try running away. There's a team of FBI agents watching you, in case you haven't noticed. Given the way things work in this town — how long things take to get done — I don't suppose you'll be meeting them until ten or eleven. If you do, Admiral, then God help you. You'll get life. I only wish they could do something worse, but you'll get life in a federal pen, with some career hood sticking it up that tight little ass of yours when the guards aren't around. I wouldn't mind seeing that either. Anyway." He retrieved the videotape, tucking it in the briefcase along with the photograph that the Bureau really shouldn't have given him — and they'd told Ryan that he'd only use it to identify Cortez. "Good day, sir."

"But you've — "

"Done what? Nobody swore me to secrecy over this. What secrets have I revealed, Admiral? You were there for all of them."

"You're Clark, aren't you?"

"Excuse me? Who?" he said on his way out. Then he was gone.

Half an hour later, Pat O'Day saw Cutter jogging down the hill toward the George Washington Parkway. One nice thing about having the President out of town, the inspector thought, was that he didn't have to shake out of the rack at 4:30 to meet the bastard. He'd been here only forty minutes, spending a lot of time with his stretching exercises, and there he was. O'Day let him pass, then moved out, keeping up easily since the man was quite a bit older. But that wasn't all. . . .

O'Day followed him for a mile, then two, approaching the Pentagon. Cutter followed the jogging path between the road and the river. Perhaps he didn't feel well. He alternately jogged and walked. Maybe he's trying to see if he has a tail, O'Day thought, but . . . Then he started moving again.

Just opposite the beginning of the northern parking lot, Cutter got off the path, heading toward the road as though to cross it. The inspector had now closed to within fifty yards. Something was wrong. He didn't know what. It was . . .

. . . the way he was looking at the traffic. He wasn't looking for openings, O'Day realized too late. A bus was coming north, a D.C. transit bus, it had just come off the 14th Street Bridge and —

"Look out!" But the man wasn't listening for that sort of warning.

Brakes screeched. The bus tried to avoid the man, slamming into another car, then five more added their mass to the pileup. O'Day approached only because he was a cop, and cops are expected to do such things. Vice Admiral James A. Cutter, Jr., USN, was still in the road, thrown fifty feet by the collision.

He'd wanted it to look like an accident, O'Day thought, *but it wasn't*. The agent didn't notice a passerby in a cheap-bodied government car who came down the other side of the parkway, rubbernecking at the accident scene like many others, but with a look of satisfaction instead of horror at the sight.

Ryan was waiting at the White House. The President had flown home because of the death of his aide, but he was still President, and there was still work to be done, and if the DDI said that he needed to meet with the President, then it had to be important. The President was puzzled to see that along with Ryan were Al Trent and Sam Fellows, co-chairmen of the House Select Committee on Intelligence Oversight.

"Come on in," he said, guiding them regally into the Oval Office. "What's so important?"

"Mr. President, it has to do with some covert operations, especially one called SHOWBOAT."

"What's that?" the President asked, on guard. Ryan explained for a minute or so.

"Oh, that. Very well. SHOWBOAT was given to these two men personally by Judge Moore under his hazardous-operations rule."

"Dr. Ryan tells us that there are some other things we need to know about also. Other operations related to SHOWBOAT," Congressman Fellows said.

"I don't know about any of that."

"Yes, you do, Mr. President," Ryan said quietly. "You authorized it. It is my duty under the law to report on these matters to Congress. Before I do so, I felt it necessary to notify you. I asked the two congressmen here to witness my doing so."

"Mr. Trent, Mr. Fellows, could you please excuse me for a moment? There are some things going on that I don't know about. Will you allow me to question Dr. Ryan in private for a moment?"

Say no! Ryan wished as hard as he could, but one does not deny such requests to the President, and in a moment he and Ryan were alone.

"What are you hiding, Ryan?" the President asked. "I know you're hiding some things."

"Yes, sir, I am and I will. The identities of some of our people, CIA and military, who acted on what they thought was proper authority." Ryan explained further, wondering what of it the President knew and what he didn't. It was something he was sure he'd never fully know. Most of the really important secrets Cutter had taken to his grave. Ryan suspected what had happened there, but . . . but had decided to let that sleeping dog lie, too. *Was it possible to be connected with something like this,* he asked himself, *and not be corrupted by it?*

"What Cutter did, what you *say* he did — I didn't know. I'm sorry. I'm especially sorry about those soldiers."

"We got about half of them out, sir. I was there. That's the part I cannot forgive. Cutter deliberately cut them off with the intention of giving you a political — "

"*I never authorized that!*" he almost screamed.

1130

"You allowed it to happen, sir." Ryan tried to look him straight in the eye, and on the moment of wavering, it was the President who looked away. "My God, sir, how could you do it?"

"The people want us to stop the flow of drugs."

"Then do it, do just what you tried to do, but do it in accordance with the law."

"It won't work that way."

"Why not?" Ryan asked. "Have the American people ever objected when we used force to protect our interests?"

"But what we had to do here could never be public."

"In that case, sir, all you needed to do was make the appropriate notification of the Congress and do it covertly. You got partial approval for the operation, politics would not necessarily have come into play, but in breaking the rules, sir, you took a national-security issue and made it into a political one."

"Ryan, you're smart and clever and good at what you do, but you're naïve."

Jack wasn't that naïve: "What are you asking me to do, sir?"

"How much does the Congress really need to know?"

"Are you asking me to lie for you, sir? You called me naïve, Mr. President. I had a man die in my arms two days ago, a sergeant in the Air Force who left seven children behind. Tell me, sir, am I naïve to let that weigh upon my thinking?"

"You can't talk to me that way."

"I take no pleasure in it, sir. But I will not lie for you."

"But you are willing to conceal the identities of people who — "

"Who followed your orders in good faith. Yes, Mr. President, I am willing to do that."

"What happens to the country, Jack?"

"I agree with you that we do not need another scandal, but that is a political question. On that, sir, you have to talk to the men outside. My function is to provide information for the government, and to perform certain tasks for the government. I am an instrument of policy. So were those people who died for their country, sir, and they had a right to expect that their lives would be given greater value by the government they served. They were people, Mr. President, young kids for the most part who went off to do a job because their country — you, sir — thought it important that they do so. What they didn't know was that there were enemies in Washington. They never suspected that, and that's why most of them died. Sir, the oath our people take when they put the uniform on requires them to bear 'true faith and allegiance' to their country. Isn't it written down somewhere that the country owes them the same thing? It's not the first time this has happened, but I wasn't part of it before, and I will not lie about it, sir, not to protect you or anyone else."

"I didn't know that, Jack. Honestly, I didn't know."

"Mr. President, I choose to believe that you are an honorable man. What you just said, sir, is that really an excuse?" Jack paused, and was fully answered by silence.

"Do you wish to meet with the congressmen before I brief them, sir?"

"Yes. Why don't you wait outside for us."

"Thank you, Mr. President."

Jack waited for an hour of discomfort before Trent and Fellows reappeared. They drove with him to Langley in silence, and the three walked into the office of the Director of Central Intelligence.

"Judge," Trent said, "that may have been the greatest service you have ever done your country."

"Under the circumstances — " Moore paused. "What else could I have done?"

"You could have left them to die, you could have warned the opposition that we were coming in," Jack said. "In that case I wouldn't be here. And for that, Judge, I am in your debt. You could have stuck with the lie."

"And live with myself?" Moore smiled in a very strange way and shook his head.

"And the operations?" Ryan asked. Exactly what had been discussed in the Oval Office he didn't know, and he told himself not to make any guesses.

"Never happened," Fellows said. "Under the hazardous-operations rule, you have done what you needed to do — granted, a little late, but we have been notified. We don't need another scandal like this, and with the way things are going, the situation will settle itself. Politically it's shaky, but legally you can argue that it's all according to Hoyle."

"The craziest part of all is, it almost worked," Trent observed. "Your CAPER operation was brilliant, and I assume it'll be kept going."

"It will. The whole operation did work," Ritter said for the first time. "It really did. We did start a war within the Cartel, and Escobedo's killing was just the last act—or maybe not if it goes on further. With that many chieftains gone, maybe Colombia will be able to do a little better. We need that capability. We can't have it stripped away from us."

"I agree," Ryan said. "We need the capability, but you don't make public policy this way, damn it!"

"Jack, tell me what right and wrong is?" Moore asked. "You seem to be the expert today," he added without very much irony.

"This is supposed to be a democracy. We let the people know something, or at least we let *them* know." He waved at the congressmen. "When a government decides to kill people who threaten its interests or its citizens, it doesn't have to be murder. Not always. I'm just not sure where the line is. But I don't have to be sure. Other people are supposed to tell us that."

"Well, come January, it won't be us," Moore observed. "It's agreed, then? It stays here. No political footballs?"

Trent and Fellows could scarcely have been further apart politically, the gay New Englander and the tough-minded Mormon from Arizona. They nodded agreement.

"No games on this," Trent said.

"It would just hurt the country," Fellows concurred.

"And what we've just done . . ." Ryan murmured. *Whatever the hell it was . . .*

"You didn't do it," Trent said. "The rest of us did."

"Right," Jack snorted. "Well, I'm gone soon, too."

"Think so?" Fellows asked.

"Not so, Dr. Ryan. We don't know who Fowler is going to appoint, probably some political lawyer he likes. I know the names on the list," Trent said.

"It sure as hell won't be me. He doesn't like me," Ryan said.

"He doesn't have to like you, and you're not going to be Director. But you will be here," Trent told him. *Deputy Director, maybe,* the congressman thought to himself.

"We'll see." Fellows said. "What if things turn out differently in November? Fowler may just screw it up yet."

"You have my word, Sam," Trent replied. "If that happens, it happens."

"There is one wild card, though," Ritter pointed out.

"I've already discussed that with Bill Shaw," Moore said. "It's funny. The only law he actually broke was illegal entry. None of the data he got out of her was technically classified. Amazing, isn't it?"

Ryan shook his head and left work early. He had an appointment with his attorney, who would soon be establishing an educational trust for seven kids living in Florida.

The infantrymen were cycled through Fort MacDill's special-operations center. Told that their operation had been a success, they were sworn to secrecy, given their promotions, and sent on to new postings. Except for one.

"Chavez?" a voice called.

"Yo, Mr. Clark."

"Buy you dinner?"

"There a good Mexican place around here?"

"Maybe I can find one."

"What's the occasion?"

"Let's talk jobs," Clark said. "There's an opening where I work. It pays better than what you do now. You'll have to go back to school for a couple of years, though."

"I've been thinkin' about that," Chavez replied. He'd been thinking that he was officer material. If he'd been in command instead of Ramirez, maybe — or maybe not. But he did want to find out.

"You're good, kid. I want you to work with me."

Chavez thought about that. At least he'd get a dinner out of the idea.

Captain Bronco Winters was dispatched to an F-15 squadron in Germany, where he distinguished himself and was soon a flight leader. He was a calmer young man now. He'd exorcised the demons of his mother's death. Winters would never look back. He'd had a job, and done it.

It was a cold, dismal fall after a hot, muggy summer in Washington. The political city emptied out for the presidential election, which shared that November with all of the House seats and a third of the Senate, plus hundreds of political-appointment slots in the executive branch. In the early fall, the FBI broke several Cuban-run spy rings, but strangely that was politically neutral. Although arresting a drug ring was a police success, arresting a spy ring was seen as a failure because of the existence of a spy ring in the first place. There was no political advantage except in the Cuban refugee community, whose votes might as well already have been cast anyway, since Fowler was talking about "opening a dialogue" with the Cuba they had left. The President regained the lead after his own convention, but ran a lackluster campaign and fired two key political advisers. But most of all, it was time for a change, and though it was close, J. Robert Fowler carried the election with a bare 2 percent advantage in the popular vote. Some called it a mandate; others called it a sloppy campaign on both sides. The latter was closer to the truth, Ryan thought after it was all over.

All over the city and its environs, displaced appointees made preparations to move home — wherever home was — or to move into law offices so that they could stay in the area. Congress hadn't changed very much, but Congress rarely did. Ryan remained in his office, wondering if he'd be confirmed as the next DDI. It was too soon to tell. One thing he did know was that the President was still President, and still a man of honor, whatever mistakes he'd made. Before he left, pardons would be issued to those who needed them. They'd go on the books, but no one was expected to notice, and after things were explained to the Fowler people — Trent would handle that — it wasn't expected that anyone ever would.

On the Saturday after the election, Dan Murray drove Moira Wolfe to Andrews Air Force Base, where a jet was waiting for them. It took just over three hours before they landed at Guantánamo. A leftover from the Spanish-American War, Gitmo, as it's called, is the only American military installation on Communist soil, a thorn stuck in Castro's side that rankled him as much as he rankled his oversized neighbor across the Florida Strait.

Moira was doing well at the Department of Agriculture, executive secretary to one of the department's top career executives. She was thinner now, but Murray wasn't concerned about that. She'd taken up walking for exercise, and was doing well with her psychological counseling. She was the last of the victims, and he hoped that this trip would help.

So this was the day, Cortez thought. He was surprised and disappointed at his fate, but resigned to it. He'd gambled greatly and lost greatly. He feared his fate, but he wouldn't let that show, not to Americans. They loaded him into the back of a sedan and drove toward the gate. He saw another car ahead of his, but made no special note of it.

And there it was, the tall barbed-wire fence, manned on one side by American Marines in their multicolor fatigues — they called them "utilities," Cortez had learned — and on the other by Cubans in their battle dress. Perhaps, just perhaps, Cortez thought, he might talk his way out of this. The car halted fifty meters from the gate. The corporal to his left pulled him out of the car and unlocked his handcuffs, lest he take them across and so enrich a Communist country. *Such trivial nonsense,* Félix thought.

"Come on, Pancho," the black corporal said. "Time to go home."

Even without the cuffs, both Marines grabbed him by the arms to help him walk to his mother country. There at the gate he saw two officers waiting for him, impassively for now. They would probably embrace him when he came across, which wouldn't mean a thing. In either case, Cortez was determined to meet his fate like a man. He straightened his back and smiled at those waiting for him as though they were family members waiting at the airport gate.

"Cortez," a man's voice called.

They stepped out of the guard shack, just inside the gate. He didn't know the man, but the woman . . .

Félix stopped, and the motion of the two Marines nearly toppled him. She just stood there, staring at him. She didn't speak a word, and Cortez didn't know what to say. The smile vanished from his lips. The look in her eyes made him shrink within himself. He'd never meant to hurt her. To use her, yes, of course, but never really . . .

"Come on, Pancho," the corporal said, heaving the man forward. They were just at the gate.

"Oh, by the way, this here's yours, Pancho," the corporal said, tucking a videocassette in his belt. "Welcome home, asshole." A final push.

"Welcome home, *Colonel*," the senior of the two Cubans said. He embraced his former comrade and whispered: "You have much to answer for!"

But before they dragged him off, Félix turned one last time, seeing Moira, just standing there with the man he didn't know, and his last thought as he turned away was that once again she'd understood: silence was the greatest passion of all.